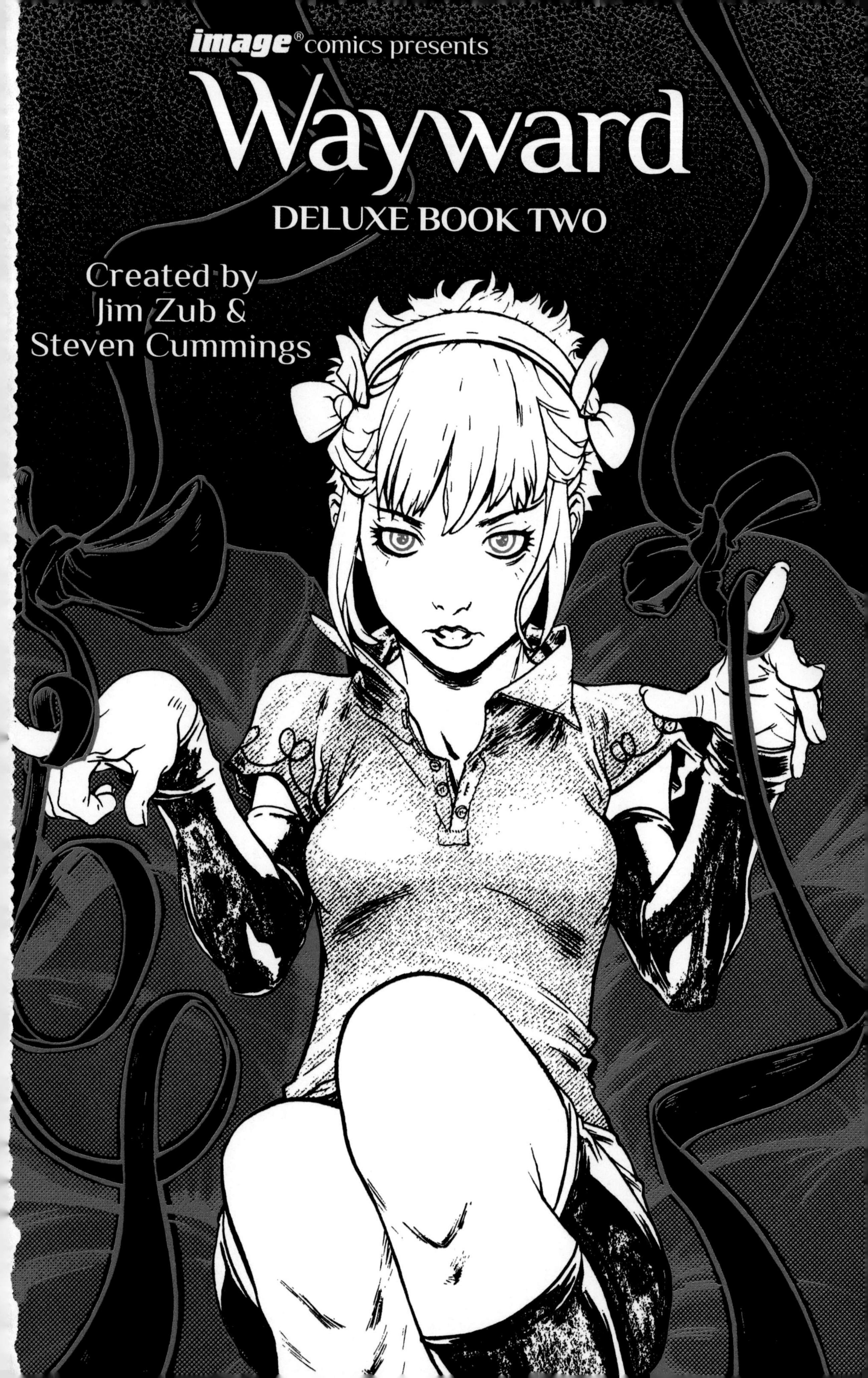
image® comics presents
Wayward
DELUXE BOOK TWO
Created by
Jim Zub &
Steven Cummings

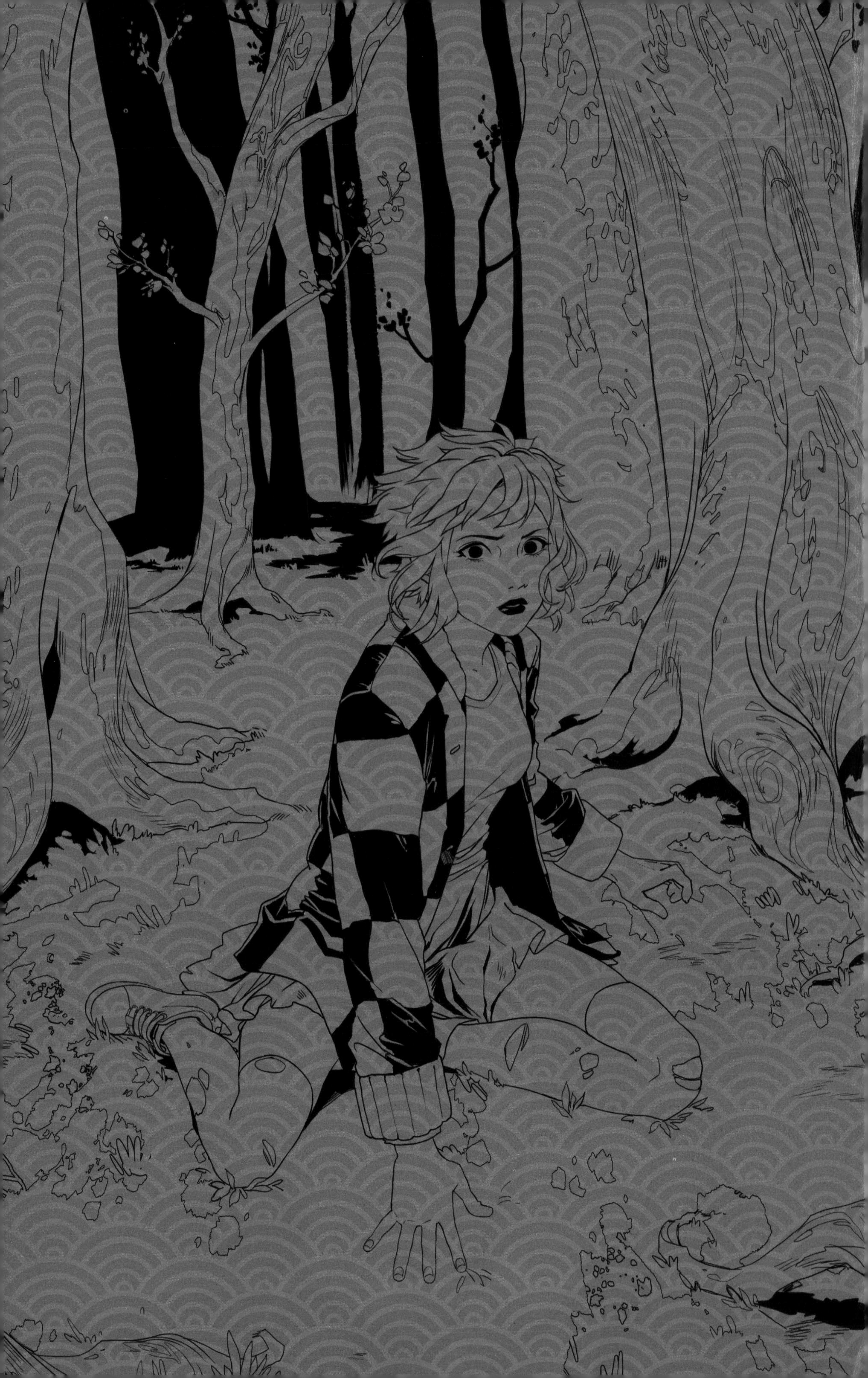

Chapter Eleven

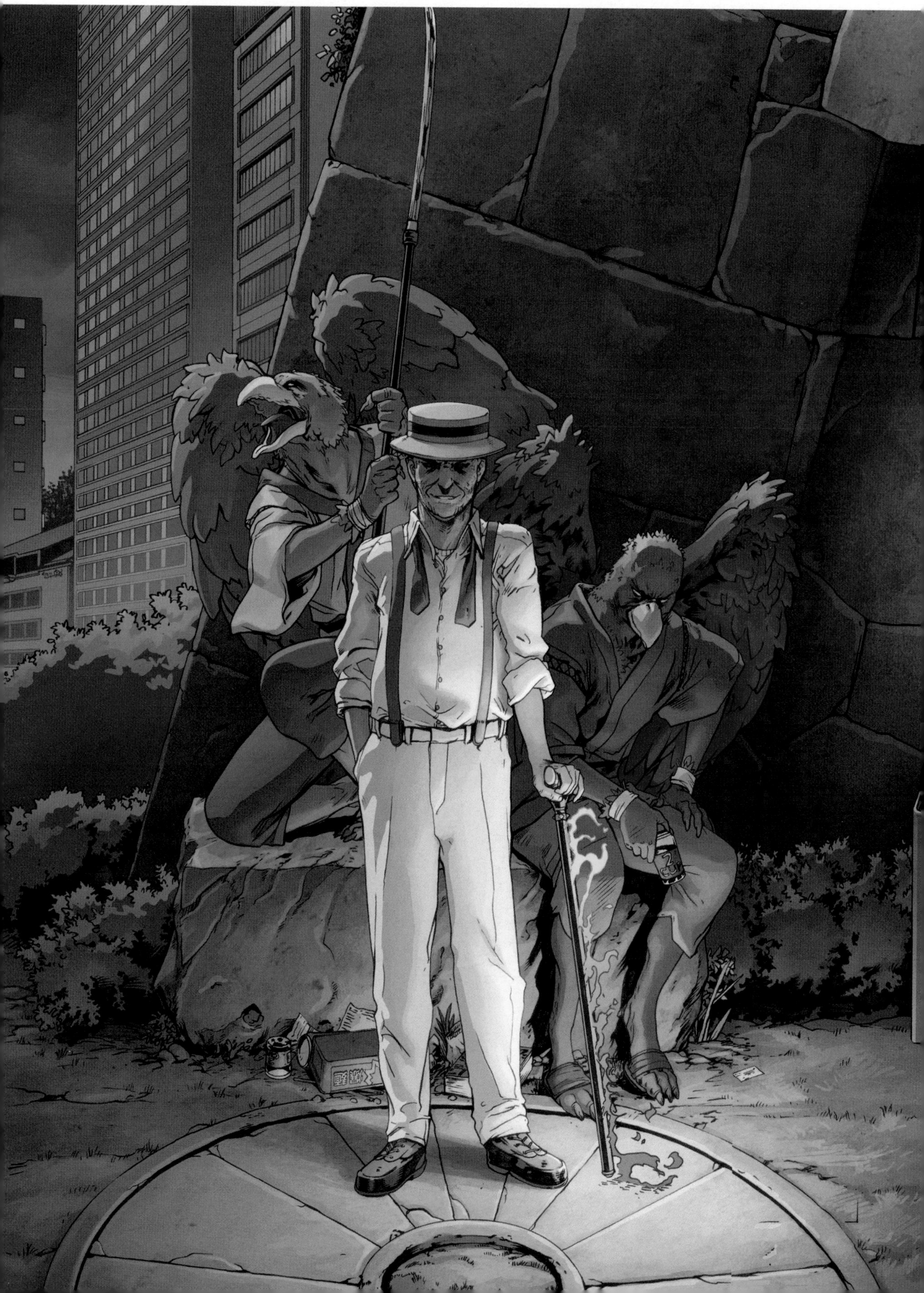

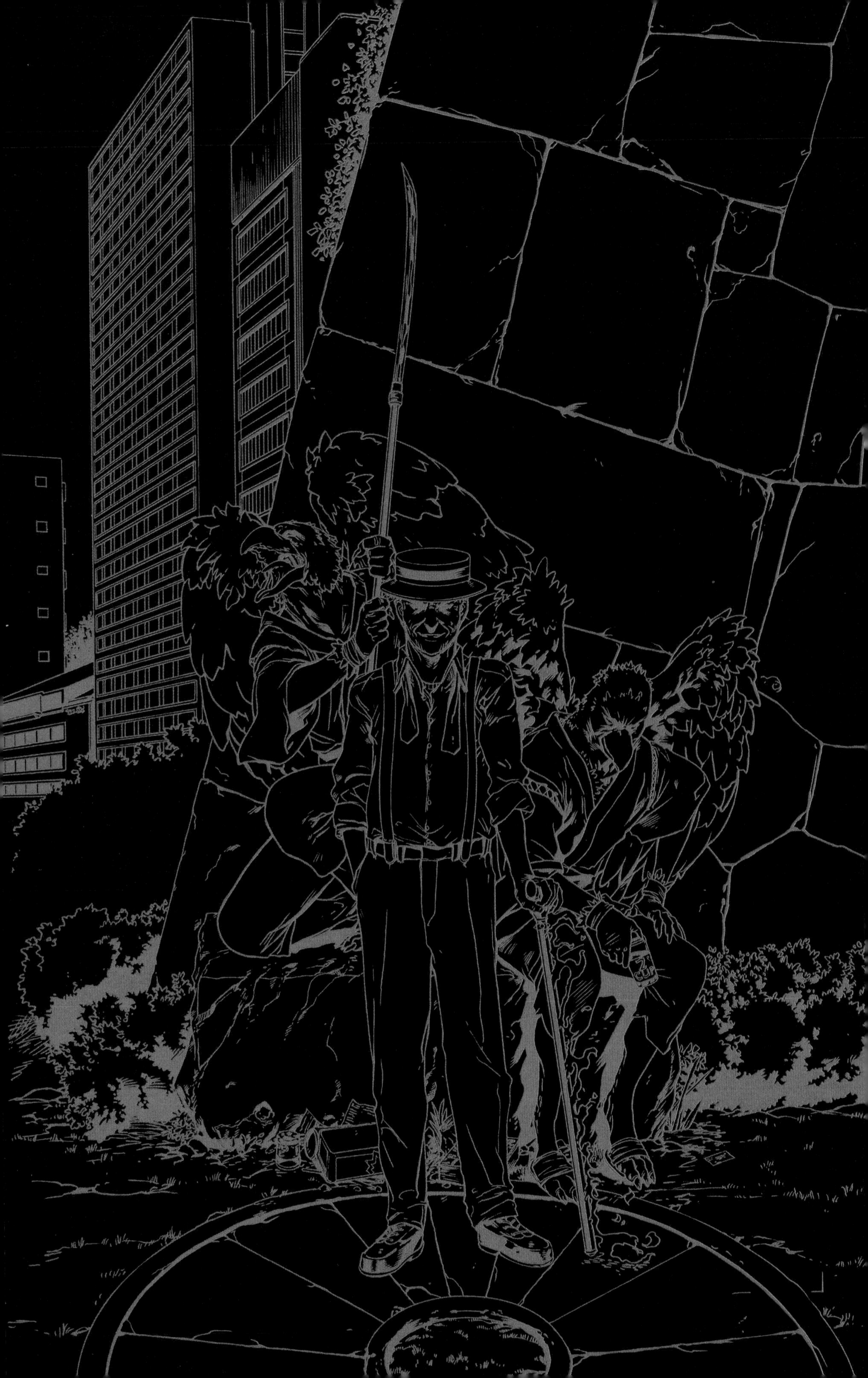

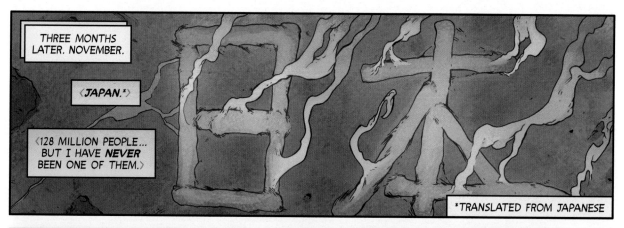

THREE MONTHS LATER. NOVEMBER.

⟨JAPAN.*⟩

⟨128 MILLION PEOPLE... BUT I HAVE **NEVER** BEEN ONE OF THEM.⟩

*TRANSLATED FROM JAPANESE

⟨THIS LAND IS **HOME**.⟩

⟨IT IS WHERE WE ARE MEANT TO BE.⟩

⟨AS THE RISING SUN SHIMMERS IN THE DISTANCE BEYOND THESE HUMAN EDIFICES OF SHELTER AND COMMERCE, I FEEL A **RAGE** CHURNING WITHIN ME.⟩

⟨FRUSTRATION, FUTILITY...⟩

⟨...CHANGES I CAN NO LONGER CONTROL.⟩

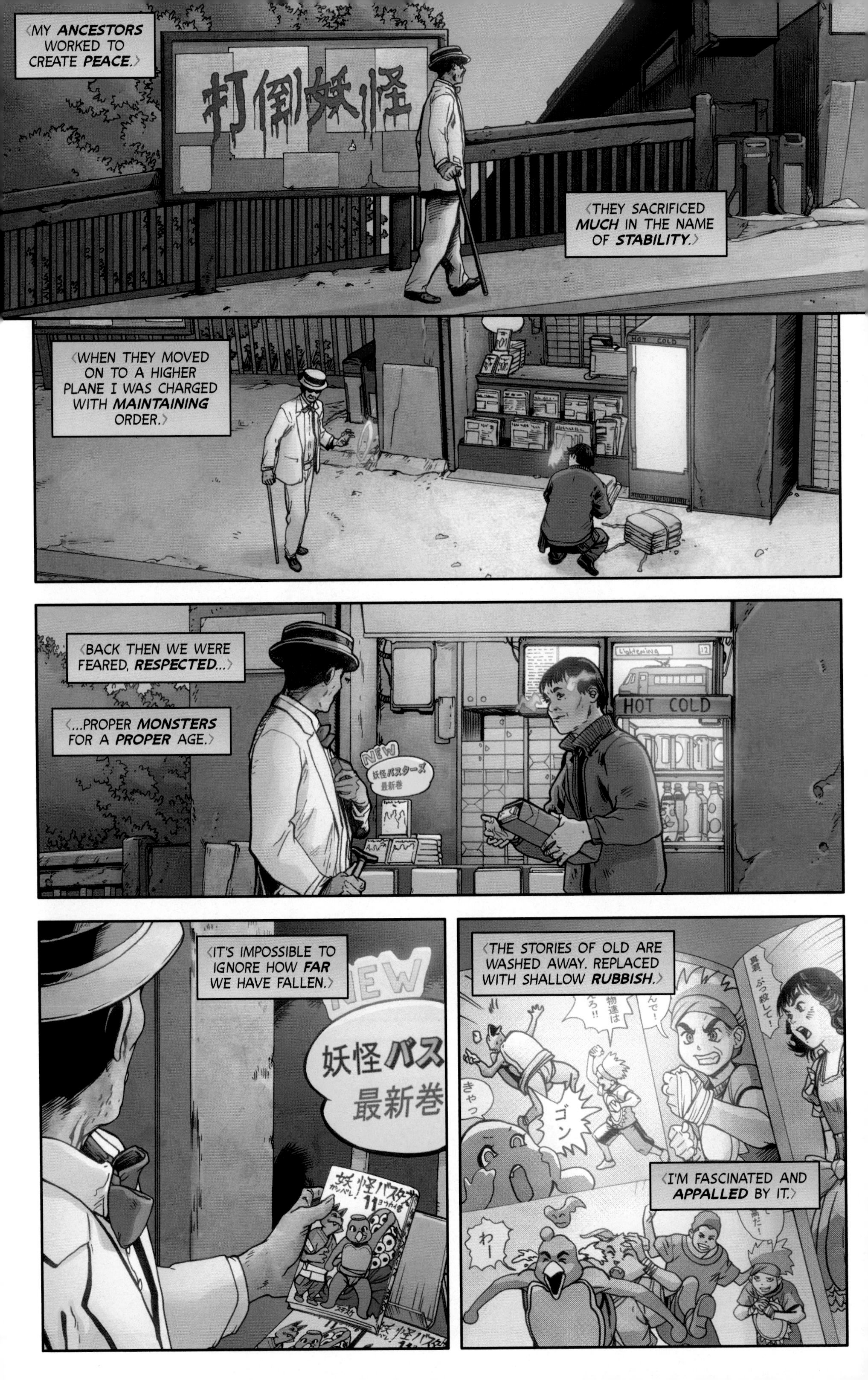

‹MY ANCESTORS WORKED TO CREATE PEACE.›
打倒妖怪
‹THEY SACRIFICED MUCH IN THE NAME OF STABILITY.›
‹WHEN THEY MOVED ON TO A HIGHER PLANE I WAS CHARGED WITH MAINTAINING ORDER.›
‹BACK THEN WE WERE FEARED, RESPECTED...›
‹...PROPER MONSTERS FOR A PROPER AGE.›
NEW
妖怪バスターズ
最新巻
HOT COLD
‹IT'S IMPOSSIBLE TO IGNORE HOW FAR WE HAVE FALLEN.›
NEW
妖怪バス
最新巻
‹THE STORIES OF OLD ARE WASHED AWAY. REPLACED WITH SHALLOW RUBBISH.›
きゃっ
ゴン
‹I'M FASCINATED AND APPALLED BY IT.›
わー

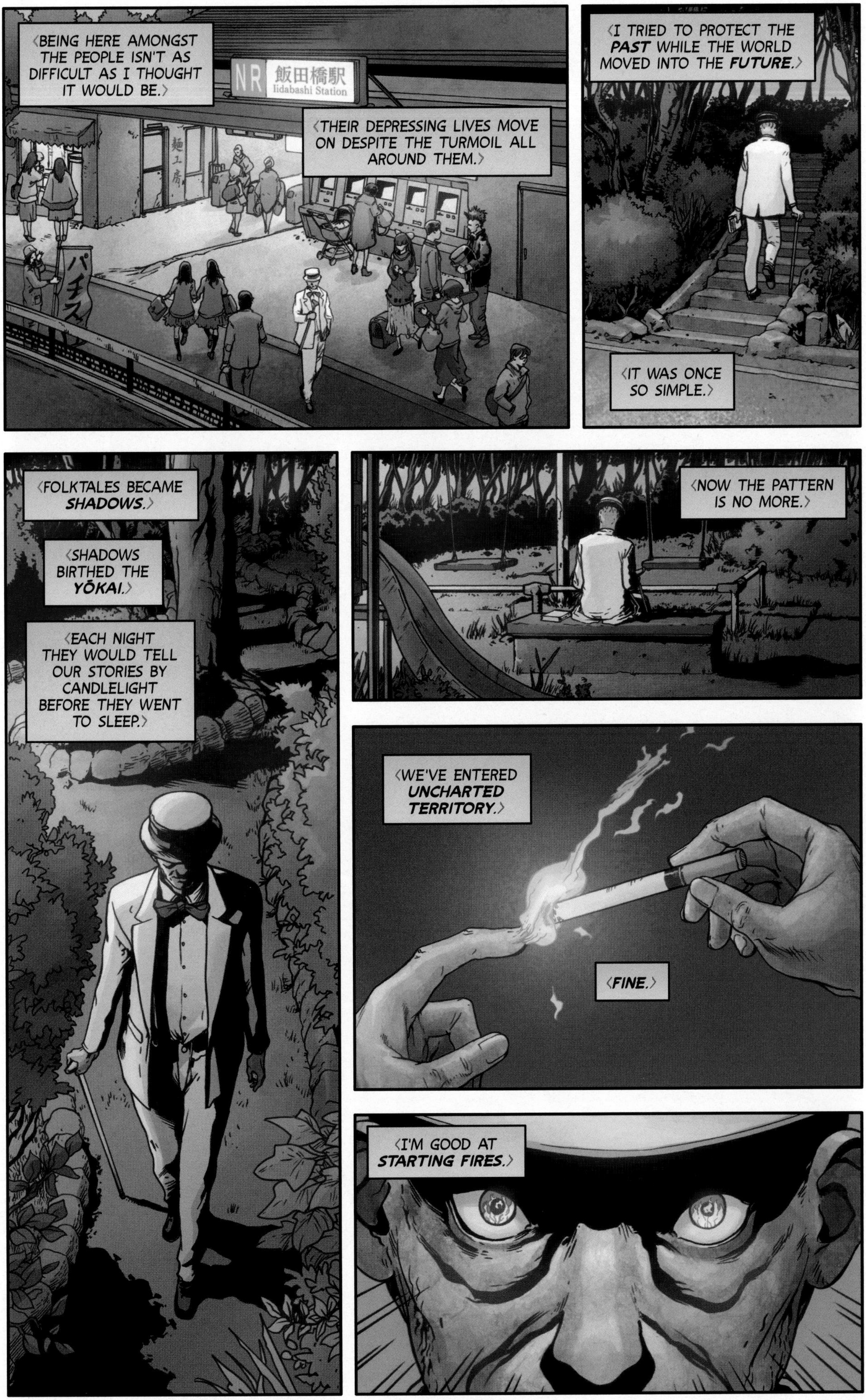
〈BEING HERE AMONGST THE PEOPLE ISN'T AS DIFFICULT AS I THOUGHT IT WOULD BE.〉
NR 飯田橋駅 Iidabashi Station
〈THEIR DEPRESSING LIVES MOVE ON DESPITE THE TURMOIL ALL AROUND THEM.〉
〈I TRIED TO PROTECT THE PAST WHILE THE WORLD MOVED INTO THE FUTURE.〉
〈IT WAS ONCE SO SIMPLE.〉
〈FOLKTALES BECAME SHADOWS.〉
〈SHADOWS BIRTHED THE YŌKAI.〉
〈EACH NIGHT THEY WOULD TELL OUR STORIES BY CANDLELIGHT BEFORE THEY WENT TO SLEEP.〉
〈NOW THE PATTERN IS NO MORE.〉
〈WE'VE ENTERED UNCHARTED TERRITORY.〉
〈FINE.〉
〈I'M GOOD AT STARTING FIRES.〉

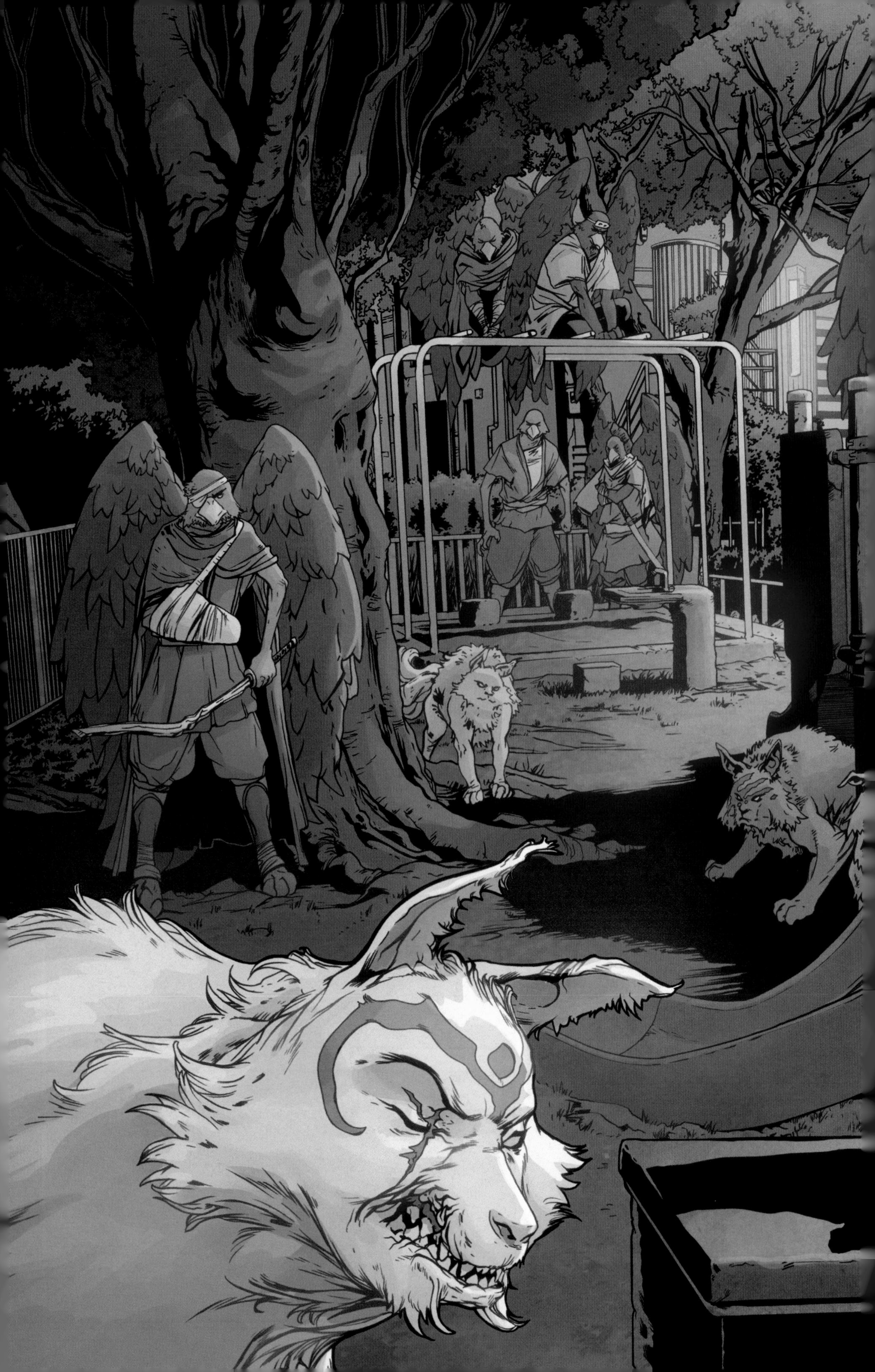

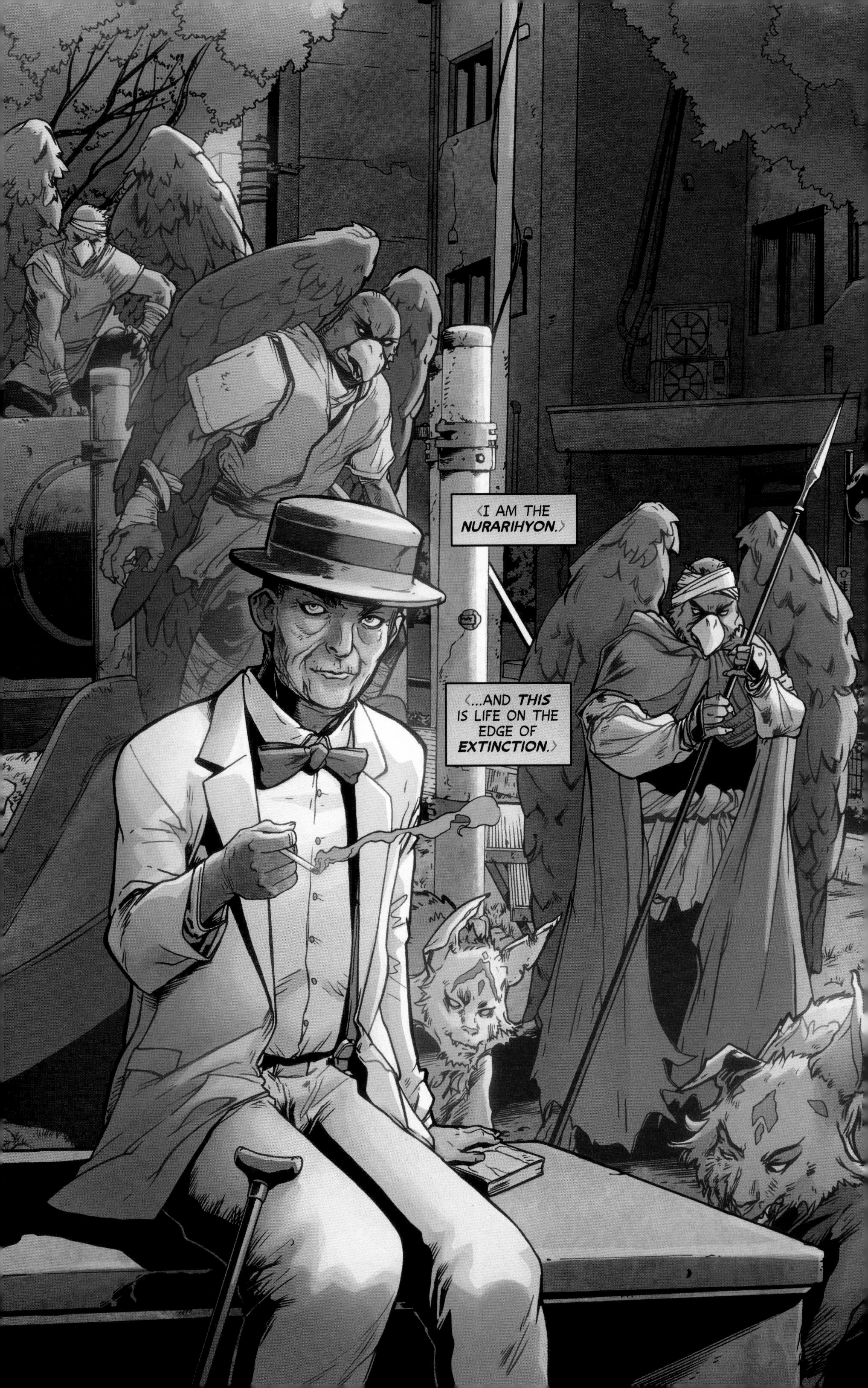

⟨I AM THE NURARIHYON.⟩
⟨...AND THIS IS LIFE ON THE EDGE OF EXTINCTION.⟩

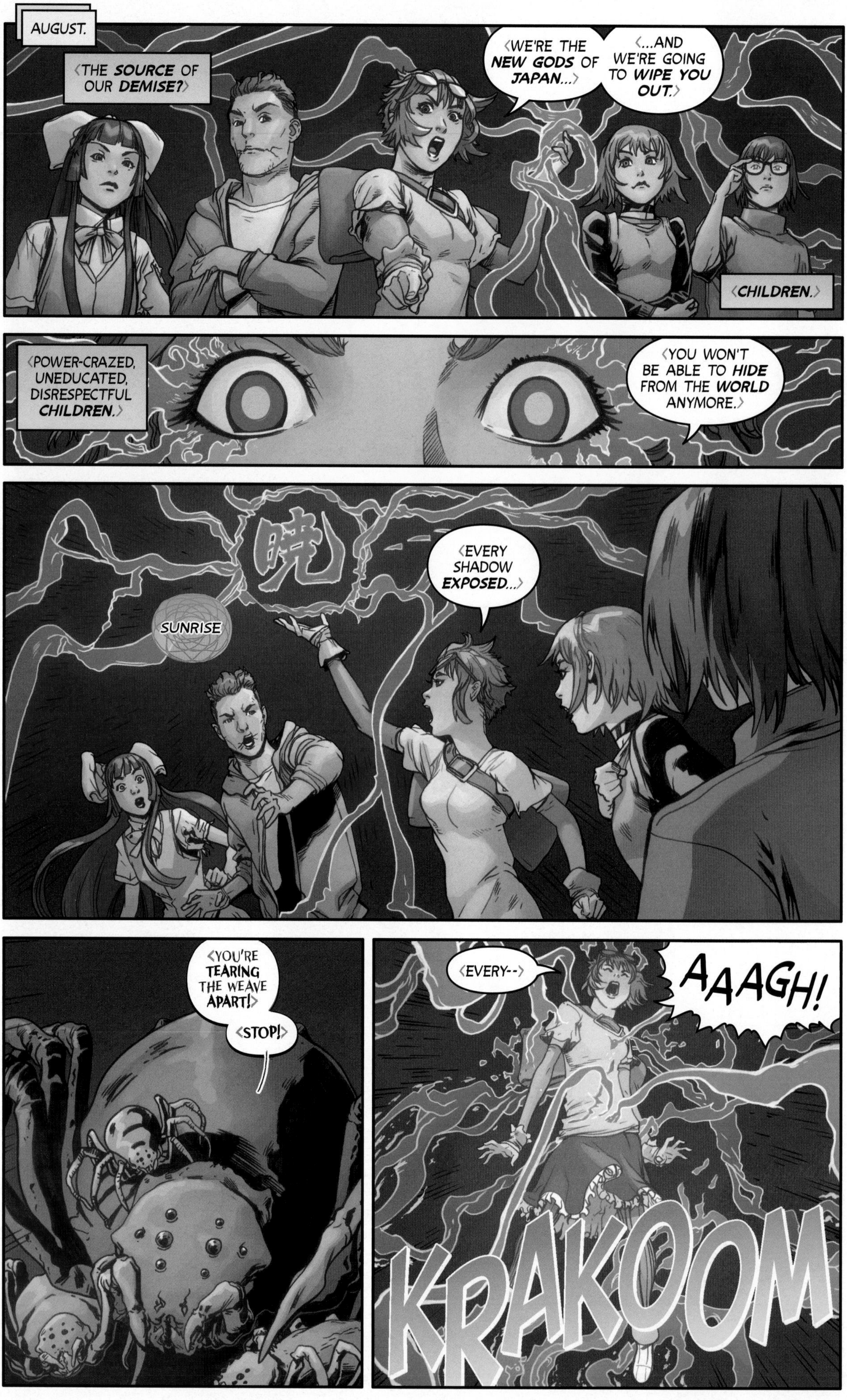
AUGUST.
‹THE SOURCE OF OUR DEMISE?›
‹WE'RE THE NEW GODS OF JAPAN...›
‹...AND WE'RE GOING TO WIPE YOU OUT.›
‹CHILDREN.›
‹POWER-CRAZED, UNEDUCATED, DISRESPECTFUL CHILDREN.›
‹YOU WON'T BE ABLE TO HIDE FROM THE WORLD ANYMORE.›
暁
SUNRISE
‹EVERY SHADOW EXPOSED...›
‹YOU'RE TEARING THE WEAVE APART!›
‹STOP!›
‹EVERY--›
AAAGH!
KRAKOOM

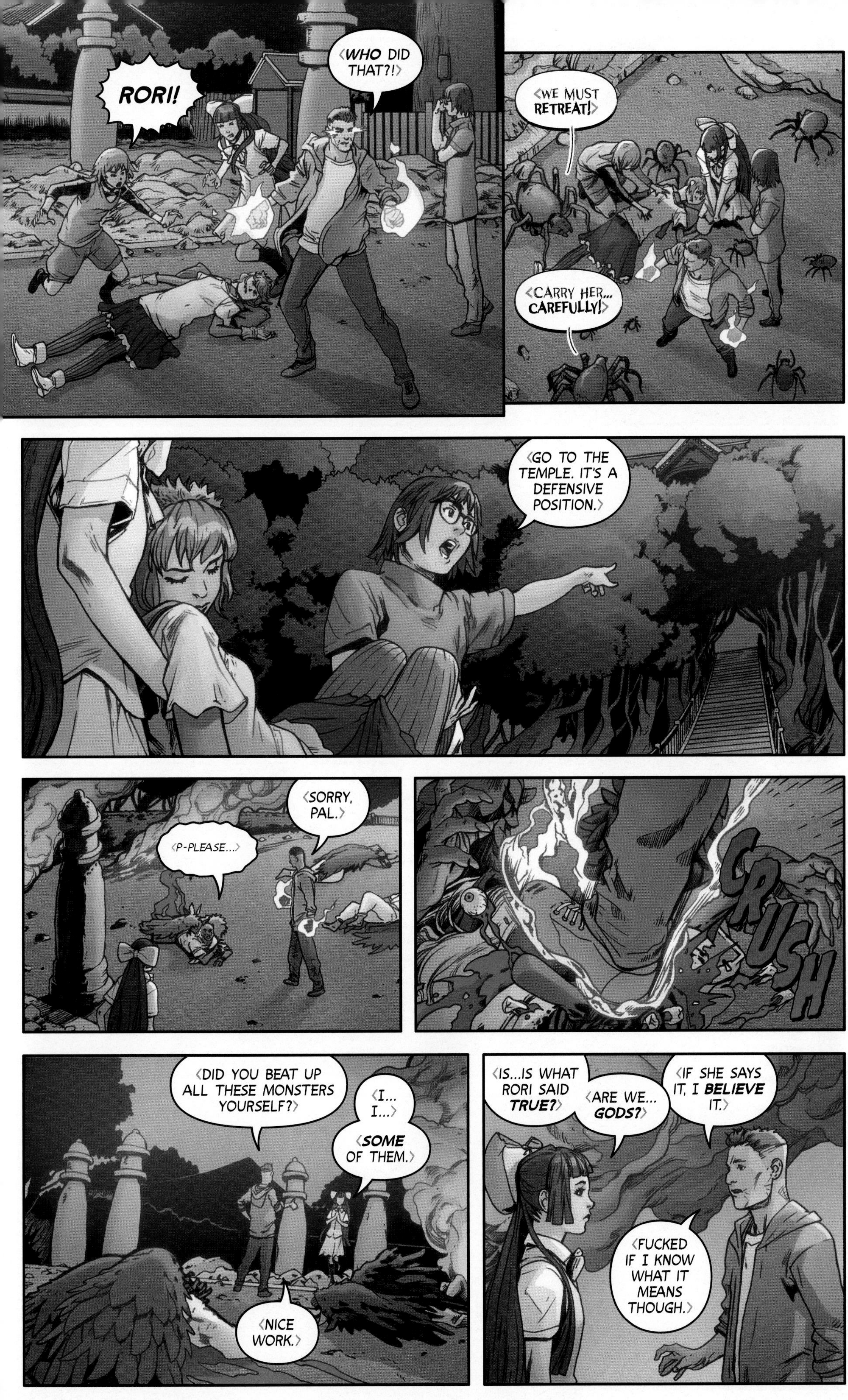
RORI!
<WHO DID THAT?!>
<WE MUST RETREAT!>
<CARRY HER... CAREFULLY!>
<GO TO THE TEMPLE. IT'S A DEFENSIVE POSITION.>
<P-PLEASE...>
<SORRY, PAL.>
CRUSH
<DID YOU BEAT UP ALL THESE MONSTERS YOURSELF?>
<I... I...>
<SOME OF THEM.>
<NICE WORK.>
<IS...IS WHAT RORI SAID TRUE?>
<ARE WE... GODS?>
<IF SHE SAYS IT, I BELIEVE IT.>
<FUCKED IF I KNOW WHAT IT MEANS THOUGH.>

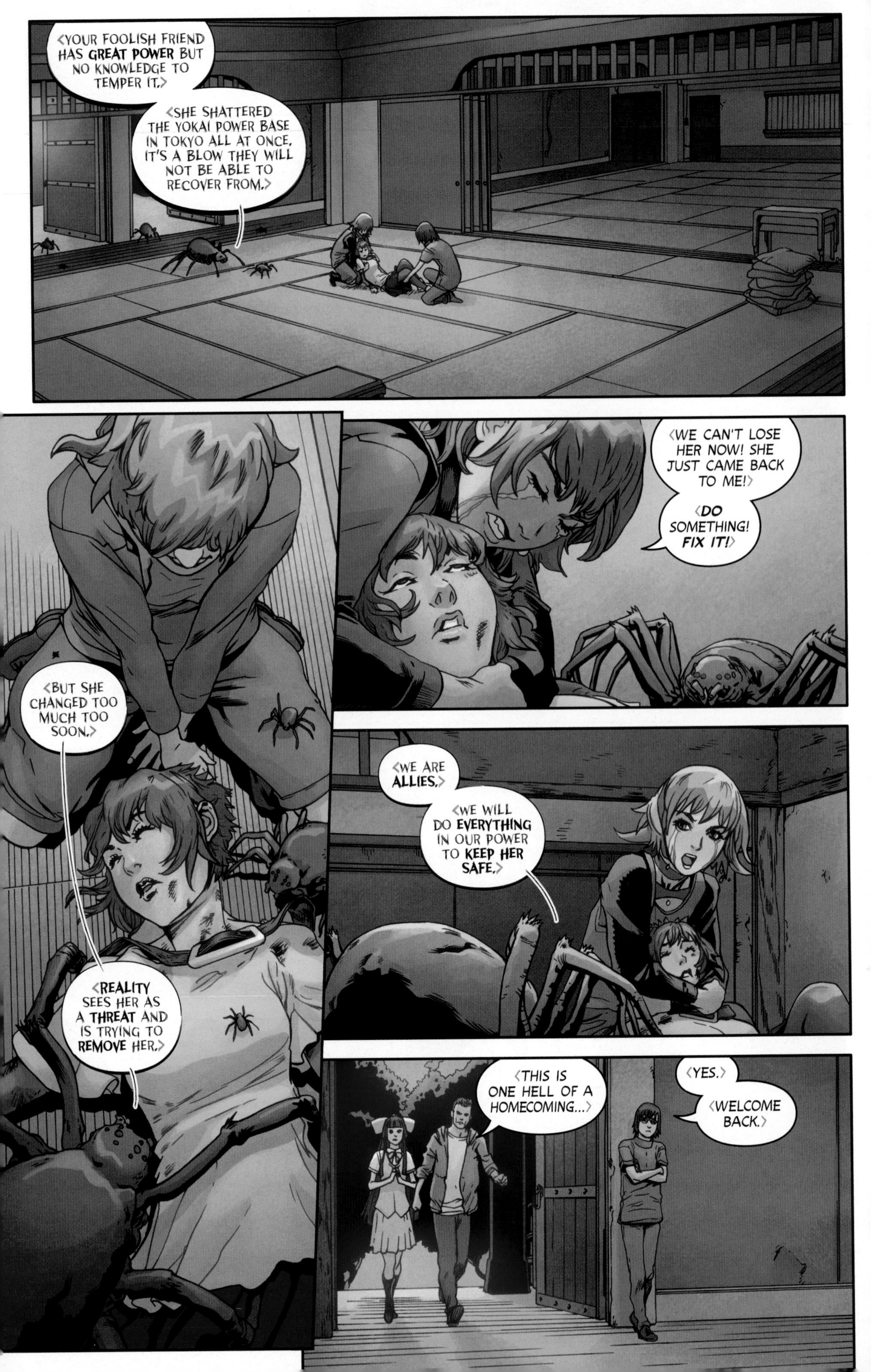

<YOUR FOOLISH FRIEND HAS GREAT POWER BUT NO KNOWLEDGE TO TEMPER IT.>
<SHE SHATTERED THE YOKAI POWER BASE IN TOKYO ALL AT ONCE. IT'S A BLOW THEY WILL NOT BE ABLE TO RECOVER FROM.>
<BUT SHE CHANGED TOO MUCH TOO SOON.>
<REALITY SEES HER AS A THREAT AND IS TRYING TO REMOVE HER.>
<WE CAN'T LOSE HER NOW! SHE JUST CAME BACK TO ME!>
<DO SOMETHING! FIX IT!>
<WE ARE ALLIES.>
<WE WILL DO EVERYTHING IN OUR POWER TO KEEP HER SAFE.>
<THIS IS ONE HELL OF A HOMECOMING...>
<YES.>
<WELCOME BACK.>

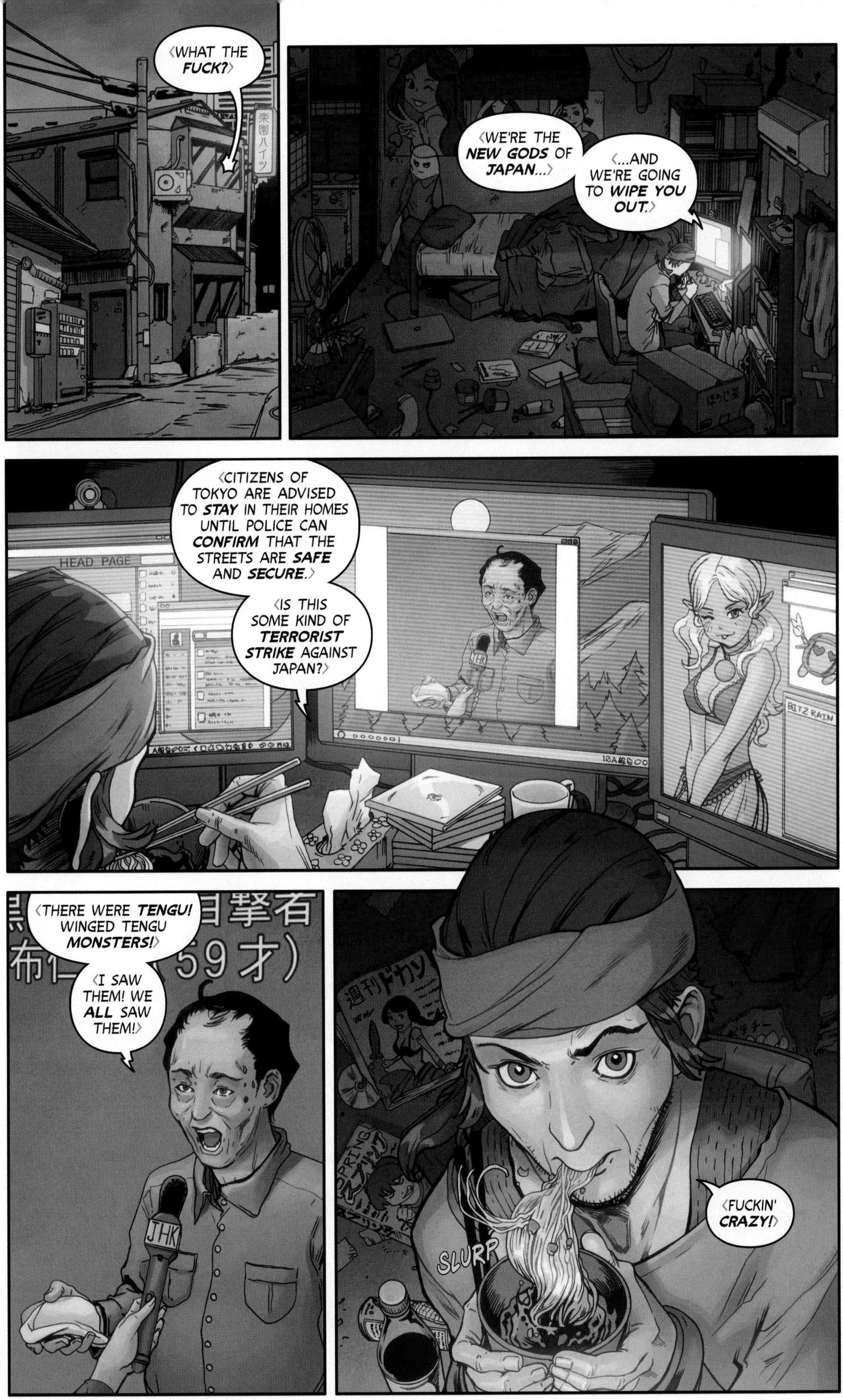

‹WHAT THE FUCK?›
楽園ハイツ
‹WE'RE THE NEW GODS OF JAPAN...›
‹...AND WE'RE GOING TO WIPE YOU OUT.›
‹CITIZENS OF TOKYO ARE ADVISED TO STAY IN THEIR HOMES UNTIL POLICE CAN CONFIRM THAT THE STREETS ARE SAFE AND SECURE.›
‹IS THIS SOME KIND OF TERRORIST STRIKE AGAINST JAPAN?›
HEAD PAGE
JHK
BITZ RAIN
目撃者
59才)
‹THERE WERE TENGU! WINGED TENGU MONSTERS!›
‹I SAW THEM! WE ALL SAW THEM!›
JHK
週刊
SLURP
‹FUCKIN' CRAZY!›

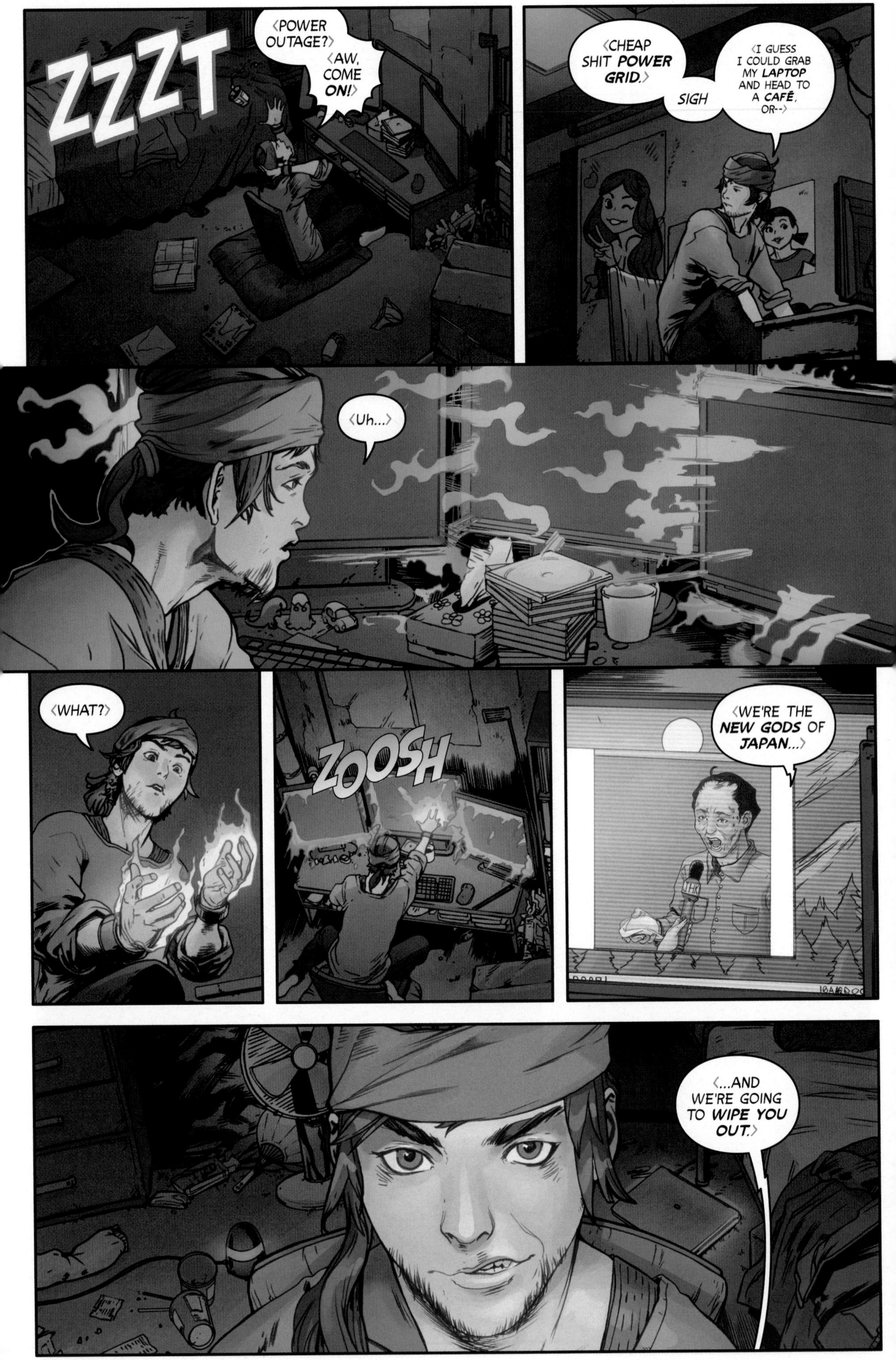
ZZZT
⟨POWER OUTAGE?⟩
⟨AW, COME ON!⟩
⟨CHEAP SHIT POWER GRID.⟩
SIGH
⟨I GUESS I COULD GRAB MY LAPTOP AND HEAD TO A CAFÉ, OR--⟩
⟨Uh...⟩
⟨WHAT?⟩
ZOOSH
⟨WE'RE THE NEW GODS OF JAPAN...⟩
⟨...AND WE'RE GOING TO WIPE YOU OUT.⟩

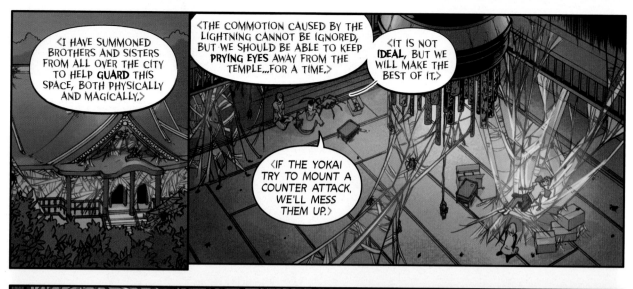

‹I HAVE SUMMONED BROTHERS AND SISTERS FROM ALL OVER THE CITY TO HELP **GUARD** THIS SPACE, BOTH PHYSICALLY AND MAGICALLY.›

‹THE COMMOTION CAUSED BY THE LIGHTNING CANNOT BE IGNORED, BUT WE SHOULD BE ABLE TO KEEP **PRYING EYES** AWAY FROM THE TEMPLE...FOR A TIME.›

‹IT IS NOT **IDEAL**, BUT WE WILL MAKE THE BEST OF IT.›

‹IF THE YOKAI TRY TO MOUNT A COUNTER ATTACK, WE'LL MESS THEM UP.›

‹OHARA, ARE YOU OKAY?›

‹I...I NEED TO SEE MY **FAMILY**, NIKAIDO, AT LEAST FOR A BIT.›

‹MOM AND DAD MUST BE WORRIED **SICK** ABOUT ME BY NOW.›

‹I DON'T WANT TO LEAVE YOU ALL HERE. THINGS ARE SO **BAD** AND I KNOW WE ALL HAVE TO--›

‹IT'S OKAY.›

‹WE ALL HAVE RESPONSIBILITIES. **FAMILY** IS ONE OF YOURS.›

‹GO AND COME BACK AS SOON AS YOU CAN.›

‹BETWEEN ME, AYANE, SHIRAI, AND THE TSUCHIGUMO WE'LL BE **ALRIGHT**.›

‹**THANK YOU**, NIKI.›

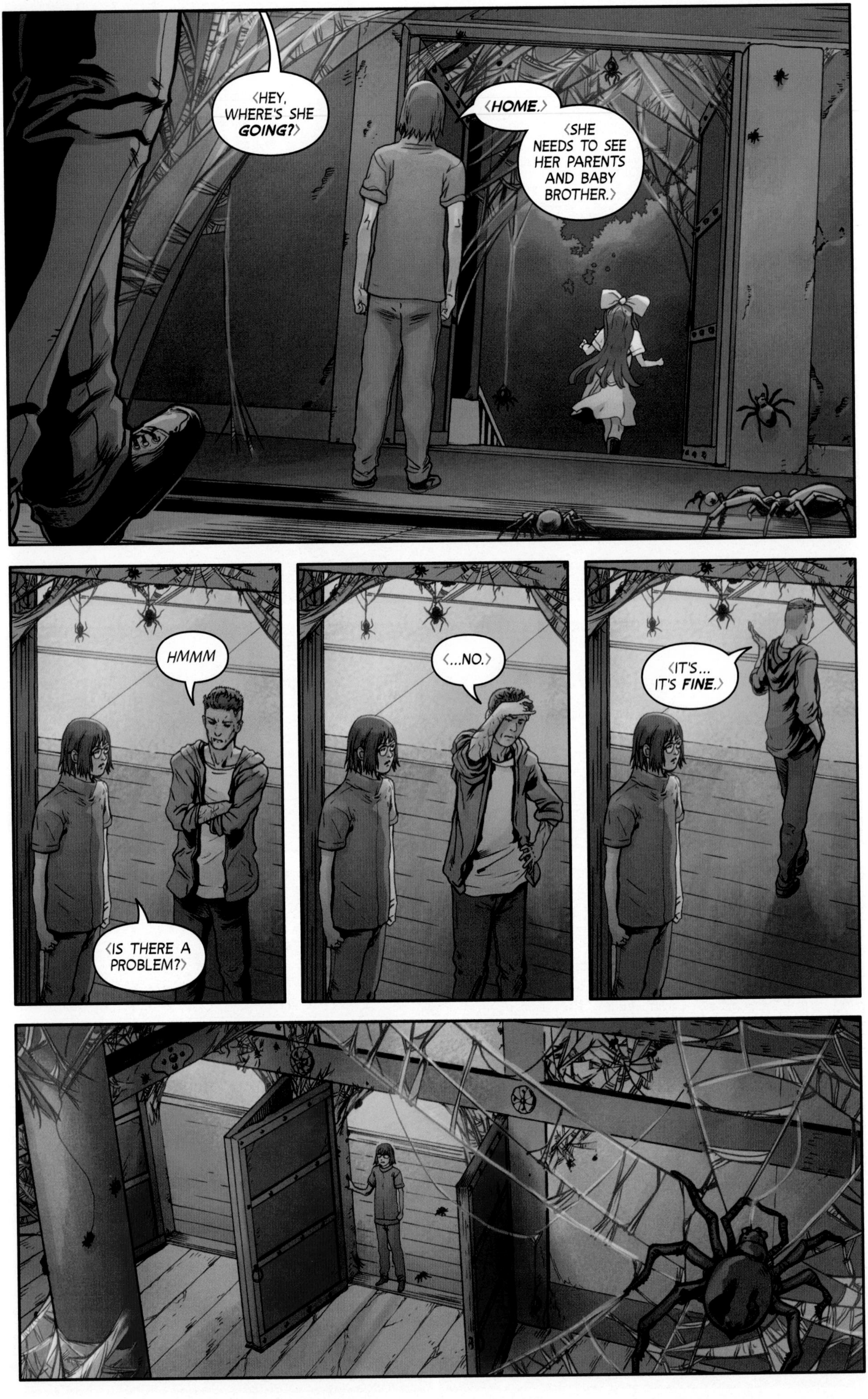

<HEY, WHERE'S SHE *GOING?*>
<***HOME.***>
<SHE NEEDS TO SEE HER PARENTS AND BABY BROTHER.>
HMMM
<IS THERE A PROBLEM?>
<...NO.>
<IT'S... IT'S ***FINE.***>

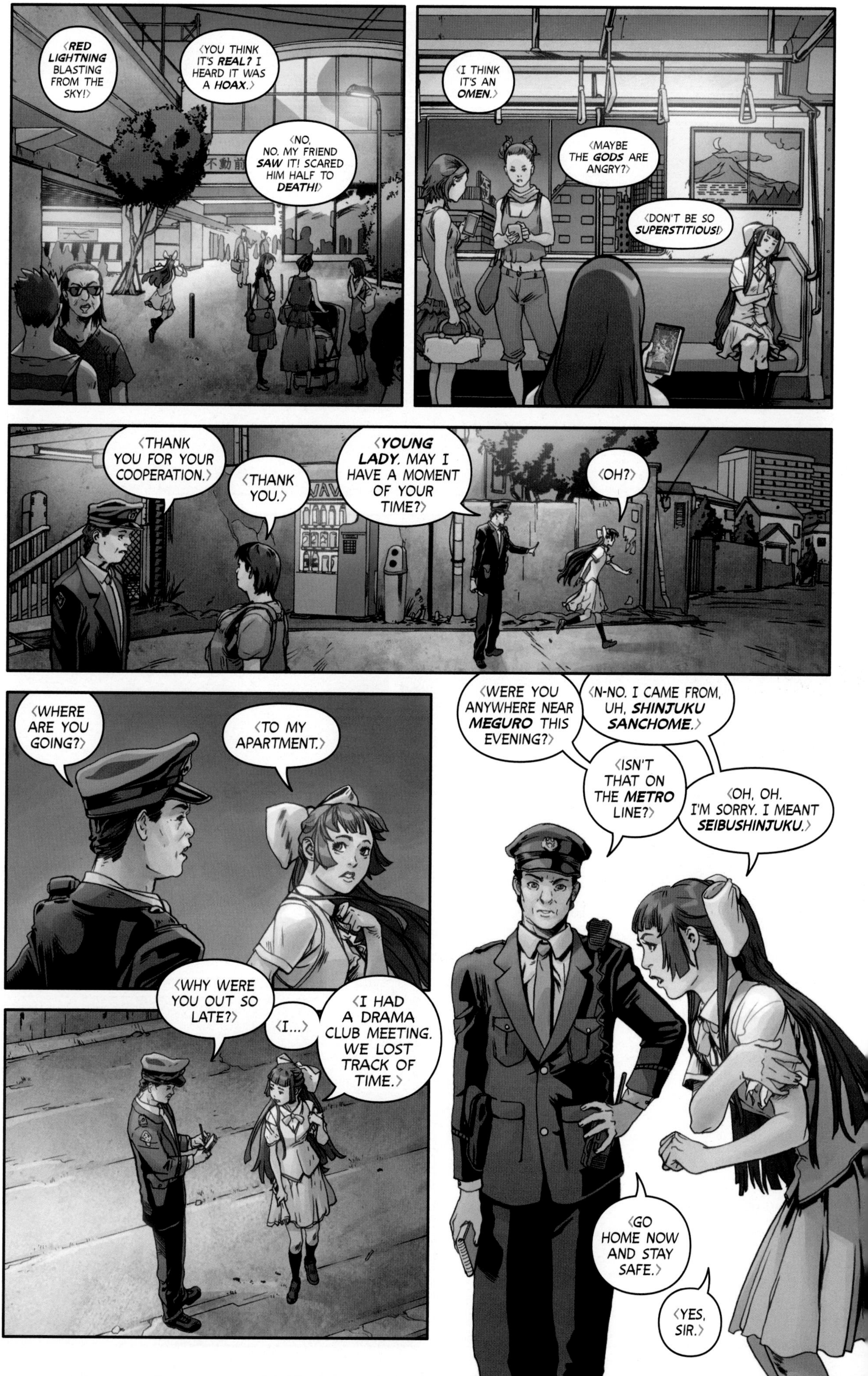
〈RED LIGHTNING BLASTING FROM THE SKY!〉
〈YOU THINK IT'S REAL? I HEARD IT WAS A HOAX.〉
不動前
〈NO, NO. MY FRIEND SAW IT! SCARED HIM HALF TO DEATH!〉
〈I THINK IT'S AN OMEN.〉
〈MAYBE THE GODS ARE ANGRY?〉
〈DON'T BE SO SUPERSTITIOUS!〉
〈THANK YOU FOR YOUR COOPERATION.〉
〈THANK YOU.〉
〈YOUNG LADY. MAY I HAVE A MOMENT OF YOUR TIME?〉
〈OH?〉
〈WHERE ARE YOU GOING?〉
〈TO MY APARTMENT.〉
〈WHY WERE YOU OUT SO LATE?〉
〈I...〉
〈I HAD A DRAMA CLUB MEETING. WE LOST TRACK OF TIME.〉
〈WERE YOU ANYWHERE NEAR MEGURO THIS EVENING?〉
〈N-NO. I CAME FROM, UH, SHINJUKU SANCHOME.〉
〈ISN'T THAT ON THE METRO LINE?〉
〈OH, OH. I'M SORRY. I MEANT SEIBUSHINJUKU.〉
〈GO HOME NOW AND STAY SAFE.〉
〈YES, SIR.〉

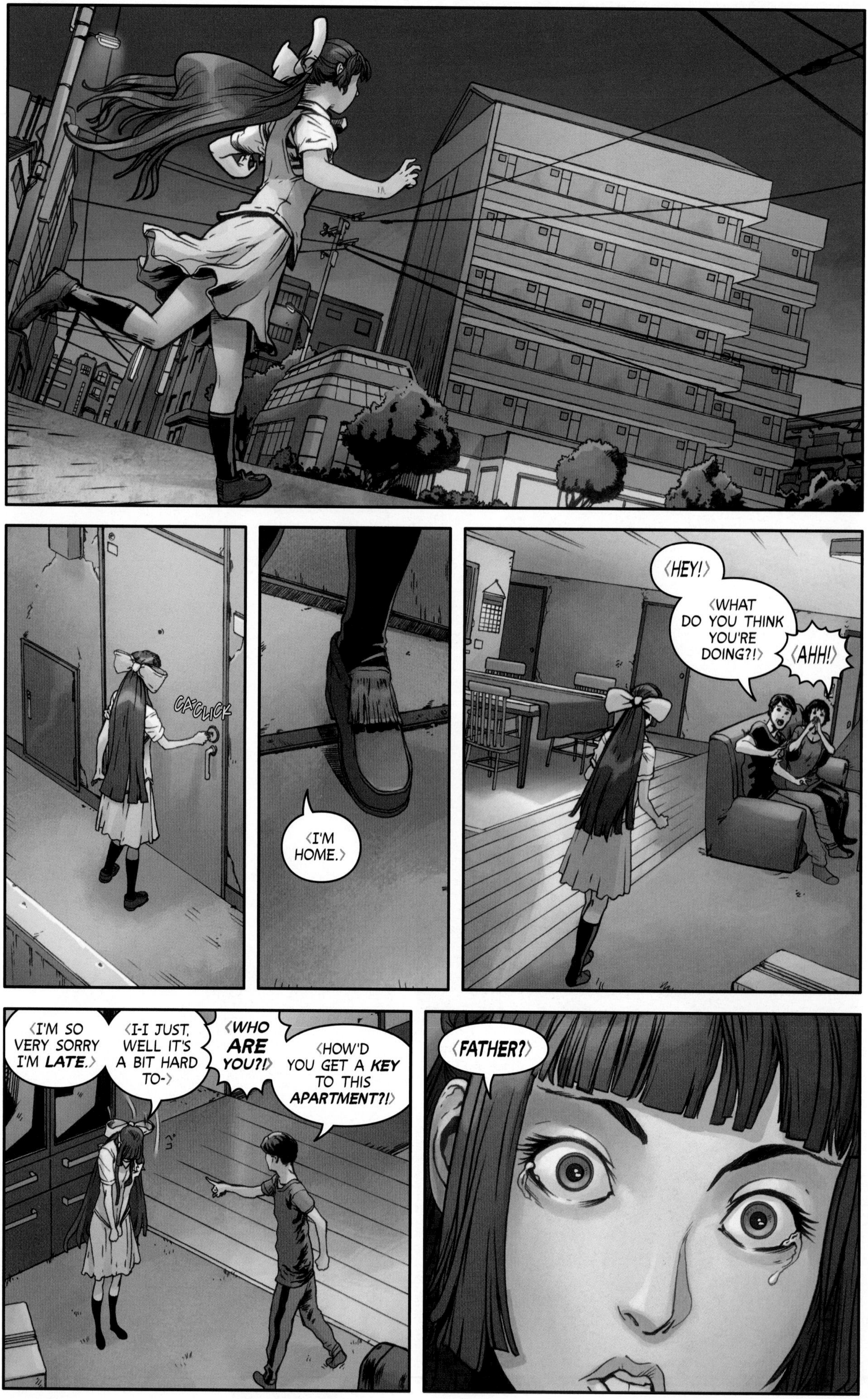
CA'CLICK
〈I'M HOME.〉
〈HEY!〉
〈WHAT DO YOU THINK YOU'RE DOING?!〉
〈AHH!〉
〈I'M SO VERY SORRY I'M LATE.〉
〈I-I JUST, WELL IT'S A BIT HARD TO-〉
〈WHO ARE YOU?!〉
〈HOW'D YOU GET A KEY TO THIS APARTMENT?!〉
〈FATHER?〉

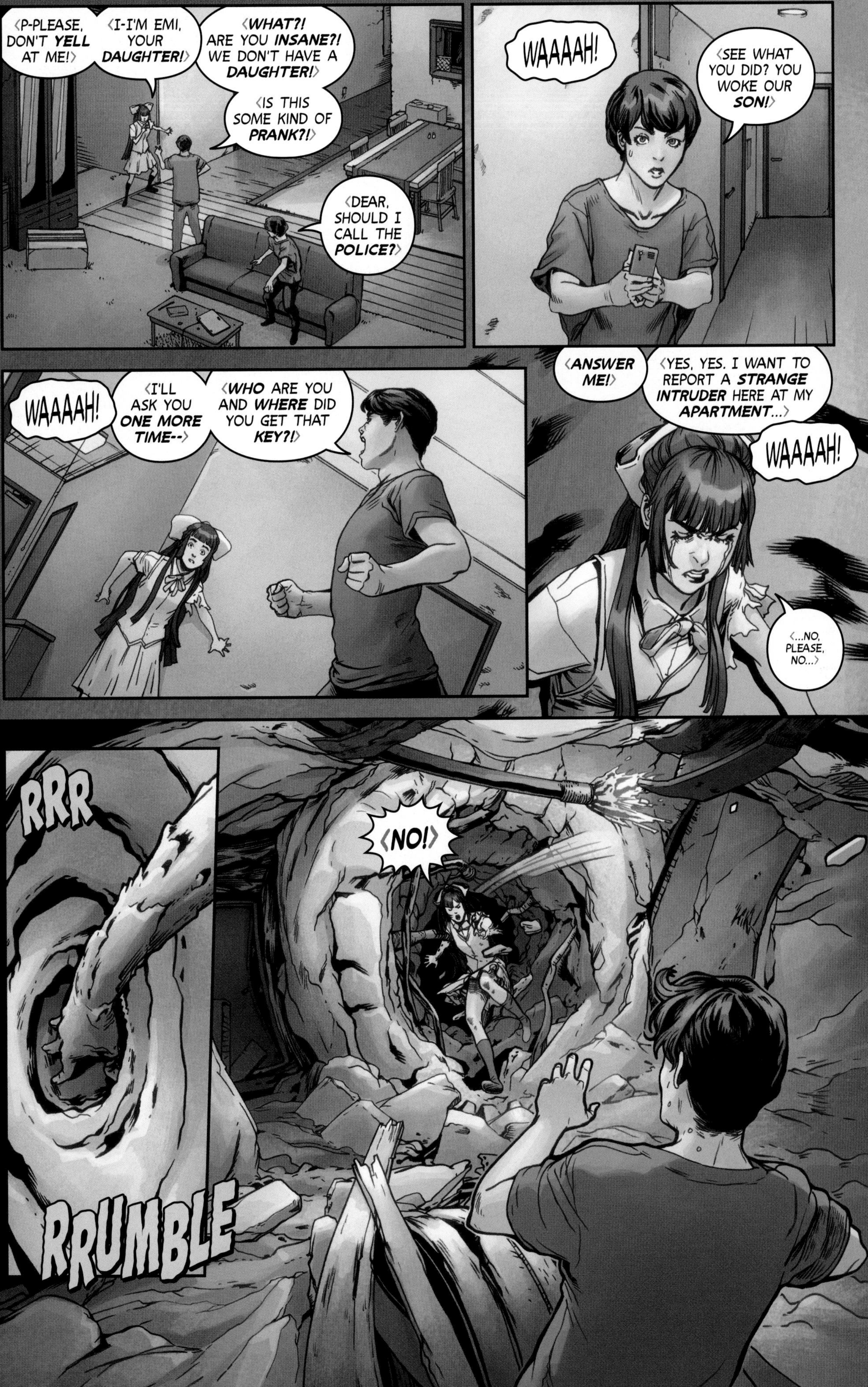

⟨P-PLEASE, DON'T YELL AT ME!⟩
⟨I-I'M EMI, YOUR DAUGHTER!⟩
⟨WHAT?! ARE YOU INSANE?! WE DON'T HAVE A DAUGHTER!⟩
⟨IS THIS SOME KIND OF PRANK?!⟩
⟨DEAR, SHOULD I CALL THE POLICE?⟩
WAAAAH!
⟨SEE WHAT YOU DID? YOU WOKE OUR SON!⟩
WAAAAH!
⟨I'LL ASK YOU ONE MORE TIME--⟩
⟨WHO ARE YOU AND WHERE DID YOU GET THAT KEY?!⟩
⟨ANSWER ME!⟩
⟨YES, YES. I WANT TO REPORT A STRANGE INTRUDER HERE AT MY APARTMENT...⟩
WAAAAH!
⟨...NO, PLEASE, NO...⟩
RRR
⟨NO!⟩
RRUMBLE

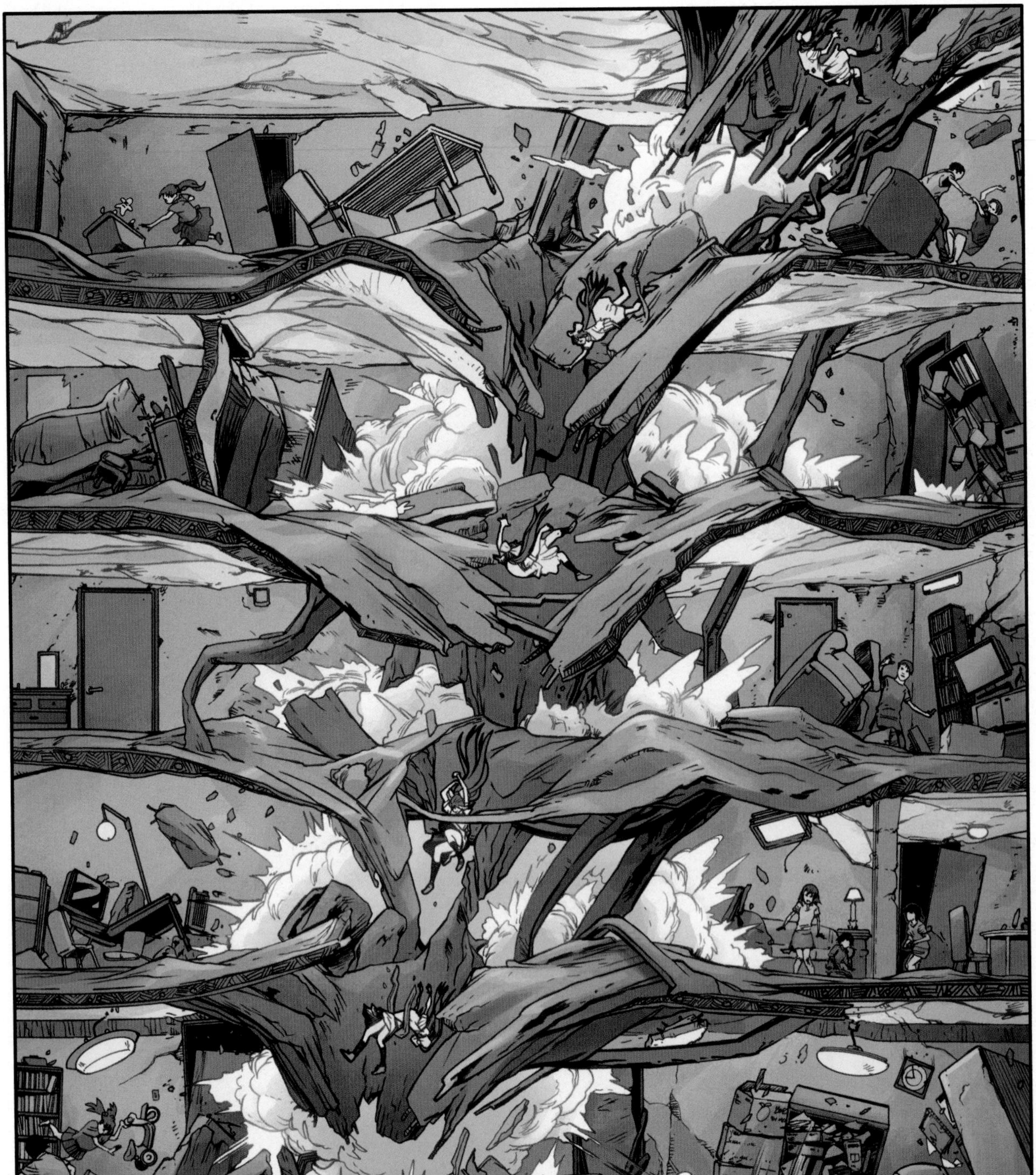

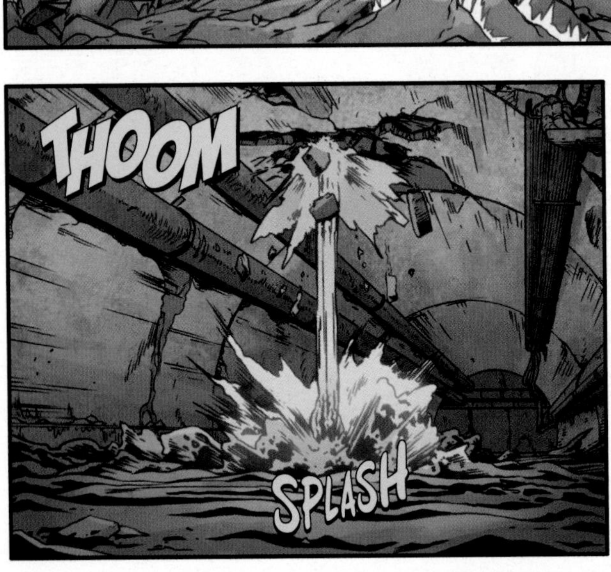
THOOM
SPLASH

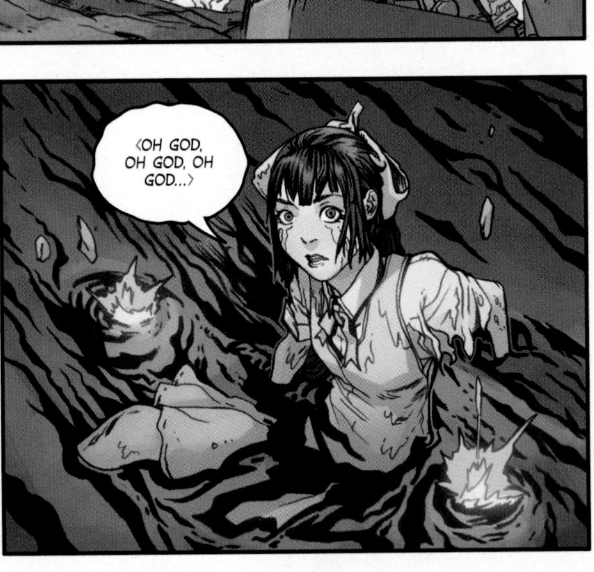
‹OH GOD, OH GOD, OH GOD...›

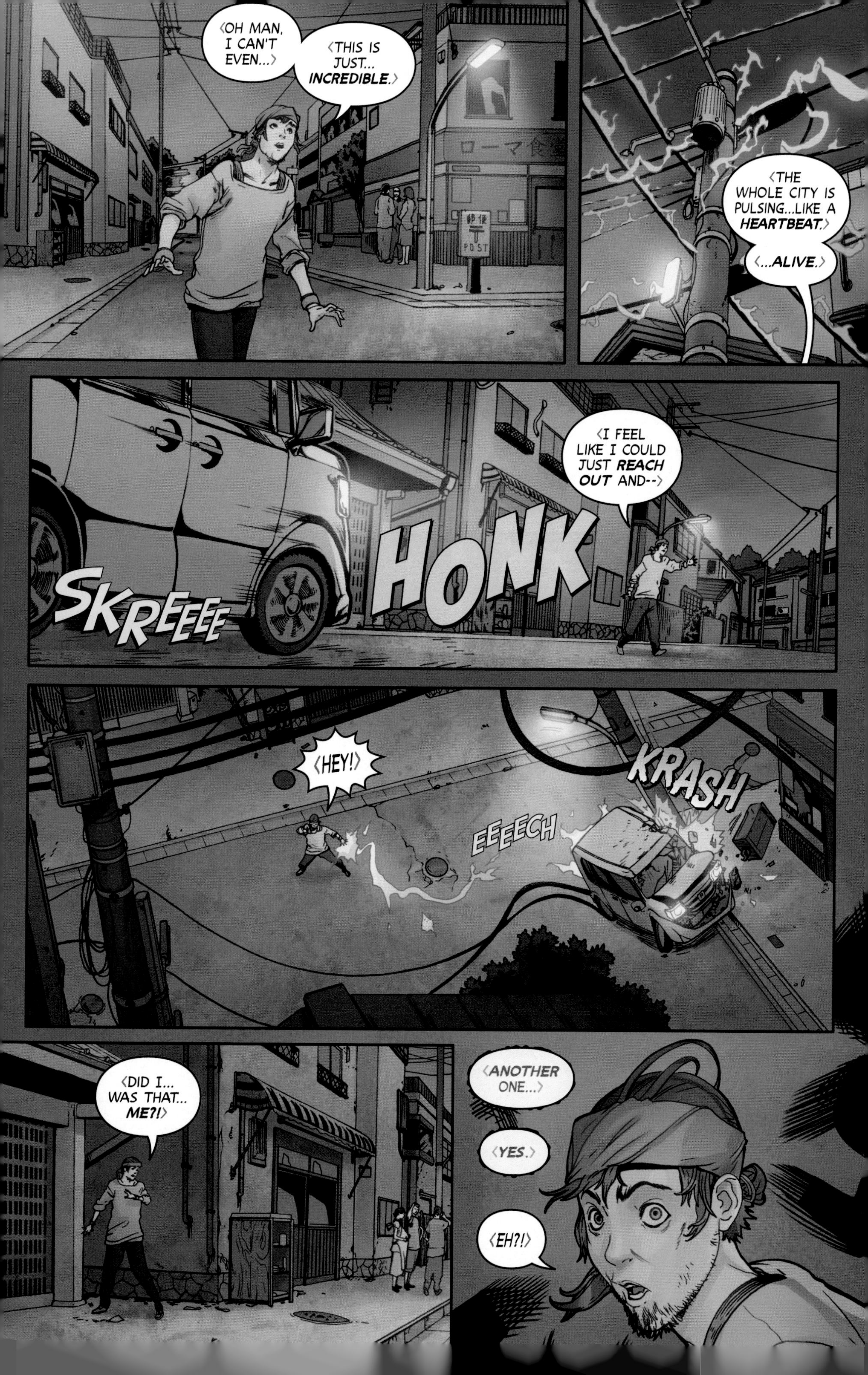

‹OH MAN, I CAN'T EVEN...›
‹THIS IS JUST... INCREDIBLE.›
‹THE WHOLE CITY IS PULSING...LIKE A HEARTBEAT.›
‹...ALIVE.›
‹I FEEL LIKE I COULD JUST REACH OUT AND--›
SKREEEEE
HONK
‹HEY!›
EEEECH
KRASH
‹DID I... WAS THAT... ME?!›
‹ANOTHER ONE...›
‹YES.›
‹EH?!›

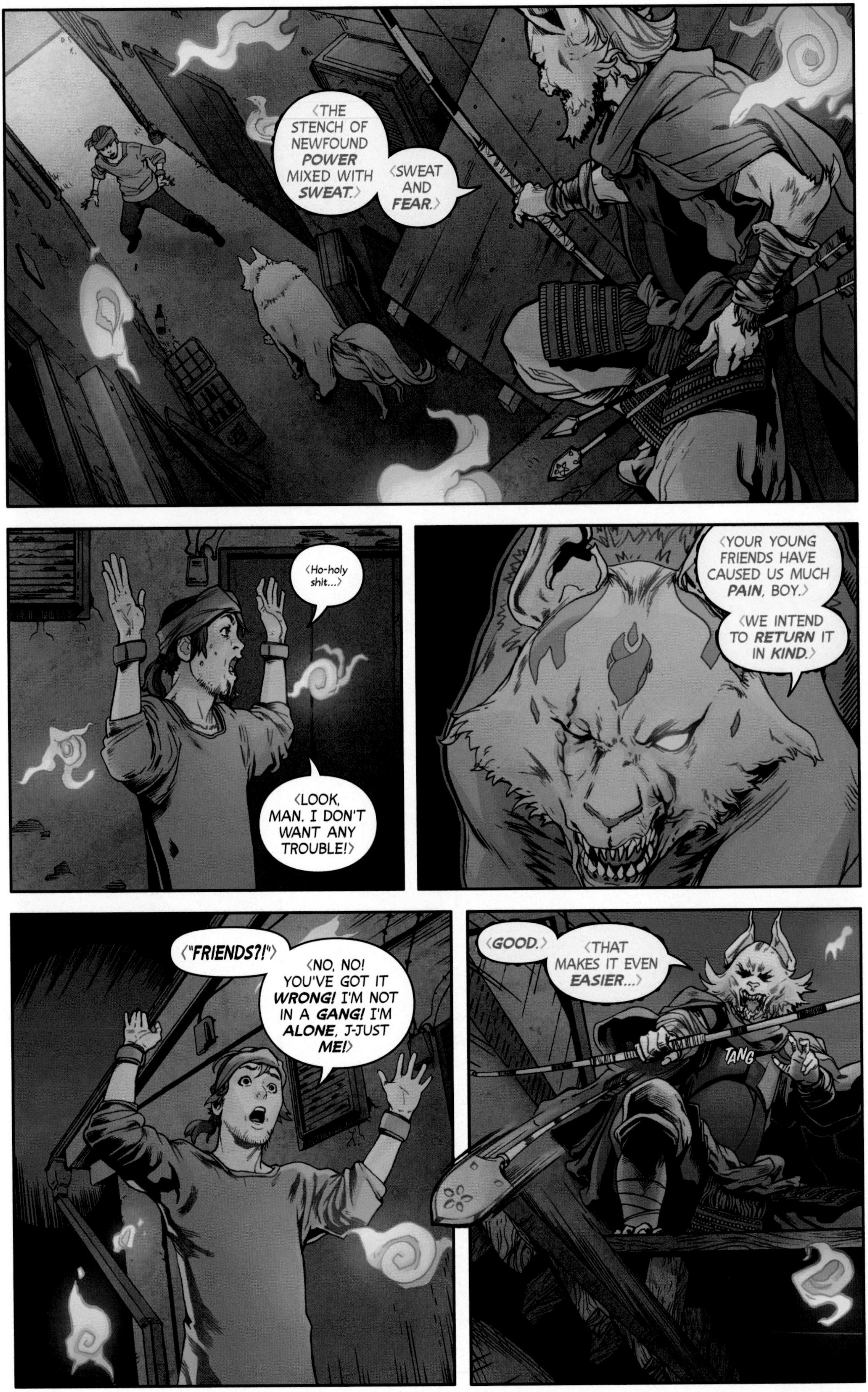
⟨THE STENCH OF NEWFOUND POWER MIXED WITH SWEAT.⟩
⟨SWEAT AND FEAR.⟩
⟨Ho-holy shit...⟩
⟨LOOK, MAN. I DON'T WANT ANY TROUBLE!⟩
⟨YOUR YOUNG FRIENDS HAVE CAUSED US MUCH PAIN, BOY.⟩
⟨WE INTEND TO RETURN IT IN KIND.⟩
⟨"FRIENDS?!"⟩
⟨NO, NO! YOU'VE GOT IT WRONG! I'M NOT IN A GANG! I'M ALONE, J-JUST ME!⟩
⟨GOOD.⟩
⟨THAT MAKES IT EVEN EASIER...⟩
TANG

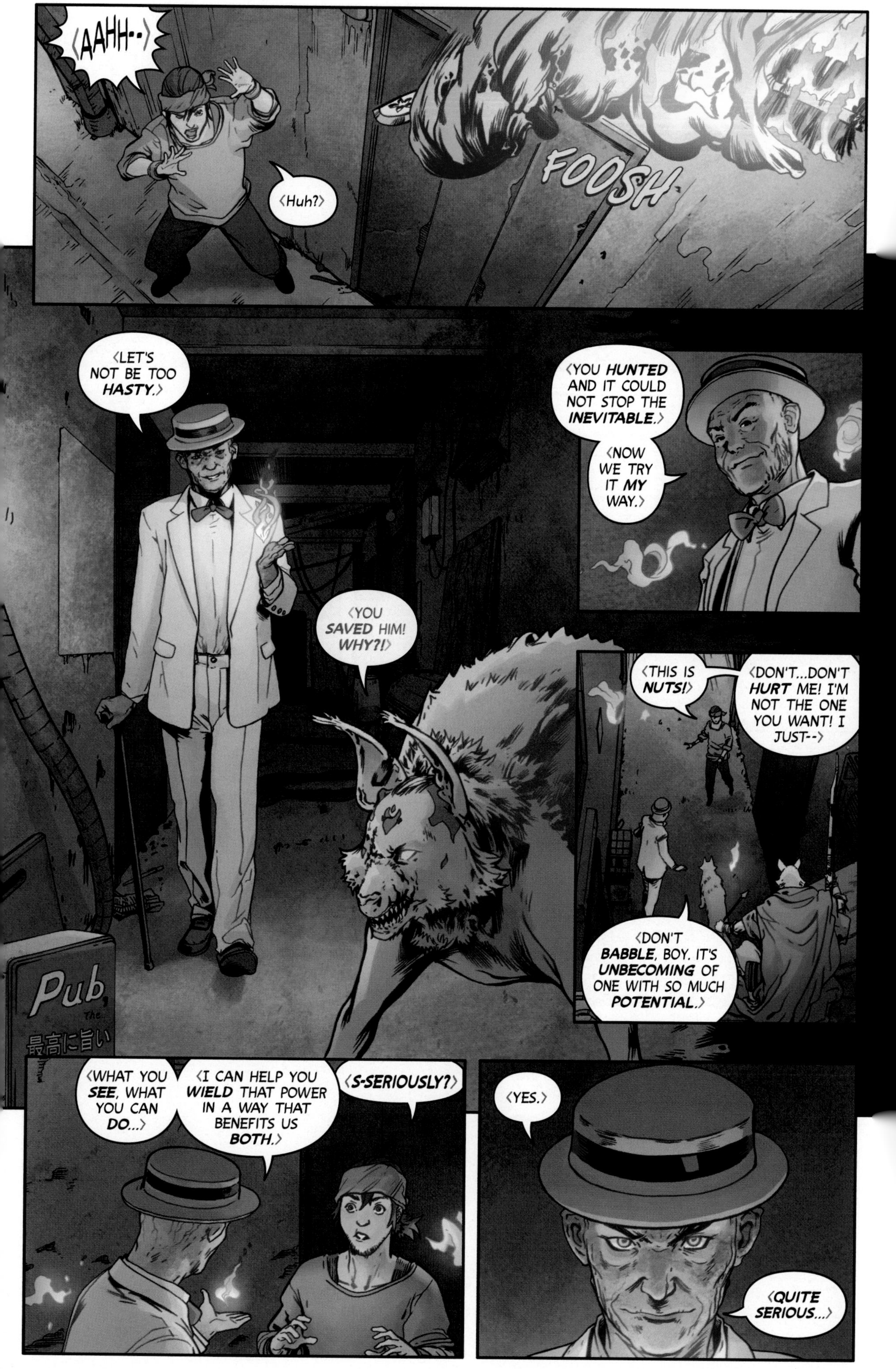
⟨AAHH--⟩
⟨Huh?⟩
FOOSH
⟨LET'S NOT BE TOO HASTY.⟩
⟨YOU SAVED HIM! WHY?!⟩
⟨YOU HUNTED AND IT COULD NOT STOP THE INEVITABLE.⟩
⟨NOW WE TRY IT MY WAY.⟩
Pub
The
最高に旨い
⟨THIS IS NUTS!⟩
⟨DON'T...DON'T HURT ME! I'M NOT THE ONE YOU WANT! I JUST--⟩
⟨DON'T BABBLE, BOY. IT'S UNBECOMING OF ONE WITH SO MUCH POTENTIAL.⟩
⟨WHAT YOU SEE, WHAT YOU CAN DO...⟩
⟨I CAN HELP YOU WIELD THAT POWER IN A WAY THAT BENEFITS US BOTH.⟩
⟨S-SERIOUSLY?⟩
⟨YES.⟩
⟨QUITE SERIOUS...⟩

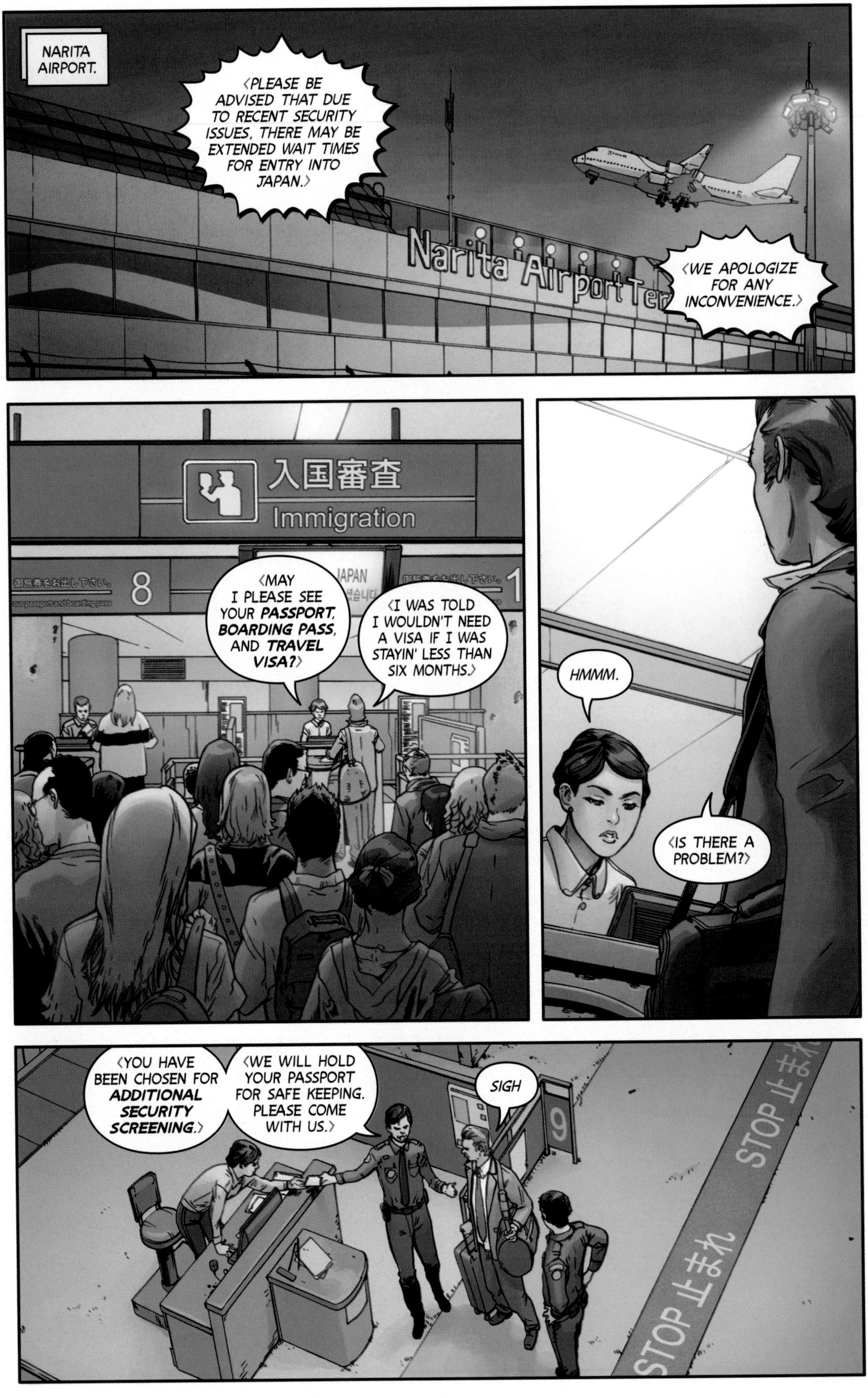
NARITA AIRPORT.
‹PLEASE BE ADVISED THAT DUE TO RECENT SECURITY ISSUES, THERE MAY BE EXTENDED WAIT TIMES FOR ENTRY INTO JAPAN.›
Narita Airport Ter
‹WE APOLOGIZE FOR ANY INCONVENIENCE.›
入国審査
Immigration
8
JAPAN
‹MAY I PLEASE SEE YOUR ***PASSPORT, BOARDING PASS***, AND ***TRAVEL VISA?***›
‹I WAS TOLD I WOULDN'T NEED A VISA IF I WAS STAYIN' LESS THAN SIX MONTHS.›
HMMM.
‹IS THERE A PROBLEM?›
‹YOU HAVE BEEN CHOSEN FOR ***ADDITIONAL SECURITY SCREENING***.›
‹WE WILL HOLD YOUR PASSPORT FOR SAFE KEEPING. PLEASE COME WITH US.›
SIGH
9
STOP 止まれ
STOP 止まれ

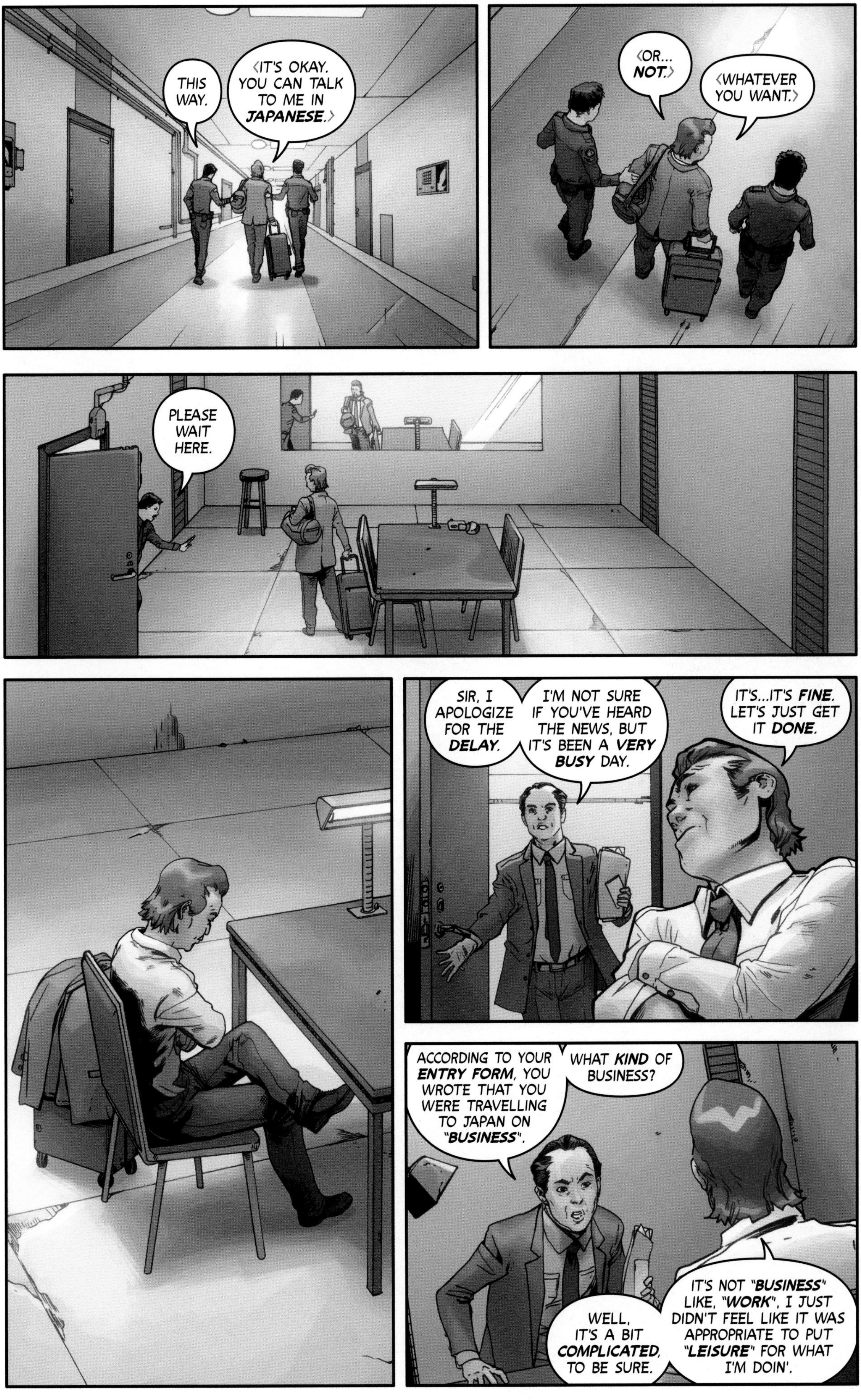
THIS WAY.
‹IT'S OKAY. YOU CAN TALK TO ME IN JAPANESE.›
‹OR... NOT.›
‹WHATEVER YOU WANT.›
PLEASE WAIT HERE.
SIR, I APOLOGIZE FOR THE DELAY.
I'M NOT SURE IF YOU'VE HEARD THE NEWS, BUT IT'S BEEN A VERY BUSY DAY.
IT'S...IT'S FINE. LET'S JUST GET IT DONE.
ACCORDING TO YOUR ENTRY FORM, YOU WROTE THAT YOU WERE TRAVELLING TO JAPAN ON "BUSINESS".
WHAT KIND OF BUSINESS?
WELL, IT'S A BIT COMPLICATED, TO BE SURE.
IT'S NOT "BUSINESS" LIKE, "WORK", I JUST DIDN'T FEEL LIKE IT WAS APPROPRIATE TO PUT "LEISURE" FOR WHAT I'M DOIN'.

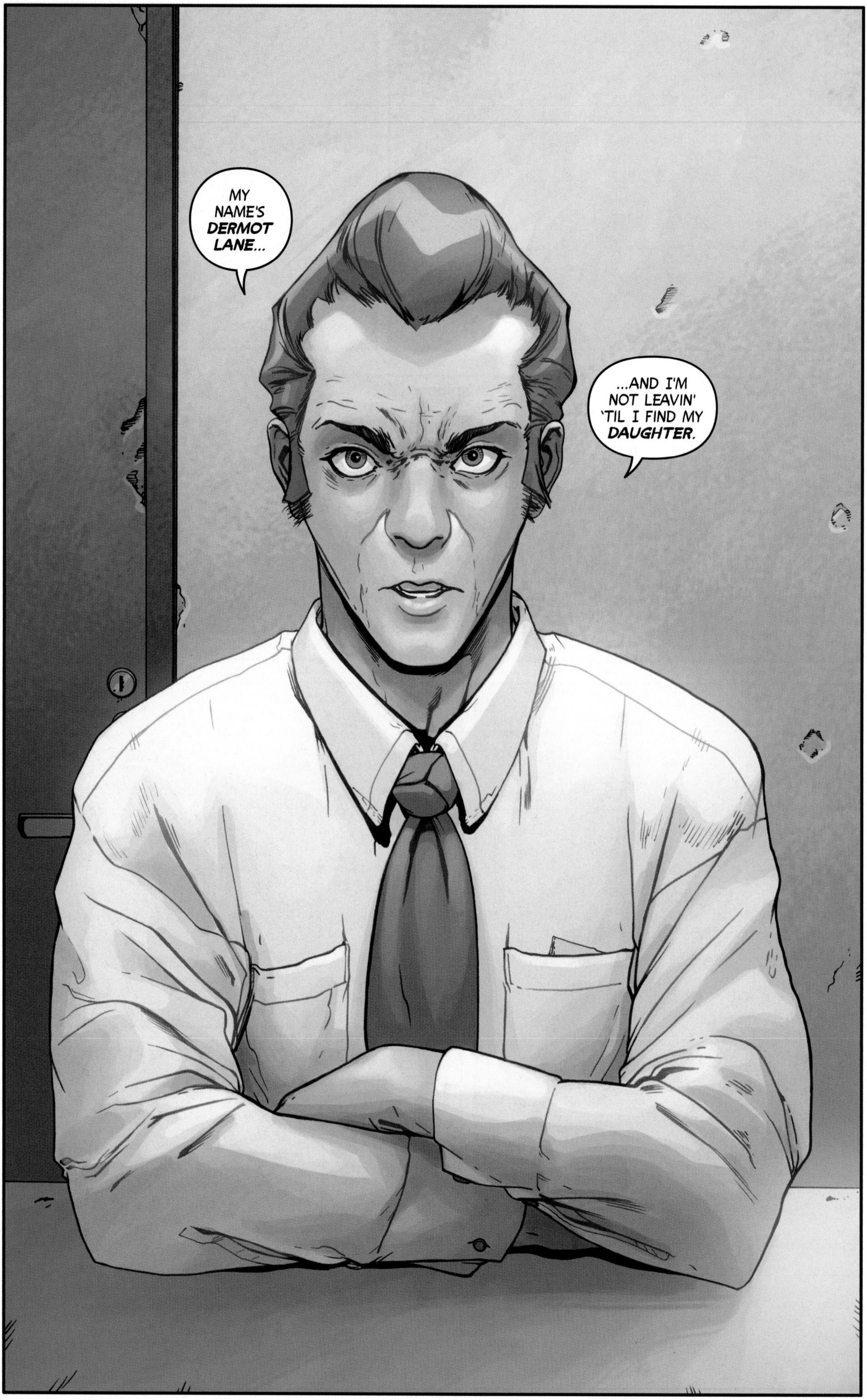
MY NAME'S **DERMOT LANE...**
...AND I'M NOT LEAVIN' 'TIL I FIND MY ***DAUGHTER.***

Chapter Twelve

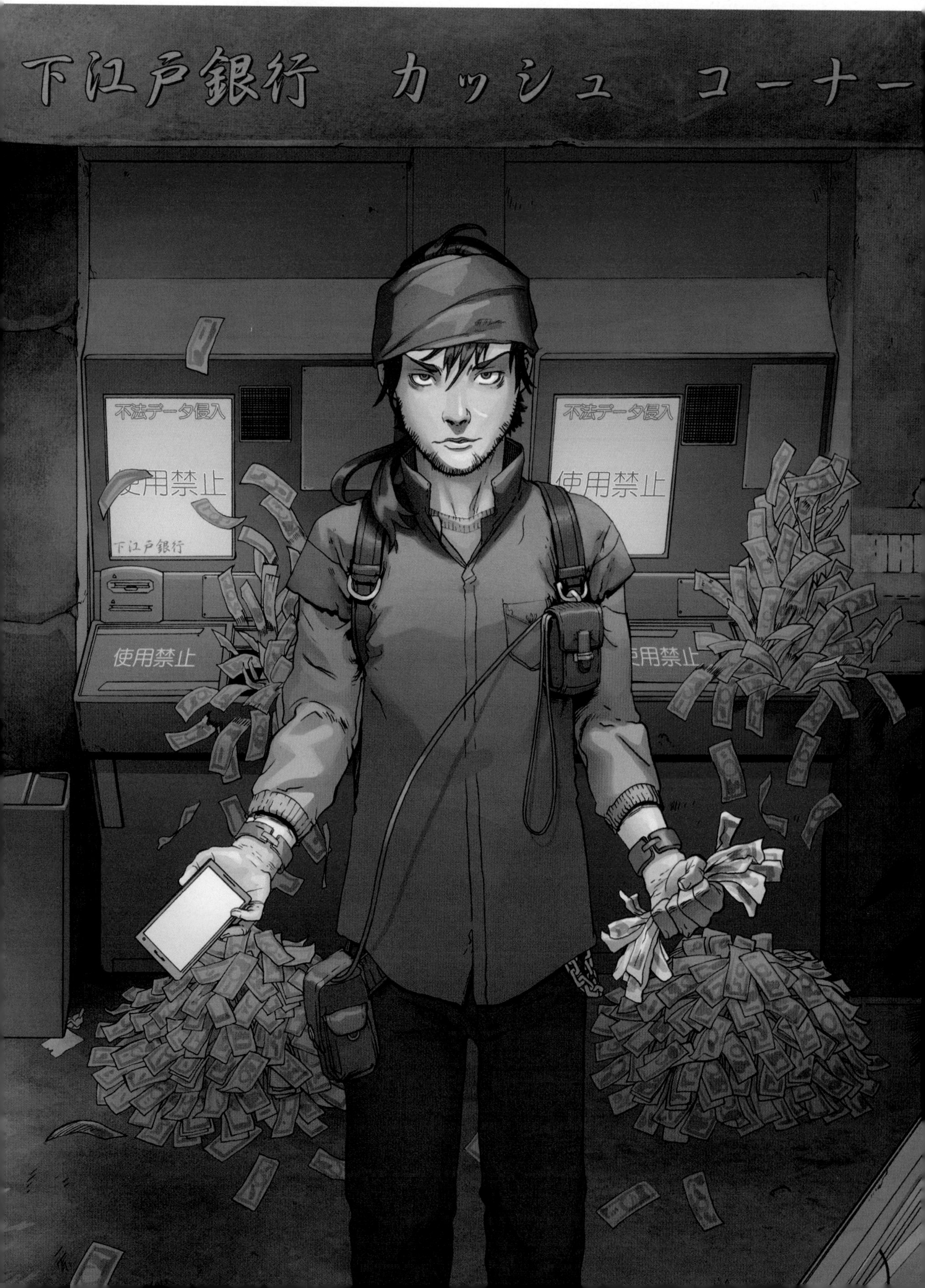
下江戸銀行　カッシュ　コーナー
不法データ侵入
使用禁止
下江戸銀行
使用禁止
不法データ侵入
使用禁止
用禁止

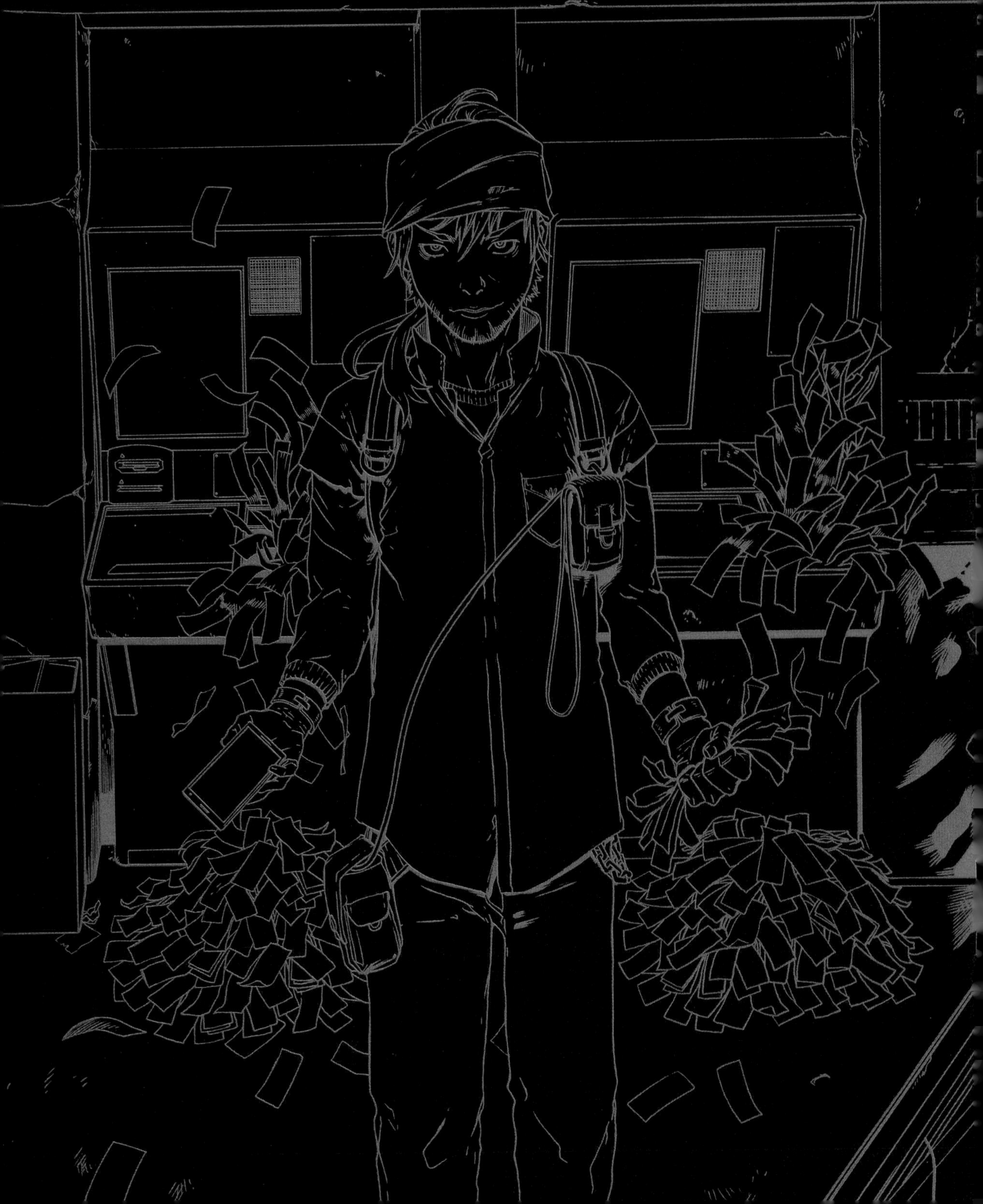

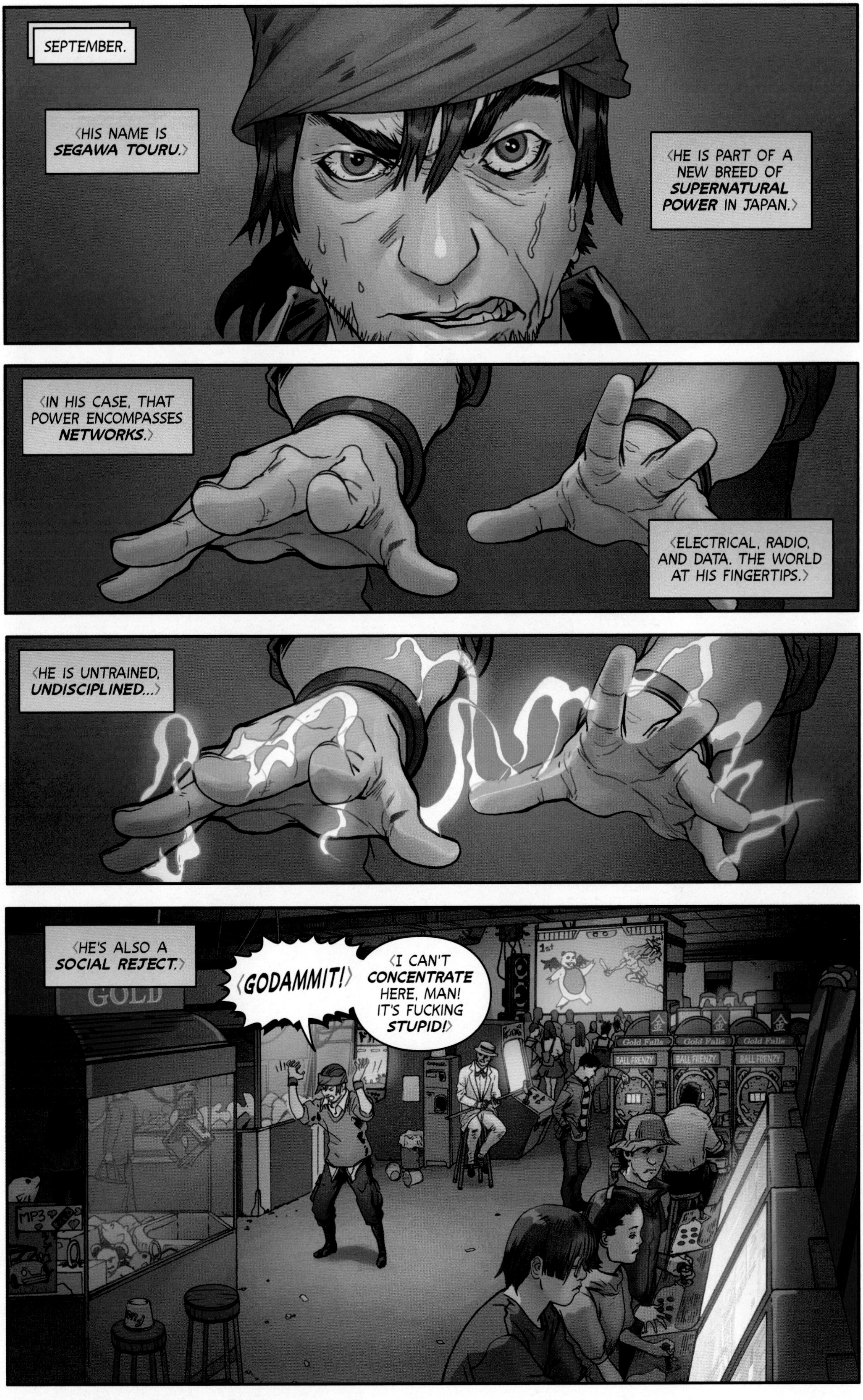
SEPTEMBER.
‹HIS NAME IS SEGAWA TOURU.›
‹HE IS PART OF A NEW BREED OF SUPERNATURAL POWER IN JAPAN.›
‹IN HIS CASE, THAT POWER ENCOMPASSES NETWORKS.›
‹ELECTRICAL, RADIO, AND DATA. THE WORLD AT HIS FINGERTIPS.›
‹HE IS UNTRAINED, UNDISCIPLINED...›
‹HE'S ALSO A SOCIAL REJECT.›
‹GODAMMIT!›
‹I CAN'T CONCENTRATE HERE, MAN! IT'S FUCKING STUPID!›
GOLD
1st
Gold Falls
Gold Falls
Gold Falls
BALL FRENZY
BALL FRENZY
BALL FRENZY
MP3

⟨I'D KILL THE LITTLE BASTARD IN AN *INSTANT* IF HE WASN'T SO *VALUABLE* TO MY CAUSE.⟩

⟨*DESPERATION* CREATES STRANGE BEDFELLOWS...⟩

⟨IT'S TOO MUCH *PRESSURE*...⟩

⟨YOU WILL NOT HAVE THE BENEFIT OF *QUIET CONTEMPLATION* IN THIS LIFE OR THE NEXT.⟩

⟨YOU MUST FIND THE *WILL* TO ENACT YOUR ABILITIES *DESPITE* THESE *DISTRACTIONS*.⟩

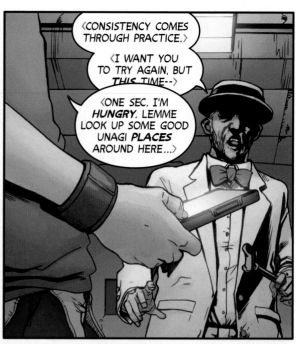

⟨CONSISTENCY COMES THROUGH PRACTICE.⟩

⟨I WANT YOU TO TRY AGAIN, BUT *THIS* TIME--⟩

⟨ONE SEC. I'M *HUNGRY*. LEMME LOOK UP SOME GOOD UNAGI *PLACES* AROUND HERE...⟩

⟨"HUNGRY?!"⟩

⟨HUNGER FOR POWER, NOT *SUSTENANCE*!⟩

⟨WE MUST FIND THE TRIGGER WITHIN YOU, THE--⟩

KRESH

⟨WHAT THE *FUCK?!*⟩

⟨YOU *BROKE* MY *PHONE!*⟩

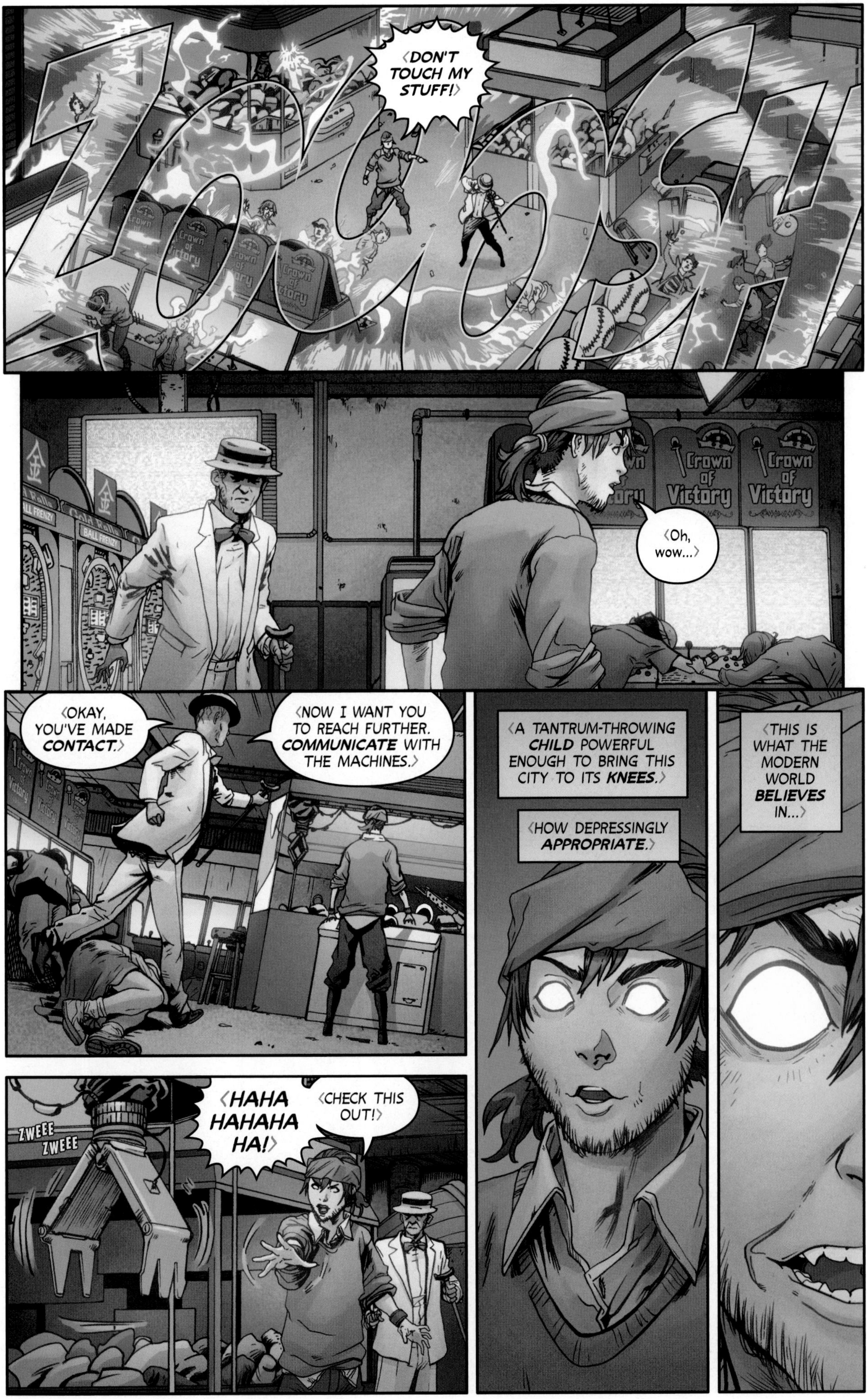
ZOOOOSH
‹DON'T TOUCH MY STUFF!›
Crown of Victory
‹Oh, wow...›
‹OKAY, YOU'VE MADE CONTACT.›
‹NOW I WANT YOU TO REACH FURTHER. COMMUNICATE WITH THE MACHINES.›
‹A TANTRUM-THROWING CHILD POWERFUL ENOUGH TO BRING THIS CITY TO ITS KNEES.›
‹HOW DEPRESSINGLY APPROPRIATE.›
‹THIS IS WHAT THE MODERN WORLD BELIEVES IN...›
ZWEEE ZWEEE
‹HAHA HAHAHA HA!›
‹CHECK THIS OUT!›

<...THESE ARE THEIR GODS OF *YOUTH* AND *MADNESS.*>

UNHHHHH!

<RORI'S *AWAKE!*>

<RORI, IT'S ME, *AYANE!*>

<DO YOU *HEAR* ME? I'M RIGHT *HERE!*>

<HER BODY IS PRESENT BUT HER MIND IS STILL *LOST* IN THE *WEAVE.* SHE CANNOT SEE OR HEAR US.>

AHHHH!

<WHAT... WHAT'S SHE DOING?!>

<YOU HAVE TO *HELP* HER!>

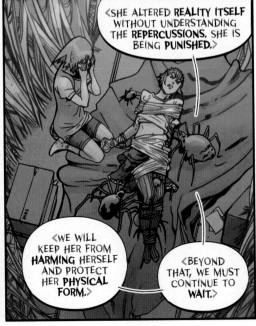

<SHE ALTERED *REALITY* ITSELF WITHOUT UNDERSTANDING THE *REPERCUSSIONS.* SHE IS BEING *PUNISHED.*>

<WE WILL KEEP HER FROM *HARMING* HERSELF AND PROTECT HER *PHYSICAL FORM.*>

<BEYOND THAT, WE MUST CONTINUE TO *WAIT.*>

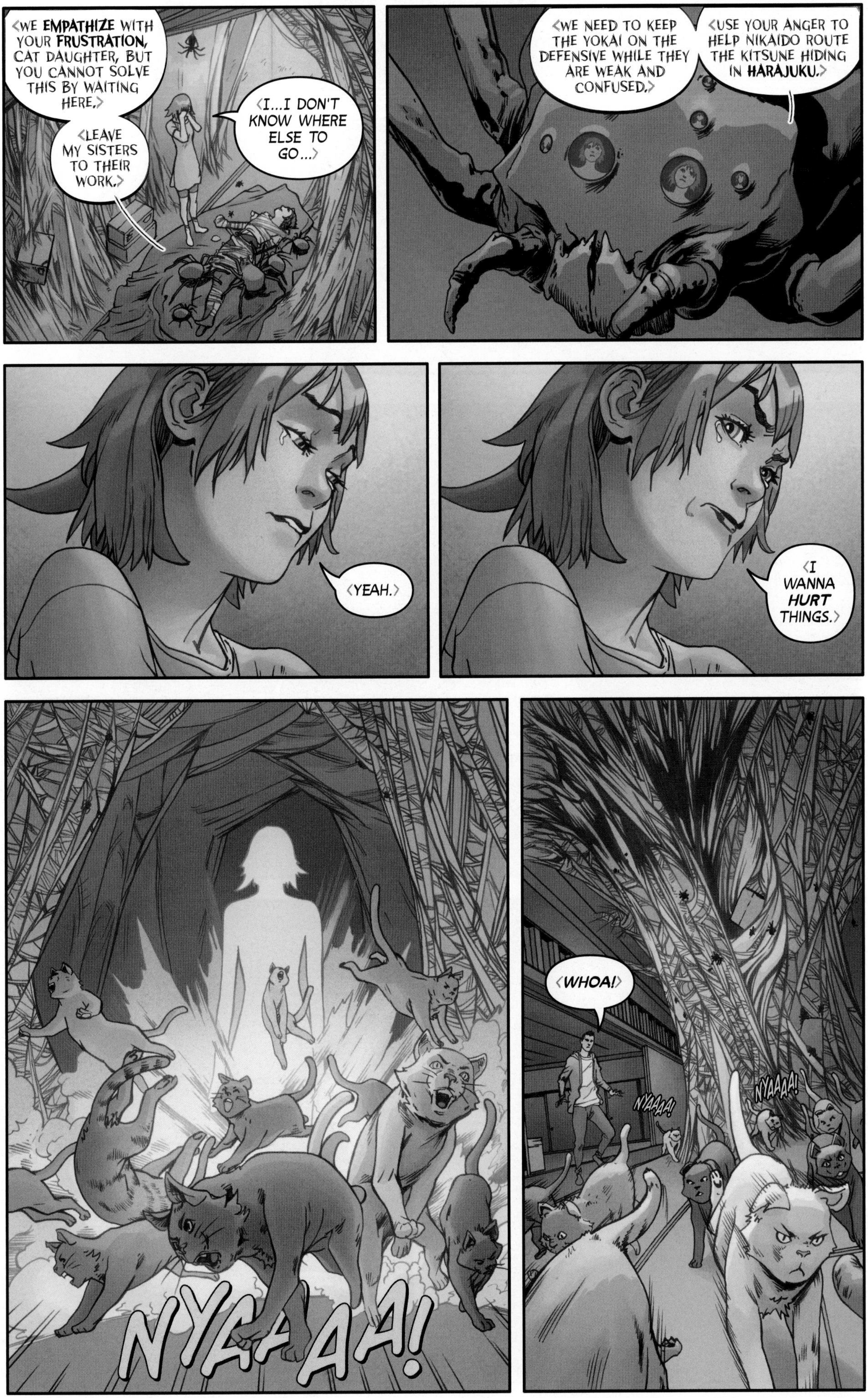
<WE EMPATHIZE WITH YOUR FRUSTRATION, CAT DAUGHTER, BUT YOU CANNOT SOLVE THIS BY WAITING HERE.>
<LEAVE MY SISTERS TO THEIR WORK.>
<I...I DON'T KNOW WHERE ELSE TO GO...>
<WE NEED TO KEEP THE YOKAI ON THE DEFENSIVE WHILE THEY ARE WEAK AND CONFUSED.>
<USE YOUR ANGER TO HELP NIKAIDO ROUTE THE KITSUNE HIDING IN HARAJUKU.>
<YEAH.>
<I WANNA HURT THINGS.>
NYAAAA!
<WHOA!>
NYAAAA!
NYAAAA!

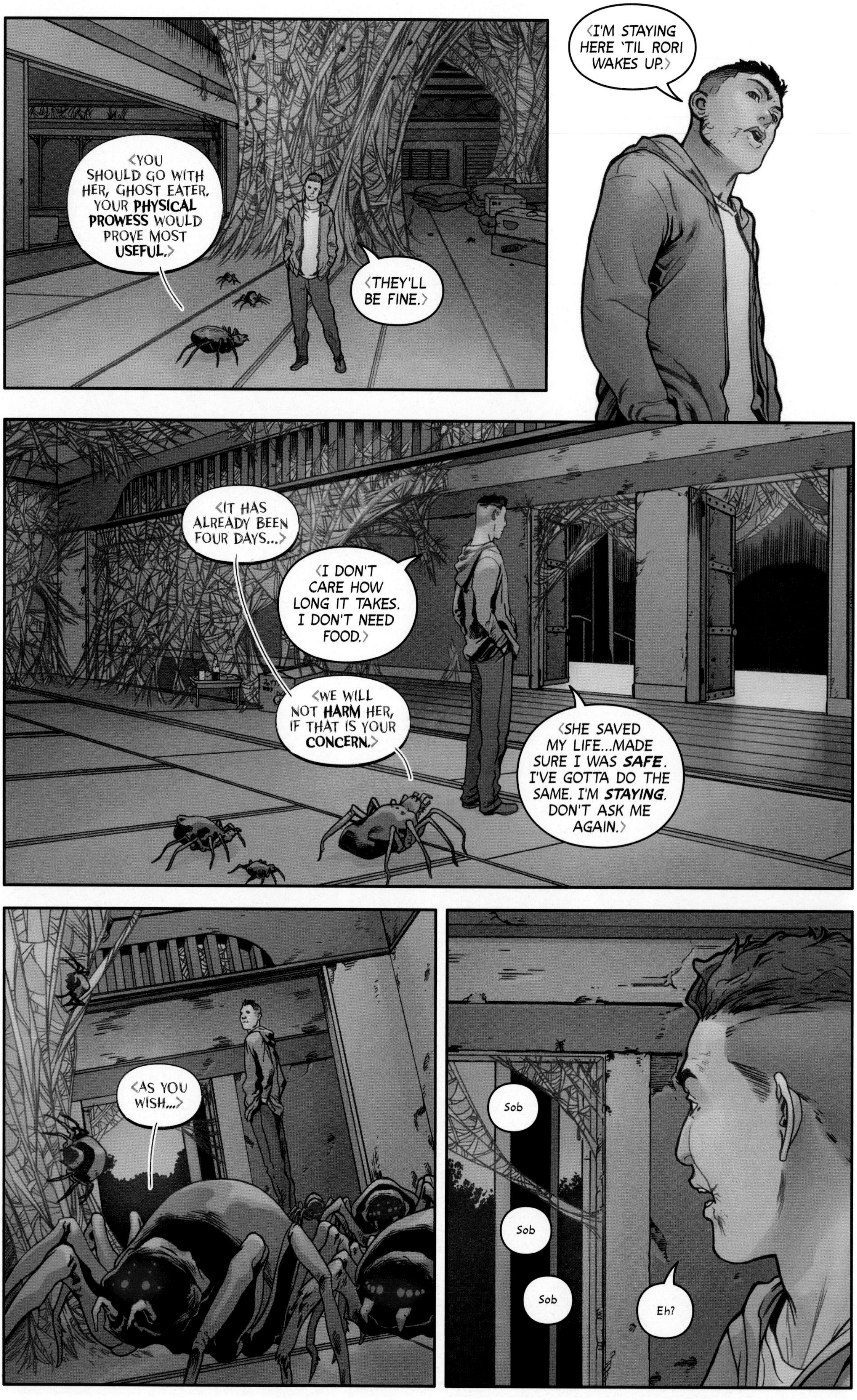
<YOU SHOULD GO WITH HER, GHOST EATER. YOUR **PHYSICAL PROWESS** WOULD PROVE MOST **USEFUL**.>
<THEY'LL BE FINE.>
<I'M STAYING HERE 'TIL RORI WAKES UP.>
<IT HAS ALREADY BEEN FOUR DAYS...>
<I DON'T CARE HOW LONG IT TAKES. I DON'T NEED FOOD.>
<WE WILL NOT **HARM** HER, IF THAT IS YOUR **CONCERN**.>
<SHE SAVED MY LIFE...MADE SURE I WAS ***SAFE***. I'VE GOTTA DO THE SAME. I'M ***STAYING***. DON'T ASK ME AGAIN.>
<AS YOU WISH...>
Sob
Sob
Sob
Eh?

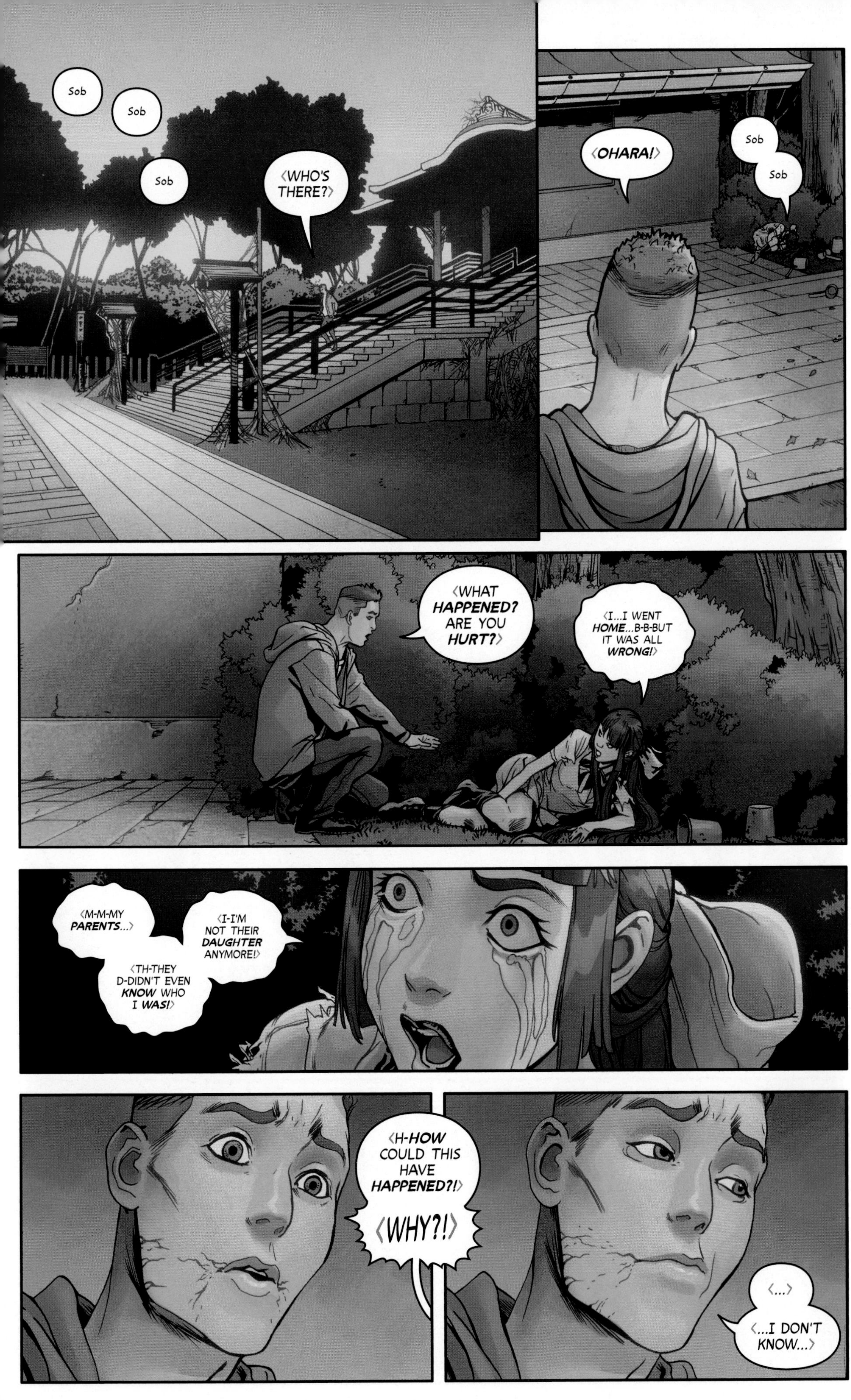
Sob
Sob
Sob
⟨WHO'S THERE?⟩
⟨OHARA!⟩
Sob
Sob
⟨WHAT HAPPENED? ARE YOU HURT?⟩
⟨I...I WENT HOME...B-B-BUT IT WAS ALL WRONG!⟩
⟨M-M-MY PARENTS...⟩
⟨TH-THEY D-DIDN'T EVEN KNOW WHO I WAS!⟩
⟨I-I'M NOT THEIR DAUGHTER ANYMORE!⟩
⟨H-HOW COULD THIS HAVE HAPPENED?!⟩
⟨WHY?!⟩
⟨...⟩
⟨...I DON'T KNOW...⟩

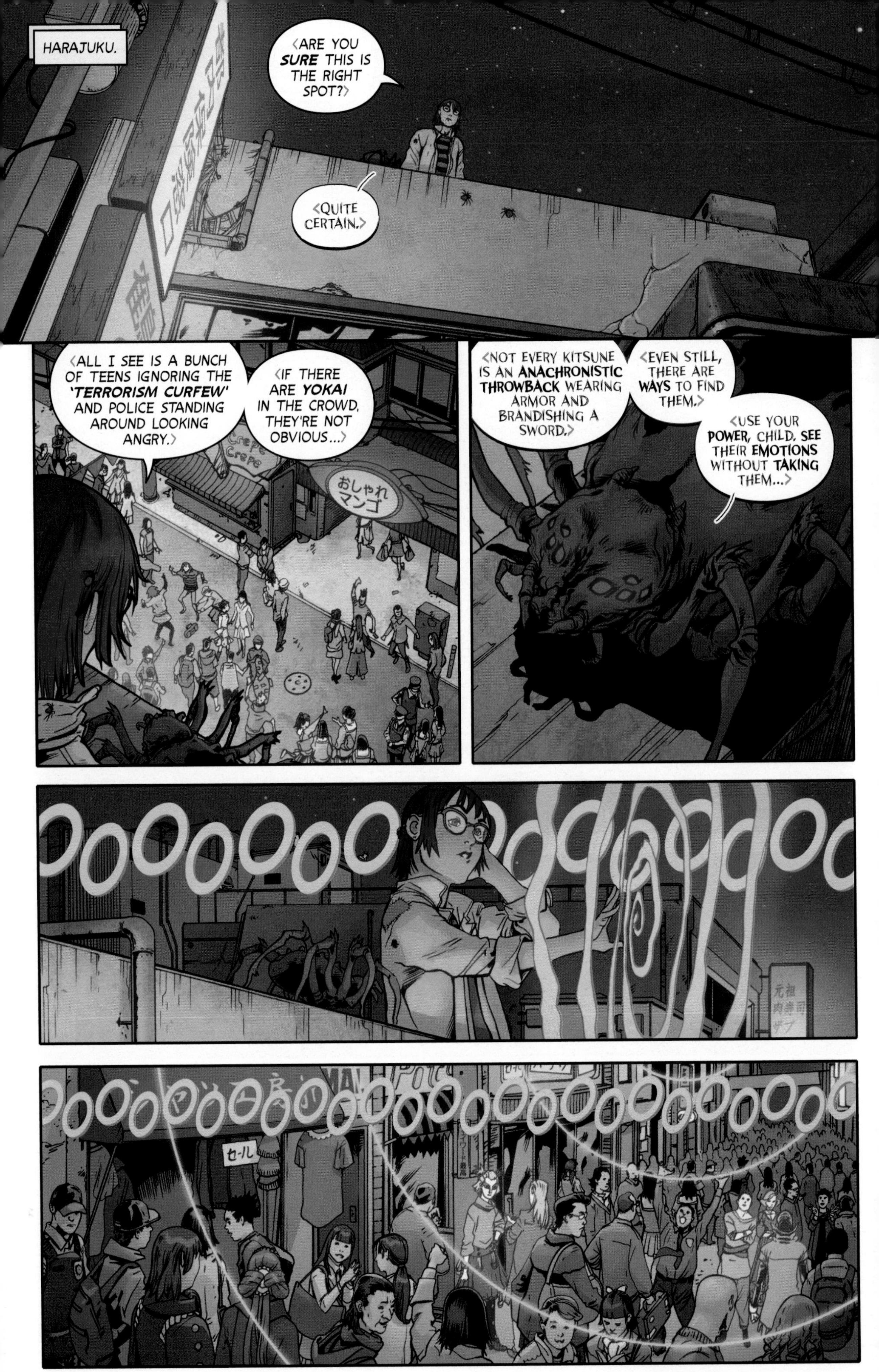
HARAJUKU.
‹ARE YOU SURE THIS IS THE RIGHT SPOT?›
‹QUITE CERTAIN.›
‹ALL I SEE IS A BUNCH OF TEENS IGNORING THE 'TERRORISM CURFEW' AND POLICE STANDING AROUND LOOKING ANGRY.›
‹IF THERE ARE YOKAI IN THE CROWD, THEY'RE NOT OBVIOUS...›
Crepe
おしゃれマンゴ
‹NOT EVERY KITSUNE IS AN ANACHRONISTIC THROWBACK WEARING ARMOR AND BRANDISHING A SWORD.›
‹EVEN STILL, THERE ARE WAYS TO FIND THEM.›
‹USE YOUR POWER, CHILD. SEE THEIR EMOTIONS WITHOUT TAKING THEM...›
セール

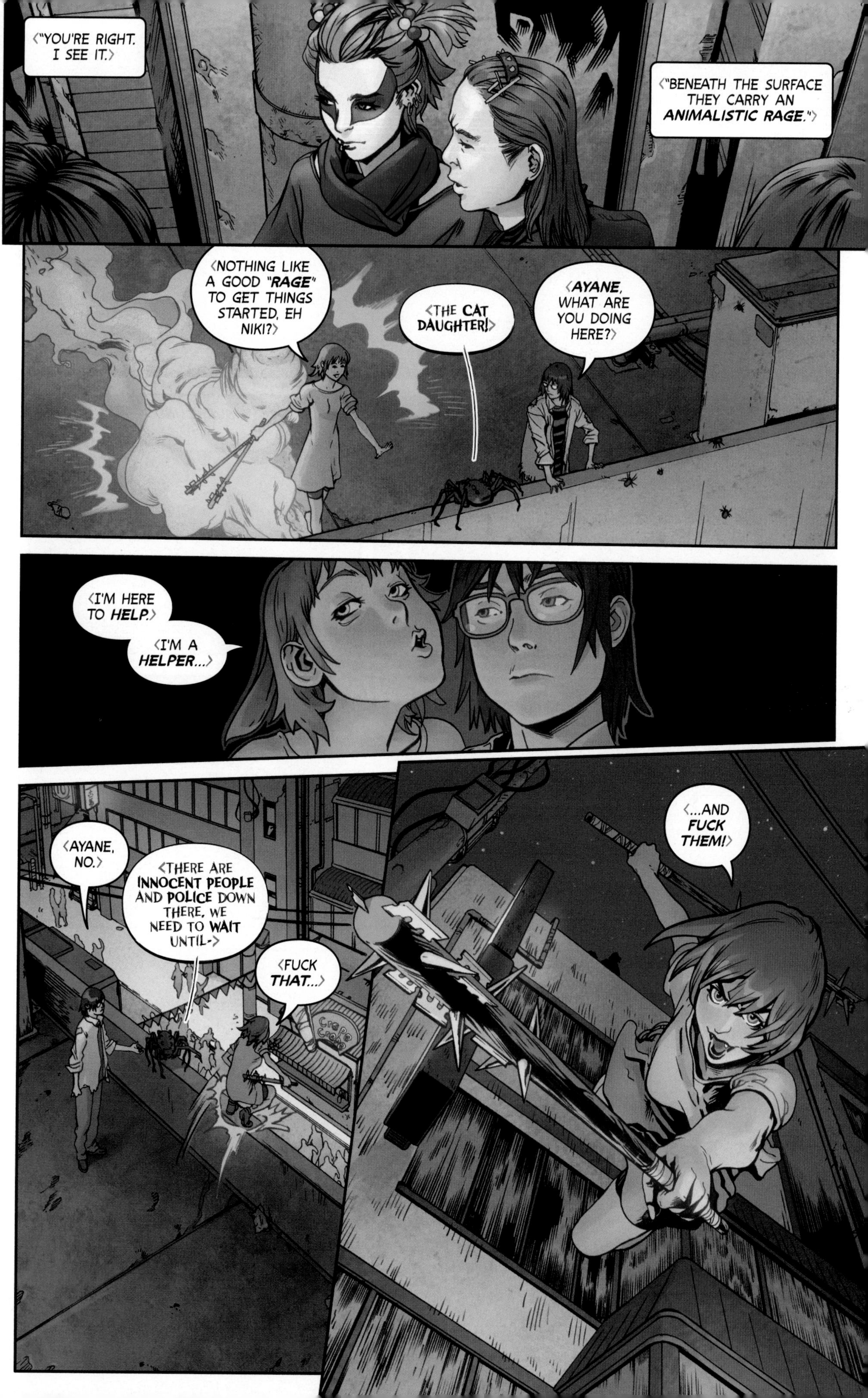
<"YOU'RE RIGHT. I SEE IT.>
<"BENEATH THE SURFACE THEY CARRY AN ANIMALISTIC RAGE.">
<NOTHING LIKE A GOOD "RAGE" TO GET THINGS STARTED, EH NIKI?>
<THE CAT DAUGHTER!>
<AYANE, WHAT ARE YOU DOING HERE?>
<I'M HERE TO HELP.>
<I'M A HELPER...>
<AYANE, NO.>
<THERE ARE INNOCENT PEOPLE AND POLICE DOWN THERE, WE NEED TO WAIT UNTIL->
<FUCK THAT...>
<...AND FUCK THEM!>

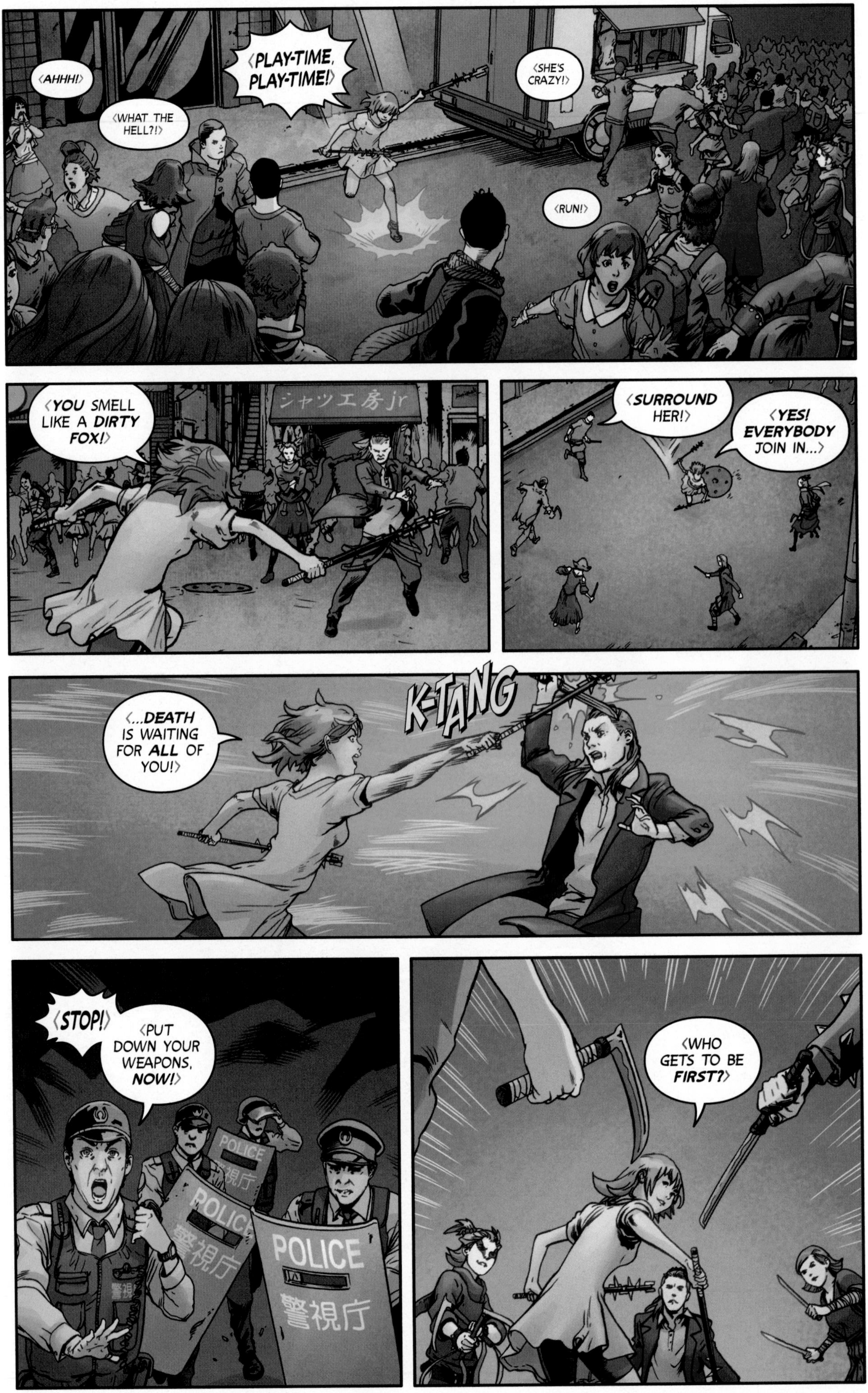

⟨AHHH!⟩
⟨WHAT THE HELL?!⟩
⟨PLAY-TIME, PLAY-TIME!⟩
⟨SHE'S CRAZY!⟩
⟨RUN!⟩
⟨YOU SMELL LIKE A DIRTY FOX!⟩
シャツ工房jr
⟨SURROUND HER!⟩
⟨YES! EVERYBODY JOIN IN...⟩
K-TANG
⟨...DEATH IS WAITING FOR ALL OF YOU!⟩
⟨STOP!⟩
⟨PUT DOWN YOUR WEAPONS, NOW!⟩
POLICE
警視庁
POLICE
警視庁
POLICE
警視庁
⟨WHO GETS TO BE FIRST?⟩

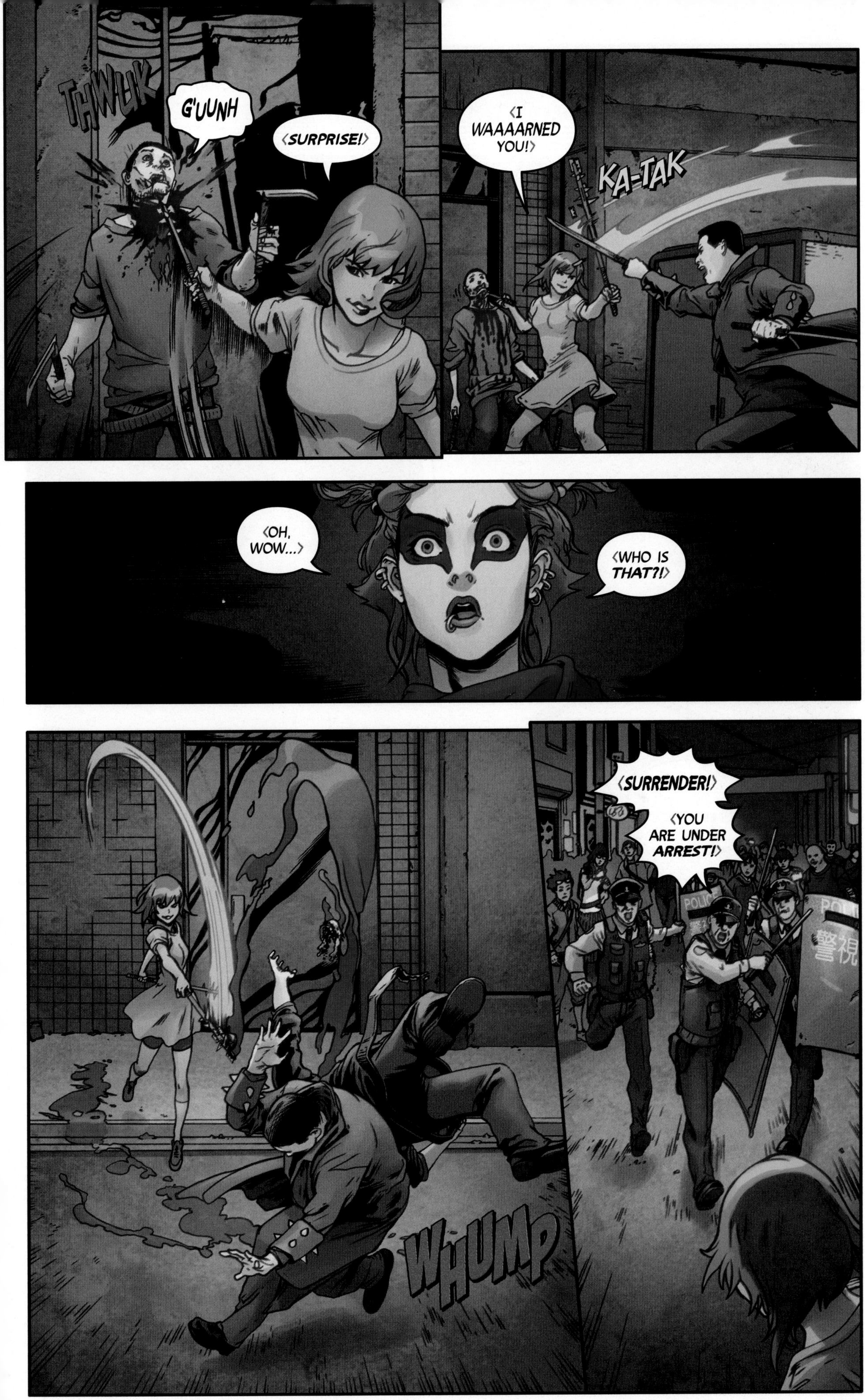
THWUK
G'UUNH
〈SURPRISE!〉
〈I WAAAARNED YOU!〉
KA-TAK
〈OH, WOW...〉
〈WHO IS THAT?!〉
WHUMP
〈SURRENDER!〉
〈YOU ARE UNDER ARREST!〉
POLICE
警視

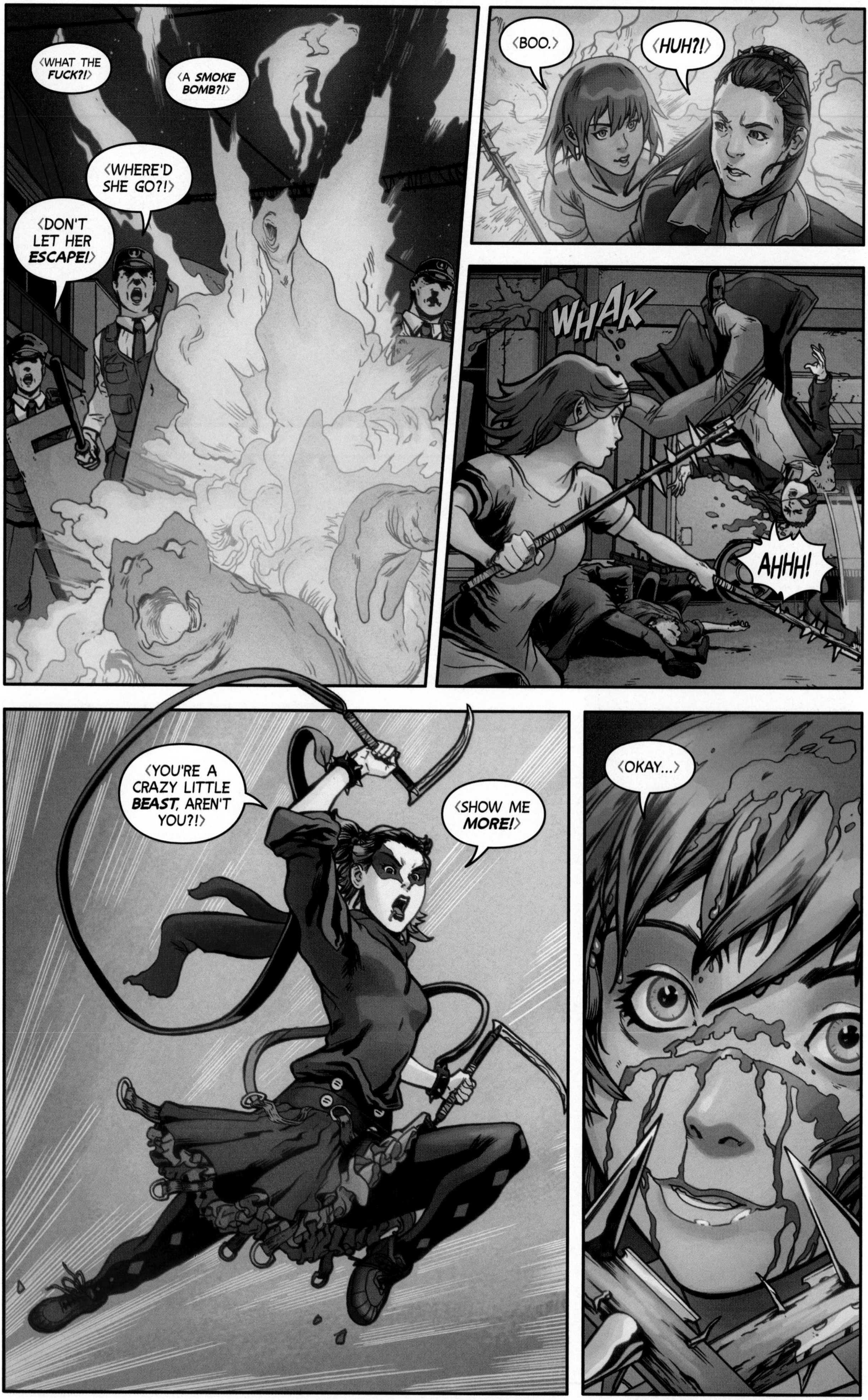

⟨WHAT THE FUCK?!⟩
⟨A SMOKE BOMB?!⟩
⟨WHERE'D SHE GO?!⟩
⟨DON'T LET HER ESCAPE!⟩
⟨BOO.⟩
⟨HUH?!⟩
WHAK
AHHH!
⟨YOU'RE A CRAZY LITTLE BEAST, AREN'T YOU?!⟩
⟨SHOW ME MORE!⟩
⟨OKAY...⟩

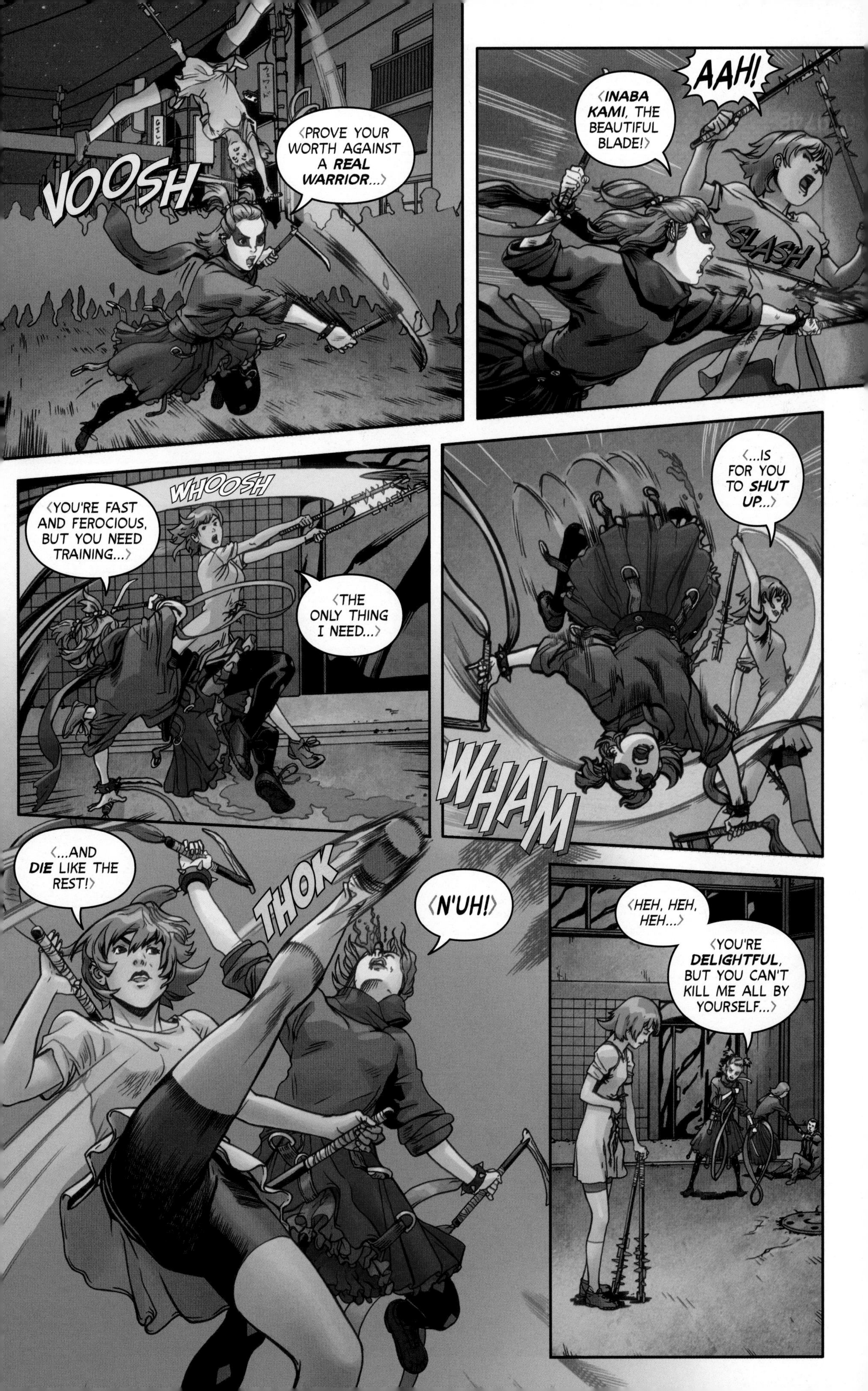
VOOSH
‹PROVE YOUR WORTH AGAINST A *REAL WARRIOR*...›
‹*INABA KAMI*, THE BEAUTIFUL BLADE!›
AAH!
SLASH
WHOOSH
‹YOU'RE FAST AND FEROCIOUS, BUT YOU NEED TRAINING...›
‹THE ONLY THING I NEED...›
‹...IS FOR YOU TO *SHUT UP*...›
WHAM
‹...AND *DIE* LIKE THE REST!›
THOK
‹N'UH!›
‹HEH, HEH, HEH...›
‹YOU'RE *DELIGHTFUL*, BUT YOU CAN'T KILL ME ALL BY YOURSELF...›

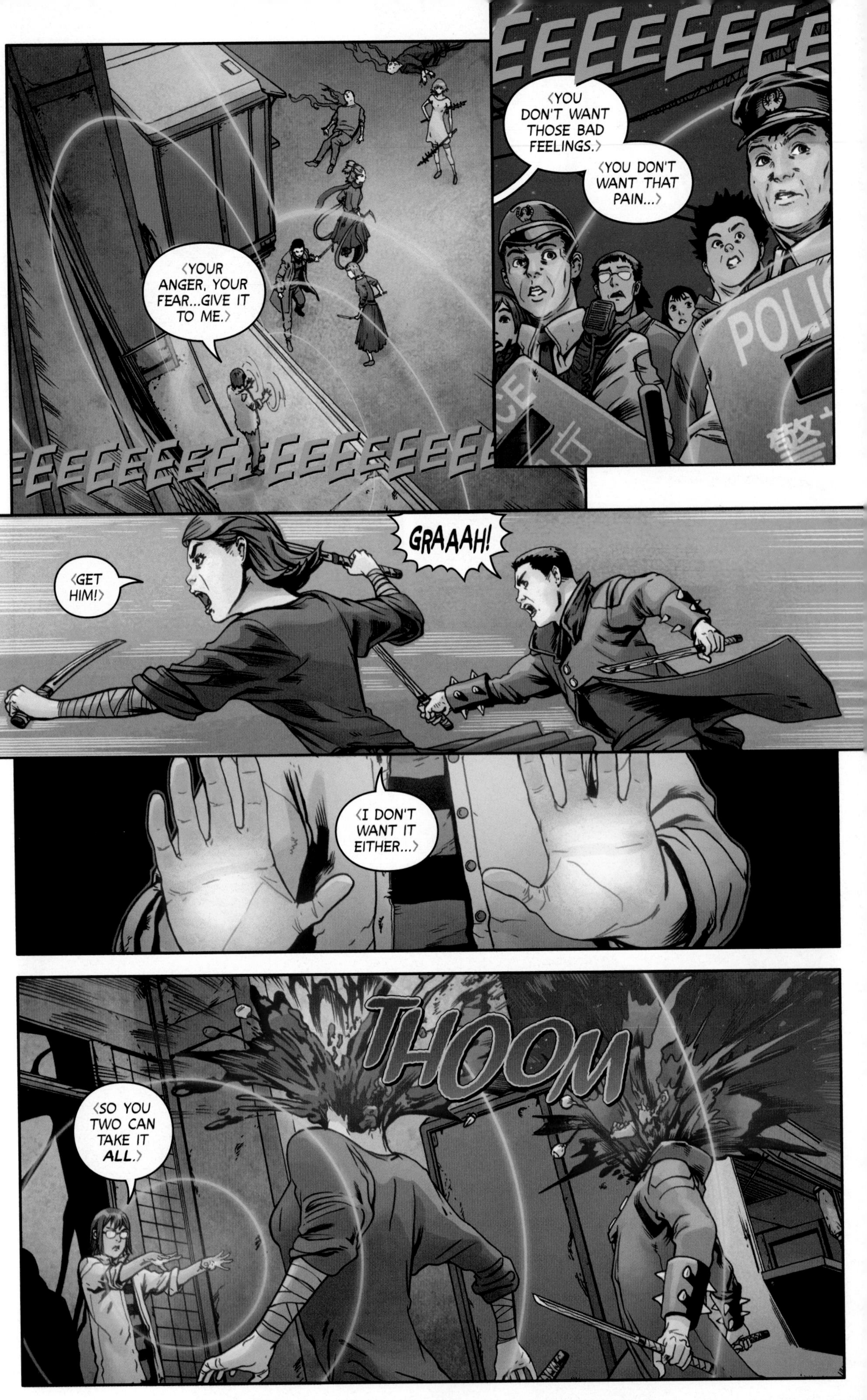
EEEEEEEEE
⟨YOU DON'T WANT THOSE BAD FEELINGS.⟩
⟨YOU DON'T WANT THAT PAIN...⟩
POLIC
⟨YOUR ANGER, YOUR FEAR...GIVE IT TO ME.⟩
EEEEEEEEEEEEEEEEE
⟨GET HIM!⟩
GRAAAH!
⟨I DON'T WANT IT EITHER...⟩
THOOM
⟨SO YOU TWO CAN TAKE IT ALL.⟩

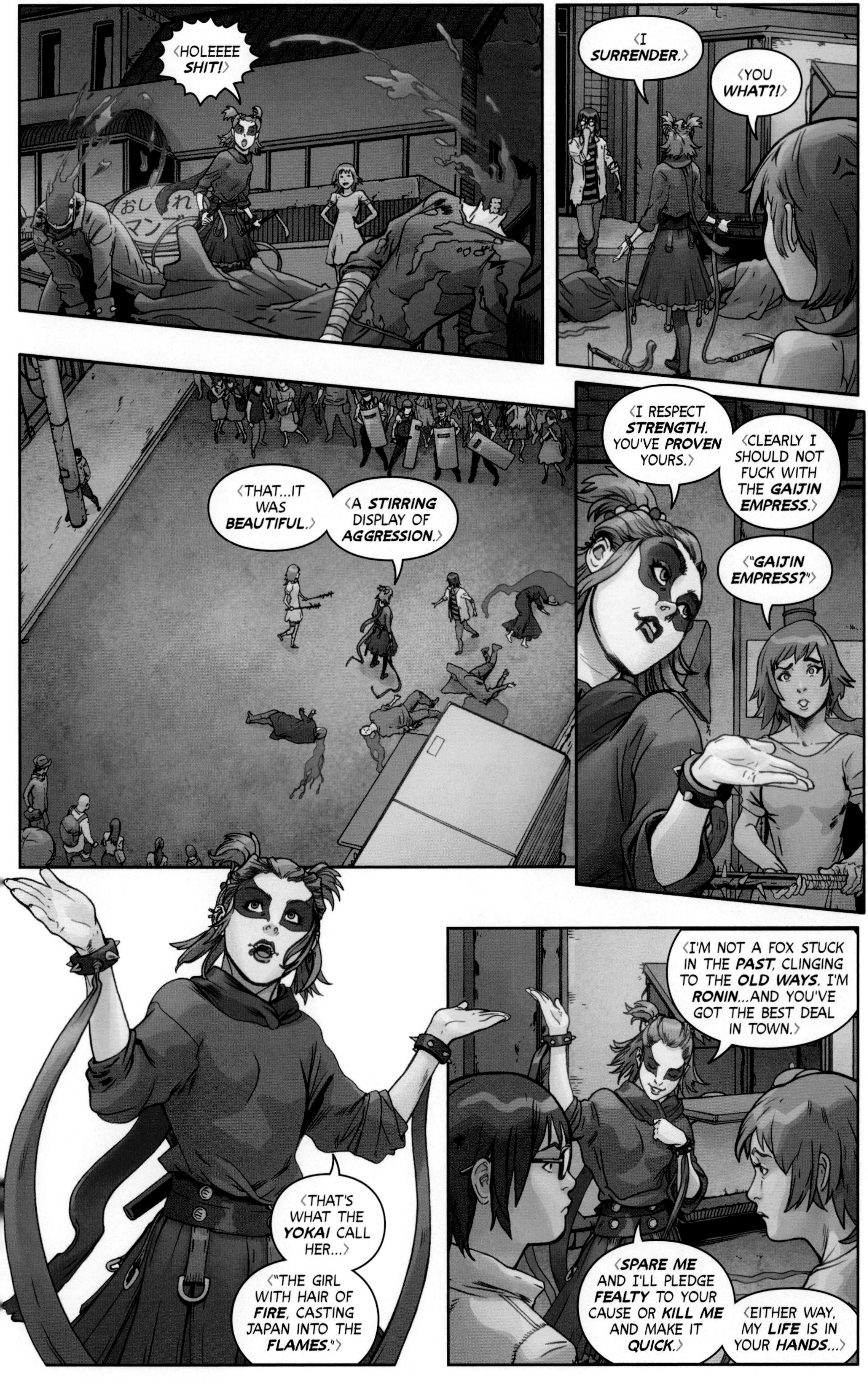

‹HOLEEEE SHIT!›
‹I SURRENDER.›
‹YOU WHAT?!›
‹THAT...IT WAS BEAUTIFUL.›
‹A STIRRING DISPLAY OF AGGRESSION.›
‹I RESPECT STRENGTH. YOU'VE PROVEN YOURS.›
‹CLEARLY I SHOULD NOT FUCK WITH THE GAIJIN EMPRESS.›
‹"GAIJIN EMPRESS?"›
‹THAT'S WHAT THE YOKAI CALL HER...›
‹"THE GIRL WITH HAIR OF FIRE, CASTING JAPAN INTO THE FLAMES."›
‹I'M NOT A FOX STUCK IN THE PAST, CLINGING TO THE OLD WAYS. I'M RONIN...AND YOU'VE GOT THE BEST DEAL IN TOWN.›
‹SPARE ME AND I'LL PLEDGE FEALTY TO YOUR CAUSE OR KILL ME AND MAKE IT QUICK.›
‹EITHER WAY, MY LIFE IS IN YOUR HANDS...›

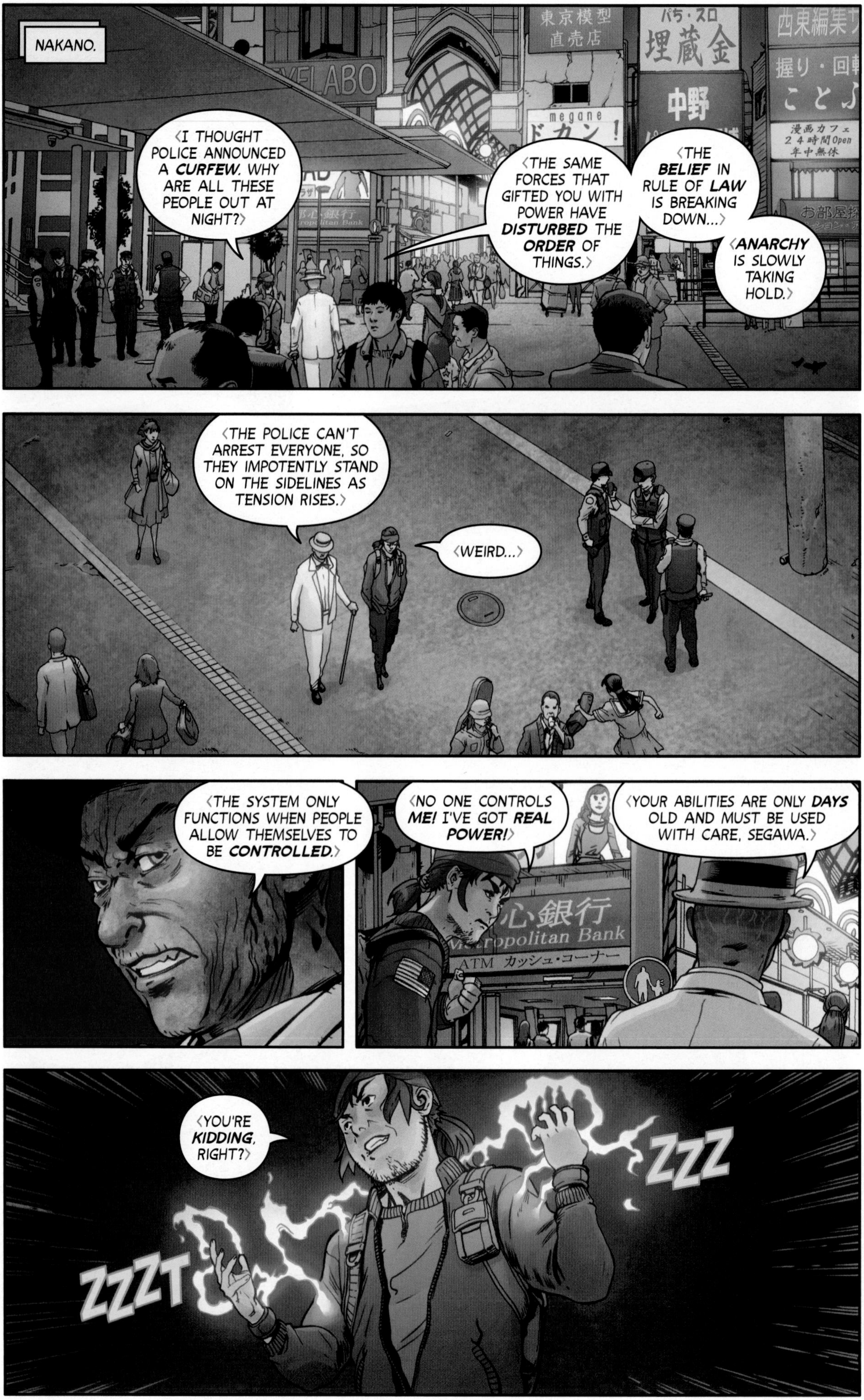
NAKANO.
東京模型 直売店
パチ・スロ 埋蔵金
中野
megane ドカン!
漫画カフェ 24時間Open 年中無休
‹I THOUGHT POLICE ANNOUNCED A *CURFEW*. WHY ARE ALL THESE PEOPLE OUT AT NIGHT?›
‹THE SAME FORCES THAT GIFTED YOU WITH POWER HAVE *DISTURBED* THE *ORDER* OF THINGS.›
‹THE *BELIEF* IN RULE OF *LAW* IS BREAKING DOWN...›
‹*ANARCHY* IS SLOWLY TAKING HOLD.›
‹THE POLICE CAN'T ARREST EVERYONE, SO THEY IMPOTENTLY STAND ON THE SIDELINES AS TENSION RISES.›
‹WEIRD...›
‹THE SYSTEM ONLY FUNCTIONS WHEN PEOPLE ALLOW THEMSELVES TO BE *CONTROLLED*.›
‹NO ONE CONTROLS *ME!* I'VE GOT *REAL POWER!*›
‹YOUR ABILITIES ARE ONLY *DAYS* OLD AND MUST BE USED WITH CARE, SEGAWA.›
心銀行
Metropolitan Bank
ATM カッシュ・コーナー
‹YOU'RE *KIDDING*, RIGHT?›
ZZZ
ZZZT

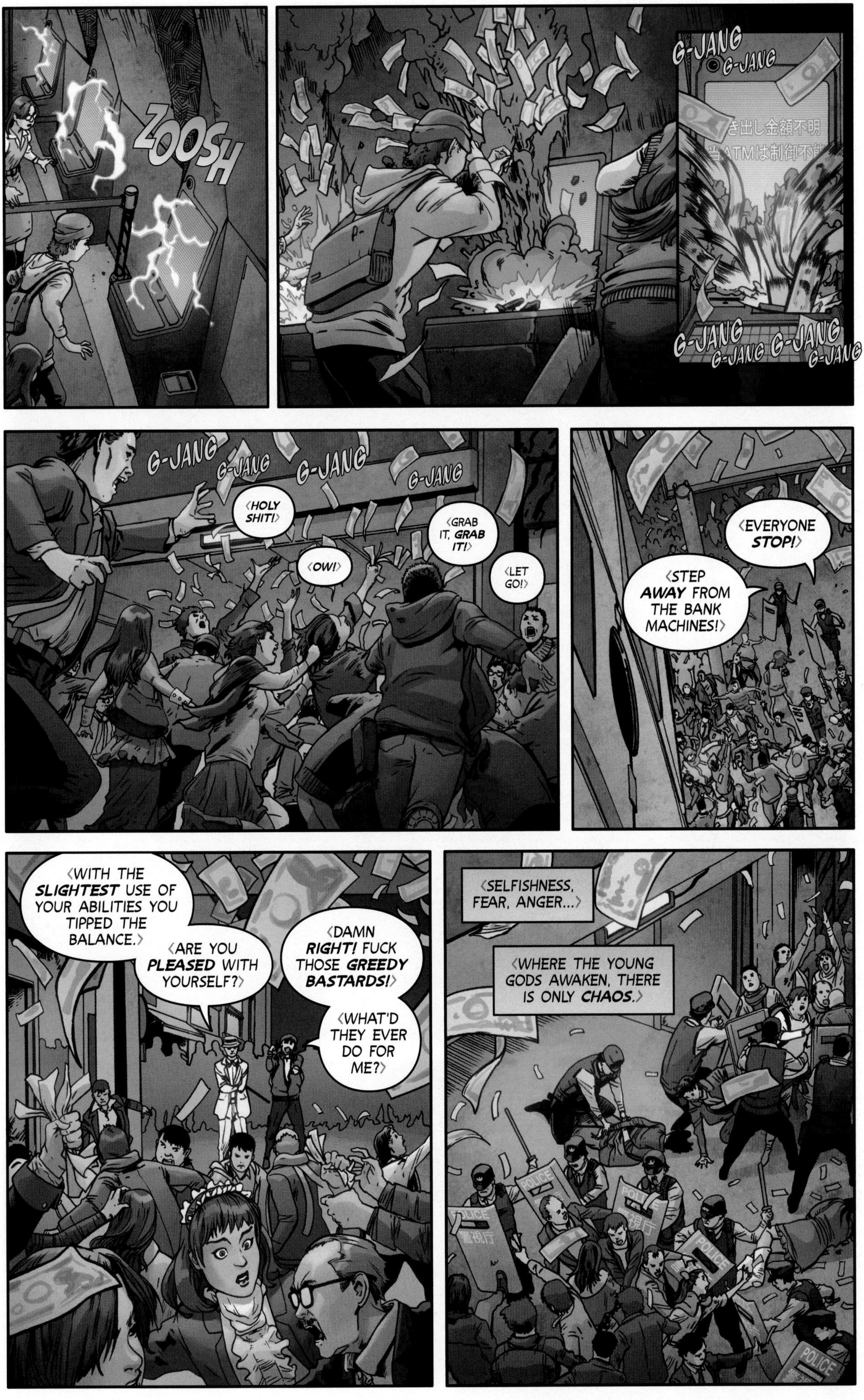
ZOOSH
G-JANG
G-JANG
き出し金額不明
当ATMは制御不
G-JANG
G-JANG
G-JANG
G-JANG
G-JANG
G-JANG
G-JANG
G-JANG
〈HOLY SHIT!〉
〈GRAB IT, GRAB IT!〉
〈OW!〉
〈LET GO!〉
〈EVERYONE STOP!〉
〈STEP AWAY FROM THE BANK MACHINES!〉
〈WITH THE SLIGHTEST USE OF YOUR ABILITIES YOU TIPPED THE BALANCE.〉
〈ARE YOU PLEASED WITH YOURSELF?〉
〈DAMN RIGHT! FUCK THOSE GREEDY BASTARDS!〉
〈WHAT'D THEY EVER DO FOR ME?〉
〈SELFISHNESS, FEAR, ANGER...〉
〈WHERE THE YOUNG GODS AWAKEN, THERE IS ONLY CHAOS.〉
POLICE
POLICE
POLICE
POLICE

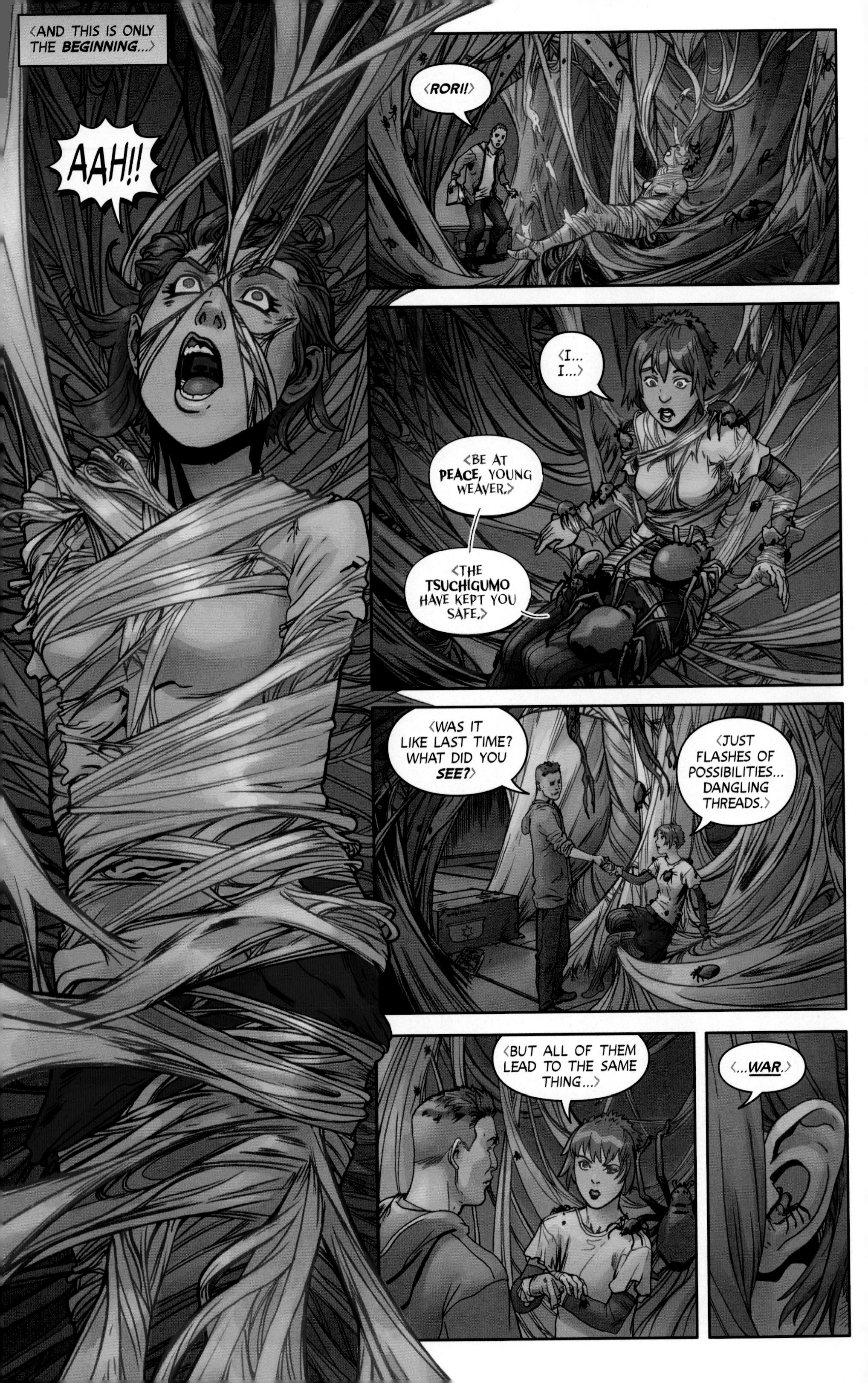
<AND THIS IS ONLY THE BEGINNING...>
AAH!!
<RORI!>
<I... I...>
<BE AT PEACE, YOUNG WEAVER.>
<THE TSUCHIGUMO HAVE KEPT YOU SAFE.>
<WAS IT LIKE LAST TIME? WHAT DID YOU SEE?>
<JUST FLASHES OF POSSIBILITIES... DANGLING THREADS.>
<BUT ALL OF THEM LEAD TO THE SAME THING...>
<...WAR.>

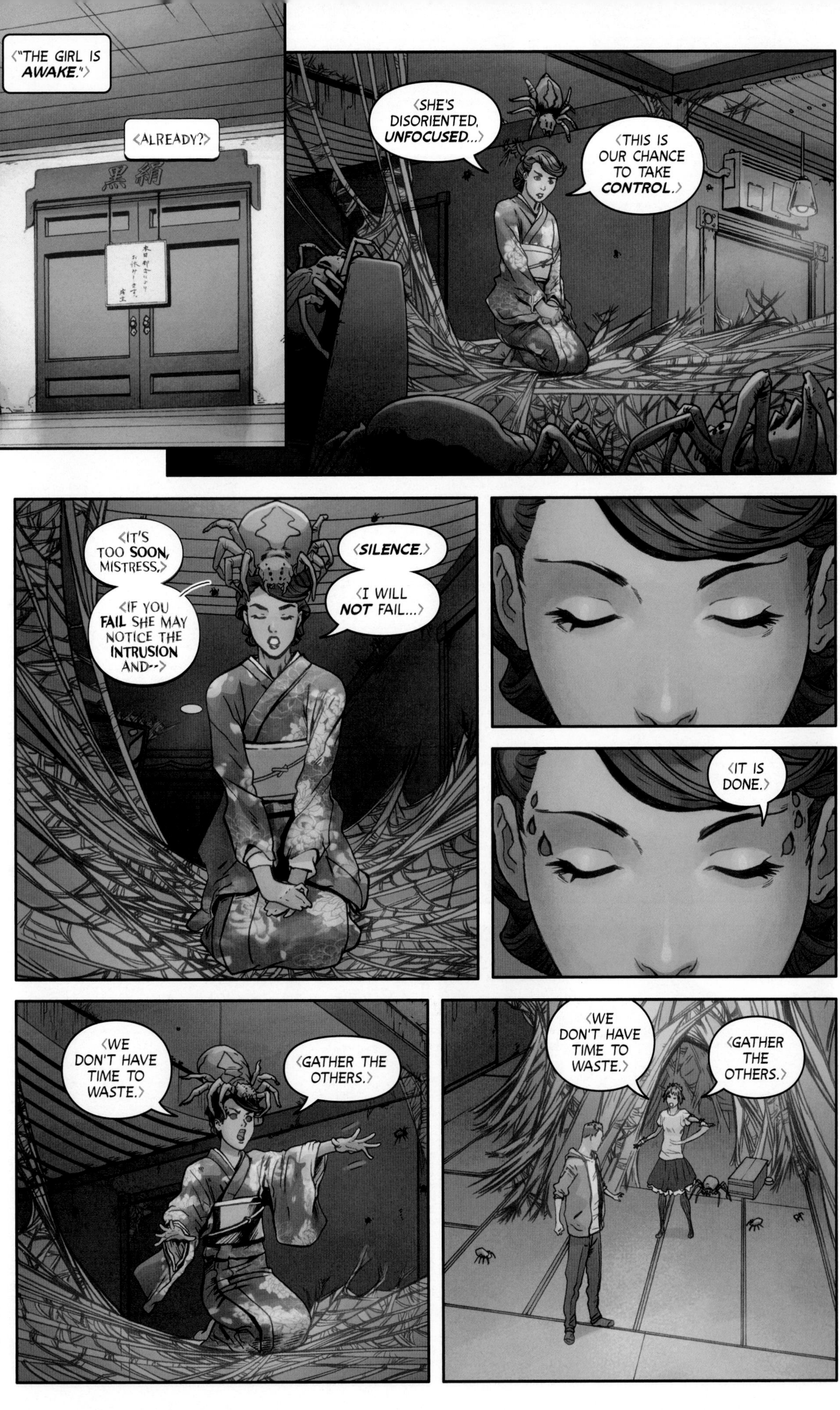

<"THE GIRL IS AWAKE.">
<ALREADY?>
<SHE'S DISORIENTED, UNFOCUSED...>
<THIS IS OUR CHANCE TO TAKE CONTROL.>
<IT'S TOO SOON, MISTRESS.>
<IF YOU FAIL SHE MAY NOTICE THE INTRUSION AND-->
<SILENCE.>
<I WILL NOT FAIL...>
<IT IS DONE.>
<WE DON'T HAVE TIME TO WASTE.>
<GATHER THE OTHERS.>
<WE DON'T HAVE TIME TO WASTE.>
<GATHER THE OTHERS.>

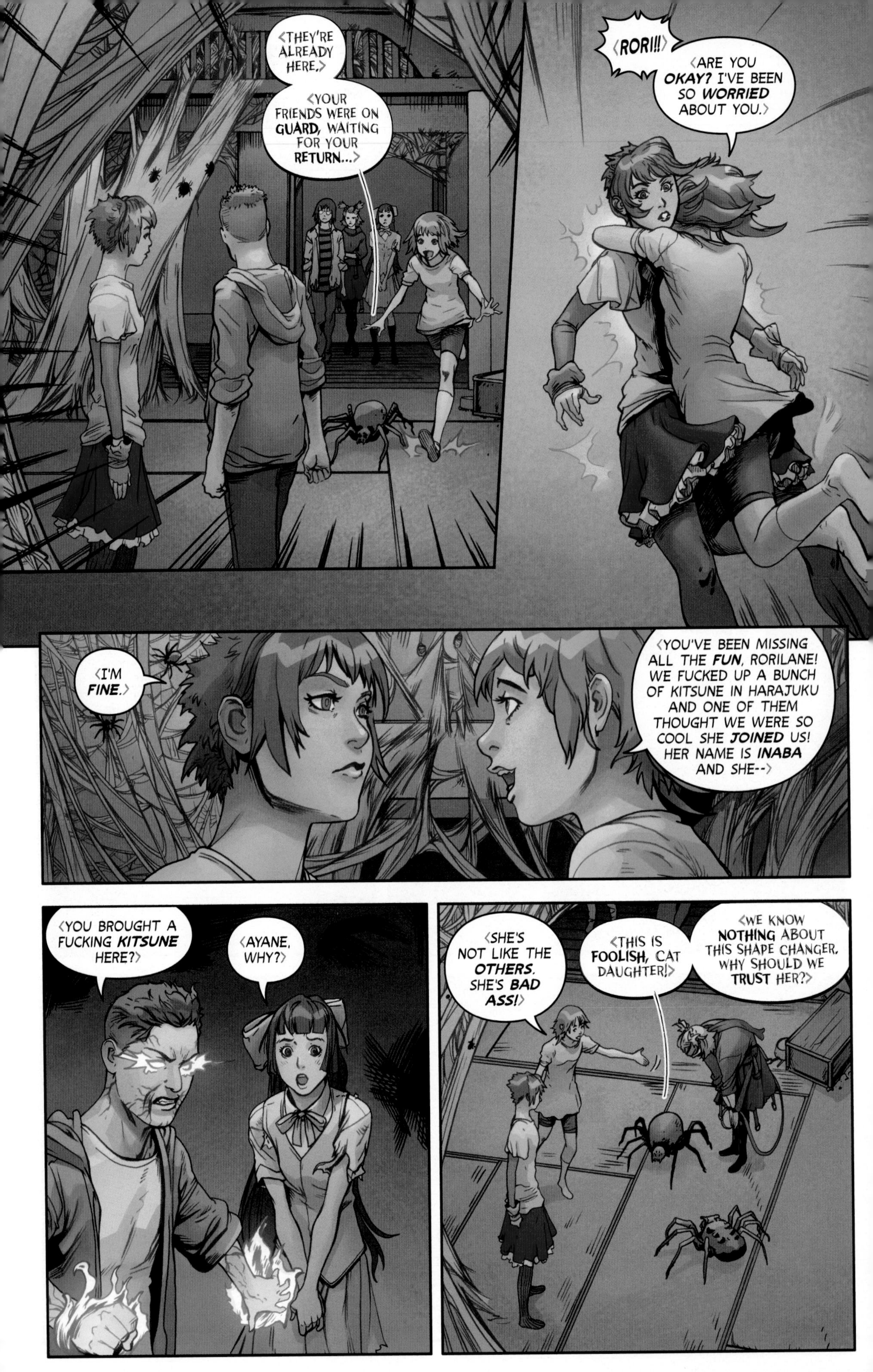

<THEY'RE ALREADY HERE.>
<YOUR FRIENDS WERE ON GUARD, WAITING FOR YOUR RETURN...>
<RORI!!>
<ARE YOU OKAY? I'VE BEEN SO WORRIED ABOUT YOU.>
<I'M FINE.>
<YOU'VE BEEN MISSING ALL THE FUN, RORILANE! WE FUCKED UP A BUNCH OF KITSUNE IN HARAJUKU AND ONE OF THEM THOUGHT WE WERE SO COOL SHE JOINED US! HER NAME IS INABA AND SHE-->
<YOU BROUGHT A FUCKING KITSUNE HERE?>
<AYANE, WHY?>
<SHE'S NOT LIKE THE OTHERS. SHE'S BAD ASS!>
<THIS IS FOOLISH, CAT DAUGHTER!>
<WE KNOW NOTHING ABOUT THIS SHAPE CHANGER. WHY SHOULD WE TRUST HER?>

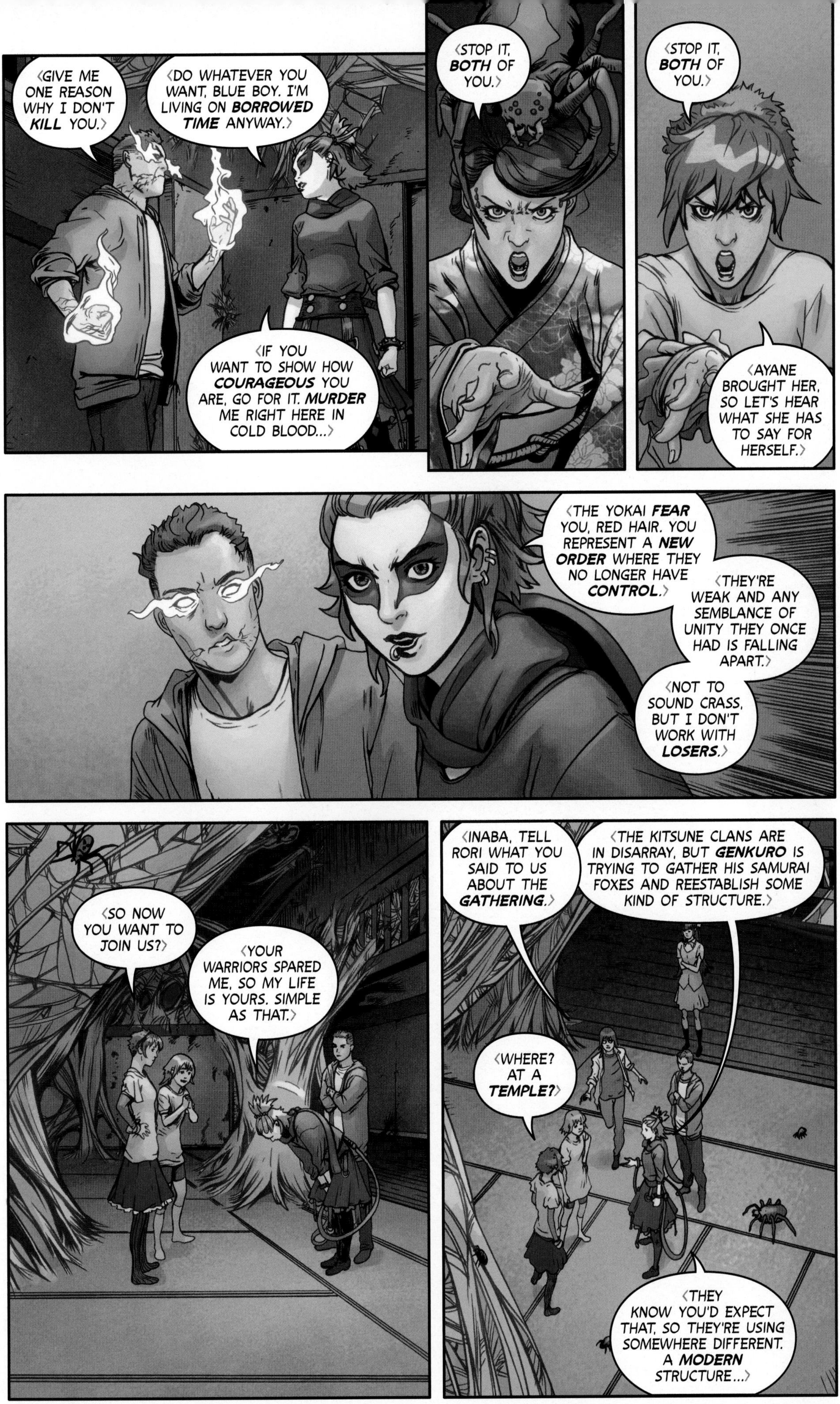

〈GIVE ME ONE REASON WHY I DON'T **KILL** YOU.〉
〈DO WHATEVER YOU WANT, BLUE BOY. I'M LIVING ON **BORROWED TIME** ANYWAY.〉
〈IF YOU WANT TO SHOW HOW **COURAGEOUS** YOU ARE, GO FOR IT. **MURDER** ME RIGHT HERE IN COLD BLOOD...〉
〈STOP IT, **BOTH** OF YOU.〉
〈STOP IT, **BOTH** OF YOU.〉
〈AYANE BROUGHT HER, SO LET'S HEAR WHAT SHE HAS TO SAY FOR HERSELF.〉
〈THE YOKAI **FEAR** YOU, RED HAIR. YOU REPRESENT A **NEW ORDER** WHERE THEY NO LONGER HAVE **CONTROL**.〉
〈THEY'RE WEAK AND ANY SEMBLANCE OF UNITY THEY ONCE HAD IS FALLING APART.〉
〈NOT TO SOUND CRASS, BUT I DON'T WORK WITH **LOSERS**.〉
〈SO NOW YOU WANT TO JOIN US?〉
〈YOUR WARRIORS SPARED ME, SO MY LIFE IS YOURS. SIMPLE AS THAT.〉
〈INABA, TELL RORI WHAT YOU SAID TO US ABOUT THE **GATHERING**.〉
〈THE KITSUNE CLANS ARE IN DISARRAY, BUT **GENKURO** IS TRYING TO GATHER HIS SAMURAI FOXES AND REESTABLISH SOME KIND OF STRUCTURE.〉
〈WHERE? AT A **TEMPLE**?〉
〈THEY KNOW YOU'D EXPECT THAT, SO THEY'RE USING SOMEWHERE DIFFERENT. A **MODERN** STRUCTURE...〉

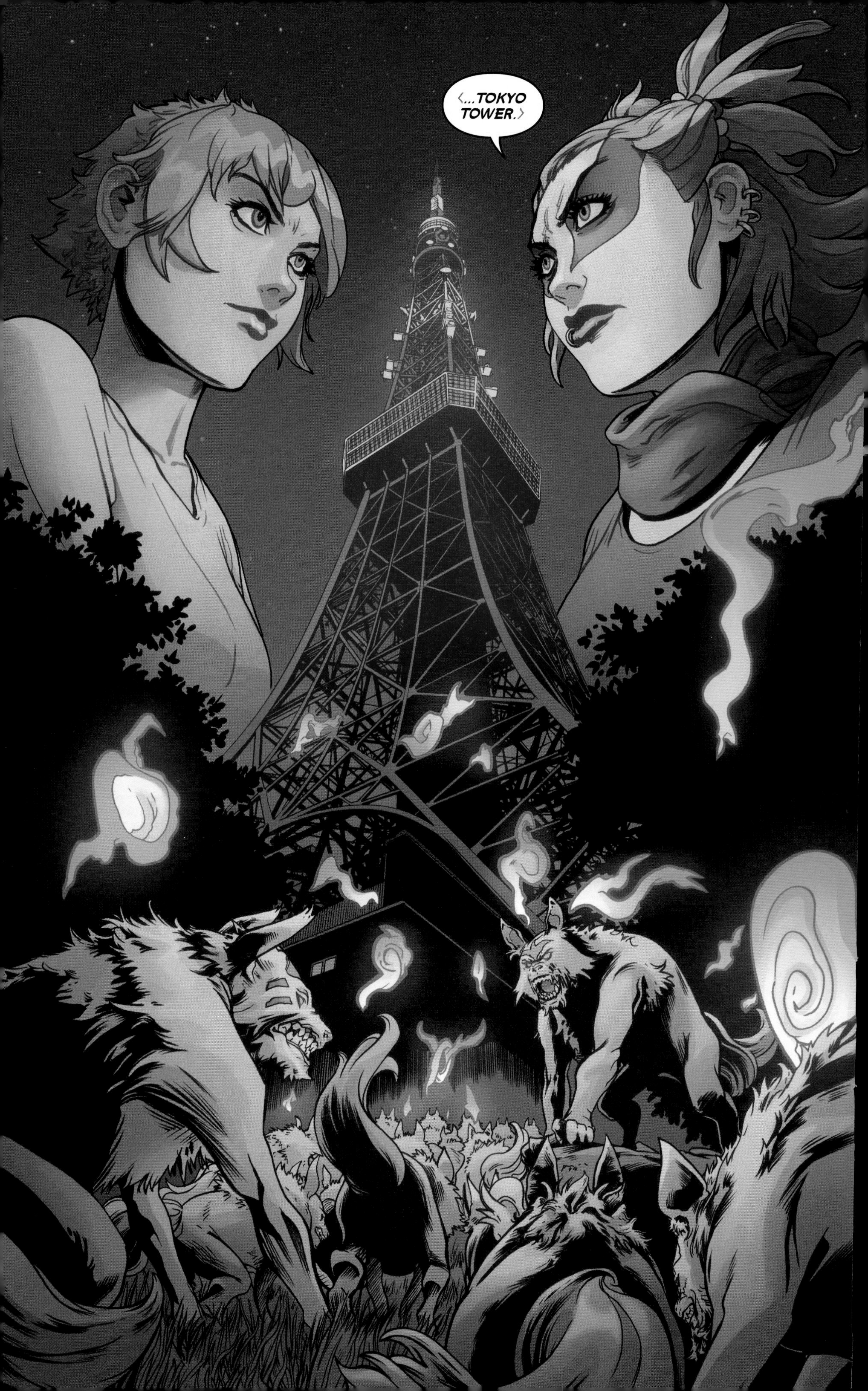

‹...TOKYO TOWER.›

Chapter Thirteen

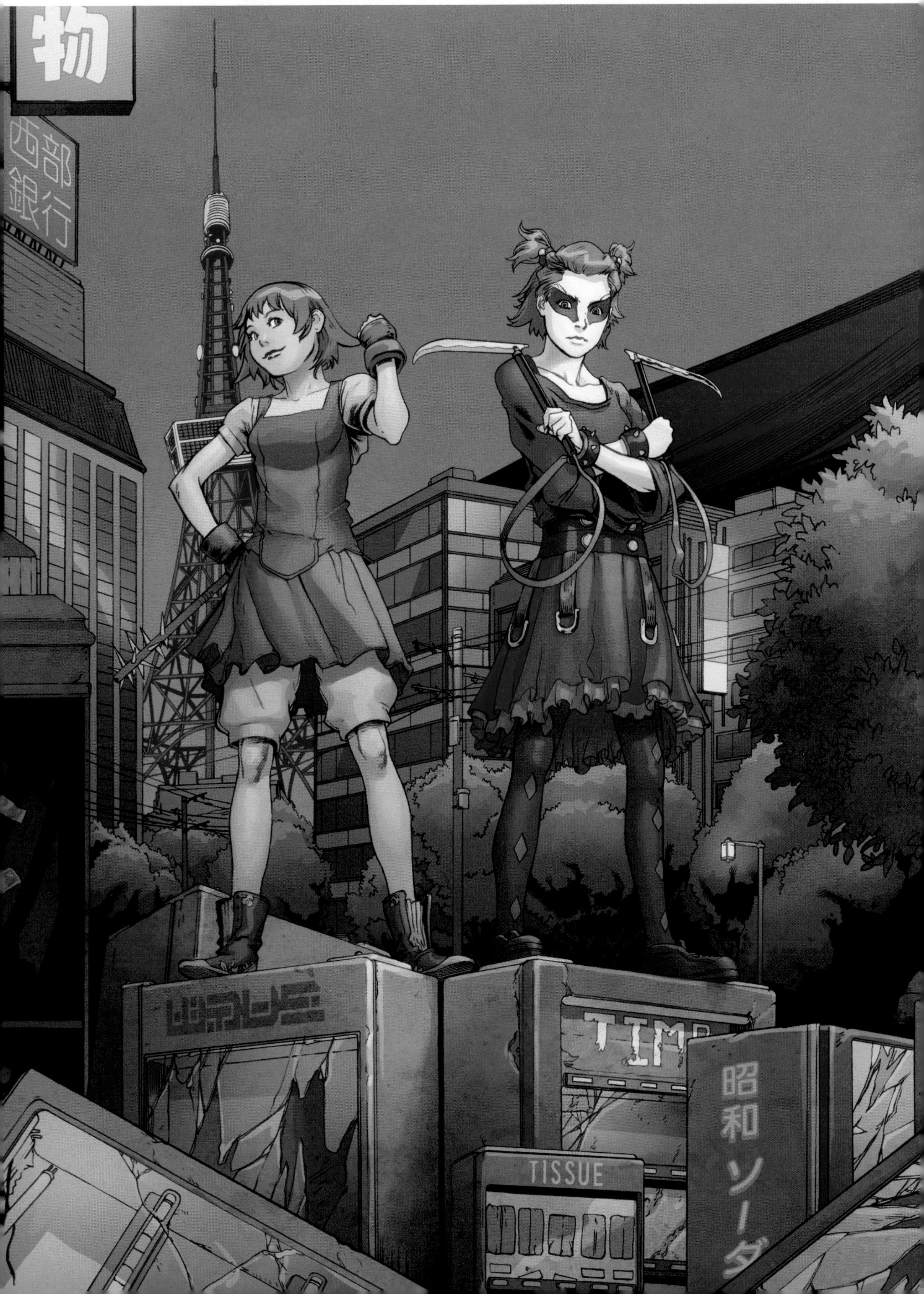
物
西部銀行
TISSUE
昭和ソーダ

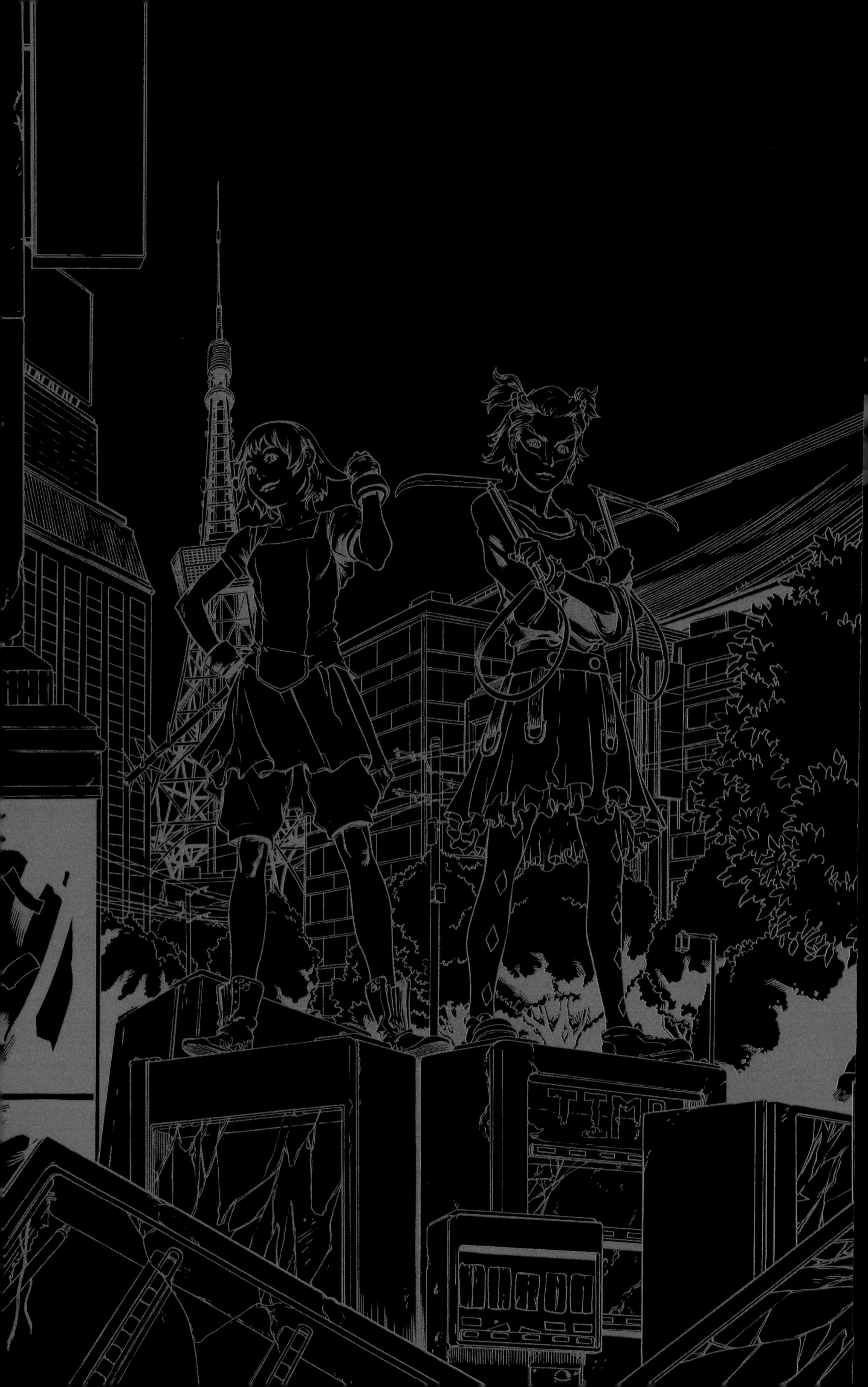

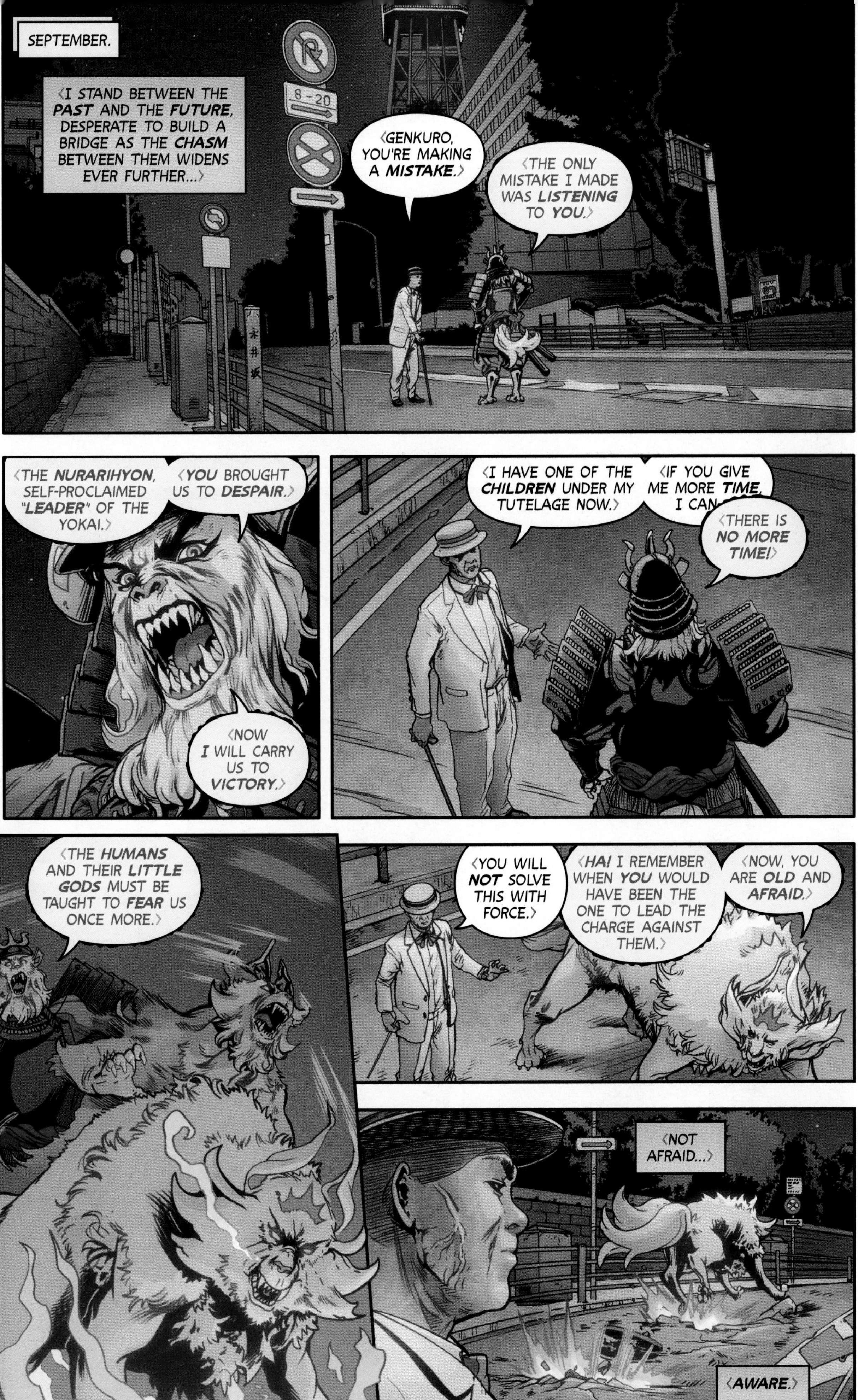
SEPTEMBER.
〈I STAND BETWEEN THE PAST AND THE FUTURE, DESPERATE TO BUILD A BRIDGE AS THE CHASM BETWEEN THEM WIDENS EVER FURTHER...〉
8 - 20
〈GENKURO, YOU'RE MAKING A MISTAKE.〉
〈THE ONLY MISTAKE I MADE WAS LISTENING TO YOU.〉
〈THE NURARIHYON, SELF-PROCLAIMED "LEADER" OF THE YOKAI.〉
〈YOU BROUGHT US TO DESPAIR.〉
〈NOW I WILL CARRY US TO VICTORY.〉
〈I HAVE ONE OF THE CHILDREN UNDER MY TUTELAGE NOW.〉
〈IF YOU GIVE ME MORE TIME, I CAN-
〈THERE IS NO MORE TIME!〉
〈THE HUMANS AND THEIR LITTLE GODS MUST BE TAUGHT TO FEAR US ONCE MORE.〉
〈YOU WILL NOT SOLVE THIS WITH FORCE.〉
〈HA! I REMEMBER WHEN YOU WOULD HAVE BEEN THE ONE TO LEAD THE CHARGE AGAINST THEM.〉
〈NOW, YOU ARE OLD AND AFRAID.〉
〈NOT AFRAID...〉
〈AWARE.〉

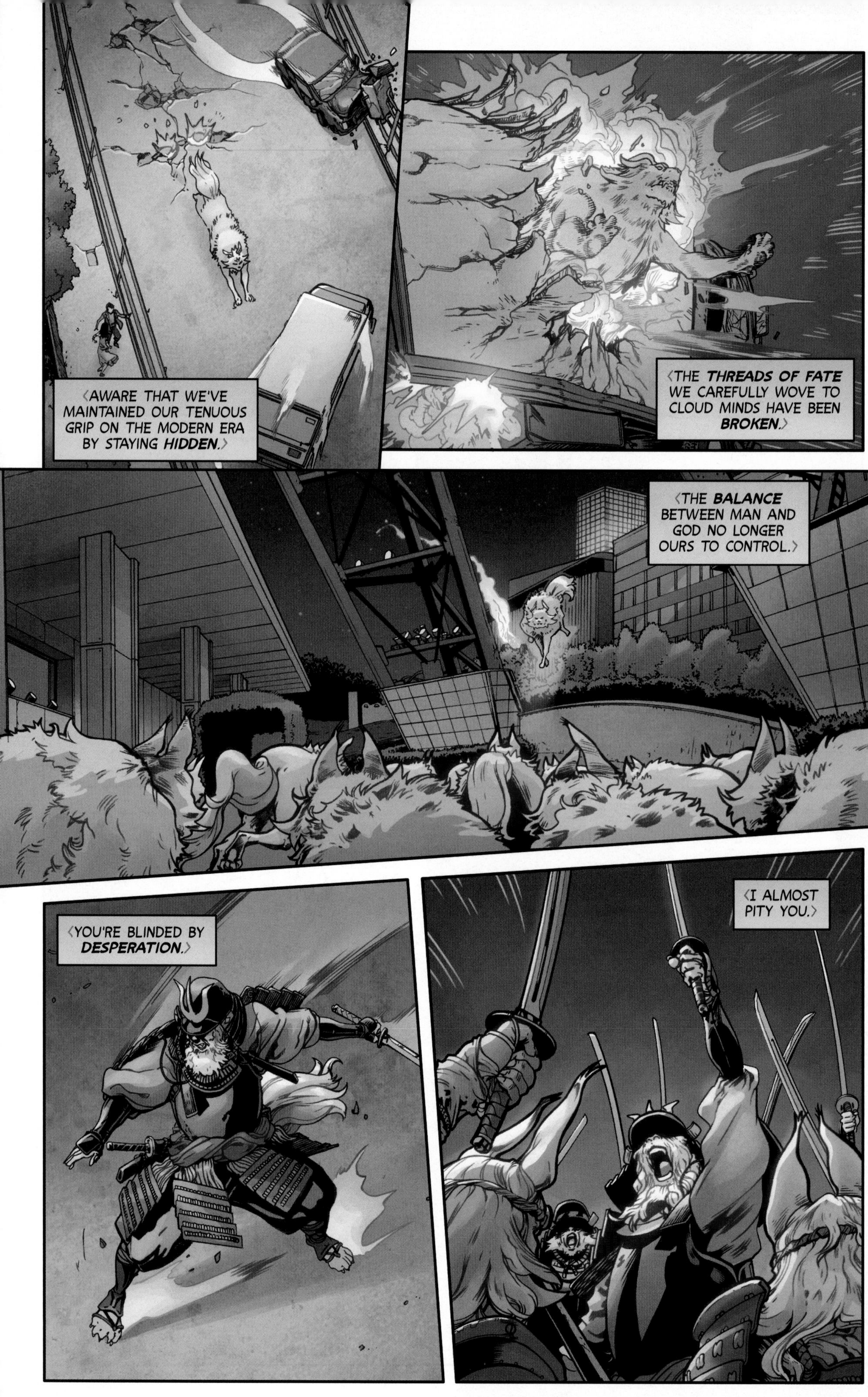
‹AWARE THAT WE'VE MAINTAINED OUR TENUOUS GRIP ON THE MODERN ERA BY STAYING *HIDDEN*.›
‹THE ***THREADS OF FATE*** WE CAREFULLY WOVE TO CLOUD MINDS HAVE BEEN ***BROKEN***.›
‹THE ***BALANCE*** BETWEEN MAN AND GOD NO LONGER OURS TO CONTROL.›
‹YOU'RE BLINDED BY ***DESPERATION***.›
‹I ALMOST PITY YOU.›

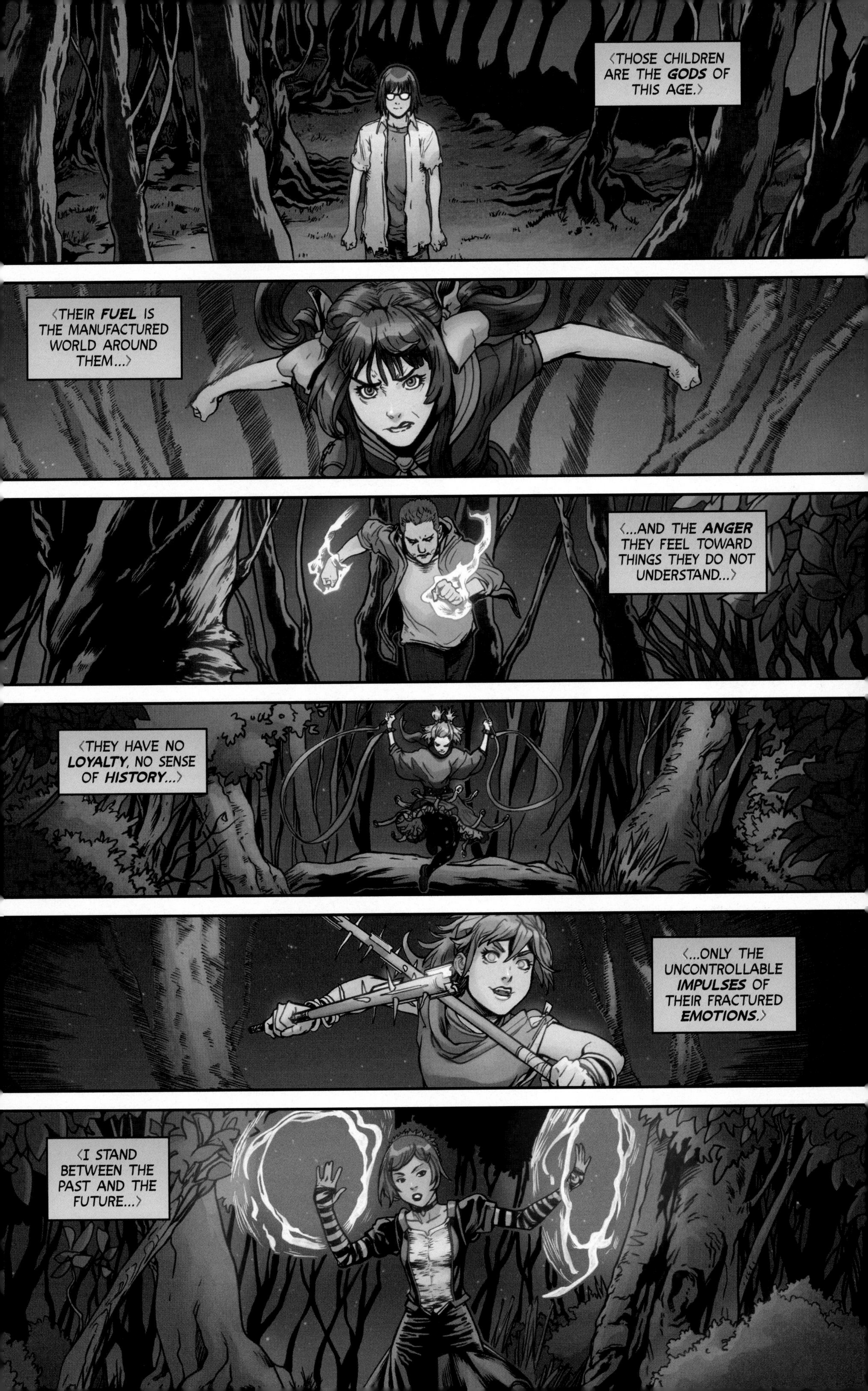
〈THOSE CHILDREN ARE THE **GODS** OF THIS AGE.〉
〈THEIR **FUEL** IS THE MANUFACTURED WORLD AROUND THEM...〉
〈...AND THE **ANGER** THEY FEEL TOWARD THINGS THEY DO NOT UNDERSTAND...〉
〈THEY HAVE NO **LOYALTY**, NO SENSE OF **HISTORY**...〉
〈...ONLY THE UNCONTROLLABLE **IMPULSES** OF THEIR FRACTURED **EMOTIONS**.〉
〈I STAND BETWEEN THE PAST AND THE FUTURE...〉

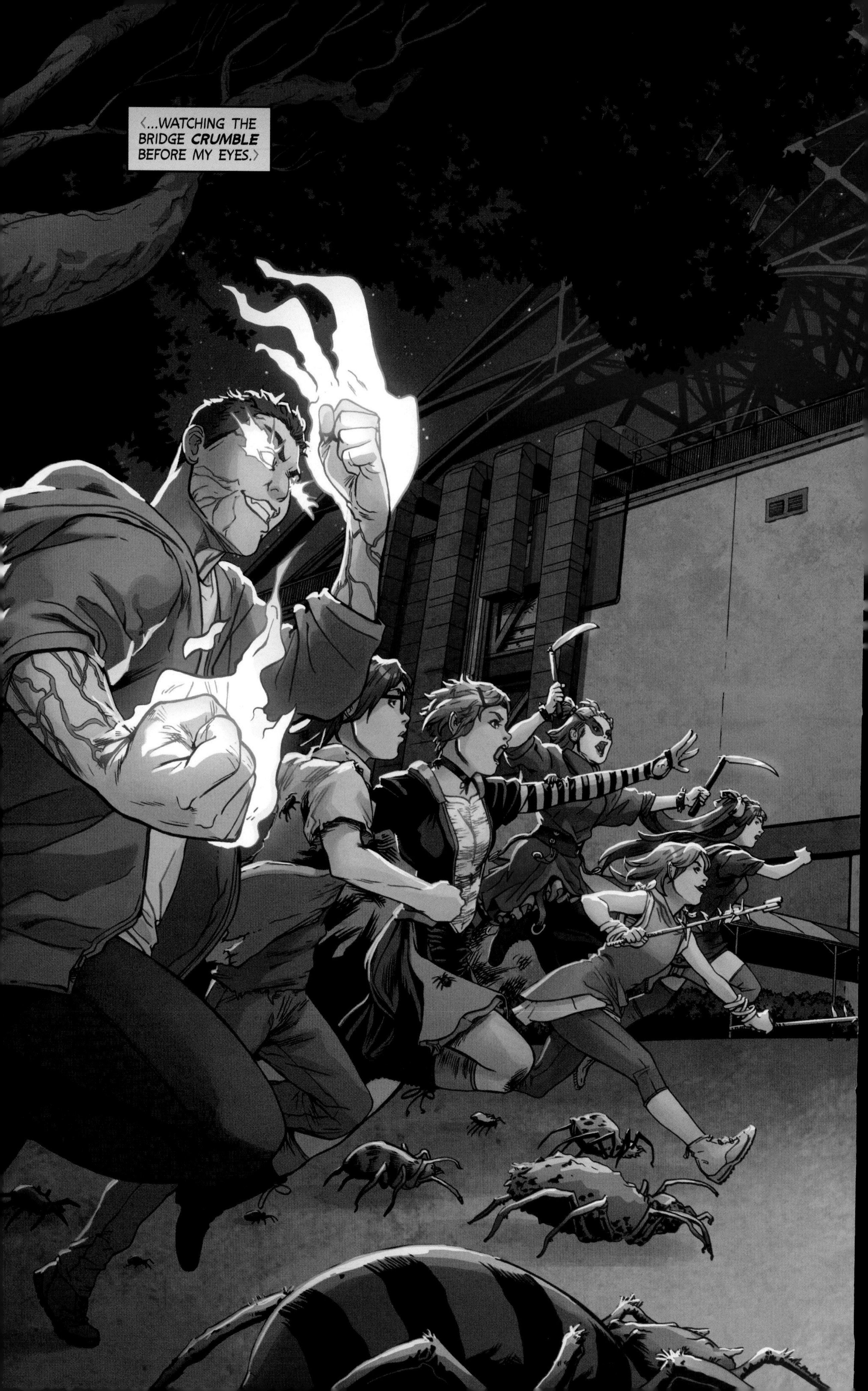
<...WATCHING THE BRIDGE **CRUMBLE** BEFORE MY EYES.>

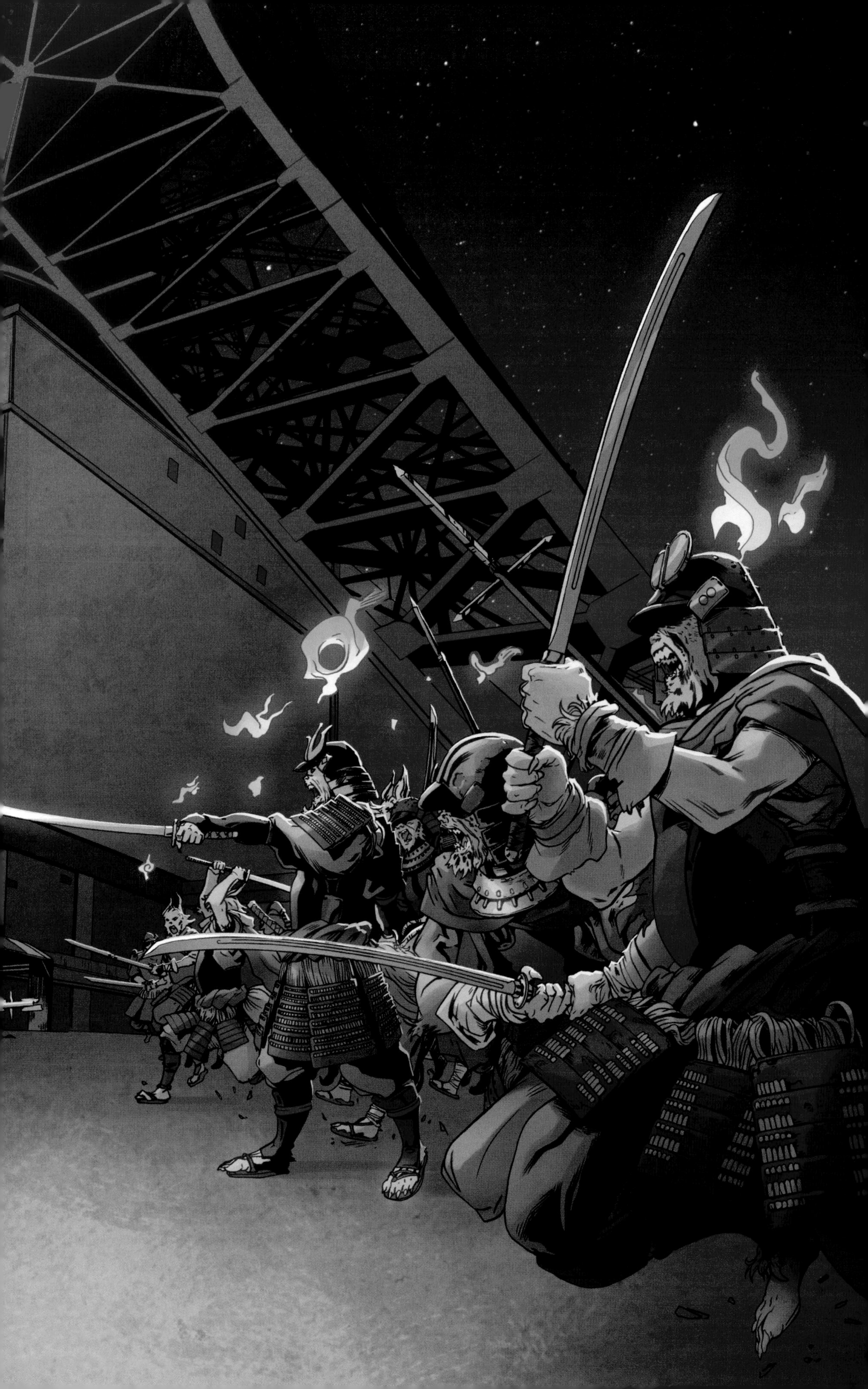

⟨*THIS* IS WHAT I'VE BEEN WAITING FOR...⟩

SHOKOOOM

THOOM

⟨...A CHANCE TO *CUT LOOSE!*⟩

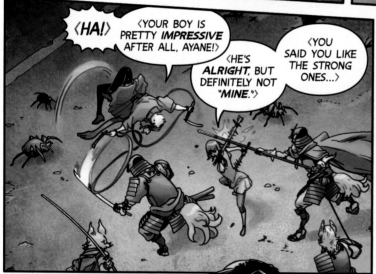

⟨*HA!*⟩

⟨YOUR BOY IS PRETTY *IMPRESSIVE* AFTER ALL, AYANE!⟩

⟨HE'S *ALRIGHT*, BUT DEFINITELY NOT "*MINE*."⟩

⟨YOU SAID YOU LIKE THE STRONG ONES...⟩

⟨*TAKE* HIM IF YOU WANT.⟩

THOK

⟨HMMM...IT'S *TEMPTING*...⟩

⟨...BUT I'LL *PASS*.⟩

SHUNK

EEEEEEEEEEEEEEEEEEEEE

⟨RAGE WILL NEVER GET YOU WHAT YOU WANT...⟩

⟨...YOU'RE JUST WASTING ENERGY.⟩

⟨NIKAIDO, WHY DO YOU KEEP TALKING TO THEM?⟩

⟨YOU KNOW YOU WON'T BE ABLE TO CONVINCE THEM, RIGHT?⟩

⟨I KNOW...⟩

⟨...IT'S JUST A BAD HABIT.⟩

FoOOM

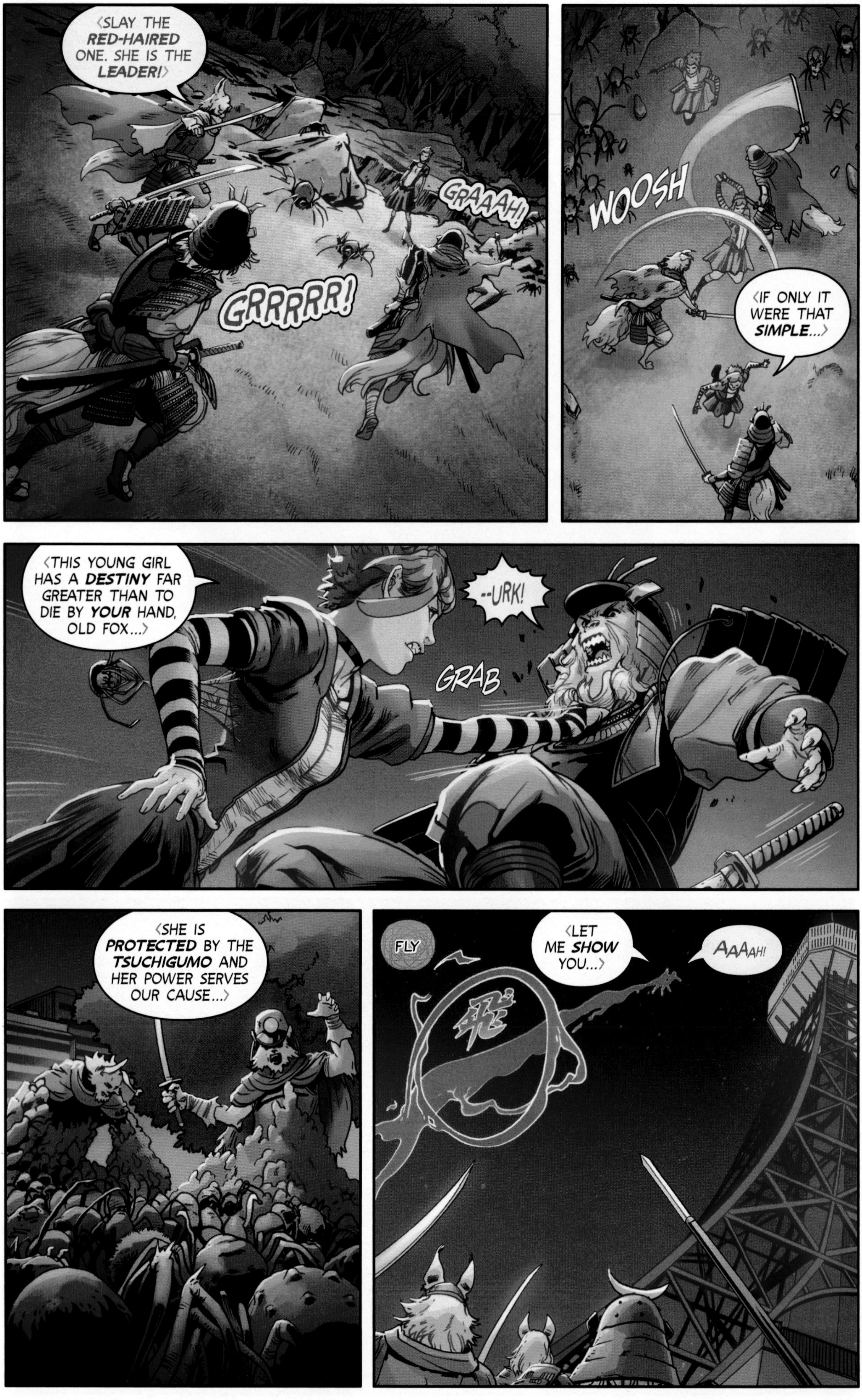

<SLAY THE RED-HAIRED ONE. SHE IS THE LEADER!>
GRAAAH!
GRRRRR!
WOOSH
<IF ONLY IT WERE THAT SIMPLE...>
<THIS YOUNG GIRL HAS A DESTINY FAR GREATER THAN TO DIE BY YOUR HAND, OLD FOX...>
--URK!
GRAB
<SHE IS PROTECTED BY THE TSUCHIGUMO AND HER POWER SERVES OUR CAUSE...>
FLY
<LET ME SHOW YOU...>
AAAAH!

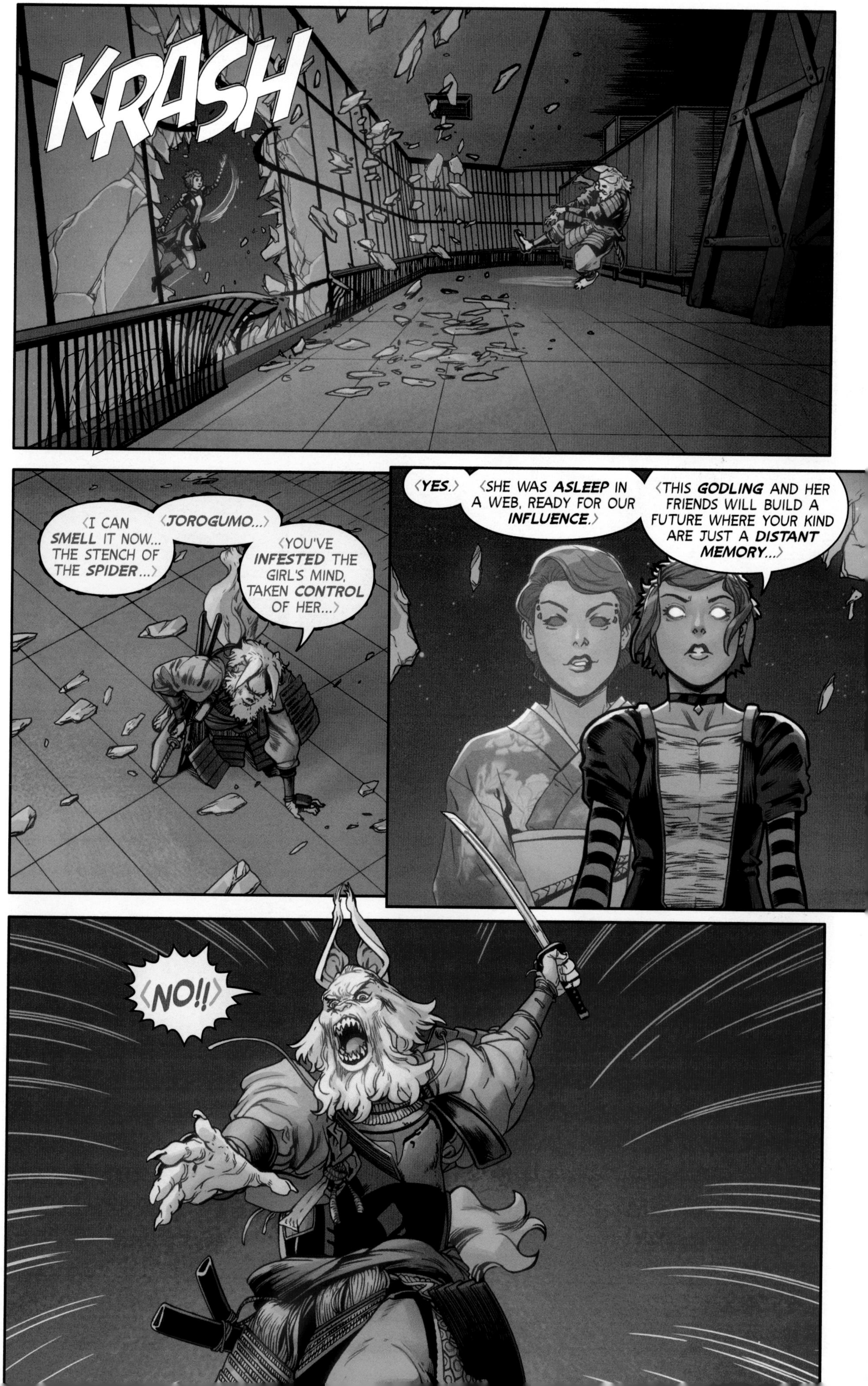
KRASH
‹I CAN SMELL IT NOW... THE STENCH OF THE SPIDER...›
‹JOROGUMO...›
‹YOU'VE INFESTED THE GIRL'S MIND, TAKEN CONTROL OF HER...›
‹YES.›
‹SHE WAS ASLEEP IN A WEB, READY FOR OUR INFLUENCE.›
‹THIS GODLING AND HER FRIENDS WILL BUILD A FUTURE WHERE YOUR KIND ARE JUST A DISTANT MEMORY...›
‹NO!!›

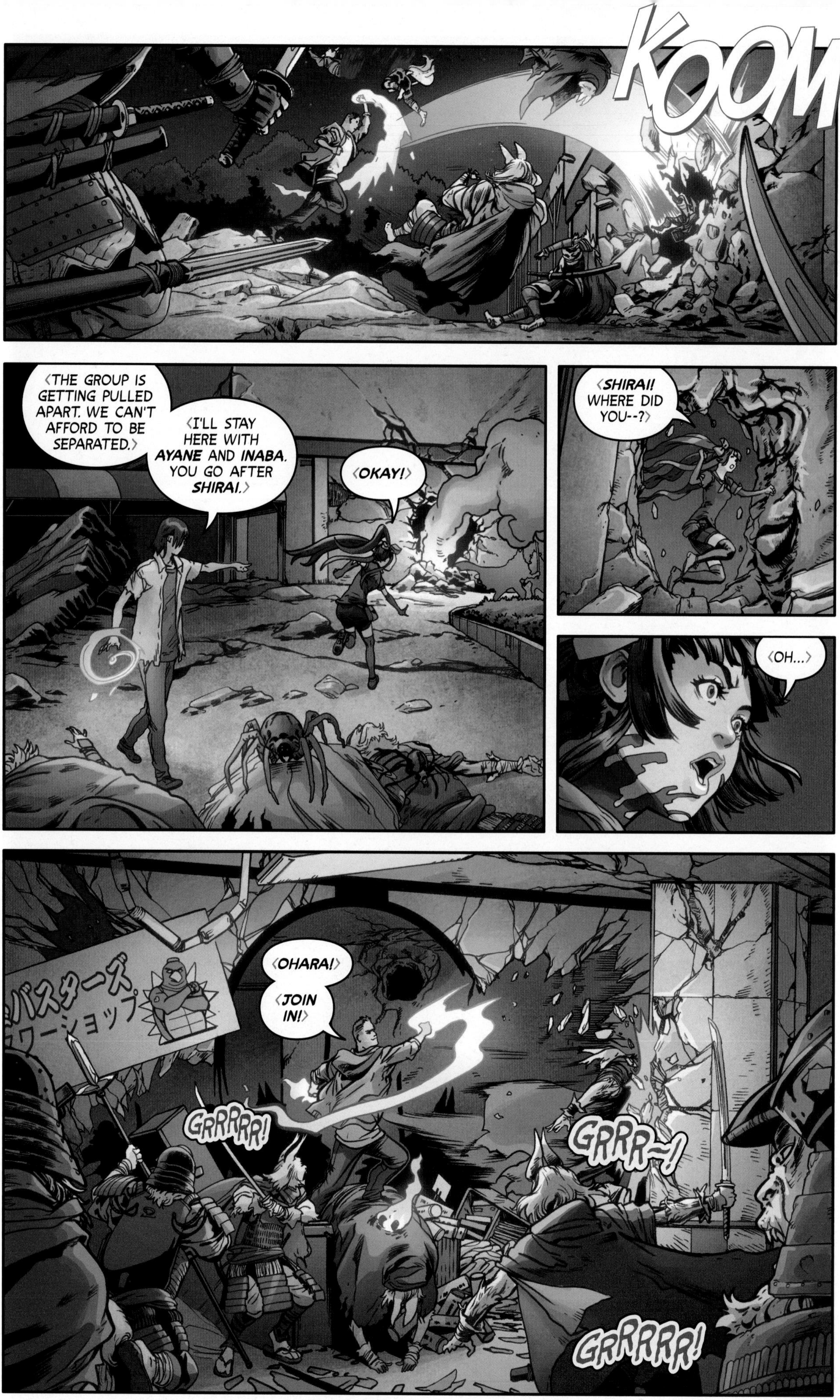
KOOM
‹THE GROUP IS GETTING PULLED APART. WE CAN'T AFFORD TO BE SEPARATED.›
‹I'LL STAY HERE WITH AYANE AND INABA. YOU GO AFTER SHIRAI.›
‹OKAY!›
‹SHIRAI! WHERE DID YOU--?›
‹OH...›
‹OHARA!›
‹JOIN IN!›
GRRRRR!
GRRR--!
GRRRRR!

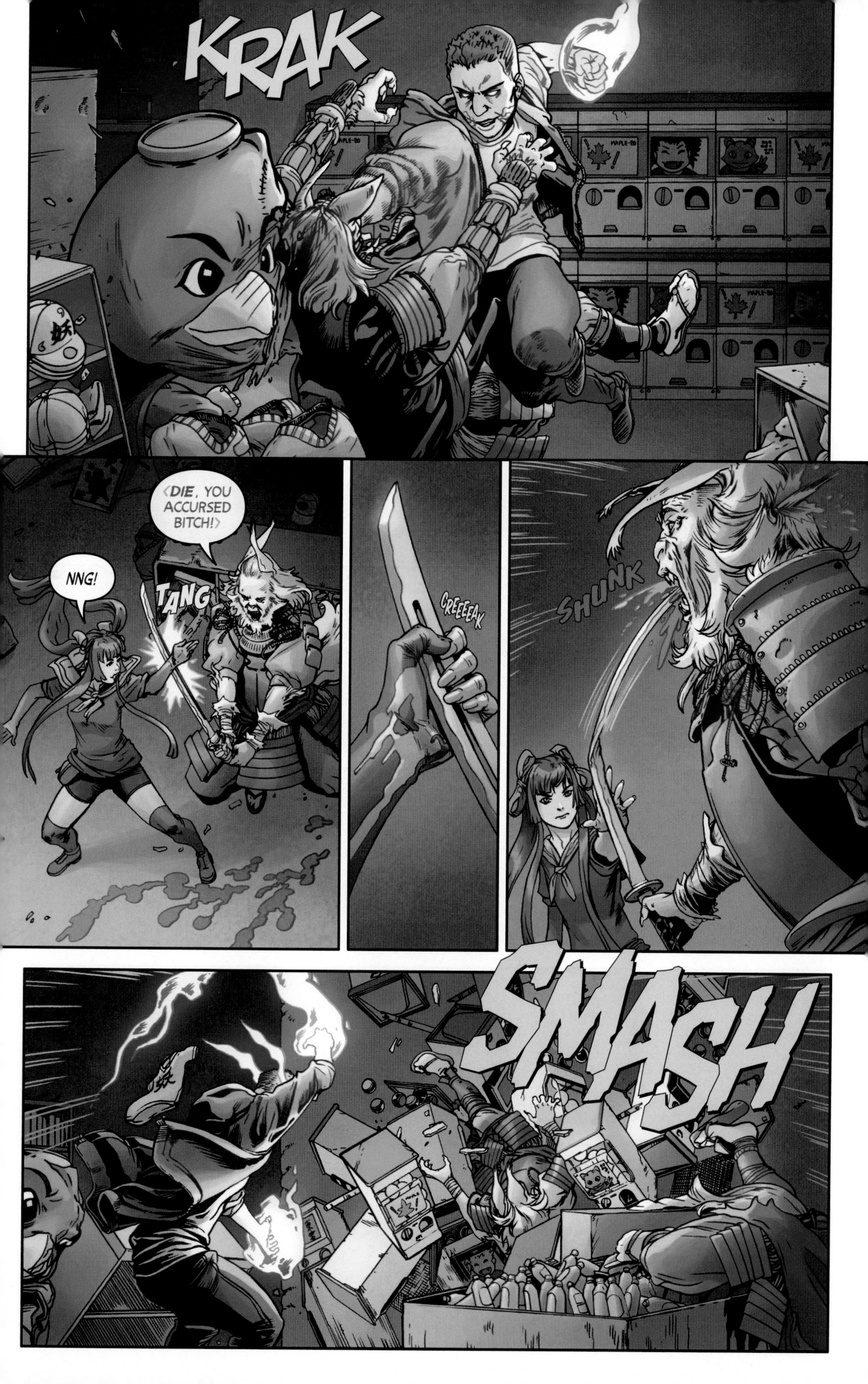
KRAK
NNG!
‹DIE, YOU ACCURSED BITCH!›
TANG
CREEEEAK
SHUNK
SMASH

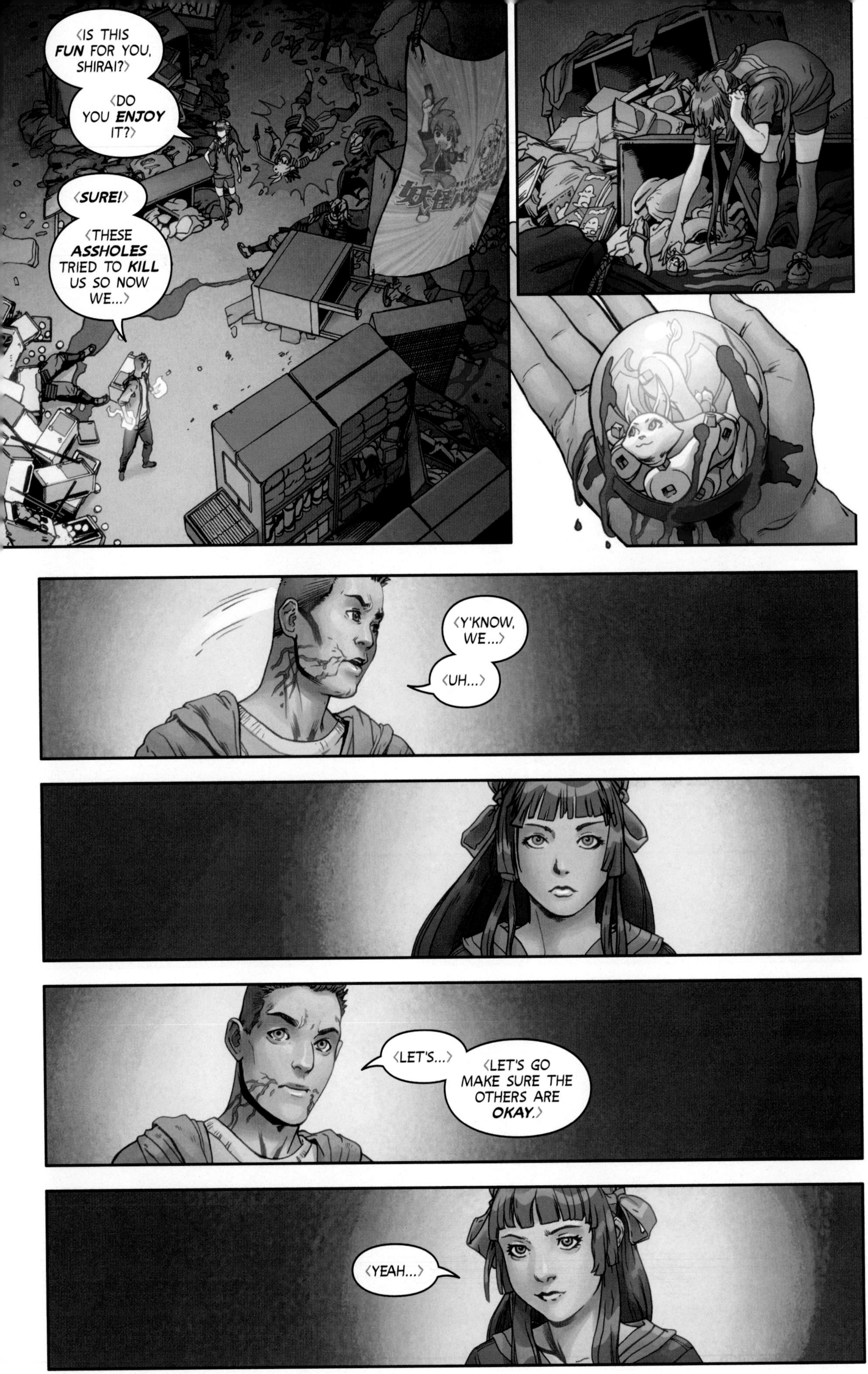
‹IS THIS FUN FOR YOU, SHIRAI?›
‹DO YOU ENJOY IT?›
‹SURE!›
‹THESE ASSHOLES TRIED TO KILL US SO NOW WE...›
‹Y'KNOW, WE...›
‹UH...›
‹LET'S...›
‹LET'S GO MAKE SURE THE OTHERS ARE OKAY.›
‹YEAH...›

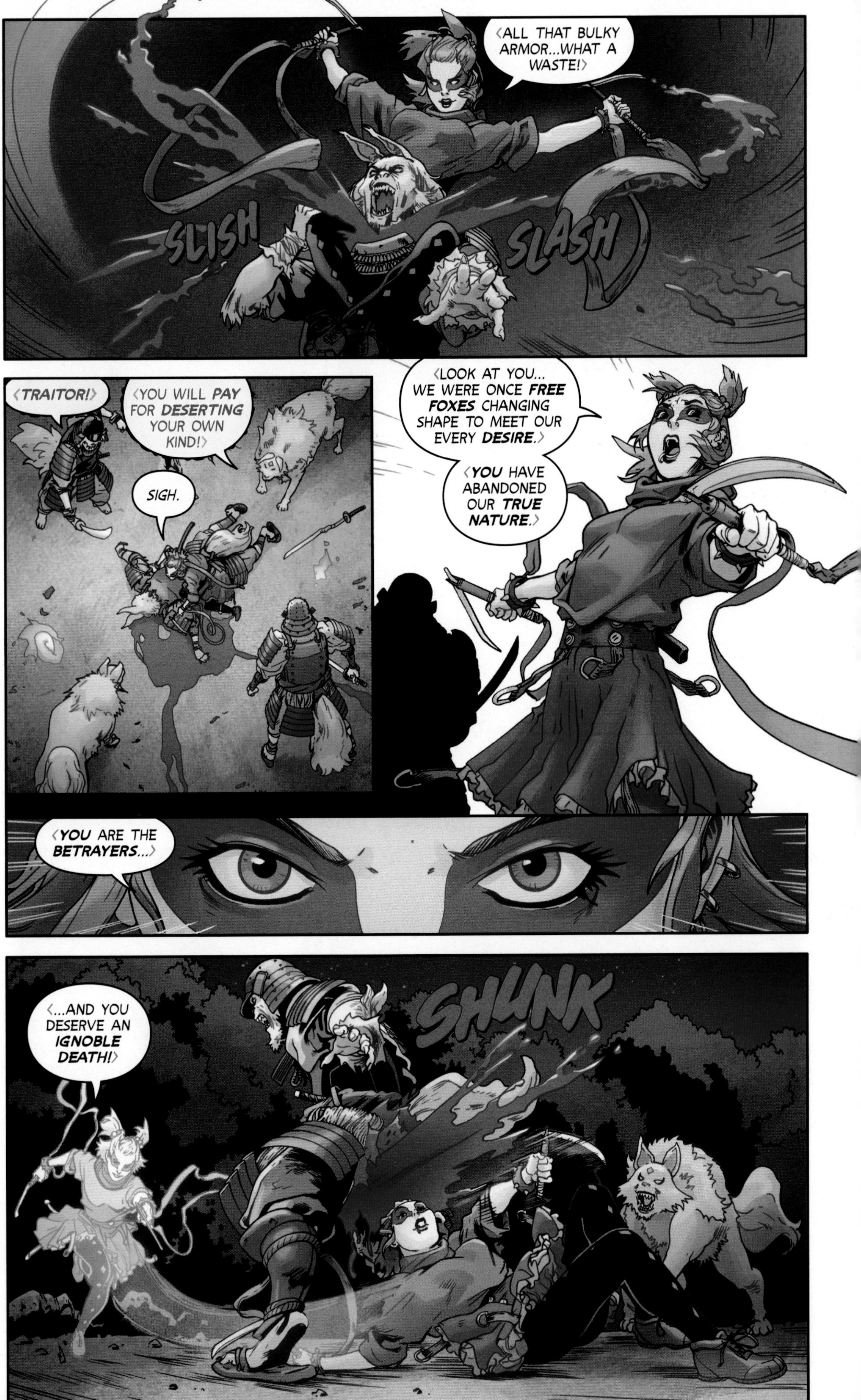
‹ALL THAT BULKY ARMOR...WHAT A WASTE!›
SLISH
SLASH
‹TRAITOR!›
‹YOU WILL PAY FOR DESERTING YOUR OWN KIND!›
SIGH.
‹LOOK AT YOU... WE WERE ONCE FREE FOXES CHANGING SHAPE TO MEET OUR EVERY DESIRE.›
‹YOU HAVE ABANDONED OUR TRUE NATURE.›
‹YOU ARE THE BETRAYERS...›
SHUNK
‹...AND YOU DESERVE AN IGNOBLE DEATH!›

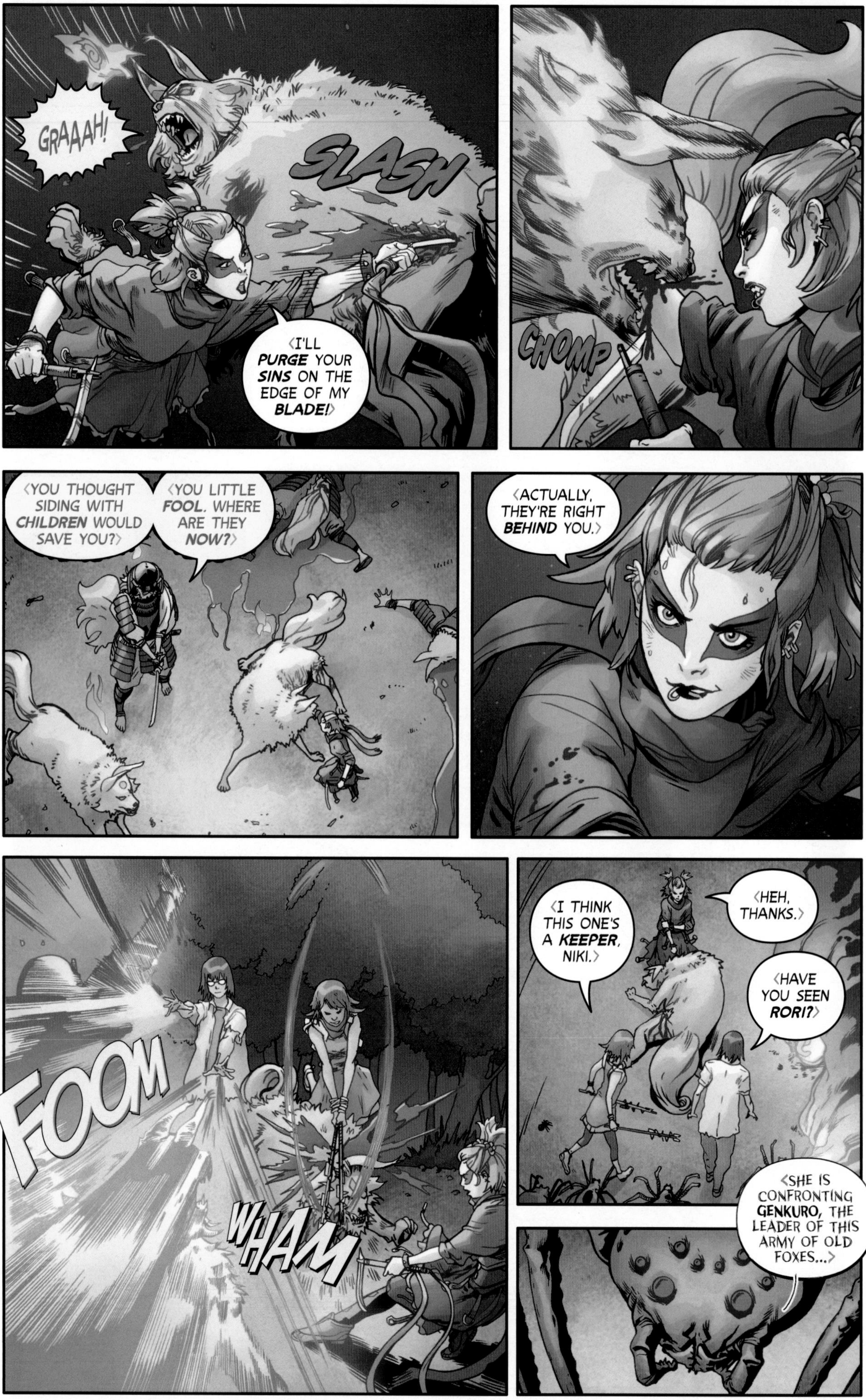
GRAAAH!
SLASH
<I'LL PURGE YOUR SINS ON THE EDGE OF MY BLADE!>
CHOMP
<YOU THOUGHT SIDING WITH CHILDREN WOULD SAVE YOU?>
<YOU LITTLE FOOL. WHERE ARE THEY NOW?>
<ACTUALLY, THEY'RE RIGHT BEHIND YOU.>
FOOM
WHAM
<I THINK THIS ONE'S A KEEPER, NIKI.>
<HEH, THANKS.>
<HAVE YOU SEEN RORI?>
<SHE IS CONFRONTING GENKURO, THE LEADER OF THIS ARMY OF OLD FOXES...>

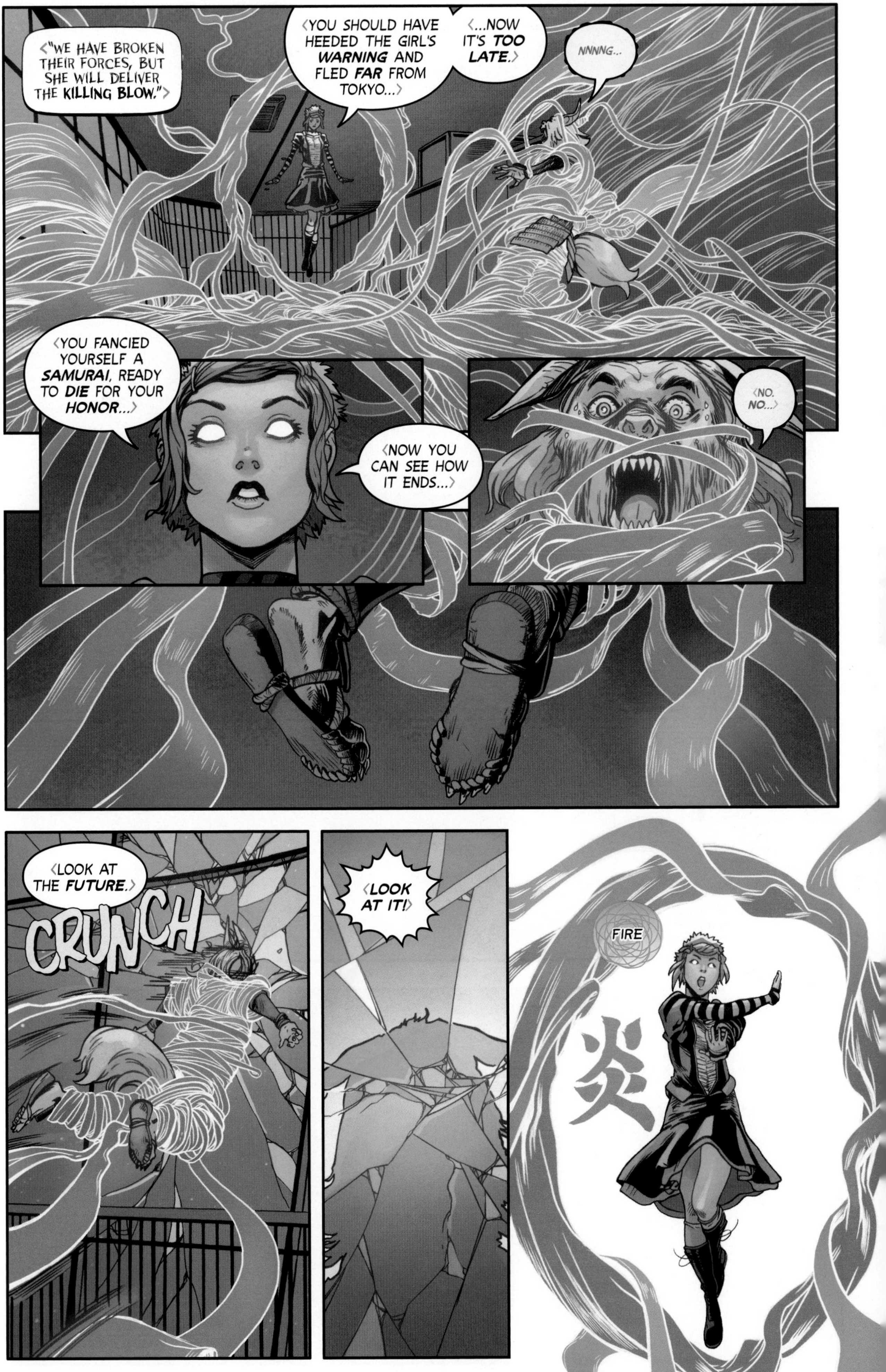
<"WE HAVE BROKEN THEIR FORCES, BUT SHE WILL DELIVER THE KILLING BLOW.">
<YOU SHOULD HAVE HEEDED THE GIRL'S WARNING AND FLED FAR FROM TOKYO...>
<...NOW IT'S TOO LATE.>
NNNNG...
<YOU FANCIED YOURSELF A SAMURAI, READY TO DIE FOR YOUR HONOR...>
<NOW YOU CAN SEE HOW IT ENDS...>
<NO. NO...>
<LOOK AT THE FUTURE.>
CRUNCH
<LOOK AT IT!>
FIRE
炎

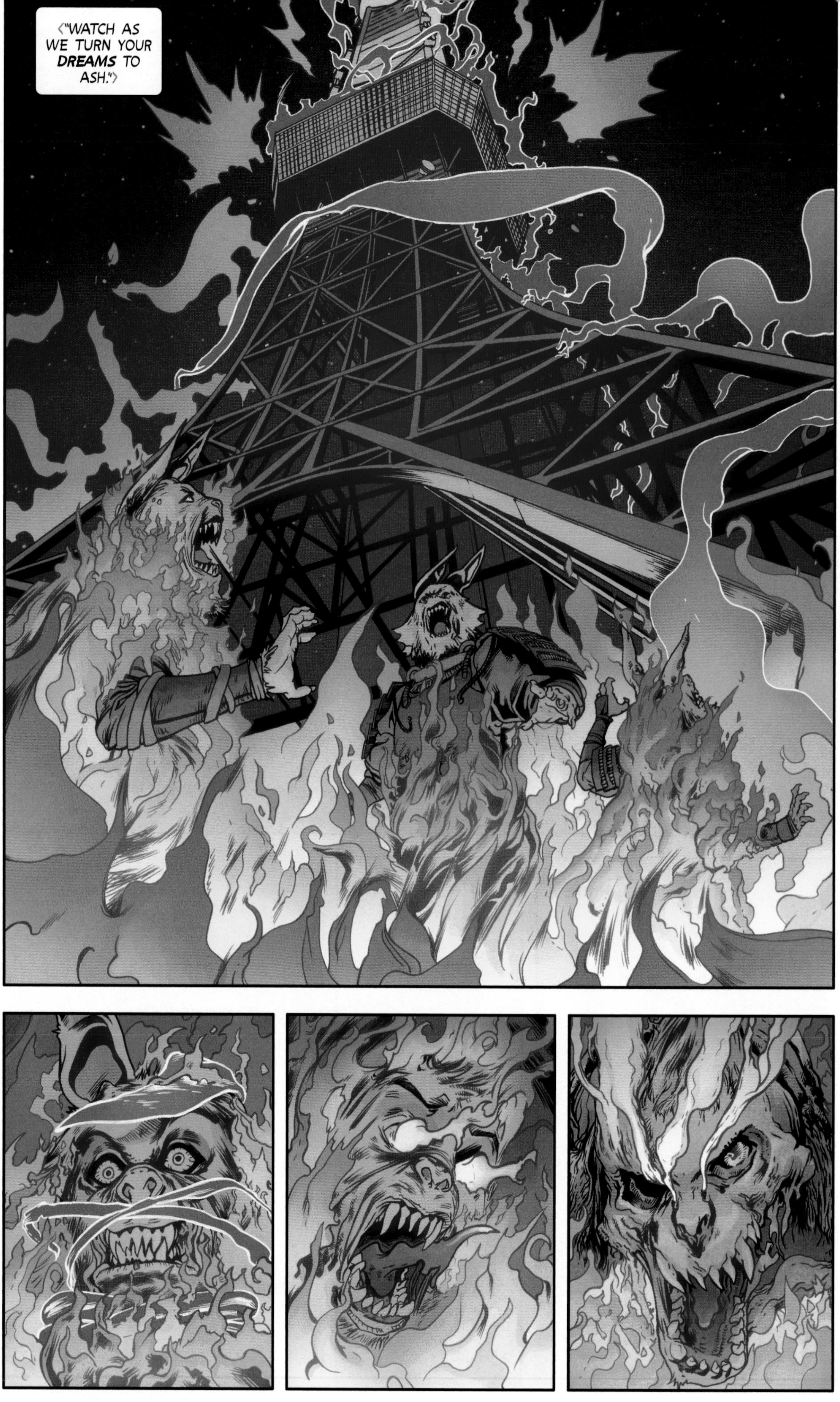
<"WATCH AS WE TURN YOUR DREAMS TO ASH.">

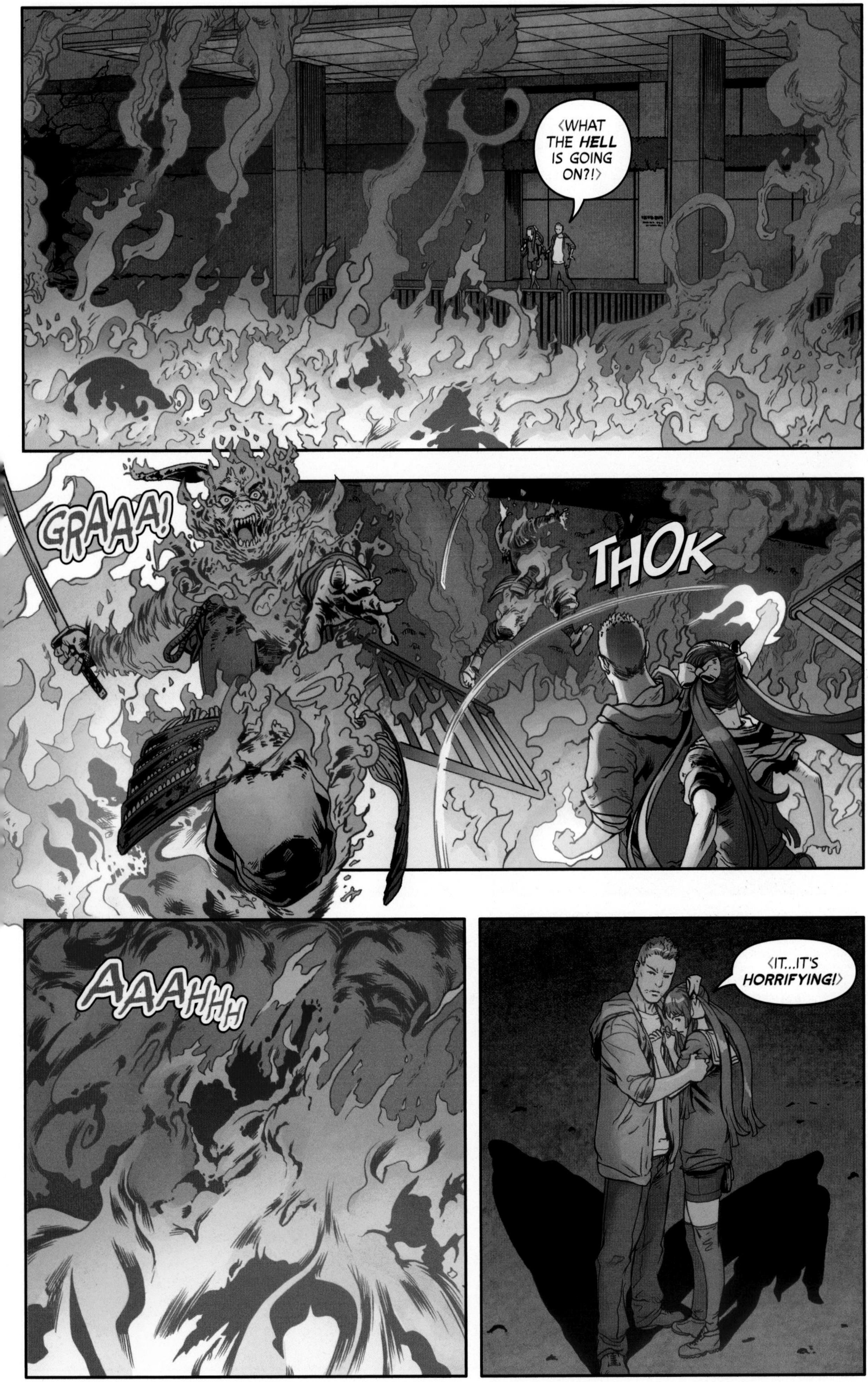

‹WHAT THE HELL IS GOING ON?!›
GRAAA!
THOK
AAAHHH
‹IT...IT'S HORRIFYING!›

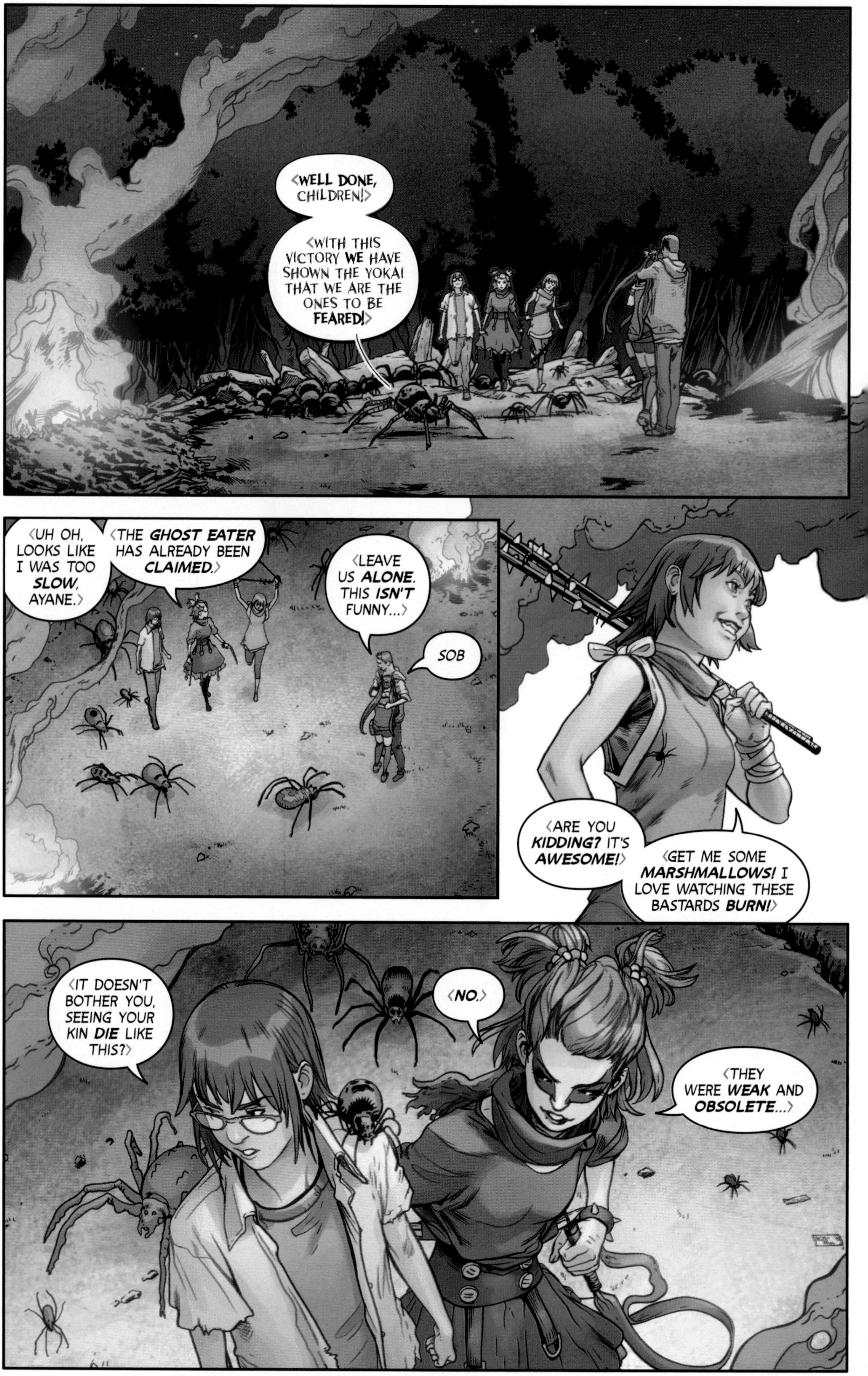

‹WELL DONE, CHILDREN!›
‹WITH THIS VICTORY WE HAVE SHOWN THE YOKAI THAT WE ARE THE ONES TO BE FEARED!›
‹UH OH, LOOKS LIKE I WAS TOO SLOW, AYANE.›
‹THE GHOST EATER HAS ALREADY BEEN CLAIMED.›
‹LEAVE US ALONE. THIS ISN'T FUNNY...›
SOB
‹ARE YOU KIDDING? IT'S AWESOME!›
‹GET ME SOME MARSHMALLOWS! I LOVE WATCHING THESE BASTARDS BURN!›
‹IT DOESN'T BOTHER YOU, SEEING YOUR KIN DIE LIKE THIS?›
‹NO.›
‹THEY WERE WEAK AND OBSOLETE...›

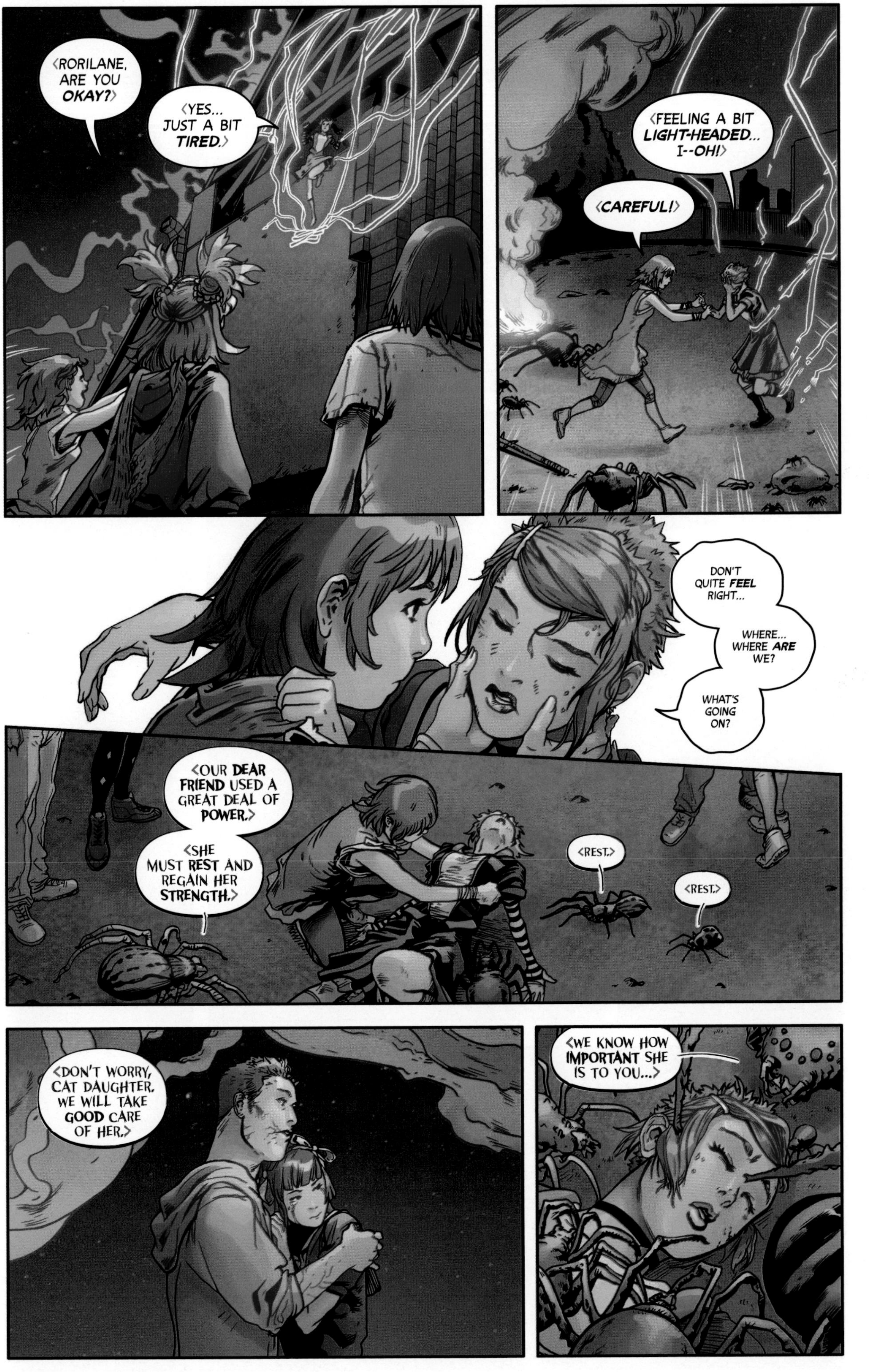

<RORILANE, ARE YOU OKAY?>
<YES... JUST A BIT TIRED.>
<FEELING A BIT LIGHT-HEADED... I--OH!>
<CAREFUL!>
DON'T QUITE FEEL RIGHT...
WHERE... WHERE ARE WE?
WHAT'S GOING ON?
<OUR DEAR FRIEND USED A GREAT DEAL OF POWER.>
<SHE MUST REST AND REGAIN HER STRENGTH.>
<REST.>
<REST.>
<DON'T WORRY, CAT DAUGHTER, WE WILL TAKE GOOD CARE OF HER.>
<WE KNOW HOW IMPORTANT SHE IS TO YOU...>

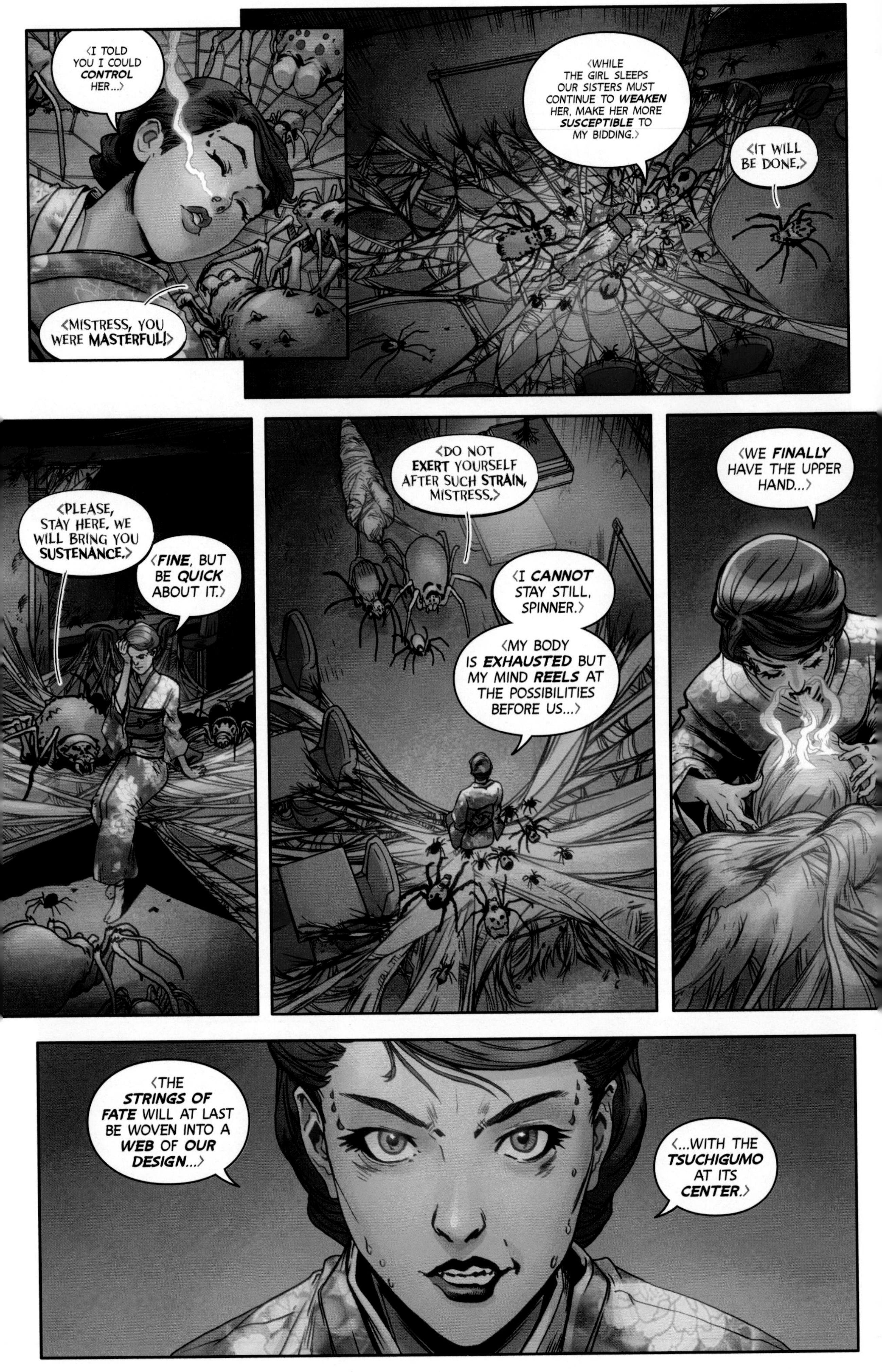

<I TOLD YOU I COULD CONTROL HER...>
<MISTRESS, YOU WERE MASTERFUL!>
<WHILE THE GIRL SLEEPS OUR SISTERS MUST CONTINUE TO WEAKEN HER, MAKE HER MORE SUSCEPTIBLE TO MY BIDDING.>
<IT WILL BE DONE.>
<PLEASE, STAY HERE. WE WILL BRING YOU SUSTENANCE.>
<FINE, BUT BE QUICK ABOUT IT.>
<DO NOT EXERT YOURSELF AFTER SUCH STRAIN, MISTRESS.>
<I CANNOT STAY STILL, SPINNER.>
<MY BODY IS EXHAUSTED BUT MY MIND REELS AT THE POSSIBILITIES BEFORE US...>
<WE FINALLY HAVE THE UPPER HAND...>
<THE STRINGS OF FATE WILL AT LAST BE WOVEN INTO A WEB OF OUR DESIGN...>
<...WITH THE TSUCHIGUMO AT ITS CENTER.>

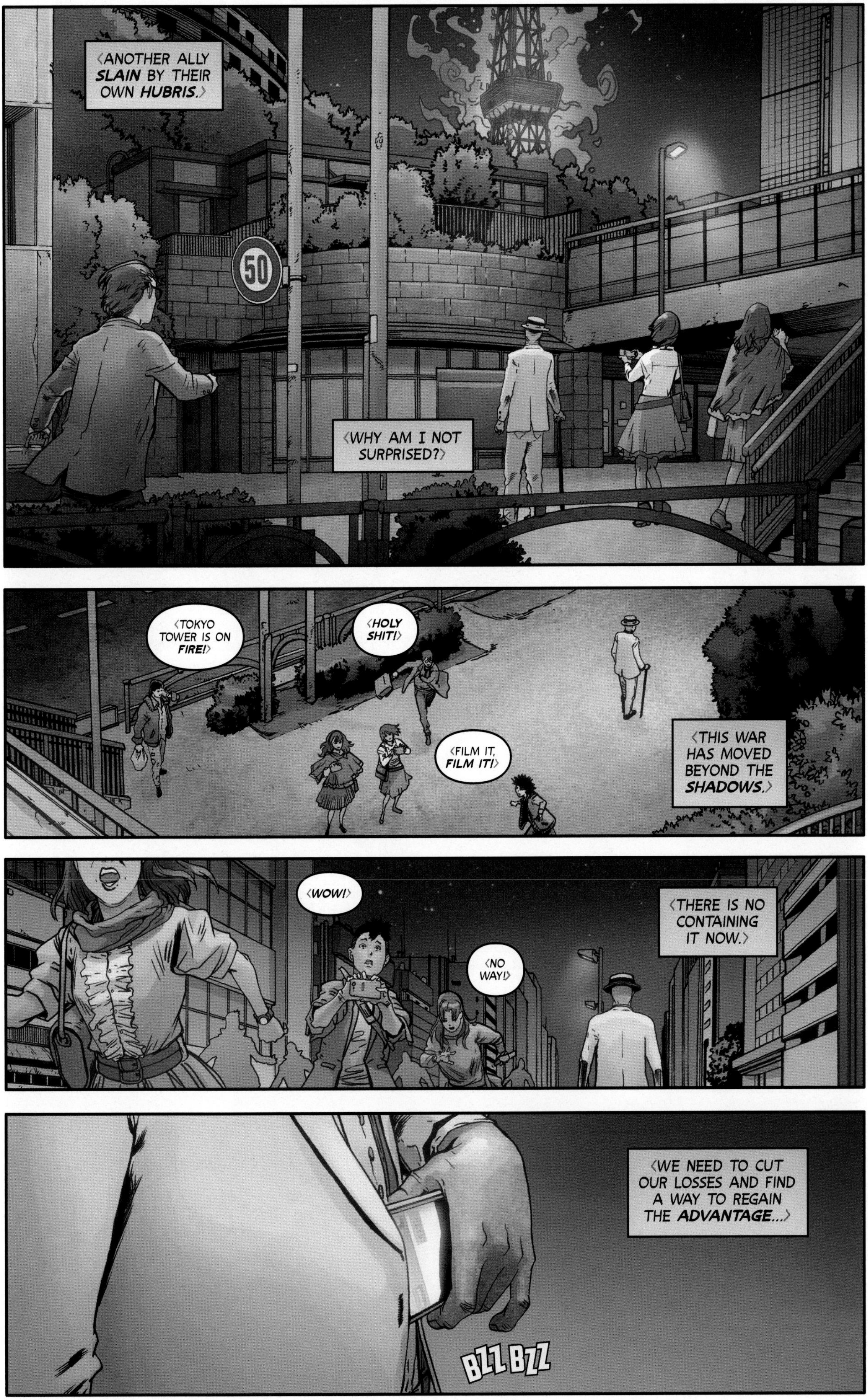

⟨ANOTHER ALLY SLAIN BY THEIR OWN HUBRIS.⟩
⟨WHY AM I NOT SURPRISED?⟩
⟨TOKYO TOWER IS ON FIRE!⟩
⟨HOLY SHIT!⟩
⟨FILM IT, FILM IT!⟩
⟨THIS WAR HAS MOVED BEYOND THE SHADOWS.⟩
⟨WOW!⟩
⟨NO WAY!⟩
⟨THERE IS NO CONTAINING IT NOW.⟩
⟨WE NEED TO CUT OUR LOSSES AND FIND A WAY TO REGAIN THE ADVANTAGE...⟩
BZZ BZZ

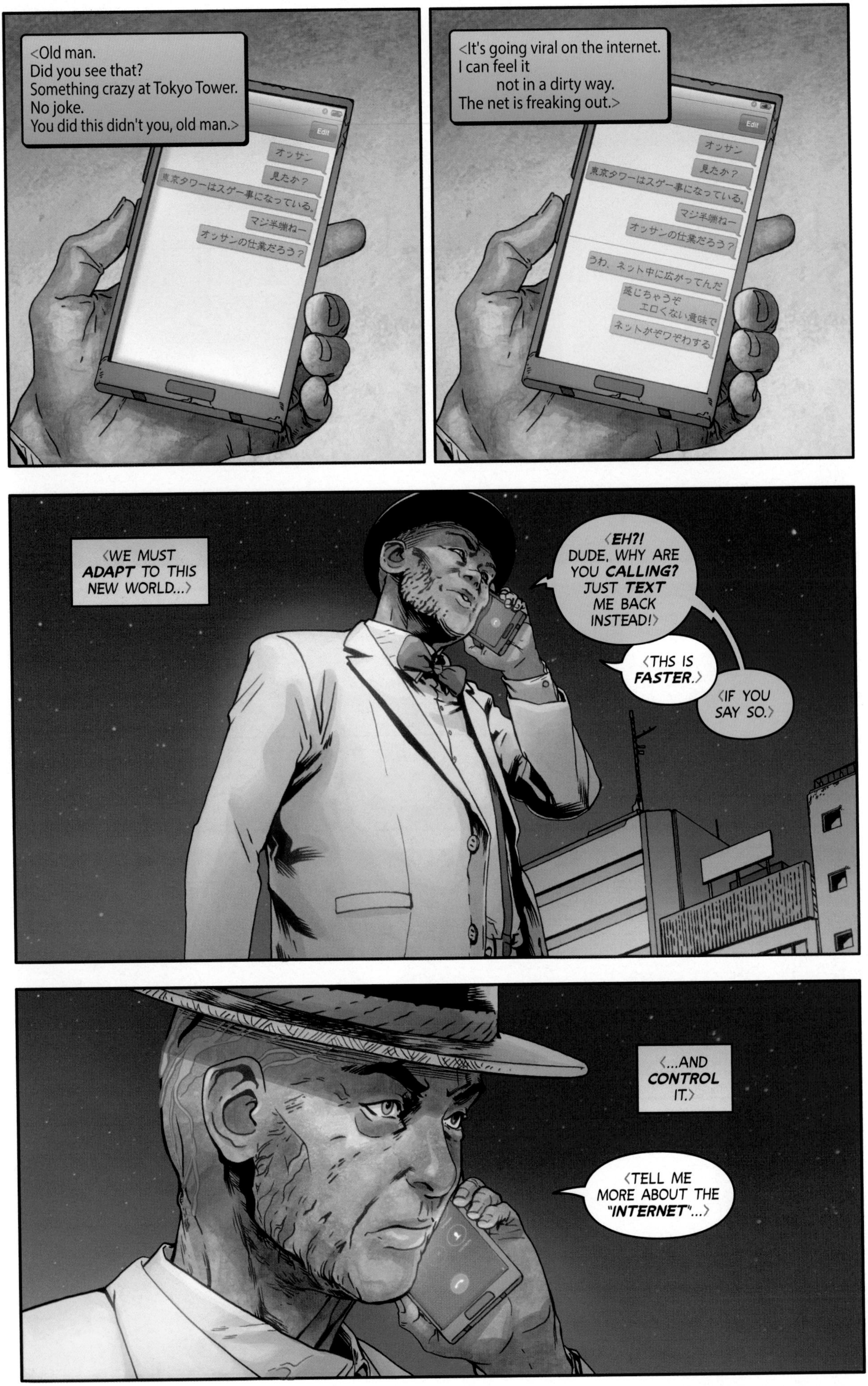
<Old man.
Did you see that?
Something crazy at Tokyo Tower.
No joke.
You did this didn't you, old man.>
Edit
オッサン
見たか？
東京タワーはスゲー事になっている。
マジ半端ねー
オッサンの仕業だろう？
<It's going viral on the internet.
I can feel it
not in a dirty way.
The net is freaking out.>
Edit
オッサン
見たか？
東京タワーはスゲー事になっている。
マジ半端ねー
オッサンの仕業だろう？
うわ、ネット中に広がってんだ
感じちゃうぞ
エロくない意味で
ネットがゾワゾワする
〈WE MUST ADAPT TO THIS NEW WORLD...〉
〈EH?! DUDE, WHY ARE YOU CALLING? JUST TEXT ME BACK INSTEAD!〉
〈THS IS FASTER.〉
〈IF YOU SAY SO.〉
〈...AND CONTROL IT.〉
〈TELL ME MORE ABOUT THE "INTERNET"...〉

Chapter Fourteen

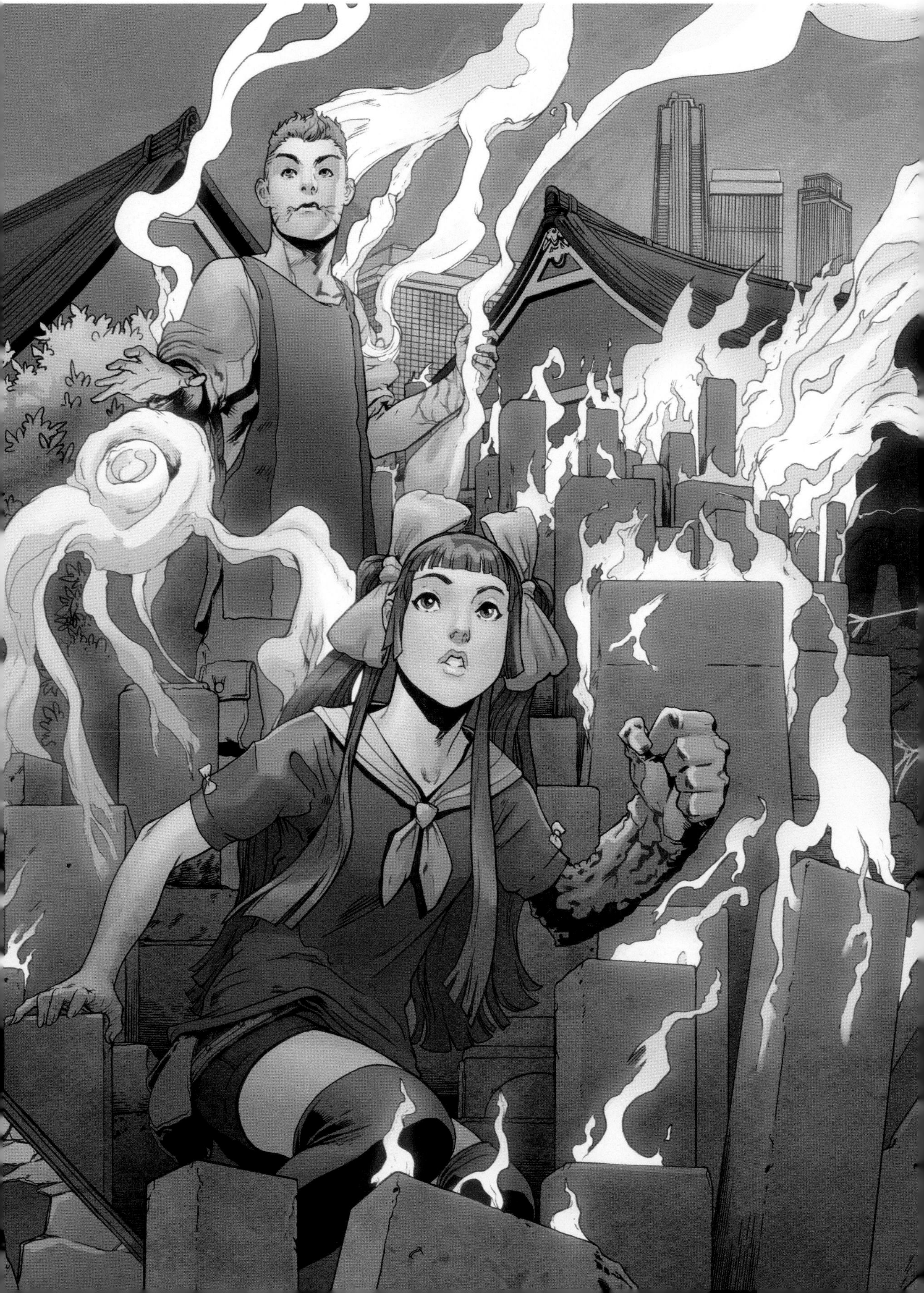

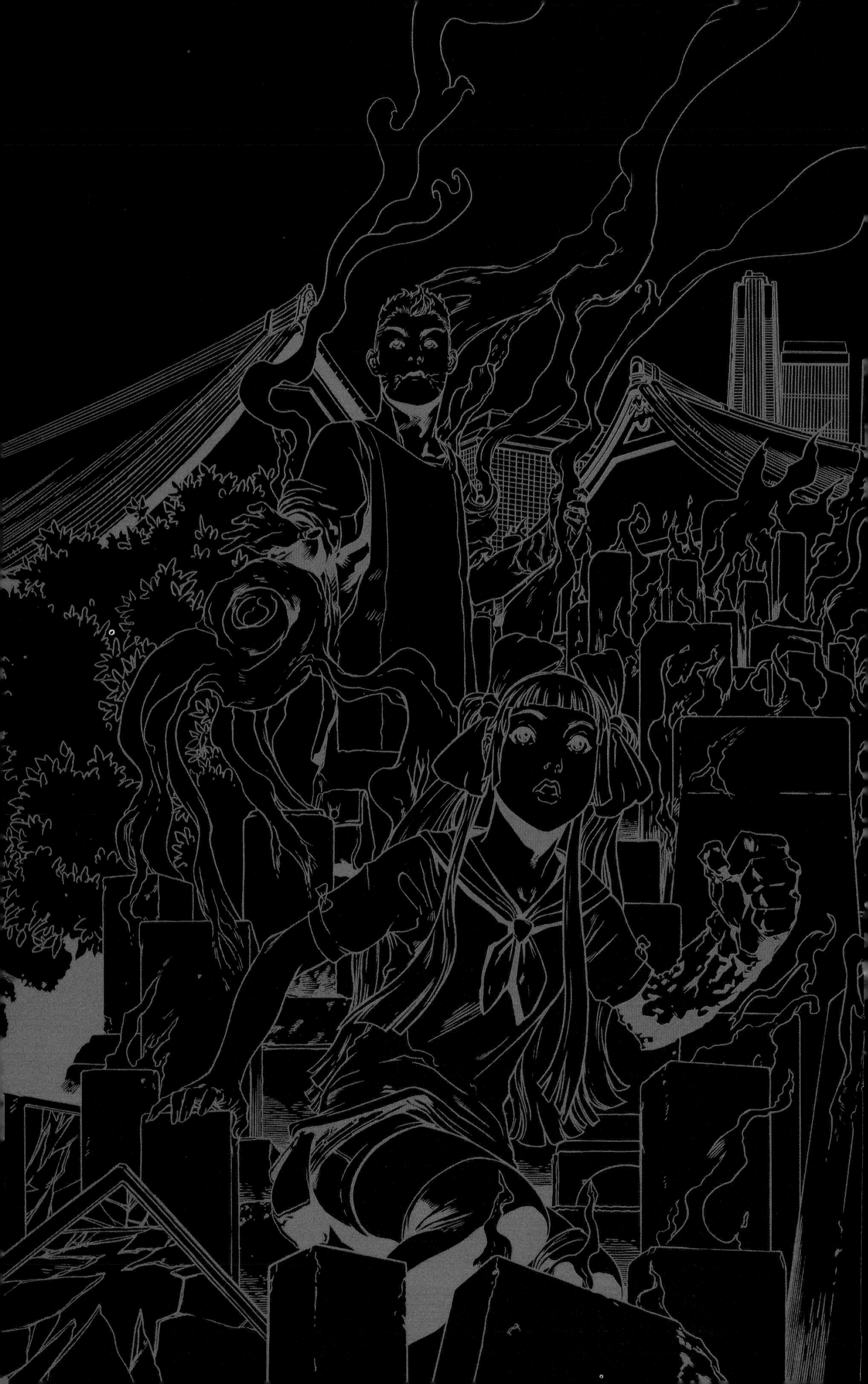

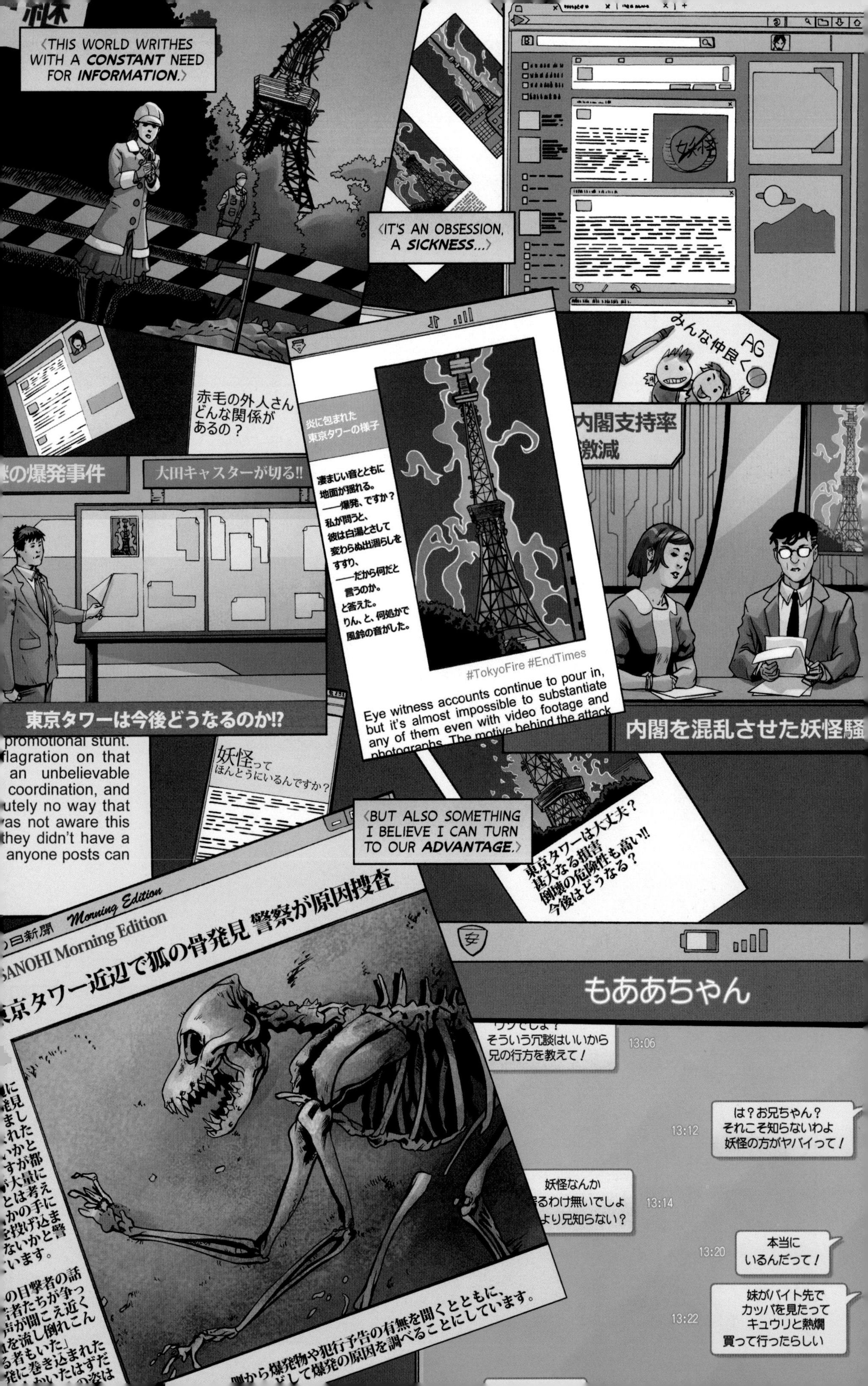
‹THIS WORLD WRITHES WITH A *CONSTANT* NEED FOR *INFORMATION*.›
‹IT'S AN OBSESSION, A *SICKNESS*...›
みんな仲良く
AG
赤毛の外人さん どんな関係が あるの？
炎に包まれた 東京タワーの様子
凄まじい音とともに 地面が揺れる。 ――爆発、ですか？ 私が問うと、 彼は白湯とさして 変わらぬ出涸らしを すすり、 ――だから何だと 言うのか。 と答えた。 りん、と、何処かで 風鈴の音がした。
#TokyoFire #EndTimes
Eye witness accounts continue to pour in, but it's almost impossible to substantiate any of them even with video footage and
内閣支持率 激減
の爆発事件
大田キャスターが切る!!
東京タワーは今後どうなるのか!?
内閣を混乱させた妖怪騒
promotional stunt. flagration on that an unbelievable coordination, and utely no way that as not aware this they didn't have a anyone posts can
妖怪って ほんとうにいるんですか？
‹BUT ALSO SOMETHING I BELIEVE I CAN TURN TO OUR *ADVANTAGE*.›
東京タワーは大丈夫？ 甚大なる損害 倒壊の危険性も高い!! 今後はどうなる？
Morning Edition
SANOHI Morning Edition
東京タワー近辺で狐の骨発見 警察が原因捜査
もああちゃん
そういう冗談はいいから 兄の行方を教えて！
13:06
は？お兄ちゃん？ それこそ知らないわよ 妖怪の方がヤバイって！
13:12
妖怪なんか
より兄知らない？
13:14
本当に いるんだって！
13:20
妹がバイト先で カッパを見たって キュウリと熱燗 買って行ったらしい
13:22

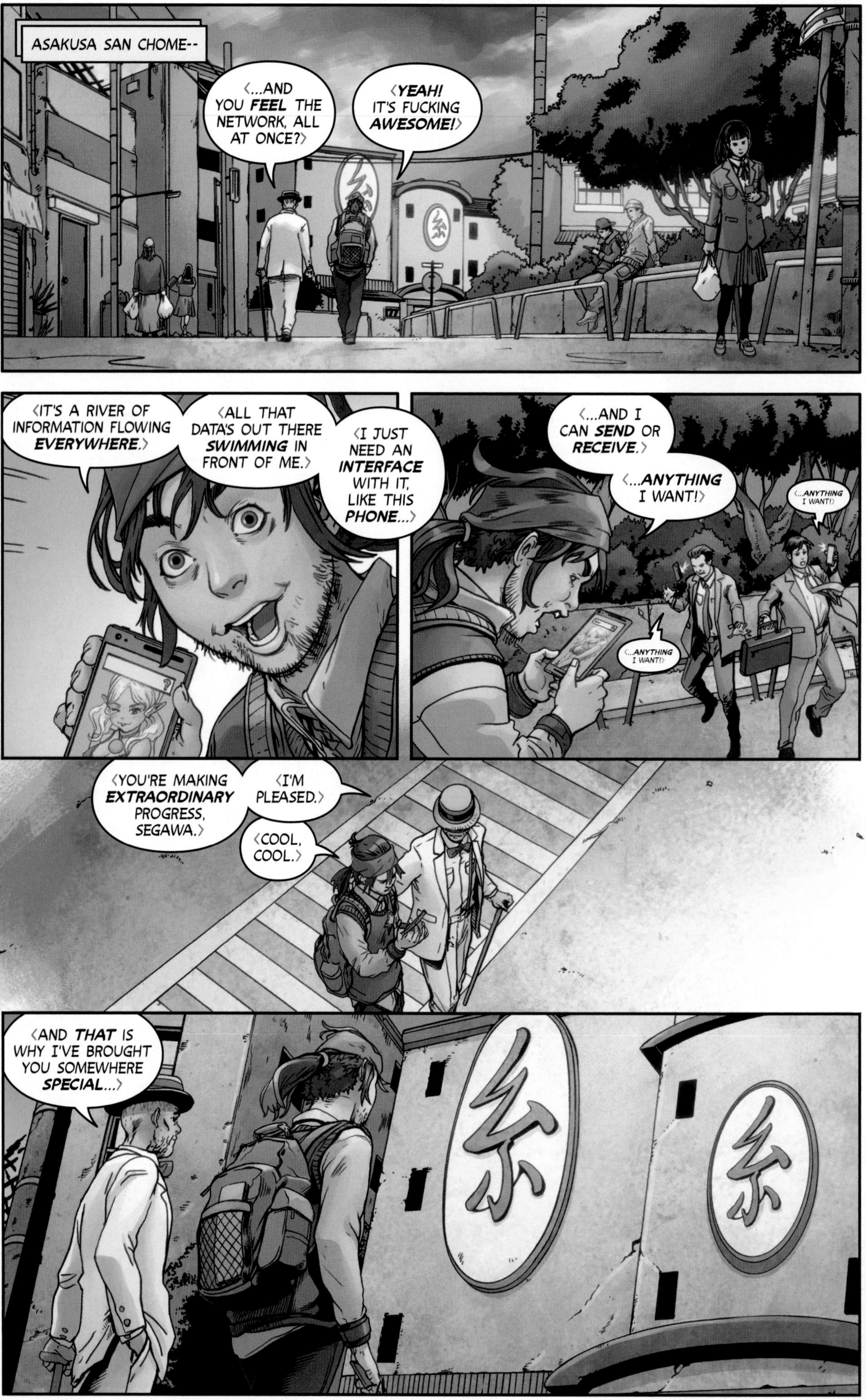
ASAKUSA SAN CHOME--
<...AND YOU FEEL THE NETWORK, ALL AT ONCE?>
<YEAH! IT'S FUCKING AWESOME!>
<IT'S A RIVER OF INFORMATION FLOWING EVERYWHERE.>
<ALL THAT DATA'S OUT THERE SWIMMING IN FRONT OF ME.>
<I JUST NEED AN INTERFACE WITH IT, LIKE THIS PHONE...>
<...AND I CAN SEND OR RECEIVE.>
<...ANYTHING I WANT!>
<...ANYTHING I WANT!>
<...ANYTHING I WANT!>
<YOU'RE MAKING EXTRAORDINARY PROGRESS, SEGAWA.>
<I'M PLEASED.>
<COOL, COOL.>
<AND THAT IS WHY I'VE BROUGHT YOU SOMEWHERE SPECIAL...>

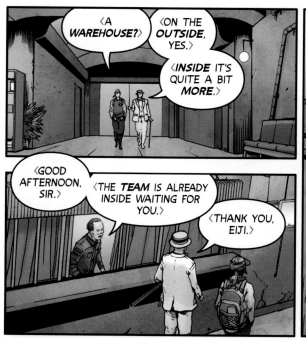

〈A WAREHOUSE?〉 〈ON THE OUTSIDE, YES.〉

〈INSIDE IT'S QUITE A BIT MORE.〉

〈GOOD AFTERNOON, SIR.〉 〈THE TEAM IS ALREADY INSIDE WAITING FOR YOU.〉

〈THANK YOU, EIJI.〉

〈YOUR ABILITY TO CONTACT AND INFLUENCE NETWORKS IS ALREADY IMPRESSIVE, BUT I WANT TO SEE IF WE CAN TAKE IT EVEN FURTHER...〉

〈THIS IS THE LOOM.〉

〈IT'S A MAGIC-POWERED MACHINE THAT CAN PERCEIVE THE STRINGS OF FATE.〉

〈IT'S TAKEN MANY YEARS, BUT WITH GREAT EFFORT WE'VE BEEN ABLE TO INTERPRET AND REWEAVE SOME OF THE STRINGS TO OUR BENEFIT.〉

〈CRAZY, BUT WHAT DOES THIS HAVE TO DO WITH ME?〉

〈I WANT YOU TO CONNECT TO IT.〉

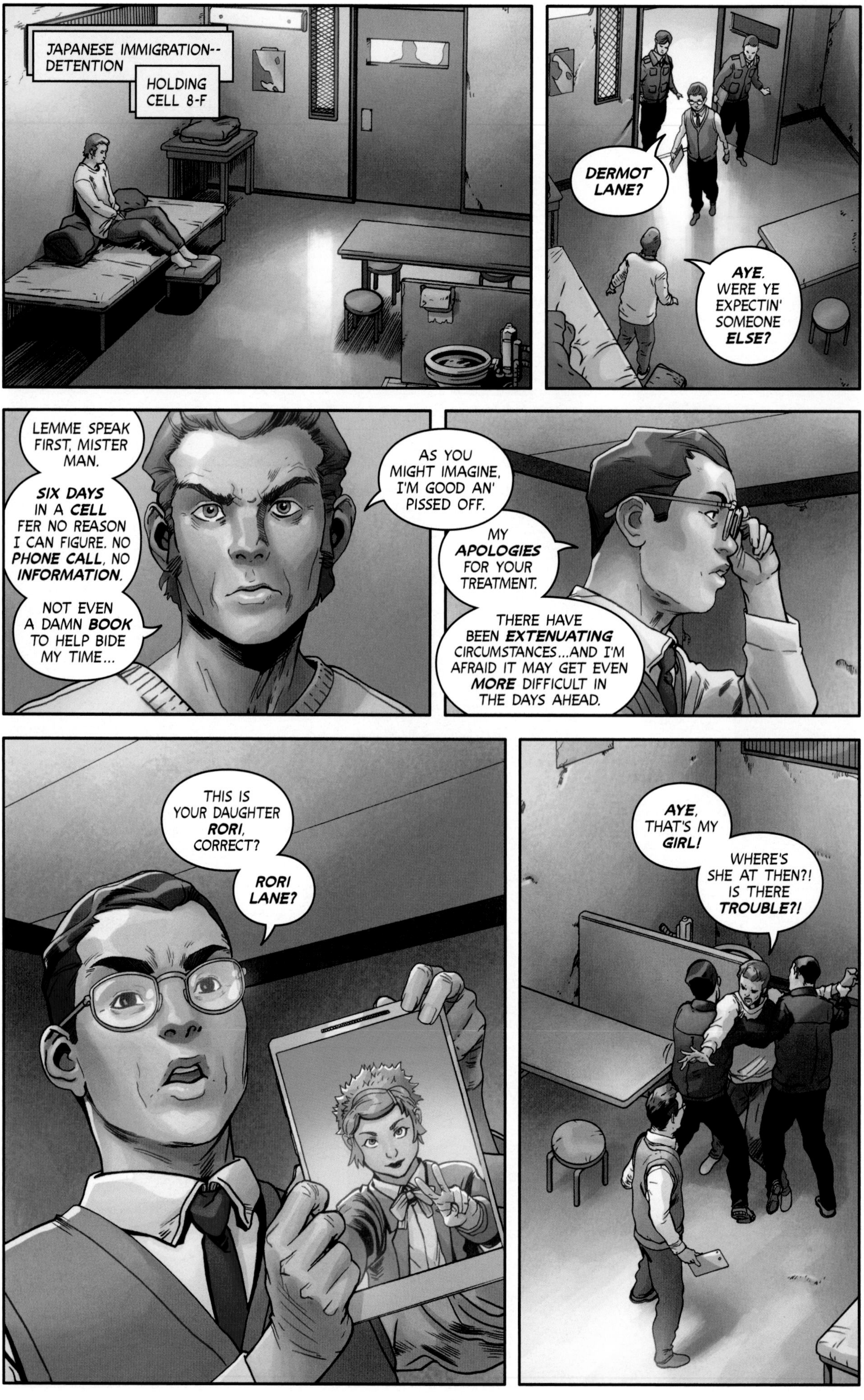

JAPANESE IMMIGRATION--DETENTION
HOLDING CELL 8-F
DERMOT LANE?
AYE. WERE YE EXPECTIN' SOMEONE ELSE?
LEMME SPEAK FIRST, MISTER MAN.
SIX DAYS IN A CELL FER NO REASON I CAN FIGURE. NO PHONE CALL, NO INFORMATION.
NOT EVEN A DAMN BOOK TO HELP BIDE MY TIME...
AS YOU MIGHT IMAGINE, I'M GOOD AN' PISSED OFF.
MY APOLOGIES FOR YOUR TREATMENT.
THERE HAVE BEEN EXTENUATING CIRCUMSTANCES...AND I'M AFRAID IT MAY GET EVEN MORE DIFFICULT IN THE DAYS AHEAD.
THIS IS YOUR DAUGHTER RORI, CORRECT?
RORI LANE?
AYE, THAT'S MY GIRL!
WHERE'S SHE AT THEN?! IS THERE TROUBLE?!

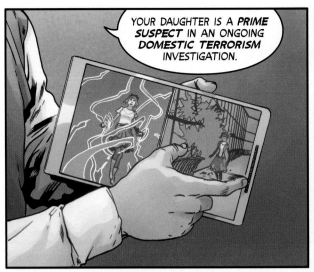

YOUR DAUGHTER IS A *PRIME SUSPECT* IN AN ONGOING *DOMESTIC TERRORISM* INVESTIGATION.

THERE HAVE BEEN MULTIPLE INCIDENTS OVER THE PAST FEW MONTHS INVOLVING *EXPLOSIVES* AND *INCENDIARY DEVICES* DEPLOYED AGAINST THE PEOPLE OF TOKYO.

MULTIPLE REPORTS PLACE *RORI* AND A GROUP OF OTHER *ANARCHISTS* AT EACH LOCATION.

YOU CAN'T BE *SERIOUS!* SHE-SHE'S JUST A *CHILD!*

EXACTLY. THAT'S WHY WE BELIEVE SHE MAY BE RECEIVING ORDERS FROM A *LARGER ORGANIZATION.* POSSIBLY ONE OF *FOREIGN* ORIGIN...

SO YOU THINK I'M SUM KINDA FUCKIN' *TERRORIST* THEN?

PERHAPS. PERHAPS NOT.

UNTIL WE CAN DETERMINE YOUR *INNOCENCE* OR VERIFY HER *LOCATION,* YOU WILL BE DETAINED HERE IN *IMMIGRATION DETENTION.*

DO YOU KNOW *WHERE* SHE IS?

DO YOU HAVE ANY WAY TO *CONTACT* HER?

IF I DID, DO YA THINK I'D JUMP ON A *FUCKIN'* PLANE AN' COME ROUND *HERE?*

VERY WELL.

I'LL RETURN WHEN I HAVE MORE *INFORMATION...*

FWUMP

[DADDY'S LITTLE GIRL...*]

*TRANSLATED FROM IRISH.

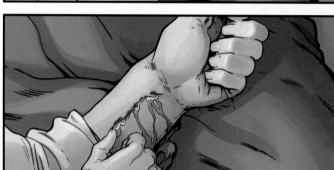

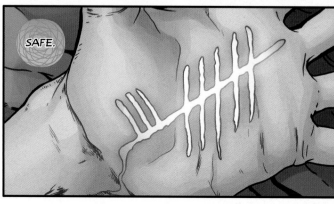

SAFE.

[KEEP HER SAFE...]

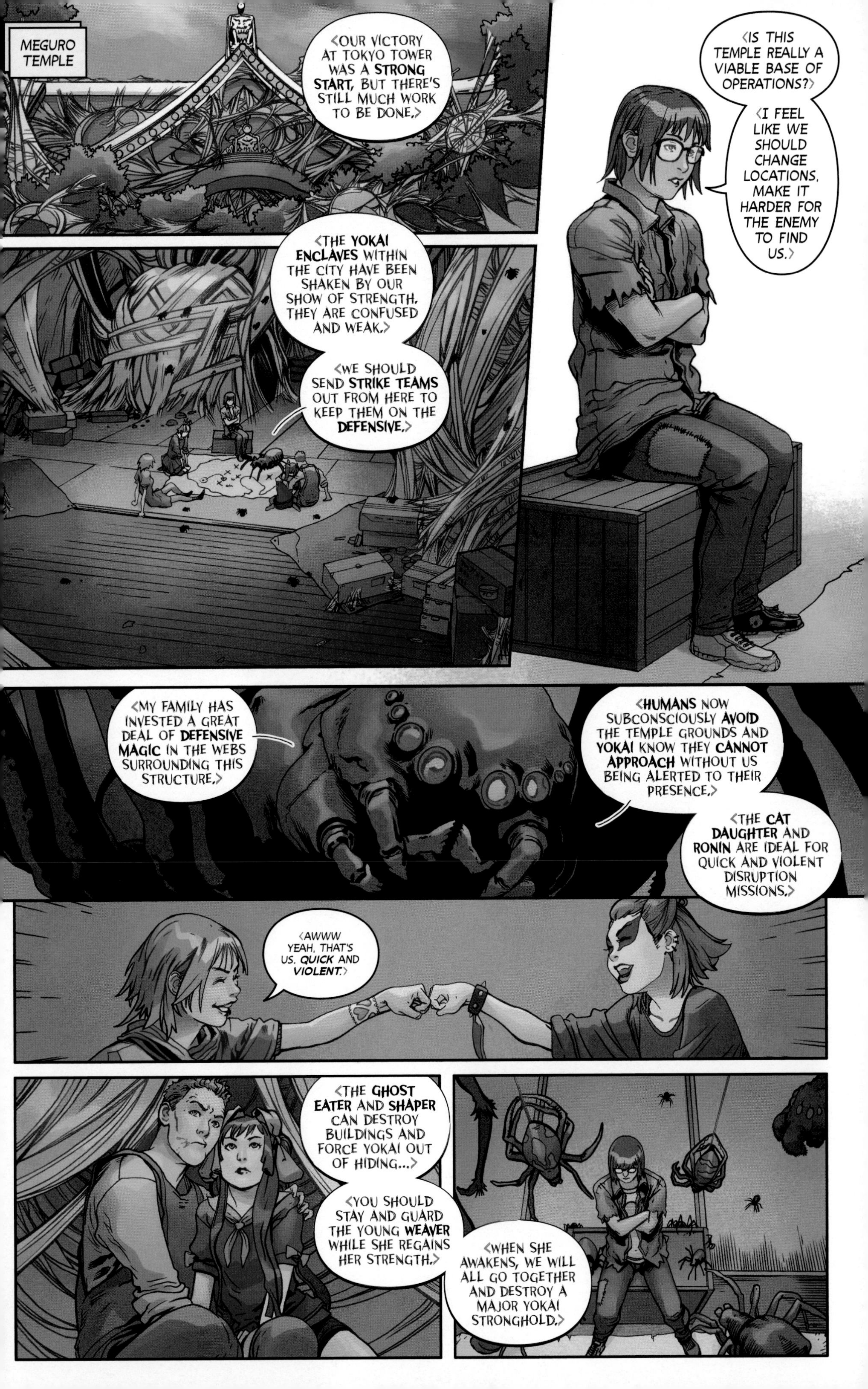
MEGURO TEMPLE
<OUR VICTORY AT TOKYO TOWER WAS A STRONG START, BUT THERE'S STILL MUCH WORK TO BE DONE.>
<IS THIS TEMPLE REALLY A VIABLE BASE OF OPERATIONS?>
<I FEEL LIKE WE SHOULD CHANGE LOCATIONS, MAKE IT HARDER FOR THE ENEMY TO FIND US.>
<THE YOKAI ENCLAVES WITHIN THE CITY HAVE BEEN SHAKEN BY OUR SHOW OF STRENGTH. THEY ARE CONFUSED AND WEAK.>
<WE SHOULD SEND STRIKE TEAMS OUT FROM HERE TO KEEP THEM ON THE DEFENSIVE.>
<MY FAMILY HAS INVESTED A GREAT DEAL OF DEFENSIVE MAGIC IN THE WEBS SURROUNDING THIS STRUCTURE.>
<HUMANS NOW SUBCONSCIOUSLY AVOID THE TEMPLE GROUNDS AND YOKAI KNOW THEY CANNOT APPROACH WITHOUT US BEING ALERTED TO THEIR PRESENCE.>
<THE CAT DAUGHTER AND RONIN ARE IDEAL FOR QUICK AND VIOLENT DISRUPTION MISSIONS.>
<AWWW YEAH, THAT'S US. QUICK AND VIOLENT.>
<THE GHOST EATER AND SHAPER CAN DESTROY BUILDINGS AND FORCE YOKAI OUT OF HIDING...>
<YOU SHOULD STAY AND GUARD THE YOUNG WEAVER WHILE SHE REGAINS HER STRENGTH.>
<WHEN SHE AWAKENS, WE WILL ALL GO TOGETHER AND DESTROY A MAJOR YOKAI STRONGHOLD.>

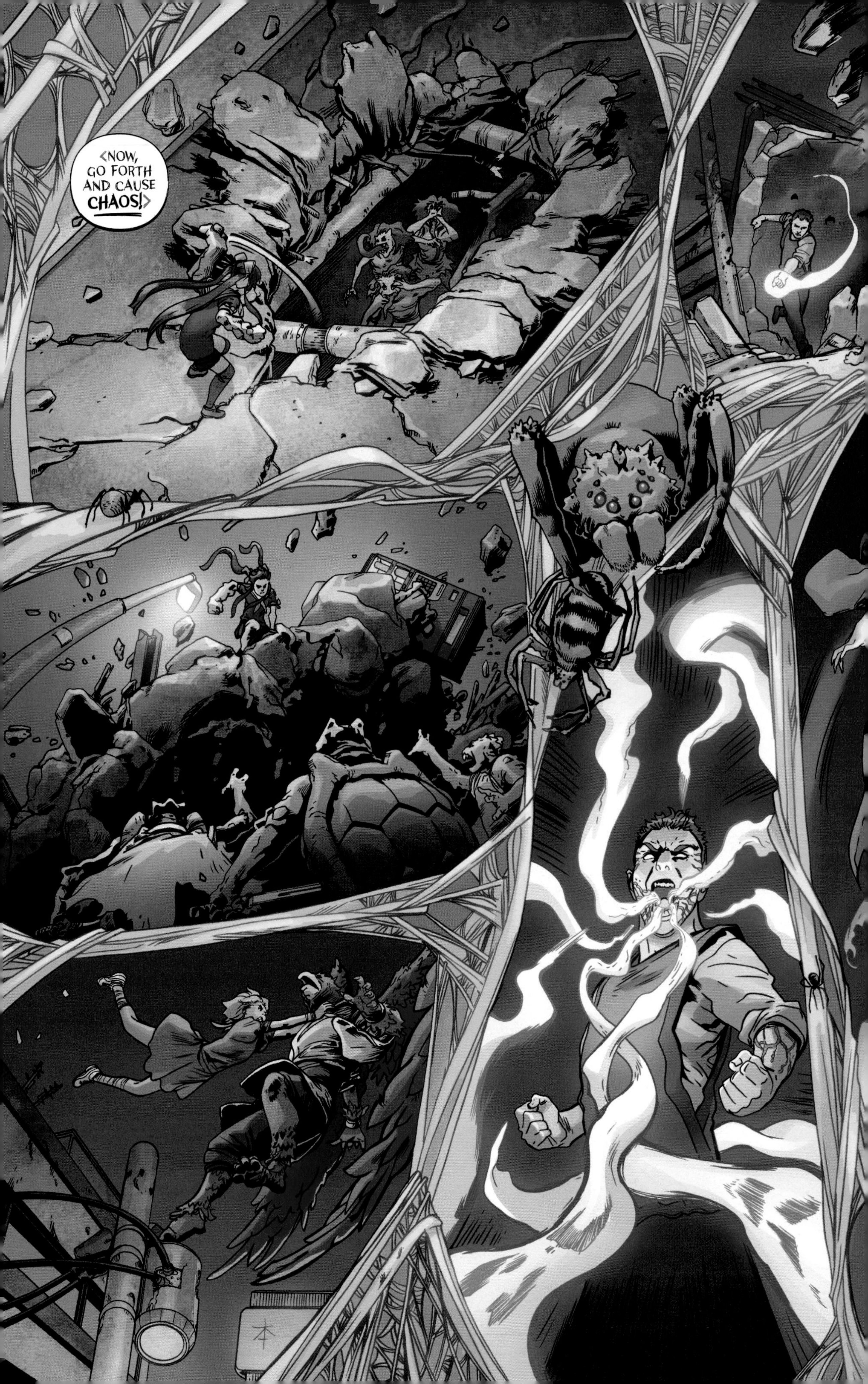
<NOW, GO FORTH AND CAUSE CHAOS!>

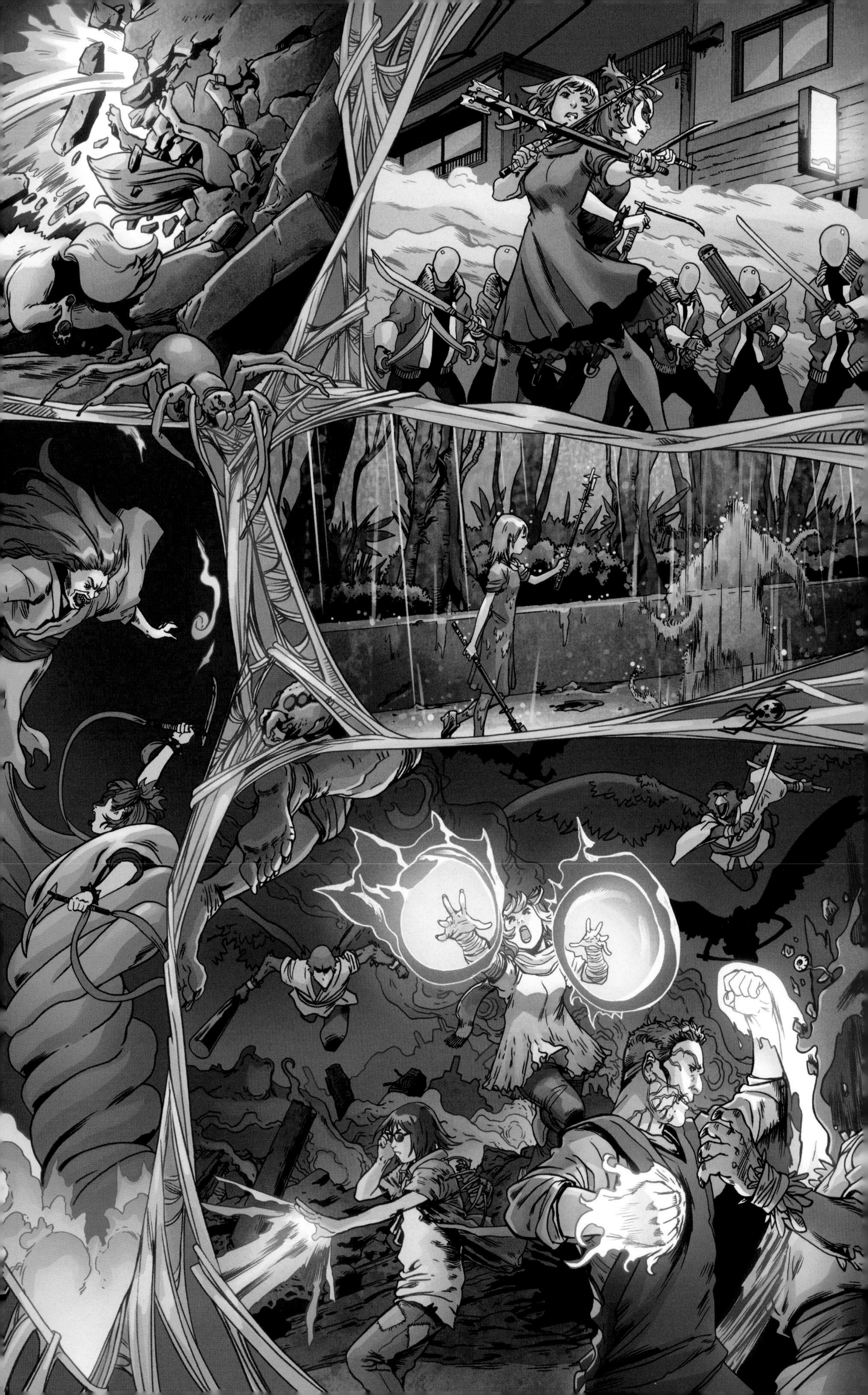

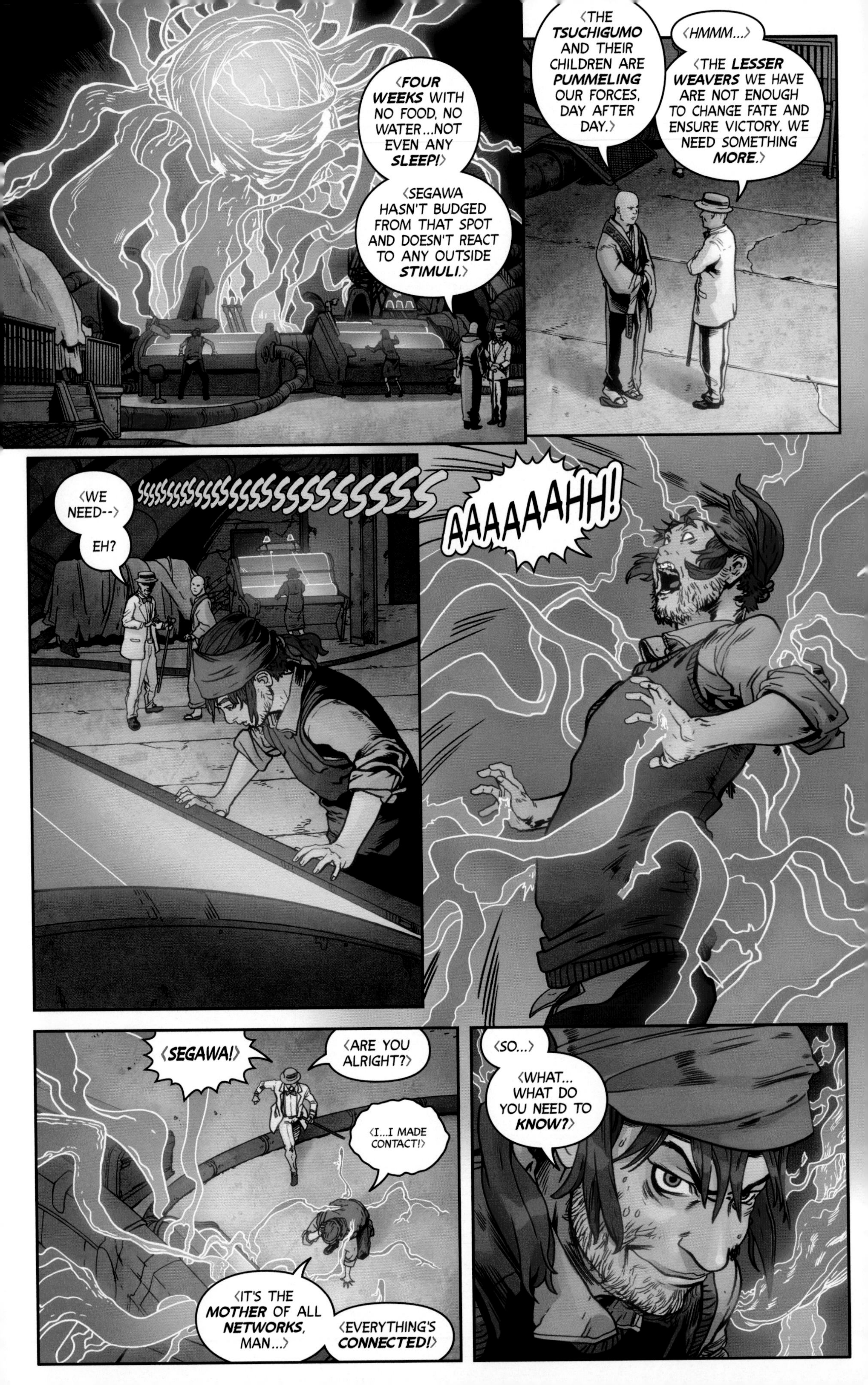

⟨FOUR WEEKS WITH NO FOOD, NO WATER...NOT EVEN ANY SLEEP!⟩
⟨SEGAWA HASN'T BUDGED FROM THAT SPOT AND DOESN'T REACT TO ANY OUTSIDE STIMULI.⟩
⟨THE TSUCHIGUMO AND THEIR CHILDREN ARE PUMMELING OUR FORCES, DAY AFTER DAY.⟩
⟨HMMM...⟩
⟨THE LESSER WEAVERS WE HAVE ARE NOT ENOUGH TO CHANGE FATE AND ENSURE VICTORY. WE NEED SOMETHING MORE.⟩
⟨WE NEED--⟩
SSSSSSSSSSSSSSSSSSSSSSSSSSSS
EH?
AAAAAAHH!
⟨SEGAWA!⟩
⟨ARE YOU ALRIGHT?⟩
⟨I...I MADE CONTACT!⟩
⟨IT'S THE MOTHER OF ALL NETWORKS, MAN...⟩
⟨EVERYTHING'S CONNECTED!⟩
⟨SO...⟩
⟨WHAT... WHAT DO YOU NEED TO KNOW?⟩

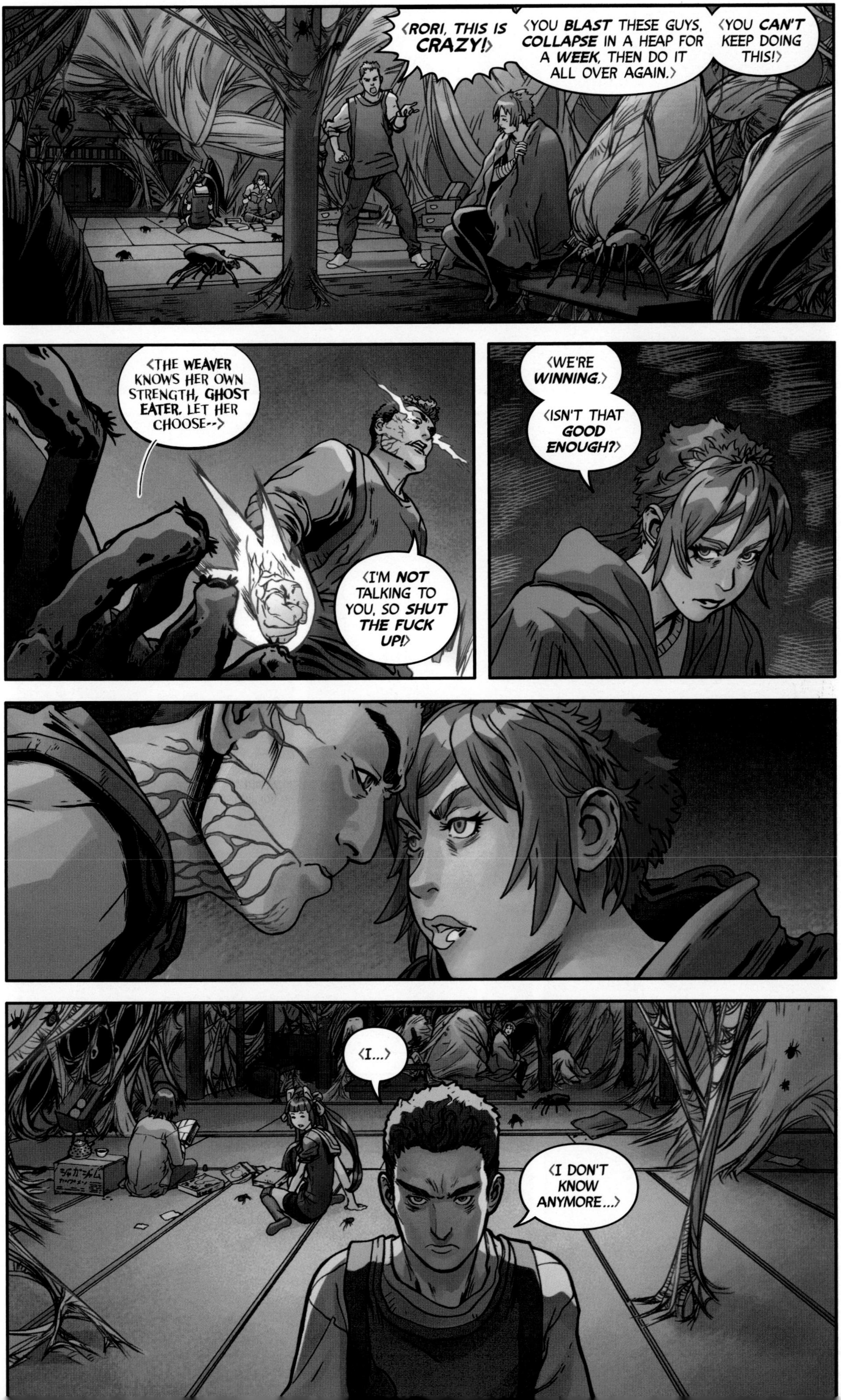
‹RORI, THIS IS CRAZY!›
‹YOU BLAST THESE GUYS, COLLAPSE IN A HEAP FOR A WEEK, THEN DO IT ALL OVER AGAIN.›
‹YOU CAN'T KEEP DOING THIS!›
‹THE WEAVER KNOWS HER OWN STRENGTH, GHOST EATER. LET HER CHOOSE--›
‹I'M NOT TALKING TO YOU, SO SHUT THE FUCK UP!›
‹WE'RE WINNING.›
‹ISN'T THAT GOOD ENOUGH?›
‹I...›
‹I DON'T KNOW ANYMORE...›

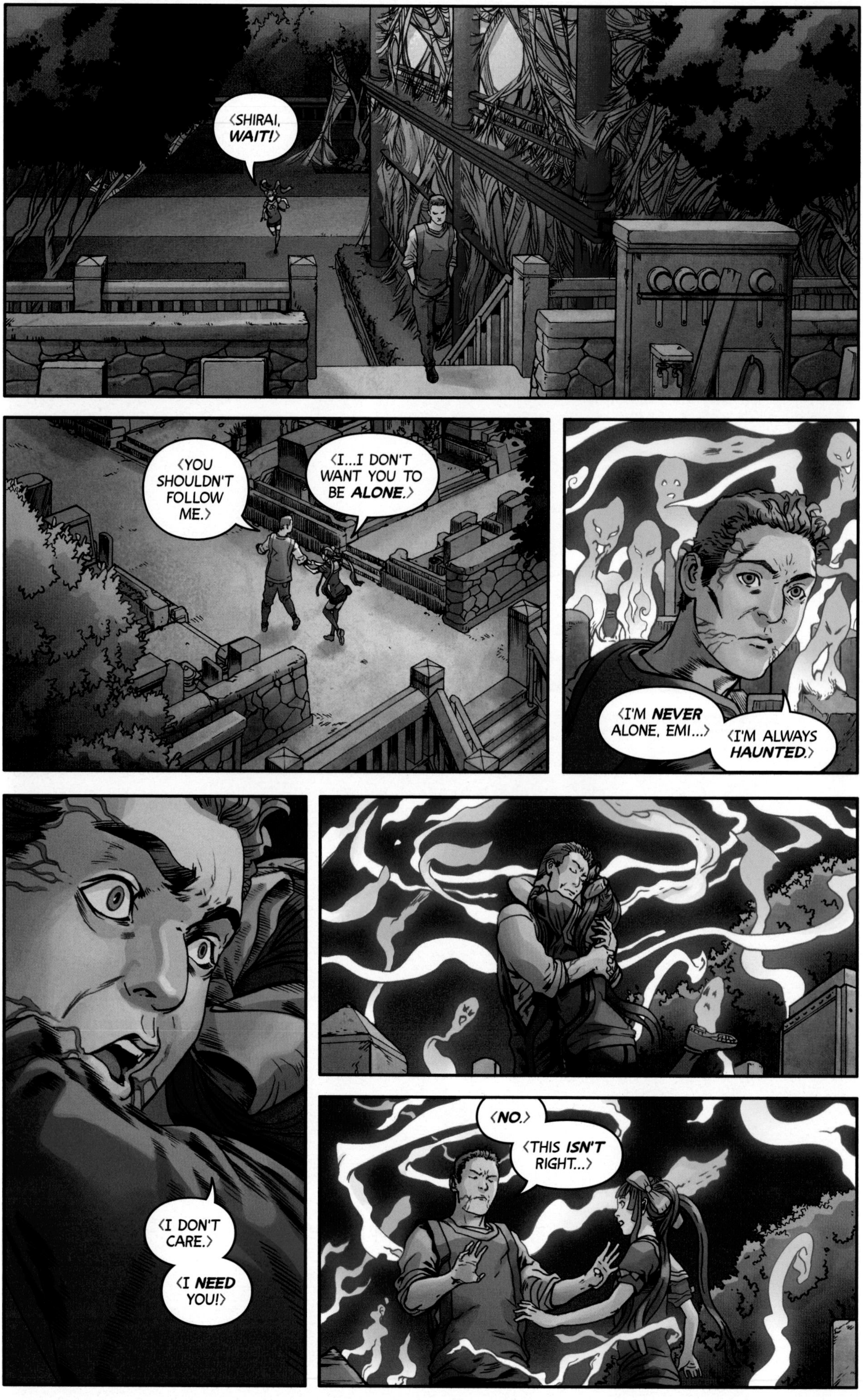

<SHIRAI, WAIT!>
<YOU SHOULDN'T FOLLOW ME.>
<I...I DON'T WANT YOU TO BE ALONE.>
<I'M NEVER ALONE, EMI...>
<I'M ALWAYS HAUNTED.>
<I DON'T CARE.>
<I NEED YOU!>
<NO.>
<THIS ISN'T RIGHT...>

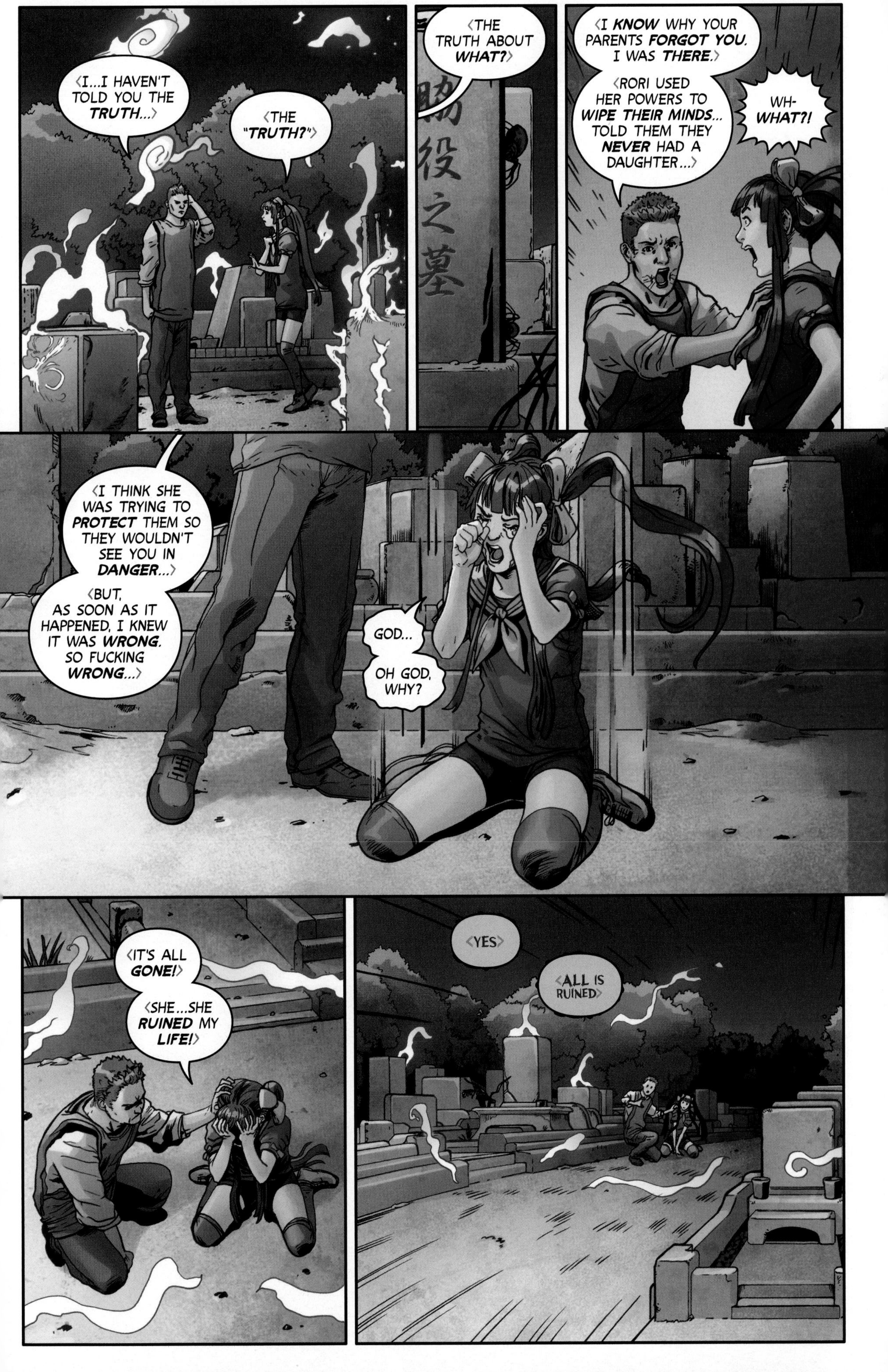

<I...I HAVEN'T TOLD YOU THE *TRUTH*...>
<THE "*TRUTH?*">
<THE TRUTH ABOUT *WHAT?*>
<I *KNOW* WHY YOUR PARENTS *FORGOT YOU*. I WAS *THERE*.>
<RORI USED HER POWERS TO *WIPE THEIR MINDS*... TOLD THEM THEY *NEVER* HAD A DAUGHTER...>
WH- *WHAT?!*
<I THINK SHE WAS TRYING TO *PROTECT* THEM SO THEY WOULDN'T SEE YOU IN *DANGER*...>
<BUT, AS SOON AS IT HAPPENED, I KNEW IT WAS *WRONG*. SO FUCKING *WRONG*...>
GOD...
OH GOD, WHY?
<IT'S ALL *GONE!*>
<SHE...SHE *RUINED* MY *LIFE!*>
<YES>
<ALL IS RUINED>

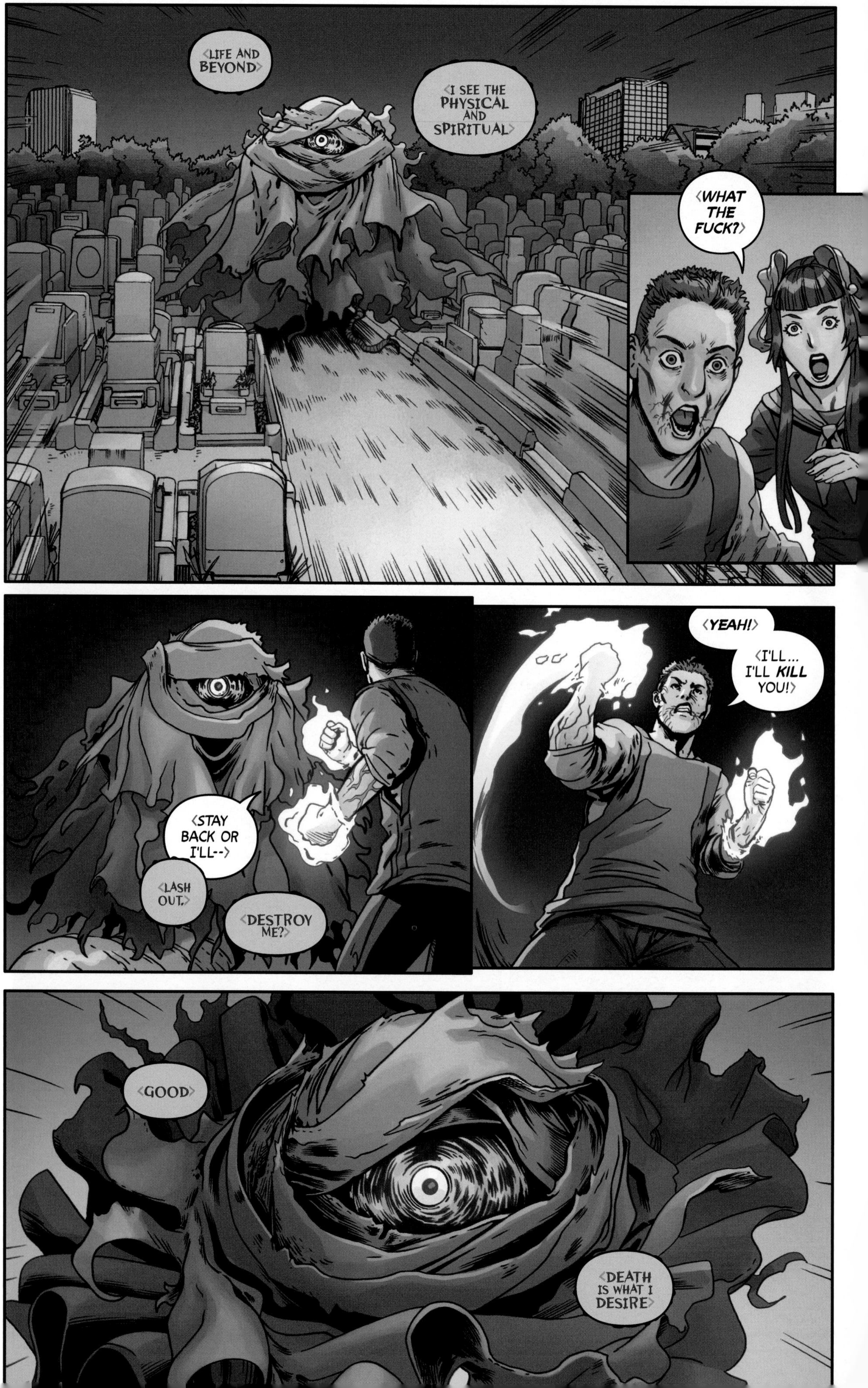
<LIFE AND BEYOND>
<I SEE THE PHYSICAL AND SPIRITUAL>
<WHAT THE FUCK?>
<STAY BACK OR I'LL-->
<LASH OUT.>
<DESTROY ME?>
<YEAH!>
<I'LL... I'LL KILL YOU!>
<GOOD>
<DEATH IS WHAT I DESIRE>

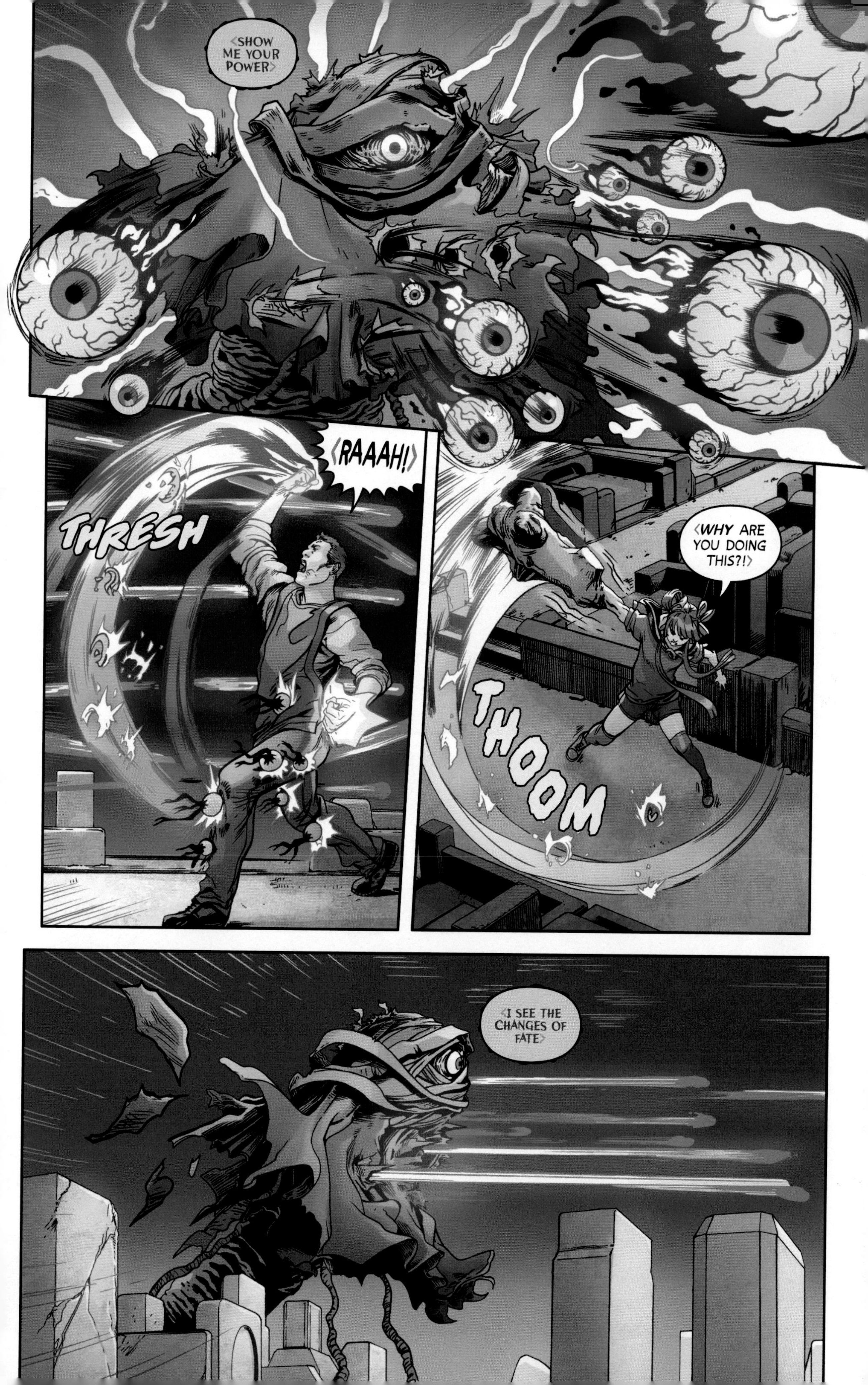
⟨SHOW ME YOUR POWER⟩
⟨RAAAH!⟩
THRESH
⟨WHY ARE YOU DOING THIS?!⟩
THOOM
⟨I SEE THE CHANGES OF FATE⟩

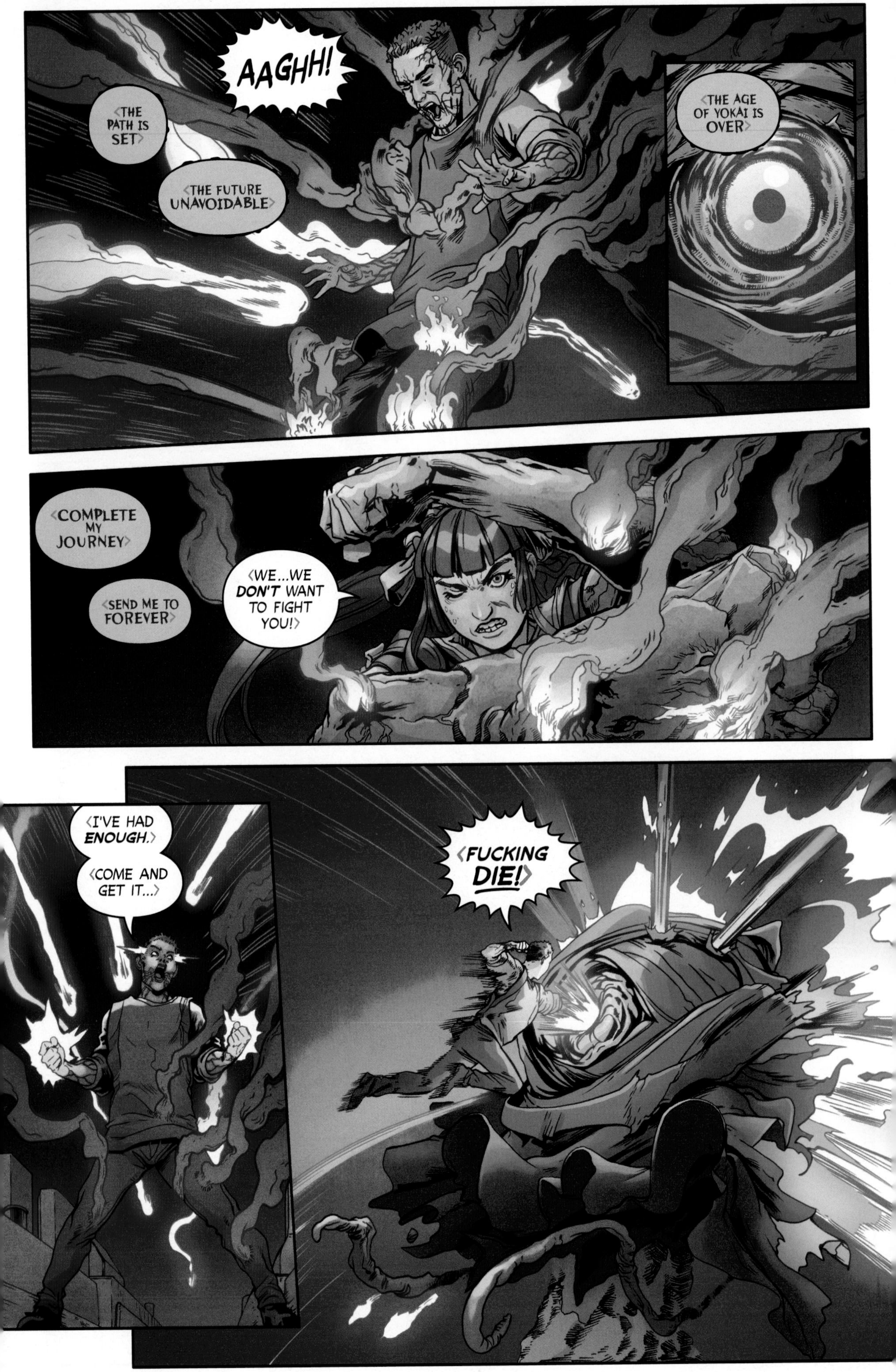

AAGHH!
‹THE PATH IS SET›
‹THE FUTURE UNAVOIDABLE›
‹THE AGE OF YOKAI IS OVER›
‹COMPLETE MY JOURNEY›
‹SEND ME TO FOREVER›
‹WE...WE DON'T WANT TO FIGHT YOU!›
‹I'VE HAD ENOUGH.›
‹COME AND GET IT...›
‹FUCKING DIE!›

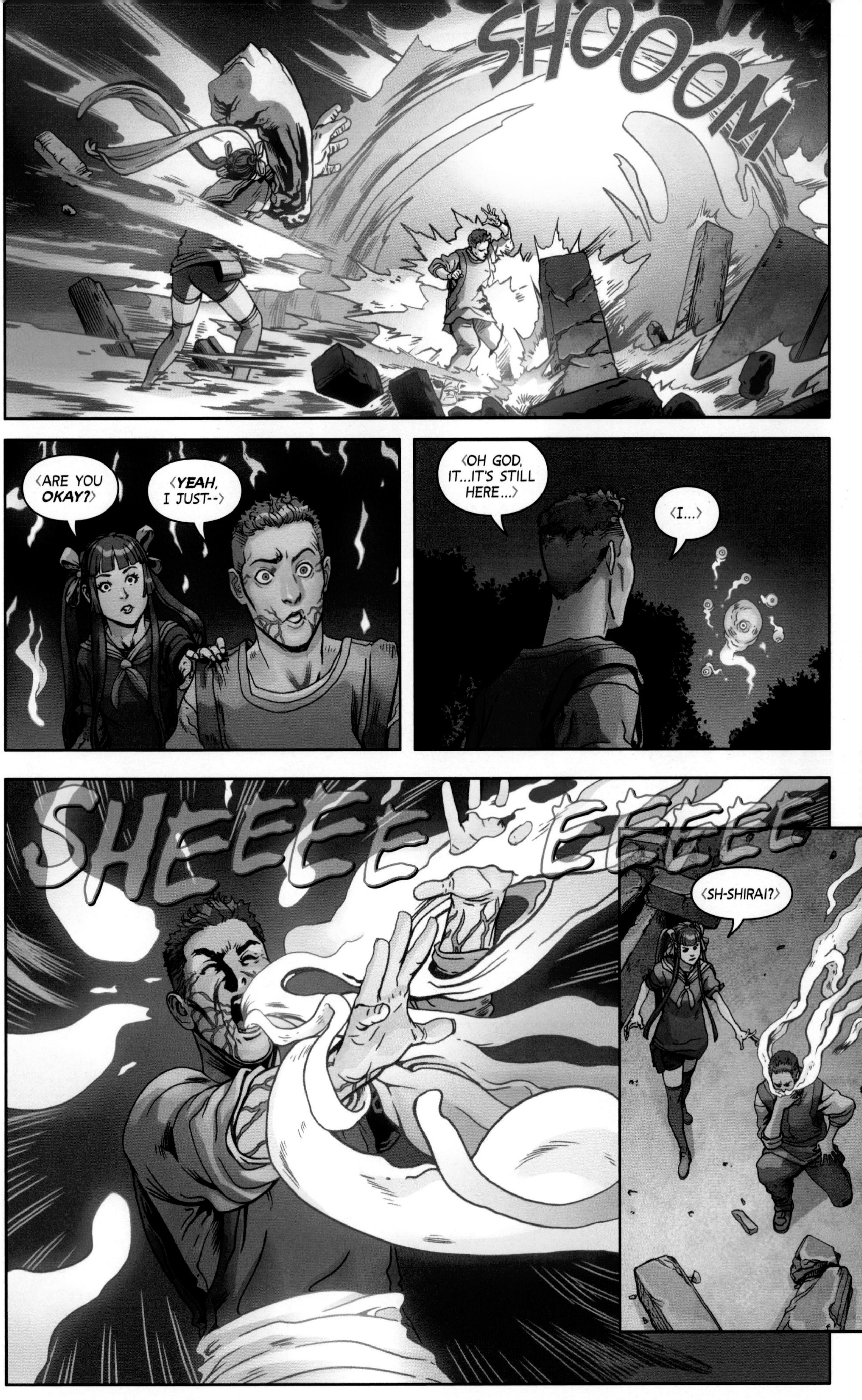
SHOOOM
‹ARE YOU OKAY?›
‹YEAH, I JUST--›
‹OH GOD, IT...IT'S STILL HERE...›
‹I...›
SHEEEE EEEEE
‹SH-SHIRAI?›

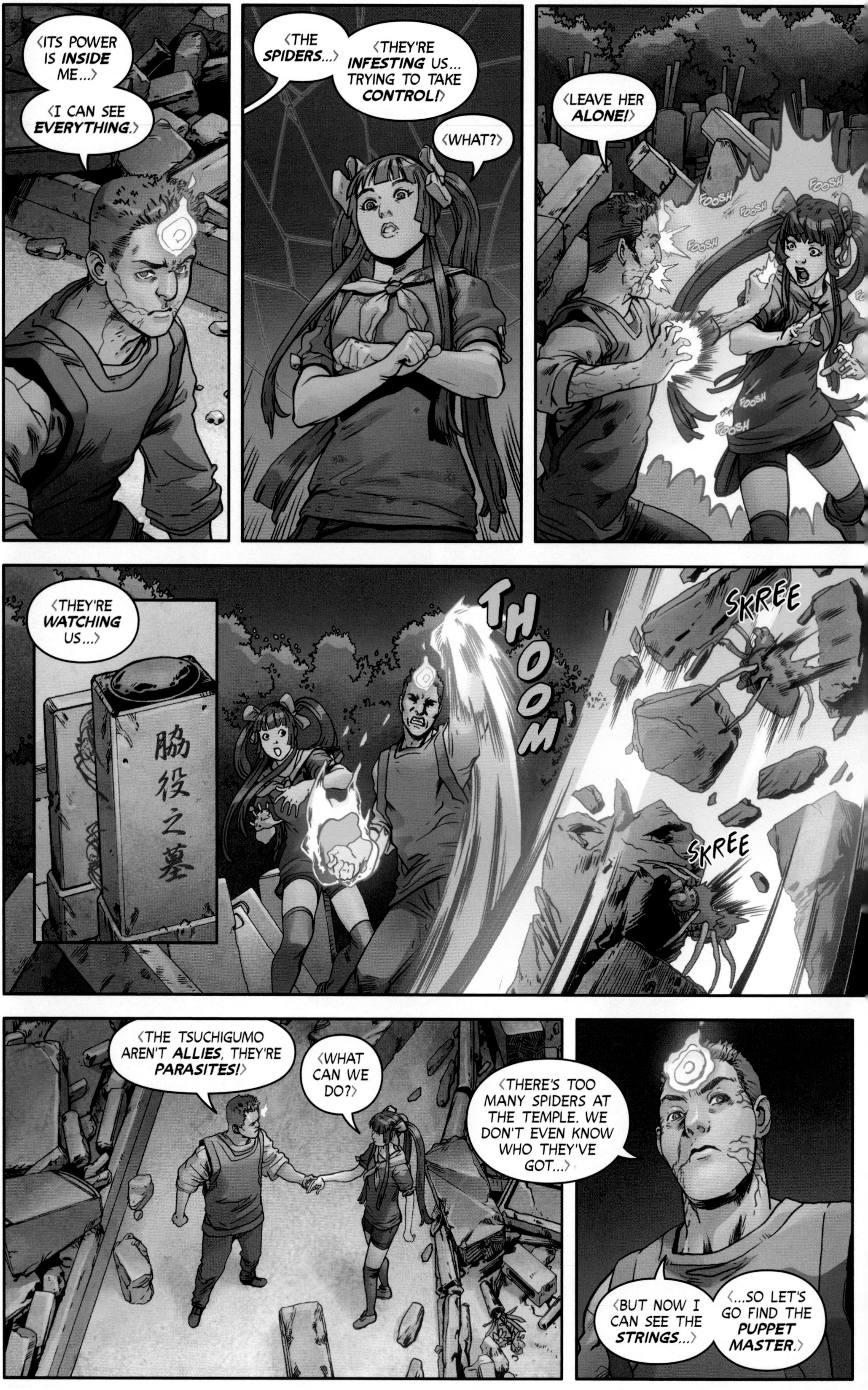

‹ITS POWER IS INSIDE ME...›
‹I CAN SEE EVERYTHING.›
‹THE SPIDERS...›
‹THEY'RE INFESTING US... TRYING TO TAKE CONTROL!›
‹WHAT?›
‹LEAVE HER ALONE!›
FOOSH
FOOSH
FOOSH
FOOSH
FOOSH
FOOSH
‹THEY'RE WATCHING US...›
脇役之墓
THOOOM
SKREE
SKREE
‹THE TSUCHIGUMO AREN'T ALLIES, THEY'RE PARASITES!›
‹WHAT CAN WE DO?›
‹THERE'S TOO MANY SPIDERS AT THE TEMPLE. WE DON'T EVEN KNOW WHO THEY'VE GOT...›
‹BUT NOW I CAN SEE THE STRINGS...›
‹...SO LET'S GO FIND THE PUPPET MASTER.›

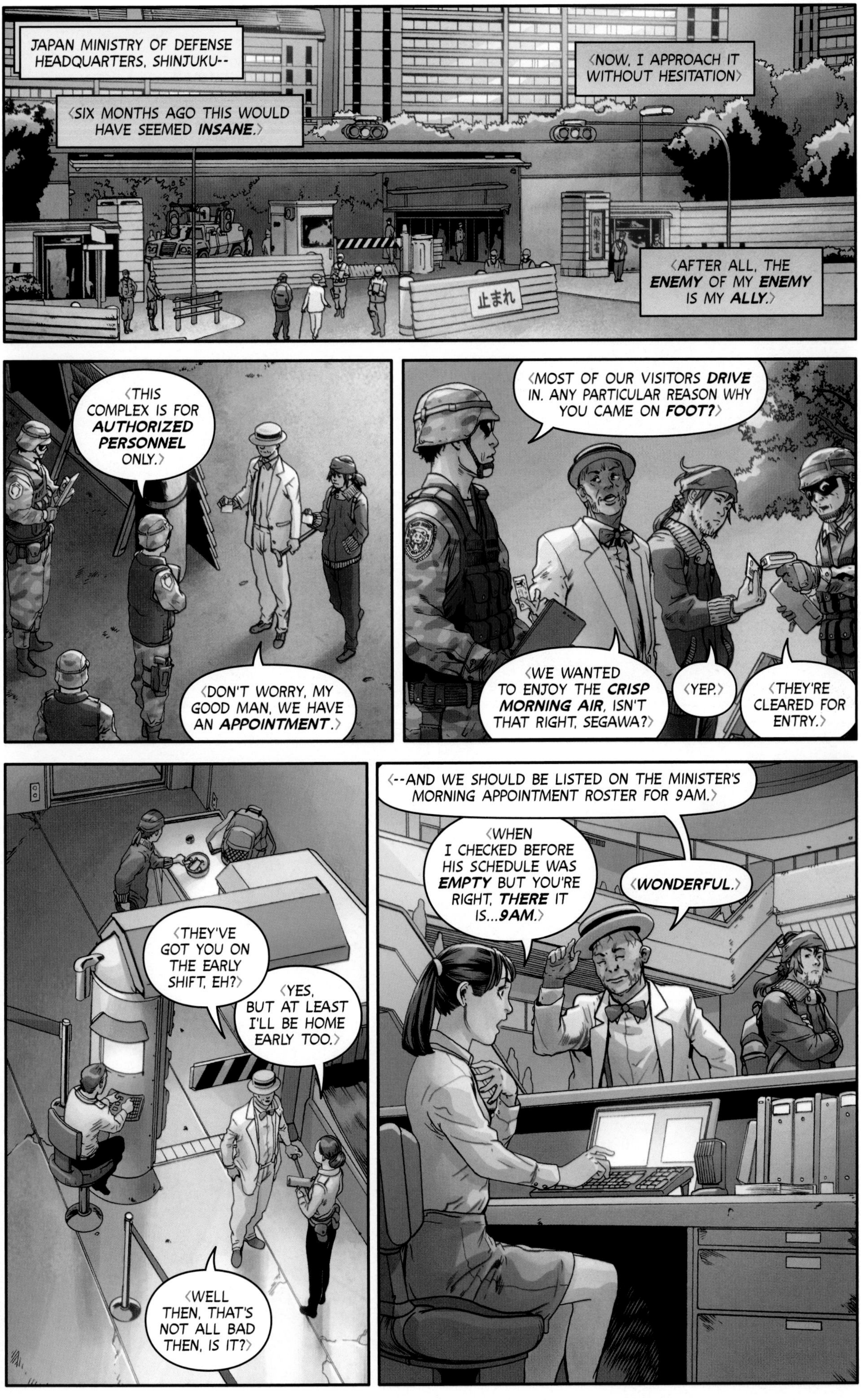
JAPAN MINISTRY OF DEFENSE HEADQUARTERS, SHINJUKU--
⟨SIX MONTHS AGO THIS WOULD HAVE SEEMED **INSANE**.⟩
⟨NOW, I APPROACH IT WITHOUT HESITATION⟩
止まれ
⟨AFTER ALL, THE **ENEMY** OF MY **ENEMY** IS MY **ALLY**.⟩
⟨THIS COMPLEX IS FOR **AUTHORIZED PERSONNEL** ONLY.⟩
⟨DON'T WORRY, MY GOOD MAN, WE HAVE AN **APPOINTMENT**.⟩
⟨MOST OF OUR VISITORS **DRIVE** IN. ANY PARTICULAR REASON WHY YOU CAME ON **FOOT?**⟩
⟨WE WANTED TO ENJOY THE **CRISP MORNING AIR**, ISN'T THAT RIGHT, SEGAWA?⟩
⟨YEP.⟩
⟨THEY'RE CLEARED FOR ENTRY.⟩
⟨THEY'VE GOT YOU ON THE EARLY SHIFT, EH?⟩
⟨YES, BUT AT LEAST I'LL BE HOME EARLY TOO.⟩
⟨WELL THEN, THAT'S NOT ALL BAD THEN, IS IT?⟩
⟨--AND WE SHOULD BE LISTED ON THE MINISTER'S MORNING APPOINTMENT ROSTER FOR 9AM.⟩
⟨WHEN I CHECKED BEFORE HIS SCHEDULE WAS **EMPTY** BUT YOU'RE RIGHT, **THERE** IT IS...**9AM**.⟩
⟨**WONDERFUL**.⟩

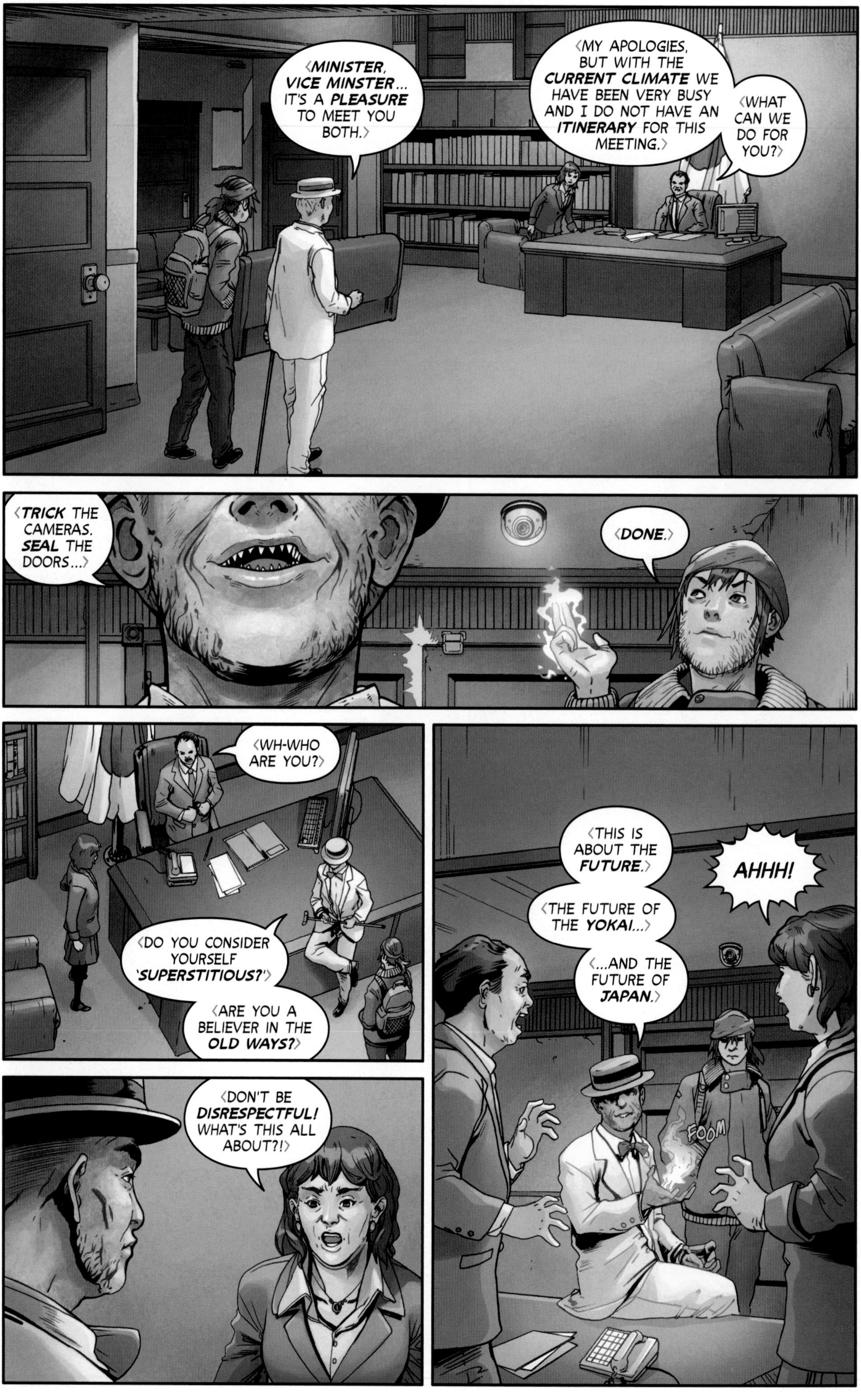
‹MINISTER, VICE MINSTER... IT'S A PLEASURE TO MEET YOU BOTH.›
‹MY APOLOGIES, BUT WITH THE CURRENT CLIMATE WE HAVE BEEN VERY BUSY AND I DO NOT HAVE AN ITINERARY FOR THIS MEETING.›
‹WHAT CAN WE DO FOR YOU?›
‹TRICK THE CAMERAS. SEAL THE DOORS...›
‹DONE.›
‹WH-WHO ARE YOU?›
‹DO YOU CONSIDER YOURSELF 'SUPERSTITIOUS?'›
‹ARE YOU A BELIEVER IN THE OLD WAYS?›
‹DON'T BE DISRESPECTFUL! WHAT'S THIS ALL ABOUT?!›
‹THIS IS ABOUT THE FUTURE.›
‹THE FUTURE OF THE YOKAI...›
‹...AND THE FUTURE OF JAPAN.›
AHHH!
FOOM

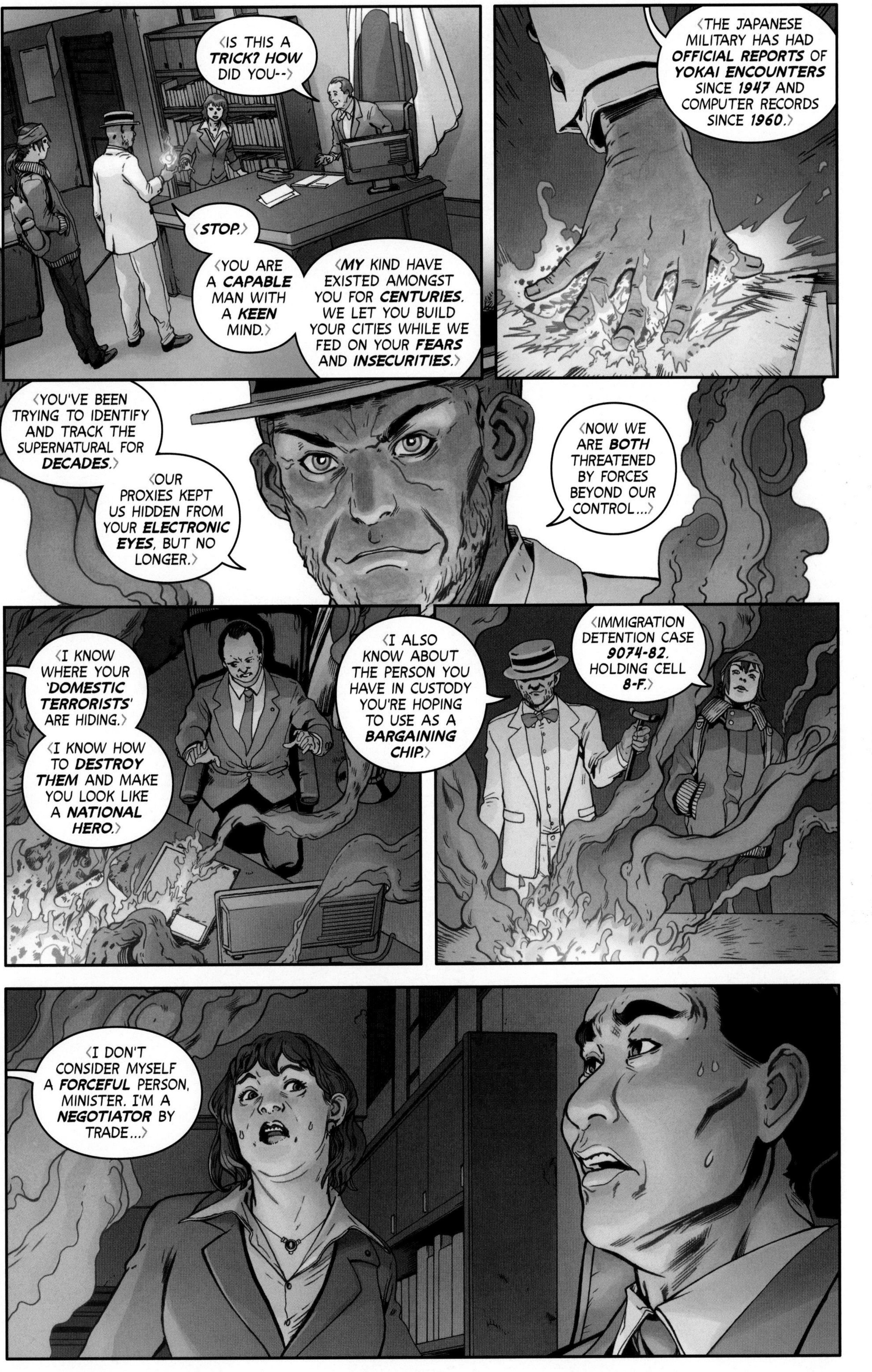
‹IS THIS A TRICK? HOW DID YOU--›
‹STOP.›
‹YOU ARE A CAPABLE MAN WITH A KEEN MIND.›
‹MY KIND HAVE EXISTED AMONGST YOU FOR CENTURIES. WE LET YOU BUILD YOUR CITIES WHILE WE FED ON YOUR FEARS AND INSECURITIES.›
‹THE JAPANESE MILITARY HAS HAD OFFICIAL REPORTS OF YOKAI ENCOUNTERS SINCE 1947 AND COMPUTER RECORDS SINCE 1960.›
‹YOU'VE BEEN TRYING TO IDENTIFY AND TRACK THE SUPERNATURAL FOR DECADES.›
‹OUR PROXIES KEPT US HIDDEN FROM YOUR ELECTRONIC EYES, BUT NO LONGER.›
‹NOW WE ARE BOTH THREATENED BY FORCES BEYOND OUR CONTROL...›
‹I KNOW WHERE YOUR 'DOMESTIC TERRORISTS' ARE HIDING.›
‹I KNOW HOW TO DESTROY THEM AND MAKE YOU LOOK LIKE A NATIONAL HERO.›
‹I ALSO KNOW ABOUT THE PERSON YOU HAVE IN CUSTODY YOU'RE HOPING TO USE AS A BARGAINING CHIP.›
‹IMMIGRATION DETENTION CASE 9074-82. HOLDING CELL 8-F.›
‹I DON'T CONSIDER MYSELF A FORCEFUL PERSON, MINISTER. I'M A NEGOTIATOR BY TRADE...›

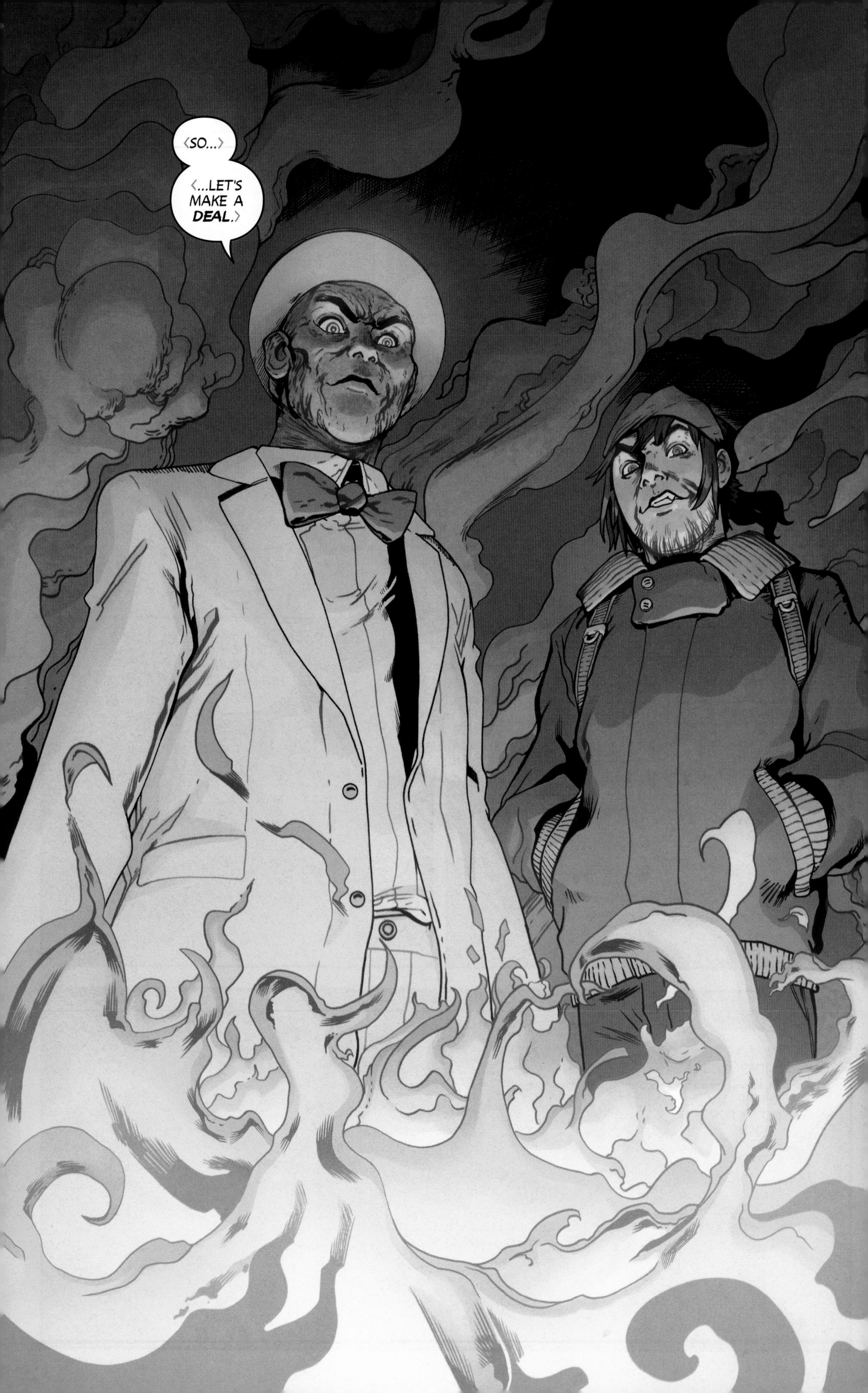

⟨SO...⟩
⟨...LET'S MAKE A **DEAL**.⟩

Chapter Fifteen

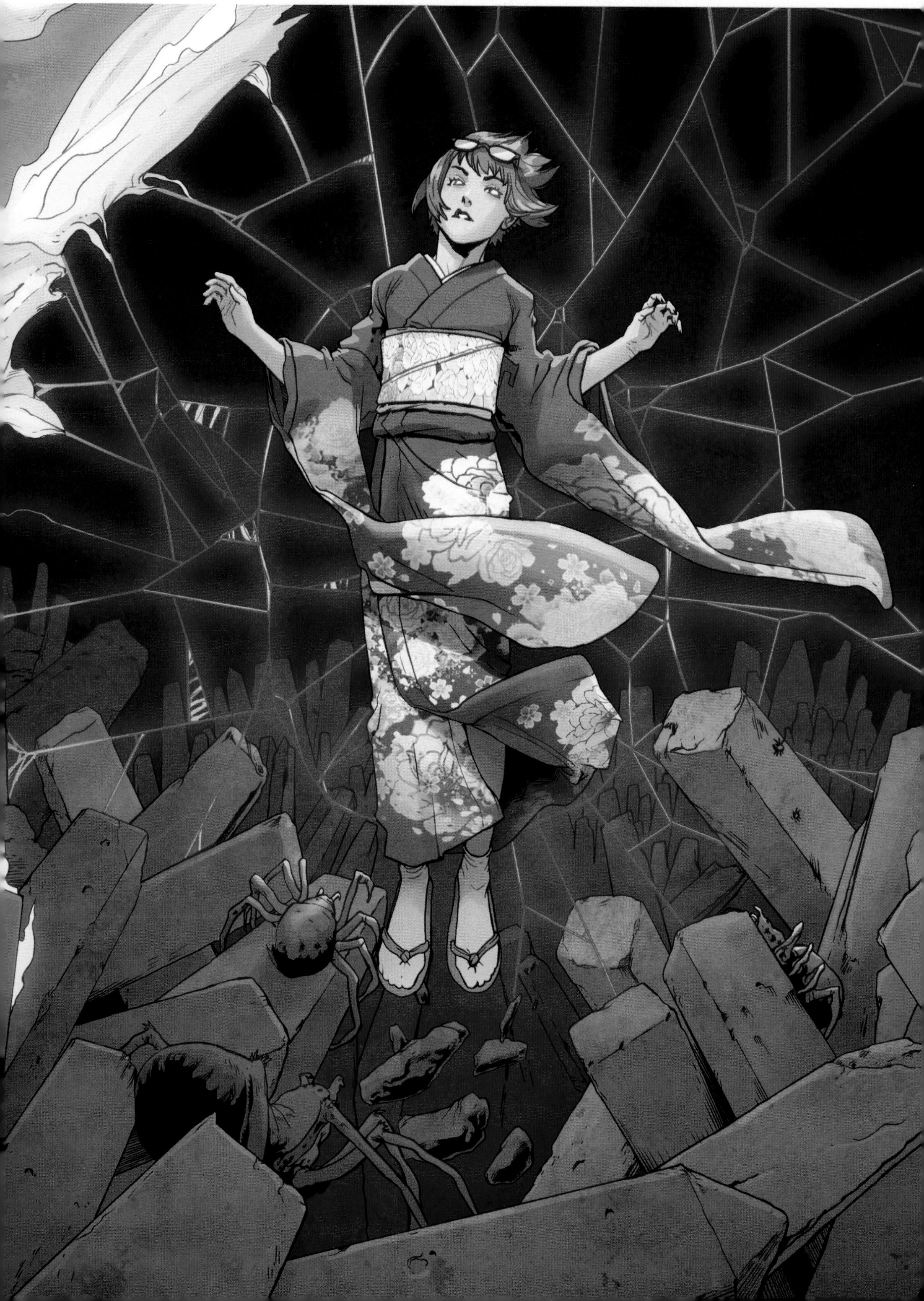

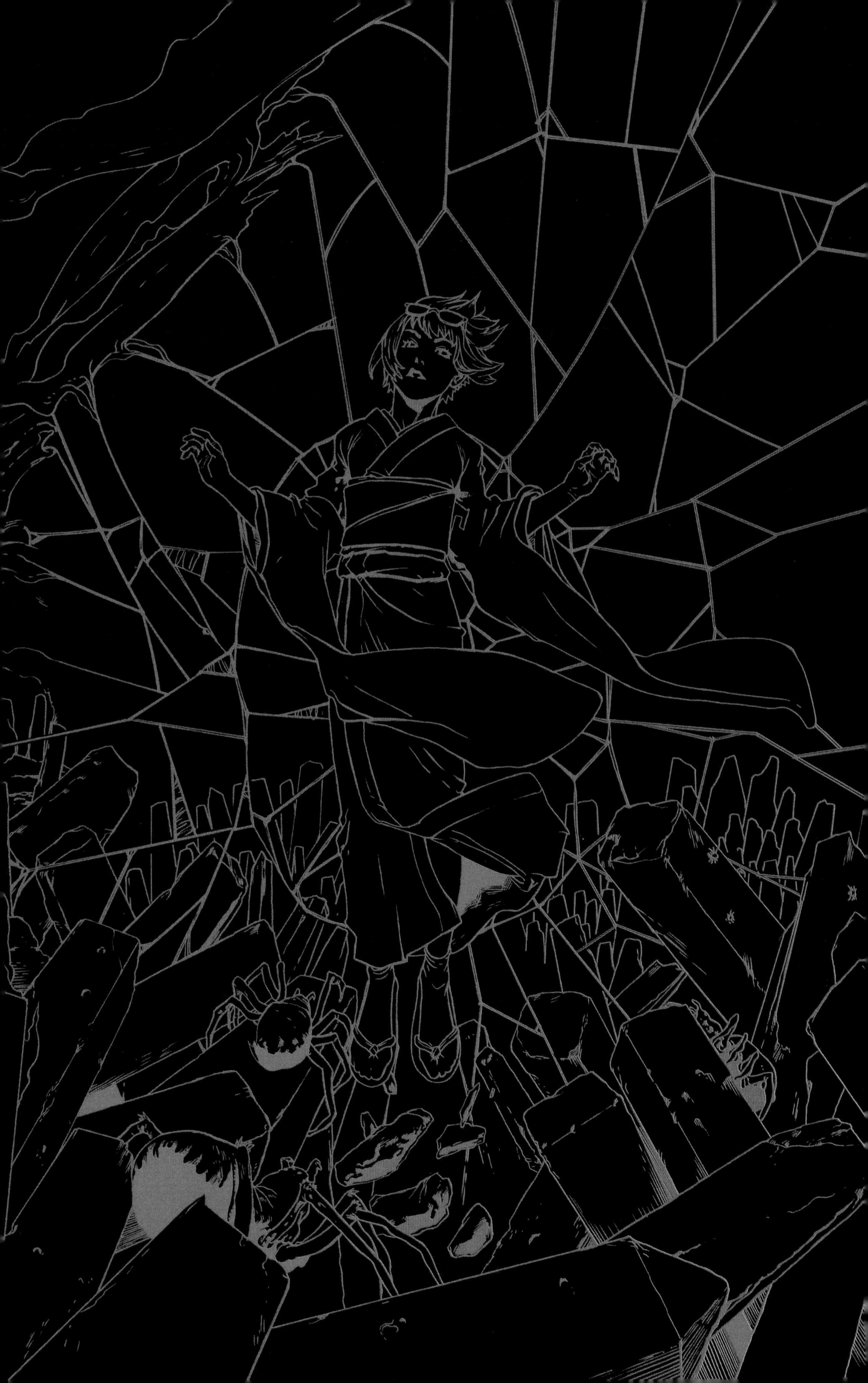

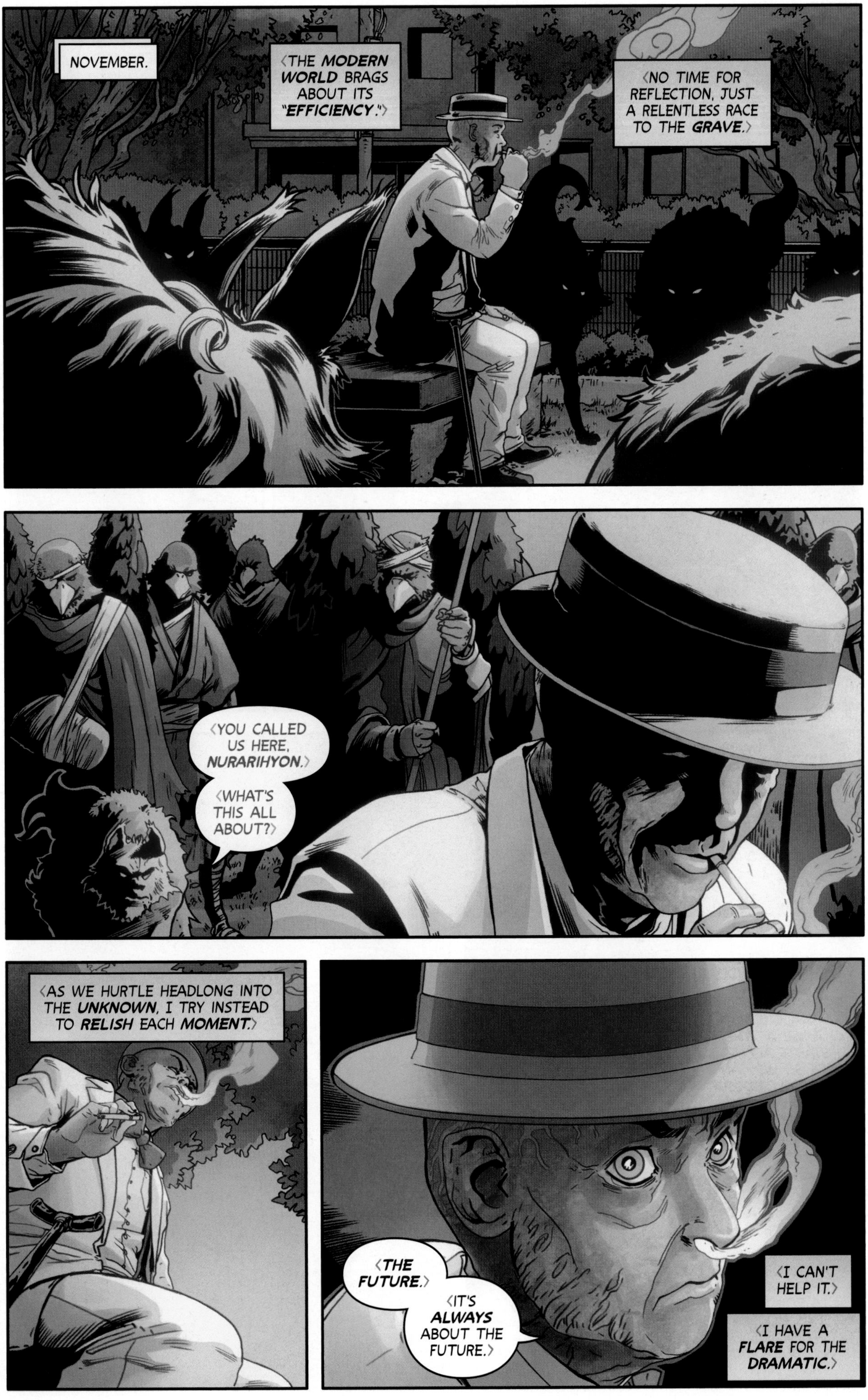
NOVEMBER.
‹THE MODERN WORLD BRAGS ABOUT ITS "EFFICIENCY".›
‹NO TIME FOR REFLECTION, JUST A RELENTLESS RACE TO THE GRAVE.›
‹YOU CALLED US HERE, NURARIHYON.›
‹WHAT'S THIS ALL ABOUT?›
‹AS WE HURTLE HEADLONG INTO THE UNKNOWN, I TRY INSTEAD TO RELISH EACH MOMENT.›
‹THE FUTURE.›
‹IT'S ALWAYS ABOUT THE FUTURE.›
‹I CAN'T HELP IT.›
‹I HAVE A FLARE FOR THE DRAMATIC.›

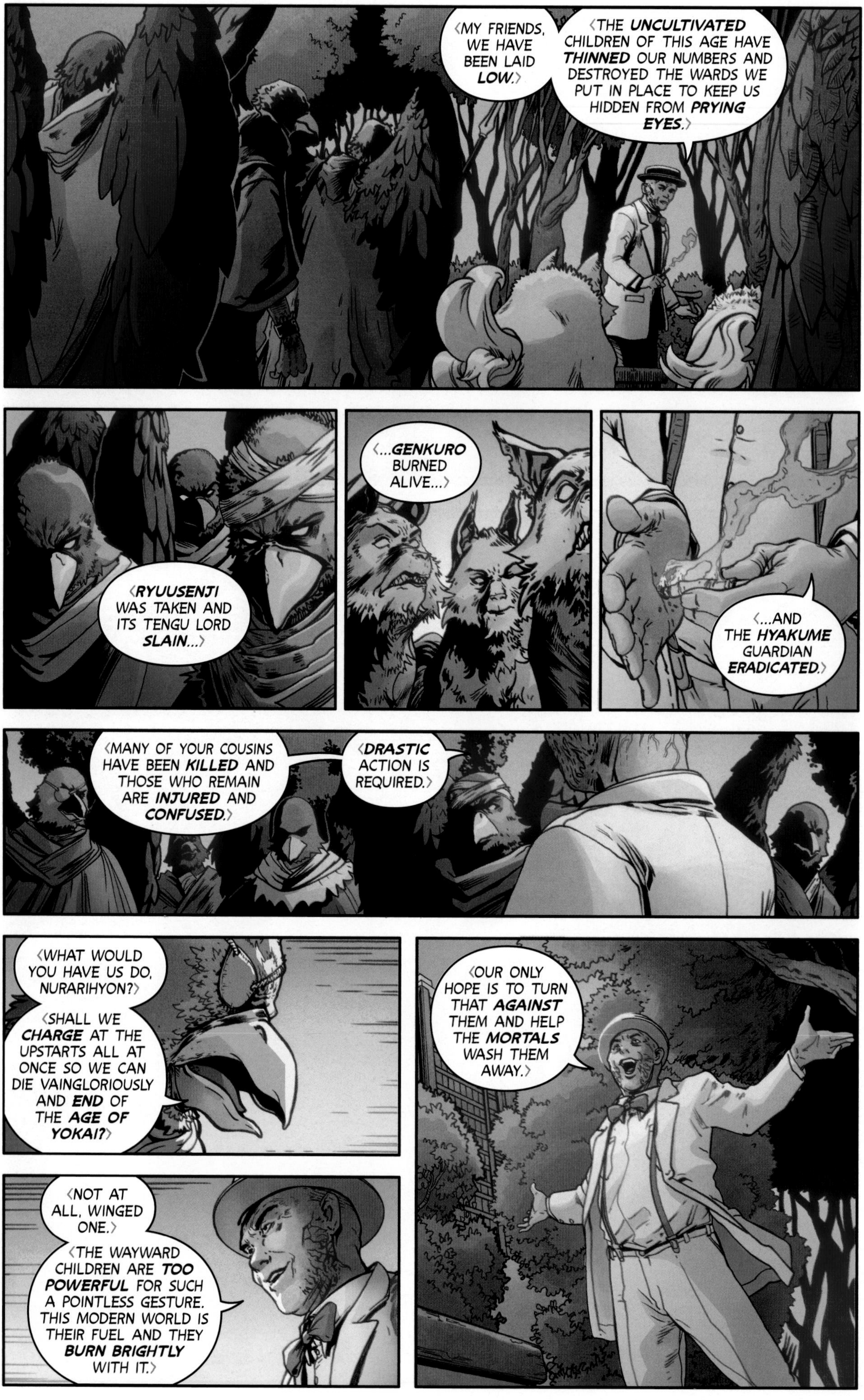
‹MY FRIENDS, WE HAVE BEEN LAID LOW.›
‹THE UNCULTIVATED CHILDREN OF THIS AGE HAVE THINNED OUR NUMBERS AND DESTROYED THE WARDS WE PUT IN PLACE TO KEEP US HIDDEN FROM PRYING EYES.›
‹RYUUSENJI WAS TAKEN AND ITS TENGU LORD SLAIN...›
‹...GENKURO BURNED ALIVE...›
‹...AND THE HYAKUME GUARDIAN ERADICATED.›
‹MANY OF YOUR COUSINS HAVE BEEN KILLED AND THOSE WHO REMAIN ARE INJURED AND CONFUSED.›
‹DRASTIC ACTION IS REQUIRED.›
‹WHAT WOULD YOU HAVE US DO, NURARIHYON?›
‹SHALL WE CHARGE AT THE UPSTARTS ALL AT ONCE SO WE CAN DIE VAINGLORIOUSLY AND END OF THE AGE OF YOKAI?›
‹NOT AT ALL, WINGED ONE.›
‹THE WAYWARD CHILDREN ARE TOO POWERFUL FOR SUCH A POINTLESS GESTURE. THIS MODERN WORLD IS THEIR FUEL AND THEY BURN BRIGHTLY WITH IT.›
‹OUR ONLY HOPE IS TO TURN THAT AGAINST THEM AND HELP THE MORTALS WASH THEM AWAY.›

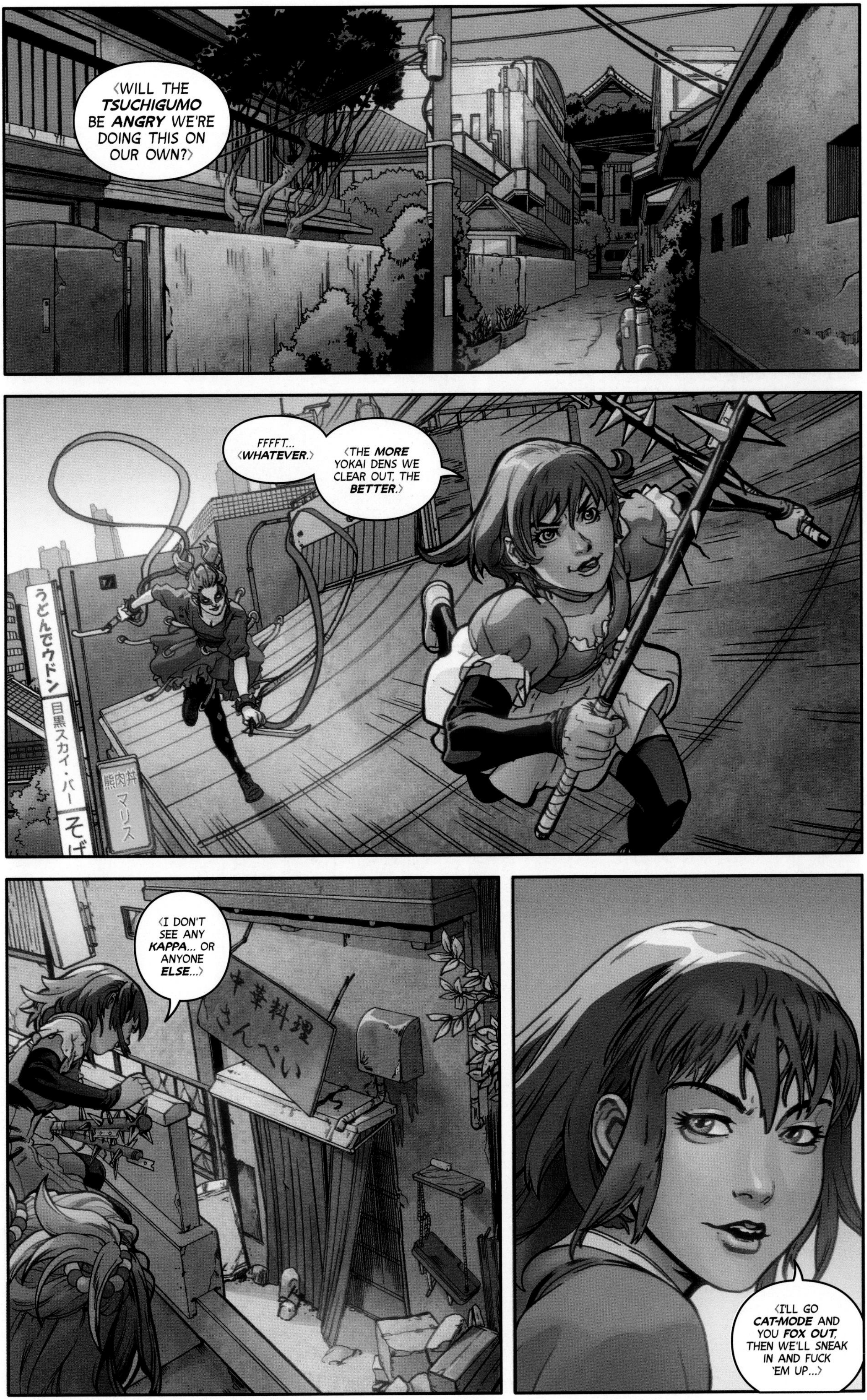
‹WILL THE TSUCHIGUMO BE ANGRY WE'RE DOING THIS ON OUR OWN?›
FFFFT... ‹WHATEVER.›
‹THE MORE YOKAI DENS WE CLEAR OUT, THE BETTER.›
うどんでウドン
目黒スカイ・バー
熊肉丼 マリス
‹I DON'T SEE ANY KAPPA... OR ANYONE ELSE...›
中華料理 さんぺい
‹I'LL GO CAT-MODE AND YOU FOX OUT, THEN WE'LL SNEAK IN AND FUCK 'EM UP...›

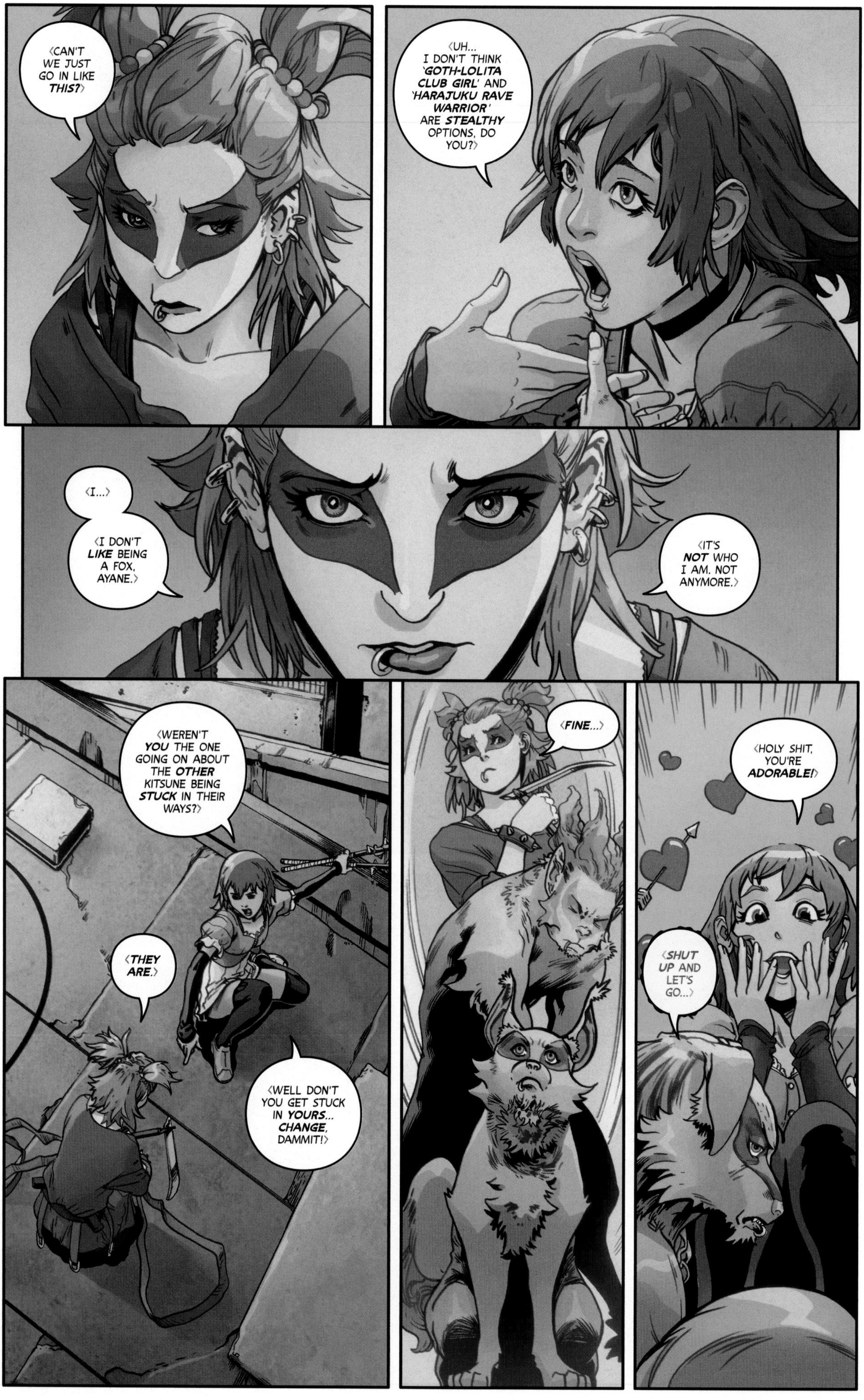

〈CAN'T WE JUST GO IN LIKE THIS?〉
〈UH... I DON'T THINK 'GOTH-LOLITA CLUB GIRL' AND 'HARAJUKU RAVE WARRIOR' ARE STEALTHY OPTIONS, DO YOU?〉
〈I...〉
〈I DON'T LIKE BEING A FOX, AYANE.〉
〈IT'S NOT WHO I AM. NOT ANYMORE.〉
〈WEREN'T YOU THE ONE GOING ON ABOUT THE OTHER KITSUNE BEING STUCK IN THEIR WAYS?〉
〈THEY ARE.〉
〈WELL DON'T YOU GET STUCK IN YOURS... CHANGE, DAMMIT!〉
〈FINE...〉
〈HOLY SHIT, YOU'RE ADORABLE!〉
〈SHUT UP AND LET'S GO...〉

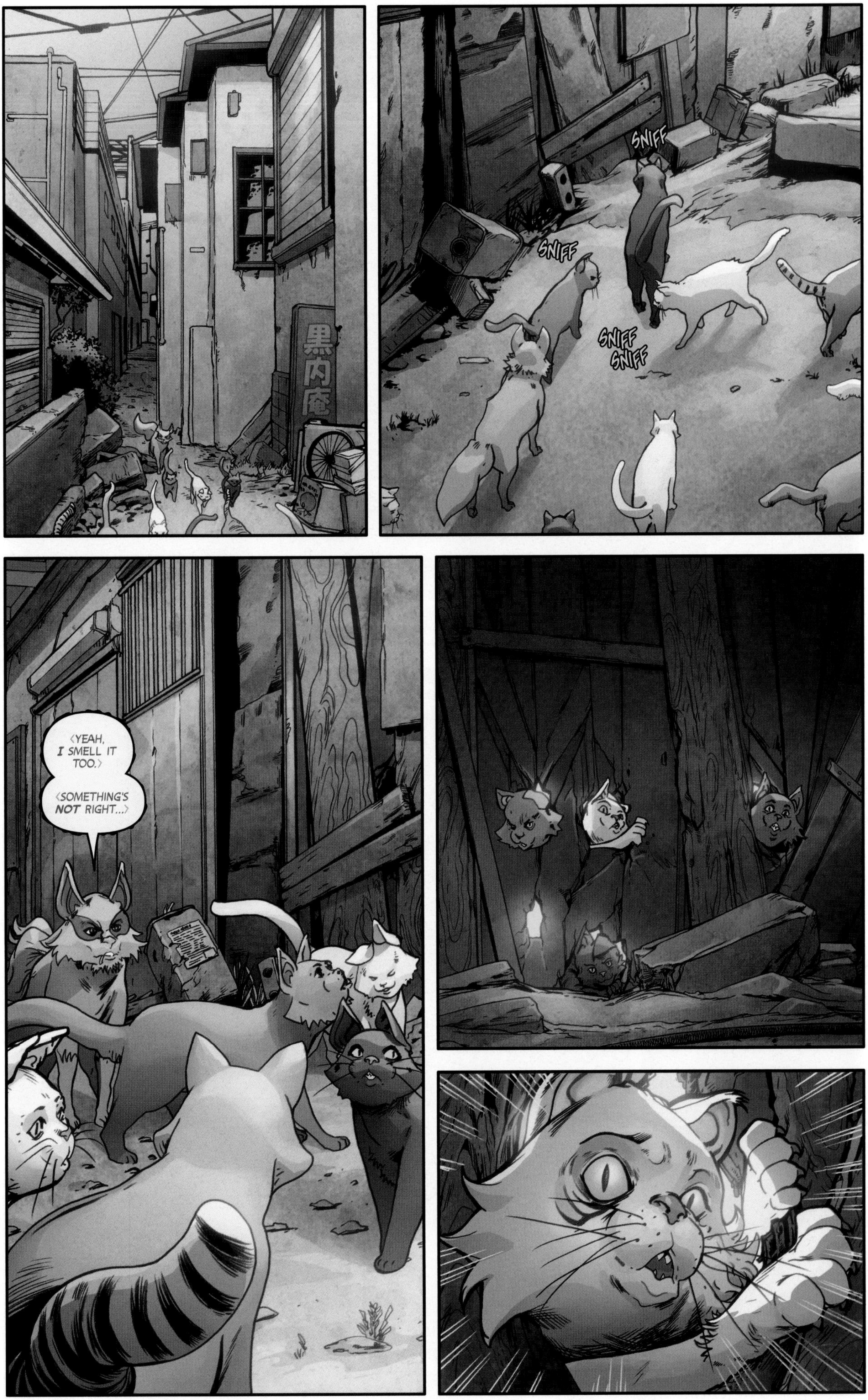
黒内庵
SNIFF
SNIFF
SNIFF SNIFF
<YEAH, I SMELL IT TOO.>
<SOMETHING'S NOT RIGHT...>

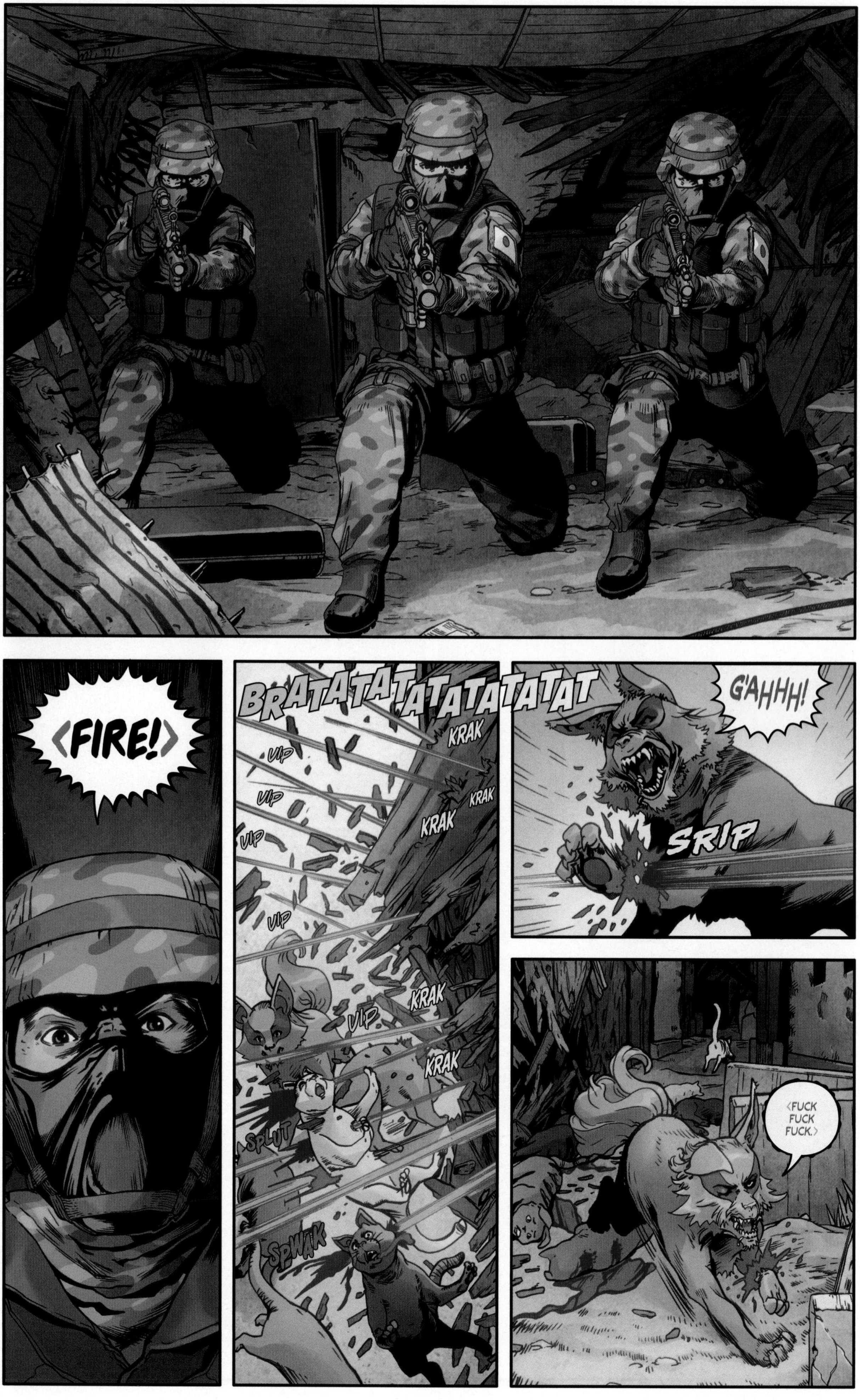
<FIRE!>
BRATATATATATATATATAT
KRAK
VIP
VIP
KRAK
KRAK
VIP
VIP
KRAK
VIP
KRAK
SPLUT
SPWAK
G'AHHH!
SRIP
<FUCK FUCK FUCK.>

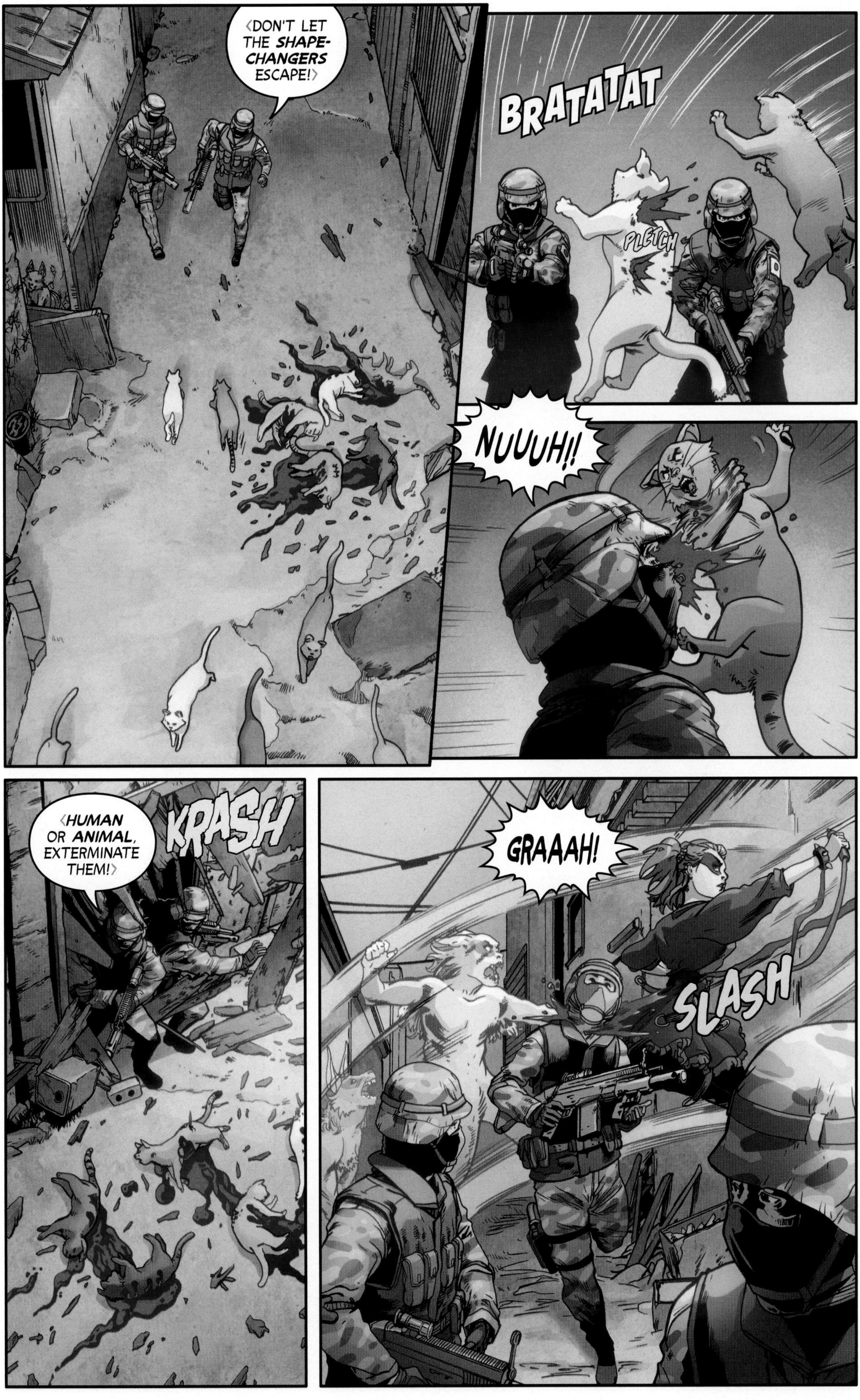

〈DON'T LET THE *SHAPE-CHANGERS* ESCAPE!〉
BRATATAT
PLETCH
NUUUH!!
〈*HUMAN* OR *ANIMAL*, EXTERMINATE THEM!〉
KRASH
GRAAAH!
SLASH

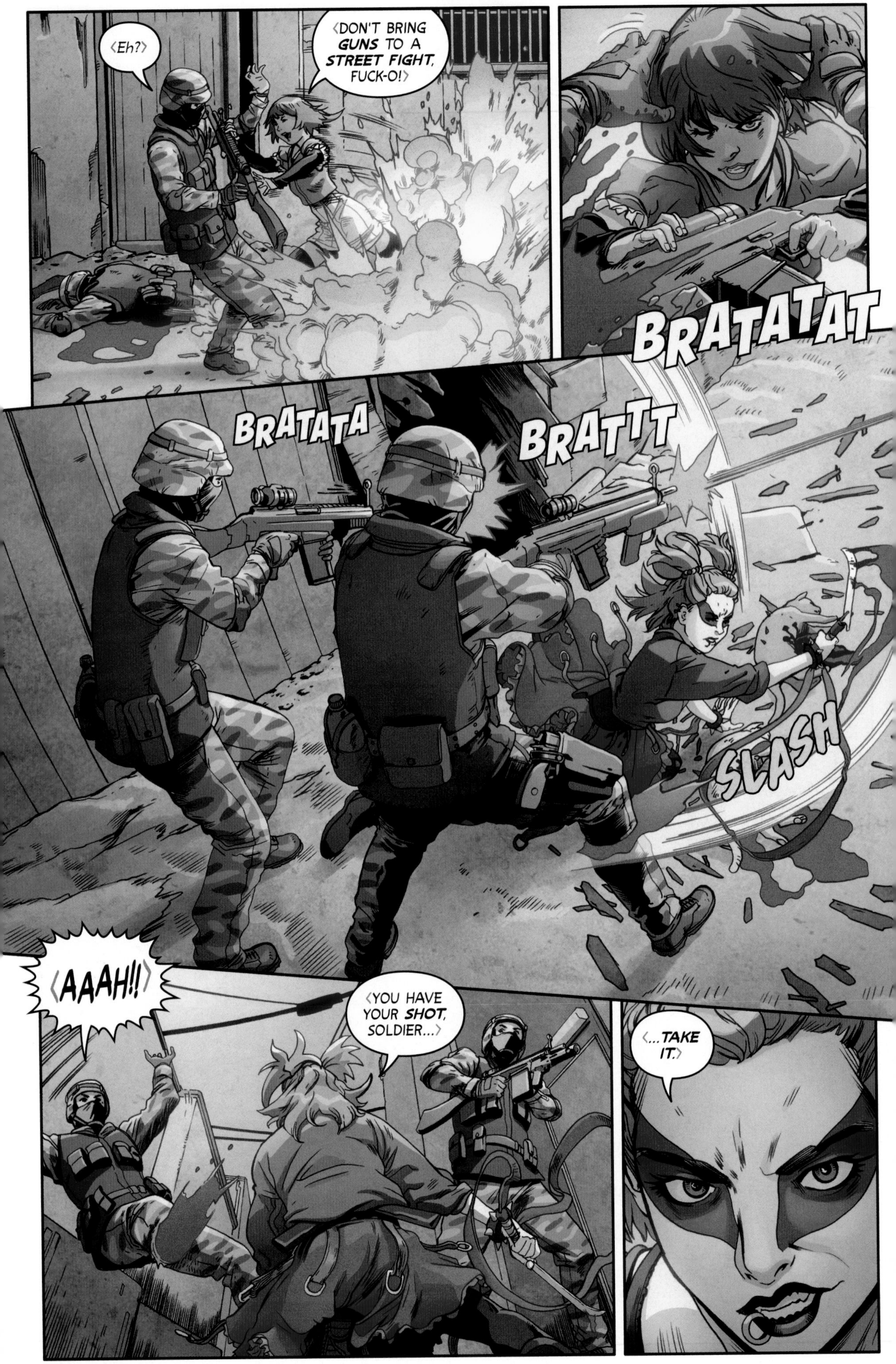

⟨Eh?⟩
⟨DON'T BRING GUNS TO A STREET FIGHT, FUCK-O!⟩
BRATATAT
BRATATA
BRATTTT
SLASH
⟨AAAH!!⟩
⟨YOU HAVE YOUR SHOT, SOLDIER...⟩
⟨...TAKE IT.⟩

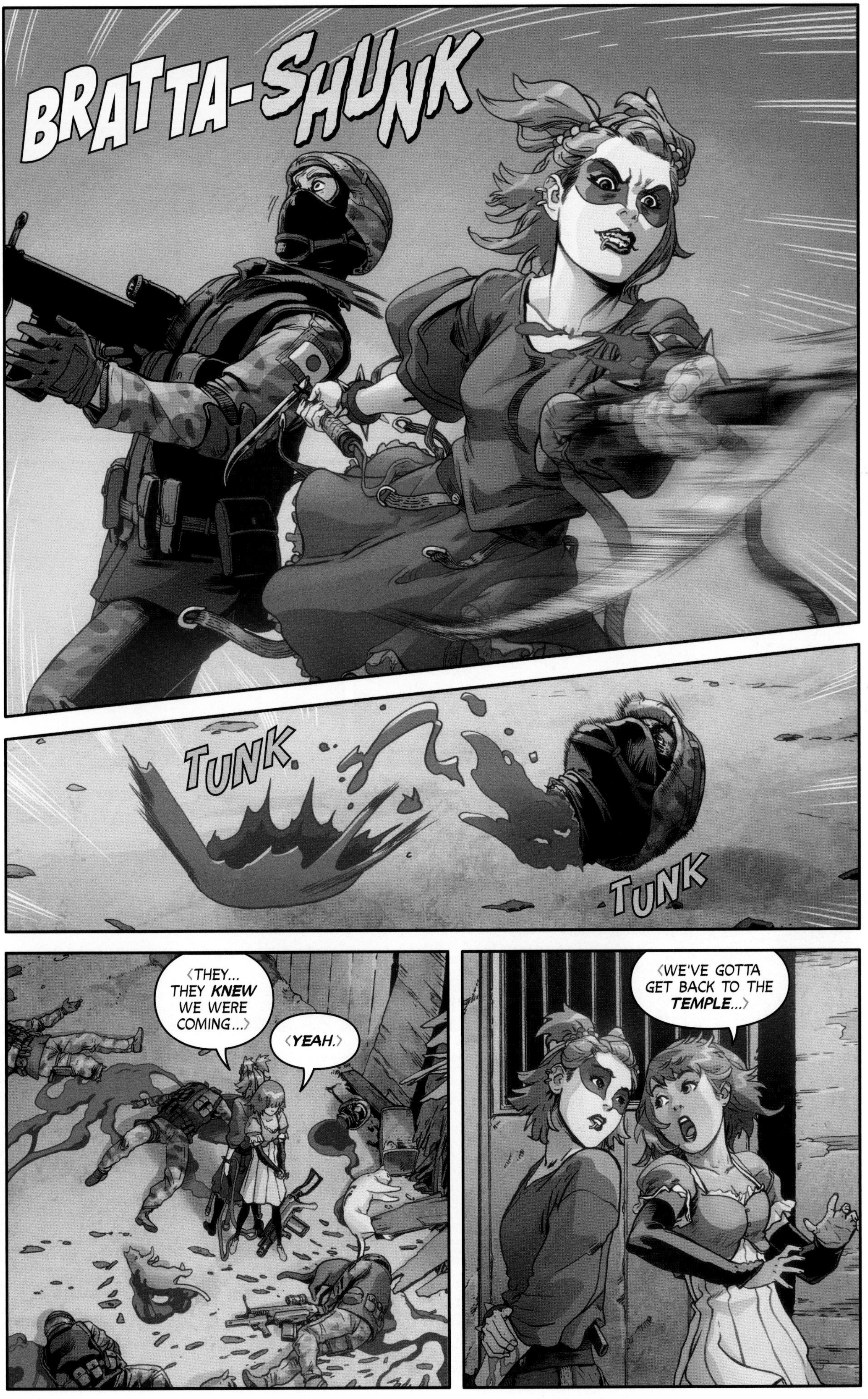
BRATTA-SHUNK
TUNK
TUNK
‹THEY... THEY *KNEW* WE WERE COMING...›
‹*YEAH.*›
‹WE'VE GOTTA GET BACK TO THE *TEMPLE*...›

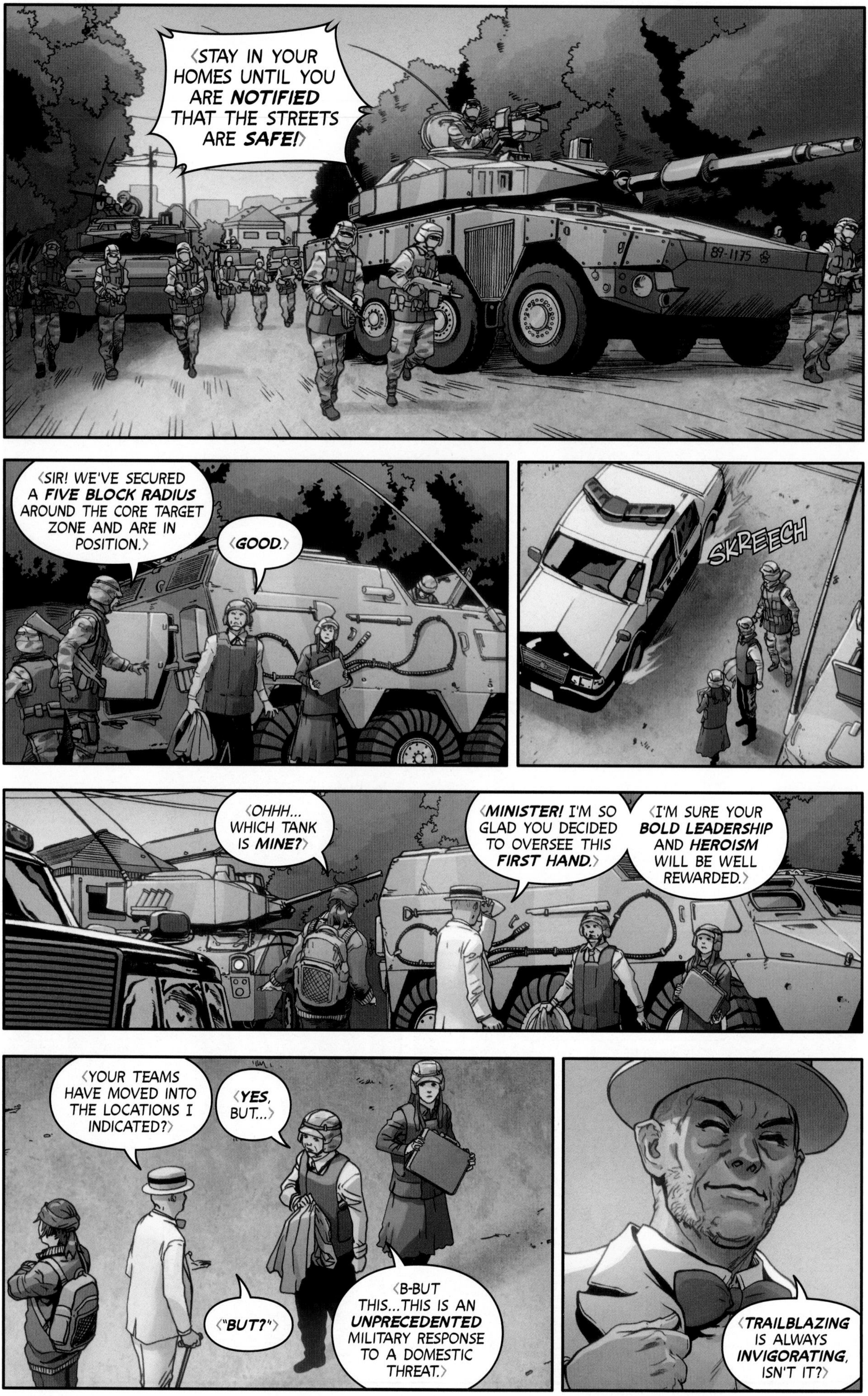

<STAY IN YOUR HOMES UNTIL YOU ARE NOTIFIED THAT THE STREETS ARE SAFE!>
87-1175
<SIR! WE'VE SECURED A FIVE BLOCK RADIUS AROUND THE CORE TARGET ZONE AND ARE IN POSITION.>
<GOOD.>
SKREECH
<OHHH... WHICH TANK IS MINE?>
<MINISTER! I'M SO GLAD YOU DECIDED TO OVERSEE THIS FIRST HAND.>
<I'M SURE YOUR BOLD LEADERSHIP AND HEROISM WILL BE WELL REWARDED.>
<YOUR TEAMS HAVE MOVED INTO THE LOCATIONS I INDICATED?>
<YES, BUT...>
<"BUT?">
<B-BUT THIS...THIS IS AN UNPRECEDENTED MILITARY RESPONSE TO A DOMESTIC THREAT.>
<TRAILBLAZING IS ALWAYS INVIGORATING, ISN'T IT?>

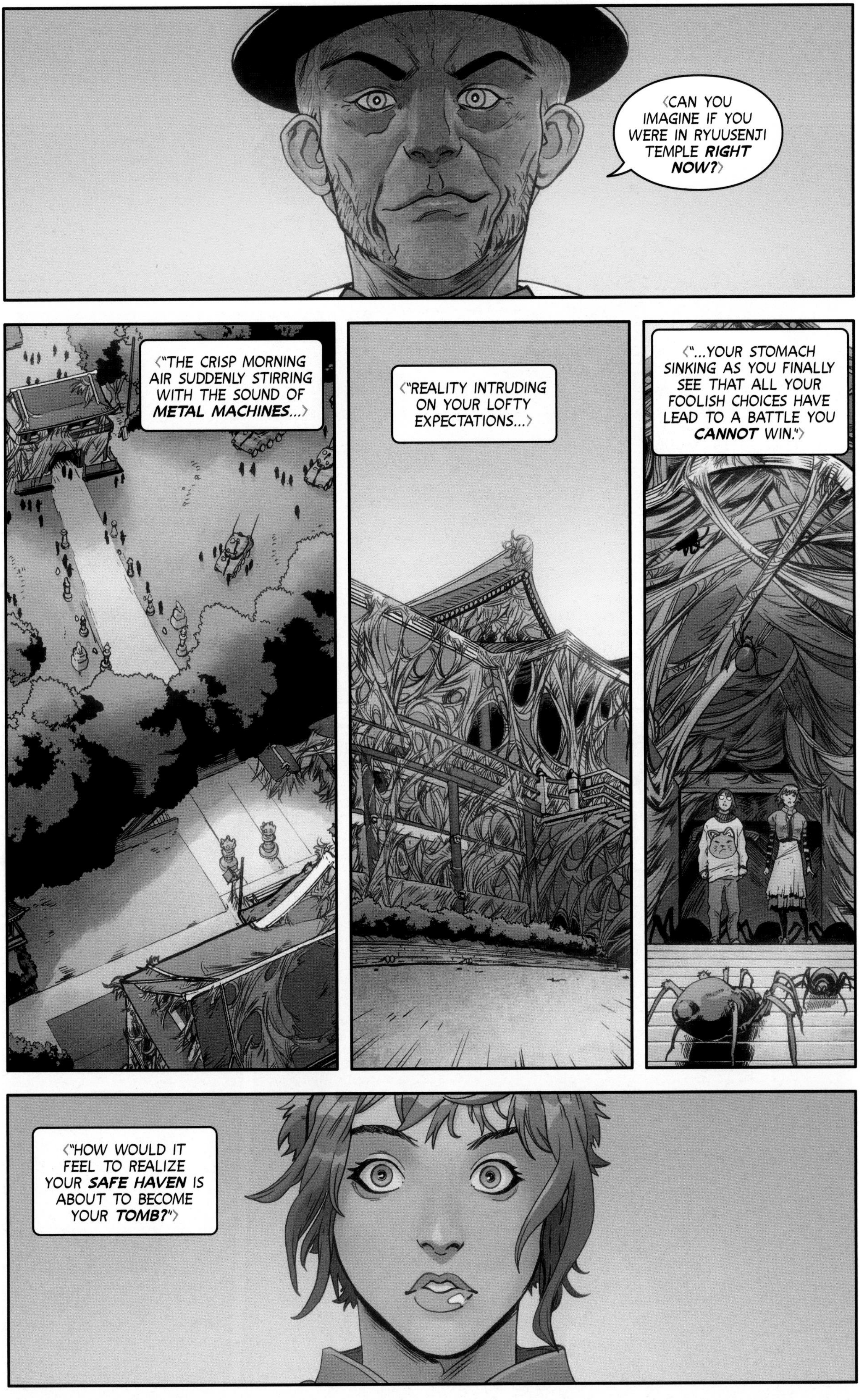
‹CAN YOU IMAGINE IF YOU WERE IN RYUUSENJI TEMPLE RIGHT NOW?›
‹"THE CRISP MORNING AIR SUDDENLY STIRRING WITH THE SOUND OF METAL MACHINES...›
‹"REALITY INTRUDING ON YOUR LOFTY EXPECTATIONS...›
‹"...YOUR STOMACH SINKING AS YOU FINALLY SEE THAT ALL YOUR FOOLISH CHOICES HAVE LEAD TO A BATTLE YOU CANNOT WIN."›
‹"HOW WOULD IT FEEL TO REALIZE YOUR SAFE HAVEN IS ABOUT TO BECOME YOUR TOMB?"›

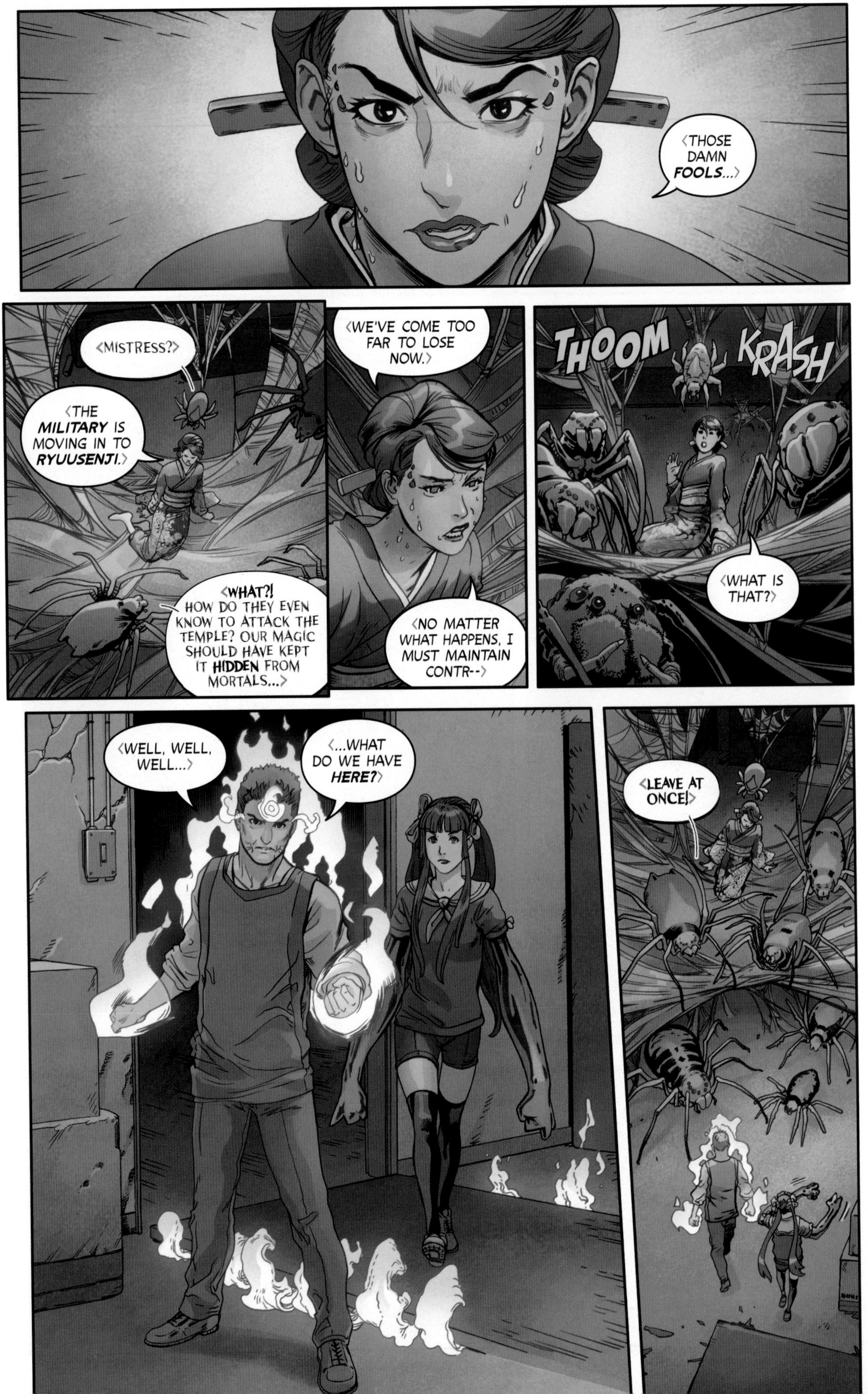
‹THOSE DAMN FOOLS...›
‹MISTRESS?›
‹THE MILITARY IS MOVING IN TO RYUUSENJI.›
‹WHAT?! HOW DO THEY EVEN KNOW TO ATTACK THE TEMPLE? OUR MAGIC SHOULD HAVE KEPT IT HIDDEN FROM MORTALS...›
‹WE'VE COME TOO FAR TO LOSE NOW.›
‹NO MATTER WHAT HAPPENS, I MUST MAINTAIN CONTR--›
THOOM
KRASH
‹WHAT IS THAT?›
‹WELL, WELL, WELL...›
‹...WHAT DO WE HAVE HERE?›
‹LEAVE AT ONCE!›

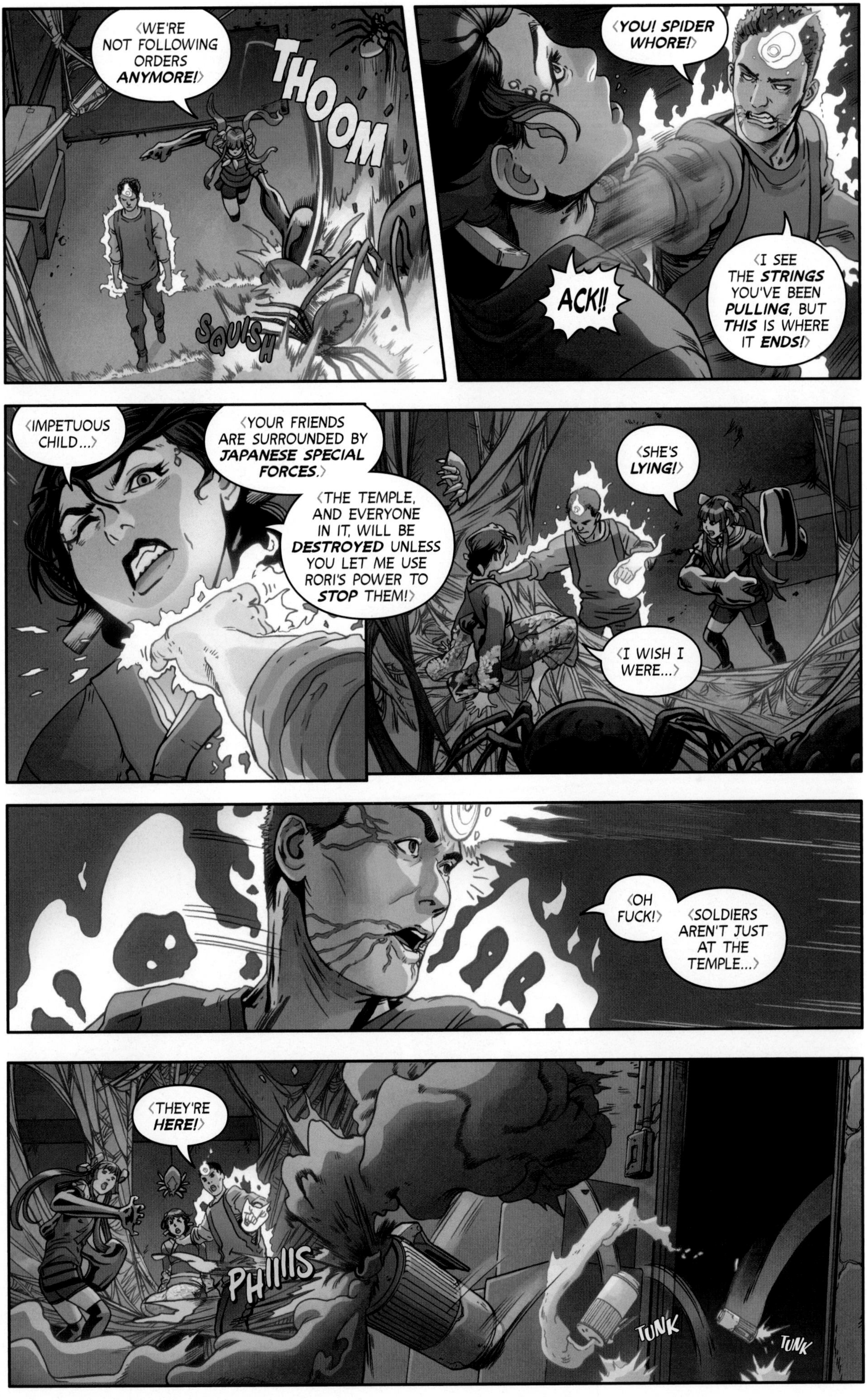

‹WE'RE NOT FOLLOWING ORDERS ANYMORE!›
THOOM
SQUISH
‹YOU! SPIDER WHORE!›
ACK!!
‹I SEE THE STRINGS YOU'VE BEEN PULLING, BUT THIS IS WHERE IT ENDS!›
‹IMPETUOUS CHILD...›
‹YOUR FRIENDS ARE SURROUNDED BY JAPANESE SPECIAL FORCES.›
‹THE TEMPLE, AND EVERYONE IN IT, WILL BE DESTROYED UNLESS YOU LET ME USE RORI'S POWER TO STOP THEM!›
‹SHE'S LYING!›
‹I WISH I WERE...›
‹OH FUCK!›
‹SOLDIERS AREN'T JUST AT THE TEMPLE...›
‹THEY'RE HERE!›
PHIIIIS
TUNK
TUNK

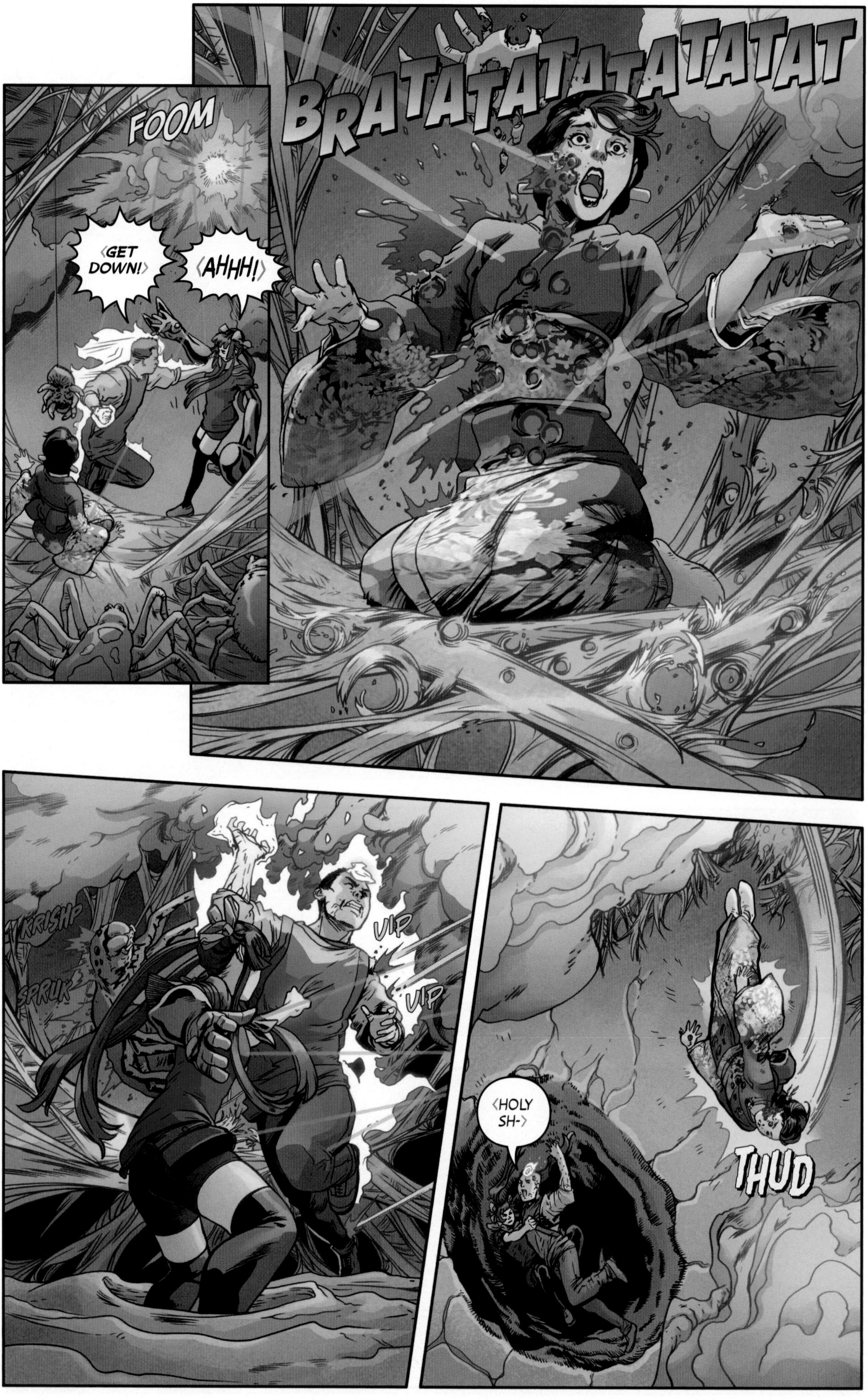
FOOM
‹GET DOWN!›
‹AHHH!›
BRATATATATATATAT
KRISHP
SPRUK
VIP
VIP
‹HOLY SH-›
THUD

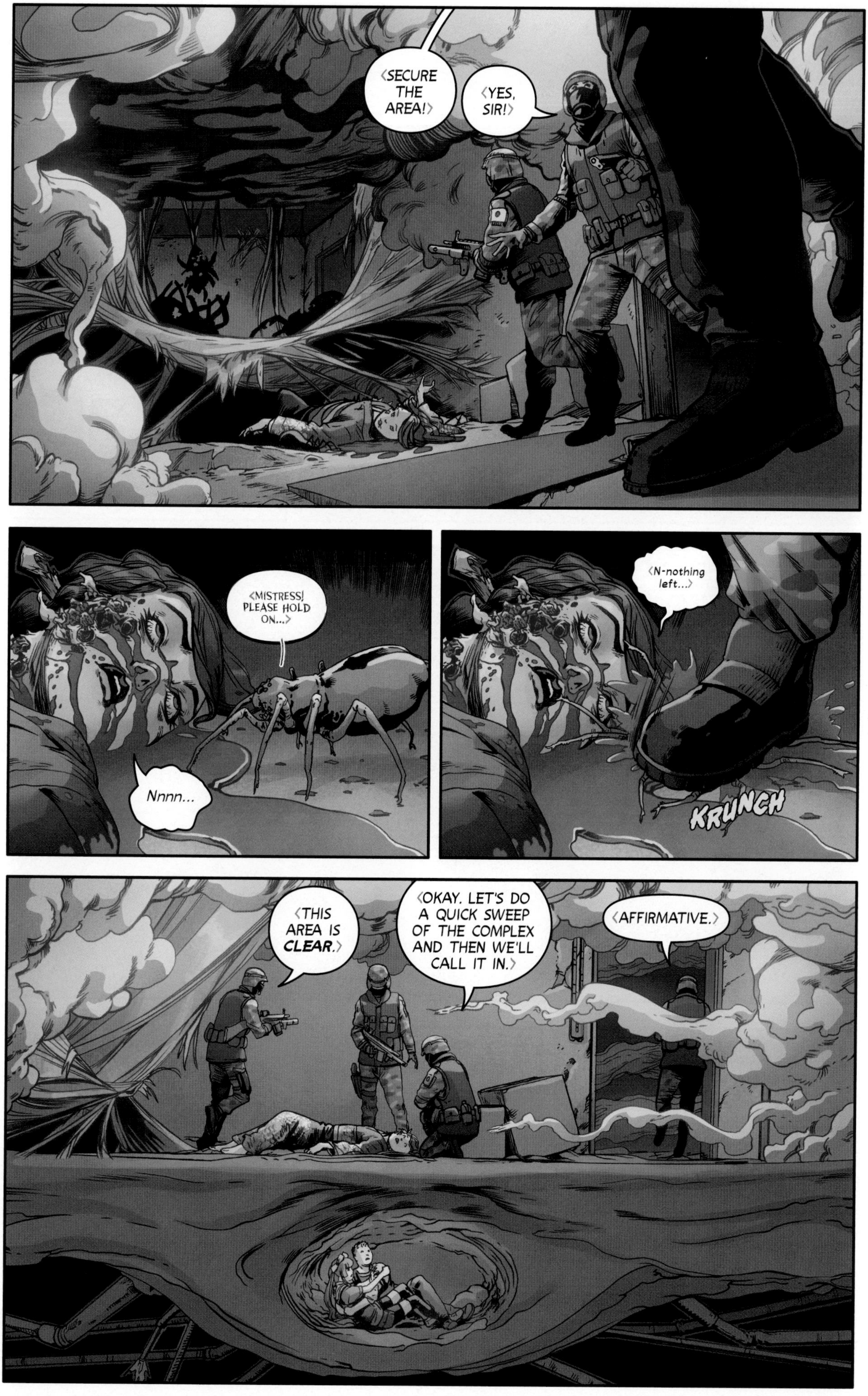

〈SECURE THE AREA!〉
〈YES, SIR!〉
〈MISTRESS! PLEASE HOLD ON...〉
Nnnn...
〈N-nothing left...〉
KRUNCH
〈THIS AREA IS CLEAR.〉
〈OKAY. LET'S DO A QUICK SWEEP OF THE COMPLEX AND THEN WE'LL CALL IT IN.〉
〈AFFIRMATIVE.〉

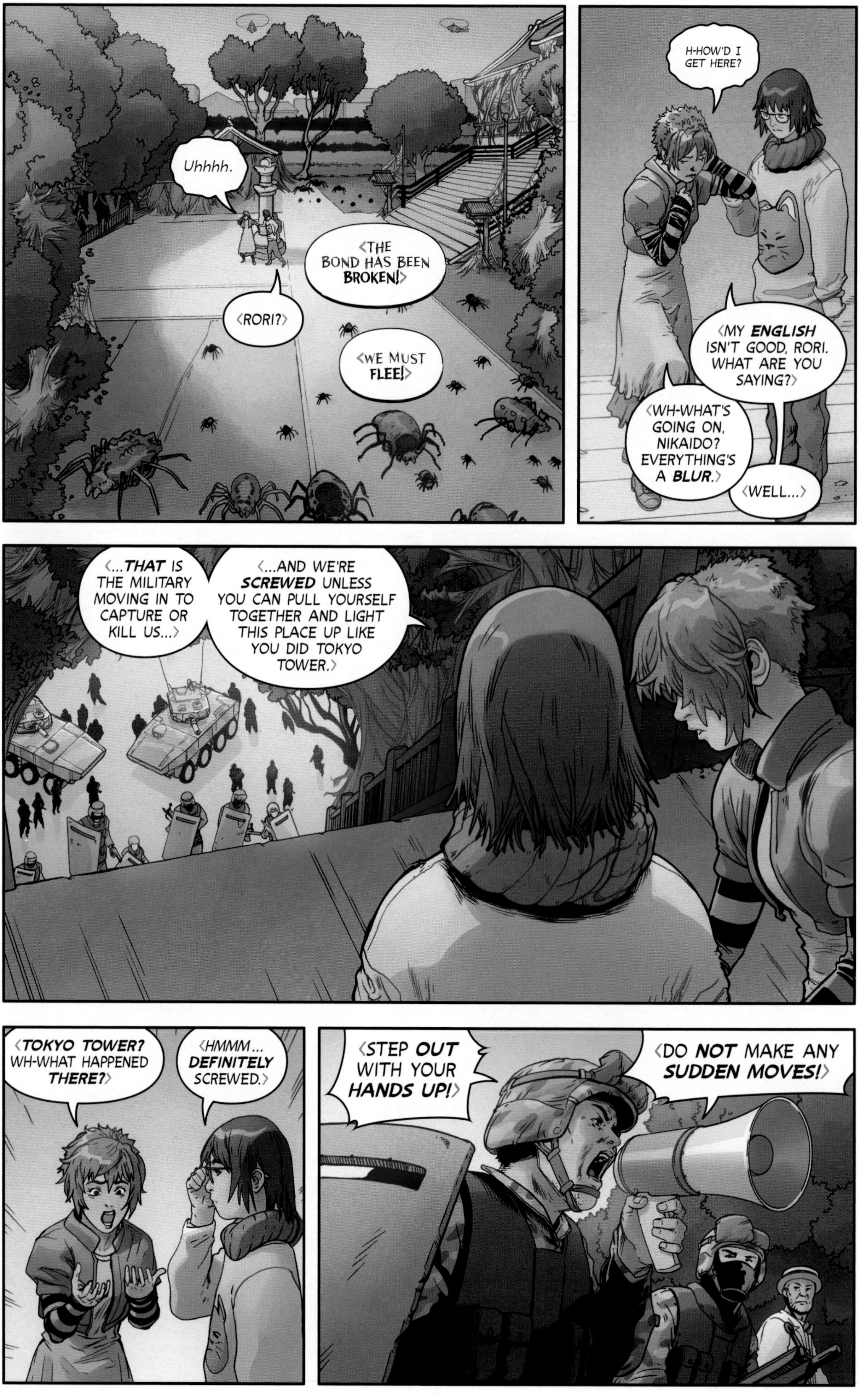
Uhhhh.
<THE BOND HAS BEEN BROKEN!>
<RORI?>
<WE MUST FLEE!>
H-HOW'D I GET HERE?
<MY ENGLISH ISN'T GOOD, RORI. WHAT ARE YOU SAYING?>
<WH-WHAT'S GOING ON, NIKAIDO? EVERYTHING'S A BLUR.>
<WELL...>
<...THAT IS THE MILITARY MOVING IN TO CAPTURE OR KILL US...>
<...AND WE'RE SCREWED UNLESS YOU CAN PULL YOURSELF TOGETHER AND LIGHT THIS PLACE UP LIKE YOU DID TOKYO TOWER.>
<TOKYO TOWER? WH-WHAT HAPPENED THERE?>
<HMMM... DEFINITELY SCREWED.>
<STEP OUT WITH YOUR HANDS UP!>
<DO NOT MAKE ANY SUDDEN MOVES!>

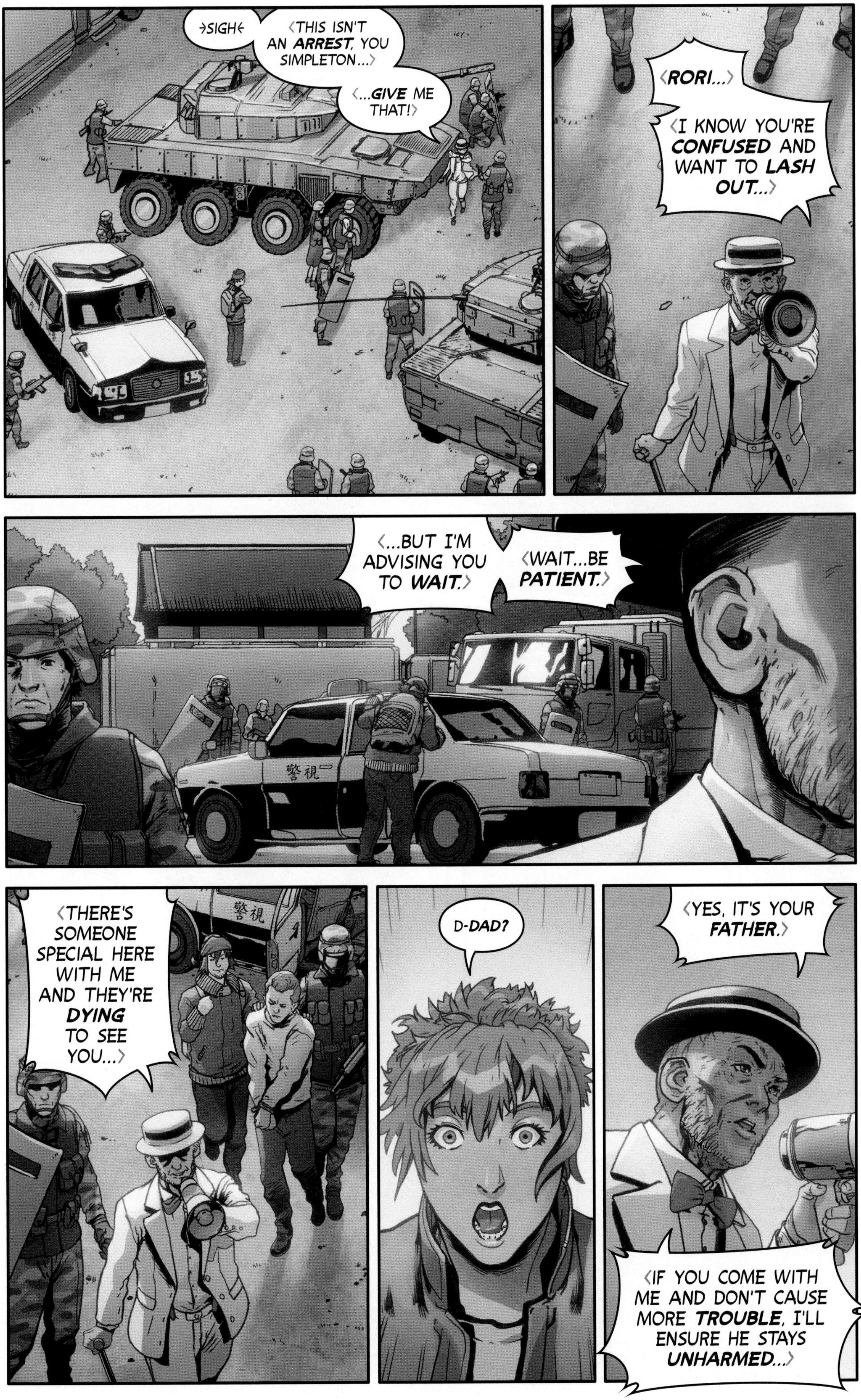
→SIGH←
‹THIS ISN'T AN ARREST, YOU SIMPLETON...›
‹...GIVE ME THAT!›
‹RORI...›
‹I KNOW YOU'RE CONFUSED AND WANT TO LASH OUT...›
‹...BUT I'M ADVISING YOU TO WAIT.›
‹WAIT...BE PATIENT.›
警視
‹THERE'S SOMEONE SPECIAL HERE WITH ME AND THEY'RE DYING TO SEE YOU...›
D-DAD?
‹YES, IT'S YOUR FATHER.›
‹IF YOU COME WITH ME AND DON'T CAUSE MORE TROUBLE, I'LL ENSURE HE STAYS UNHARMED...›

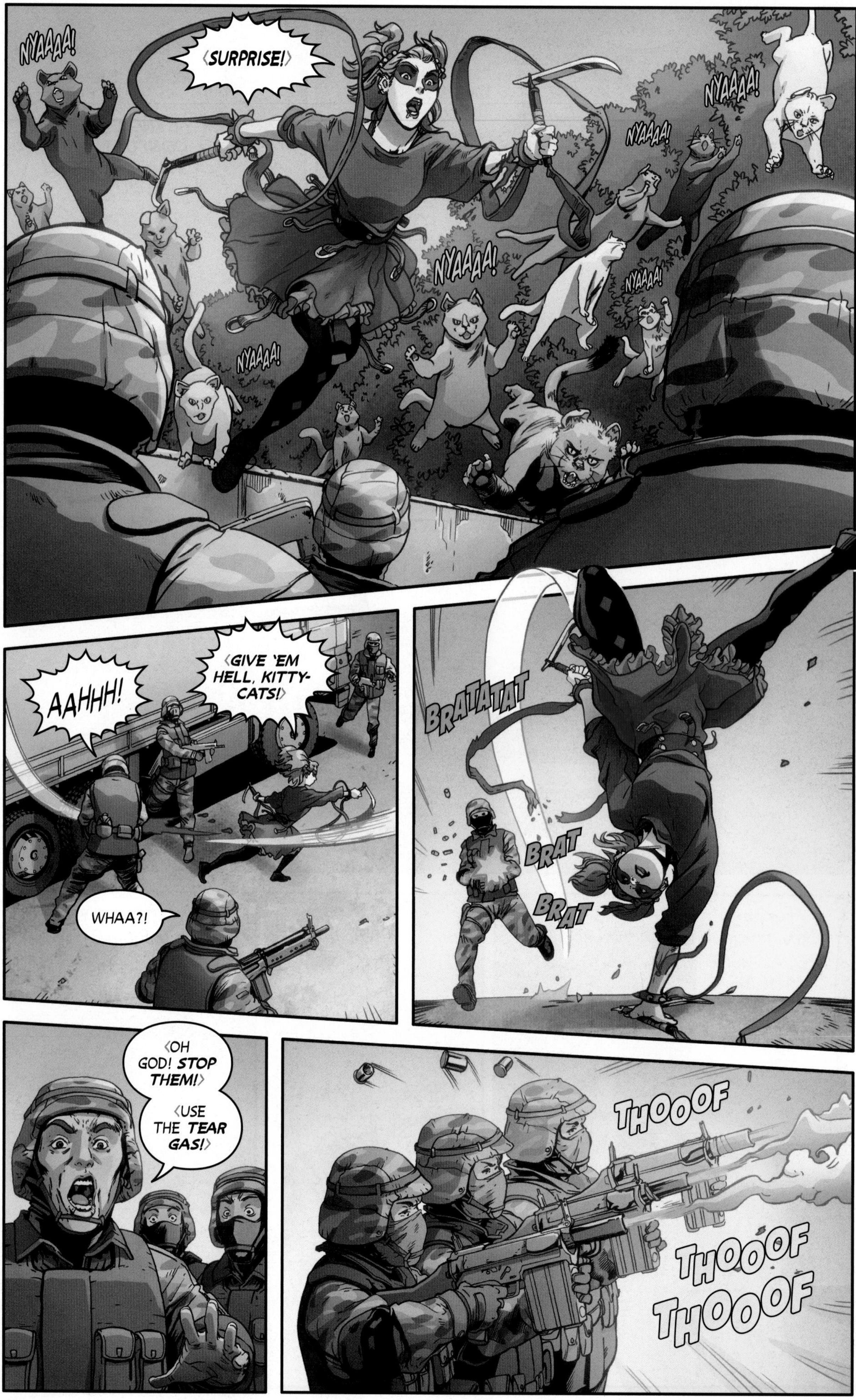
NYAAAA!
⟨SURPRISE!⟩
NYAAAA!
NYAAAA!
NYAAAA!
NYAAAA!
NYAAAA!
AAHHH!
⟨GIVE 'EM HELL, KITTY-CATS!⟩
WHAA?!
BRATATAT
BRAT
BRAT
⟨OH GOD! STOP THEM!⟩
⟨USE THE TEAR GAS!⟩
THOOOF
THOOOF
THOOOF

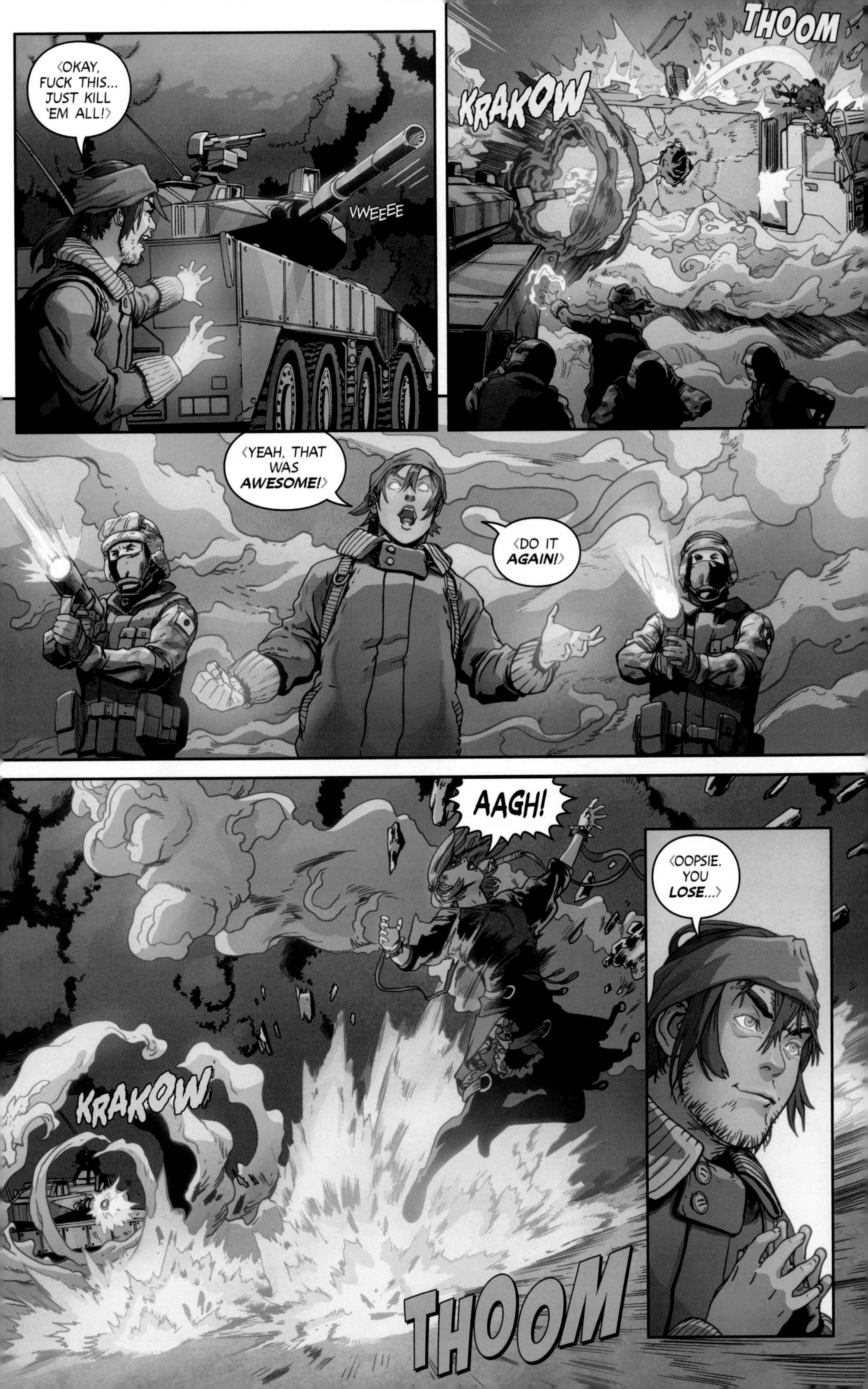
‹OKAY, FUCK THIS... JUST KILL 'EM ALL!›
VWEEEE
KRAKOW
THOOM
‹YEAH, THAT WAS **AWESOME!**›
‹DO IT **AGAIN!**›
AAGH!
KRAKOW
THOOM
‹OOPSIE. YOU **LOSE**...›

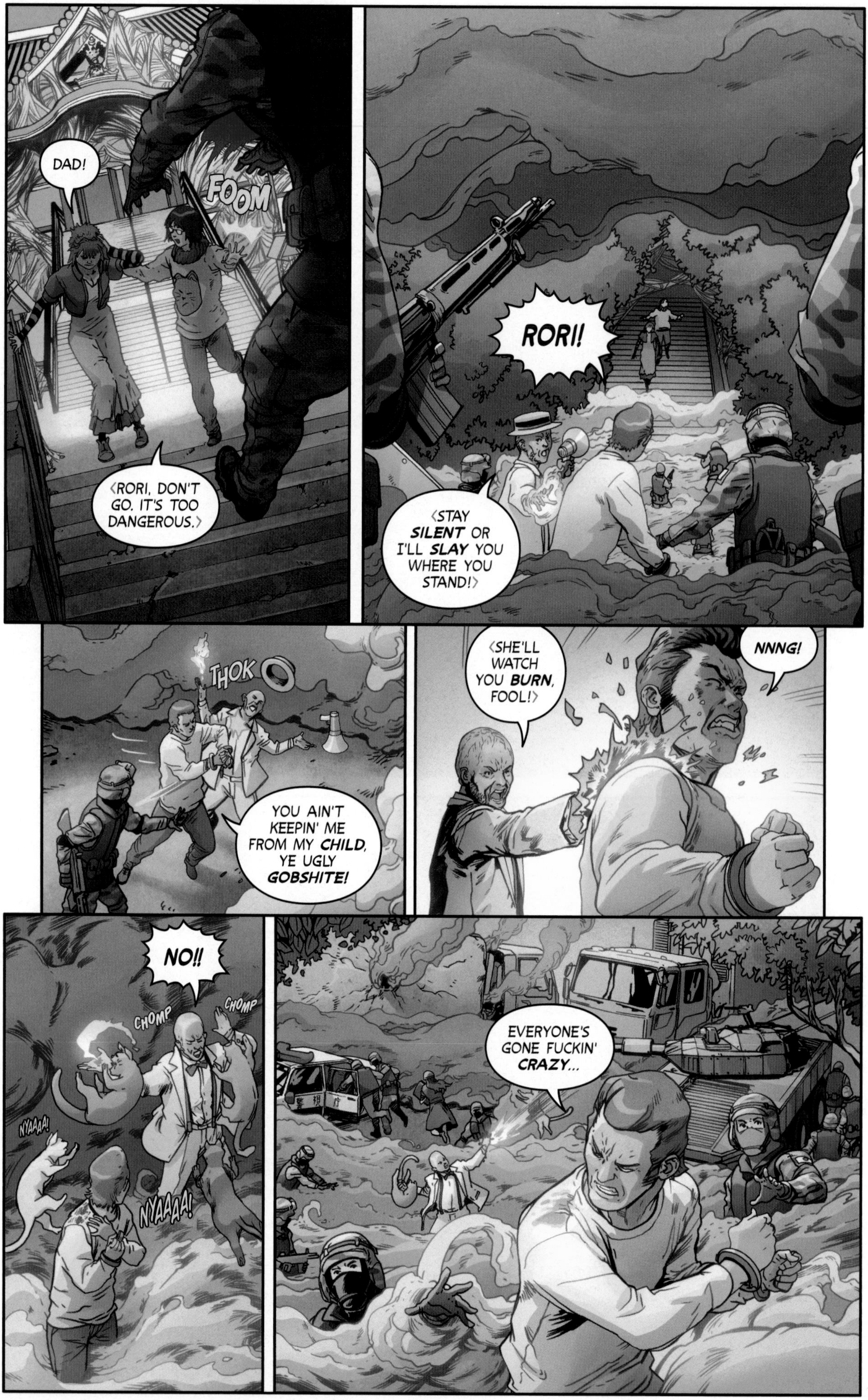
DAD!
FOOM
‹RORI, DON'T GO. IT'S TOO DANGEROUS.›
RORI!
‹STAY SILENT OR I'LL SLAY YOU WHERE YOU STAND!›
THOK
YOU AIN'T KEEPIN' ME FROM MY CHILD, YE UGLY GOBSHITE!
‹SHE'LL WATCH YOU BURN, FOOL!›
NNNG!
NO!!
CHOMP
CHOMP
NYAAAA!
NYAAAA!
EVERYONE'S GONE FUCKIN' CRAZY...

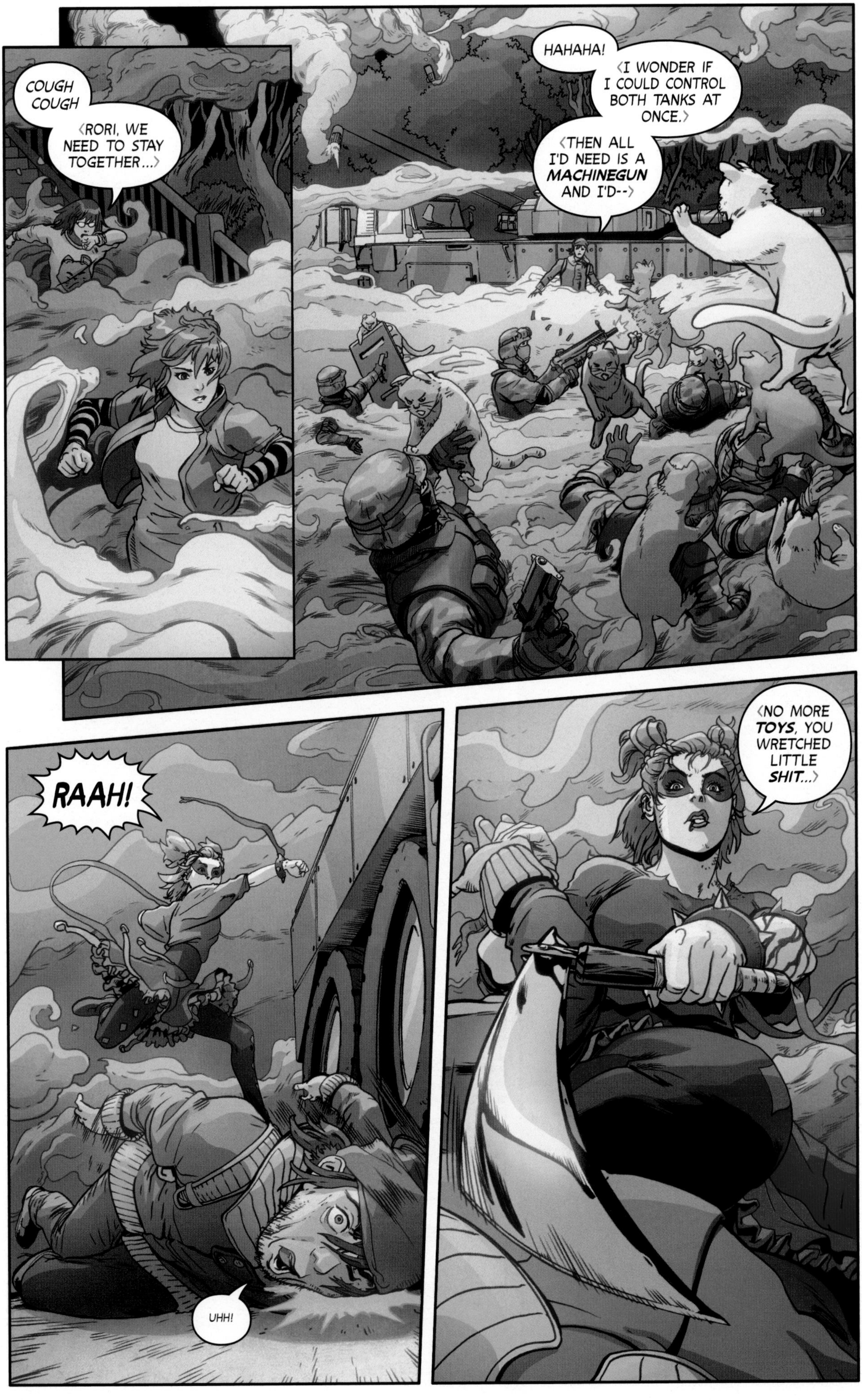
COUGH COUGH
‹RORI, WE NEED TO STAY TOGETHER...›
HAHAHA!
‹I WONDER IF I COULD CONTROL BOTH TANKS AT ONCE.›
‹THEN ALL I'D NEED IS A *MACHINEGUN* AND I'D--›
RAAH!
UHH!
‹NO MORE *TOYS*, YOU WRETCHED LITTLE *SHIT*...›

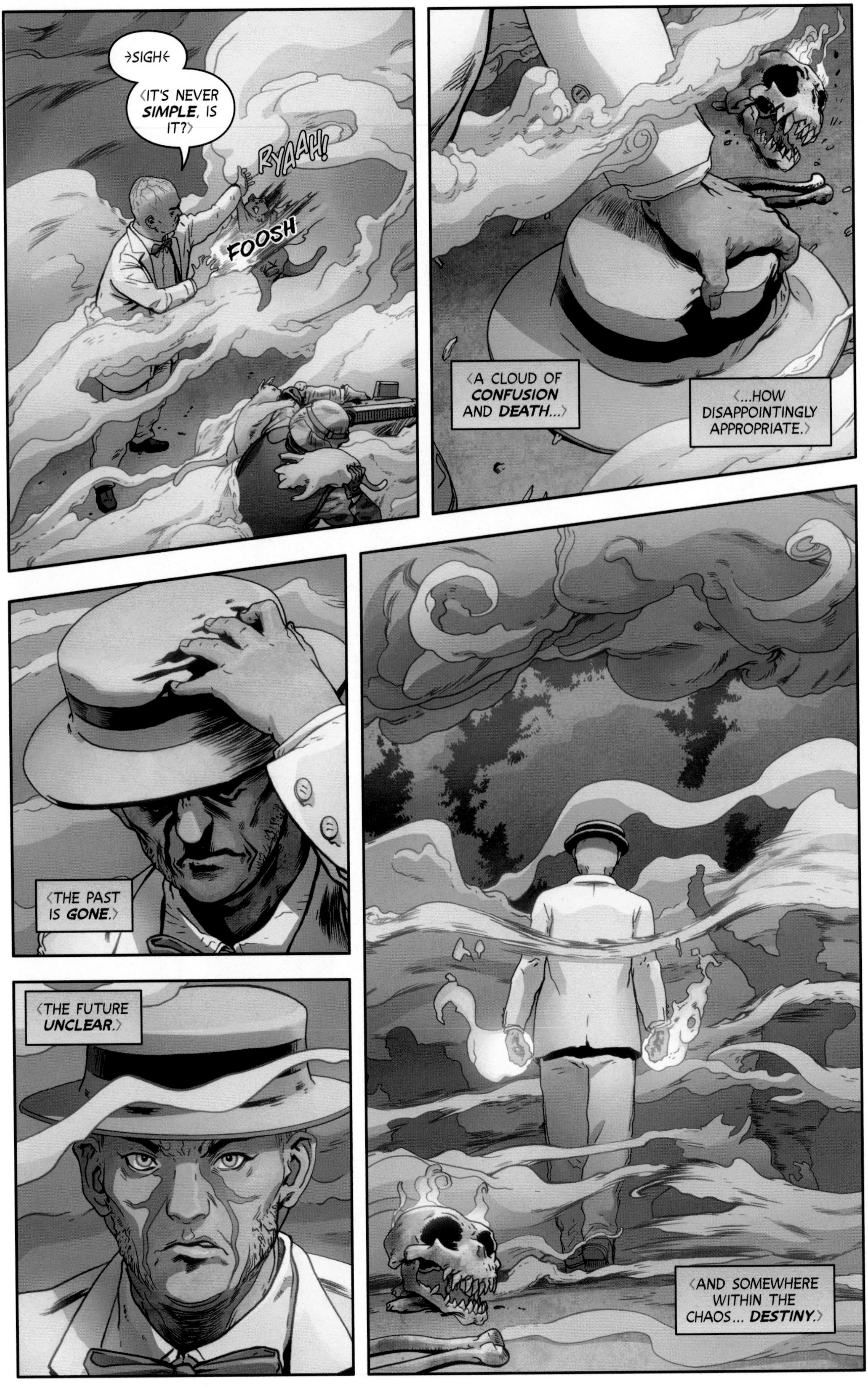

›SIGH‹
‹IT'S NEVER SIMPLE, IS IT?›
RYAAH!
FOOSH
‹A CLOUD OF CONFUSION AND DEATH...›
‹...HOW DISAPPOINTINGLY APPROPRIATE.›
‹THE PAST IS GONE.›
‹THE FUTURE UNCLEAR.›
‹AND SOMEWHERE WITHIN THE CHAOS... DESTINY.›

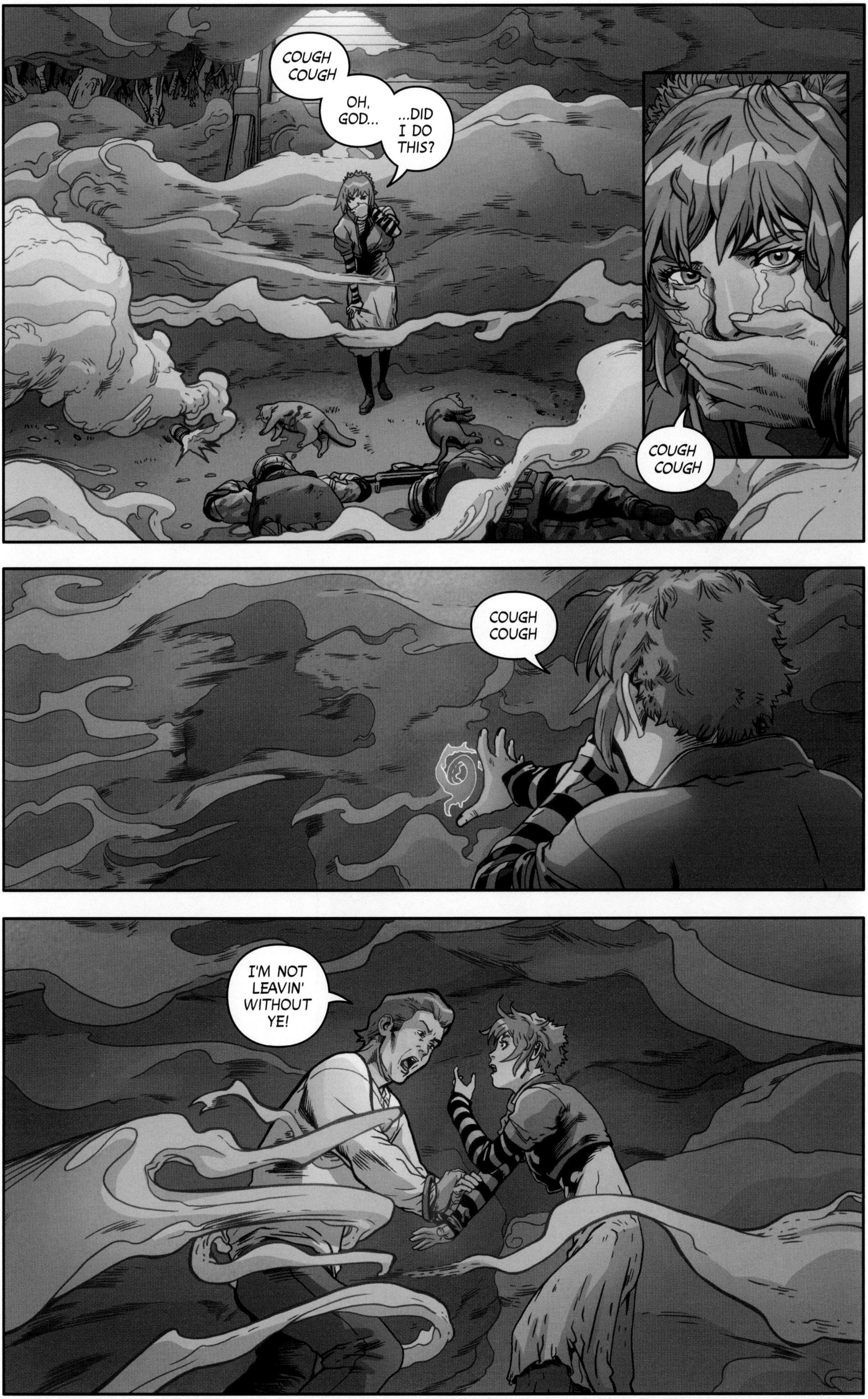
COUGH COUGH
OH, GOD...
...DID I DO THIS?
COUGH COUGH
COUGH COUGH
I'M NOT LEAVIN' WITHOUT YE!

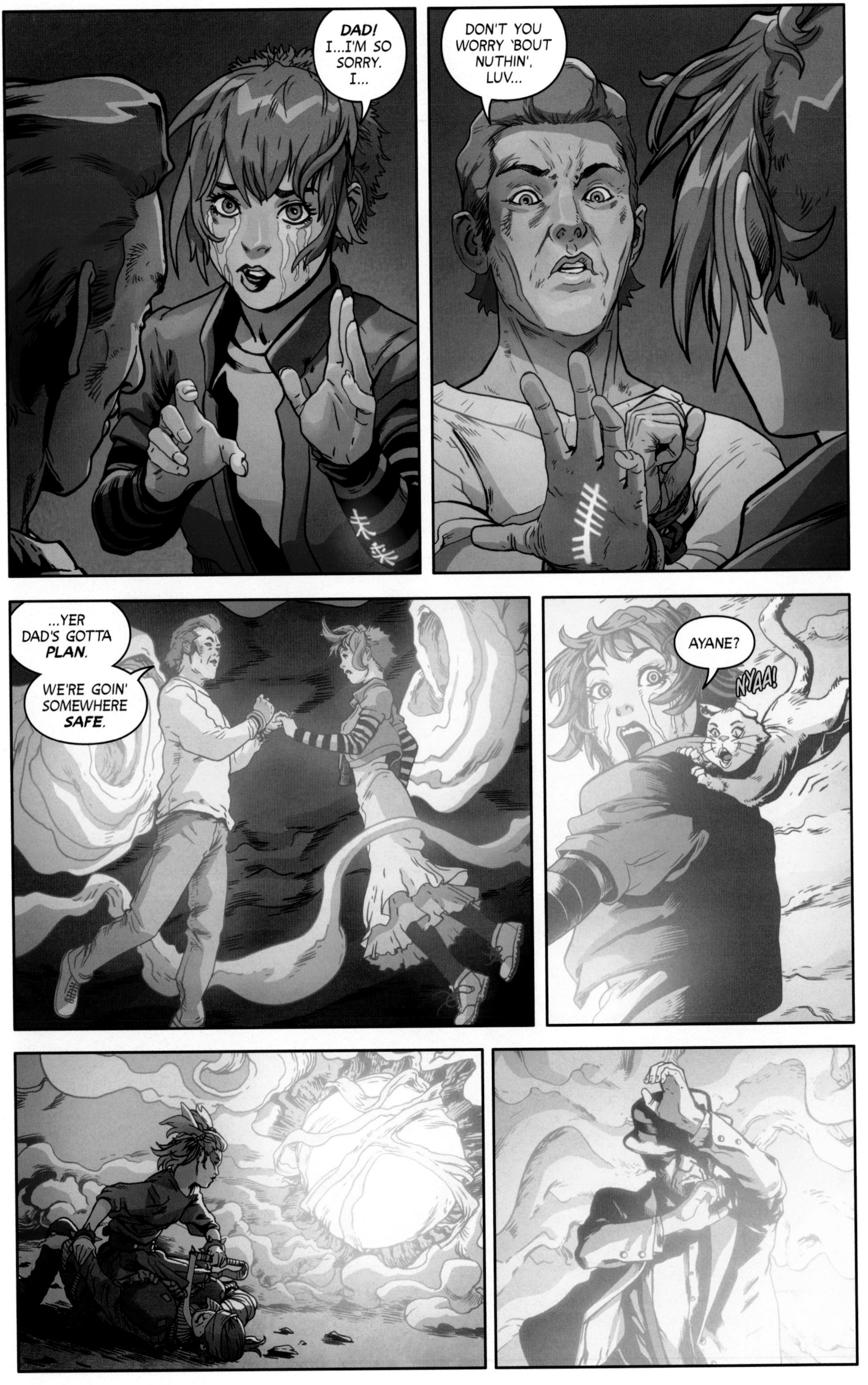
DAD! I...I'M SO SORRY. I...
DON'T YOU WORRY 'BOUT NUTHIN', LUV...
...YER DAD'S GOTTA PLAN.
WE'RE GOIN' SOMEWHERE SAFE.
AYANE?
NYAA!

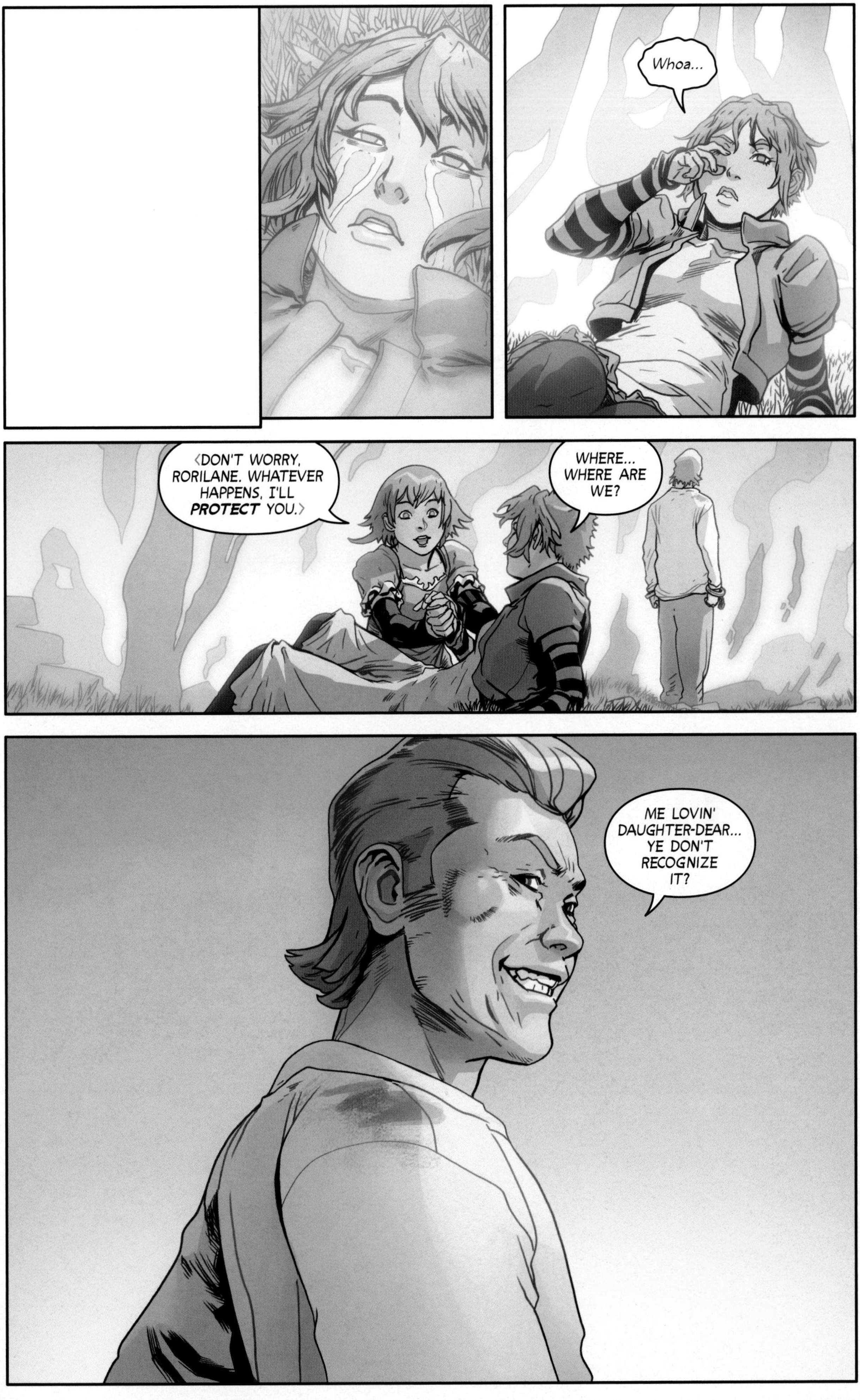

Whoa...
<DON'T WORRY, RORILANE. WHATEVER HAPPENS, I'LL **PROTECT** YOU.>
WHERE... WHERE ARE WE?
ME LOVIN' DAUGHTER-DEAR... YE DON'T RECOGNIZE IT?

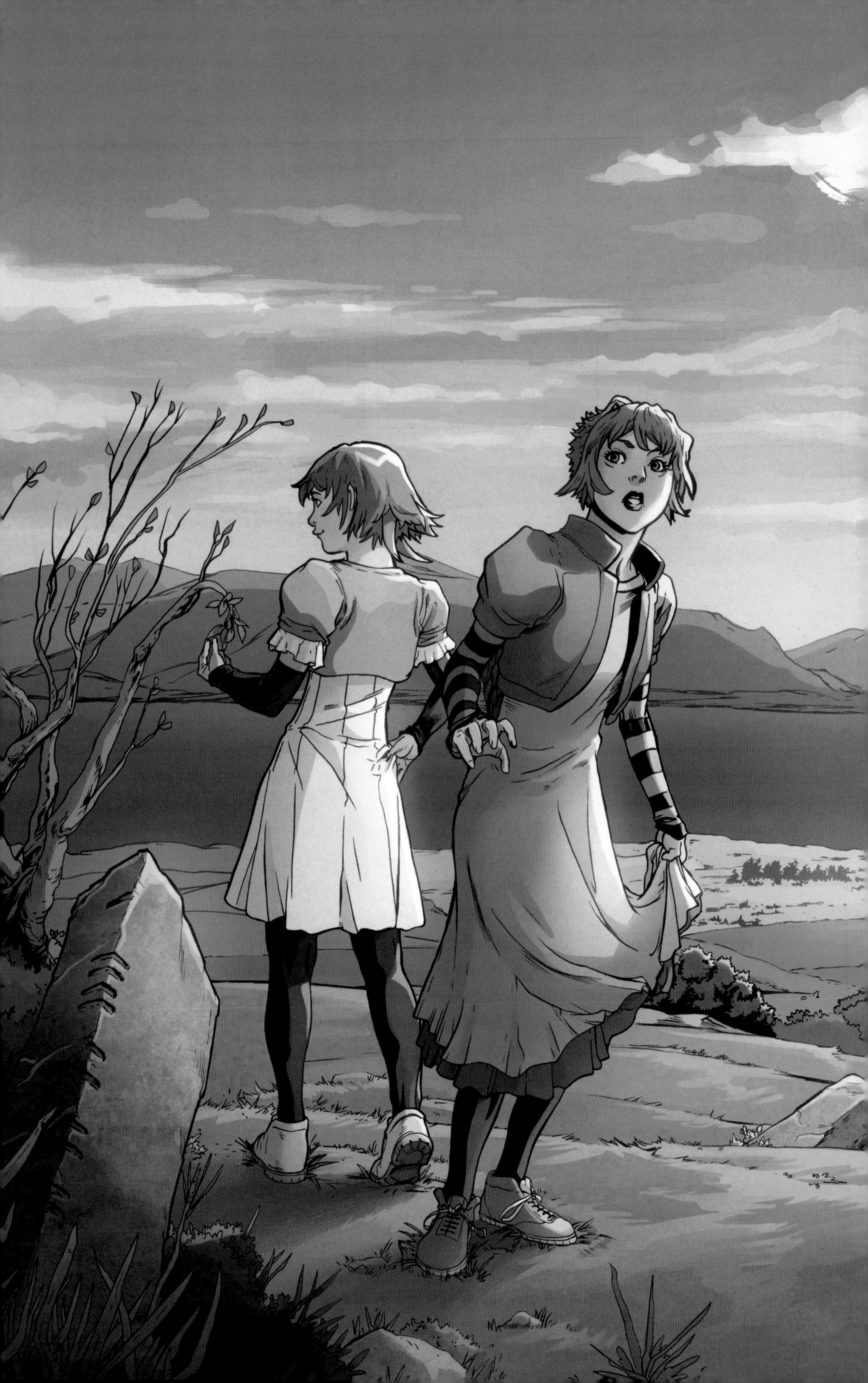

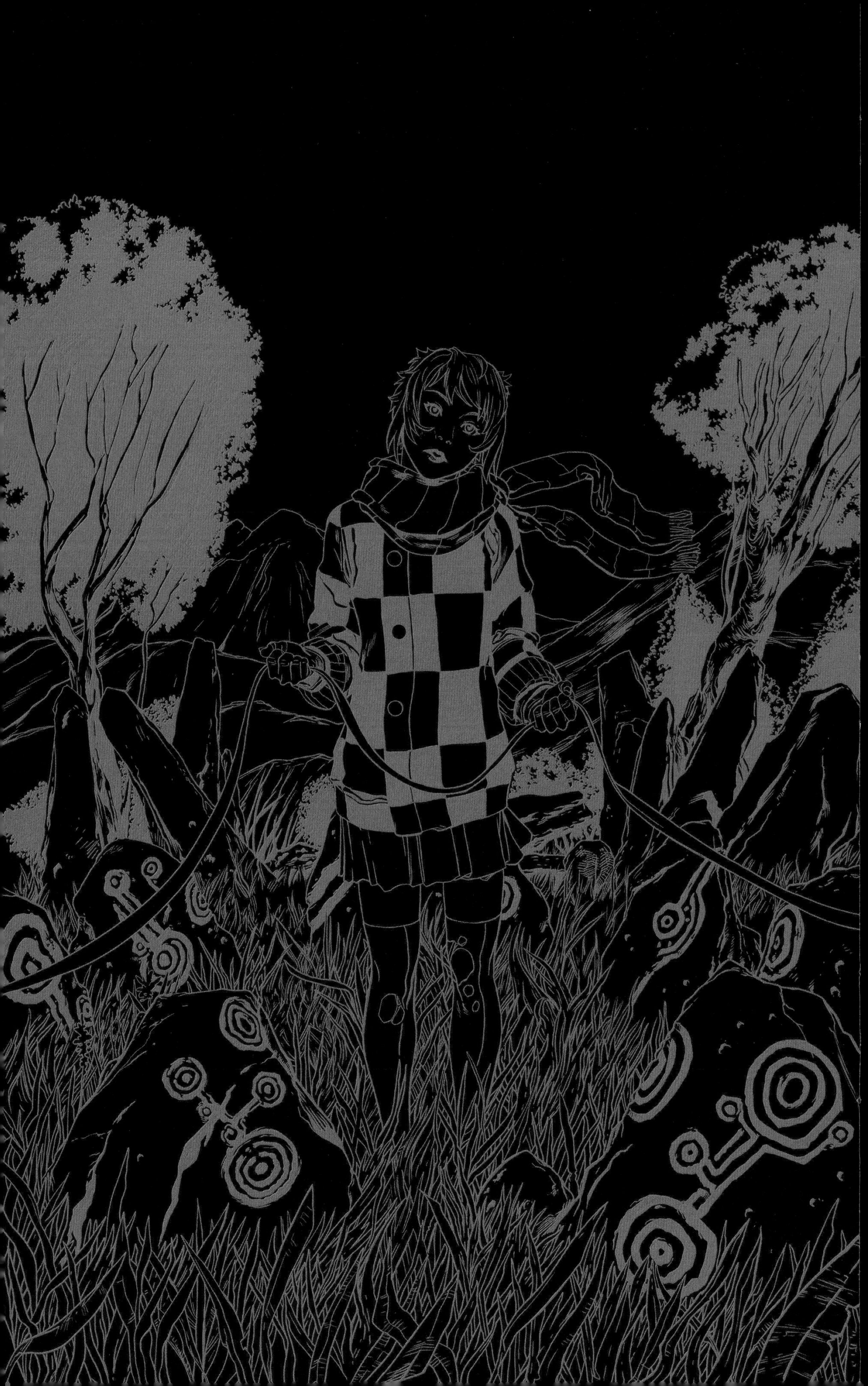

Chapter Sixteen

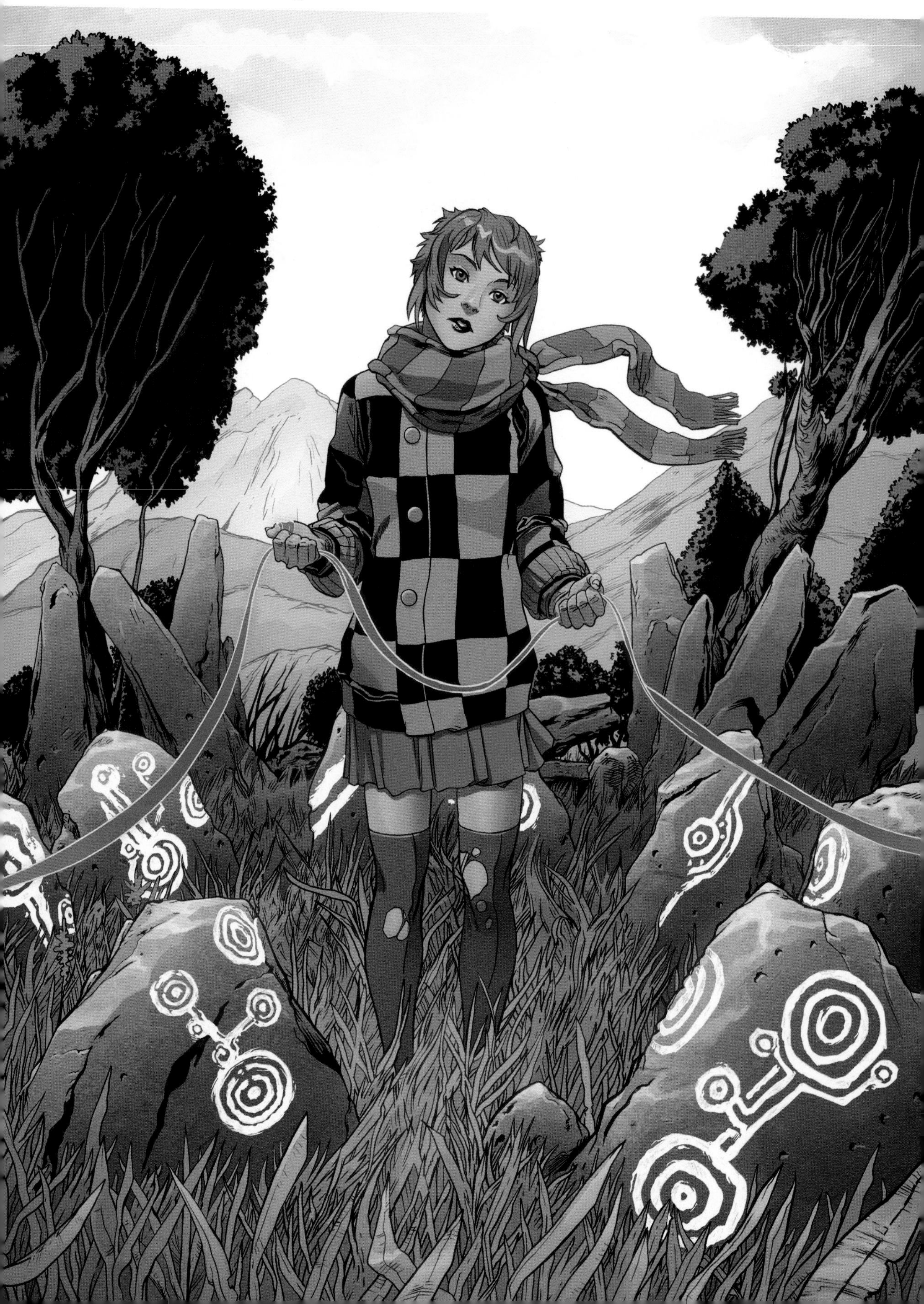

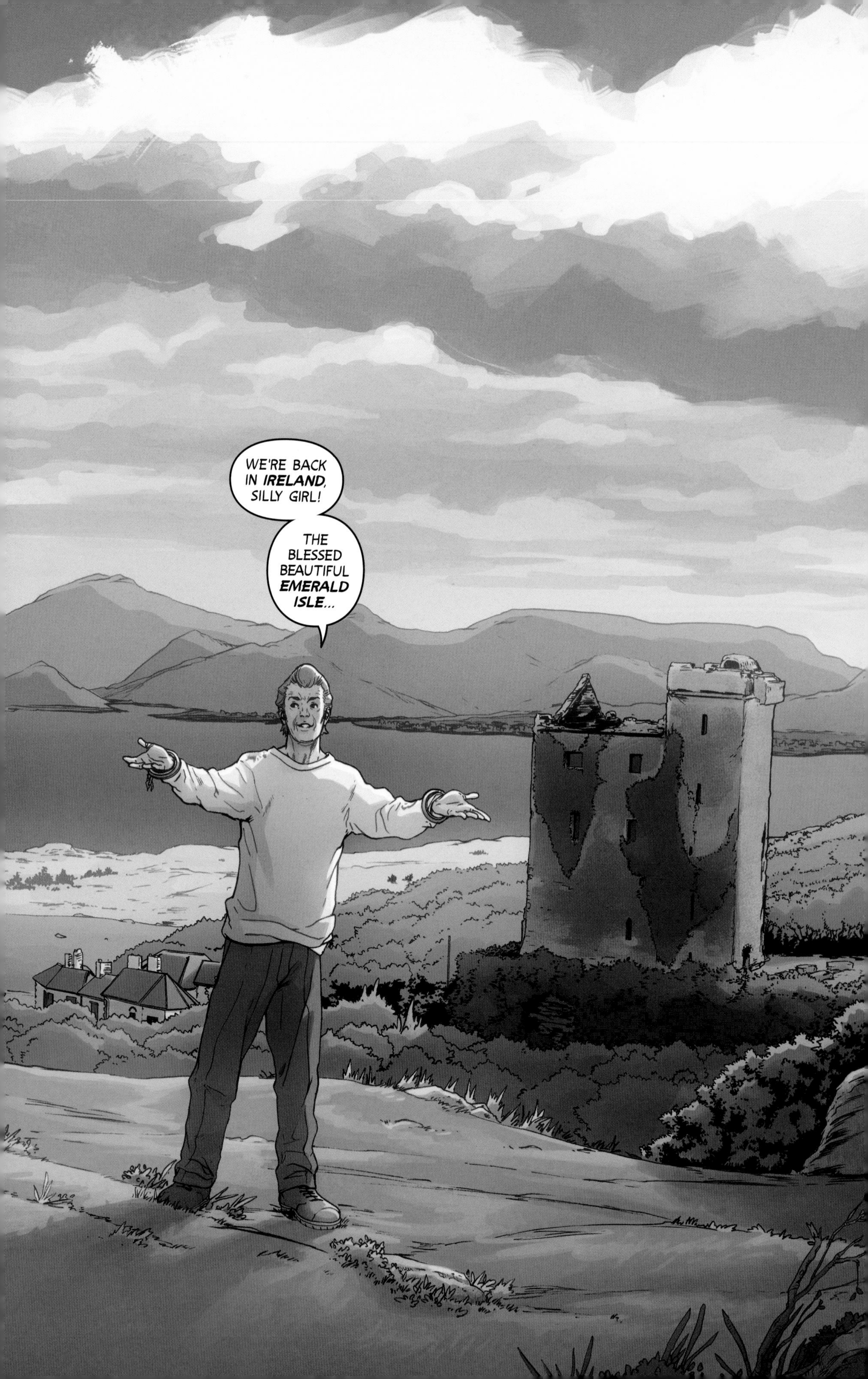
WE'RE BACK IN *IRELAND*, SILLY GIRL!
THE BLESSED BEAUTIFUL *EMERALD ISLE*...

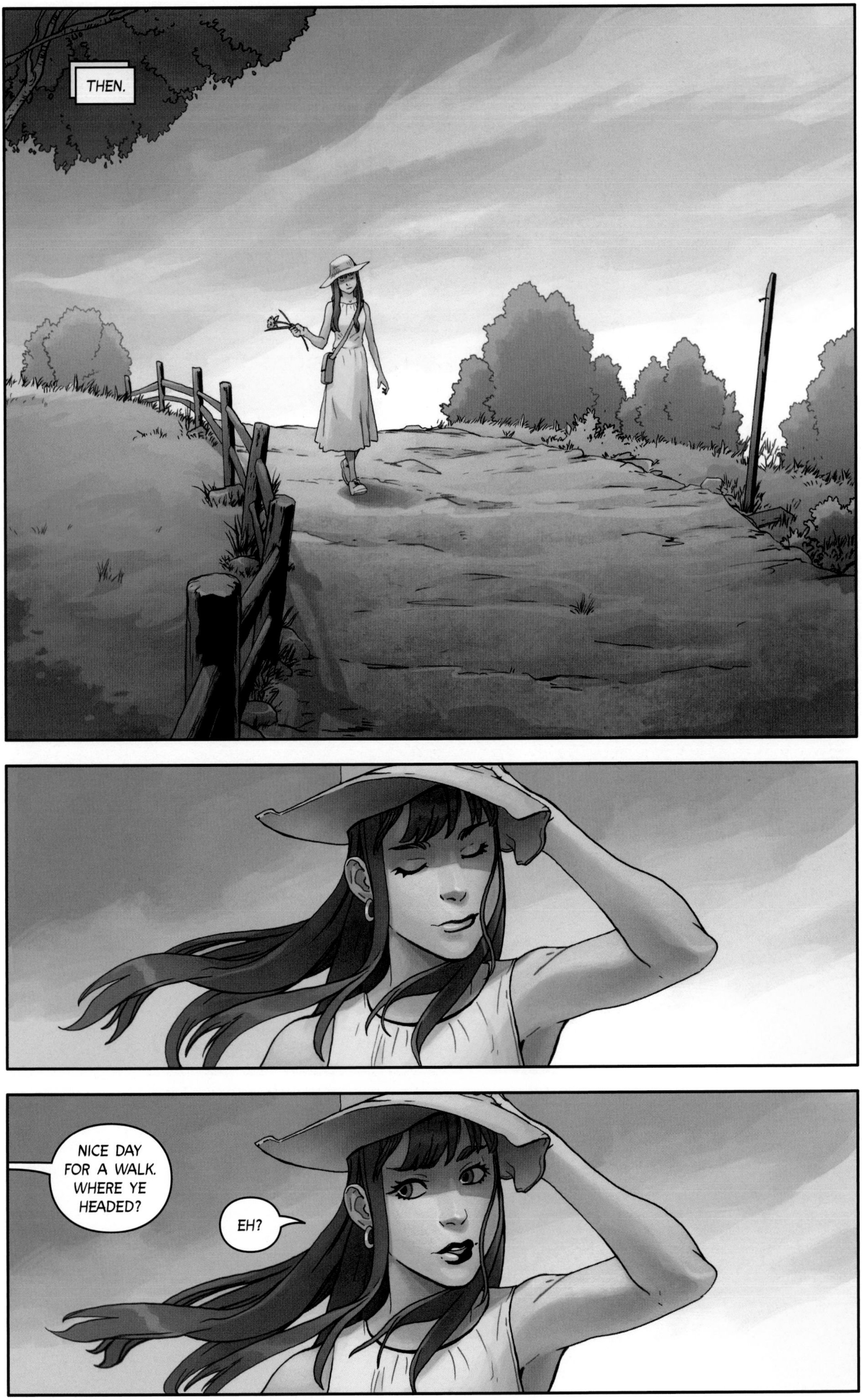
THEN.
NICE DAY FOR A WALK. WHERE YE HEADED?
EH?

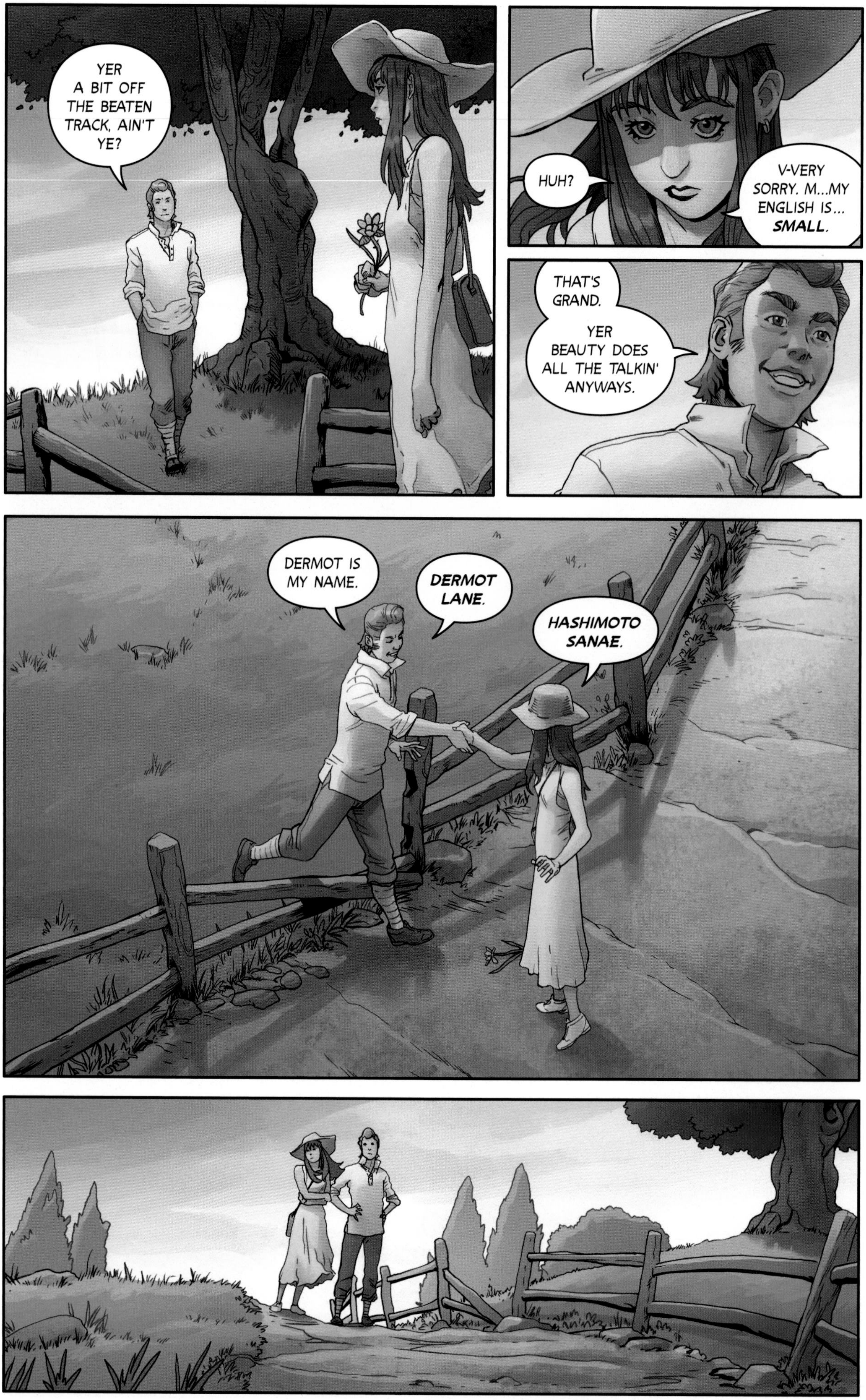
YER A BIT OFF THE BEATEN TRACK, AIN'T YE?
HUH?
V-VERY SORRY. M...MY ENGLISH IS... **SMALL.**
THAT'S GRAND.
YER BEAUTY DOES ALL THE TALKIN' ANYWAYS.
DERMOT IS MY NAME.
DERMOT LANE.
HASHIMOTO SANAE.

WHAT BRINGS YER HERE THEN? ARE YER ON *HOLS?*

"HALLS"?

UH... *VACATION.*

AH, YES, YES. SPECIAL TRIP. *ALONE.*

I NEVER LEAVE JAPAN BEFORE, BUT I SEE PICTURE.

IRELAND.

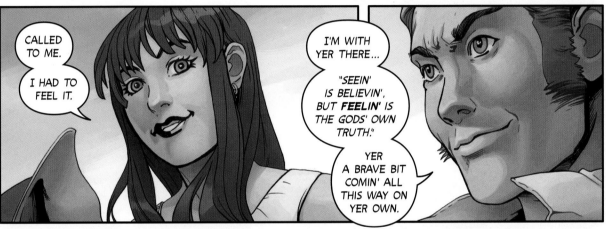

CALLED TO ME.

I HAD TO FEEL IT.

I'M WITH YER THERE...

"SEEIN' IS BELIEVIN', BUT *FEELIN'* IS THE GODS' OWN TRUTH."

YER A BRAVE BIT COMIN' ALL THIS WAY ON YER OWN.

YOU FANCY A *CUP O'TAE* THEN?

"*KAPPA TEE*"?*

JUST "*TEA*", LOVE.

WOULD YE LIKE A CUP OF *TEA?*

*KAPPA: TURTLE CREATURE IN JAPAN.

TEA? *OKAY.*

WELCOME TO THE *WILD ATLANTIC WAY...*

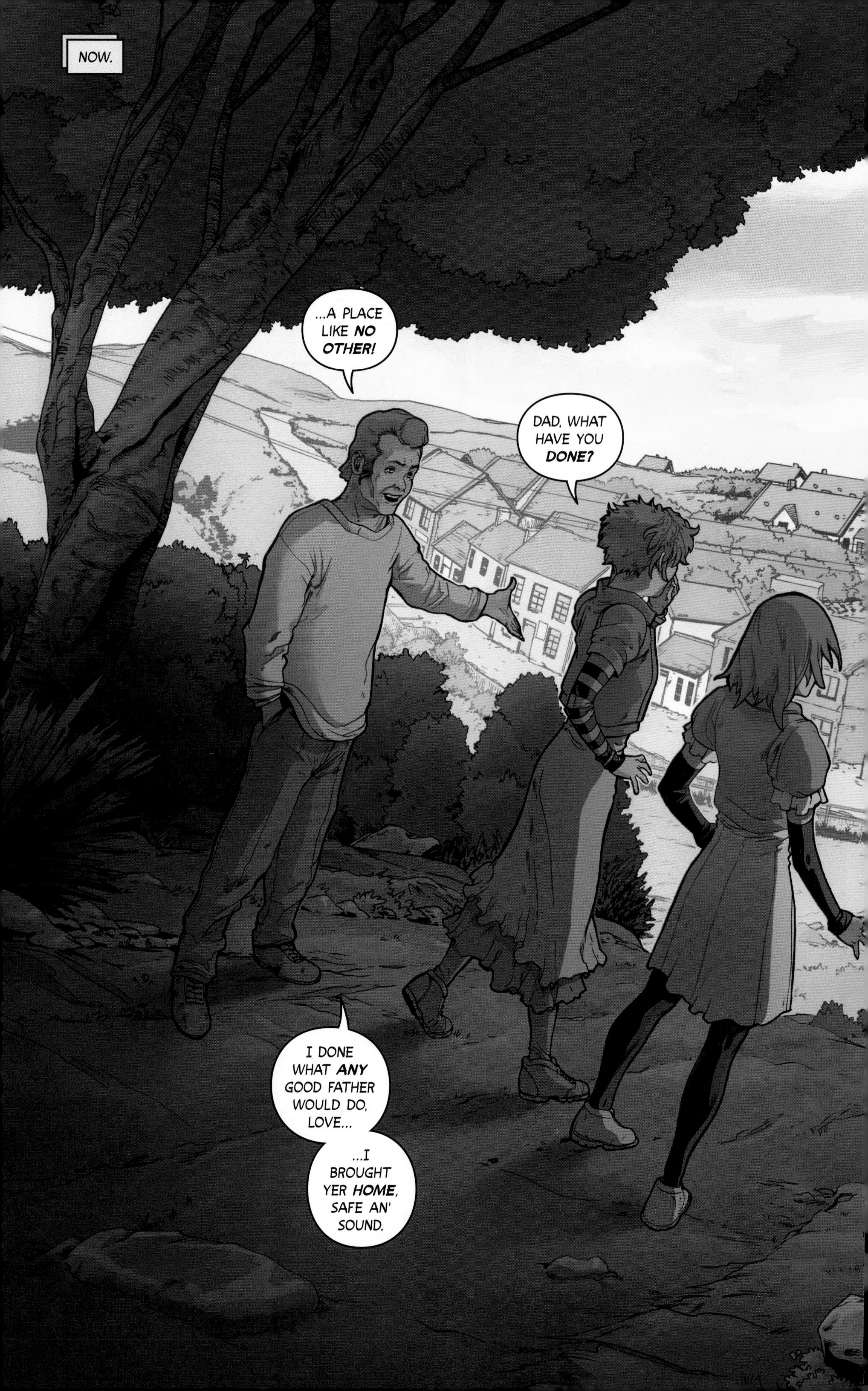
NOW.
...A PLACE LIKE **NO OTHER!**
DAD, WHAT HAVE YOU **DONE?**
I DONE WHAT **ANY** GOOD FATHER WOULD DO, LOVE...
...I BROUGHT YER **HOME**, SAFE AN' SOUND.

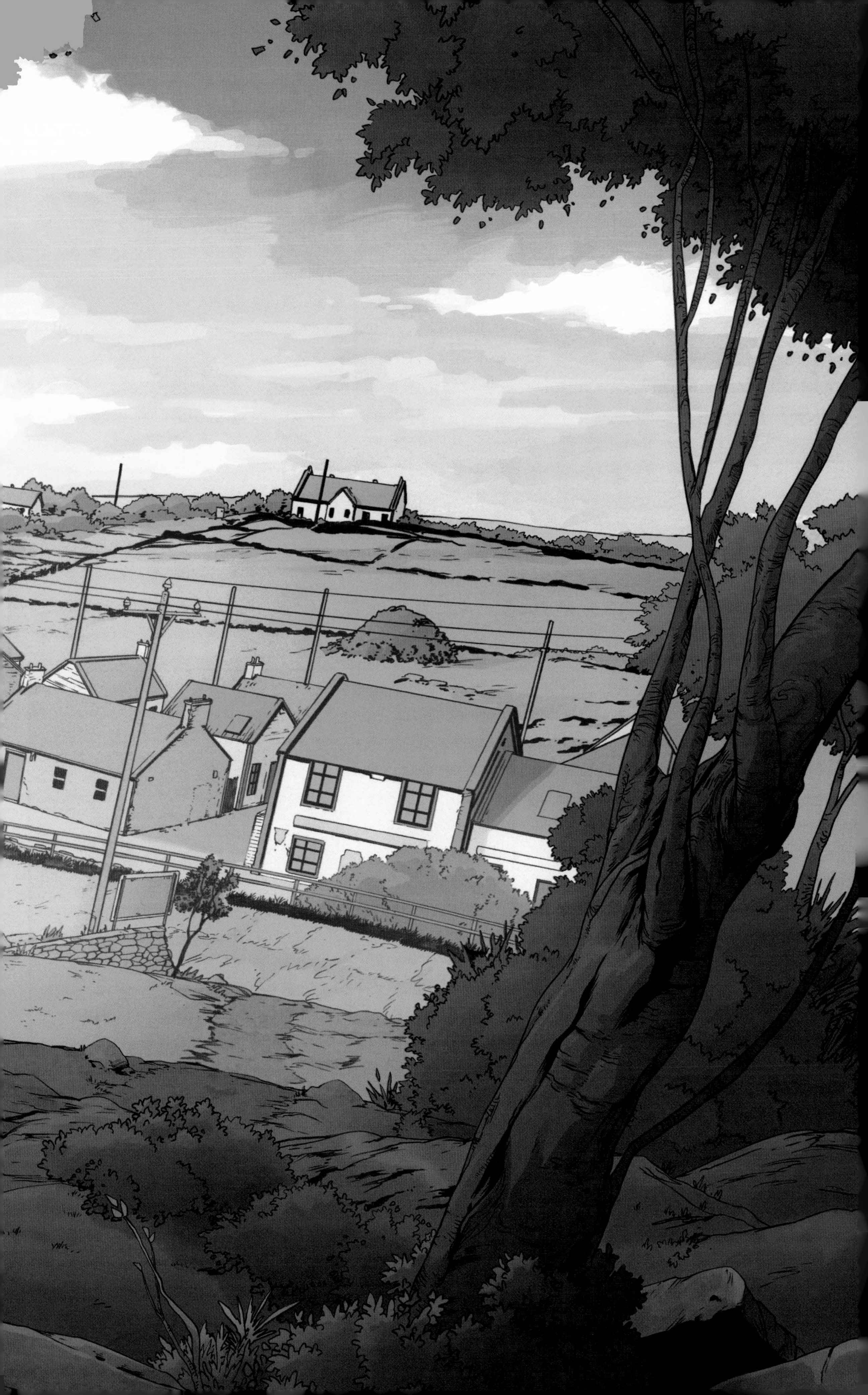

I KNOW IT'S A BIT OF A SHOCK AN' ALL, BUT DON'T CRY, RORI.

I SAVED YE.

NOW ALLS WE GOTTA DO IS GET AHOLD OF MUM AN' THEN WE CAN GET THIS FAMILY FIXED UP RIGHT.

OH GOD...

DAD...

...MOM...

SH-SH-SH...SHE'S DEAD.

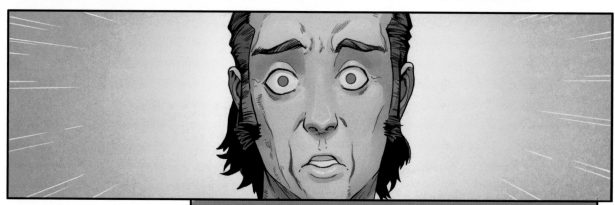

I...

W-W... WELL...

WELL, SHITE...

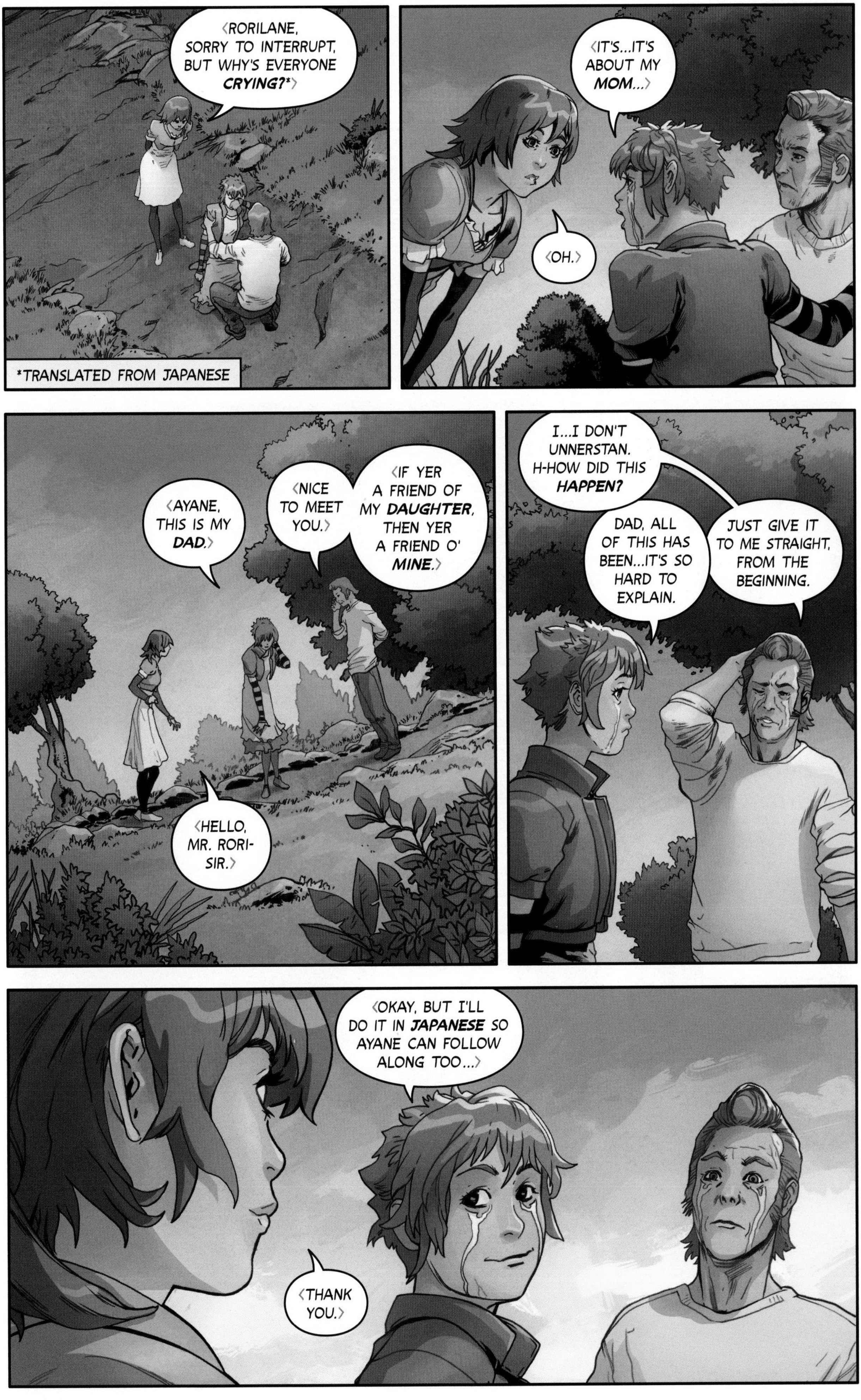

⟨RORILANE, SORRY TO INTERRUPT, BUT WHY'S EVERYONE CRYING?*⟩
*TRANSLATED FROM JAPANESE
⟨IT'S...IT'S ABOUT MY MOM...⟩
⟨OH.⟩
⟨AYANE, THIS IS MY DAD.⟩
⟨NICE TO MEET YOU.⟩
⟨IF YER A FRIEND OF MY DAUGHTER, THEN YER A FRIEND O' MINE.⟩
⟨HELLO, MR. RORI-SIR.⟩
I...I DON'T UNNERSTAN. H-HOW DID THIS HAPPEN?
DAD, ALL OF THIS HAS BEEN...IT'S SO HARD TO EXPLAIN.
JUST GIVE IT TO ME STRAIGHT, FROM THE BEGINNING.
⟨OKAY, BUT I'LL DO IT IN JAPANESE SO AYANE CAN FOLLOW ALONG TOO...⟩
⟨THANK YOU.⟩

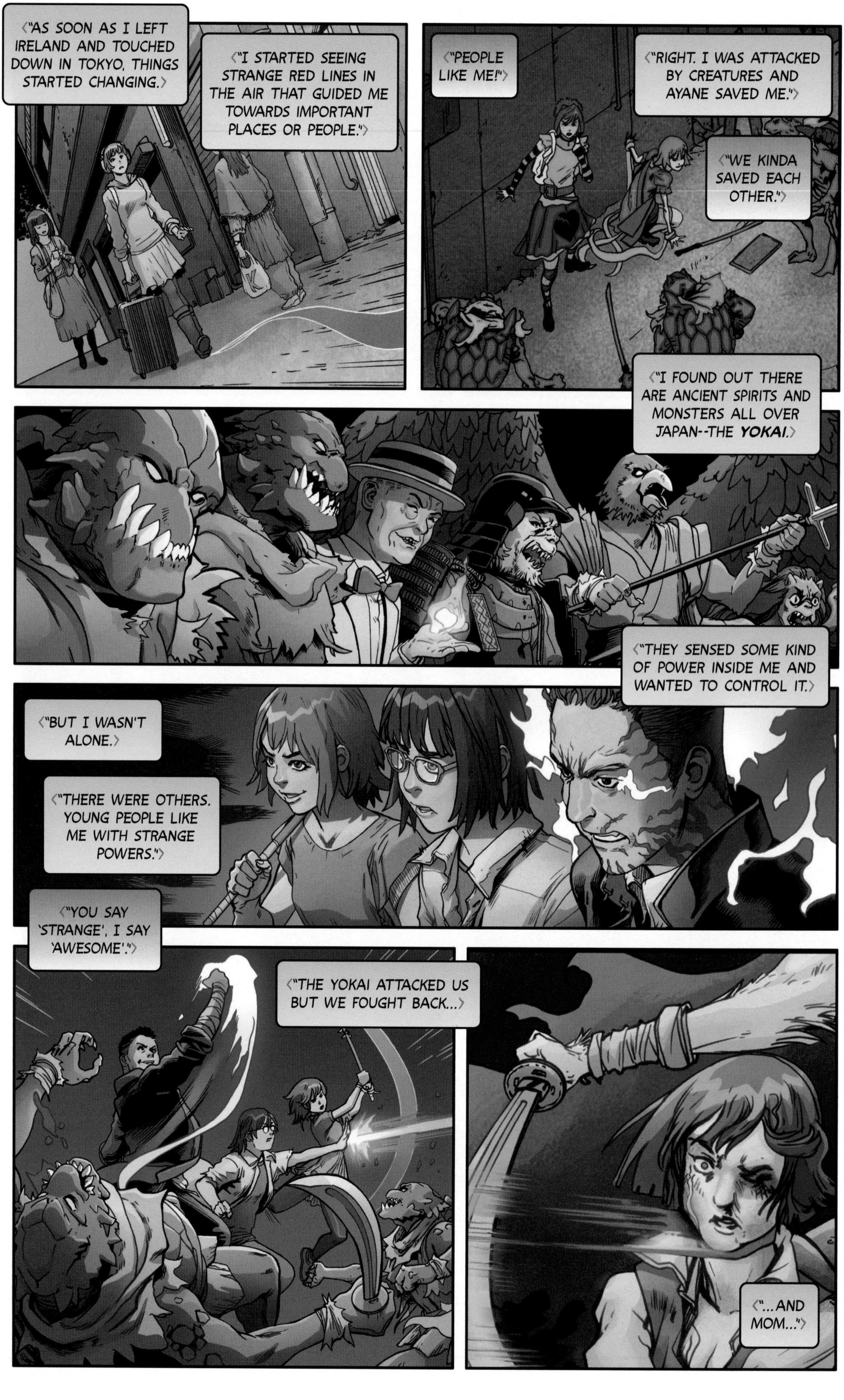
‹"AS SOON AS I LEFT IRELAND AND TOUCHED DOWN IN TOKYO, THINGS STARTED CHANGING.›
‹"I STARTED SEEING STRANGE RED LINES IN THE AIR THAT GUIDED ME TOWARDS IMPORTANT PLACES OR PEOPLE."›
‹"PEOPLE LIKE ME!"›
‹"RIGHT. I WAS ATTACKED BY CREATURES AND AYANE SAVED ME."›
‹"WE KINDA SAVED EACH OTHER."›
‹"I FOUND OUT THERE ARE ANCIENT SPIRITS AND MONSTERS ALL OVER JAPAN--THE ***YOKAI***.›
‹"THEY SENSED SOME KIND OF POWER INSIDE ME AND WANTED TO CONTROL IT.›
‹"BUT I WASN'T ALONE.›
‹"THERE WERE OTHERS. YOUNG PEOPLE LIKE ME WITH STRANGE POWERS."›
‹"YOU SAY 'STRANGE', I SAY 'AWESOME'."›
‹"THE YOKAI ATTACKED US BUT WE FOUGHT BACK...›
‹"...AND MOM..."›

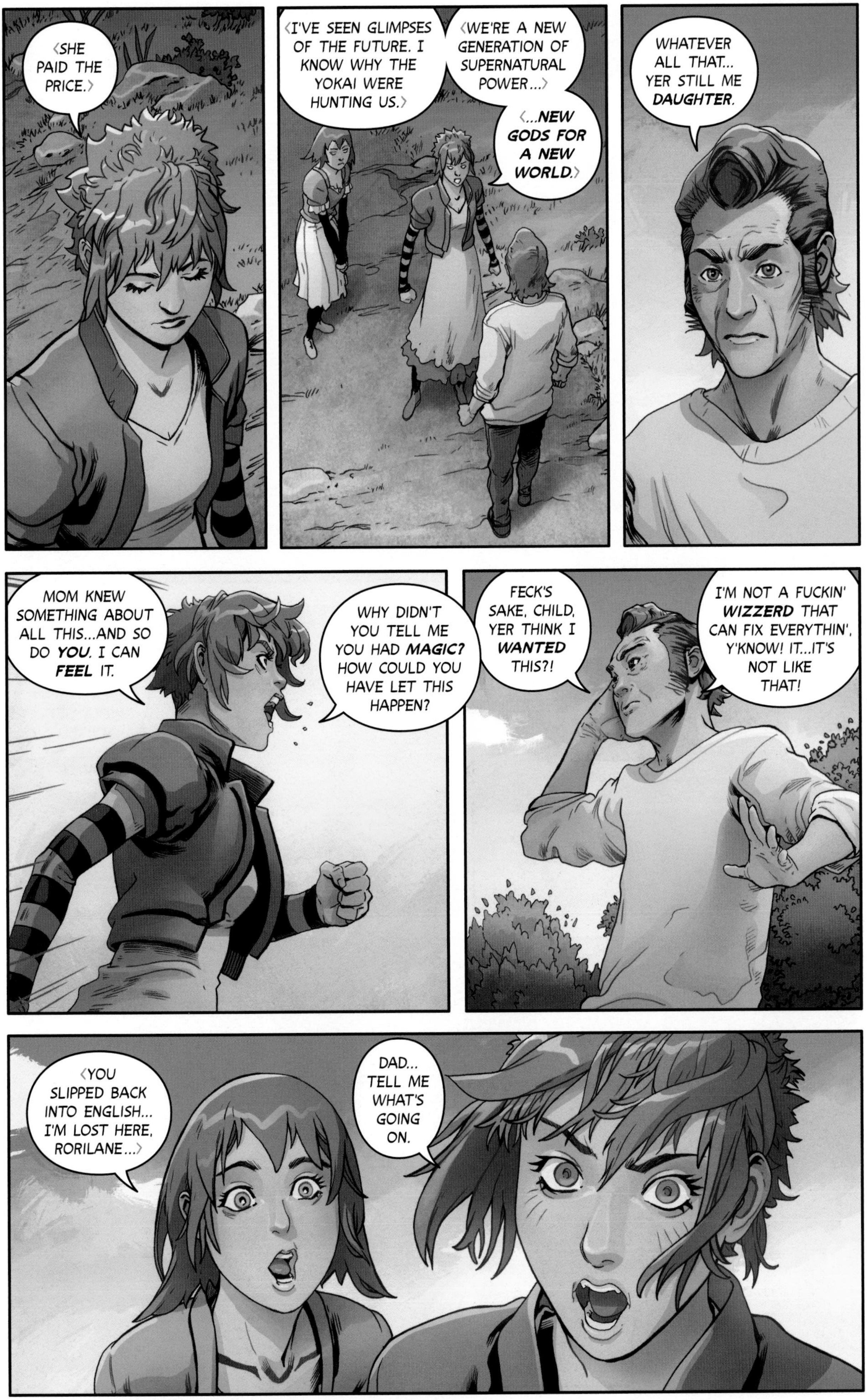

‹SHE PAID THE PRICE.›
‹I'VE SEEN GLIMPSES OF THE FUTURE. I KNOW WHY THE YOKAI WERE HUNTING US.›
‹WE'RE A NEW GENERATION OF SUPERNATURAL POWER...›
‹...NEW GODS FOR A NEW WORLD.›
WHATEVER ALL THAT... YER STILL ME DAUGHTER.
MOM KNEW SOMETHING ABOUT ALL THIS...AND SO DO YOU. I CAN FEEL IT.
WHY DIDN'T YOU TELL ME YOU HAD MAGIC? HOW COULD YOU HAVE LET THIS HAPPEN?
FECK'S SAKE, CHILD, YER THINK I WANTED THIS?!
I'M NOT A FUCKIN' WIZZERD THAT CAN FIX EVERYTHIN', Y'KNOW! IT...IT'S NOT LIKE THAT!
‹YOU SLIPPED BACK INTO ENGLISH... I'M LOST HERE, RORILANE...›
DAD... TELL ME WHAT'S GOING ON.

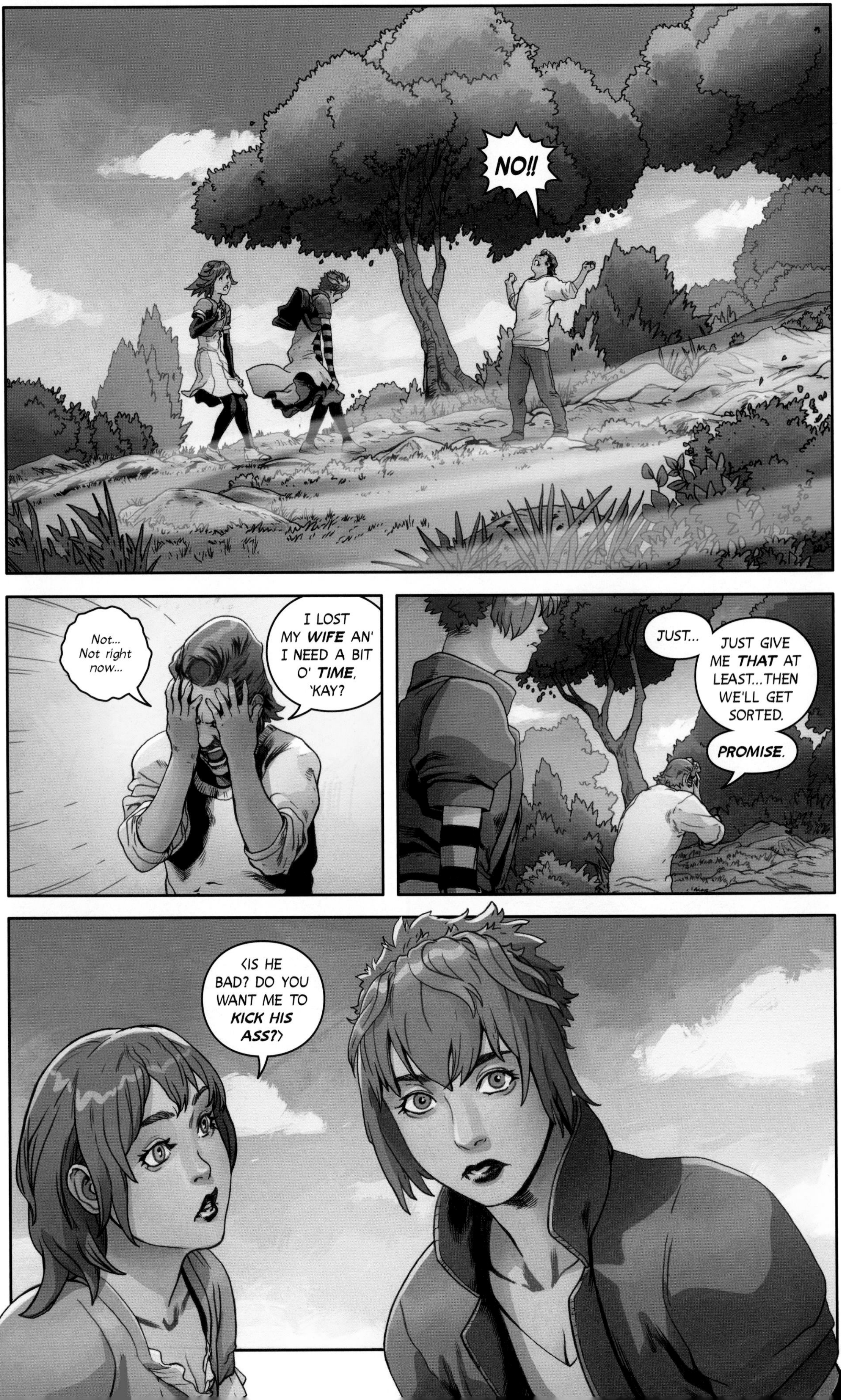
NO!!
Not... Not right now...
I LOST MY WIFE AN' I NEED A BIT O' TIME, 'KAY?
JUST...
JUST GIVE ME THAT AT LEAST...THEN WE'LL GET SORTED.
PROMISE.
<IS HE BAD? DO YOU WANT ME TO KICK HIS ASS?>

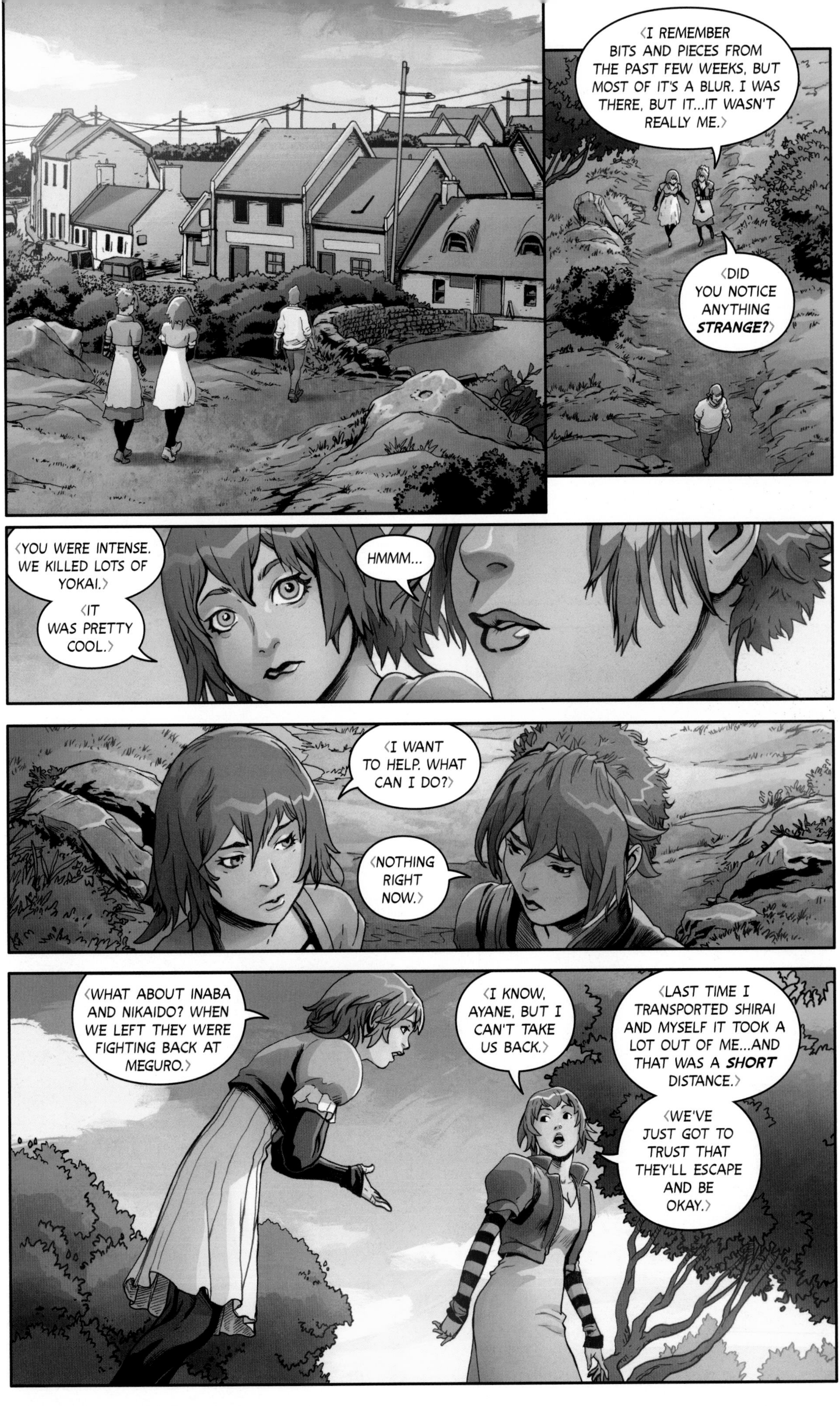

<I REMEMBER BITS AND PIECES FROM THE PAST FEW WEEKS, BUT MOST OF IT'S A BLUR. I WAS THERE, BUT IT...IT WASN'T REALLY ME.>
<DID YOU NOTICE ANYTHING ***STRANGE?***>
<YOU WERE INTENSE. WE KILLED LOTS OF YOKAI.>
<IT WAS PRETTY COOL.>
HMMM...
<I WANT TO HELP. WHAT CAN I DO?>
<NOTHING RIGHT NOW.>
<WHAT ABOUT INABA AND NIKAIDO? WHEN WE LEFT THEY WERE FIGHTING BACK AT MEGURO.>
<I KNOW, AYANE, BUT I CAN'T TAKE US BACK.>
<LAST TIME I TRANSPORTED SHIRAI AND MYSELF IT TOOK A LOT OUT OF ME...AND THAT WAS A ***SHORT*** DISTANCE.>
<WE'VE JUST GOT TO TRUST THAT THEY'LL ESCAPE AND BE OKAY.>

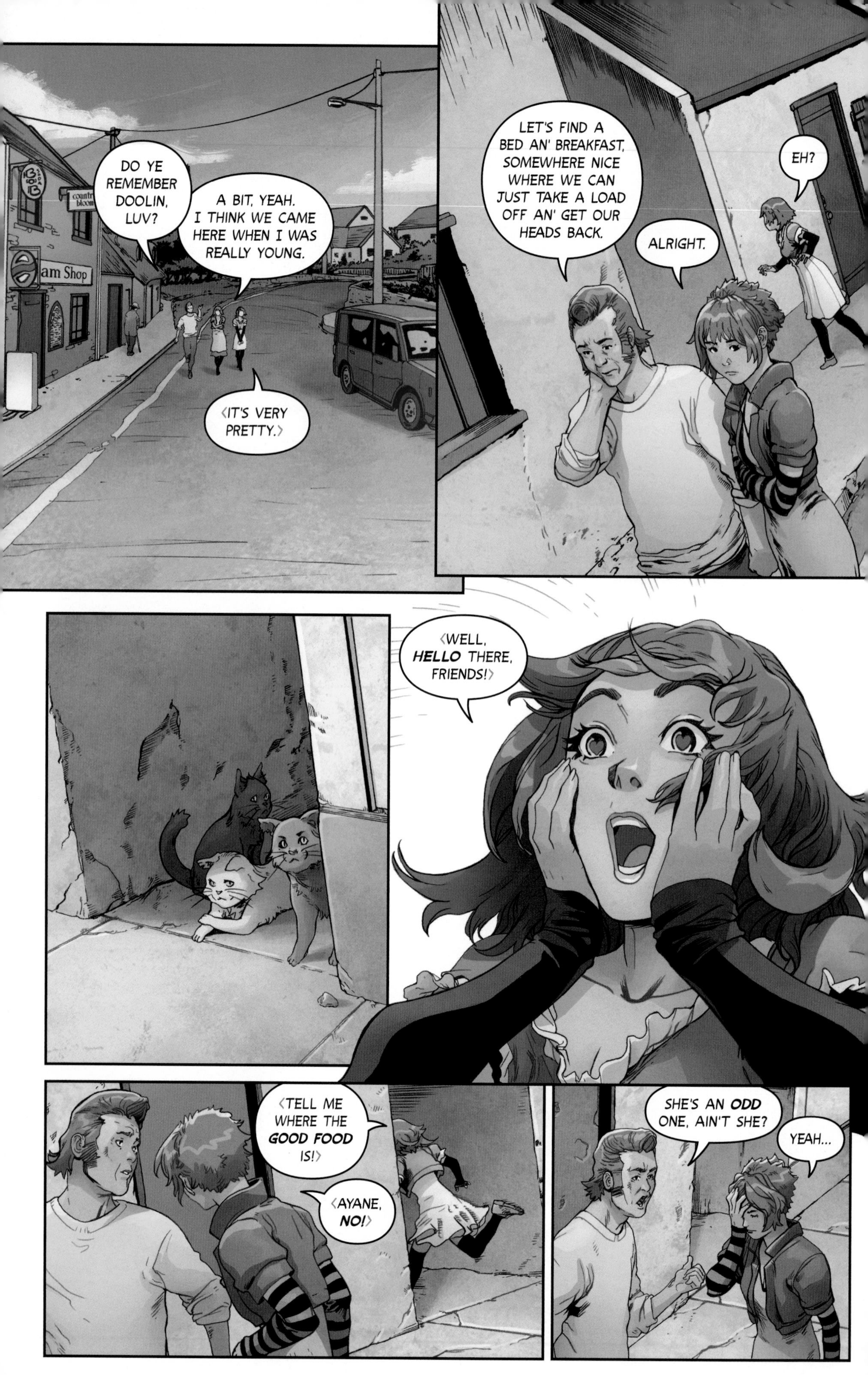

Ham Shop
DO YE REMEMBER DOOLIN, LUV?
A BIT, YEAH. I THINK WE CAME HERE WHEN I WAS REALLY YOUNG.
‹IT'S VERY PRETTY.›
LET'S FIND A BED AN' BREAKFAST, SOMEWHERE NICE WHERE WE CAN JUST TAKE A LOAD OFF AN' GET OUR HEADS BACK.
ALRIGHT.
EH?
‹WELL, **HELLO** THERE, FRIENDS!›
‹TELL ME WHERE THE **GOOD FOOD** IS!›
‹AYANE, **NO!**›
SHE'S AN **ODD** ONE, AIN'T SHE?
YEAH...

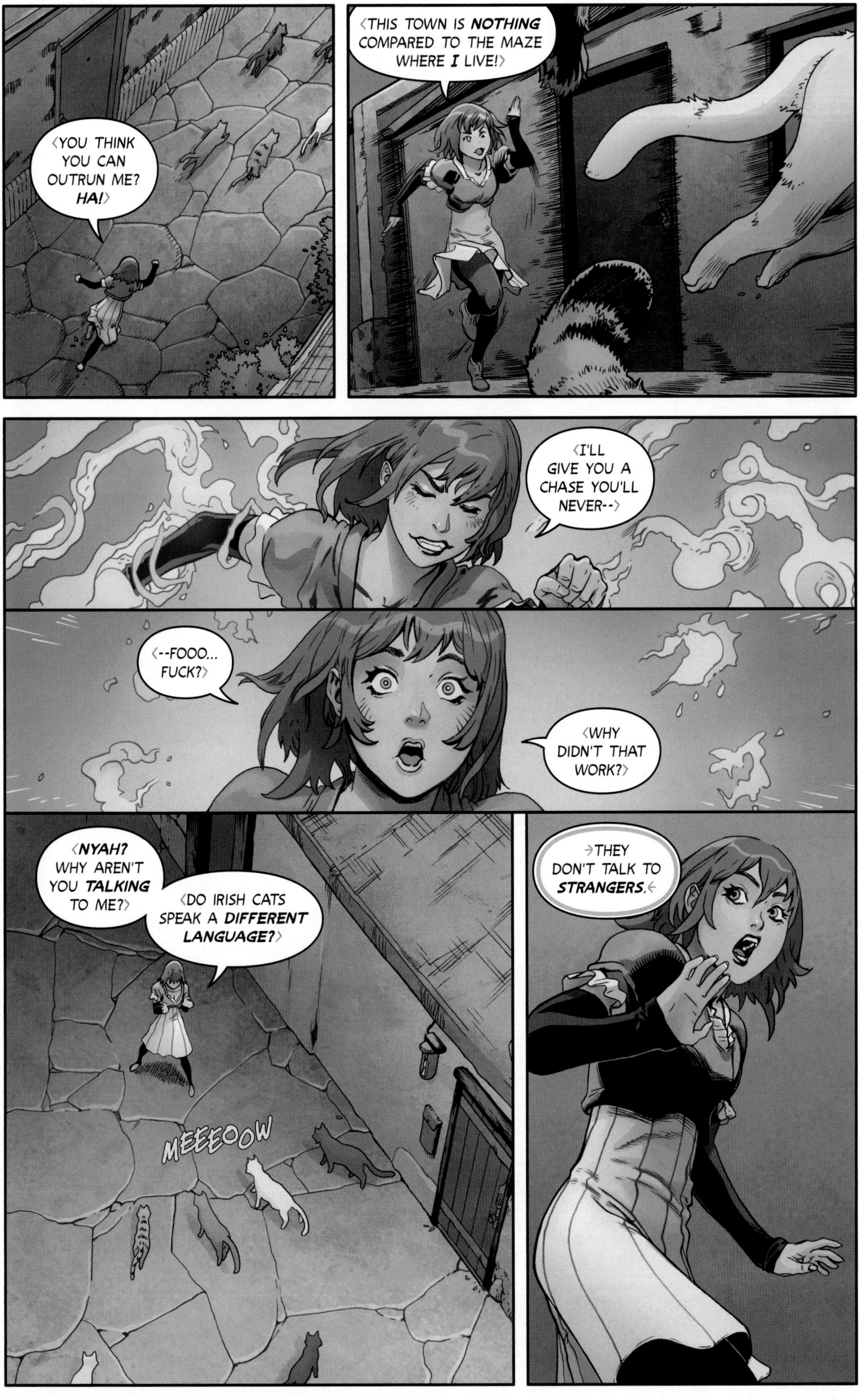

‹YOU THINK YOU CAN OUTRUN ME? **HA!**›
‹THIS TOWN IS **NOTHING** COMPARED TO THE MAZE WHERE **I** LIVE!›
‹I'LL GIVE YOU A CHASE YOU'LL NEVER--›
‹--FOOO... FUCK?›
‹WHY DIDN'T THAT WORK?›
‹**NYAH?** WHY AREN'T YOU **TALKING** TO ME?›
‹DO IRISH CATS SPEAK A **DIFFERENT LANGUAGE?**›
MEEEOOW
→THEY DON'T TALK TO **STRANGERS.**←

→WHO ARE YOU?←

⟨I'M *AYANE*. HOW 'BOUT YOU?⟩

SNIFF SNIFF SNIFF

⟨I'M NOT A *BAD GUY*, IF THAT'S WHAT YOU'RE THINKING...⟩

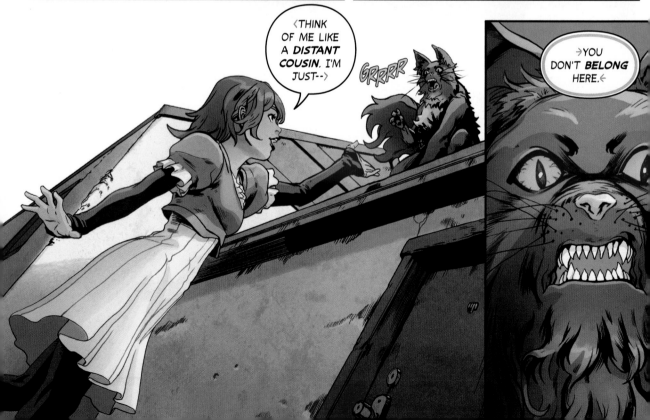

⟨THINK OF ME LIKE A *DISTANT COUSIN*. I'M JUST--⟩

GRRRR

→YOU DON'T *BELONG* HERE.←

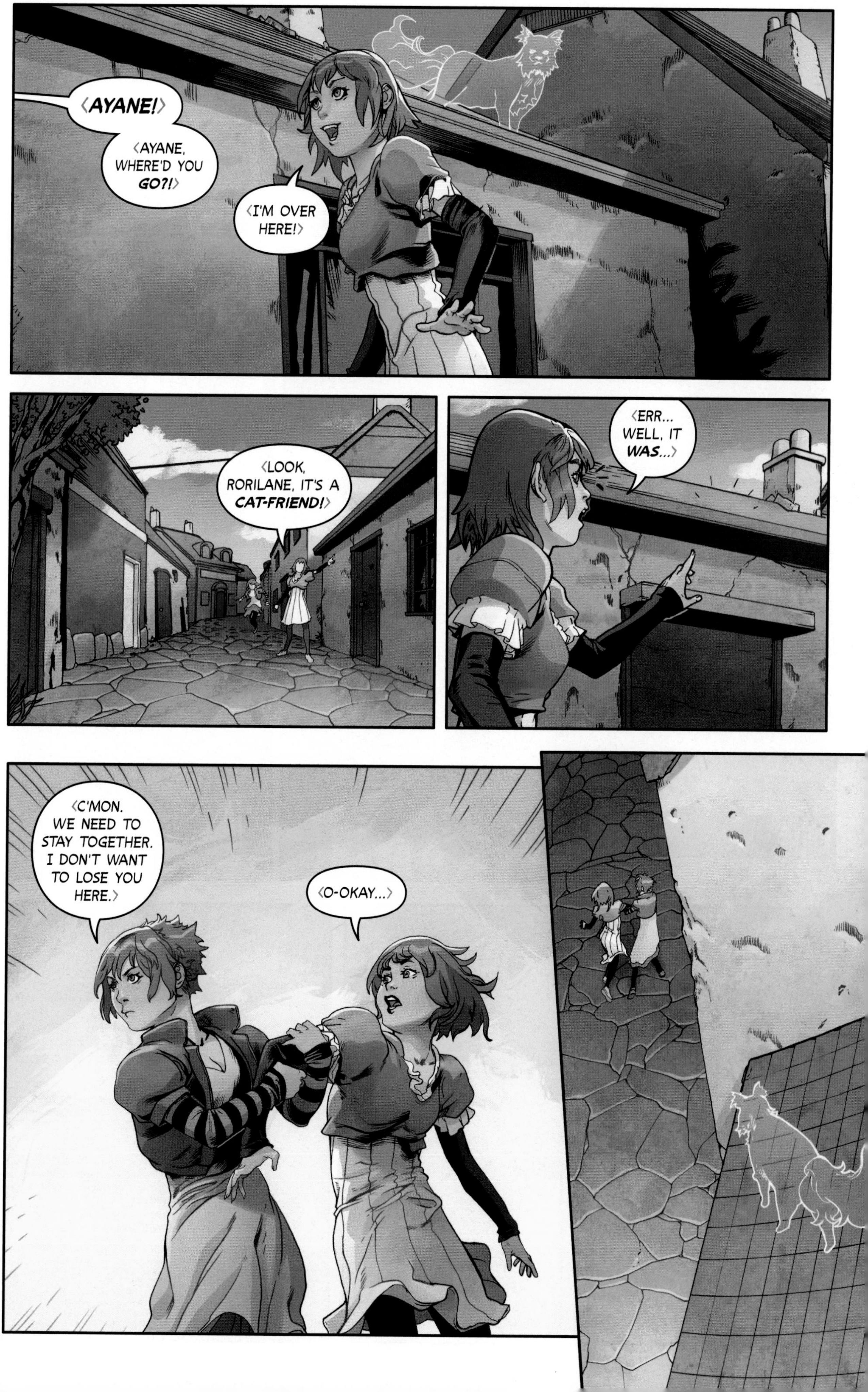
〈AYANE!〉
〈AYANE, WHERE'D YOU GO?!〉
〈I'M OVER HERE!〉
〈LOOK, RORILANE, IT'S A CAT-FRIEND!〉
〈ERR... WELL, IT WAS...〉
〈C'MON. WE NEED TO STAY TOGETHER. I DON'T WANT TO LOSE YOU HERE.〉
〈O-OKAY...〉

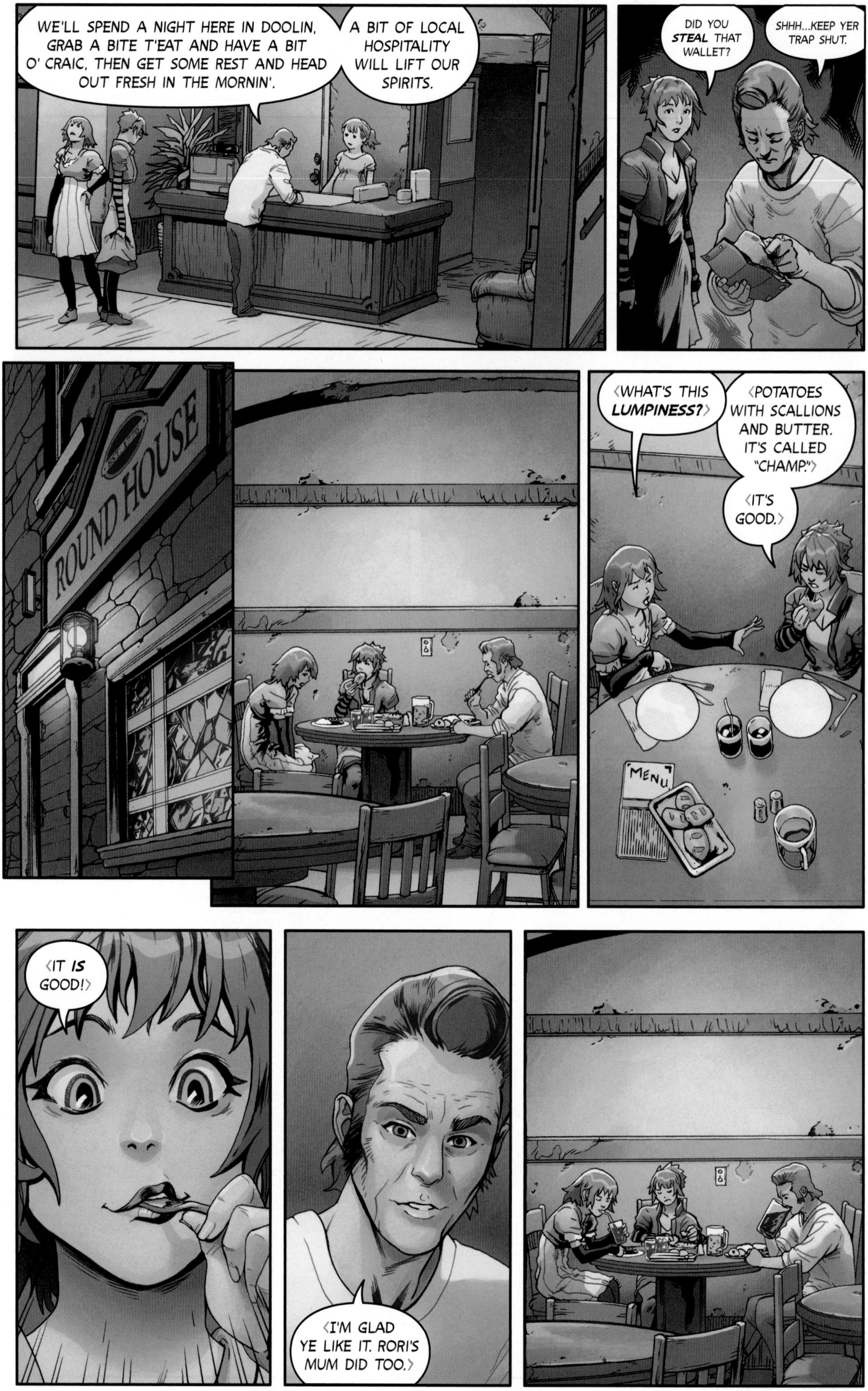
WE'LL SPEND A NIGHT HERE IN DOOLIN, GRAB A BITE T'EAT AND HAVE A BIT O' CRAIC, THEN GET SOME REST AND HEAD OUT FRESH IN THE MORNIN'.
A BIT OF LOCAL HOSPITALITY WILL LIFT OUR SPIRITS.
DID YOU STEAL THAT WALLET?
SHHH...KEEP YER TRAP SHUT.
ROUND HOUSE
⟨WHAT'S THIS LUMPINESS?⟩
⟨POTATOES WITH SCALLIONS AND BUTTER. IT'S CALLED "CHAMP."⟩
⟨IT'S GOOD.⟩
MENU
⟨IT IS GOOD!⟩
⟨I'M GLAD YE LIKE IT. RORI'S MUM DID TOO.⟩

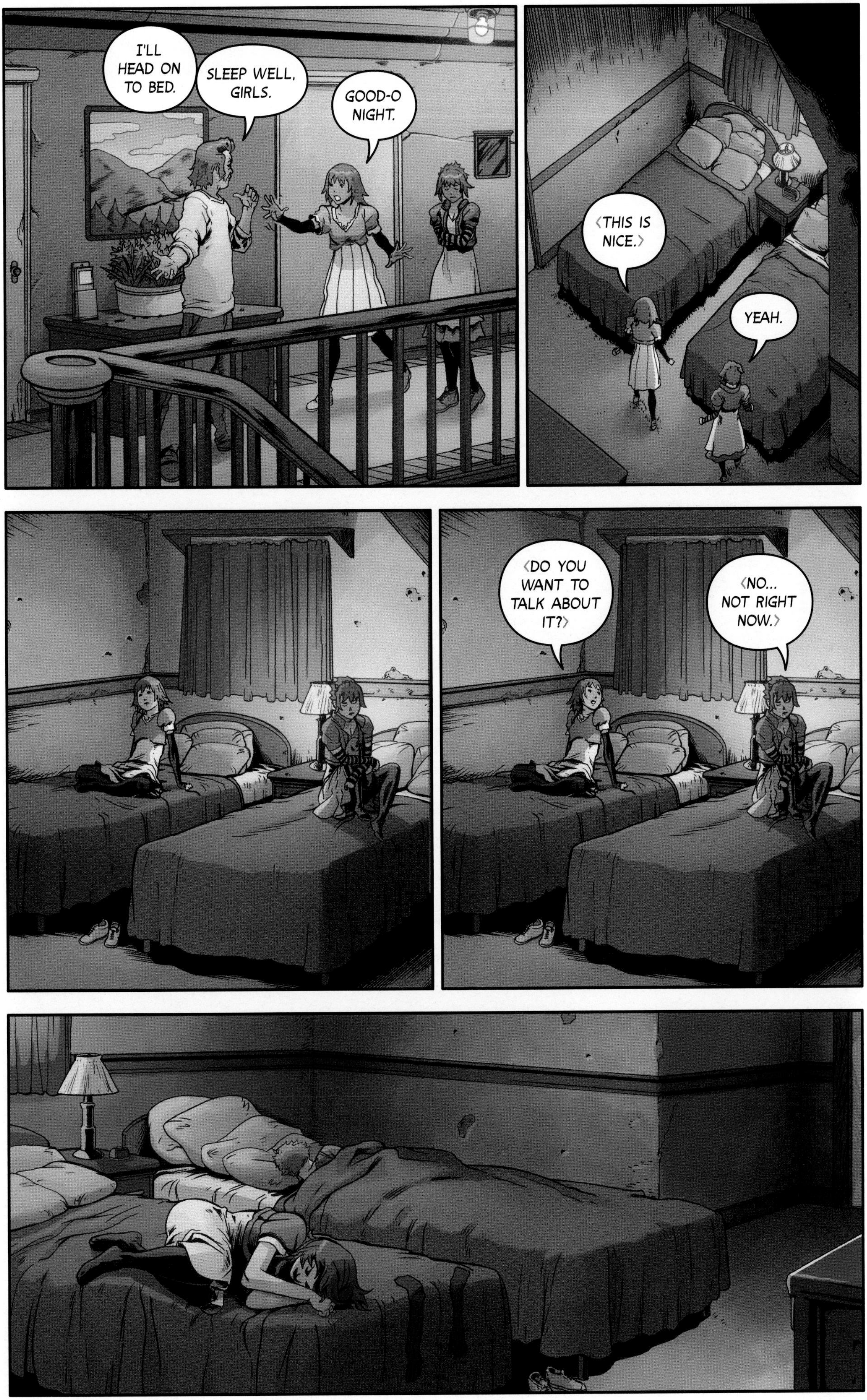
I'LL HEAD ON TO BED.
SLEEP WELL, GIRLS.
GOOD-O NIGHT.
‹THIS IS NICE.›
YEAH.
‹DO YOU WANT TO TALK ABOUT IT?›
‹NO... NOT RIGHT NOW.›

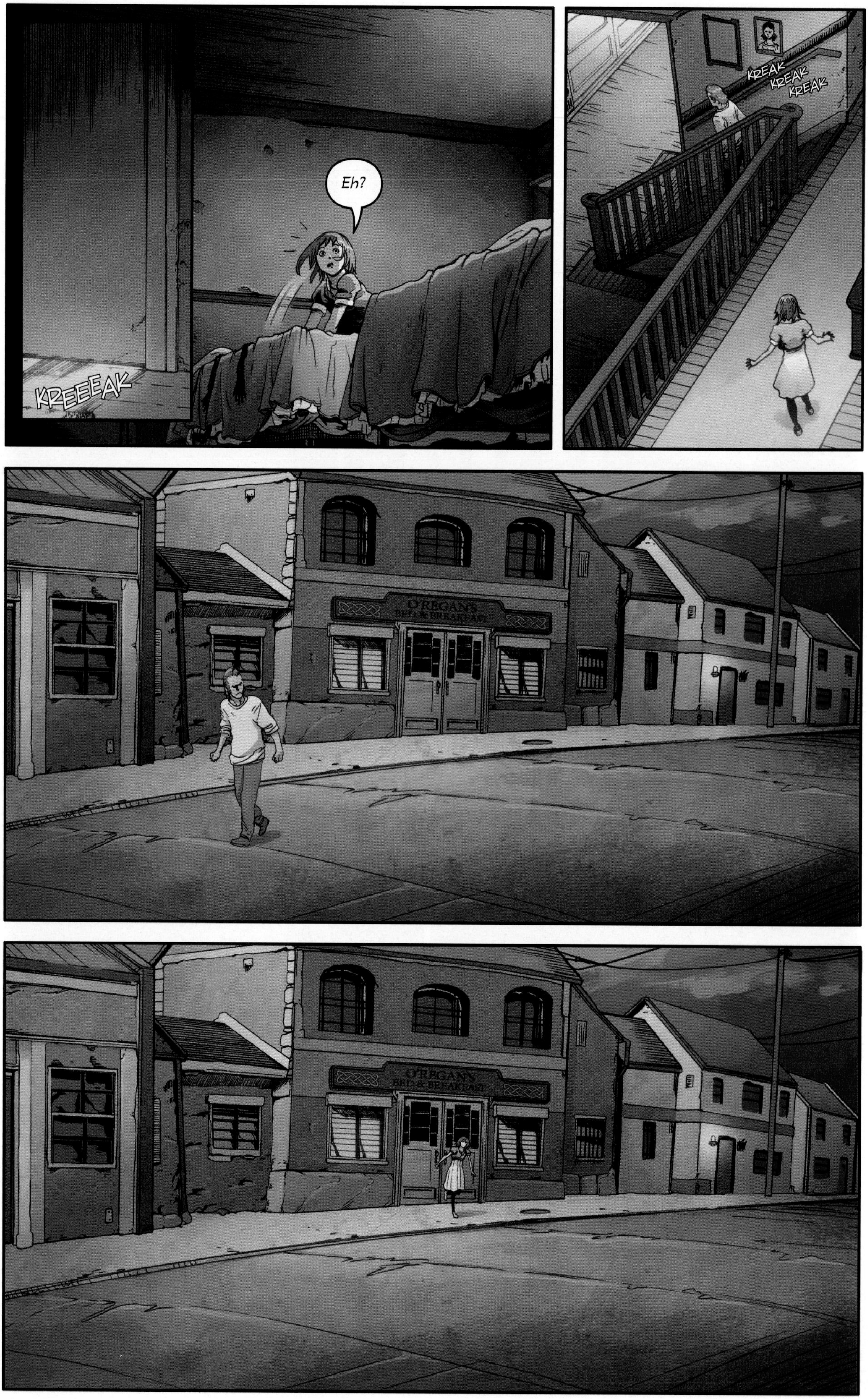

Eh?
KREEEAK
KREAK
KREAK
KREAK
O'REGAN'S BED & BREAKFAST
O'REGAN'S BED & BREAKFAST

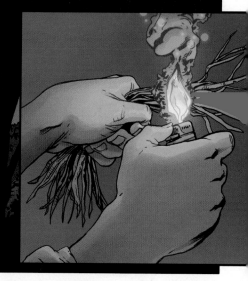

DRUÍ...

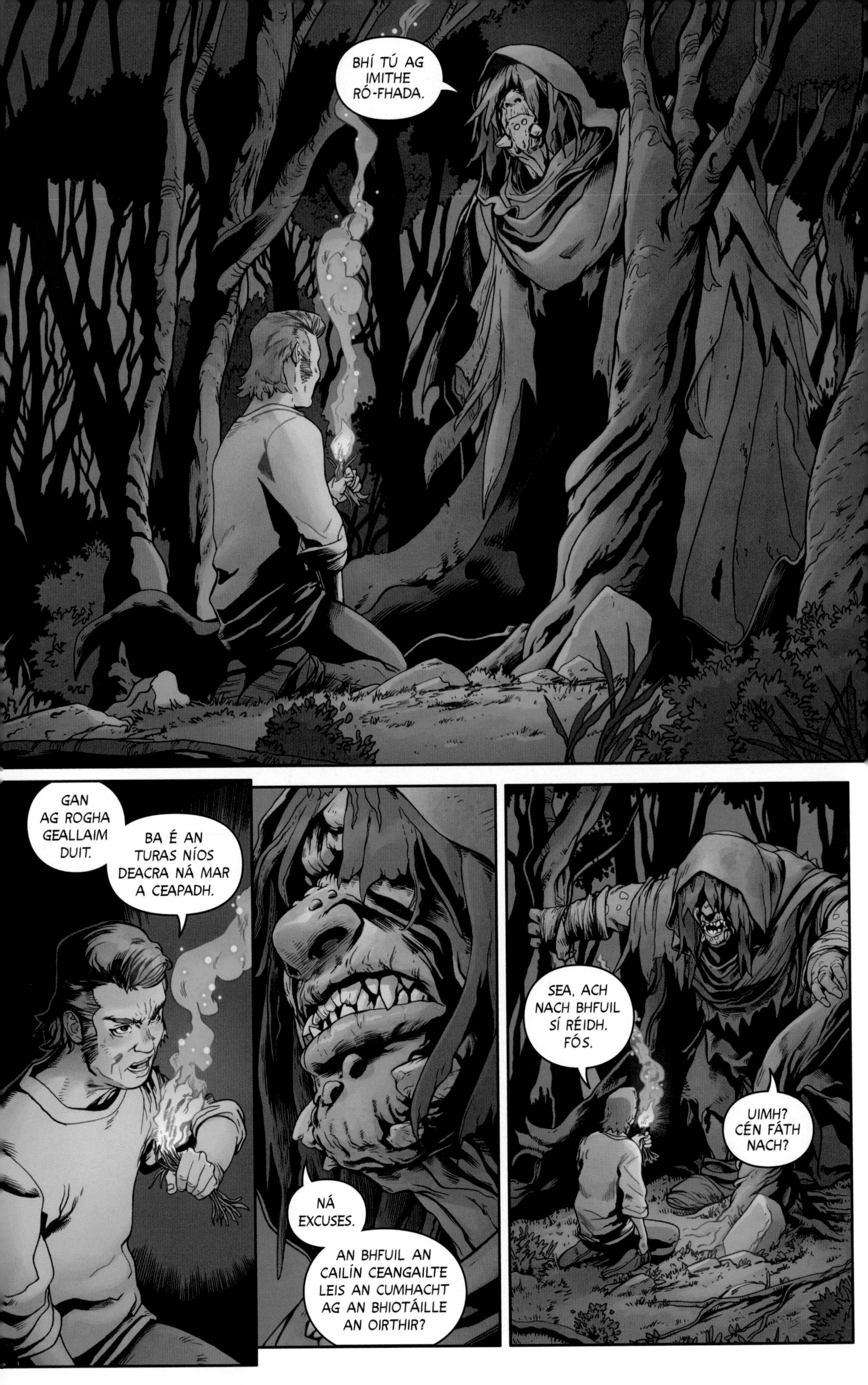
BHÍ TÚ AG IMITHE RÓ-FHADA.
GAN AG ROGHA GEALLAIM DUIT.
BA É AN TURAS NÍOS DEACRA NÁ MAR A CEAPADH.
NÁ EXCUSES.
AN BHFUIL AN CAILÍN CEANGAILTE LEIS AN CUMHACHT AG AN BHIOTÁILLE AN OIRTHIR?
SEA, ACH NACH BHFUIL SÍ RÉIDH. FÓS.
UIMH? CÉN FÁTH NACH?

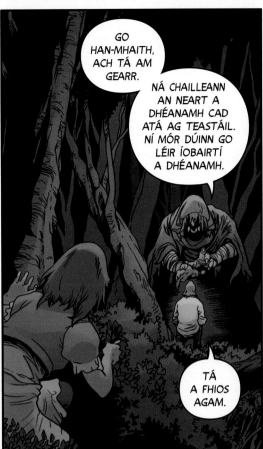

MAR TÁ SÍ MO INÍON.

DHÍTH ORM LE BEAGÁN AMA CHUN SLÁN A FHÁGÁIL.

GO HAN-MHAITH, ACH TÁ AM GEARR.

NÁ CHAILLEANN AN NEART A DHÉANAMH CAD ATÁ AG TEASTÁIL. NÍ MÓR DÚINN GO LÉIR ÍOBAIRTÍ A DHÉANAMH.

TÁ A FHIOS AGAM.

‹RORILANE, WAKE UP!›

‹I JUST SAW YOUR--›

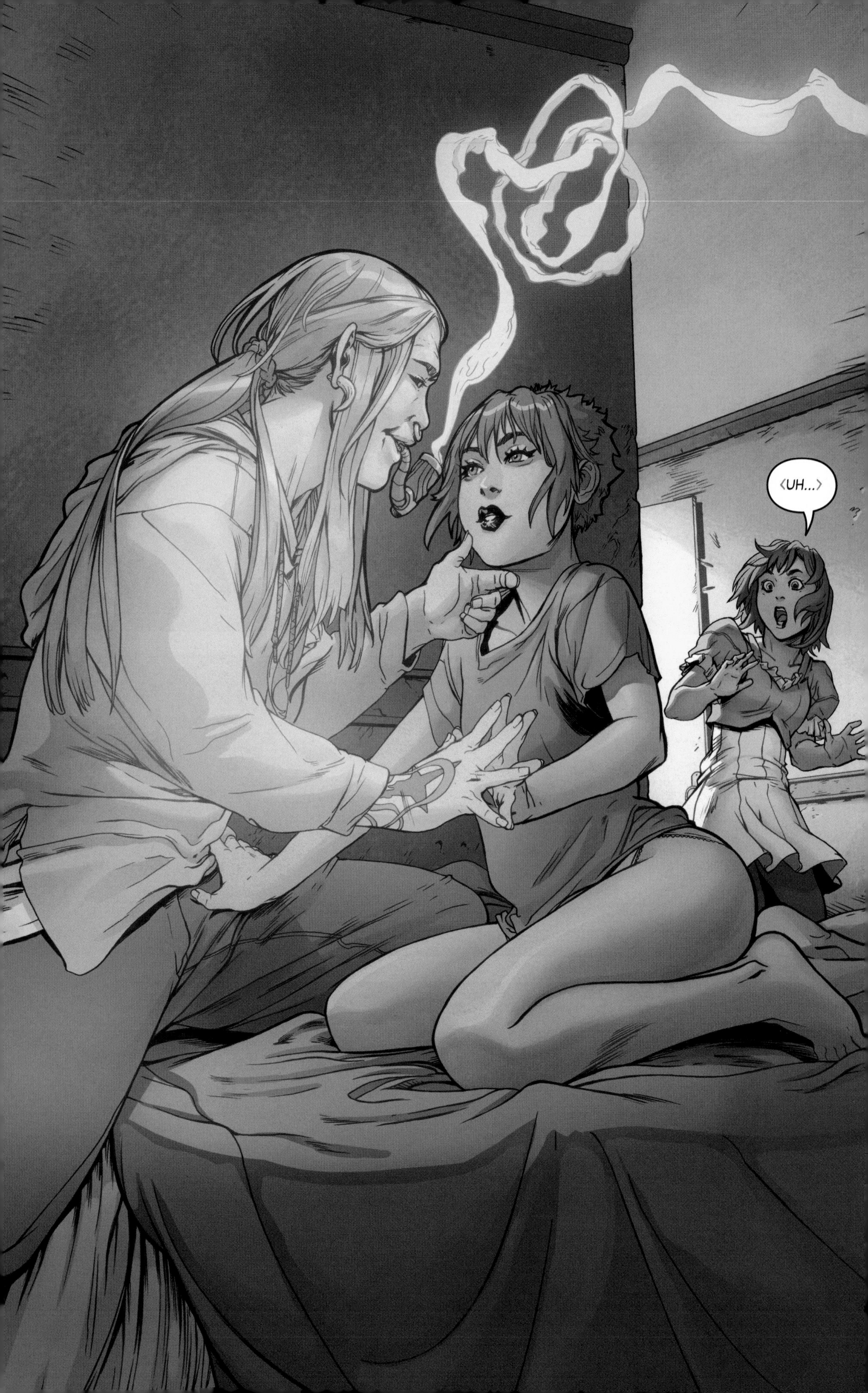
‹UH...›

Chapter Seventeen

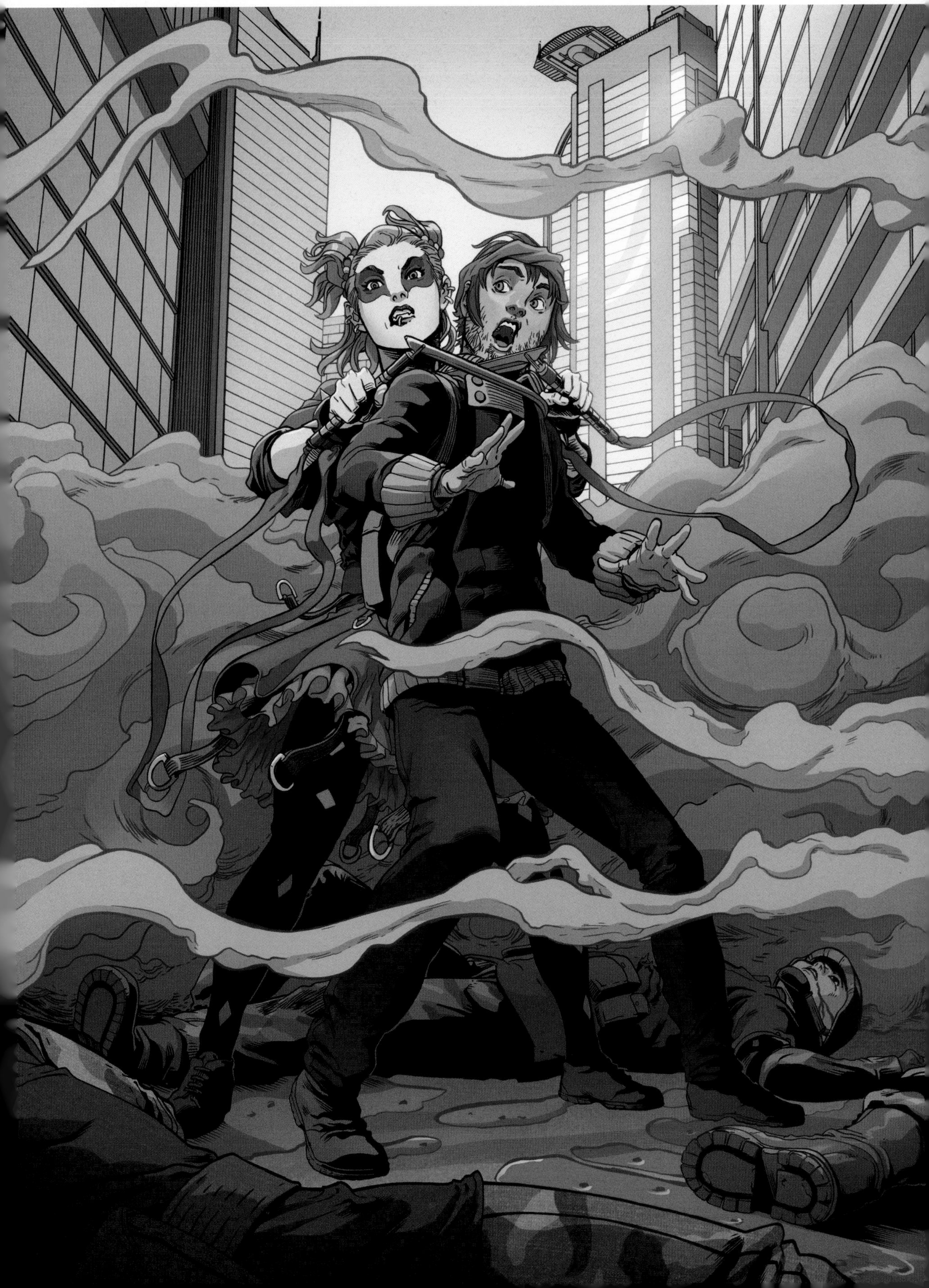

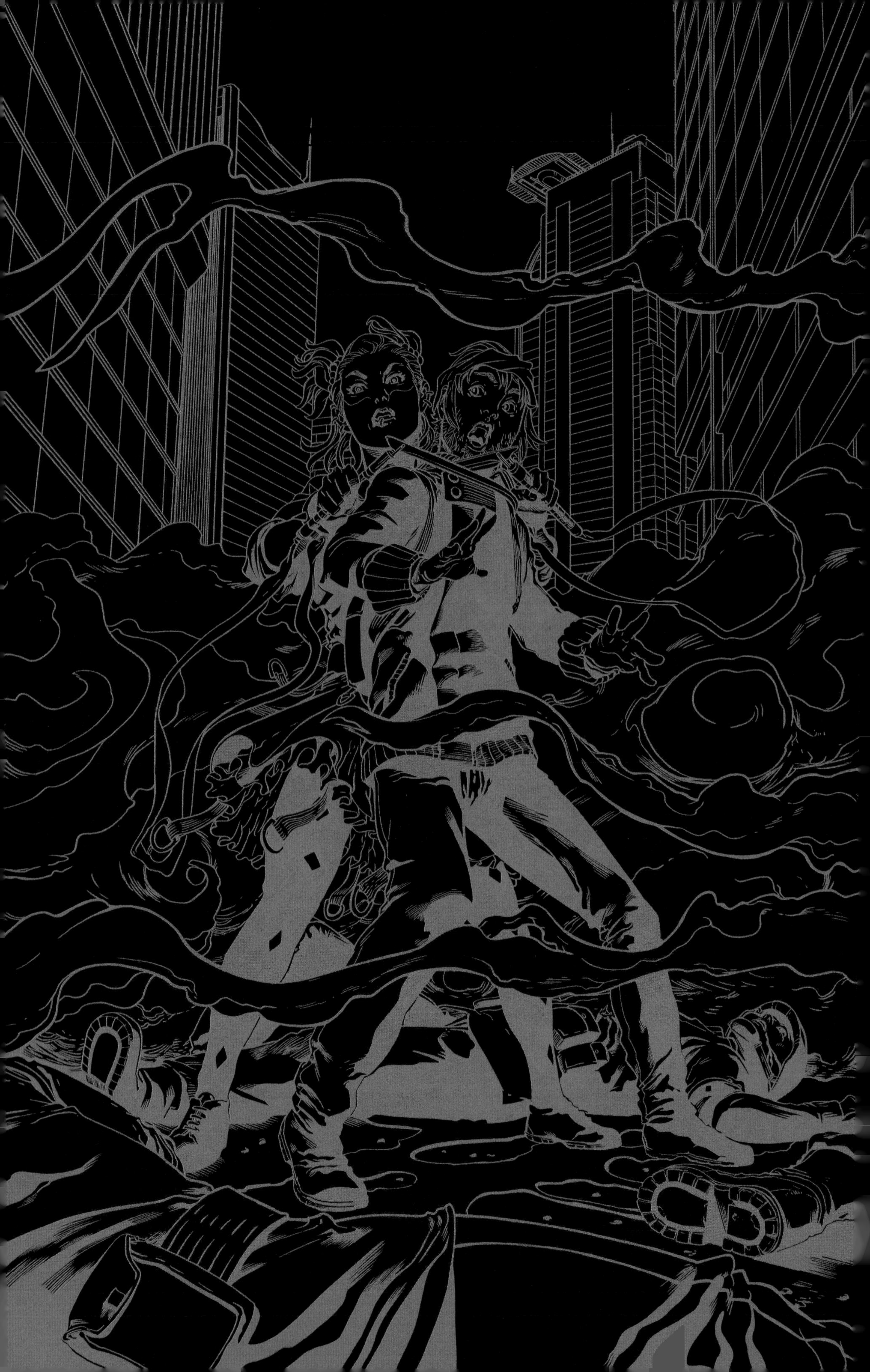

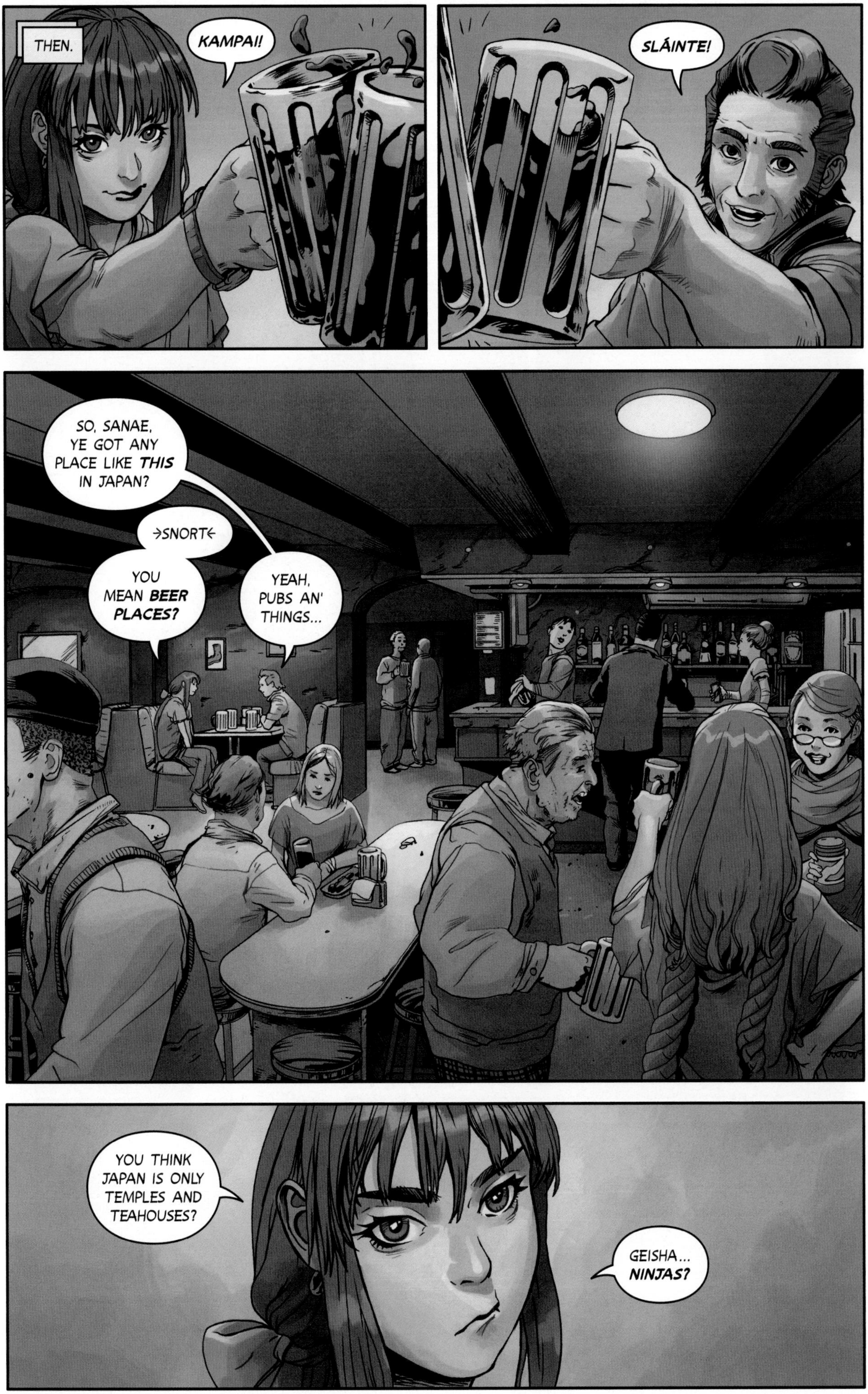
THEN.
KAMPAI!
SLÁINTE!
SO, SANAE, YE GOT ANY PLACE LIKE THIS IN JAPAN?
→SNORT←
YOU MEAN BEER PLACES?
YEAH, PUBS AN' THINGS...
YOU THINK JAPAN IS ONLY TEMPLES AND TEAHOUSES?
GEISHA... NINJAS?

GLUG GLUG

NO, NO, I JUST--

...uh...

WHAM

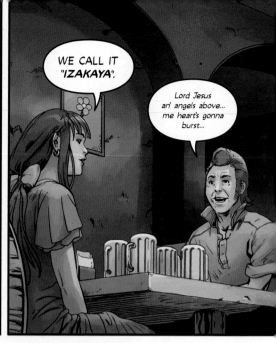

WE CALL IT "IZAKAYA".

Lord Jesus an' angels above... me heart's gonna burst...

YOU COME TO JAPAN, I SHOW YOU.

MANY IZAKAYA.

MANY DRINK.

I'D LIKE THAT.

FER NOW THOUGH, YOU'RE IN *MY* NECK OF THE WOODS SO WE'RE DOIN' IT UP *IRISH*.

O-KAY!

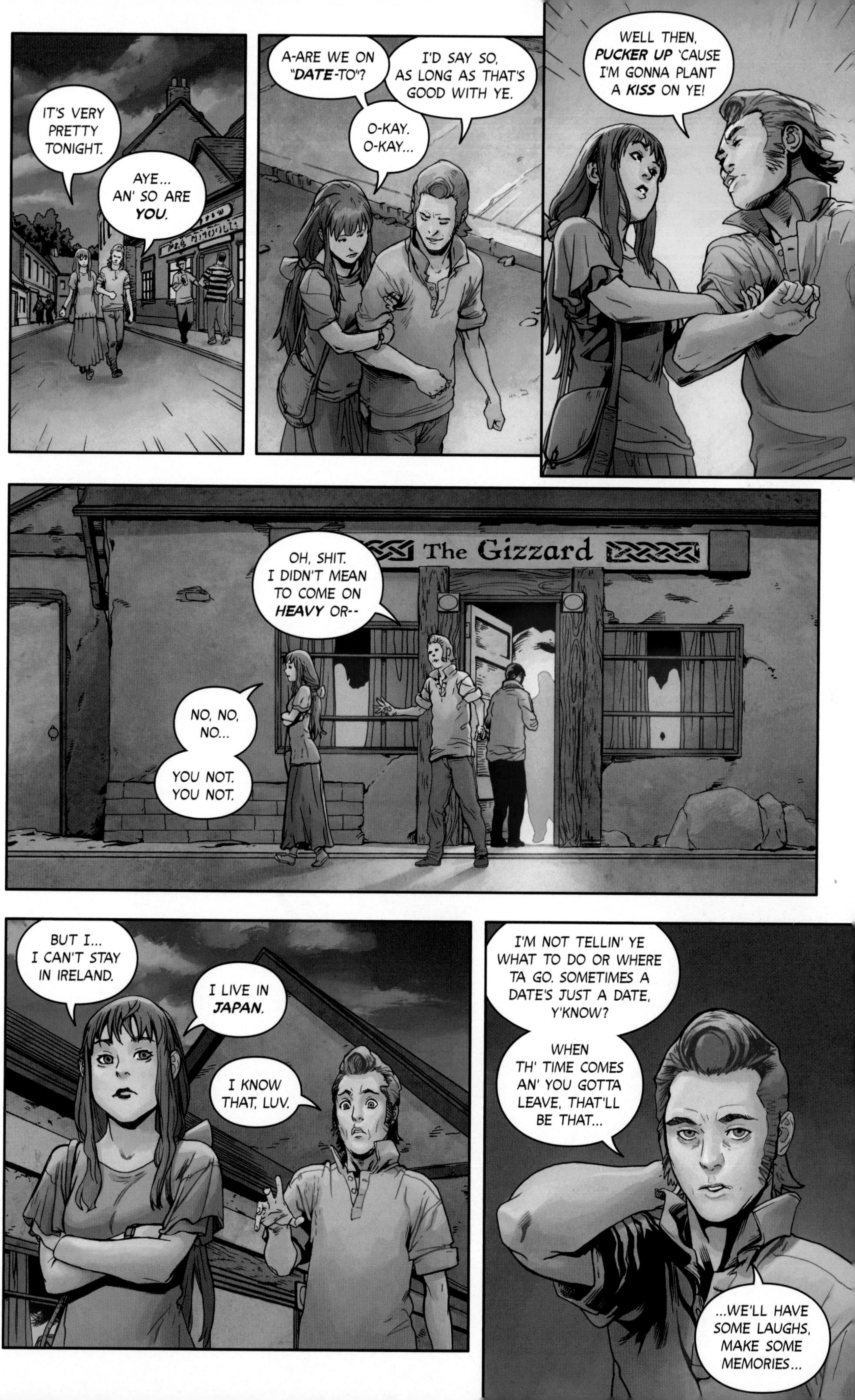
IT'S VERY PRETTY TONIGHT.
AYE... AN' SO ARE YOU.
A-ARE WE ON "DATE-TO"?
I'D SAY SO, AS LONG AS THAT'S GOOD WITH YE.
O-KAY. O-KAY...
WELL THEN, PUCKER UP 'CAUSE I'M GONNA PLANT A KISS ON YE!
The Gizzard
OH, SHIT. I DIDN'T MEAN TO COME ON HEAVY OR--
NO, NO, NO...
YOU NOT. YOU NOT.
BUT I... I CAN'T STAY IN IRELAND.
I LIVE IN JAPAN.
I KNOW THAT, LUV.
I'M NOT TELLIN' YE WHAT TO DO OR WHERE TA GO. SOMETIMES A DATE'S JUST A DATE, Y'KNOW?
WHEN TH' TIME COMES AN' YOU GOTTA LEAVE, THAT'LL BE THAT...
...WE'LL HAVE SOME LAUGHS, MAKE SOME MEMORIES...

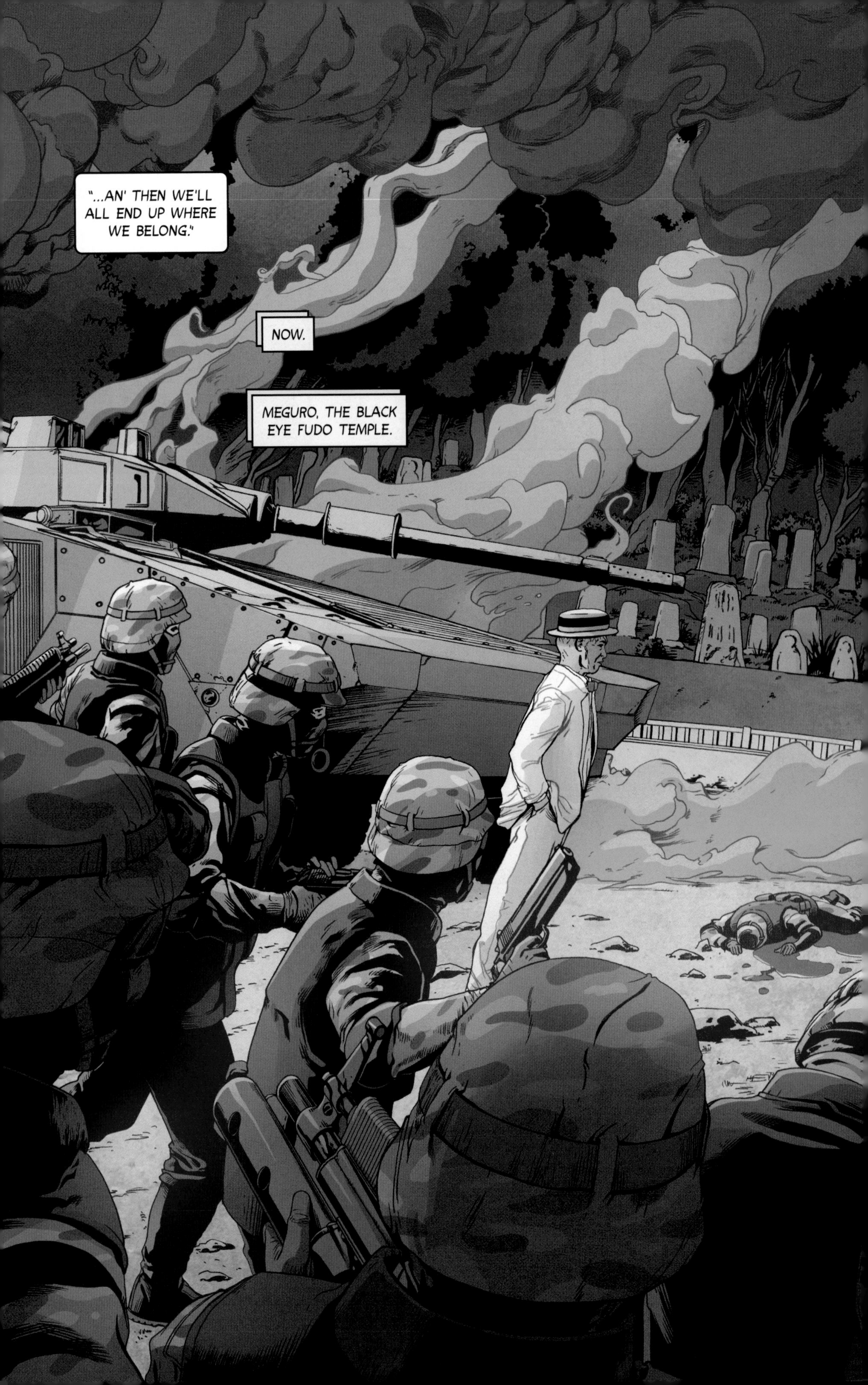
"...AN' THEN WE'LL ALL END UP WHERE WE BELONG."
NOW.
MEGURO, THE BLACK EYE FUDO TEMPLE.

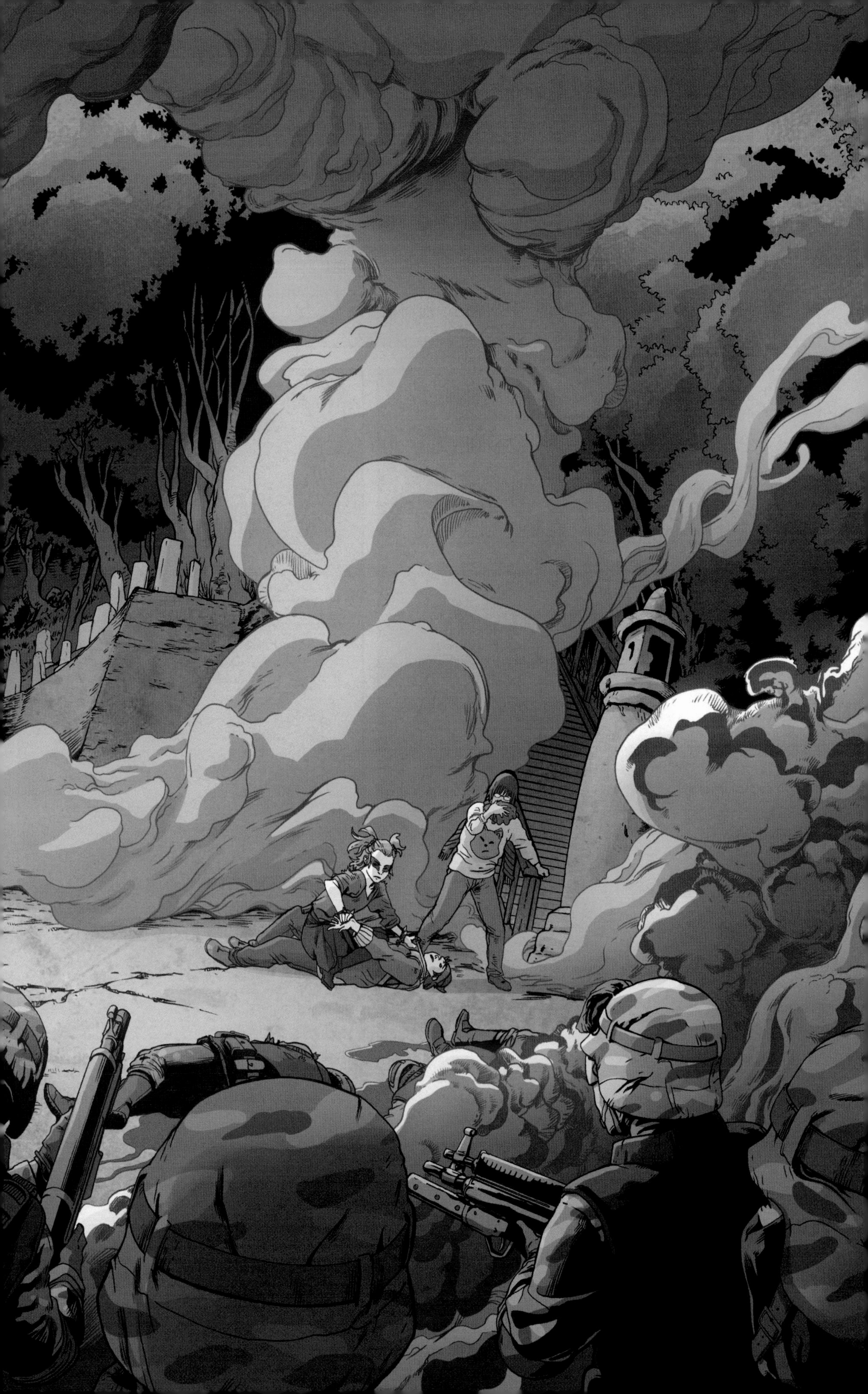

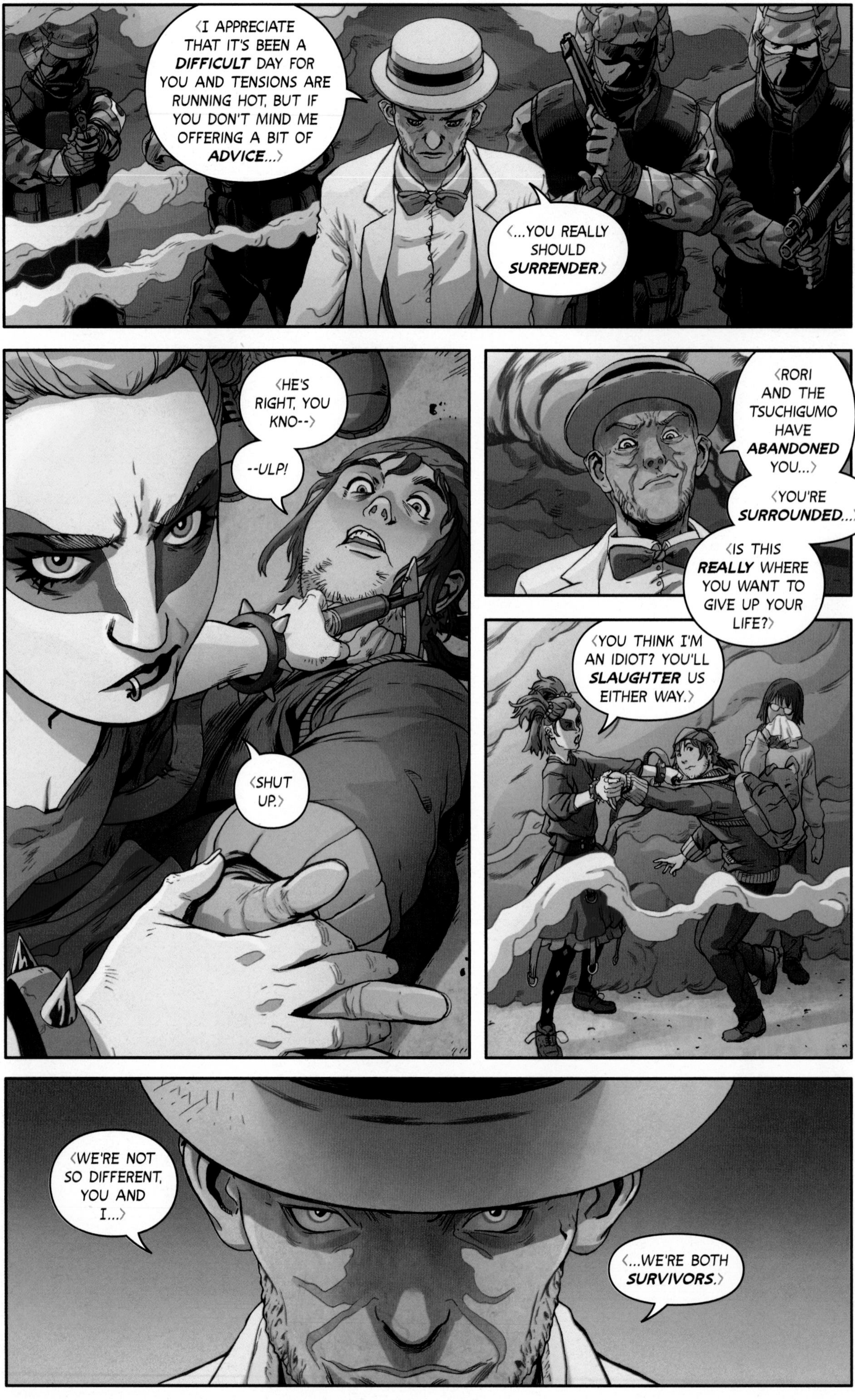
‹I APPRECIATE THAT IT'S BEEN A DIFFICULT DAY FOR YOU AND TENSIONS ARE RUNNING HOT, BUT IF YOU DON'T MIND ME OFFERING A BIT OF ADVICE...›
‹...YOU REALLY SHOULD SURRENDER.›
‹HE'S RIGHT, YOU KNO--›
--ULP!
‹SHUT UP.›
‹RORI AND THE TSUCHIGUMO HAVE ABANDONED YOU...›
‹YOU'RE SURROUNDED...›
‹IS THIS REALLY WHERE YOU WANT TO GIVE UP YOUR LIFE?›
‹YOU THINK I'M AN IDIOT? YOU'LL SLAUGHTER US EITHER WAY.›
‹WE'RE NOT SO DIFFERENT, YOU AND I...›
‹...WE'RE BOTH SURVIVORS.›

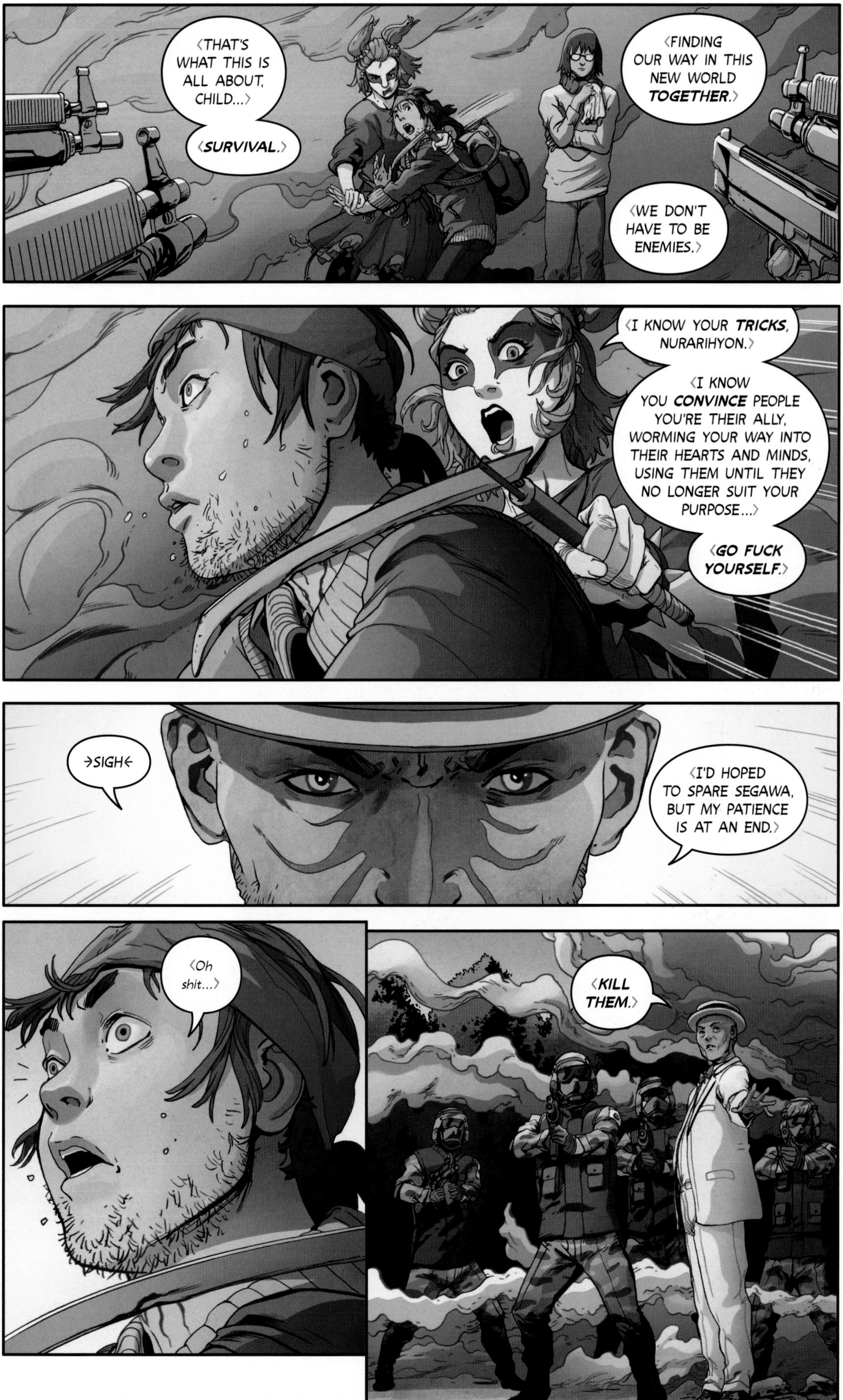
〈THAT'S WHAT THIS IS ALL ABOUT, CHILD...〉
〈SURVIVAL.〉
〈FINDING OUR WAY IN THIS NEW WORLD TOGETHER.〉
〈WE DON'T HAVE TO BE ENEMIES.〉
〈I KNOW YOUR TRICKS, NURARIHYON.〉
〈I KNOW YOU CONVINCE PEOPLE YOU'RE THEIR ALLY, WORMING YOUR WAY INTO THEIR HEARTS AND MINDS, USING THEM UNTIL THEY NO LONGER SUIT YOUR PURPOSE...〉
〈GO FUCK YOURSELF.〉
>SIGH<
〈I'D HOPED TO SPARE SEGAWA, BUT MY PATIENCE IS AT AN END.〉
〈Oh shit...〉
〈KILL THEM.〉

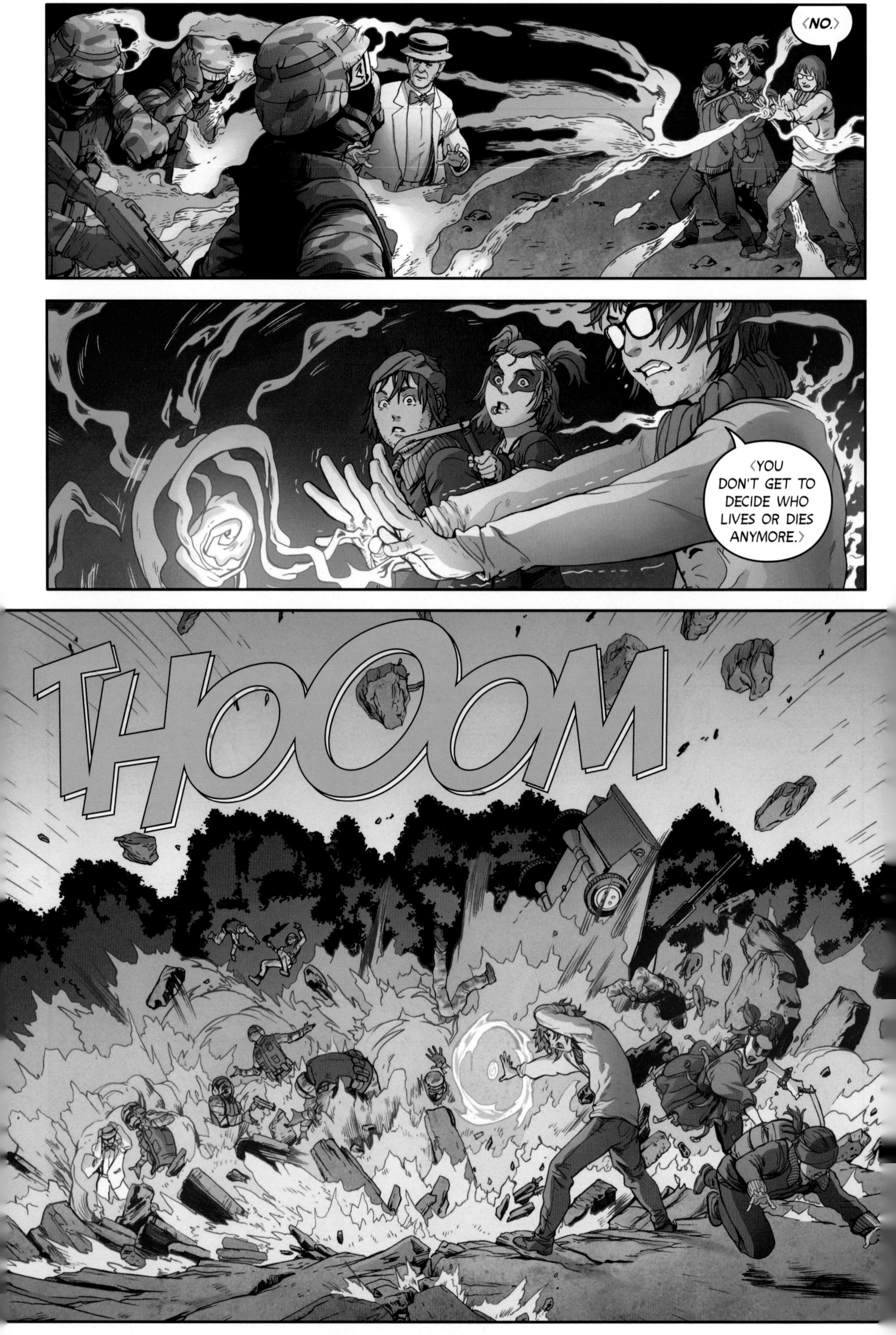

‹NO.›
‹YOU DON'T GET TO DECIDE WHO LIVES OR DIES ANYMORE.›
THOOOM

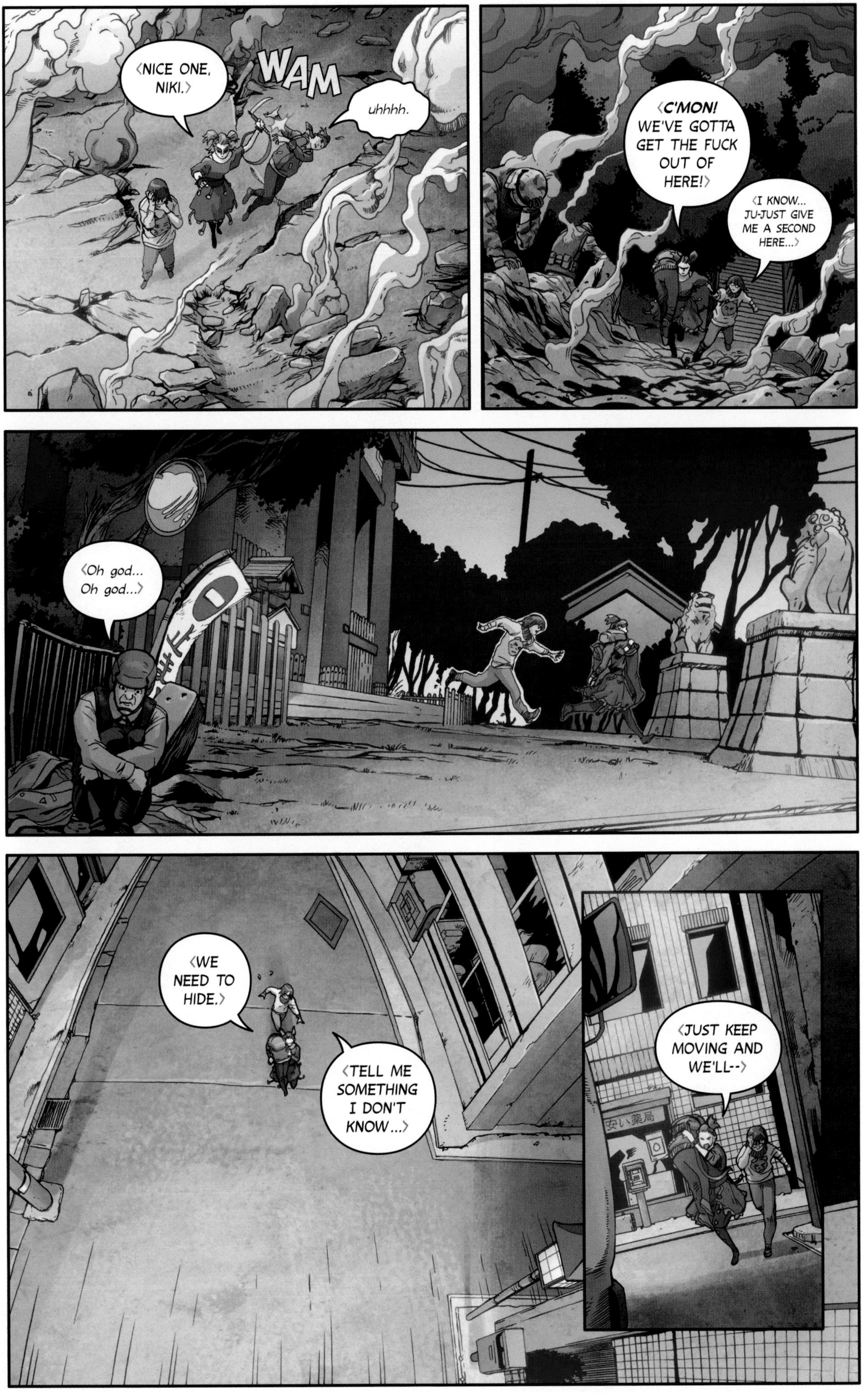
〈NICE ONE, NIKI.〉
WAM
uhhhh.
〈C'MON! WE'VE GOTTA GET THE FUCK OUT OF HERE!〉
〈I KNOW... JU-JUST GIVE ME A SECOND HERE...〉
〈Oh god... Oh god...〉
〈WE NEED TO HIDE.〉
〈TELL ME SOMETHING I DON'T KNOW...〉
〈JUST KEEP MOVING AND WE'LL--〉
安い薬局

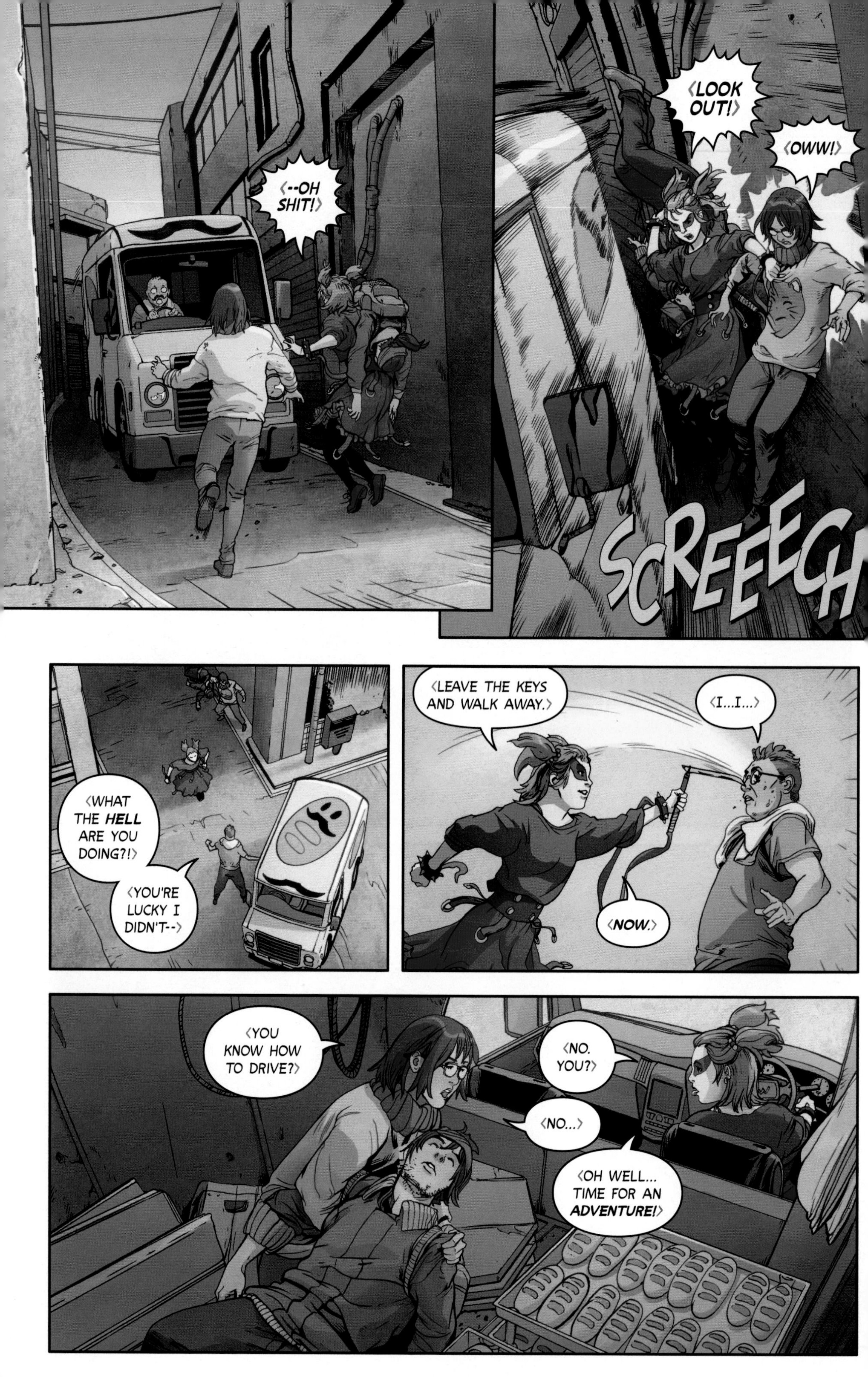

⟨--OH SHIT!⟩
⟨LOOK OUT!⟩
⟨OWW!⟩
SCREEECH
⟨WHAT THE **HELL** ARE YOU DOING?!⟩
⟨YOU'RE LUCKY I DIDN'T--⟩
⟨LEAVE THE KEYS AND WALK AWAY.⟩
⟨I...I...⟩
⟨**NOW.**⟩
⟨YOU KNOW HOW TO DRIVE?⟩
⟨NO. YOU?⟩
⟨NO...⟩
⟨OH WELL... TIME FOR AN **ADVENTURE!**⟩

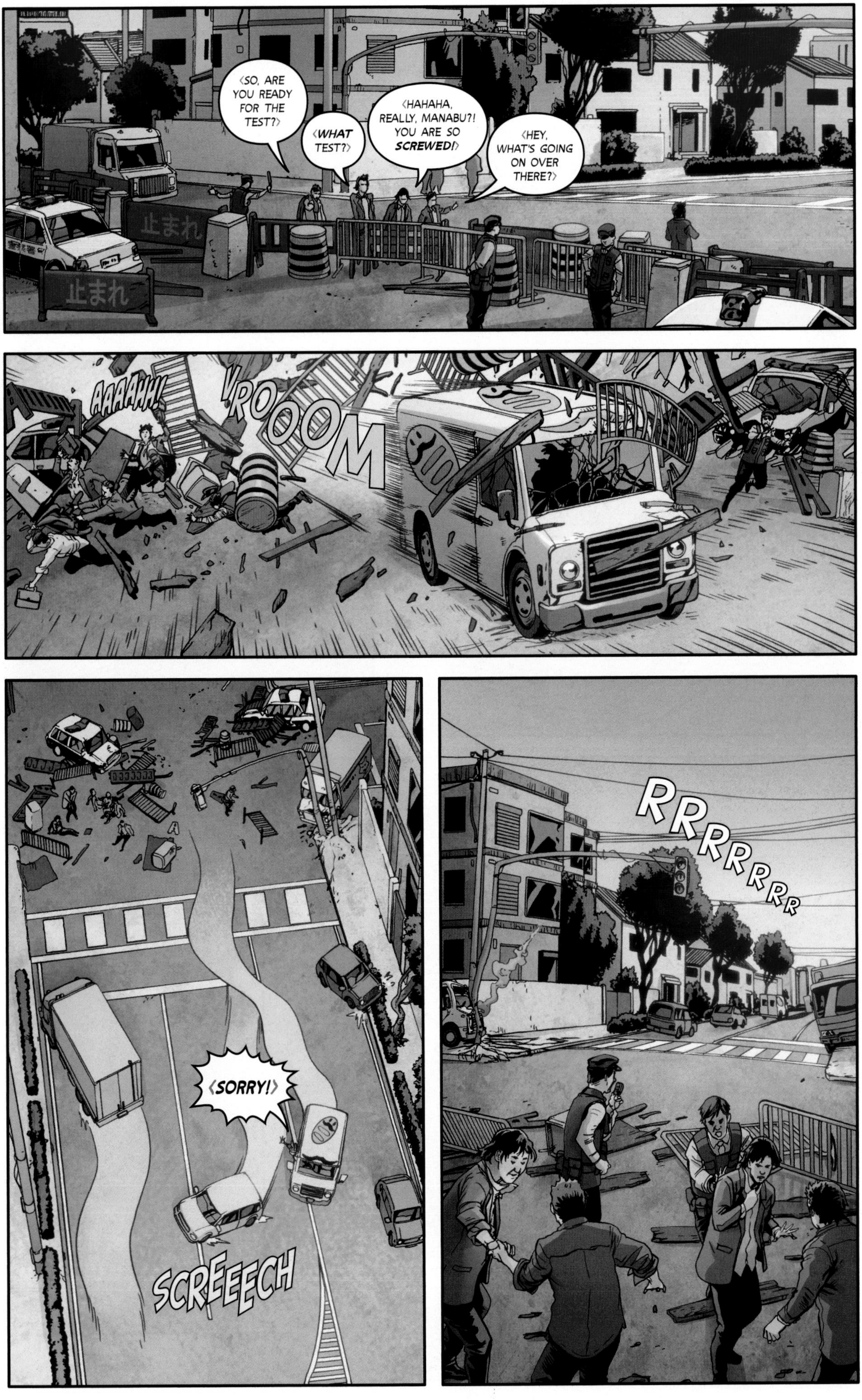
〈SO, ARE YOU READY FOR THE TEST?〉
〈WHAT TEST?〉
〈HAHAHA, REALLY, MANABU?! YOU ARE SO SCREWED!〉
〈HEY, WHAT'S GOING ON OVER THERE?〉
止まれ
止まれ
AAAAHH!
VROOOM
〈SORRY!〉
SCREEECH
RRRRRRRR

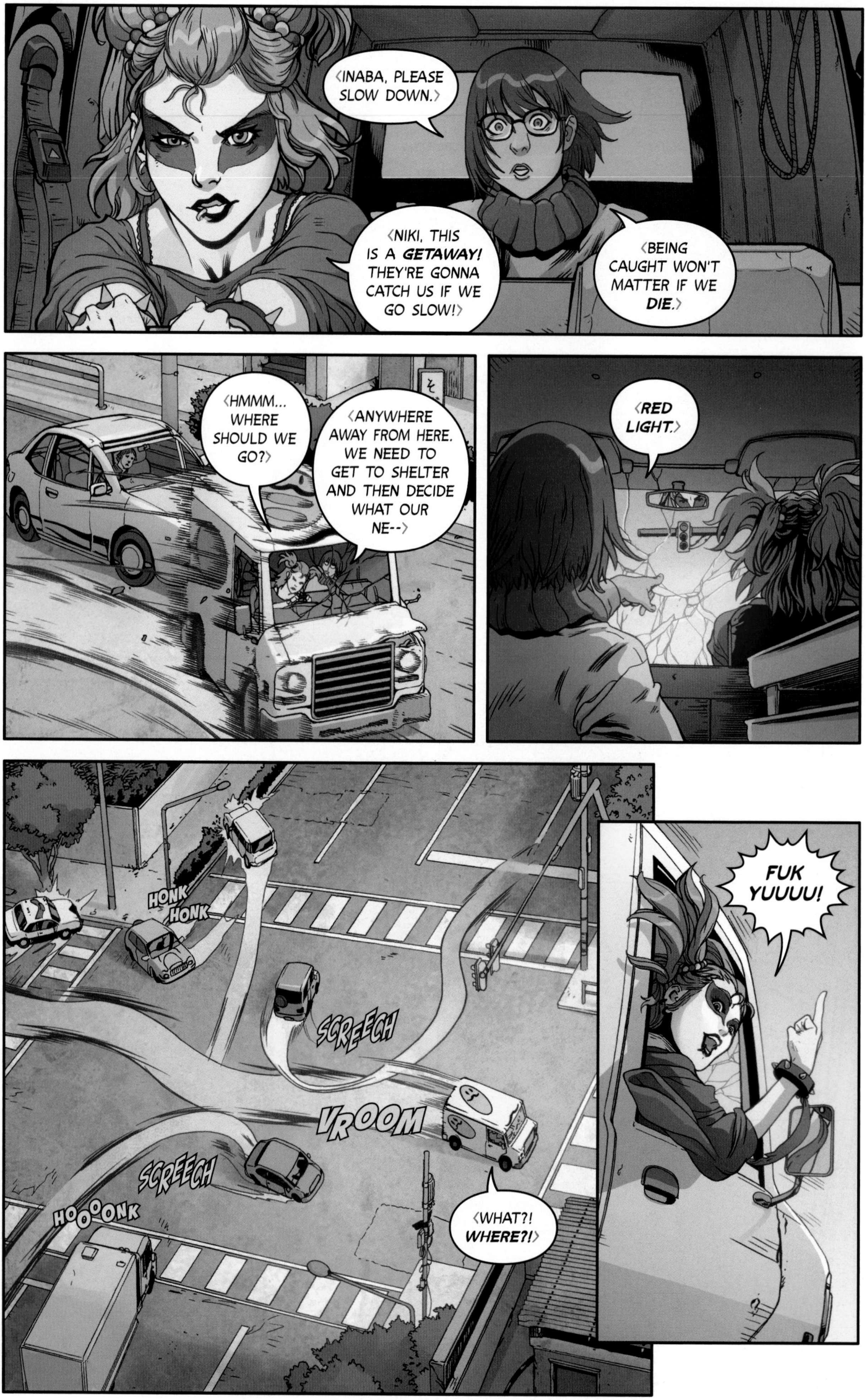

〈INABA, PLEASE SLOW DOWN.〉
〈NIKI, THIS IS A ***GETAWAY!*** THEY'RE GONNA CATCH US IF WE GO SLOW!〉
〈BEING CAUGHT WON'T MATTER IF WE ***DIE***.〉
〈HMMM... WHERE SHOULD WE GO?〉
〈ANYWHERE AWAY FROM HERE. WE NEED TO GET TO SHELTER AND THEN DECIDE WHAT OUR NE--〉
〈***RED LIGHT.***〉
HONK
HONK
SCREECH
VROOM
SCREECH
HOOOONK
〈WHAT?! ***WHERE?!***〉
FUK YUUUU!

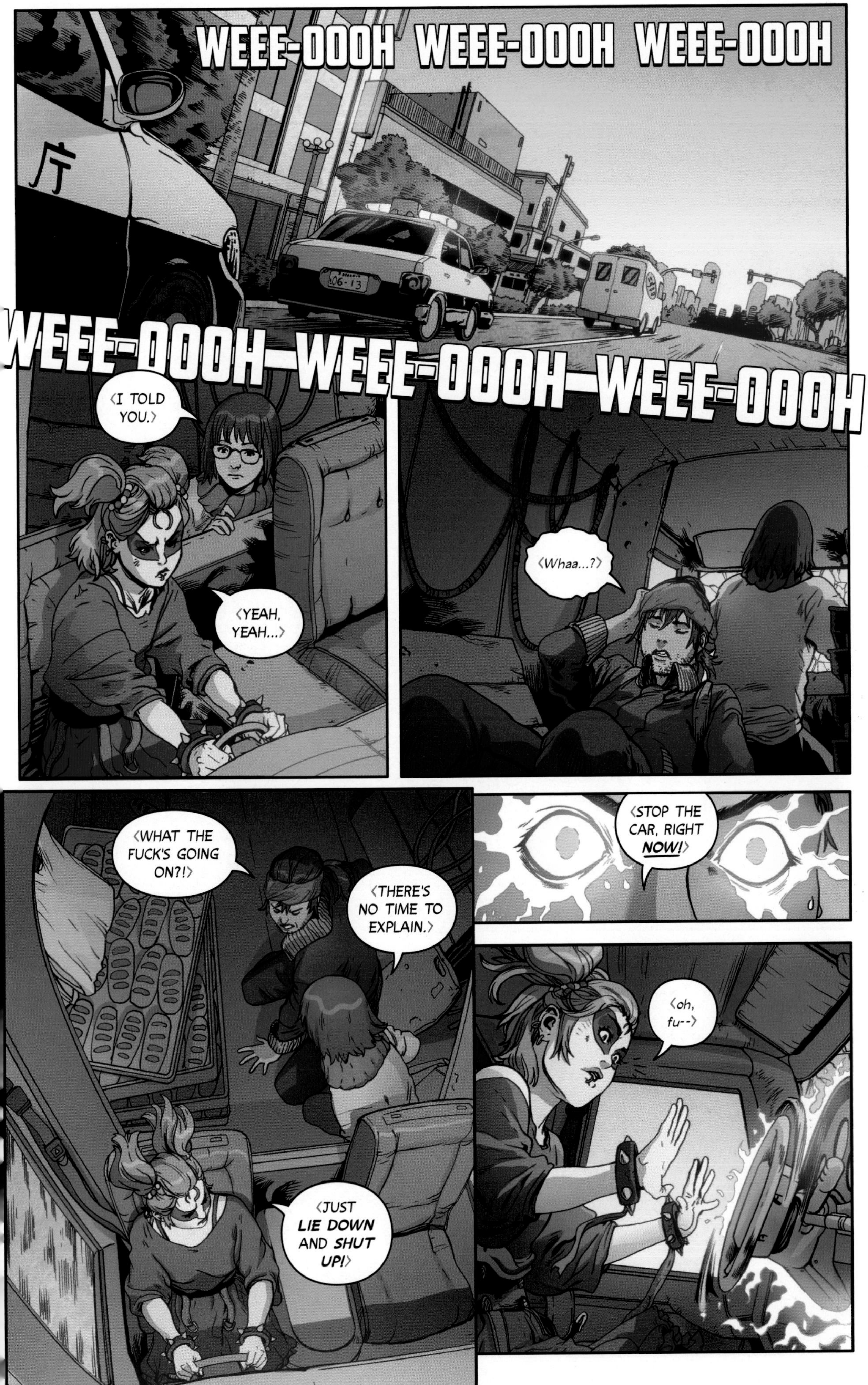

WEEE-OOOH WEEE-OOOH WEEE-OOOH
06-13
WEEE-OOOH WEEE-OOOH WEEE-OOOH
〈I TOLD YOU.〉
〈YEAH, YEAH...〉
〈Whaa...?〉
〈WHAT THE FUCK'S GOING ON?!〉
〈THERE'S NO TIME TO EXPLAIN.〉
〈JUST LIE DOWN AND SHUT UP!〉
〈STOP THE CAR, RIGHT NOW!〉
〈oh, fu--〉

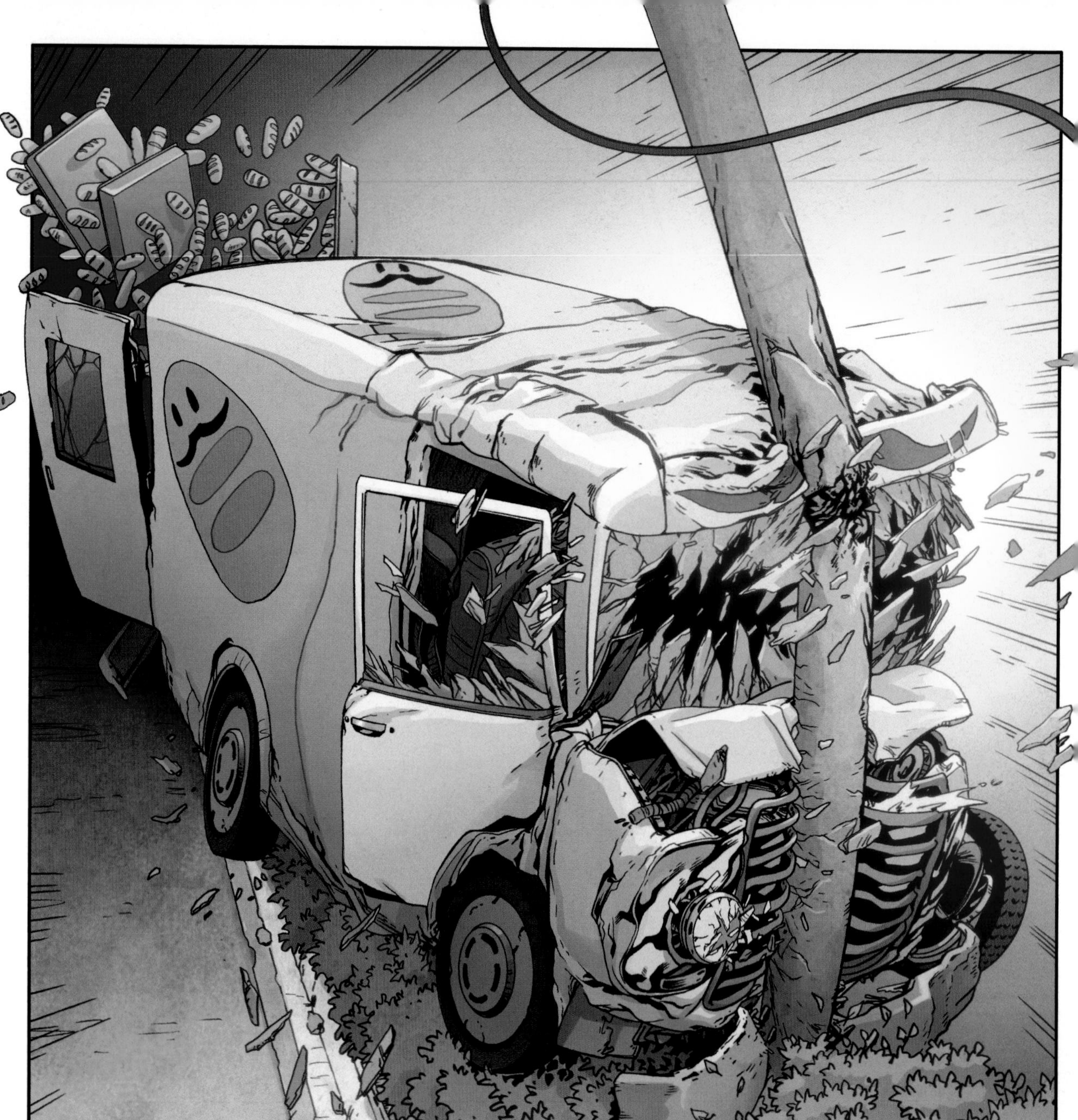
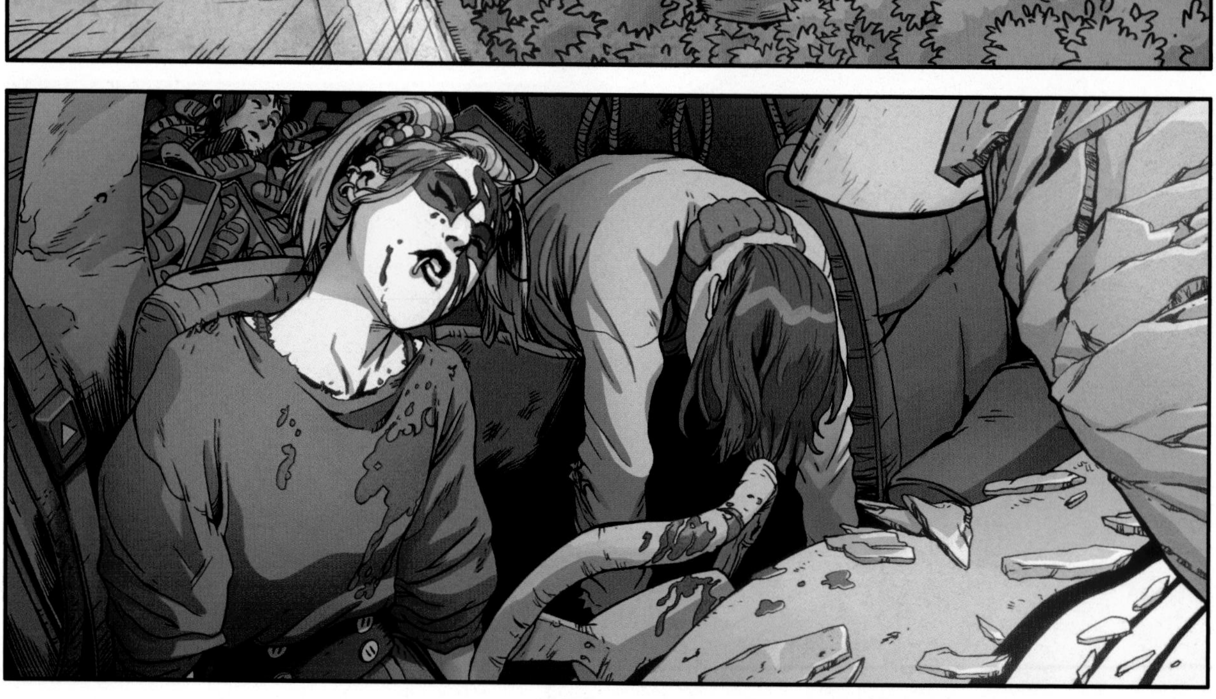

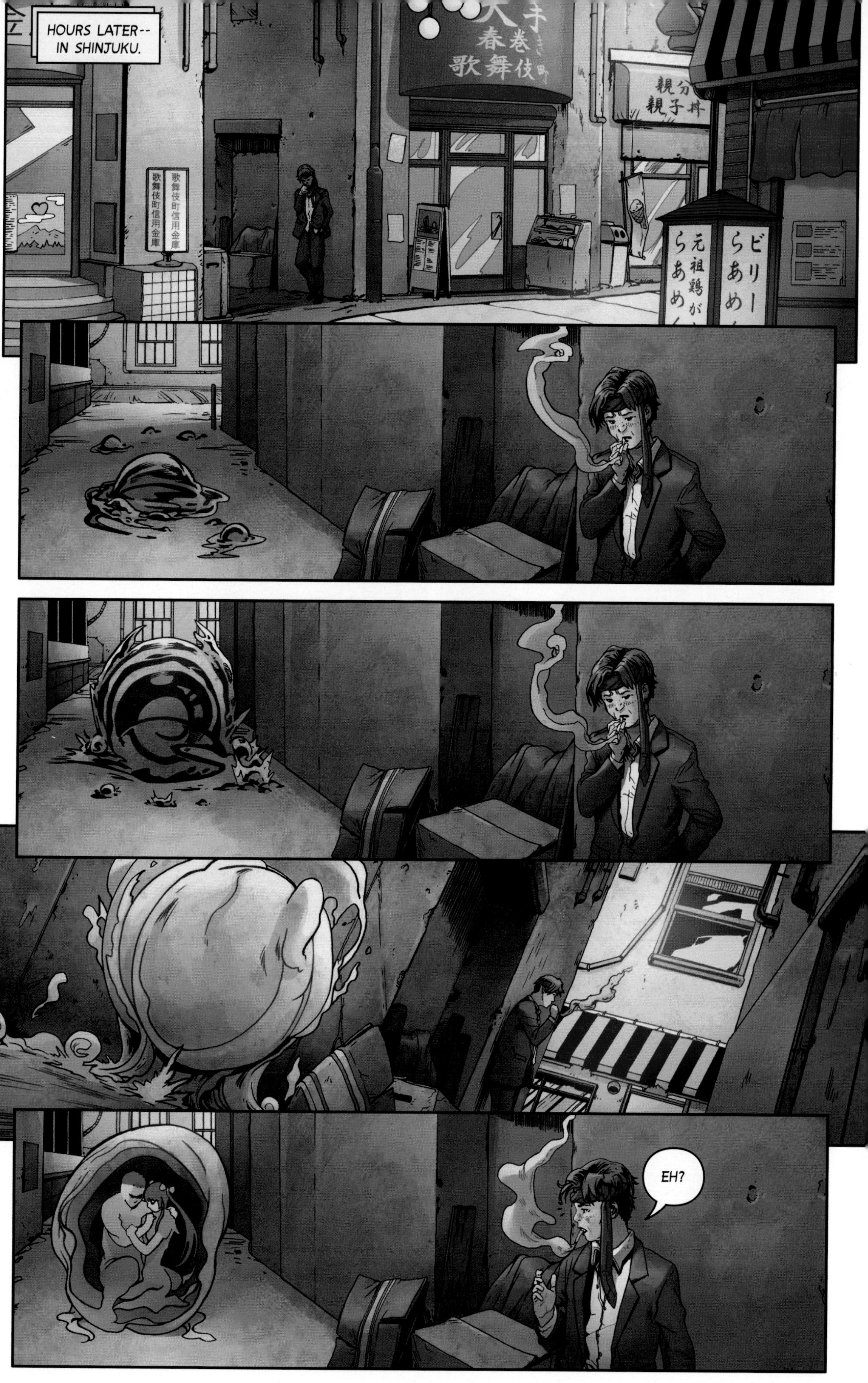
HOURS LATER--
IN SHINJUKU.
春巻き
歌舞伎町
親分
親子丼
歌舞伎町信用金庫
歌舞伎町信用金庫
EH?

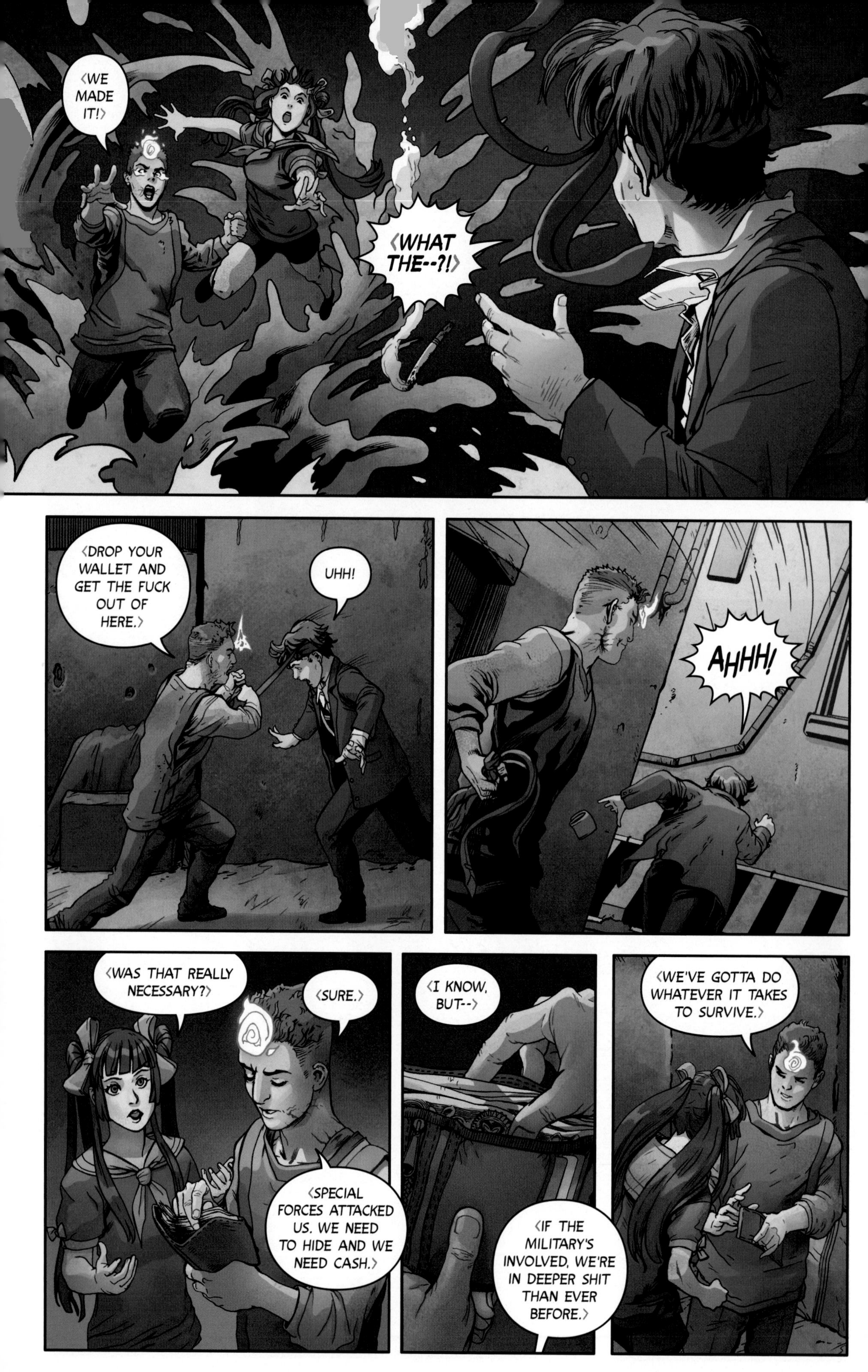

‹WE MADE IT!›
‹WHAT THE--?!›
‹DROP YOUR WALLET AND GET THE FUCK OUT OF HERE.›
UHH!
AHHH!
‹WAS THAT REALLY NECESSARY?›
‹SURE.›
‹SPECIAL FORCES ATTACKED US. WE NEED TO HIDE AND WE NEED CASH.›
‹I KNOW, BUT--›
‹IF THE MILITARY'S INVOLVED, WE'RE IN DEEPER SHIT THAN EVER BEFORE.›
‹WE'VE GOTTA DO WHATEVER IT TAKES TO SURVIVE.›

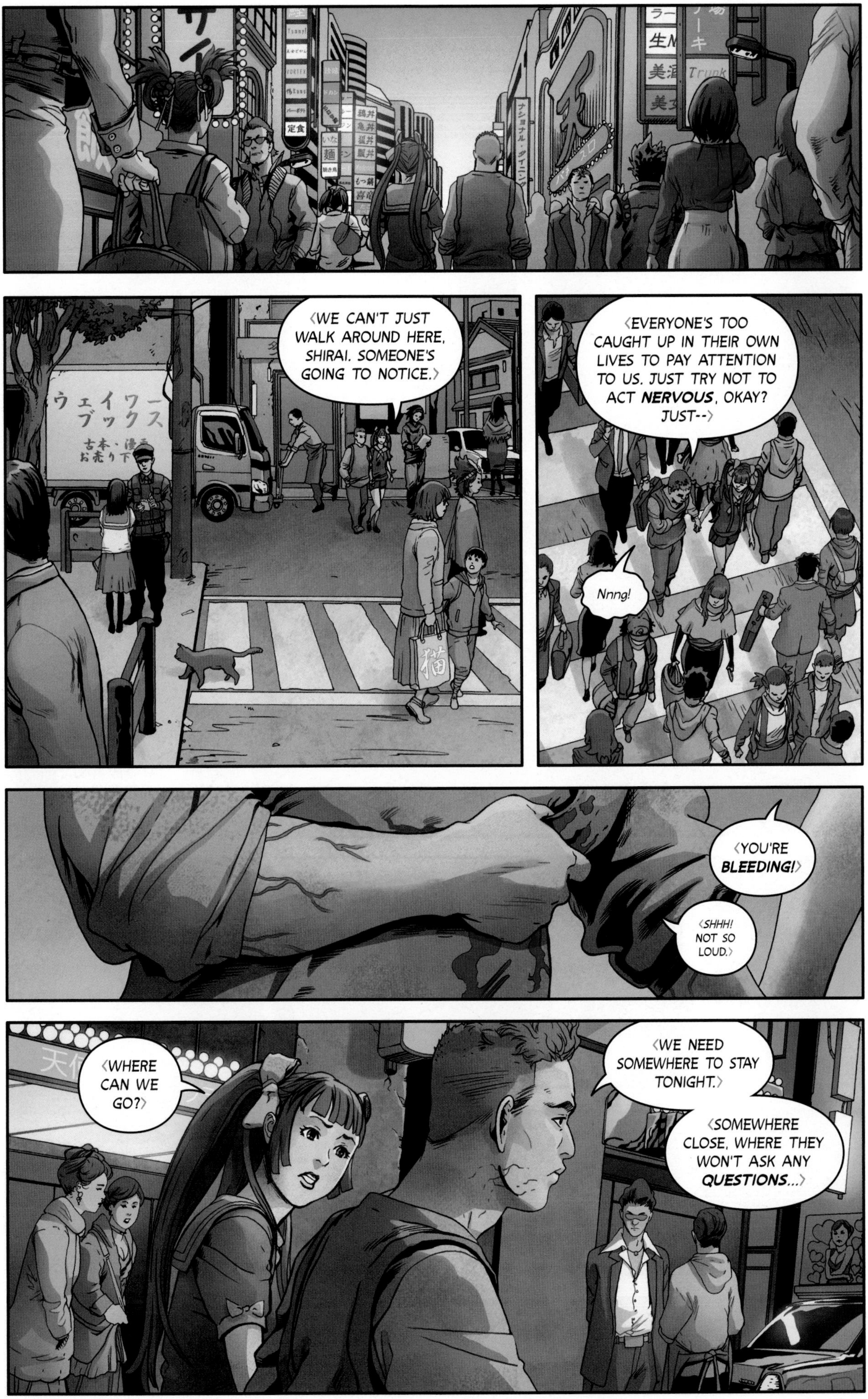

〈WE CAN'T JUST WALK AROUND HERE, SHIRAI. SOMEONE'S GOING TO NOTICE.〉
〈EVERYONE'S TOO CAUGHT UP IN THEIR OWN LIVES TO PAY ATTENTION TO US. JUST TRY NOT TO ACT NERVOUS, OKAY? JUST--〉
Nnng!
〈YOU'RE BLEEDING!〉
〈SHHH! NOT SO LOUD.〉
〈WHERE CAN WE GO?〉
〈WE NEED SOMEWHERE TO STAY TONIGHT.〉
〈SOMEWHERE CLOSE, WHERE THEY WON'T ASK ANY QUESTIONS...〉

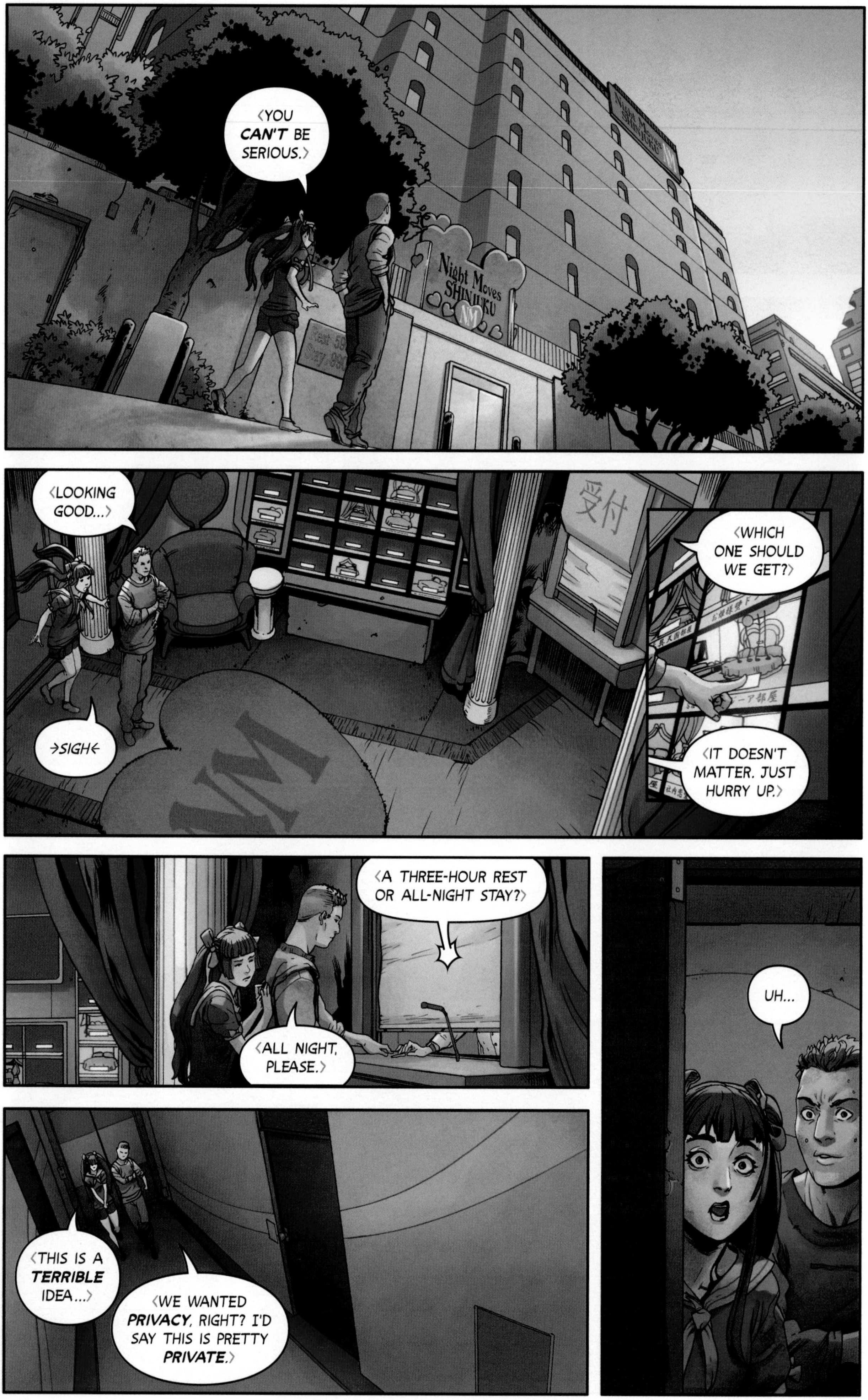

Night Moves SHINJUKU
〈YOU **CAN'T** BE SERIOUS.〉
Night Moves SHINJUKU
受付
〈LOOKING GOOD...〉
→SIGH←
〈WHICH ONE SHOULD WE GET?〉
〈IT DOESN'T MATTER. JUST HURRY UP.〉
〈A THREE-HOUR REST OR ALL-NIGHT STAY?〉
〈ALL NIGHT, PLEASE.〉
〈THIS IS A **TERRIBLE** IDEA...〉
〈WE WANTED **PRIVACY**, RIGHT? I'D SAY THIS IS PRETTY **PRIVATE**.〉
UH...

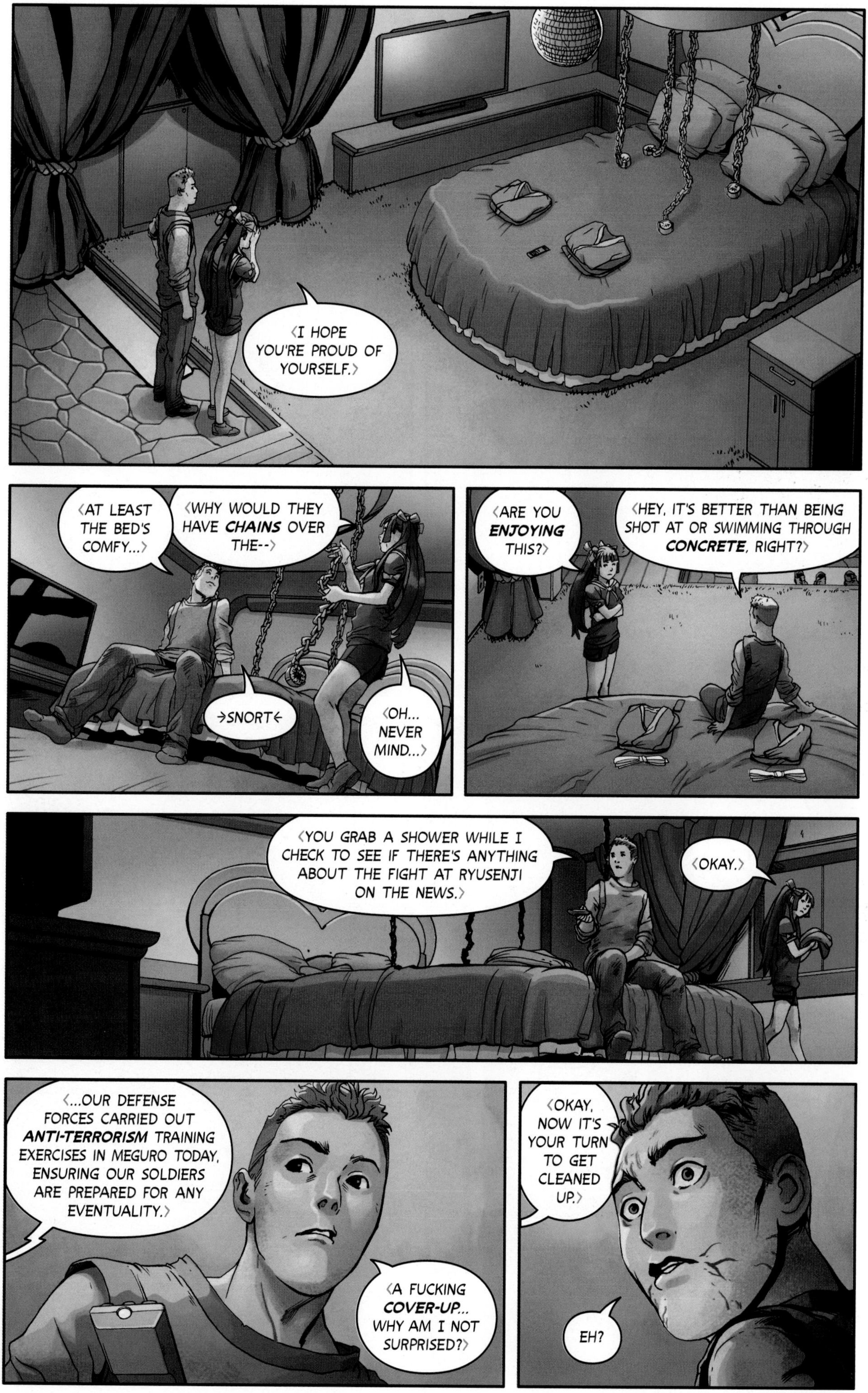

‹I HOPE YOU'RE PROUD OF YOURSELF.›
‹AT LEAST THE BED'S COMFY...›
‹WHY WOULD THEY HAVE **CHAINS** OVER THE--›
→SNORT←
‹OH... NEVER MIND...›
‹ARE YOU **ENJOYING** THIS?›
‹HEY, IT'S BETTER THAN BEING SHOT AT OR SWIMMING THROUGH **CONCRETE**, RIGHT?›
‹YOU GRAB A SHOWER WHILE I CHECK TO SEE IF THERE'S ANYTHING ABOUT THE FIGHT AT RYUSENJI ON THE NEWS.›
‹OKAY.›
‹...OUR DEFENSE FORCES CARRIED OUT **ANTI-TERRORISM** TRAINING EXERCISES IN MEGURO TODAY, ENSURING OUR SOLDIERS ARE PREPARED FOR ANY EVENTUALITY.›
‹A FUCKING **COVER-UP**... WHY AM I NOT SURPRISED?›
‹OKAY, NOW IT'S YOUR TURN TO GET CLEANED UP.›
EH?

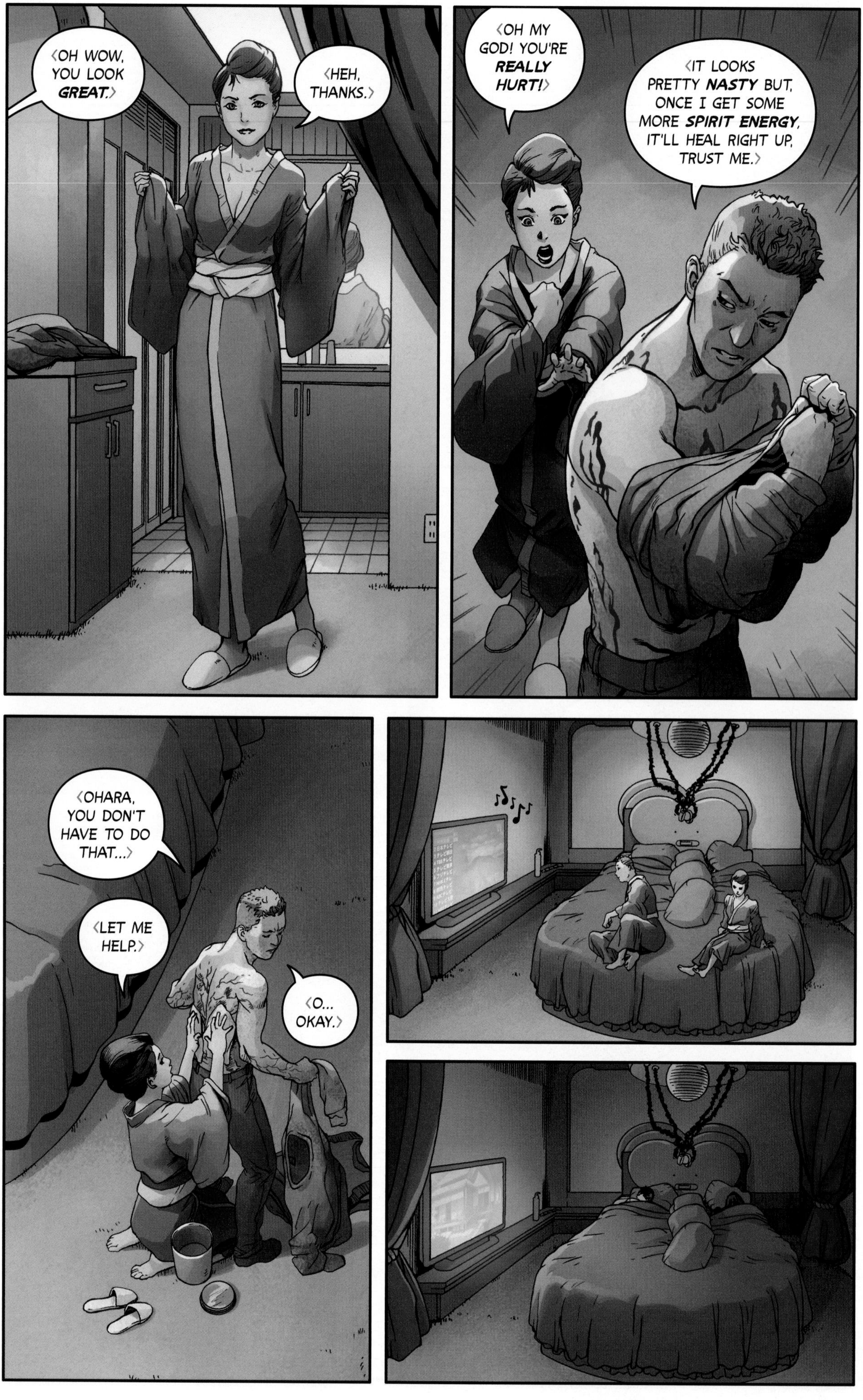

‹OH WOW, YOU LOOK **GREAT.**›
‹HEH, THANKS.›
‹OH MY GOD! YOU'RE **REALLY HURT!**›
‹IT LOOKS PRETTY **NASTY** BUT, ONCE I GET SOME MORE **SPIRIT ENERGY**, IT'LL HEAL RIGHT UP, TRUST ME.›
‹OHARA, YOU DON'T HAVE TO DO THAT...›
‹LET ME HELP.›
‹O... OKAY.›

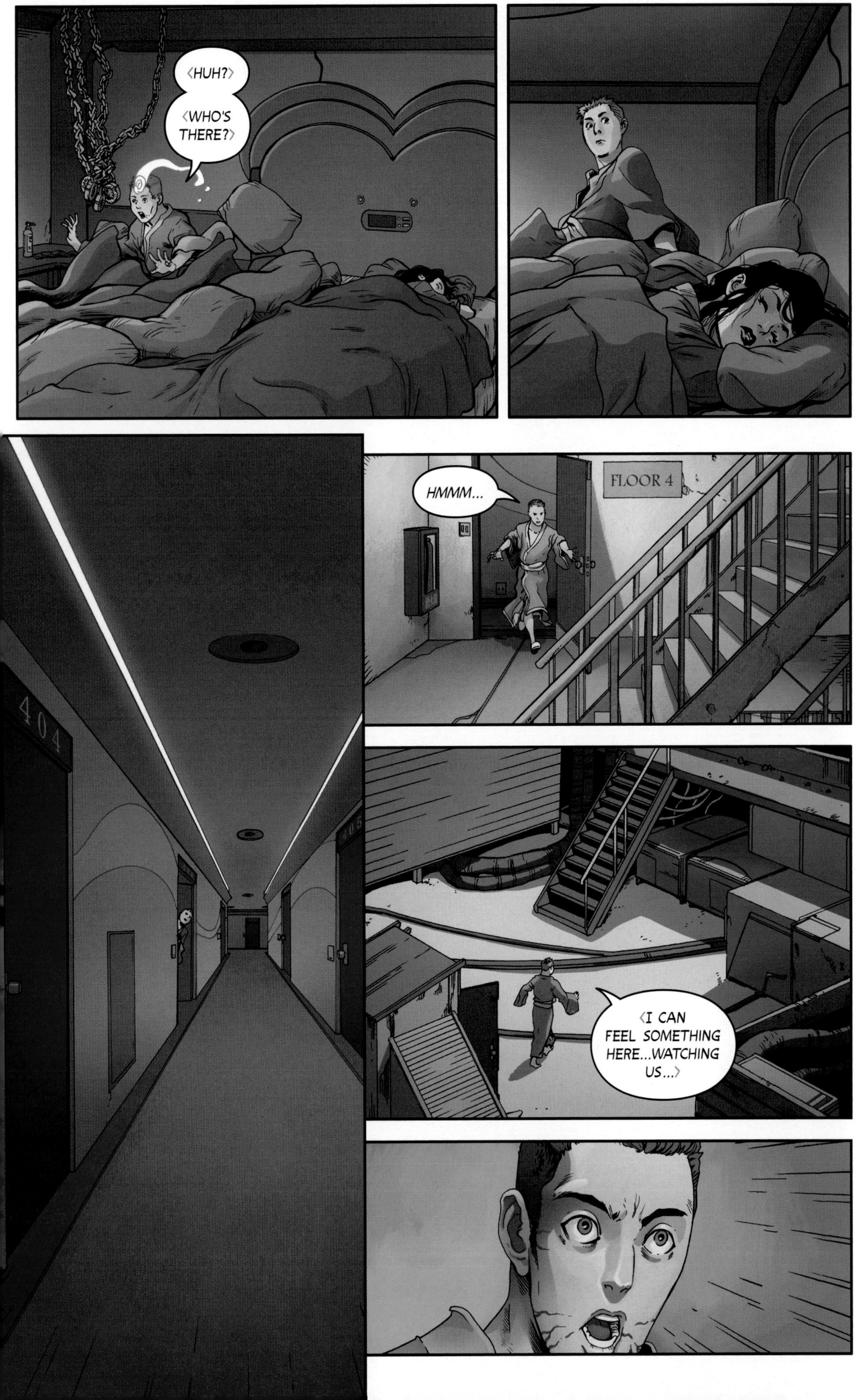

‹HUH?›
‹WHO'S THERE?›
HMMM...
FLOOR 4
404
405
‹I CAN FEEL SOMETHING HERE...WATCHING US...›

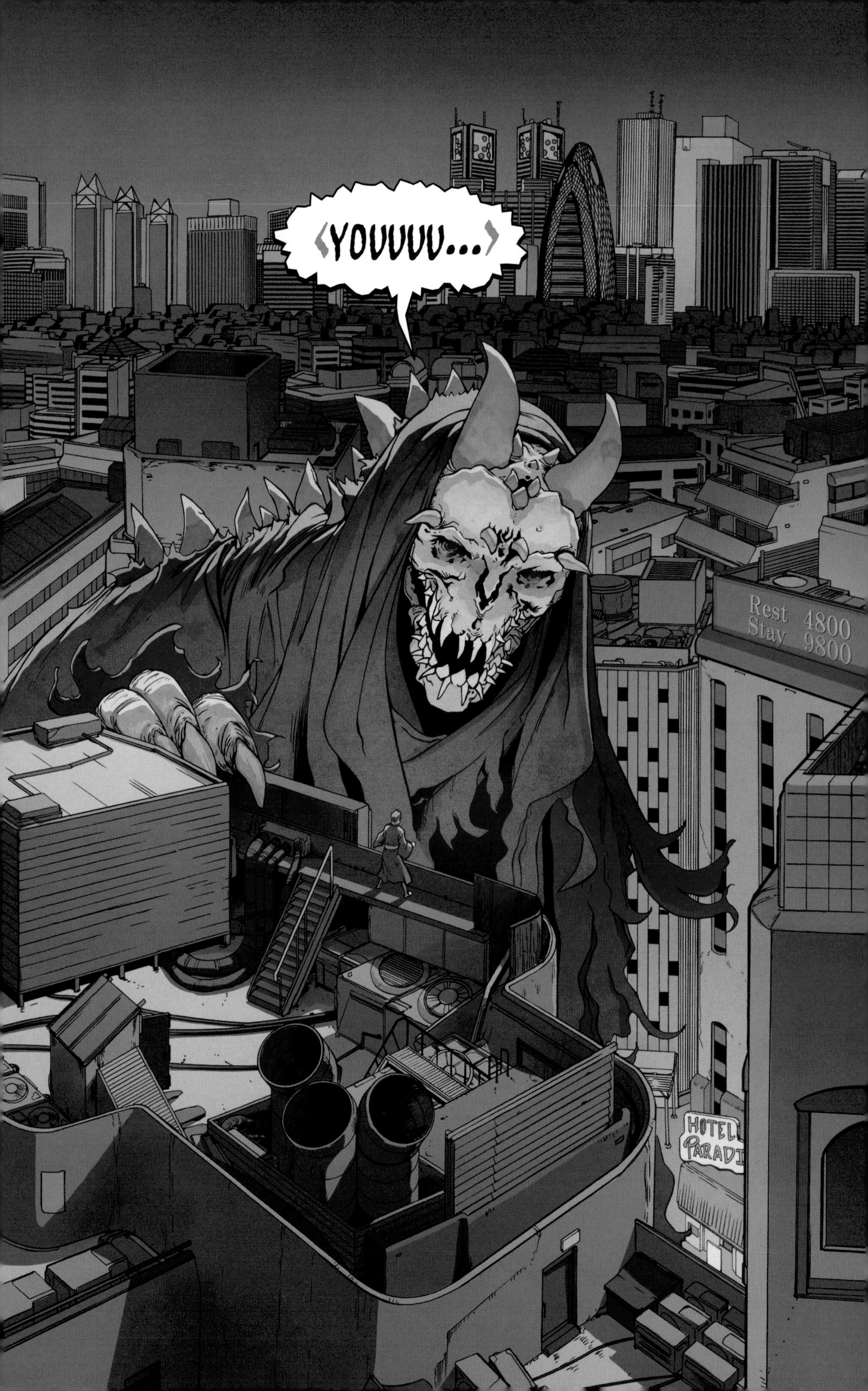

‹YOUUUU...›
Rest 4800
Stay 9800
HOTEL PARADI

Chapter Eighteen

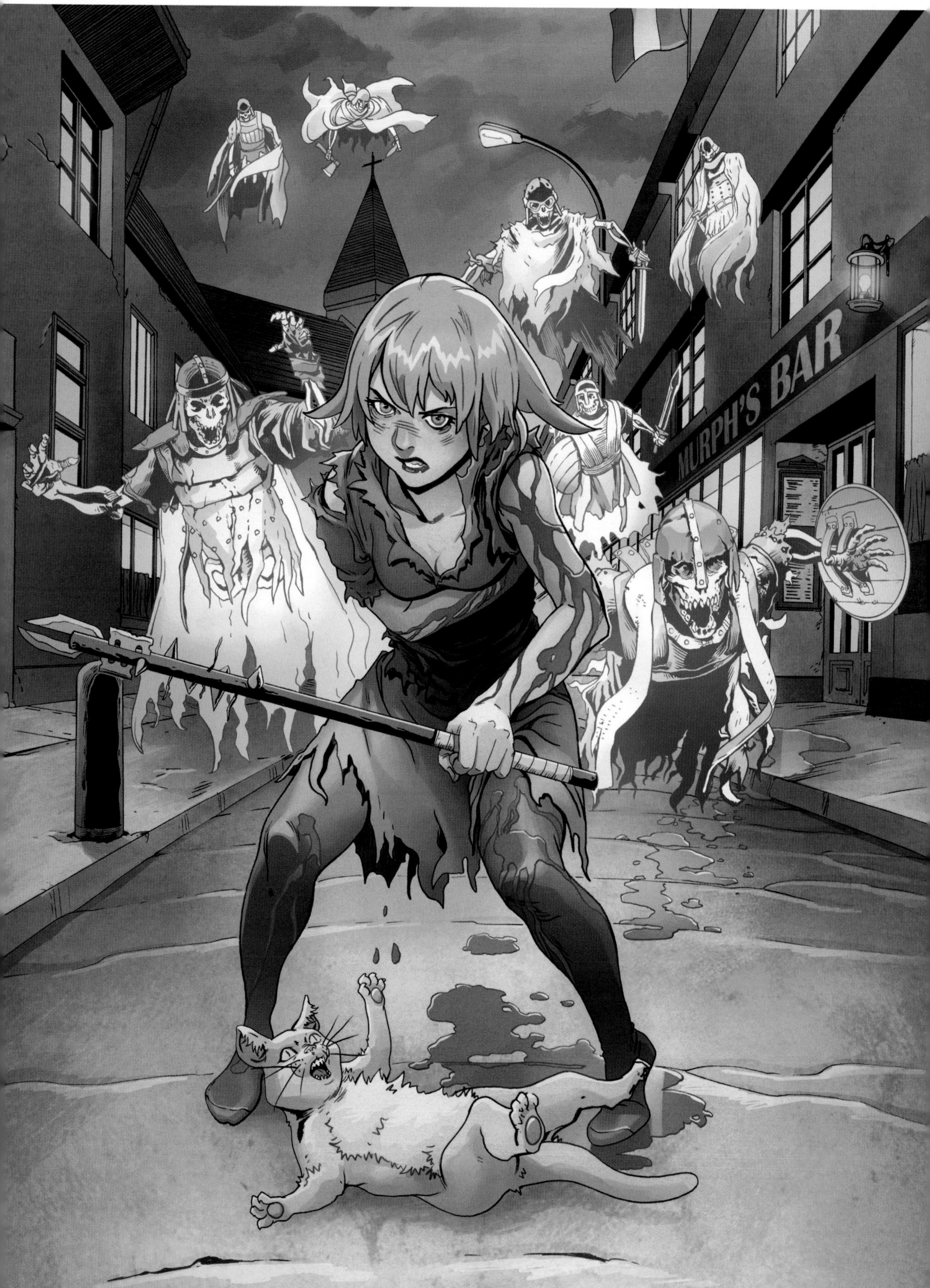
MURPH'S BAR

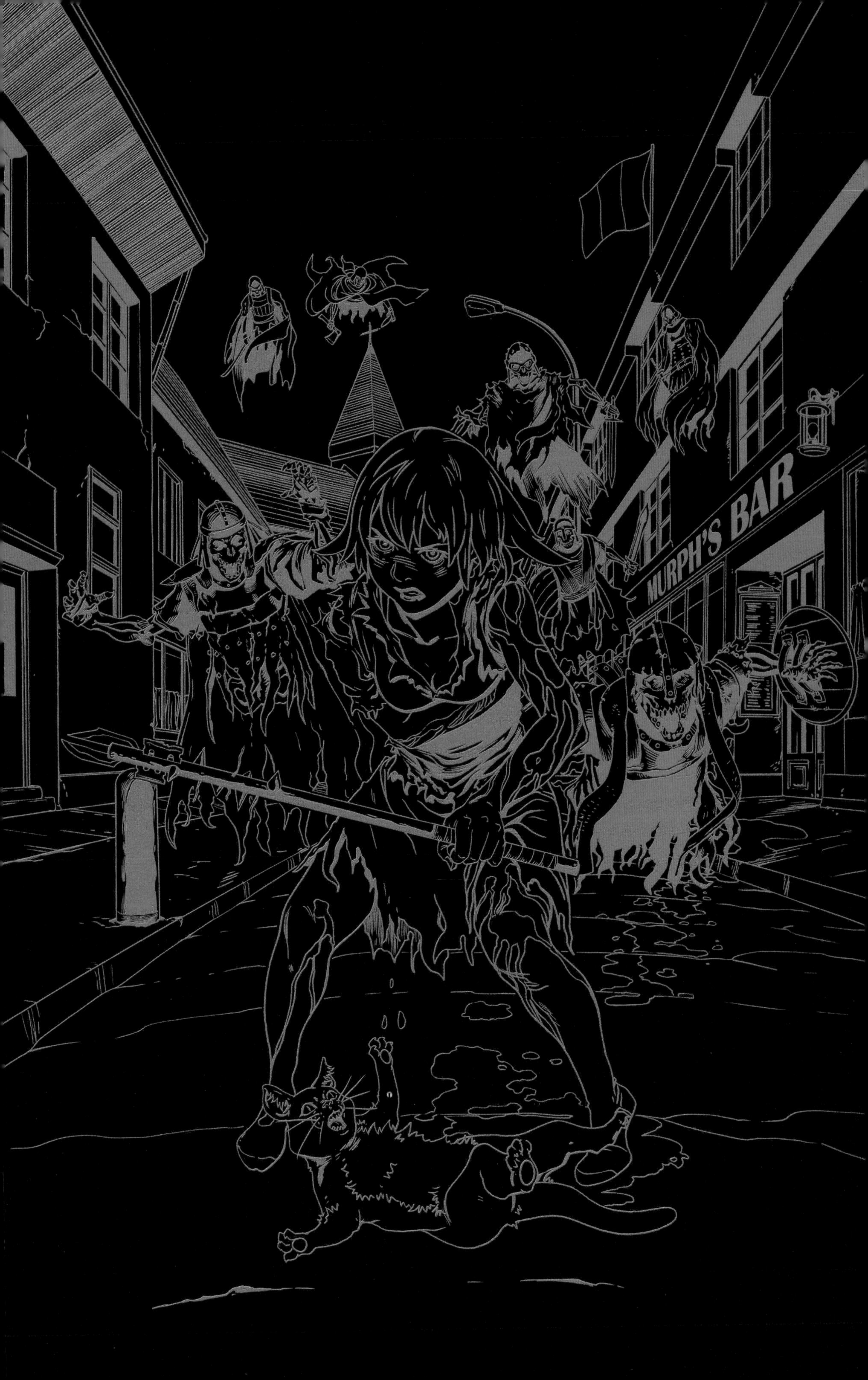
MURPH'S BAR

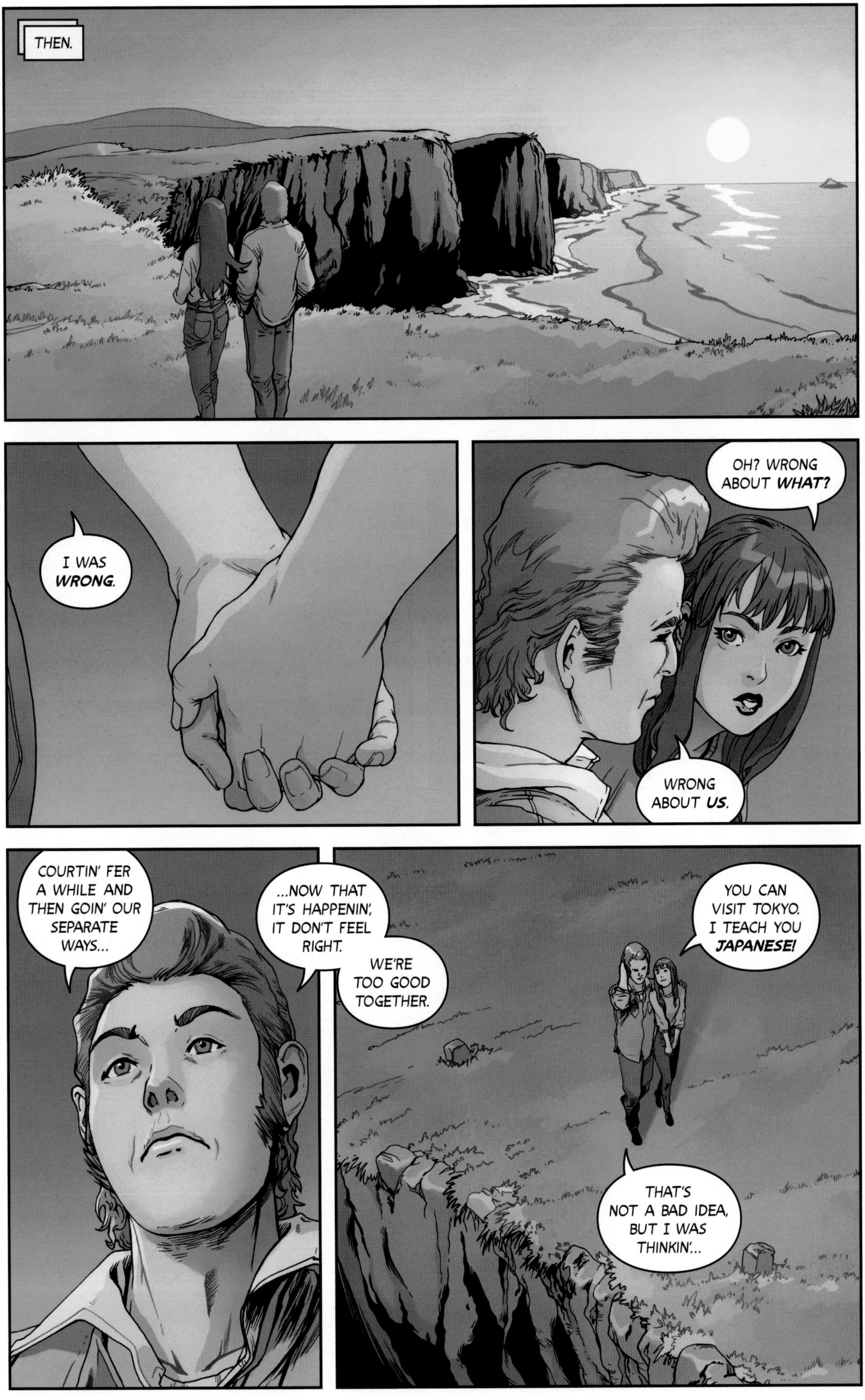
THEN.
I WAS WRONG.
OH? WRONG ABOUT WHAT?
WRONG ABOUT US.
COURTIN' FER A WHILE AND THEN GOIN' OUR SEPARATE WAYS...
...NOW THAT IT'S HAPPENIN', IT DON'T FEEL RIGHT.
WE'RE TOO GOOD TOGETHER.
YOU CAN VISIT TOKYO. I TEACH YOU JAPANESE!
THAT'S NOT A BAD IDEA, BUT I WAS THINKIN'...

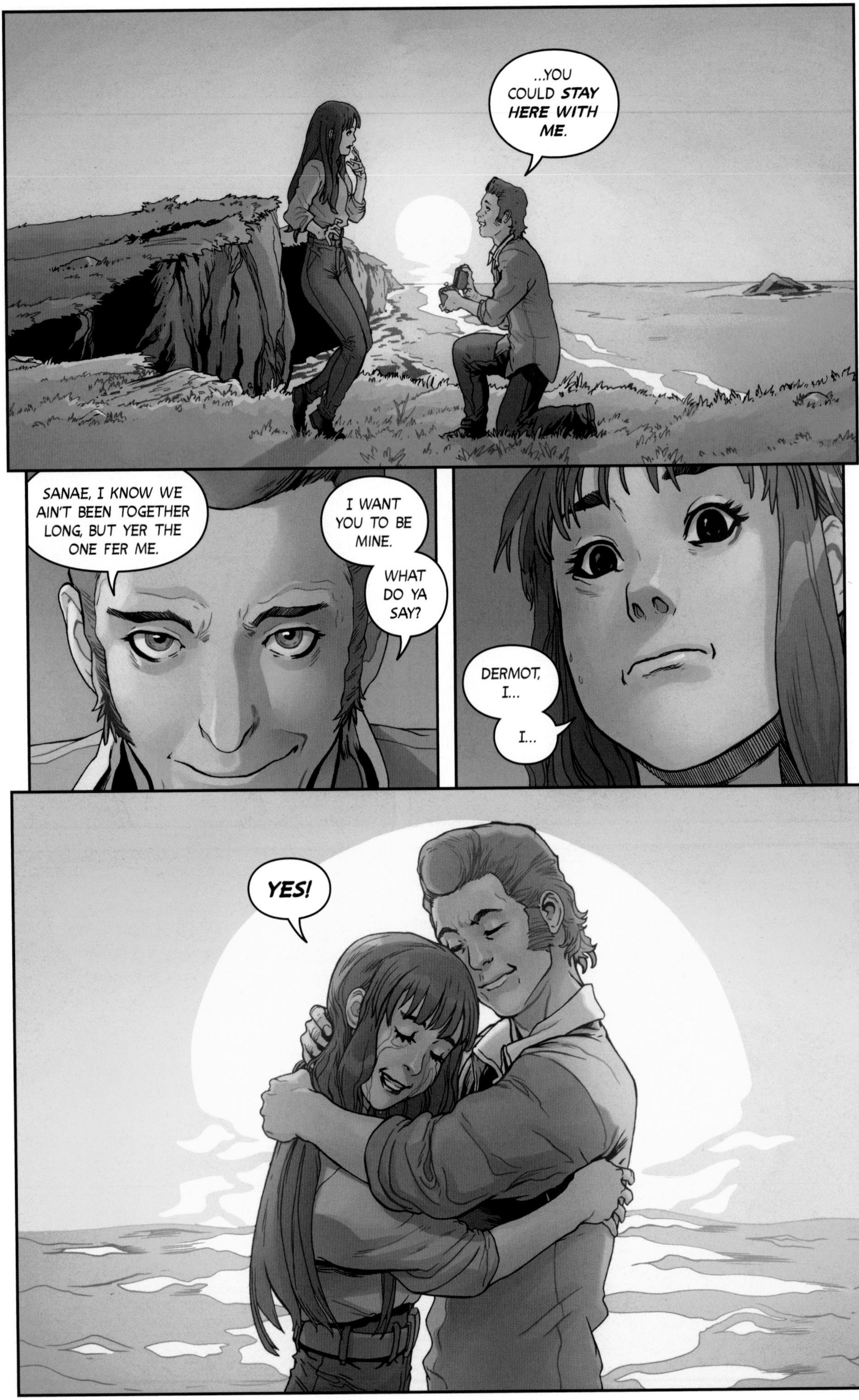
...YOU COULD STAY HERE WITH ME.
SANAE, I KNOW WE AIN'T BEEN TOGETHER LONG, BUT YER THE ONE FER ME.
I WANT YOU TO BE MINE.
WHAT DO YA SAY?
DERMOT, I...
I...
YES!

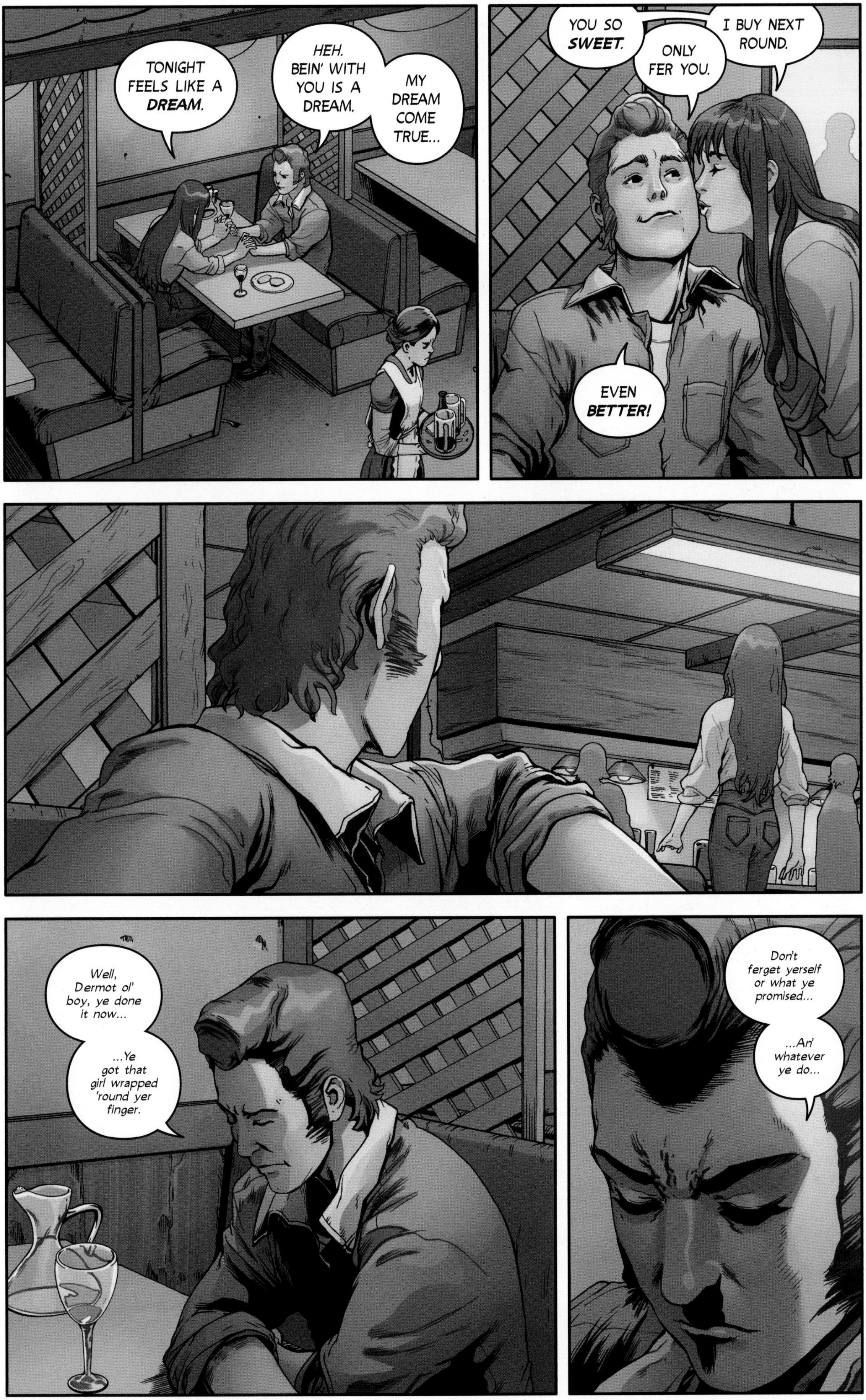
TONIGHT FEELS LIKE A DREAM.
HEH. BEIN' WITH YOU IS A DREAM.
MY DREAM COME TRUE...
YOU SO SWEET.
ONLY FER YOU.
I BUY NEXT ROUND.
EVEN BETTER!
Well, Dermot ol' boy, ye done it now...
...Ye got that girl wrapped 'round yer finger.
Don't ferget yerself or what ye promised...
...An' whatever ye do...

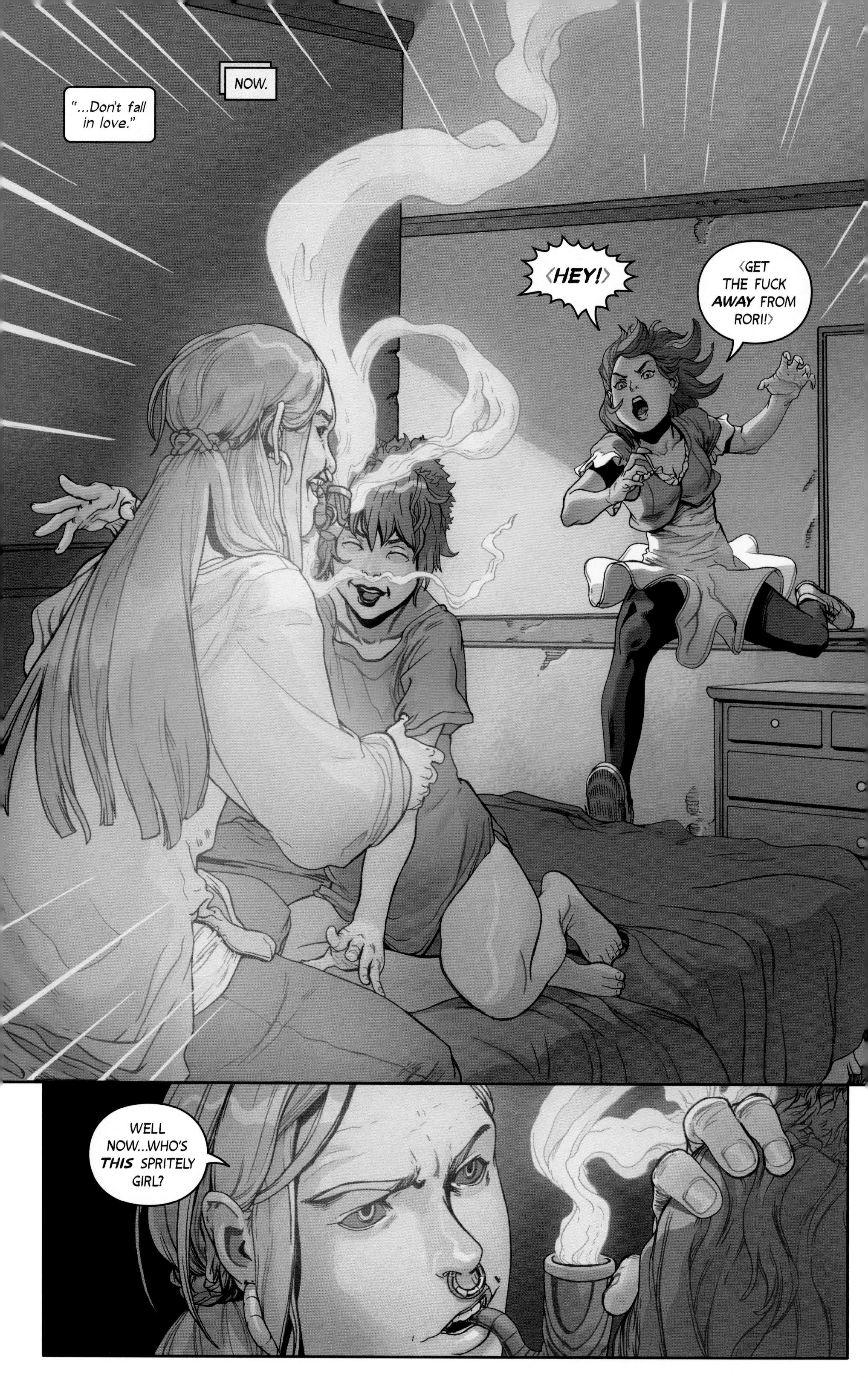
"...Don't fall in love."
NOW.
‹HEY!›
‹GET THE FUCK AWAY FROM RORI!›
WELL NOW...WHO'S THIS SPRITELY GIRL?

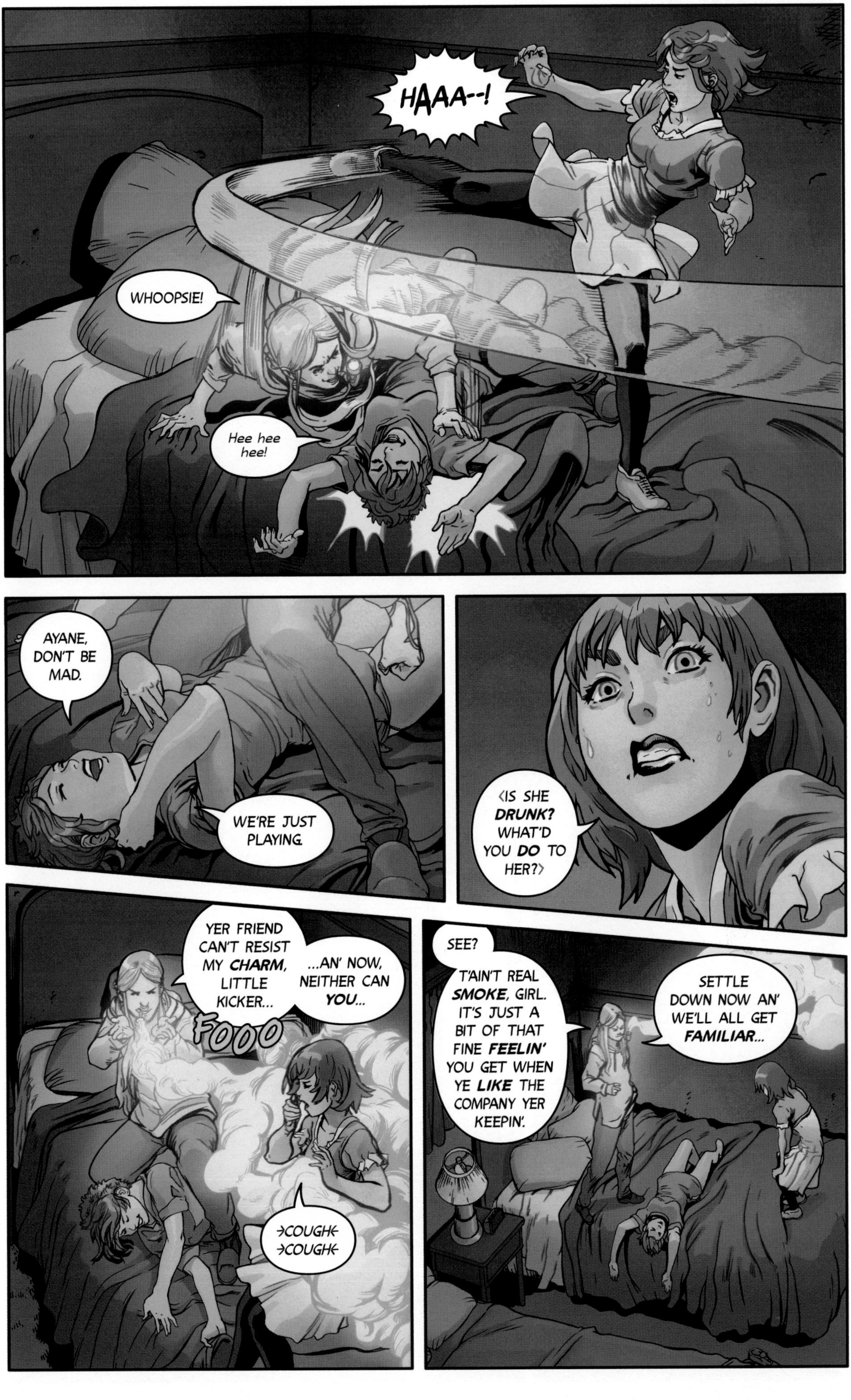
HAAA--!
WHOOPSIE!
Hee hee hee!
AYANE, DON'T BE MAD.
WE'RE JUST PLAYING.
‹IS SHE DRUNK? WHAT'D YOU DO TO HER?›
YER FRIEND CAN'T RESIST MY CHARM, LITTLE KICKER...
...AN' NOW, NEITHER CAN YOU...
FOOO
›COUGH‹ ›COUGH‹
SEE?
T'AIN'T REAL SMOKE, GIRL. IT'S JUST A BIT OF THAT FINE FEELIN' YOU GET WHEN YE LIKE THE COMPANY YER KEEPIN'.
SETTLE DOWN NOW AN' WE'LL ALL GET FAMILIAR...

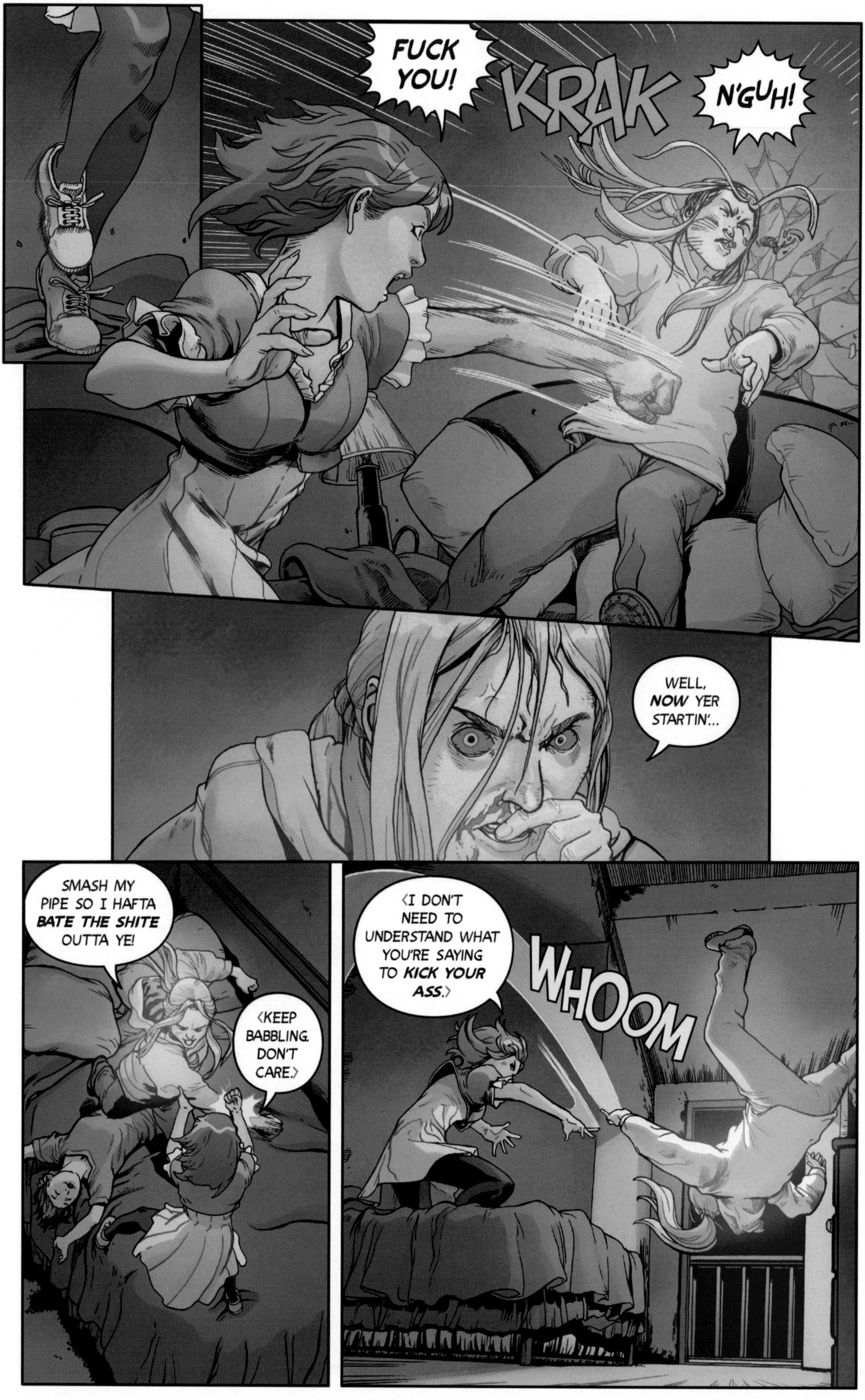
FUCK YOU!
KRAK
N'GUH!
WELL, NOW YER STARTIN'...
SMASH MY PIPE SO I HAFTA BATE THE SHITE OUTTA YE!
‹KEEP BABBLING. DON'T CARE.›
‹I DON'T NEED TO UNDERSTAND WHAT YOU'RE SAYING TO KICK YOUR ASS.›
WHOOM

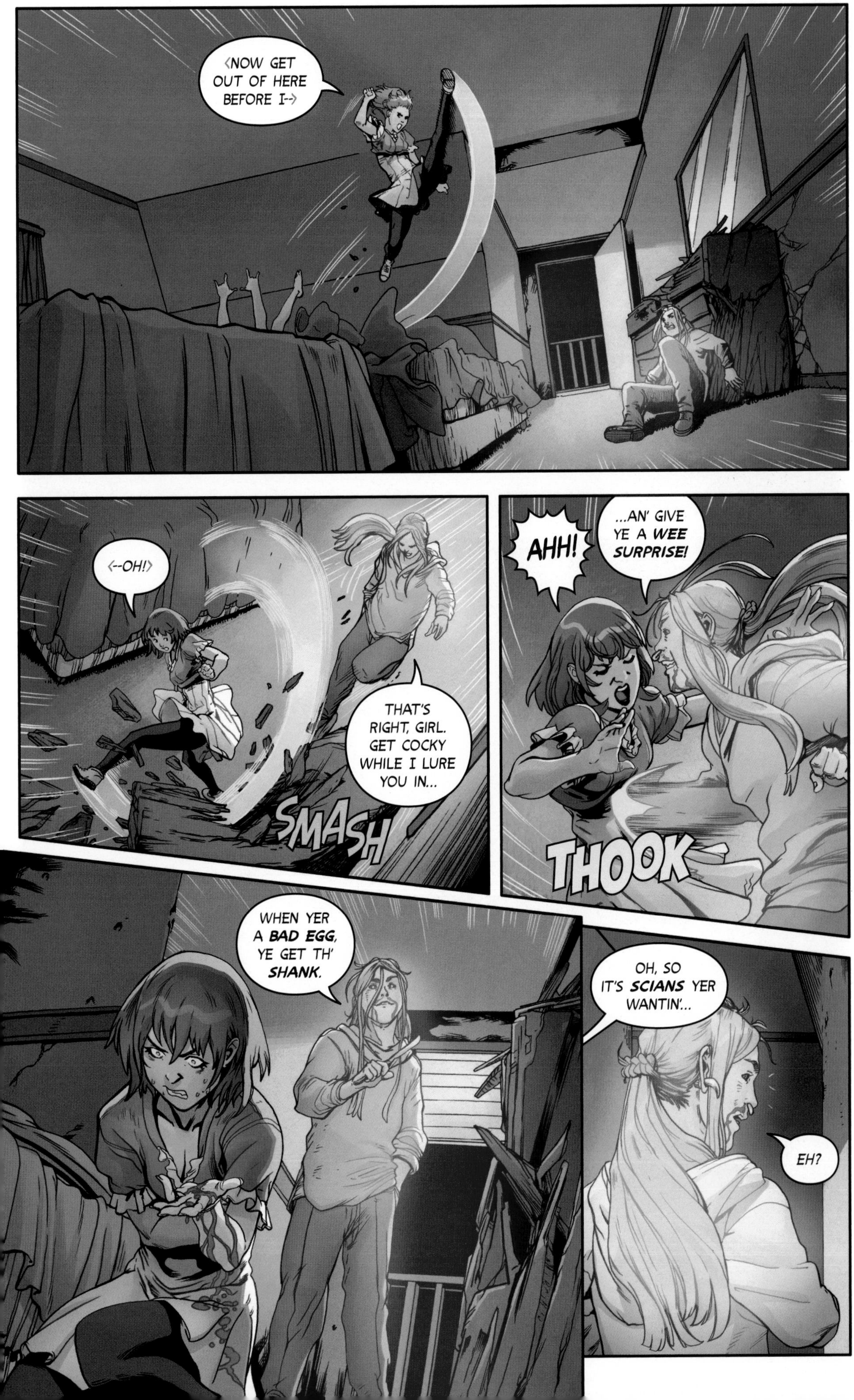

<NOW GET OUT OF HERE BEFORE I-->
<--OH!>
THAT'S RIGHT, GIRL. GET COCKY WHILE I LURE YOU IN...
SMASH
AHH!
...AN' GIVE YE A WEE SURPRISE!
THOOK
WHEN YER A BAD EGG, YE GET TH' SHANK.
OH, SO IT'S SCIANS YER WANTIN'...
EH?

...LEMME *OBLIGE* YE!

SHUNK

F-f-fek...

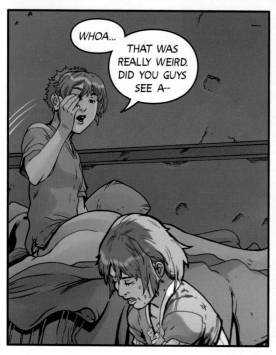

WHOA...

THAT WAS REALLY WEIRD. DID YOU GUYS SEE A--

...A...

...OH, FUCK...

⟨AYANE... YOU'RE HURT, GIRL.⟩

⟨IT'S FINE. I HEAL FAST.⟩

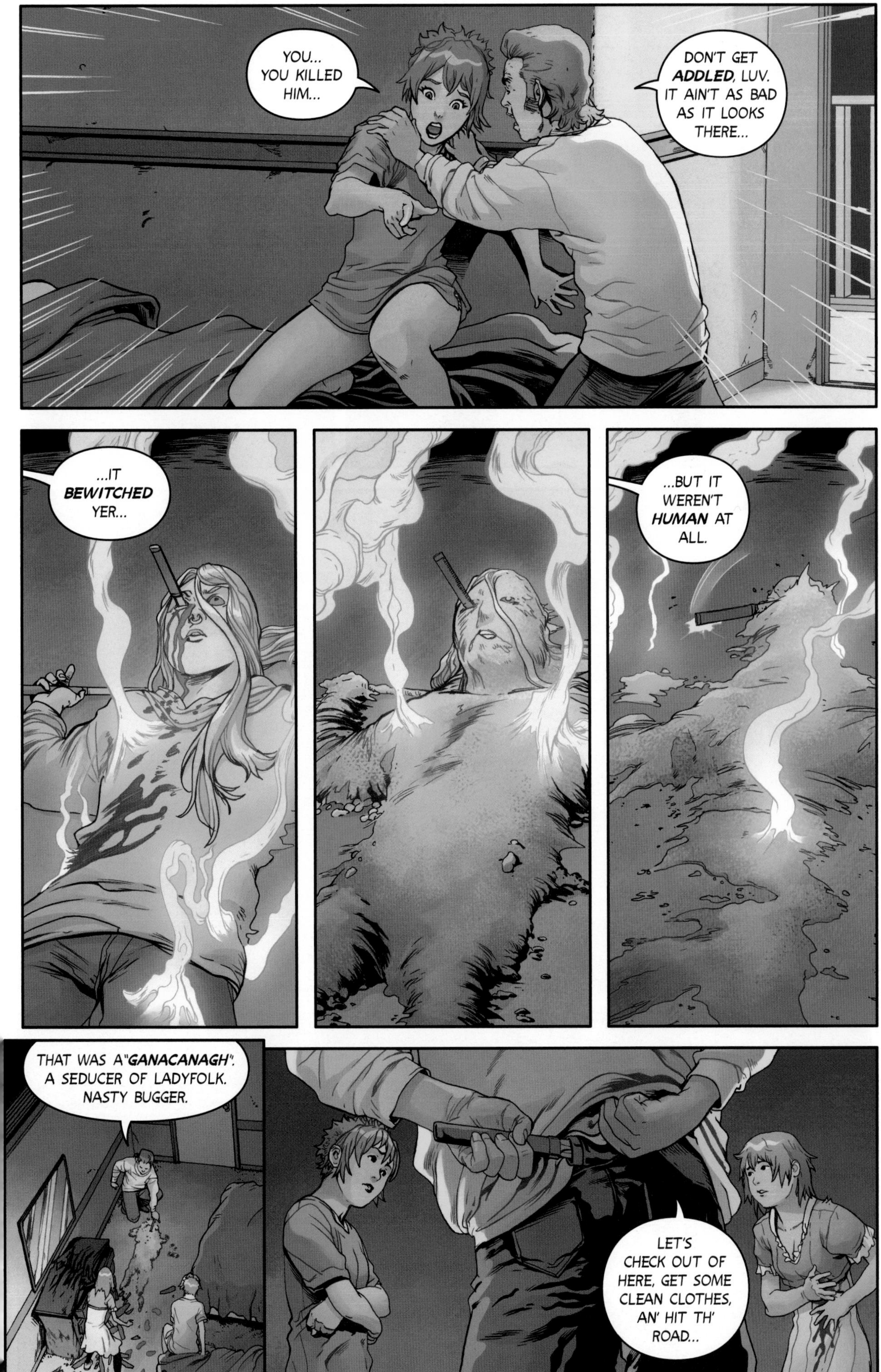
YOU... YOU KILLED HIM...
DON'T GET ADDLED, LUV. IT AIN'T AS BAD AS IT LOOKS THERE...
...IT BEWITCHED YER...
...BUT IT WEREN'T HUMAN AT ALL.
THAT WAS A "GANACANAGH". A SEDUCER OF LADYFOLK. NASTY BUGGER.
LET'S CHECK OUT OF HERE, GET SOME CLEAN CLOTHES, AN' HIT TH' ROAD...

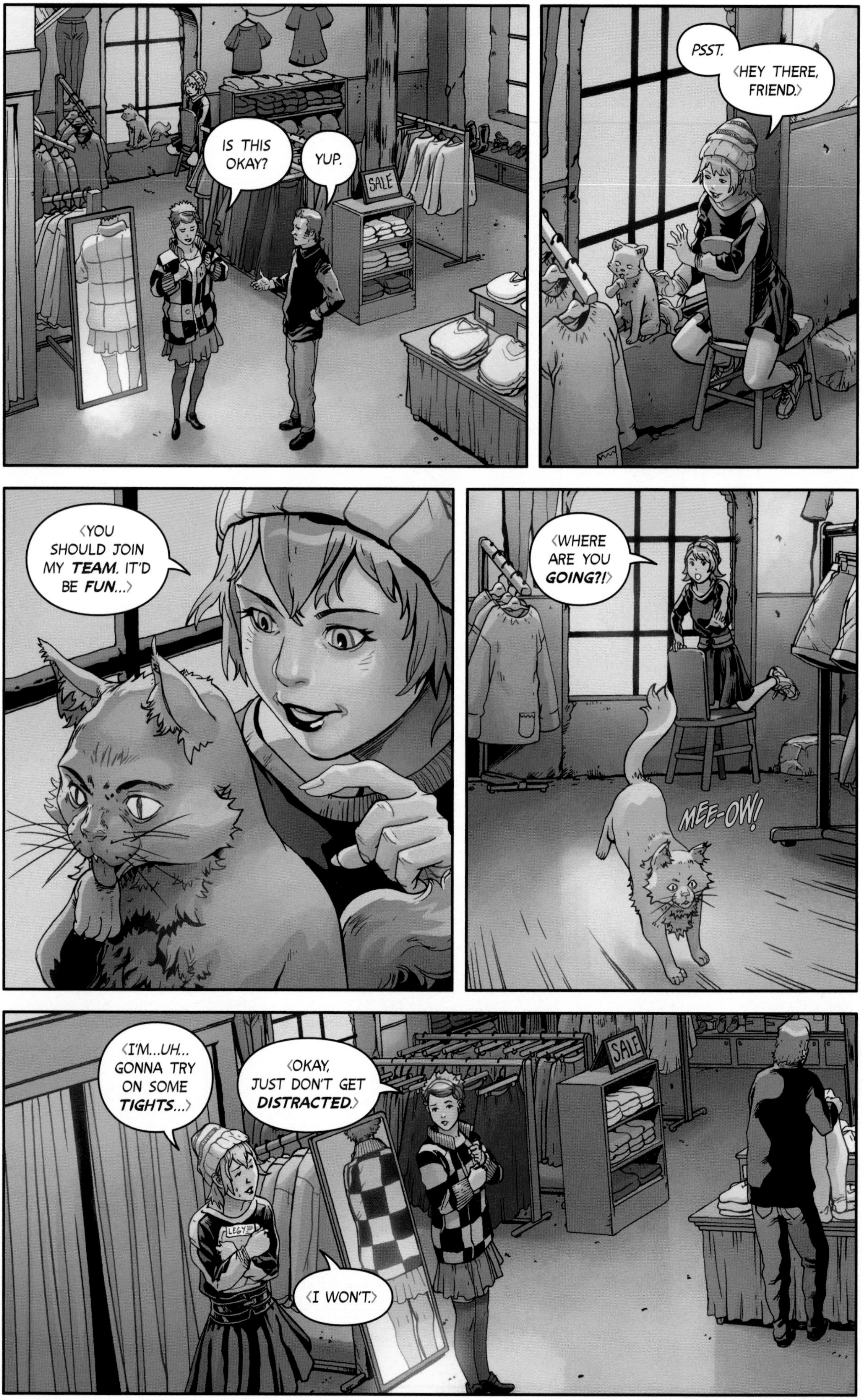
IS THIS OKAY?
YUP.
SALE
PSST.
‹HEY THERE, FRIEND.›
‹YOU SHOULD JOIN MY **TEAM**. IT'D BE **FUN**...›
‹WHERE ARE YOU **GOING?!**›
MEE-OW!
‹I'M...UH... GONNA TRY ON SOME **TIGHTS**...›
‹OKAY, JUST DON'T GET **DISTRACTED**.›
SALE
LEGY
‹I WON'T.›

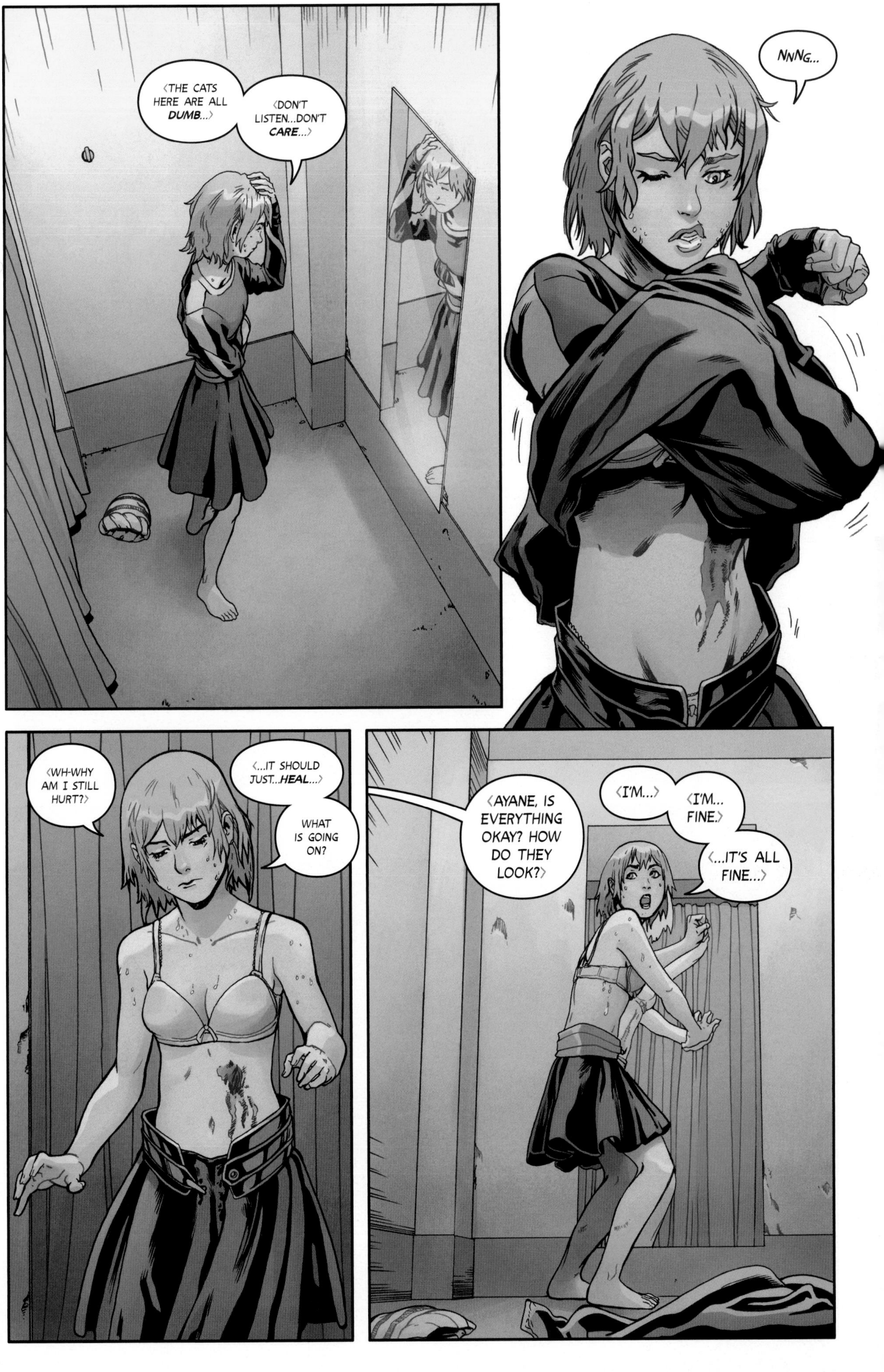

‹THE CATS HERE ARE ALL **DUMB**...›
‹DON'T LISTEN...DON'T **CARE**...›
NNNG...
‹WH-WHY AM I STILL HURT?›
‹...IT SHOULD JUST...**HEAL**...›
WHAT IS GOING ON?
‹AYANE, IS EVERYTHING OKAY? HOW DO THEY LOOK?›
‹I'M...›
‹I'M... FINE.›
‹...IT'S ALL FINE...›

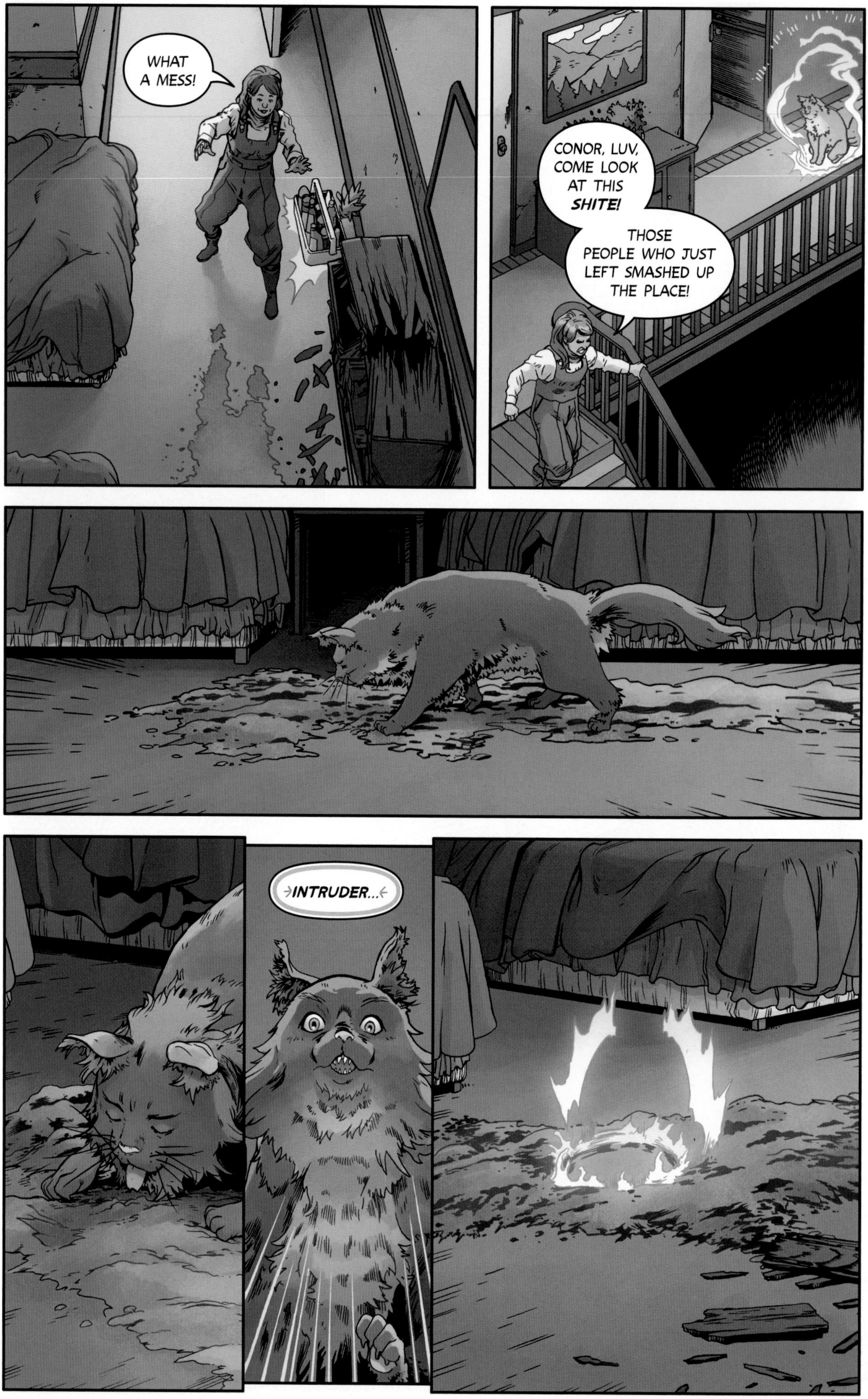
WHAT A MESS!
CONOR, LUV, COME LOOK AT THIS SHITE!
THOSE PEOPLE WHO JUST LEFT SMASHED UP THE PLACE!
INTRUDER...

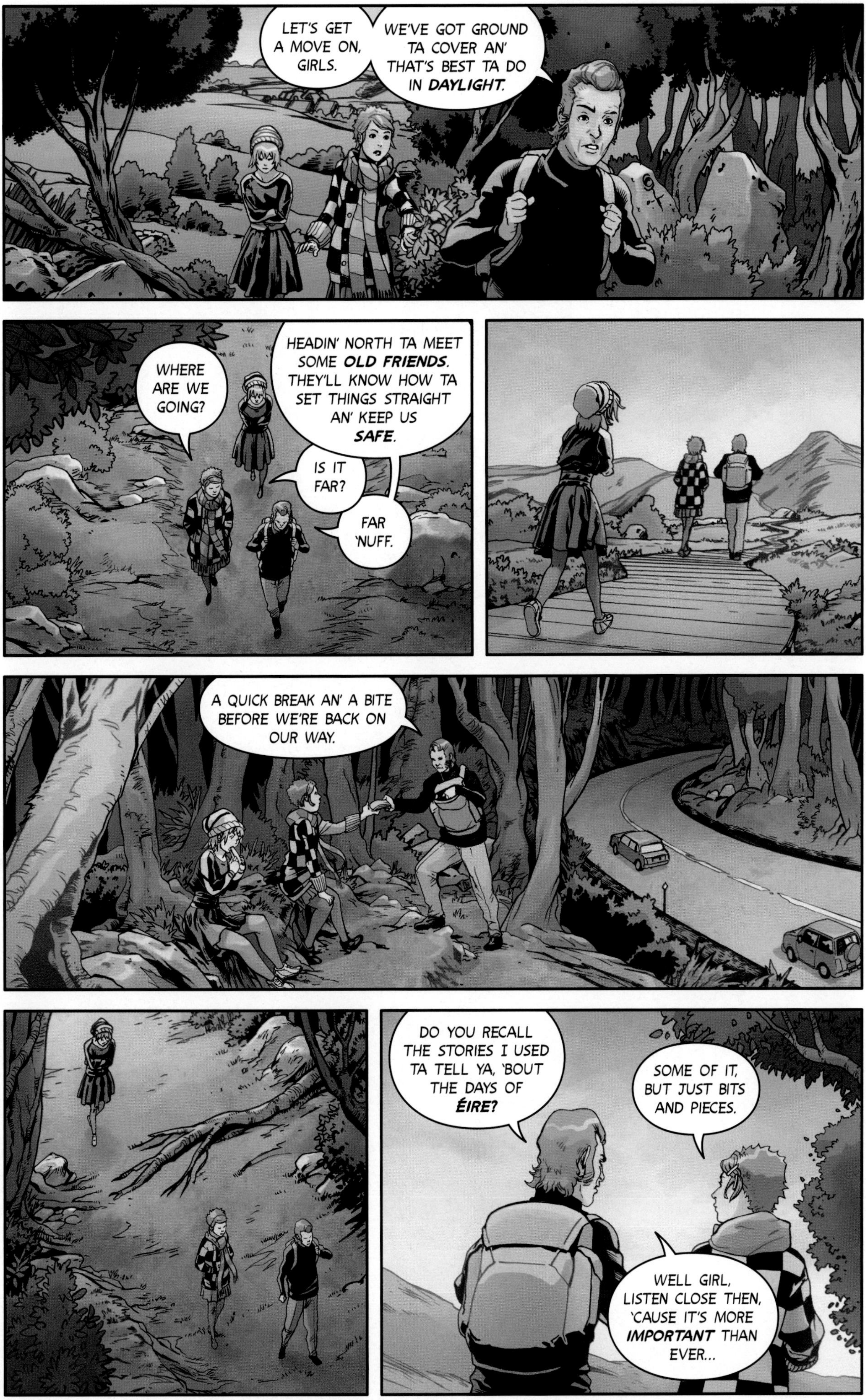
LET'S GET A MOVE ON, GIRLS.
WE'VE GOT GROUND TA COVER AN' THAT'S BEST TA DO IN *DAYLIGHT*.
WHERE ARE WE GOING?
HEADIN' NORTH TA MEET SOME *OLD FRIENDS*. THEY'LL KNOW HOW TA SET THINGS STRAIGHT AN' KEEP US *SAFE*.
IS IT FAR?
FAR 'NUFF.
A QUICK BREAK AN' A BITE BEFORE WE'RE BACK ON OUR WAY.
DO YOU RECALL THE STORIES I USED TA TELL YA, 'BOUT THE DAYS OF *ÉIRE?*
SOME OF IT, BUT JUST BITS AND PIECES.
WELL GIRL, LISTEN CLOSE THEN, 'CAUSE IT'S MORE *IMPORTANT* THAN EVER...

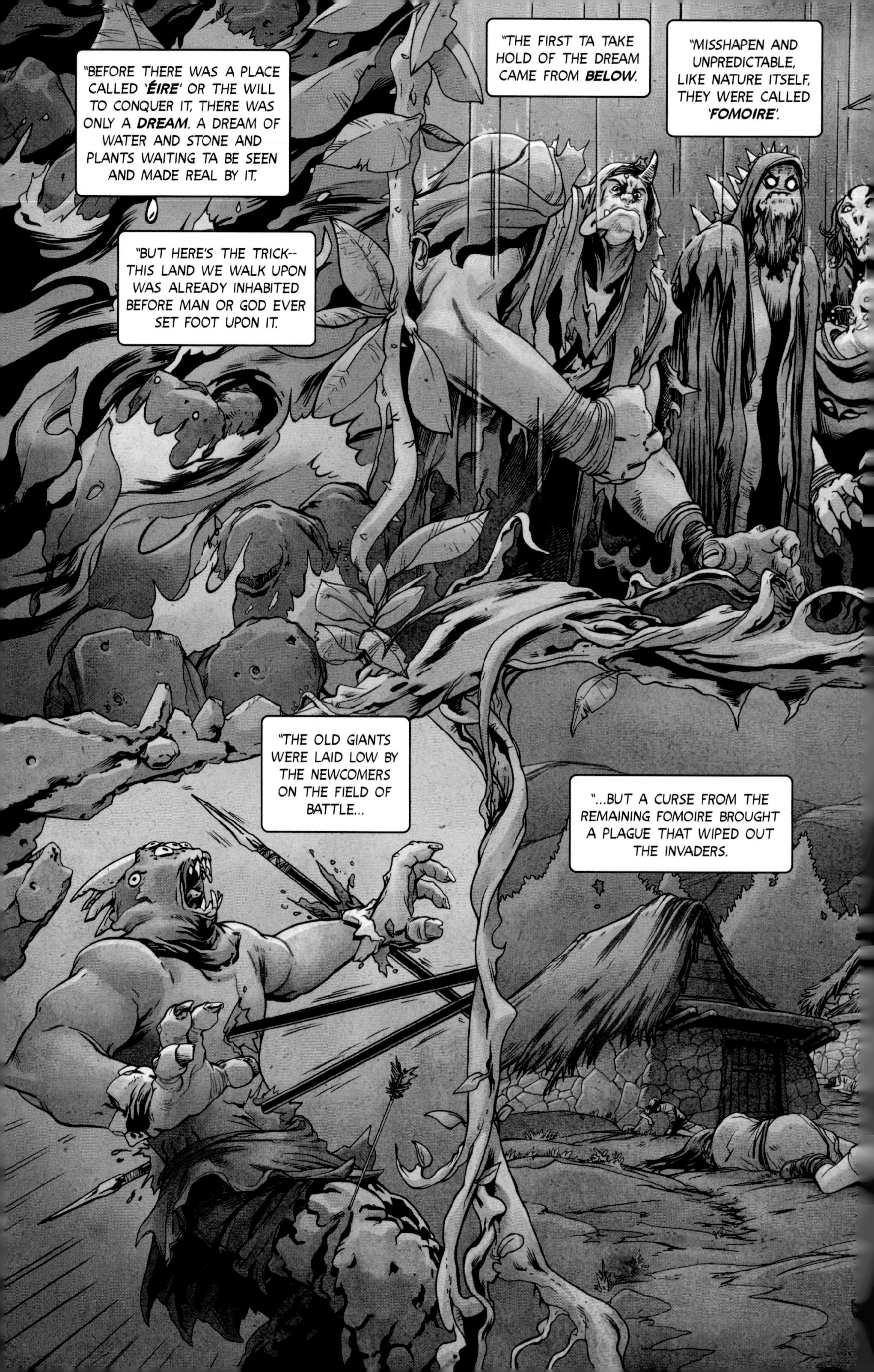
"BEFORE THERE WAS A PLACE CALLED 'ÉIRE' OR THE WILL TO CONQUER IT, THERE WAS ONLY A DREAM. A DREAM OF WATER AND STONE AND PLANTS WAITING TA BE SEEN AND MADE REAL BY IT.
"BUT HERE'S THE TRICK-- THIS LAND WE WALK UPON WAS ALREADY INHABITED BEFORE MAN OR GOD EVER SET FOOT UPON IT.
"THE FIRST TA TAKE HOLD OF THE DREAM CAME FROM BELOW.
"MISSHAPEN AND UNPREDICTABLE, LIKE NATURE ITSELF, THEY WERE CALLED 'FOMOIRE'.
"THE OLD GIANTS WERE LAID LOW BY THE NEWCOMERS ON THE FIELD OF BATTLE...
"...BUT A CURSE FROM THE REMAINING FOMOIRE BROUGHT A PLAGUE THAT WIPED OUT THE INVADERS.

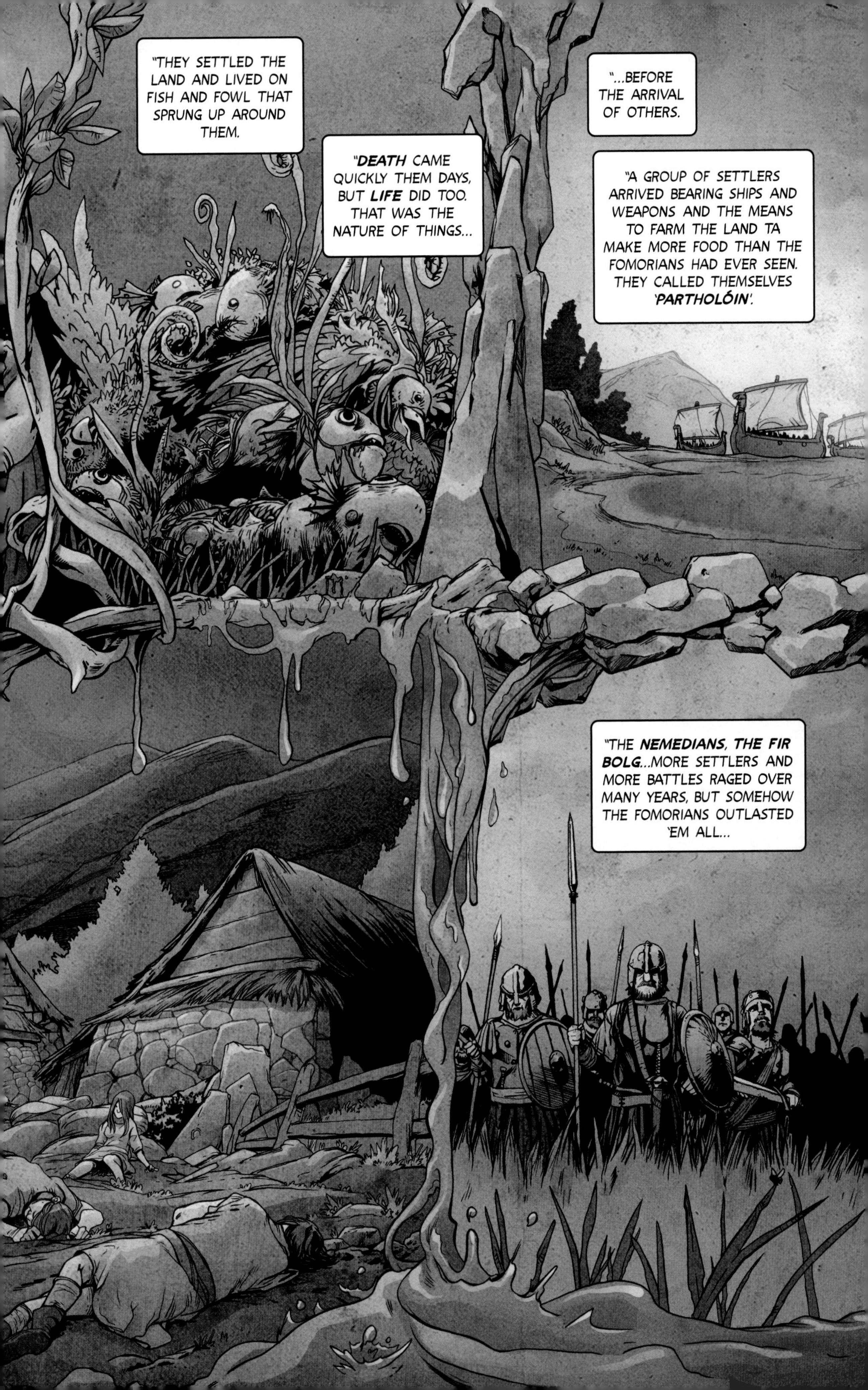
"THEY SETTLED THE LAND AND LIVED ON FISH AND FOWL THAT SPRUNG UP AROUND THEM.
"DEATH CAME QUICKLY THEM DAYS, BUT LIFE DID TOO. THAT WAS THE NATURE OF THINGS...
"...BEFORE THE ARRIVAL OF OTHERS.
"A GROUP OF SETTLERS ARRIVED BEARING SHIPS AND WEAPONS AND THE MEANS TO FARM THE LAND TA MAKE MORE FOOD THAN THE FOMORIANS HAD EVER SEEN. THEY CALLED THEMSELVES 'PARTHOLÓIN'.
"THE NEMEDIANS, THE FIR BOLG...MORE SETTLERS AND MORE BATTLES RAGED OVER MANY YEARS, BUT SOMEHOW THE FOMORIANS OUTLASTED 'EM ALL...

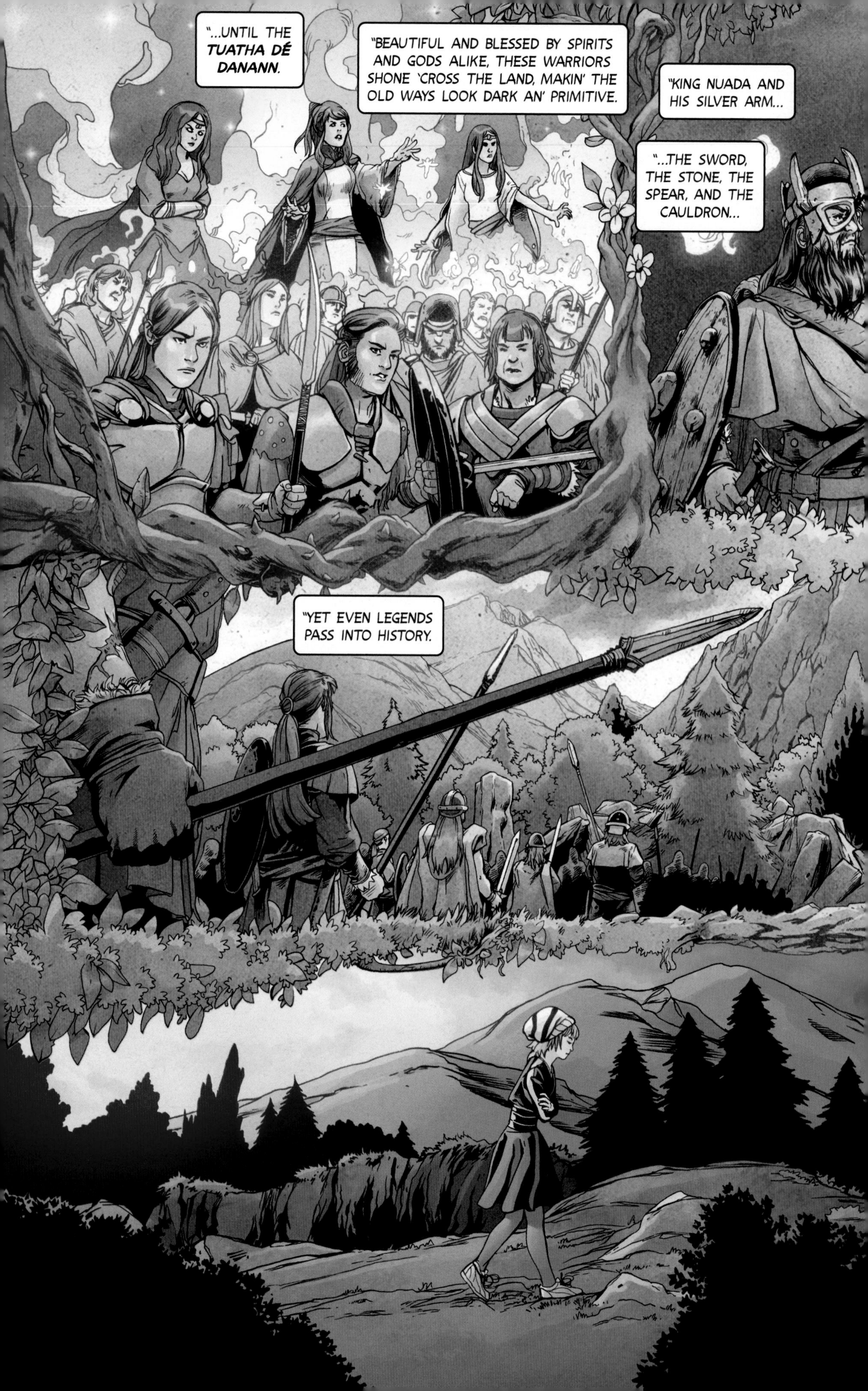
"...UNTIL THE *TUATHA DÉ DANANN.*
"BEAUTIFUL AND BLESSED BY SPIRITS AND GODS ALIKE, THESE WARRIORS SHONE 'CROSS THE LAND, MAKIN' THE OLD WAYS LOOK DARK AN' PRIMITIVE.
"KING NUADA AND HIS SILVER ARM...
"...THE SWORD, THE STONE, THE SPEAR, AND THE CAULDRON...
"YET EVEN LEGENDS PASS INTO HISTORY.

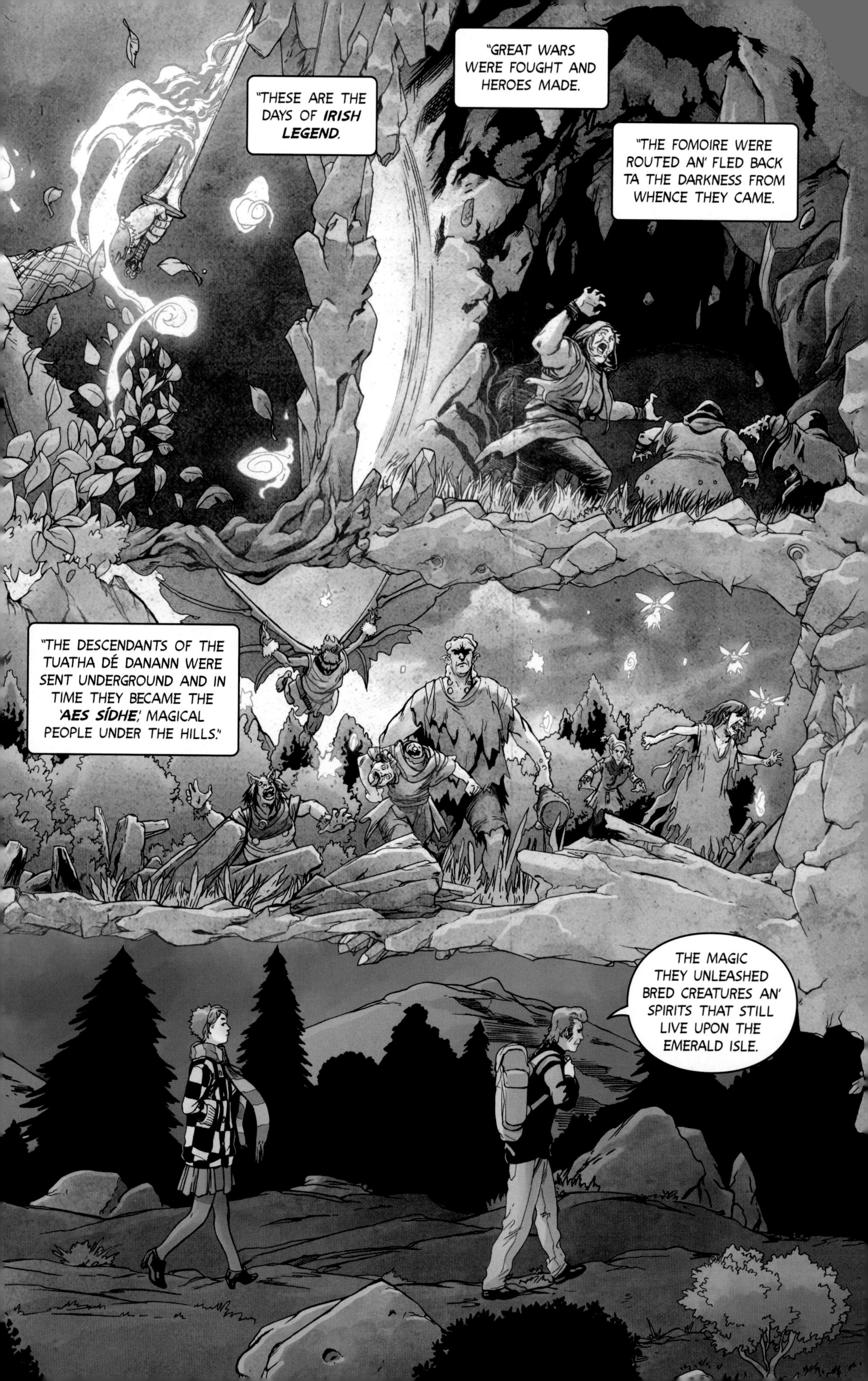
"THESE ARE THE DAYS OF IRISH LEGEND.
"GREAT WARS WERE FOUGHT AND HEROES MADE.
"THE FOMOIRE WERE ROUTED AN' FLED BACK TA THE DARKNESS FROM WHENCE THEY CAME.
"THE DESCENDANTS OF THE TUATHA DÉ DANANN WERE SENT UNDERGROUND AND IN TIME THEY BECAME THE 'AES SÍDHE,' MAGICAL PEOPLE UNDER THE HILLS."
THE MAGIC THEY UNLEASHED BRED CREATURES AN' SPIRITS THAT STILL LIVE UPON THE EMERALD ISLE.

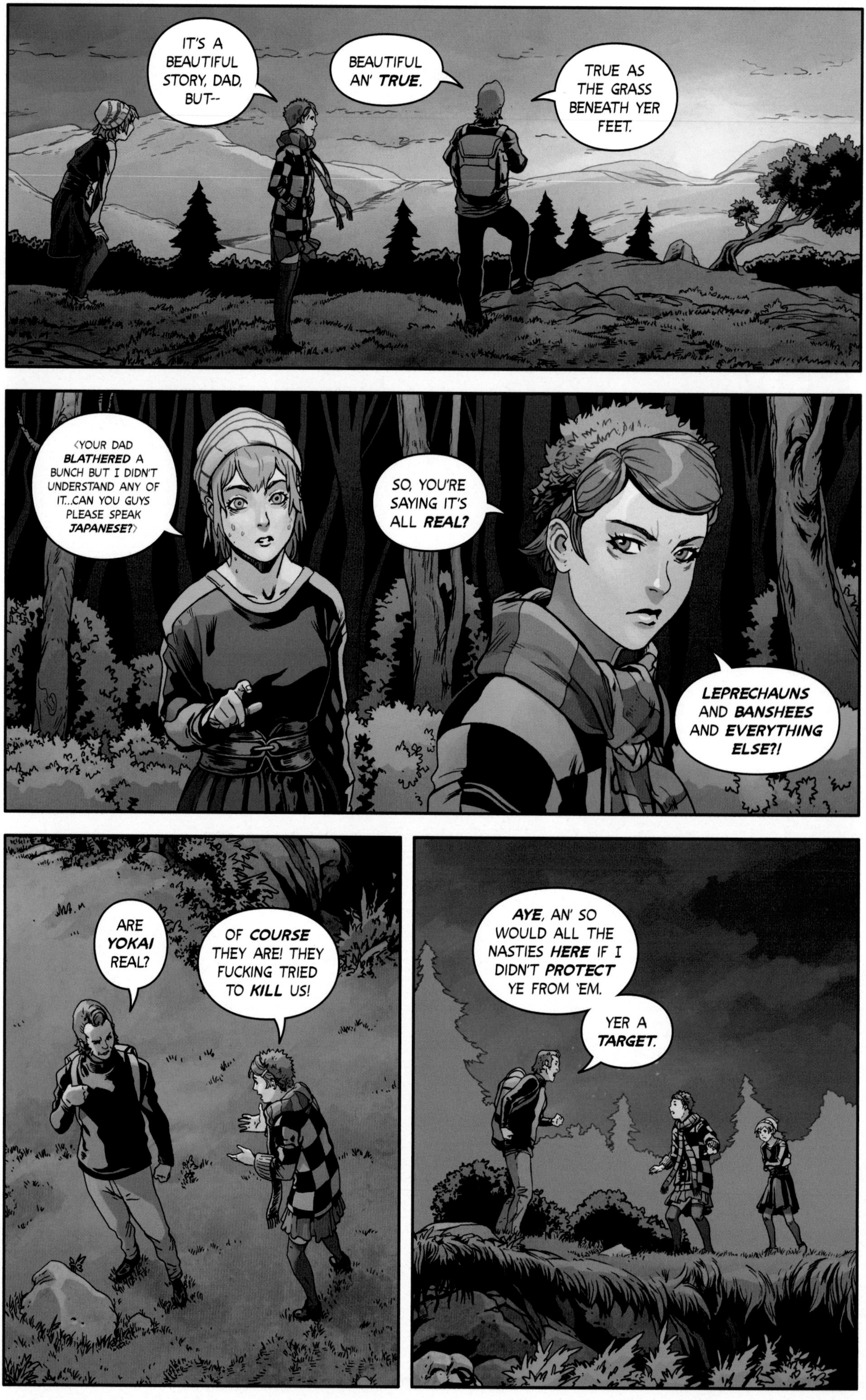
IT'S A BEAUTIFUL STORY, DAD, BUT--
BEAUTIFUL AN' TRUE.
TRUE AS THE GRASS BENEATH YER FEET.
<YOUR DAD BLATHERED A BUNCH BUT I DIDN'T UNDERSTAND ANY OF IT...CAN YOU GUYS PLEASE SPEAK JAPANESE?>
SO, YOU'RE SAYING IT'S ALL REAL?
LEPRECHAUNS AND BANSHEES AND EVERYTHING ELSE?!
ARE YOKAI REAL?
OF COURSE THEY ARE! THEY FUCKING TRIED TO KILL US!
AYE, AN' SO WOULD ALL THE NASTIES HERE IF I DIDN'T PROTECT YE FROM 'EM.
YER A TARGET.

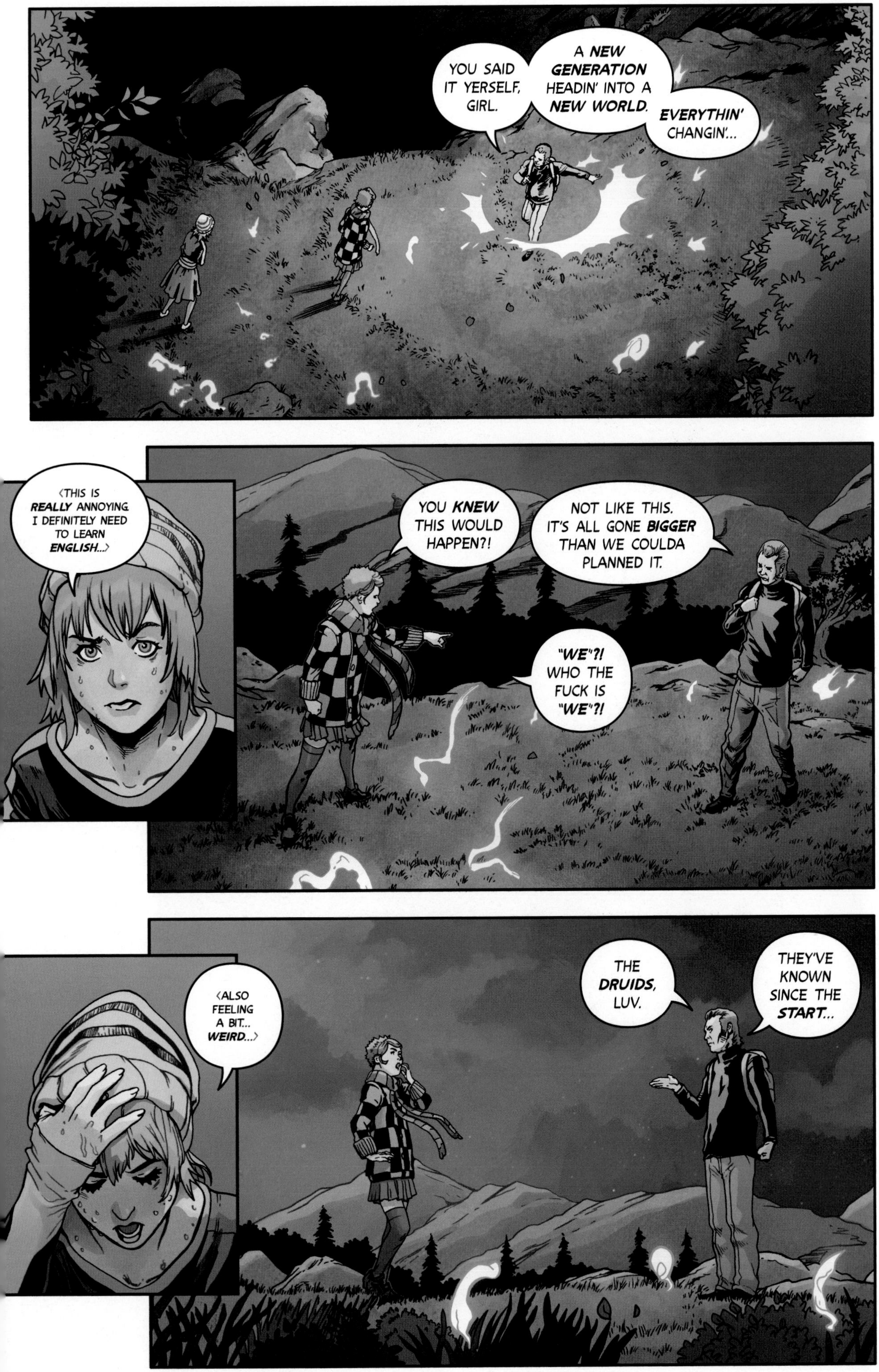
YOU SAID IT YERSELF, GIRL.
A NEW GENERATION HEADIN' INTO A NEW WORLD.
EVERYTHIN' CHANGIN'...
‹THIS IS REALLY ANNOYING. I DEFINITELY NEED TO LEARN ENGLISH...›
YOU KNEW THIS WOULD HAPPEN?!
NOT LIKE THIS. IT'S ALL GONE BIGGER THAN WE COULDA PLANNED IT.
"WE"?! WHO THE FUCK IS "WE"?!
‹ALSO FEELING A BIT... WEIRD...›
THE DRUIDS, LUV.
THEY'VE KNOWN SINCE THE START...

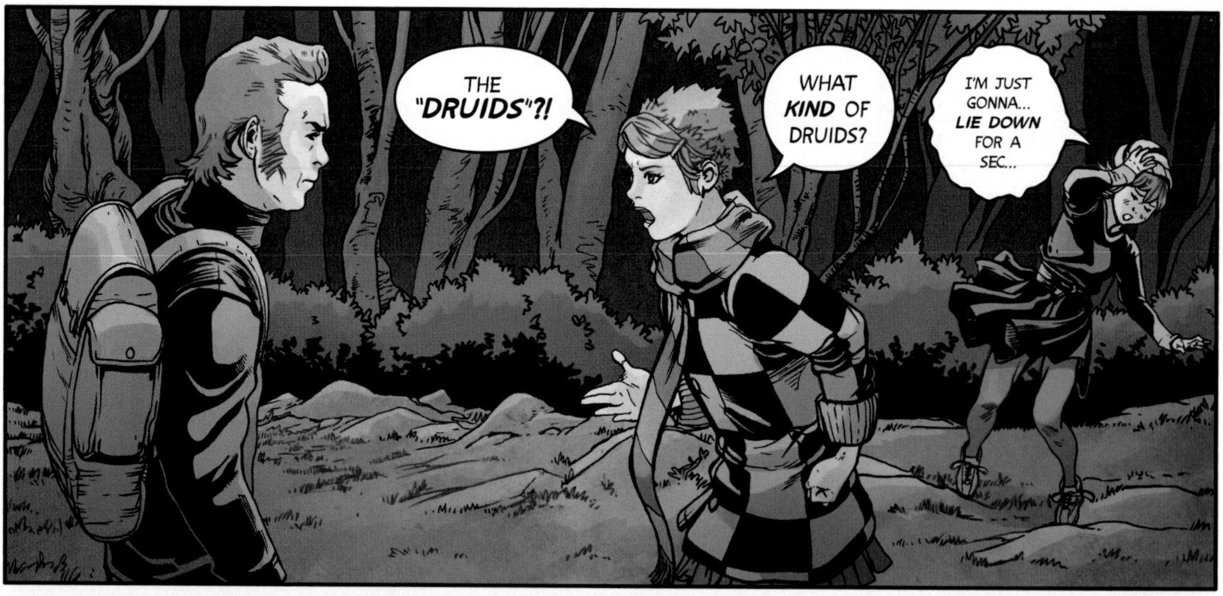
THE "DRUIDS"?!
WHAT KIND OF DRUIDS?
I'M JUST GONNA... LIE DOWN FOR A SEC...

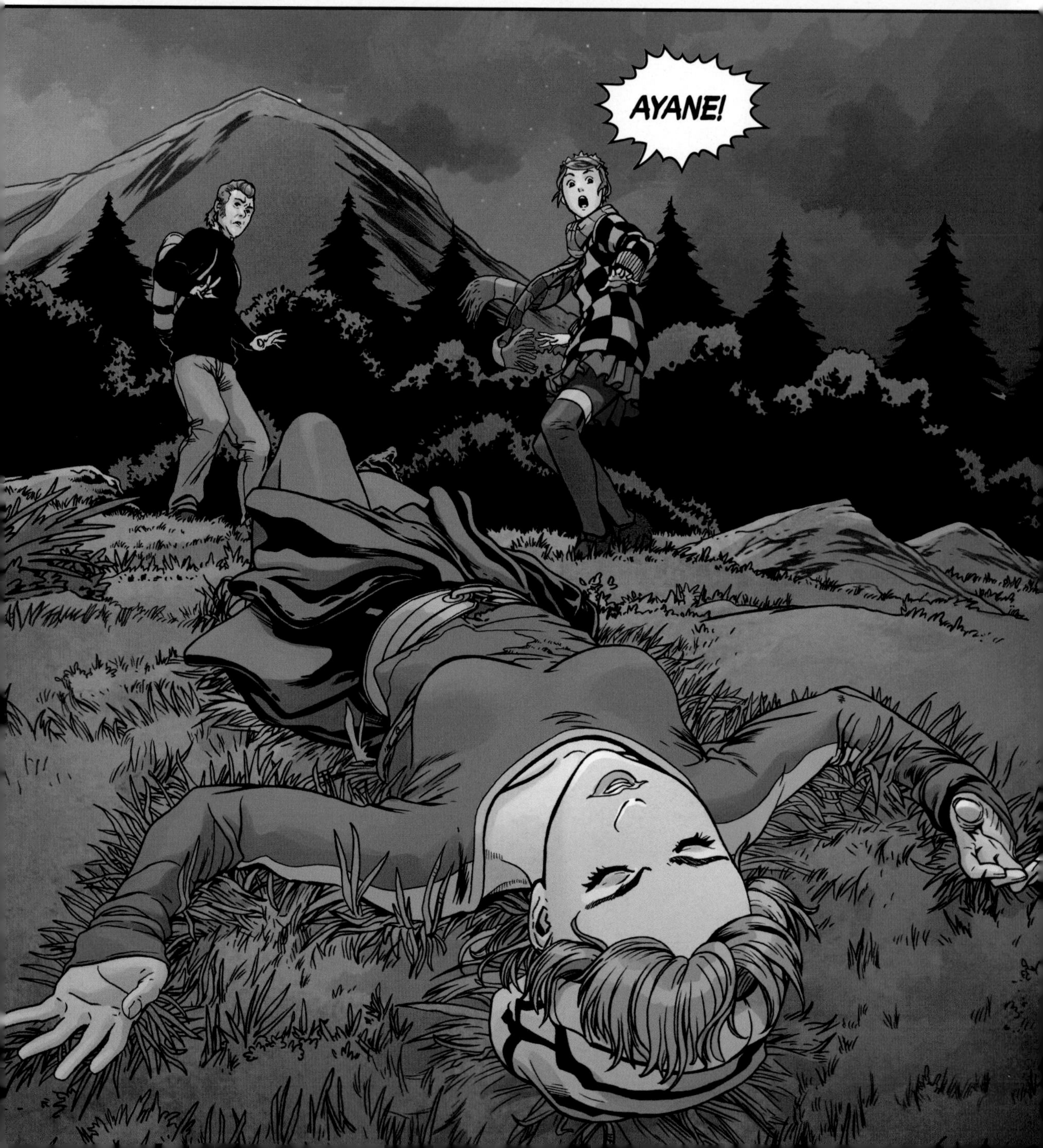
AYANE!

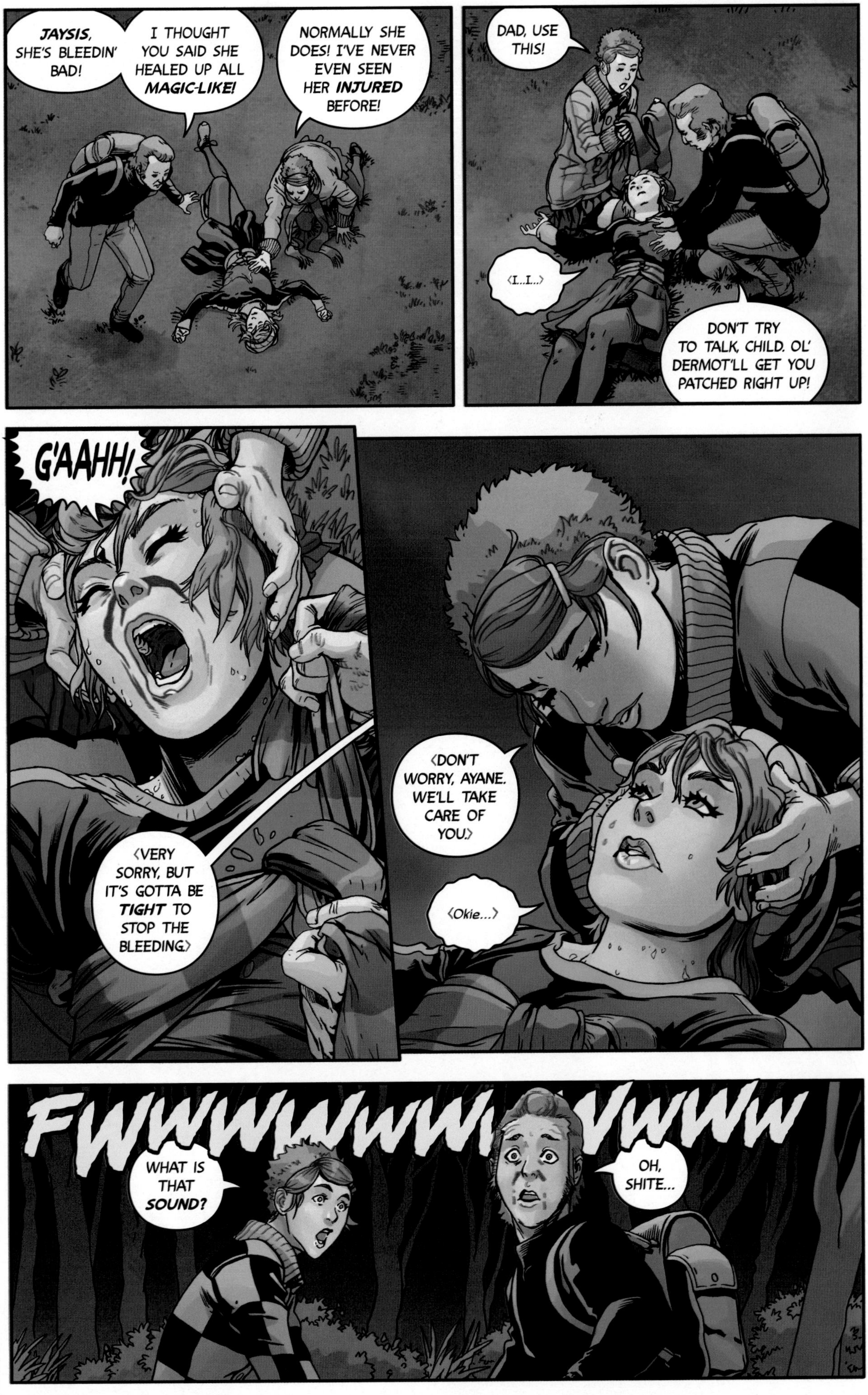

JAYSIS, SHE'S BLEEDIN' BAD!
I THOUGHT YOU SAID SHE HEALED UP ALL MAGIC-LIKE!
NORMALLY SHE DOES! I'VE NEVER EVEN SEEN HER INJURED BEFORE!
DAD, USE THIS!
‹I...I...›
DON'T TRY TO TALK, CHILD. OL' DERMOT'LL GET YOU PATCHED RIGHT UP!
G'AAHH!
‹VERY SORRY, BUT IT'S GOTTA BE TIGHT TO STOP THE BLEEDING.›
‹DON'T WORRY, AYANE. WE'LL TAKE CARE OF YOU.›
‹Okie...›
FWWWWWWWWWWWW
WHAT IS THAT SOUND?
OH, SHITE...

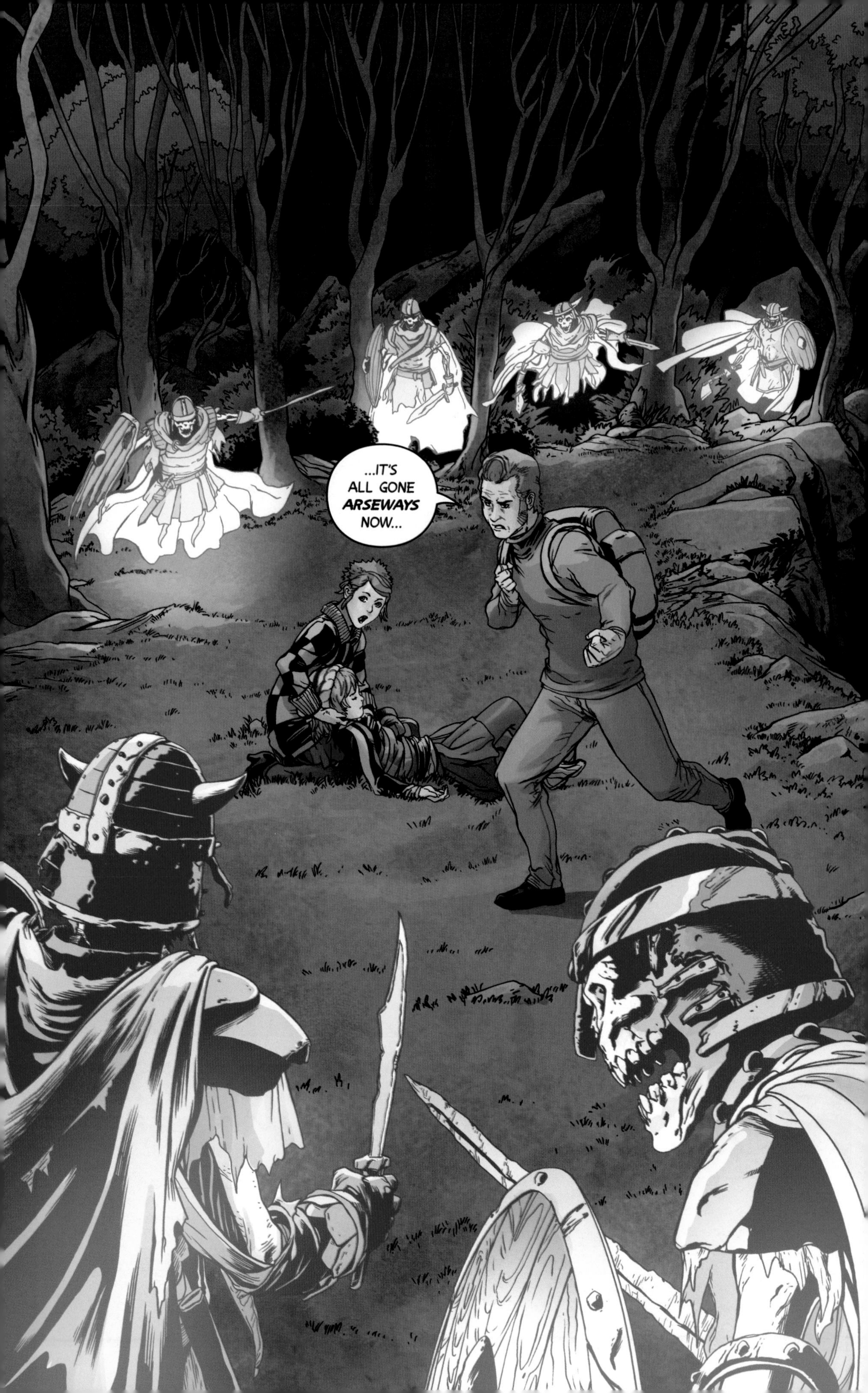
...IT'S ALL GONE ARSEWAYS NOW...

Chapter Nineteen

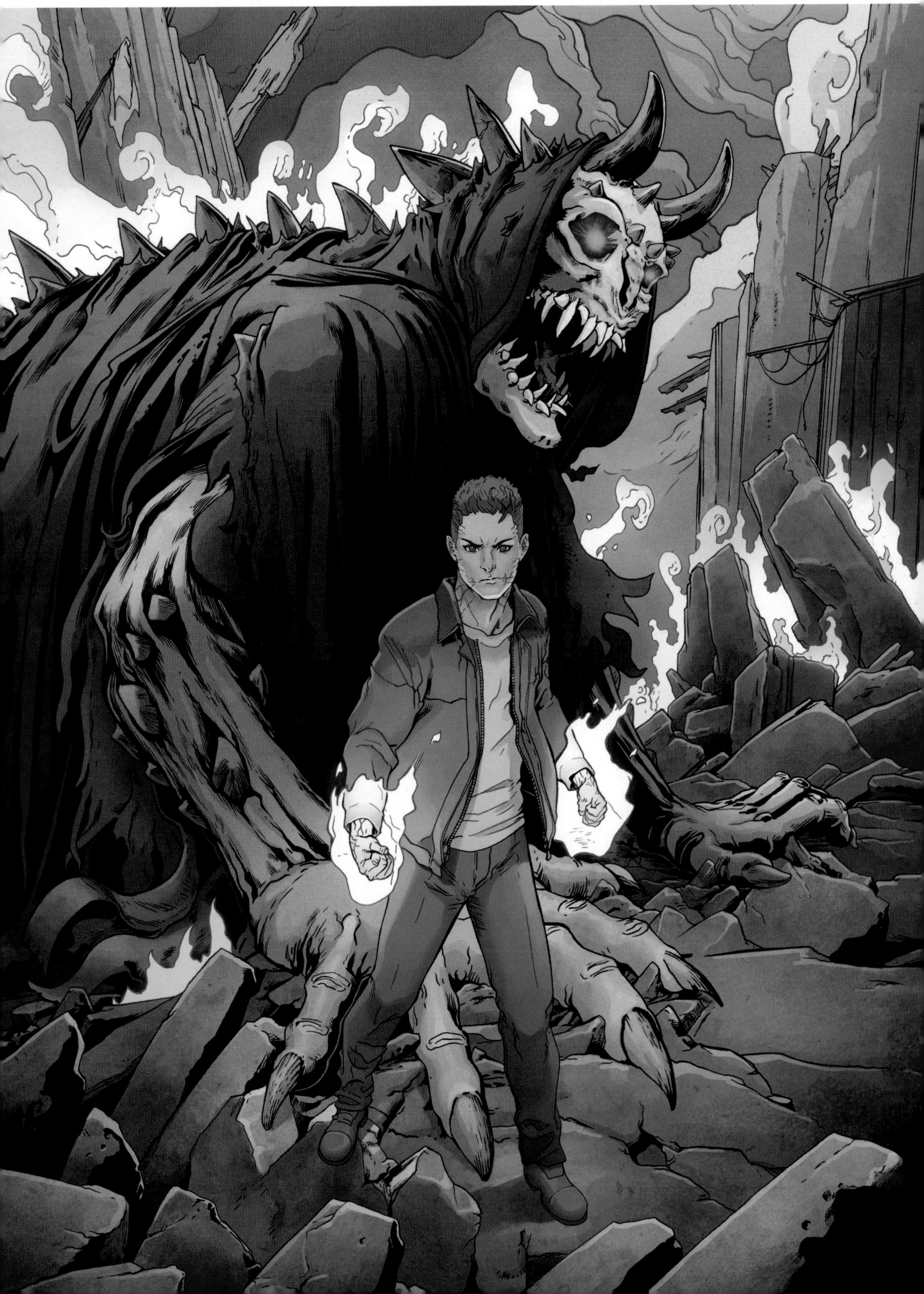

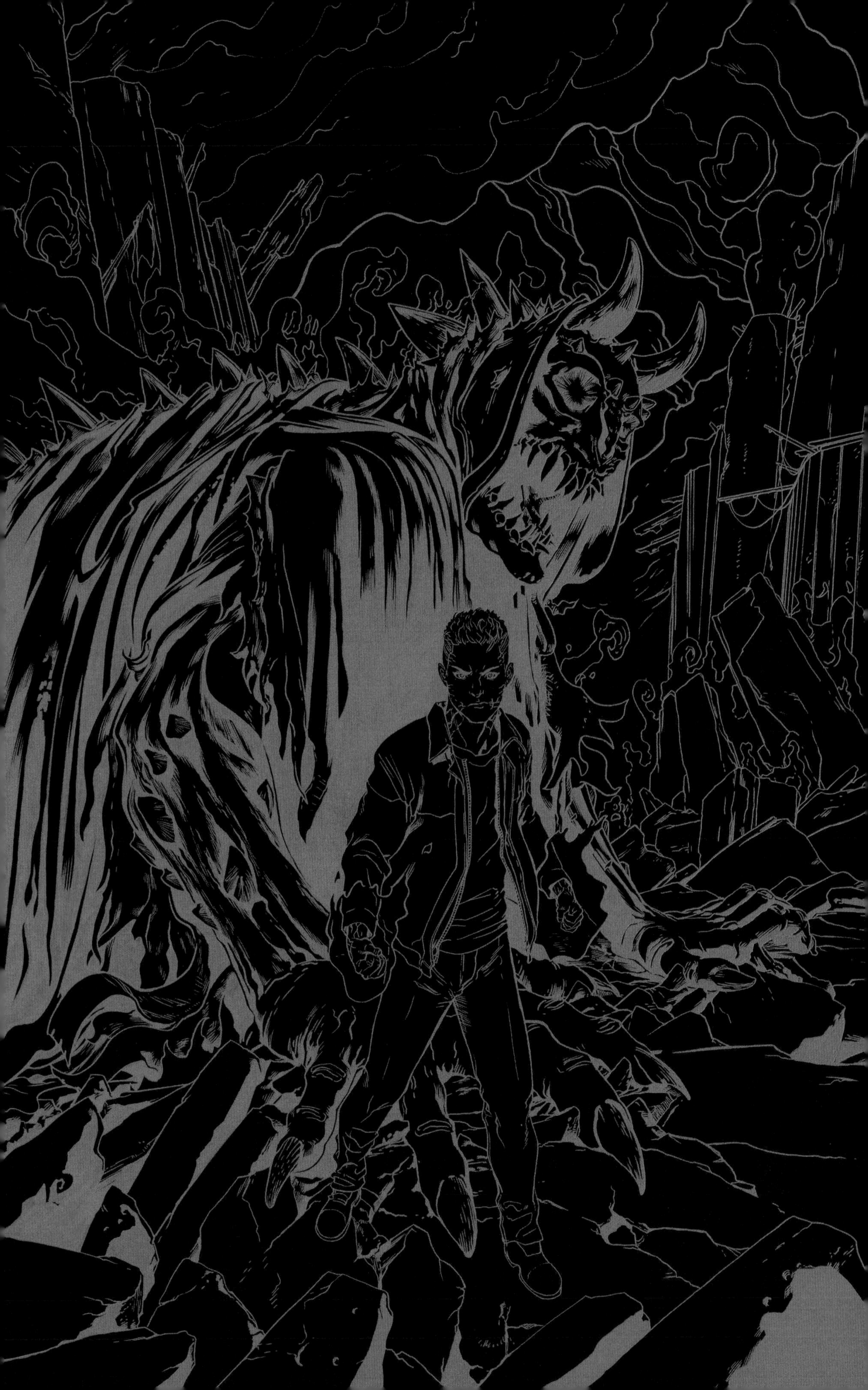

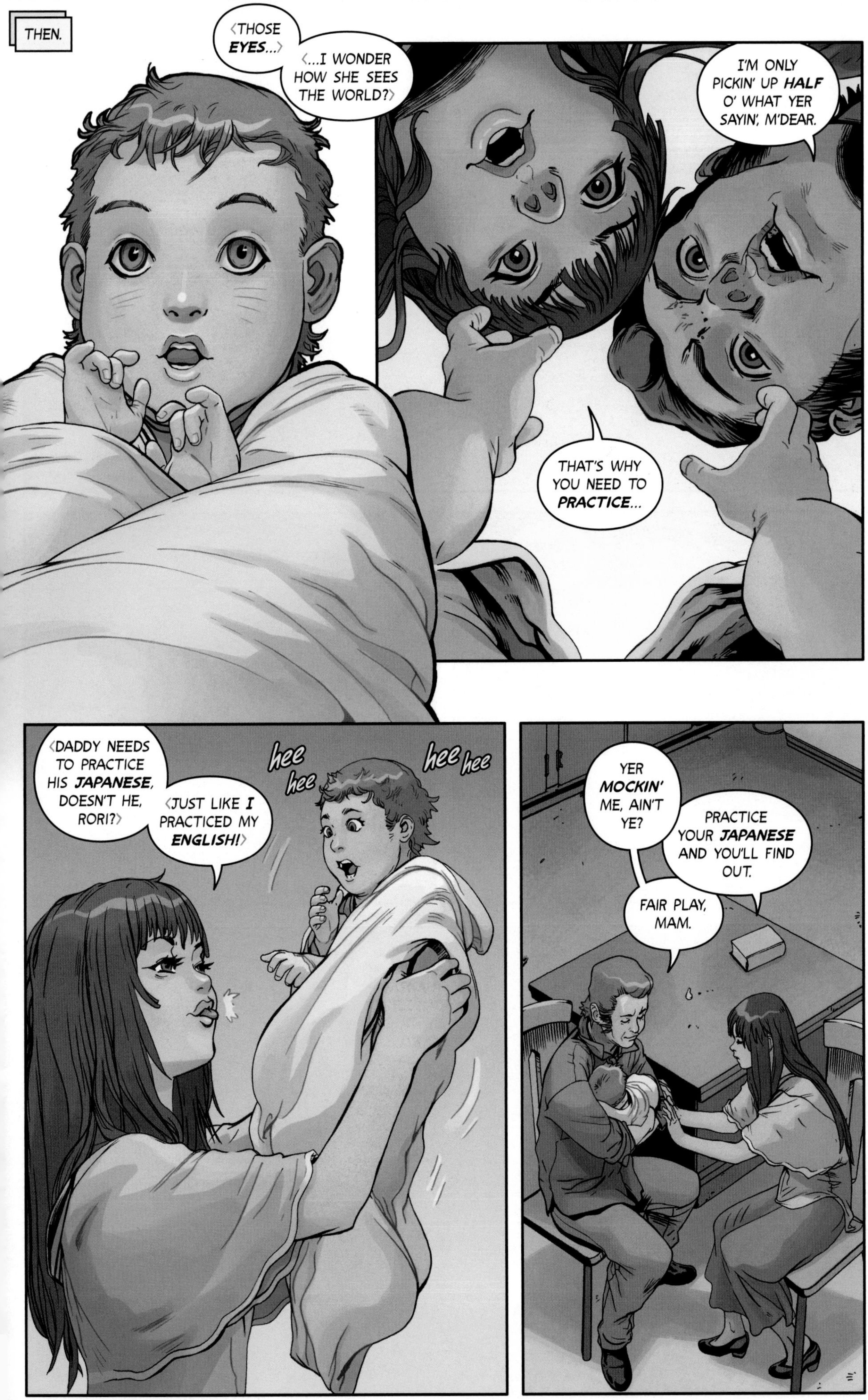
THEN.
⟨THOSE EYES...⟩
⟨...I WONDER HOW SHE SEES THE WORLD?⟩
I'M ONLY PICKIN' UP HALF O' WHAT YER SAYIN', M'DEAR.
THAT'S WHY YOU NEED TO PRACTICE...
⟨DADDY NEEDS TO PRACTICE HIS JAPANESE, DOESN'T HE, RORI?⟩
⟨JUST LIKE I PRACTICED MY ENGLISH!⟩
hee hee
hee hee
YER MOCKIN' ME, AIN'T YE?
PRACTICE YOUR JAPANESE AND YOU'LL FIND OUT.
FAIR PLAY, MAM.

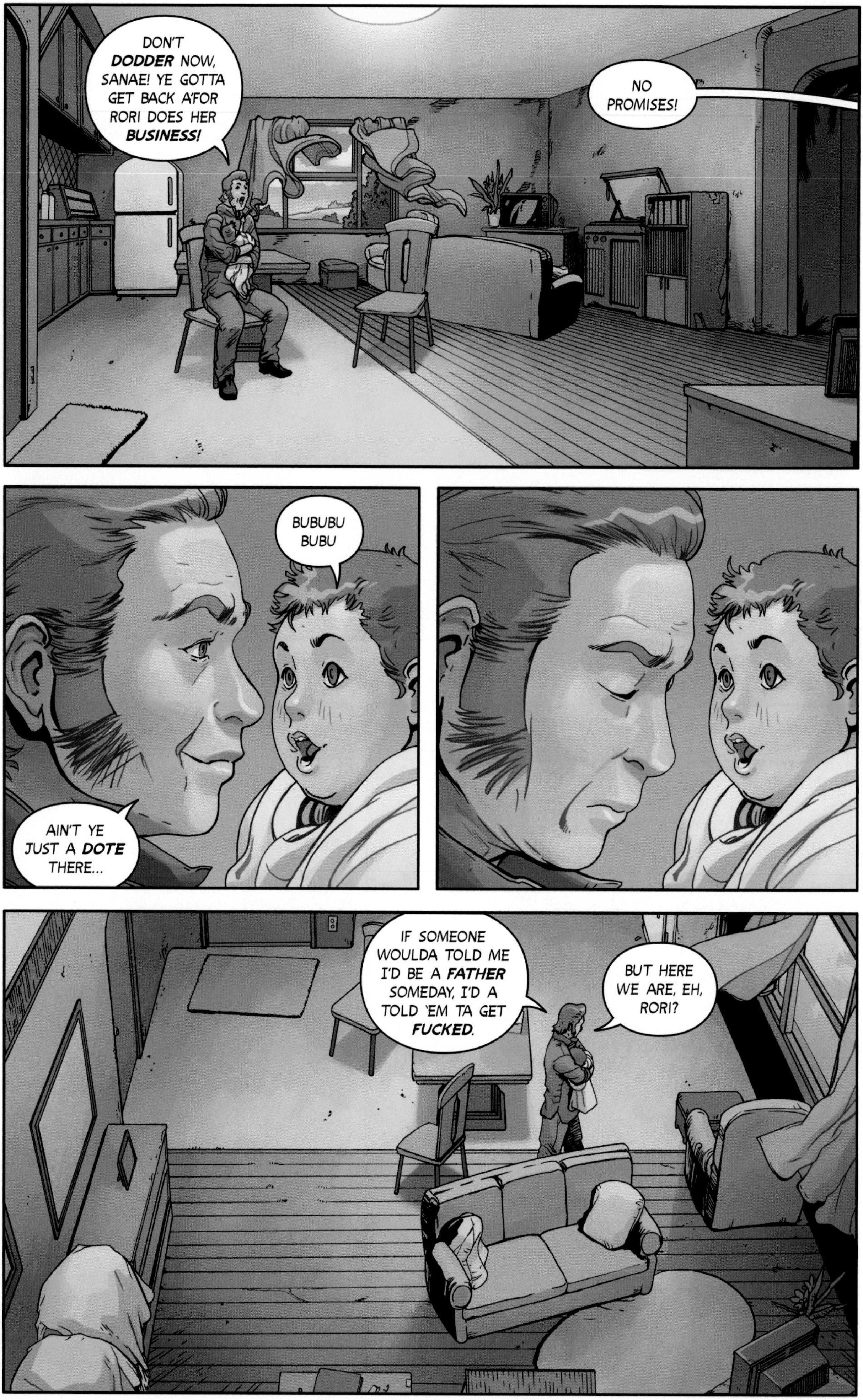

DON'T DODDER NOW, SANAE! YE GOTTA GET BACK A'FOR RORI DOES HER BUSINESS!
NO PROMISES!
BUBUBU BUBU
AIN'T YE JUST A DOTE THERE...
IF SOMEONE WOULDA TOLD ME I'D BE A FATHER SOMEDAY, I'D A TOLD 'EM TA GET FUCKED.
BUT HERE WE ARE, EH, RORI?

Y'HAVE NO IDEA HOW *PRECIOUS* Y'ARE.

INSIDE YE IS A *SPECIAL SEED,* AN' WHEN IT BLOOMS, GIRL, *EVERYTHIN'S* GONNA *CHANGE.*

FWIK

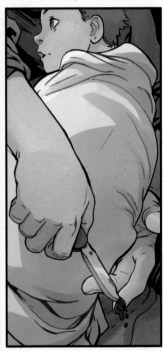

Oooo...

THAT'S WHY I'VE GOTTA MAKE SURE I KEEP YE *SAFE...*

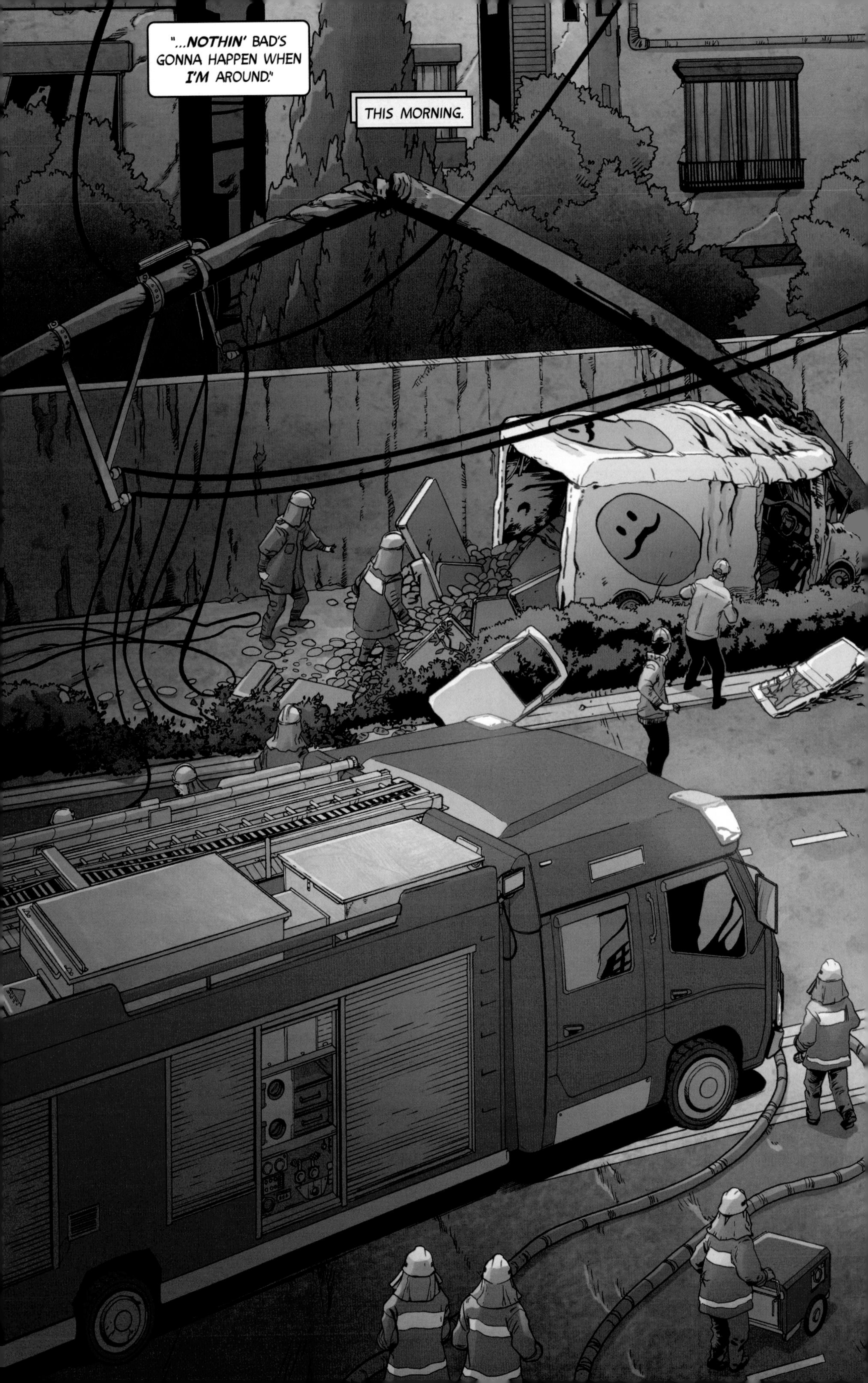
"...NOTHIN' BAD'S GONNA HAPPEN WHEN I'M AROUND."
THIS MORNING.

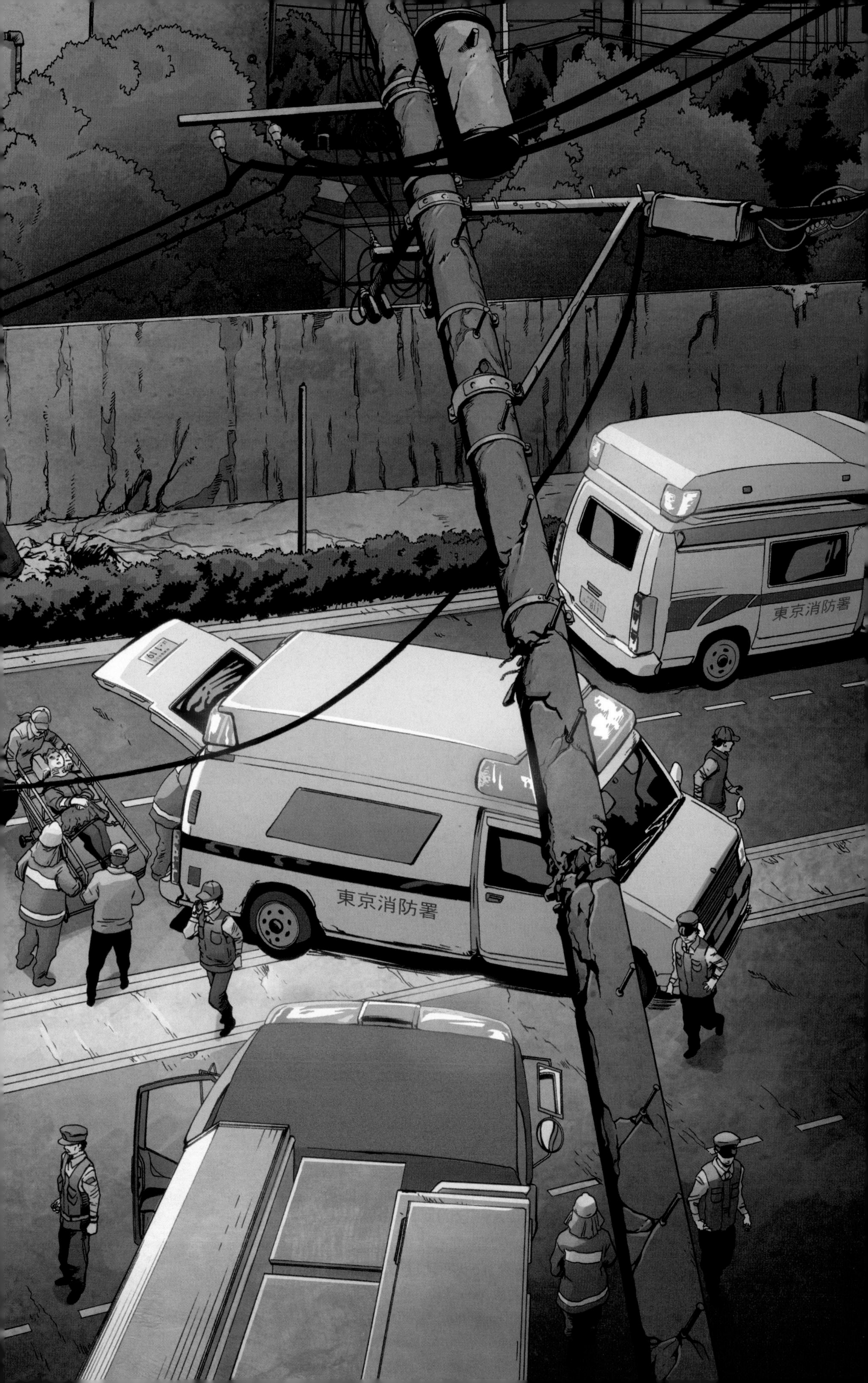
東京消防署
東京消防署

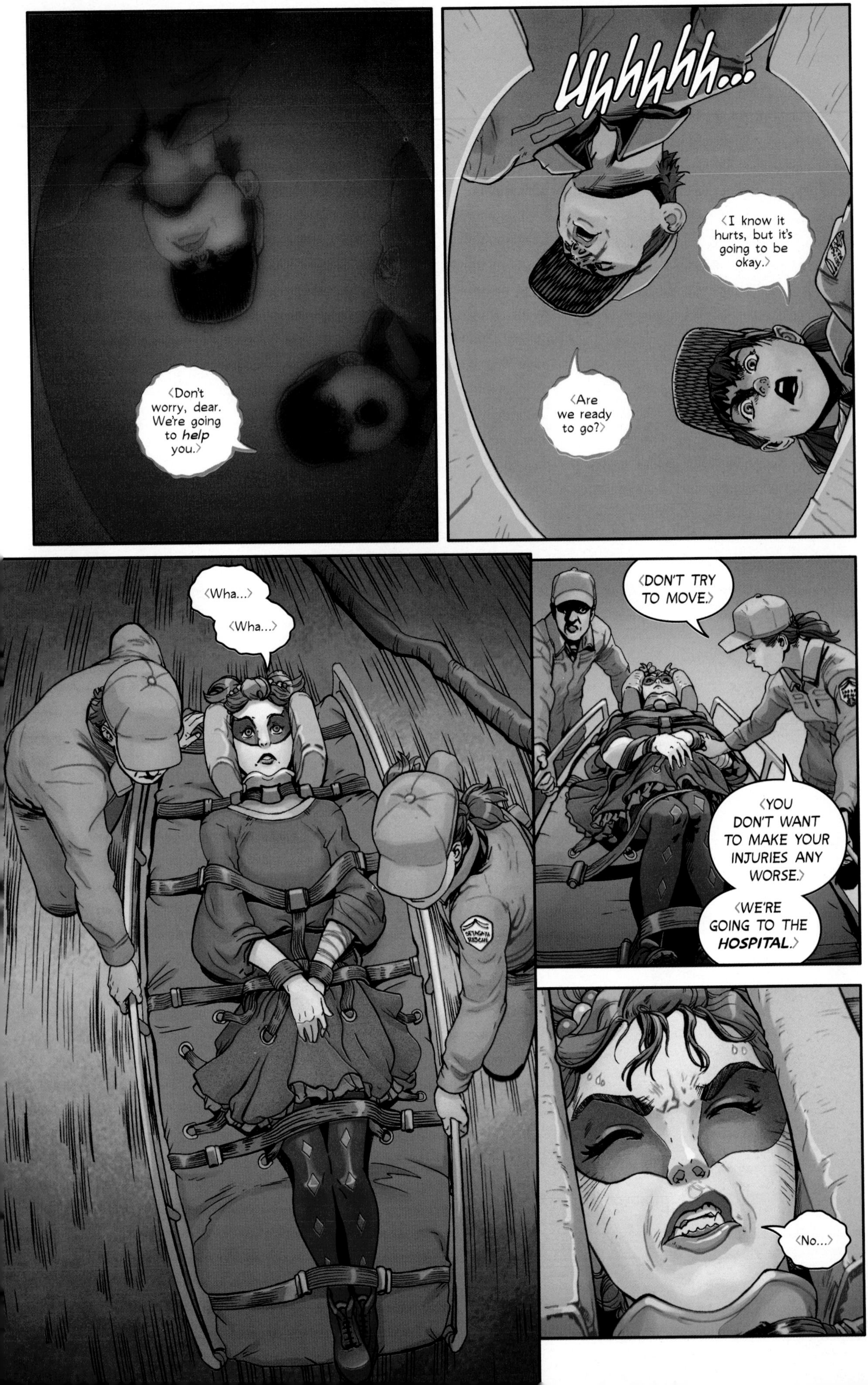

〈Don't worry, dear. We're going to *help* you.〉
Uhhhhh...
〈I know it hurts, but it's going to be okay.〉
〈Are we ready to go?〉
〈Wha...〉
〈Wha...〉
〈DON'T TRY TO MOVE.〉
〈YOU DON'T WANT TO MAKE YOUR INJURIES ANY WORSE.〉
〈WE'RE GOING TO THE *HOSPITAL*.〉
〈No...〉

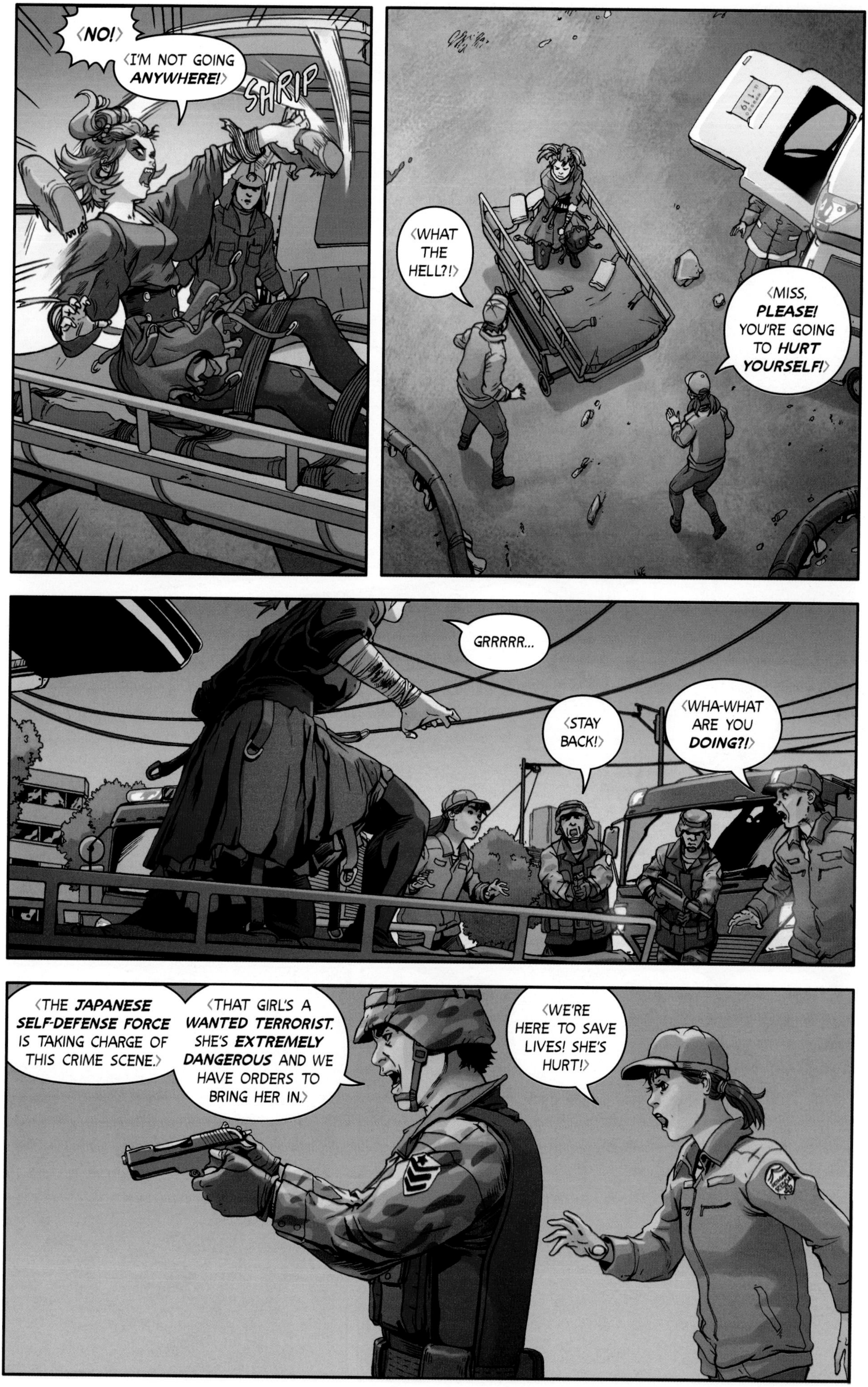

‹NO!›
‹I'M NOT GOING ANYWHERE!›
SHRIP
‹WHAT THE HELL?!›
‹MISS, PLEASE! YOU'RE GOING TO HURT YOURSELF!›
GRRRRR...
‹STAY BACK!›
‹WHA-WHAT ARE YOU DOING?!›
‹THE JAPANESE SELF-DEFENSE FORCE IS TAKING CHARGE OF THIS CRIME SCENE.›
‹THAT GIRL'S A WANTED TERRORIST. SHE'S EXTREMELY DANGEROUS AND WE HAVE ORDERS TO BRING HER IN.›
‹WE'RE HERE TO SAVE LIVES! SHE'S HURT!›

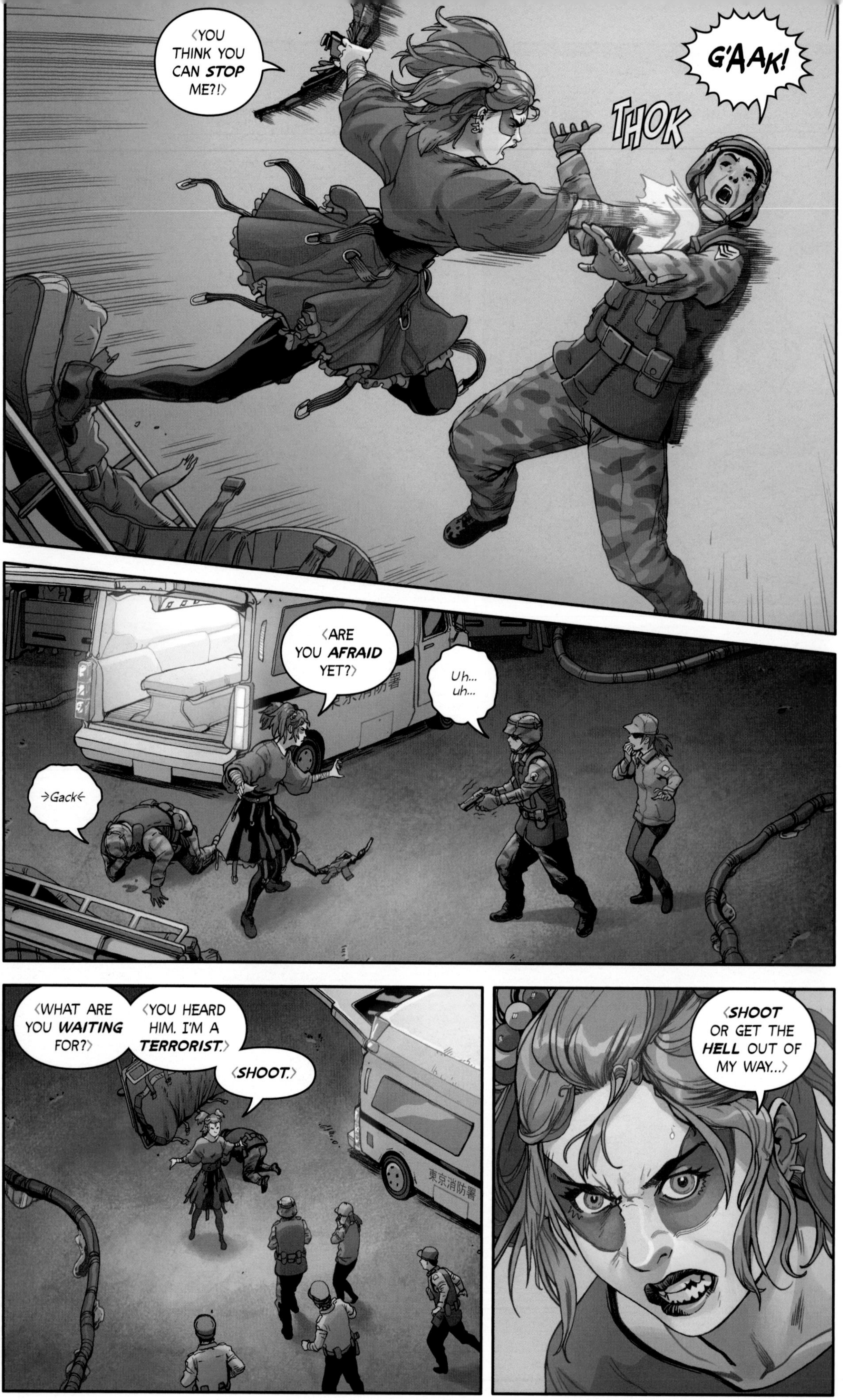

‹YOU THINK YOU CAN STOP ME?!›
THOK
G'AAK!
‹ARE YOU AFRAID YET?›
Uh... uh...
→Gack←
東京消防署
‹WHAT ARE YOU WAITING FOR?›
‹YOU HEARD HIM. I'M A TERRORIST.›
‹SHOOT.›
東京消防署
‹SHOOT OR GET THE HELL OUT OF MY WAY...›

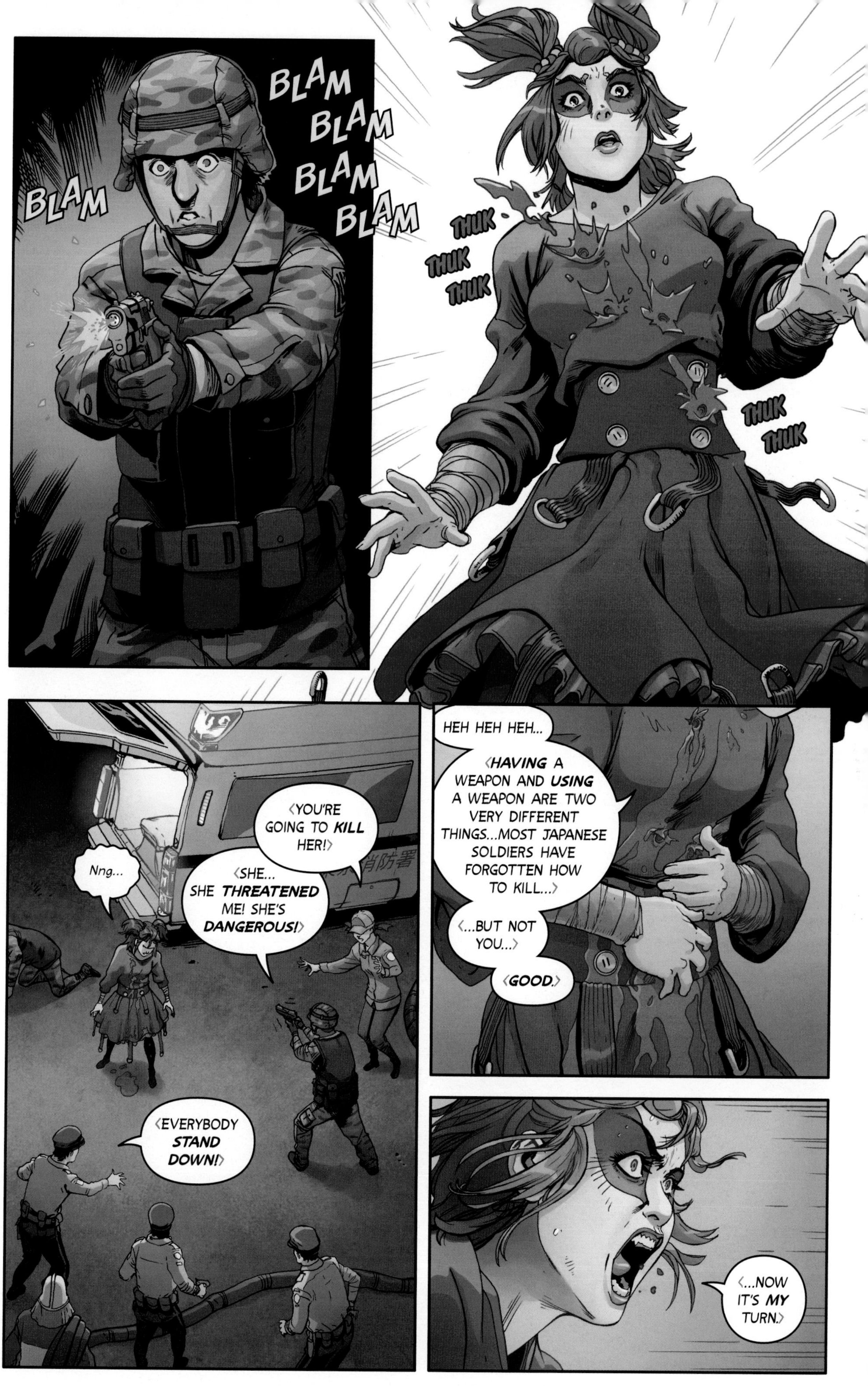
BLAM
BLAM
BLAM
BLAM
BLAM
THUK
THUK
THUK
THUK
THUK
Nng...
‹YOU'RE GOING TO **KILL** HER!›
‹SHE... SHE **THREATENED** ME! SHE'S **DANGEROUS!**›
‹EVERYBODY **STAND DOWN!**›
HEH HEH HEH...
‹**HAVING** A WEAPON AND **USING** A WEAPON ARE TWO VERY DIFFERENT THINGS...MOST JAPANESE SOLDIERS HAVE FORGOTTEN HOW TO KILL...›
‹...BUT NOT YOU...›
‹**GOOD.**›
‹...NOW IT'S **MY** TURN.›

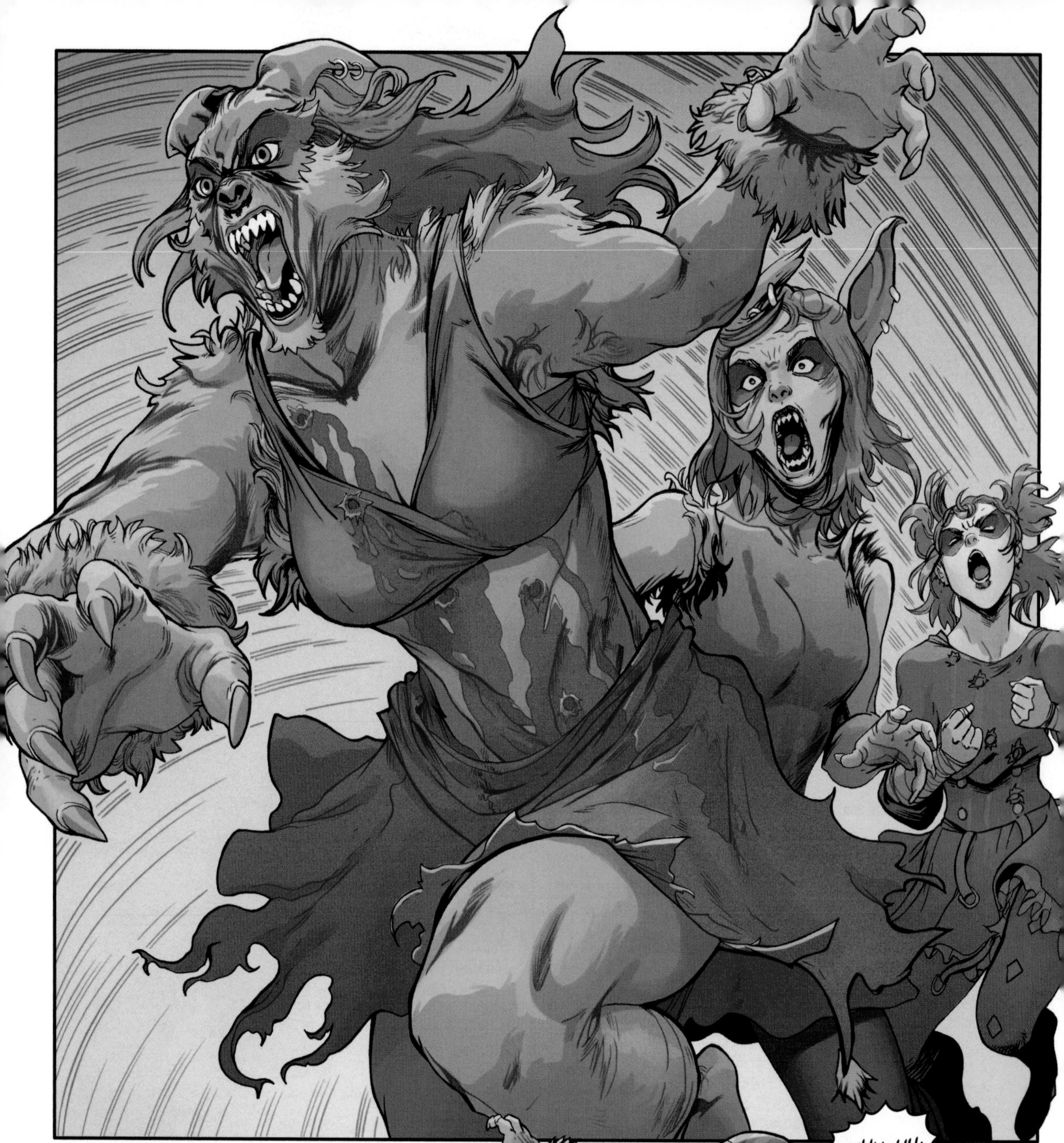

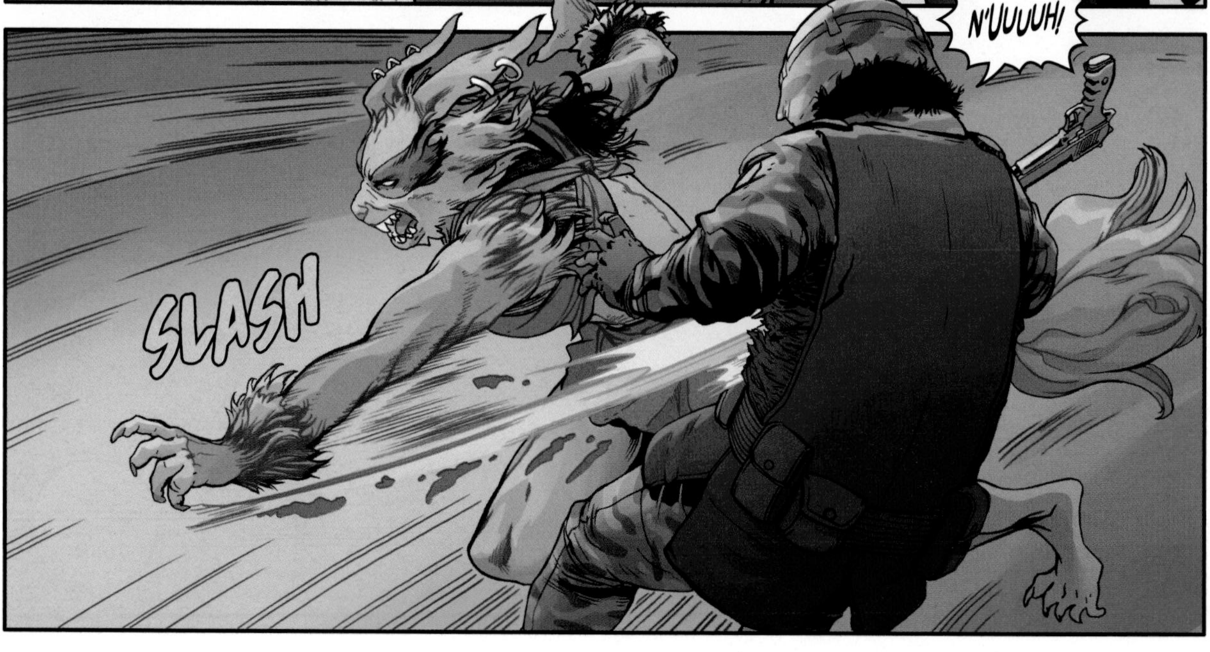
N'UUUUH!
SLASH

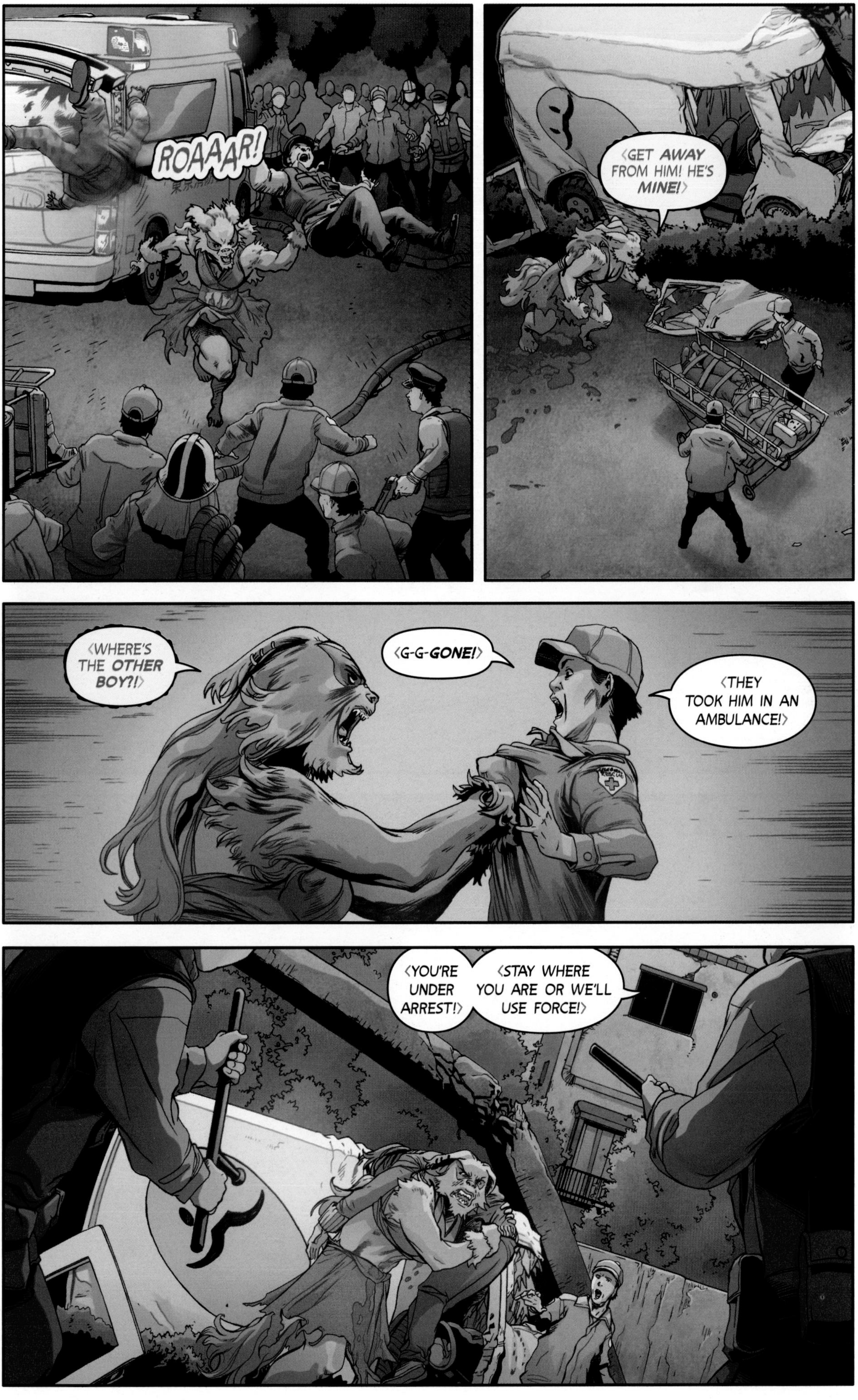
ROAAAR!
〈GET AWAY FROM HIM! HE'S MINE!〉
〈WHERE'S THE OTHER BOY?!〉
〈G-G-GONE!〉
〈THEY TOOK HIM IN AN AMBULANCE!〉
〈YOU'RE UNDER ARREST!〉
〈STAY WHERE YOU ARE OR WE'LL USE FORCE!〉

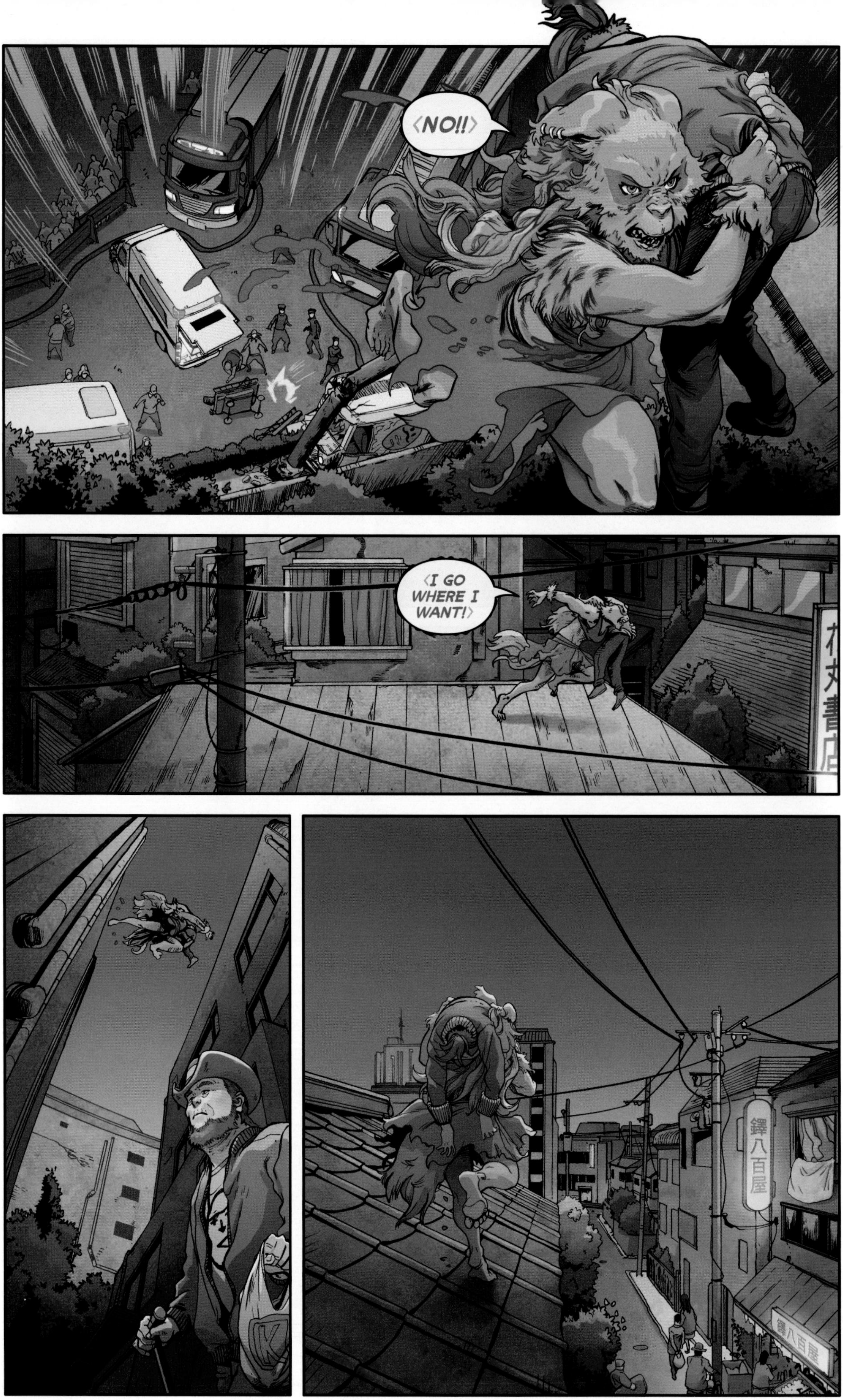

⟨NO!!⟩
⟨I GO WHERE I WANT!⟩

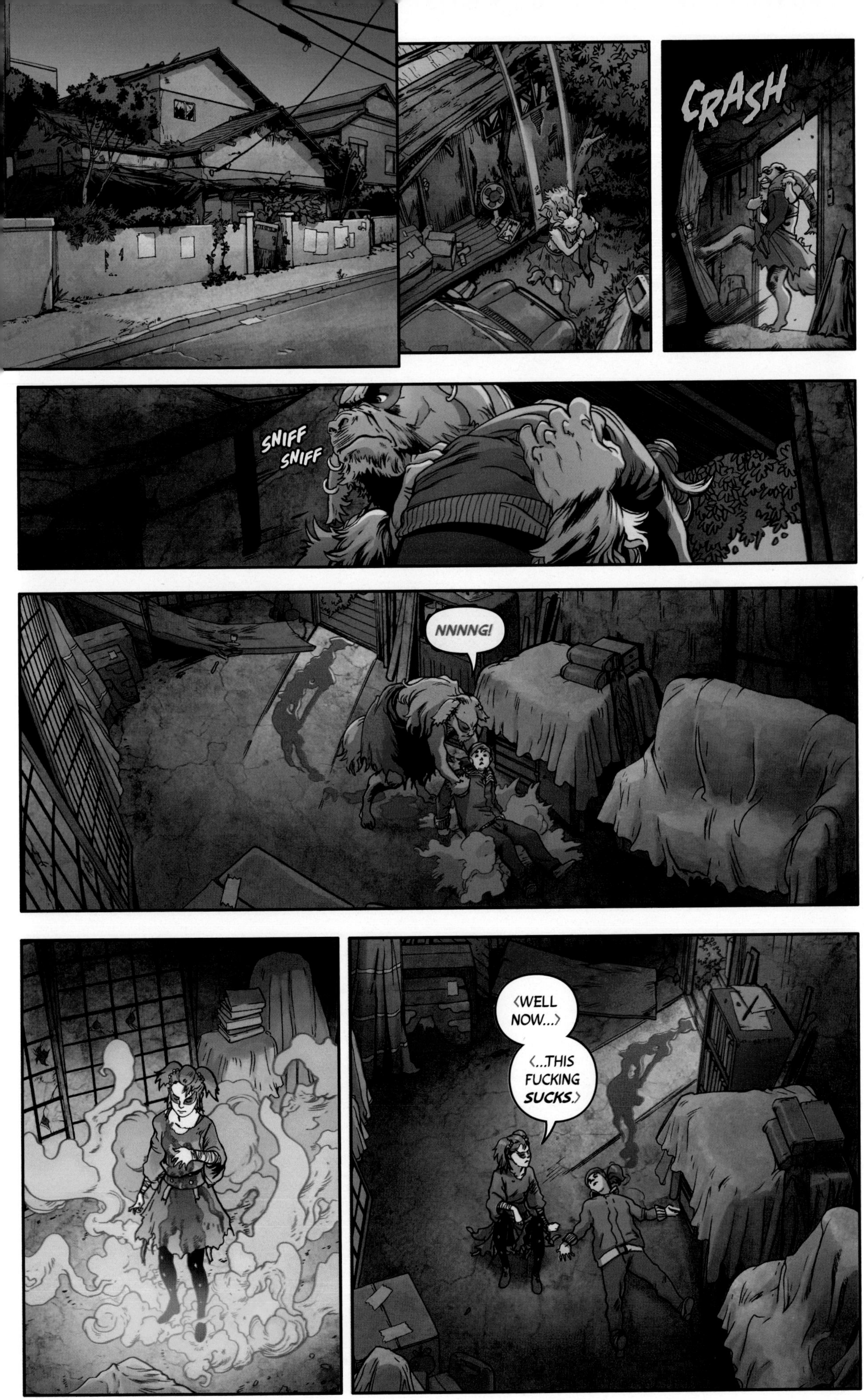
CRASH
SNIFF SNIFF
NNNNG!
‹WELL NOW...›
‹...THIS FUCKING SUCKS.›

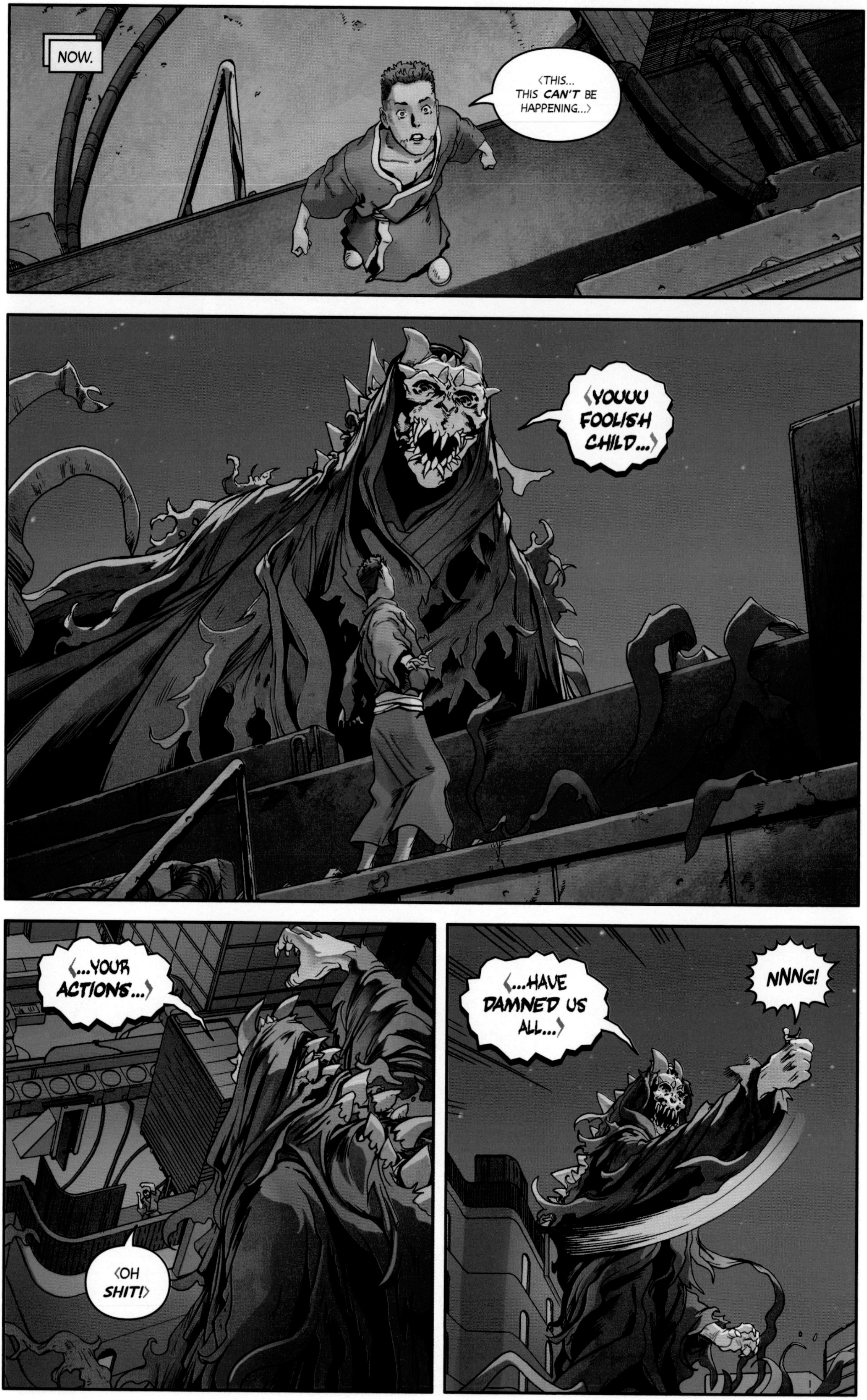
NOW.
‹THIS... THIS CAN'T BE HAPPENING...›
‹YOUUU FOOLISH CHILD...›
‹...YOUR ACTIONS...›
‹OH SHIT!›
‹...HAVE DAMNED US ALL...›
NNNG!

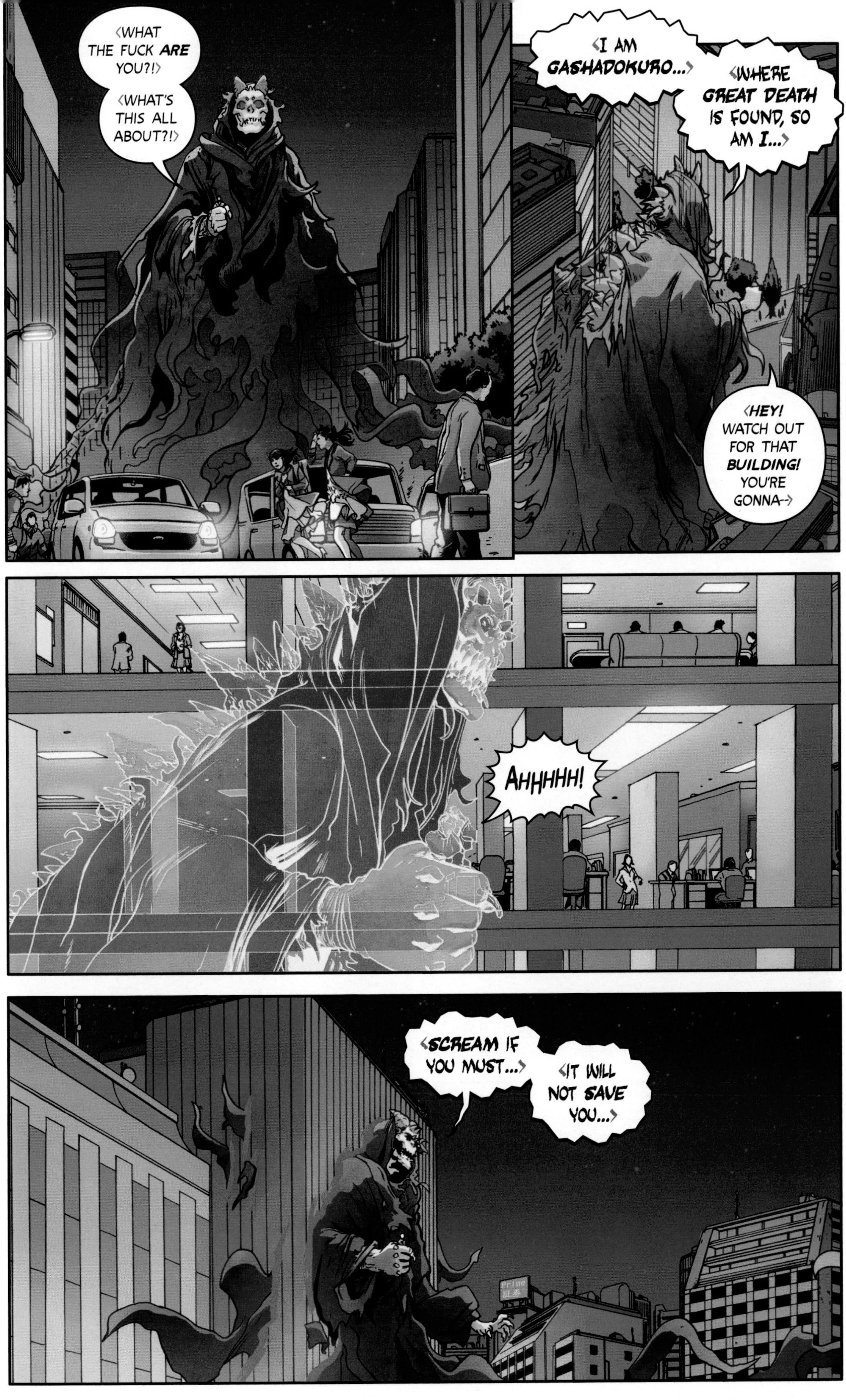
‹WHAT THE FUCK ARE YOU?!›
‹WHAT'S THIS ALL ABOUT?!›
‹I AM GASHADOKURO...›
‹WHERE GREAT DEATH IS FOUND, SO AM I...›
‹HEY! WATCH OUT FOR THAT BUILDING! YOU'RE GONNA--›
AHHHHH!
‹SCREAM IF YOU MUST...›
‹IT WILL NOT SAVE YOU...›

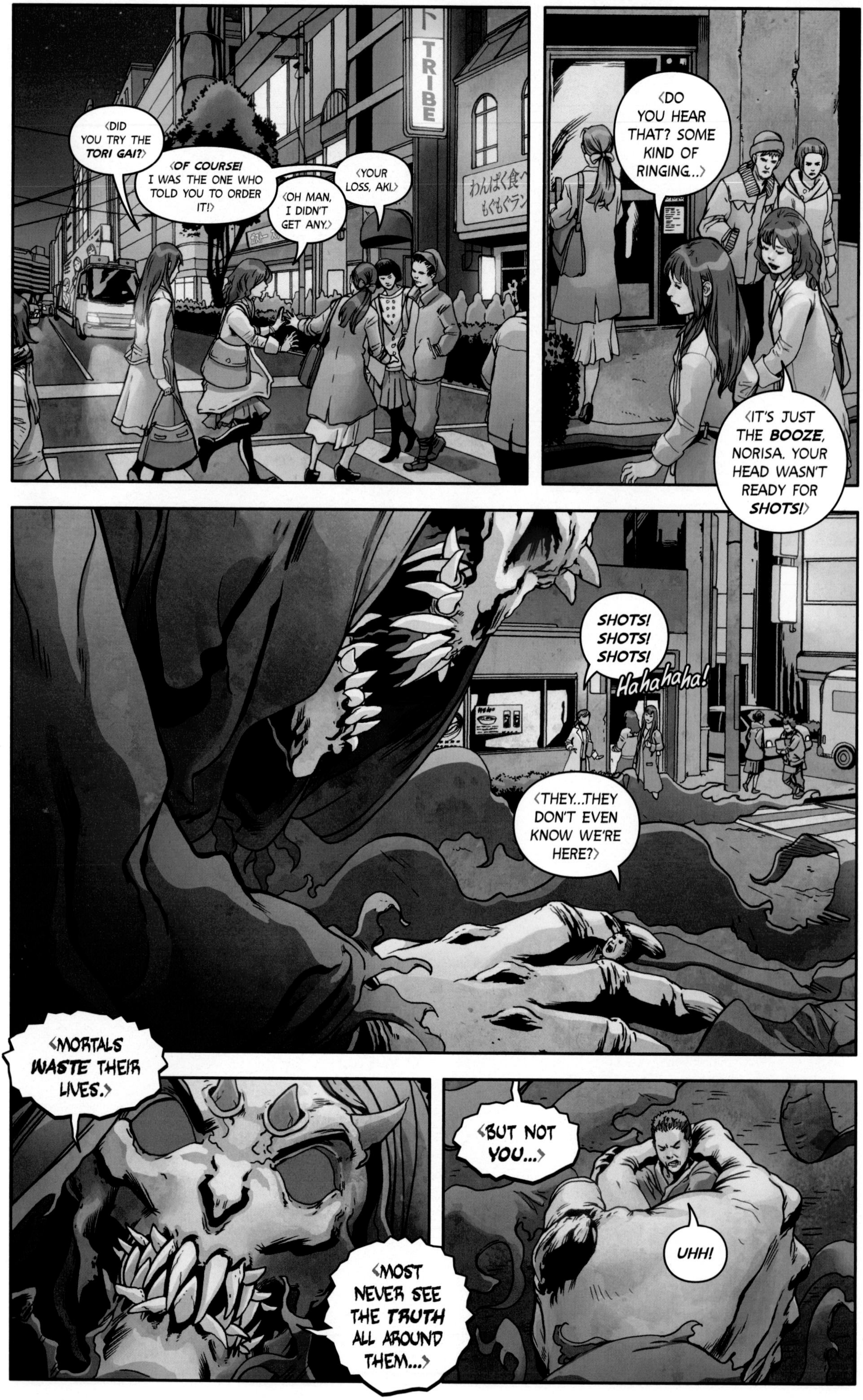
TRIBE
‹DID YOU TRY THE TORI GAI?›
‹OF COURSE! I WAS THE ONE WHO TOLD YOU TO ORDER IT!›
‹OH MAN, I DIDN'T GET ANY.›
‹YOUR LOSS, AKI.›
‹DO YOU HEAR THAT? SOME KIND OF RINGING...›
‹IT'S JUST THE BOOZE, NORISA. YOUR HEAD WASN'T READY FOR SHOTS!›
SHOTS! SHOTS! SHOTS!
Hahahaha!
‹THEY...THEY DON'T EVEN KNOW WE'RE HERE?›
‹MORTALS WASTE THEIR LIVES.›
‹MOST NEVER SEE THE TRUTH ALL AROUND THEM...›
‹BUT NOT YOU...›
UHH!

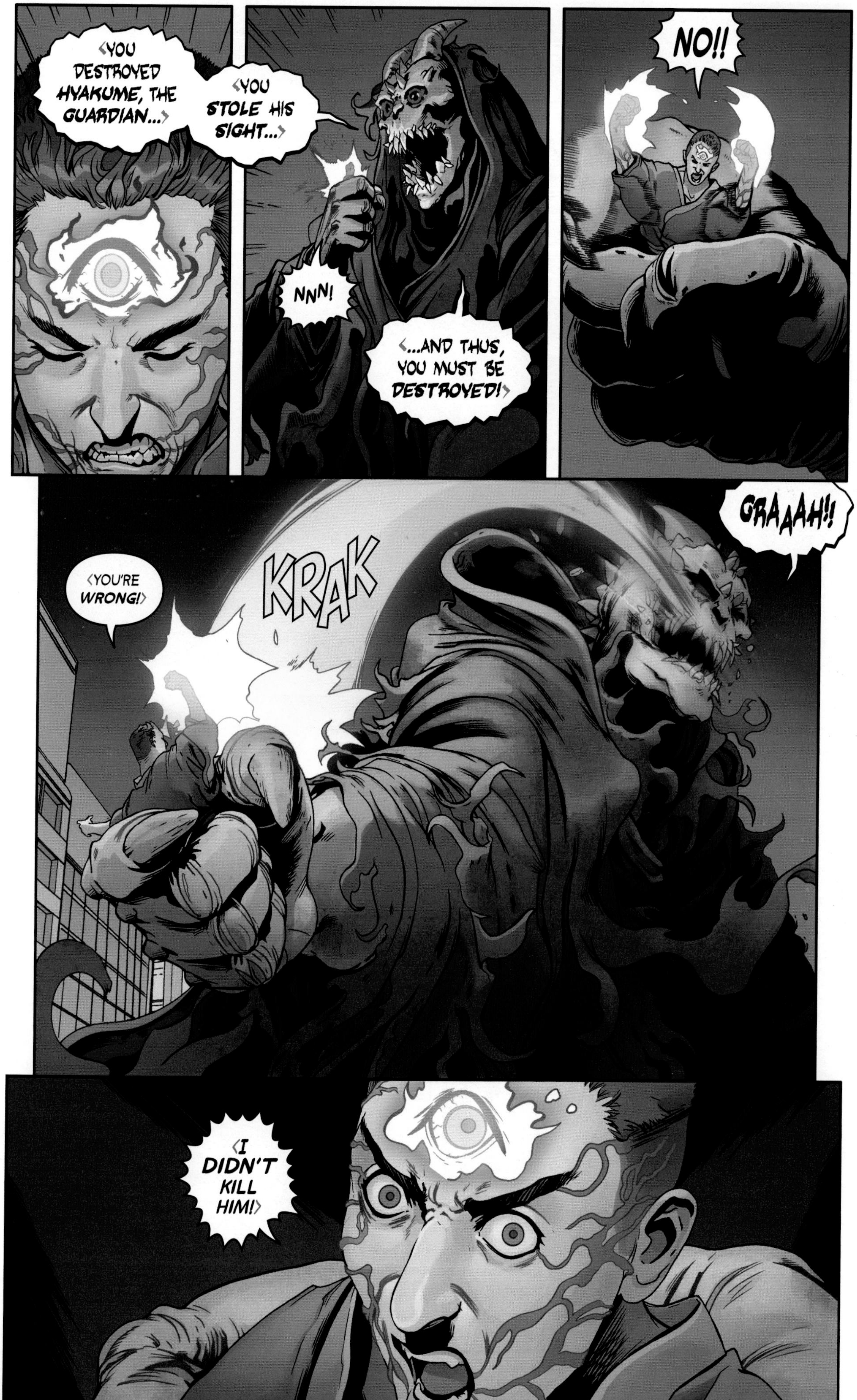

‹YOU DESTROYED HYAKUME, THE GUARDIAN...›
‹YOU STOLE HIS SIGHT...›
NNN!
‹...AND THUS, YOU MUST BE DESTROYED!›
NO!!
‹YOU'RE WRONG!›
KRAK
GRAAAH!!
‹I DIDN'T KILL HIM!›

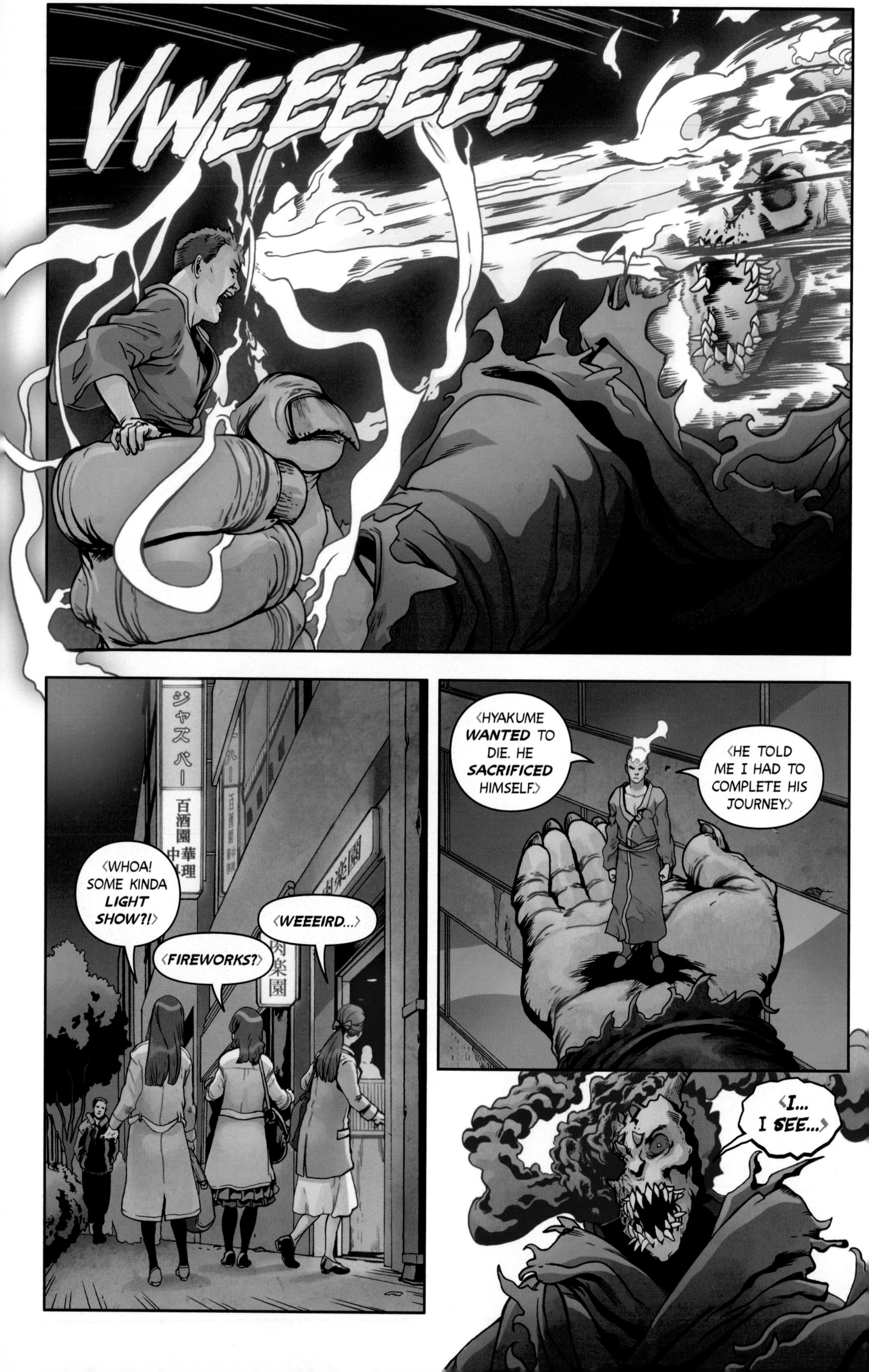
VWEEEEEE
‹WHOA! SOME KINDA **LIGHT SHOW?!**›
‹**FIREWORKS?**›
‹**WEEEIRD...**›
‹HYAKUME **WANTED** TO DIE. HE **SACRIFICED** HIMSELF.›
‹HE TOLD ME I HAD TO COMPLETE HIS JOURNEY.›
‹**I... I SEE...**›

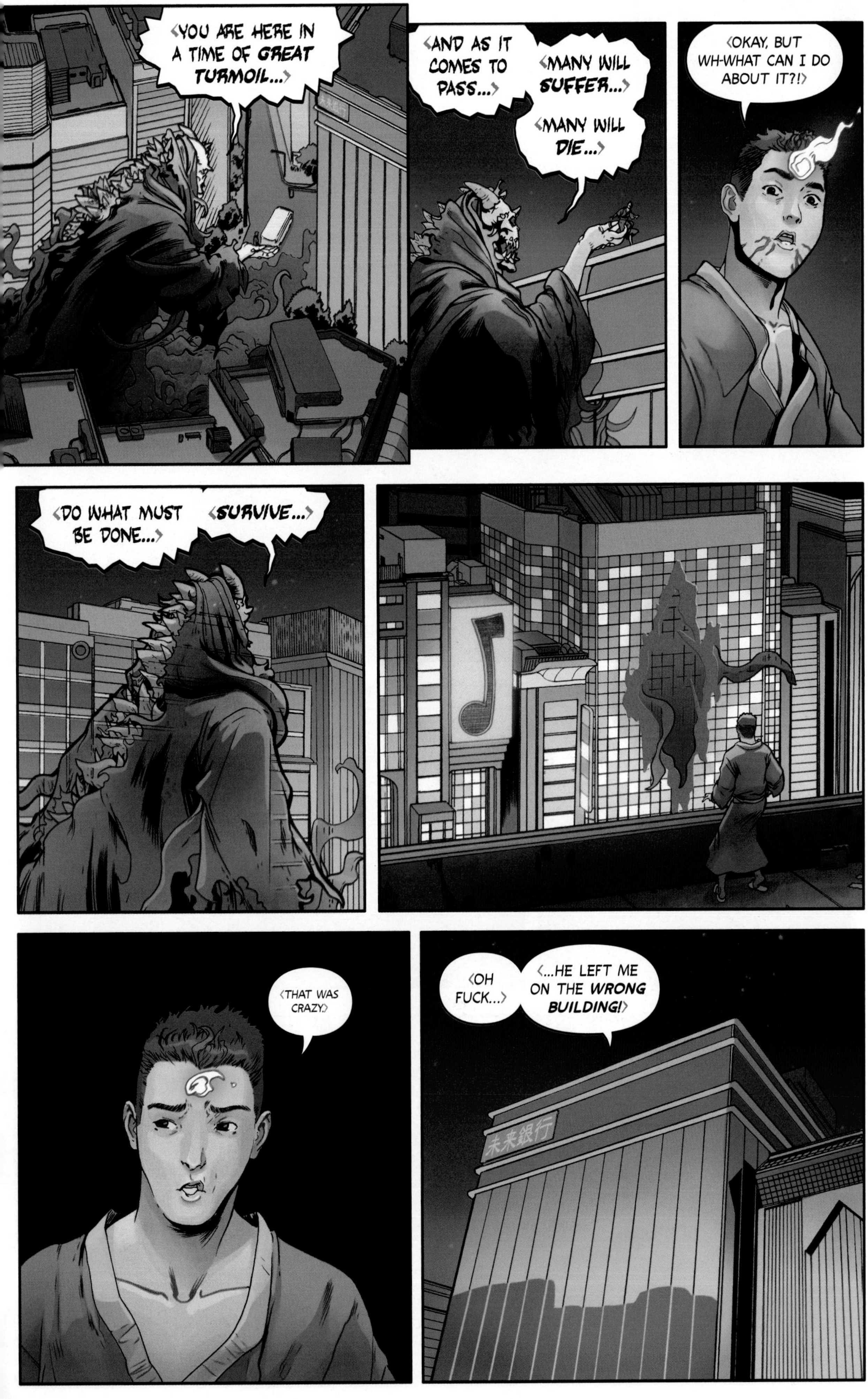

‹YOU ARE HERE IN A TIME OF GREAT TURMOIL...›
‹AND AS IT COMES TO PASS...›
‹MANY WILL SUFFER...›
‹MANY WILL DIE...›
‹OKAY, BUT WH-WHAT CAN I DO ABOUT IT?!›
‹DO WHAT MUST BE DONE...›
‹SURVIVE...›
‹THAT WAS CRAZY.›
‹OH FUCK...›
‹...HE LEFT ME ON THE WRONG BUILDING!›
未来銀行

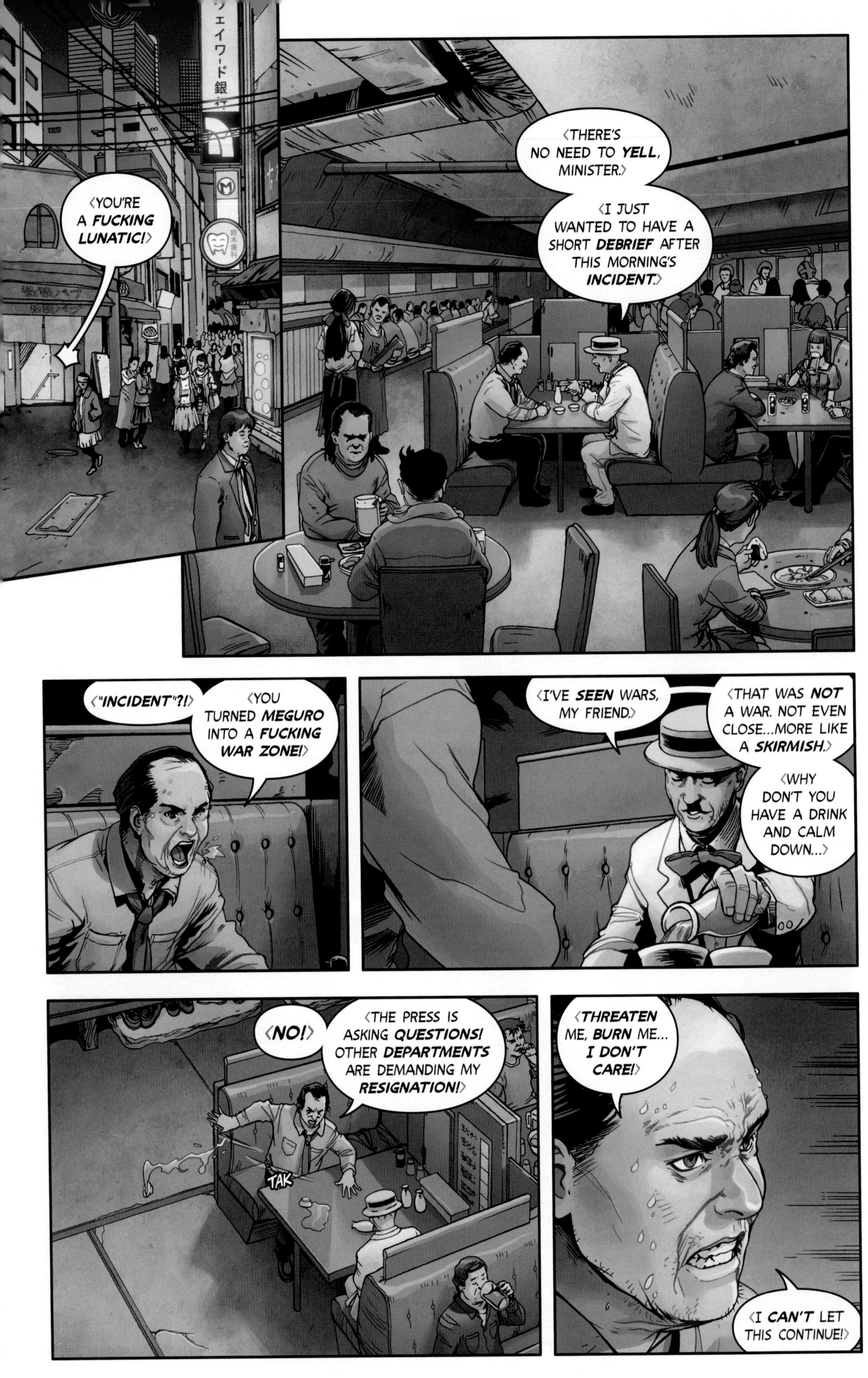
⟨YOU'RE A FUCKING LUNATIC!⟩
⟨THERE'S NO NEED TO YELL, MINISTER.⟩
⟨I JUST WANTED TO HAVE A SHORT DEBRIEF AFTER THIS MORNING'S INCIDENT.⟩
⟨"INCIDENT"?!⟩
⟨YOU TURNED MEGURO INTO A FUCKING WAR ZONE!⟩
⟨I'VE SEEN WARS, MY FRIEND.⟩
⟨THAT WAS NOT A WAR. NOT EVEN CLOSE...MORE LIKE A SKIRMISH.⟩
⟨WHY DON'T YOU HAVE A DRINK AND CALM DOWN...⟩
⟨NO!⟩
⟨THE PRESS IS ASKING QUESTIONS! OTHER DEPARTMENTS ARE DEMANDING MY RESIGNATION!⟩
TAK
⟨THREATEN ME, BURN ME... I DON'T CARE!⟩
⟨I CAN'T LET THIS CONTINUE!⟩

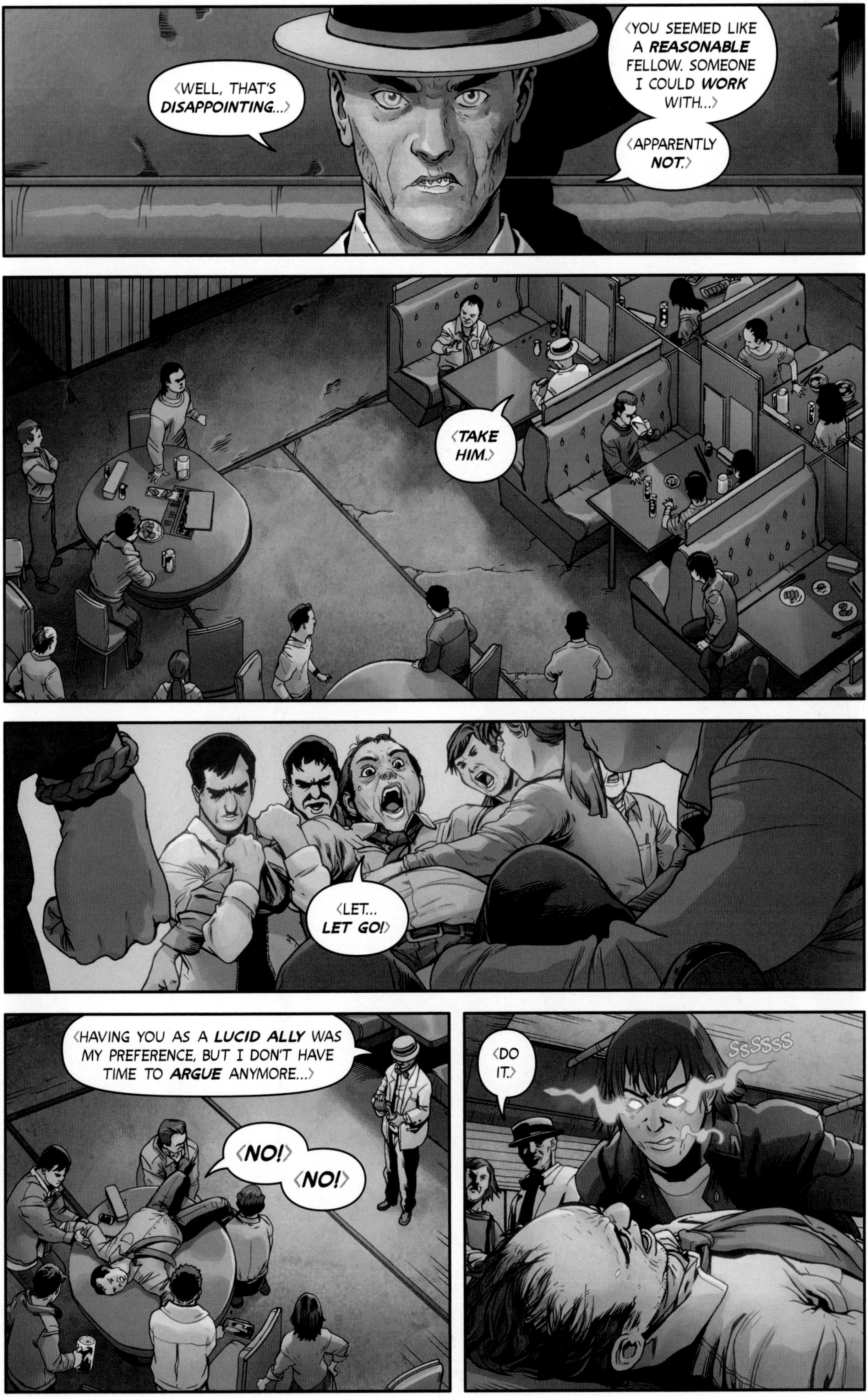
⟨WELL, THAT'S DISAPPOINTING...⟩
⟨YOU SEEMED LIKE A REASONABLE FELLOW. SOMEONE I COULD WORK WITH...⟩
⟨APPARENTLY NOT.⟩
⟨TAKE HIM.⟩
⟨LET... LET GO!⟩
⟨HAVING YOU AS A LUCID ALLY WAS MY PREFERENCE, BUT I DON'T HAVE TIME TO ARGUE ANYMORE...⟩
⟨NO!⟩
⟨NO!⟩
⟨DO IT.⟩
SSSSSS

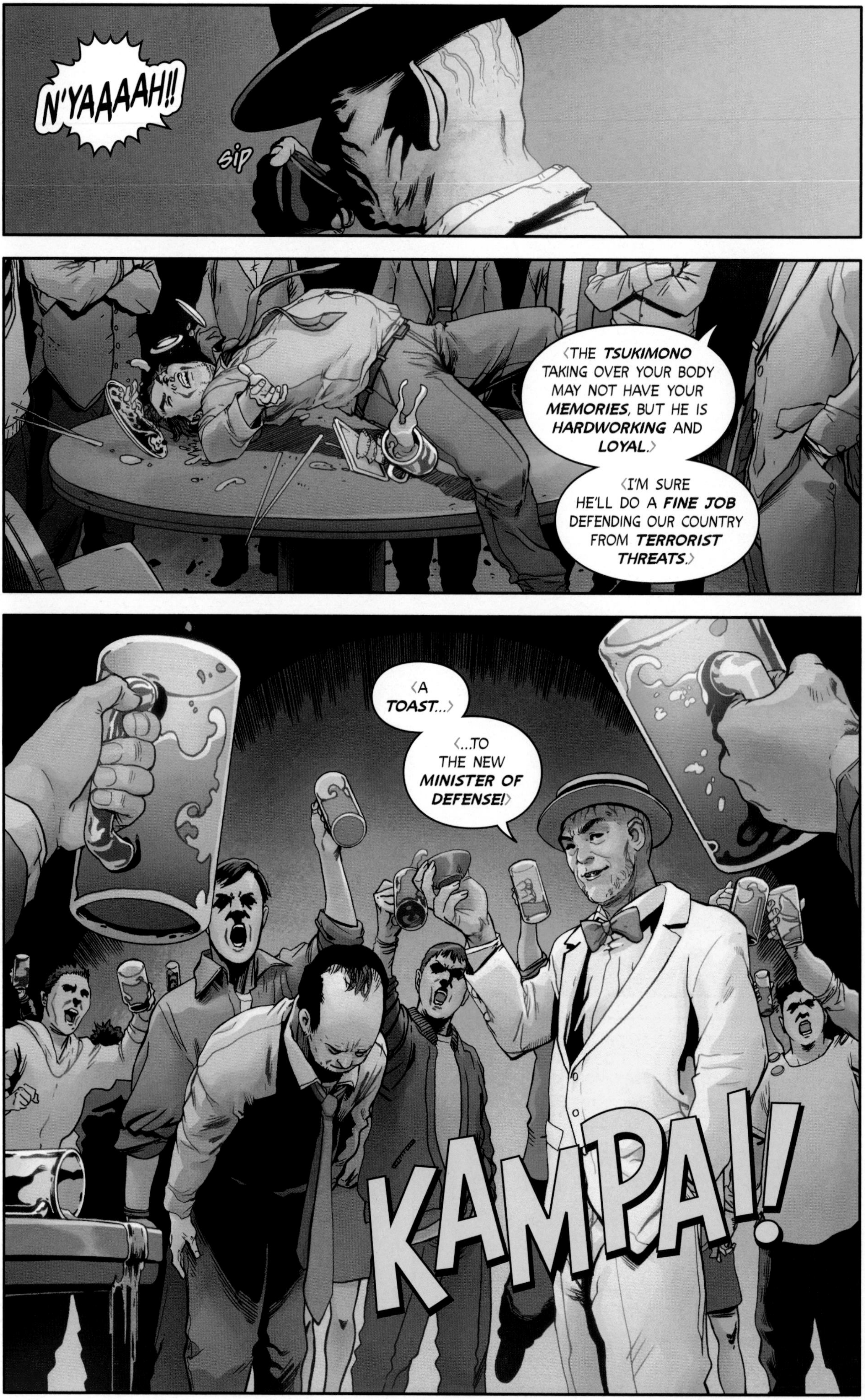
N'YAAAAH!!
sip
‹THE TSUKIMONO TAKING OVER YOUR BODY MAY NOT HAVE YOUR MEMORIES, BUT HE IS HARDWORKING AND LOYAL.›
‹I'M SURE HE'LL DO A FINE JOB DEFENDING OUR COUNTRY FROM TERRORIST THREATS.›
‹A TOAST...›
‹...TO THE NEW MINISTER OF DEFENSE!›
KAMPAI!

Chapter Twenty

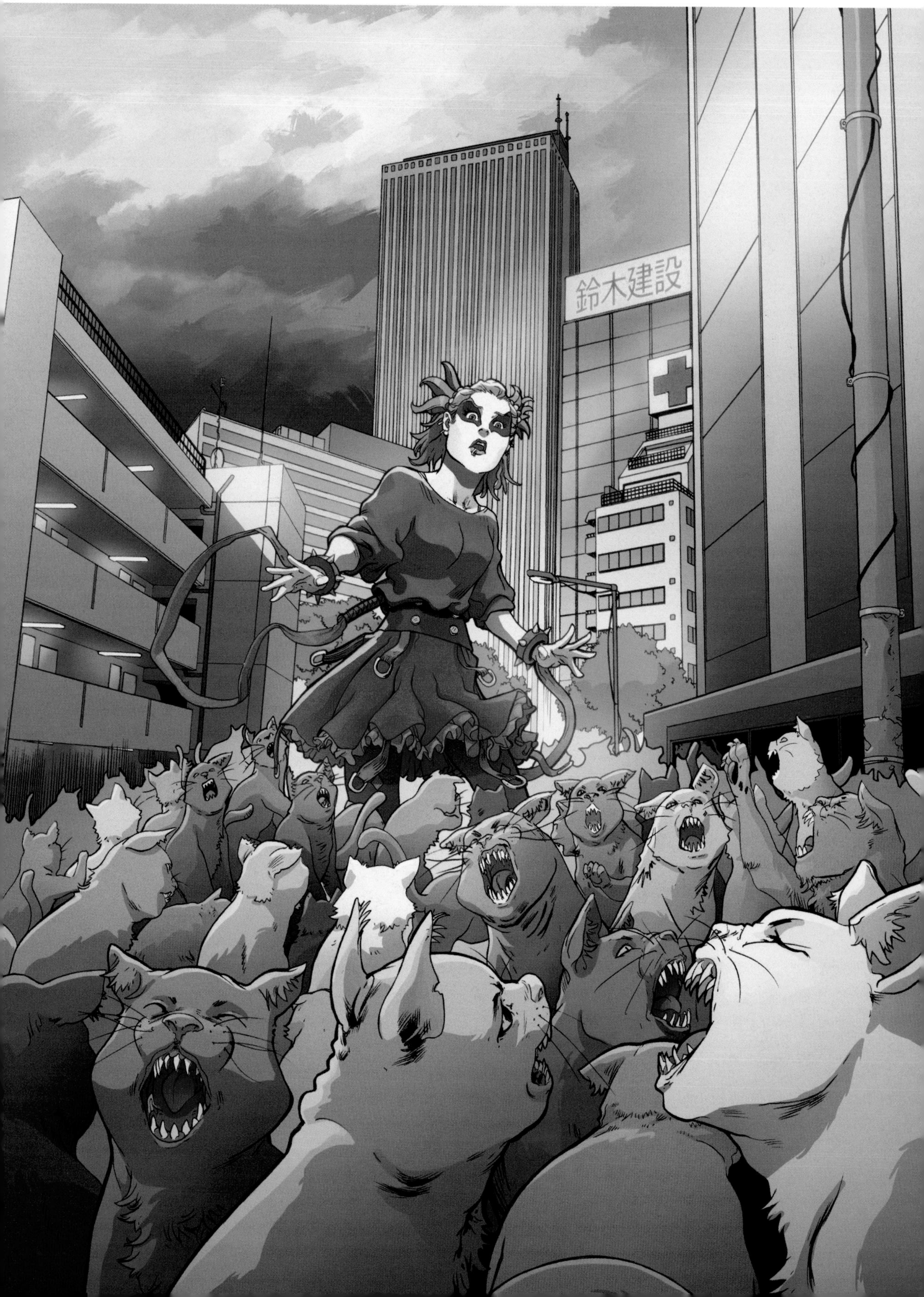

鈴木建設

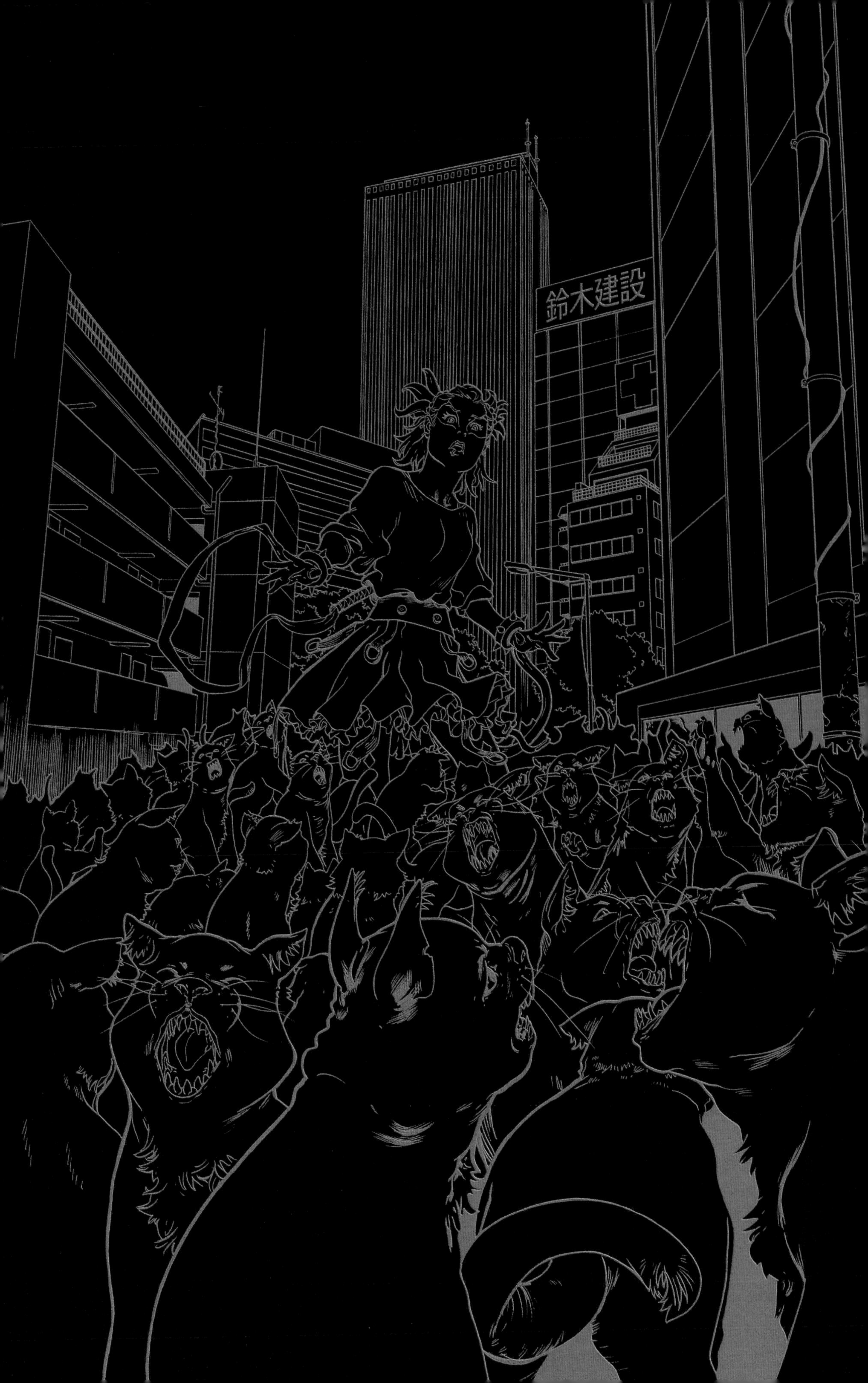
鈴木建設

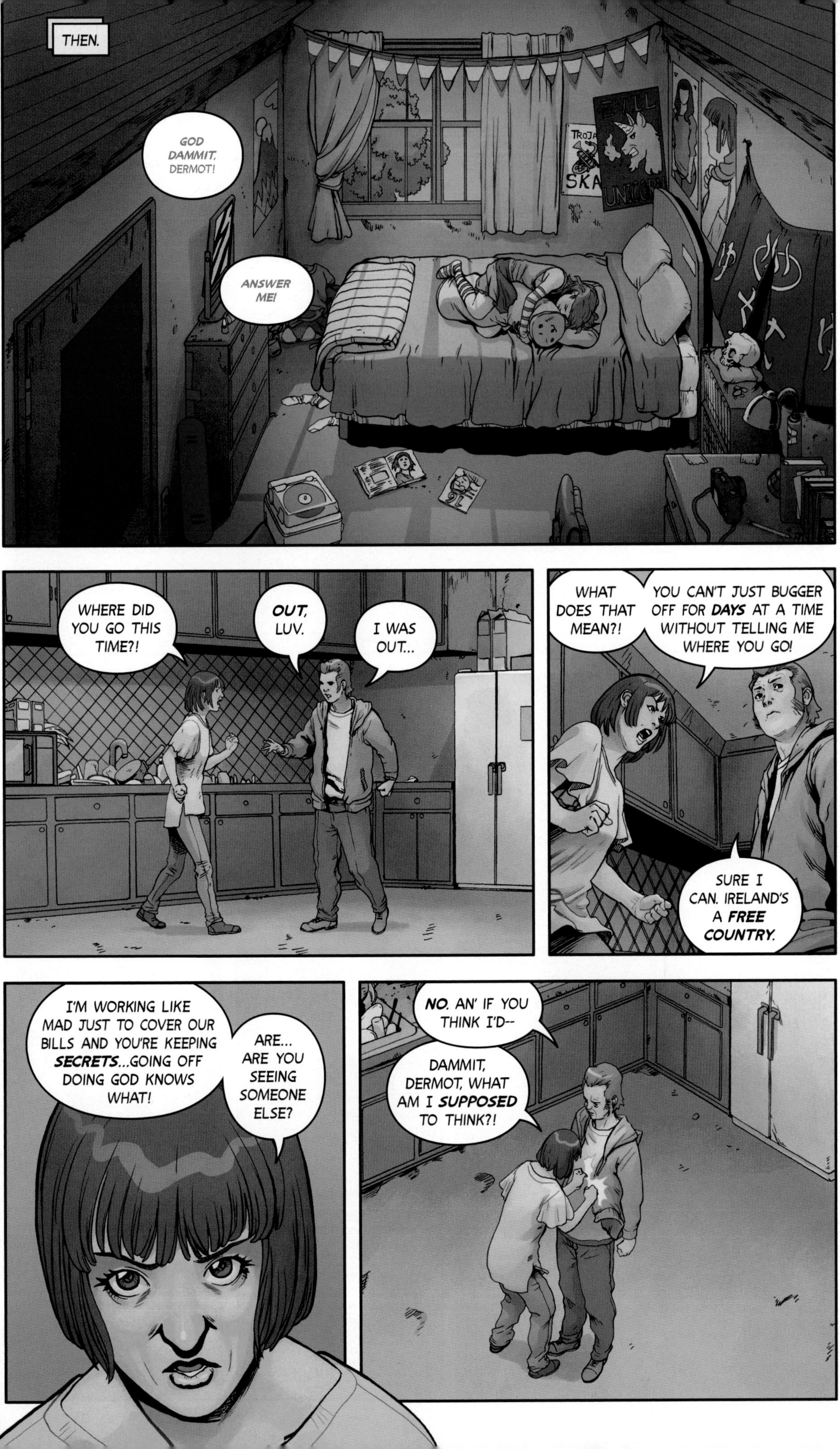
THEN.
GOD DAMMIT, DERMOT!
ANSWER ME!
TROJAN SKA
EVIL UNICORN
WHERE DID YOU GO THIS TIME?!
OUT, LUV.
I WAS OUT...
WHAT DOES THAT MEAN?!
YOU CAN'T JUST BUGGER OFF FOR DAYS AT A TIME WITHOUT TELLING ME WHERE YOU GO!
SURE I CAN. IRELAND'S A FREE COUNTRY.
I'M WORKING LIKE MAD JUST TO COVER OUR BILLS AND YOU'RE KEEPING SECRETS...GOING OFF DOING GOD KNOWS WHAT!
ARE... ARE YOU SEEING SOMEONE ELSE?
NO. AN' IF YOU THINK I'D--
DAMMIT, DERMOT, WHAT AM I SUPPOSED TO THINK?!

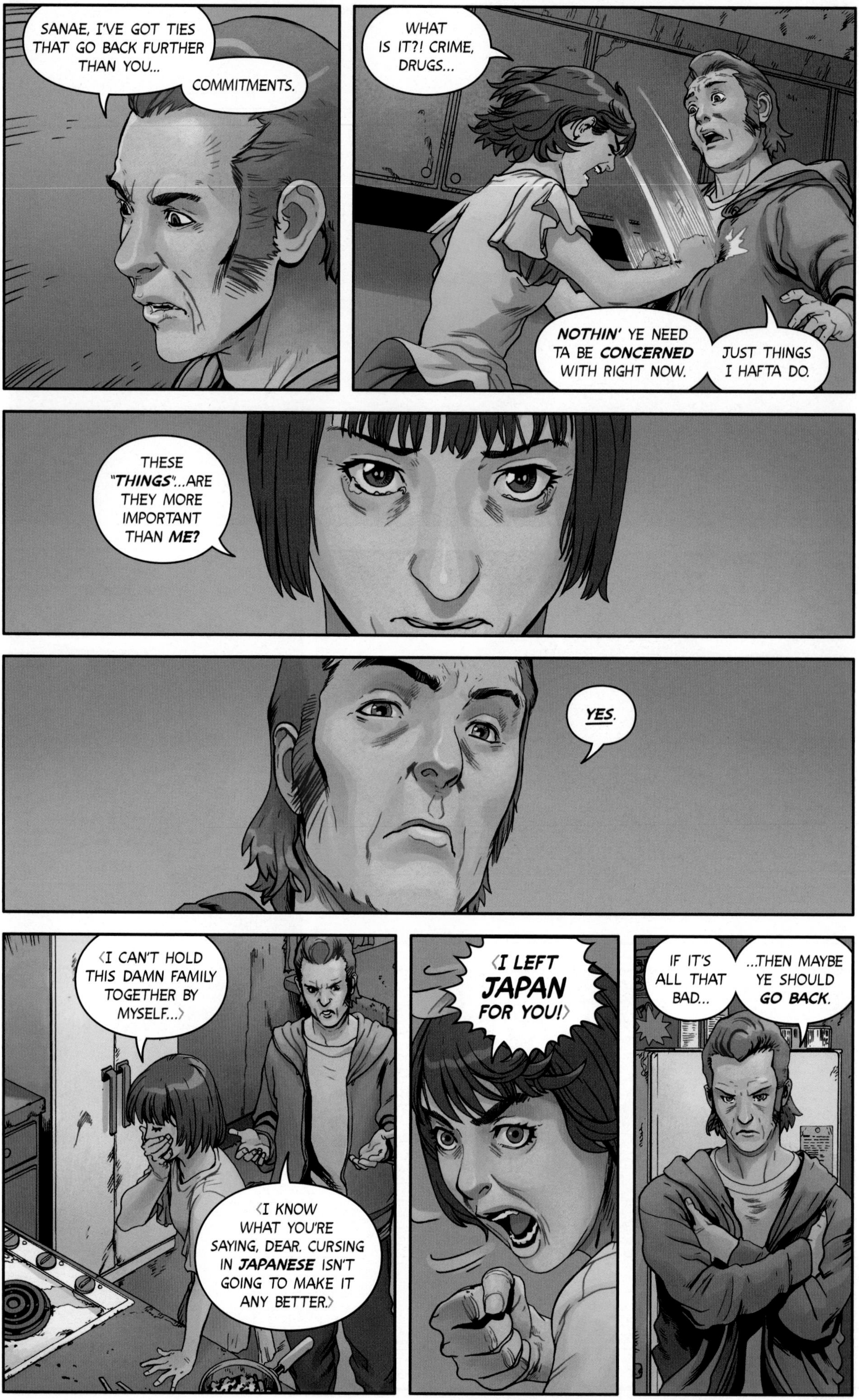
SANAE, I'VE GOT TIES THAT GO BACK FURTHER THAN YOU...
COMMITMENTS.
WHAT IS IT?! CRIME, DRUGS...
NOTHIN' YE NEED TA BE CONCERNED WITH RIGHT NOW.
JUST THINGS I HAFTA DO.
THESE "THINGS"...ARE THEY MORE IMPORTANT THAN ME?
YES.
‹I CAN'T HOLD THIS DAMN FAMILY TOGETHER BY MYSELF...›
‹I KNOW WHAT YOU'RE SAYING, DEAR. CURSING IN JAPANESE ISN'T GOING TO MAKE IT ANY BETTER.›
‹I LEFT JAPAN FOR YOU!›
IF IT'S ALL THAT BAD...
...THEN MAYBE YE SHOULD GO BACK.

I'M GOING OUT...

RORI, *WAIT!*

SLAM

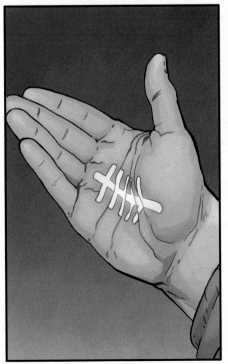

IT'S *DONE*, Y' BASTARDS.

MY FAMILY DESTROYED, JUST LIKE YE WANTED...

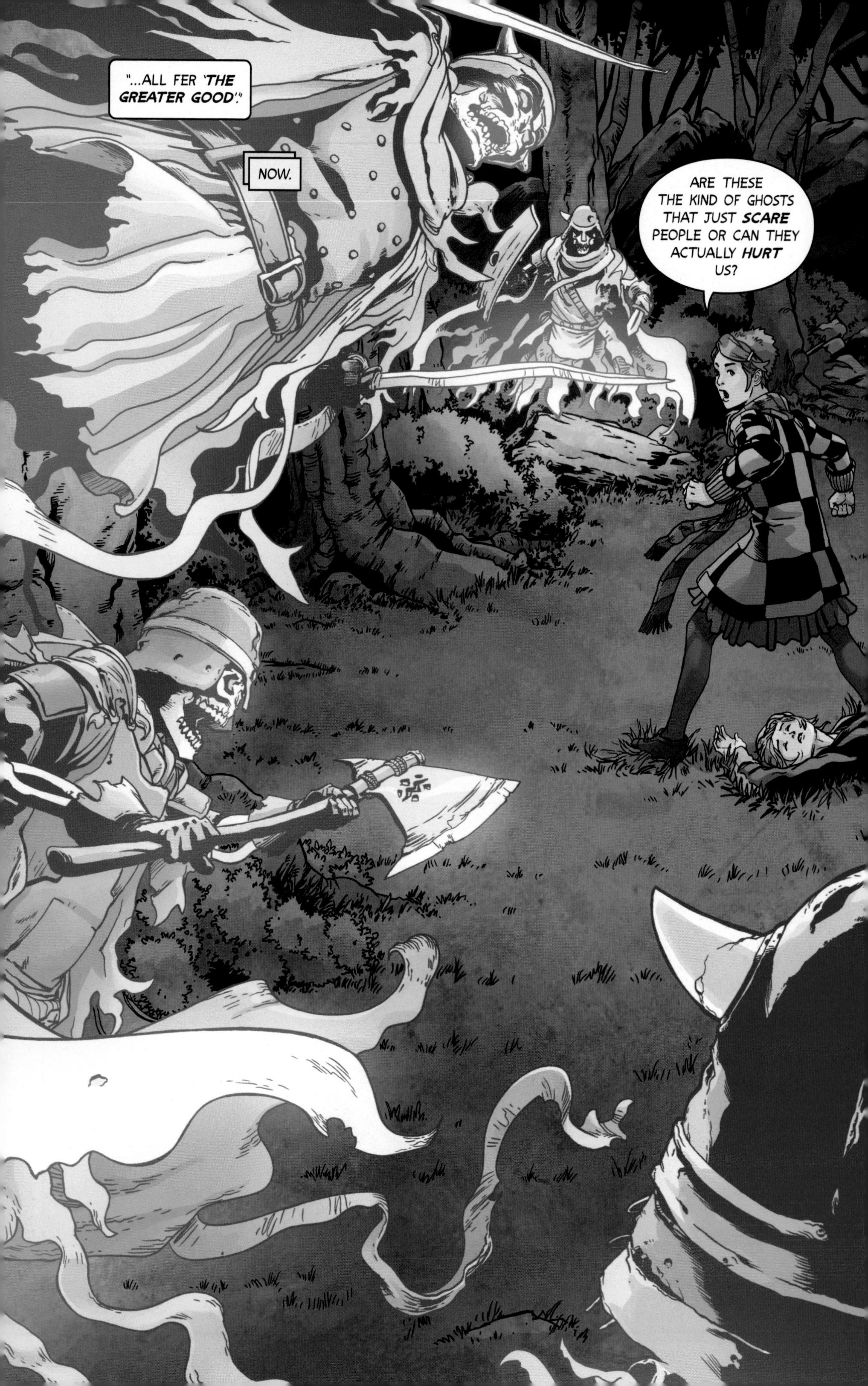
"...ALL FER 'THE GREATER GOOD'."
NOW.
ARE THESE THE KIND OF GHOSTS THAT JUST SCARE PEOPLE OR CAN THEY ACTUALLY HURT US?

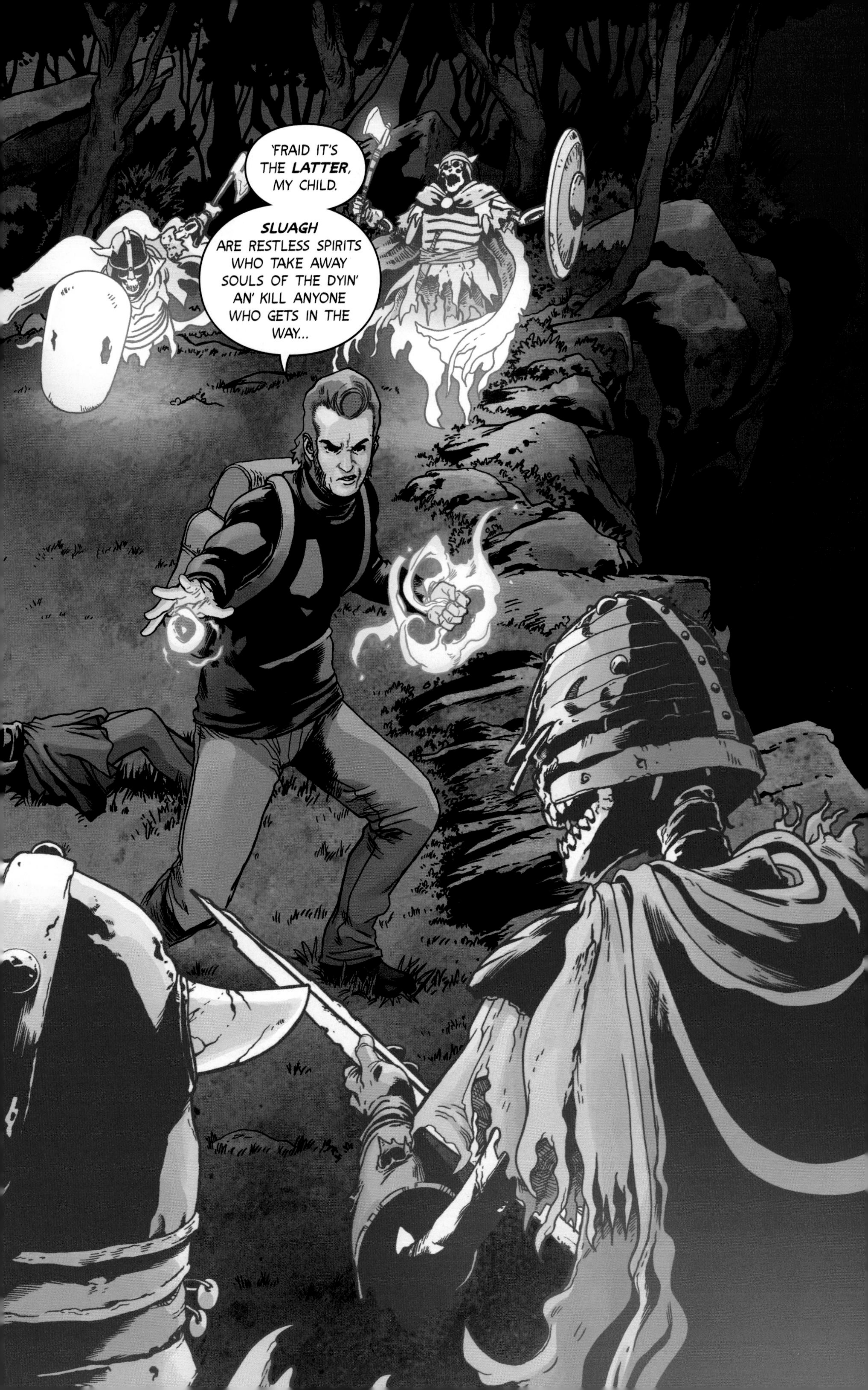
'FRAID IT'S THE **LATTER**, MY CHILD.
SLUAGH ARE RESTLESS SPIRITS WHO TAKE AWAY SOULS OF THE DYIN' AN' KILL ANYONE WHO GETS IN THE WAY...

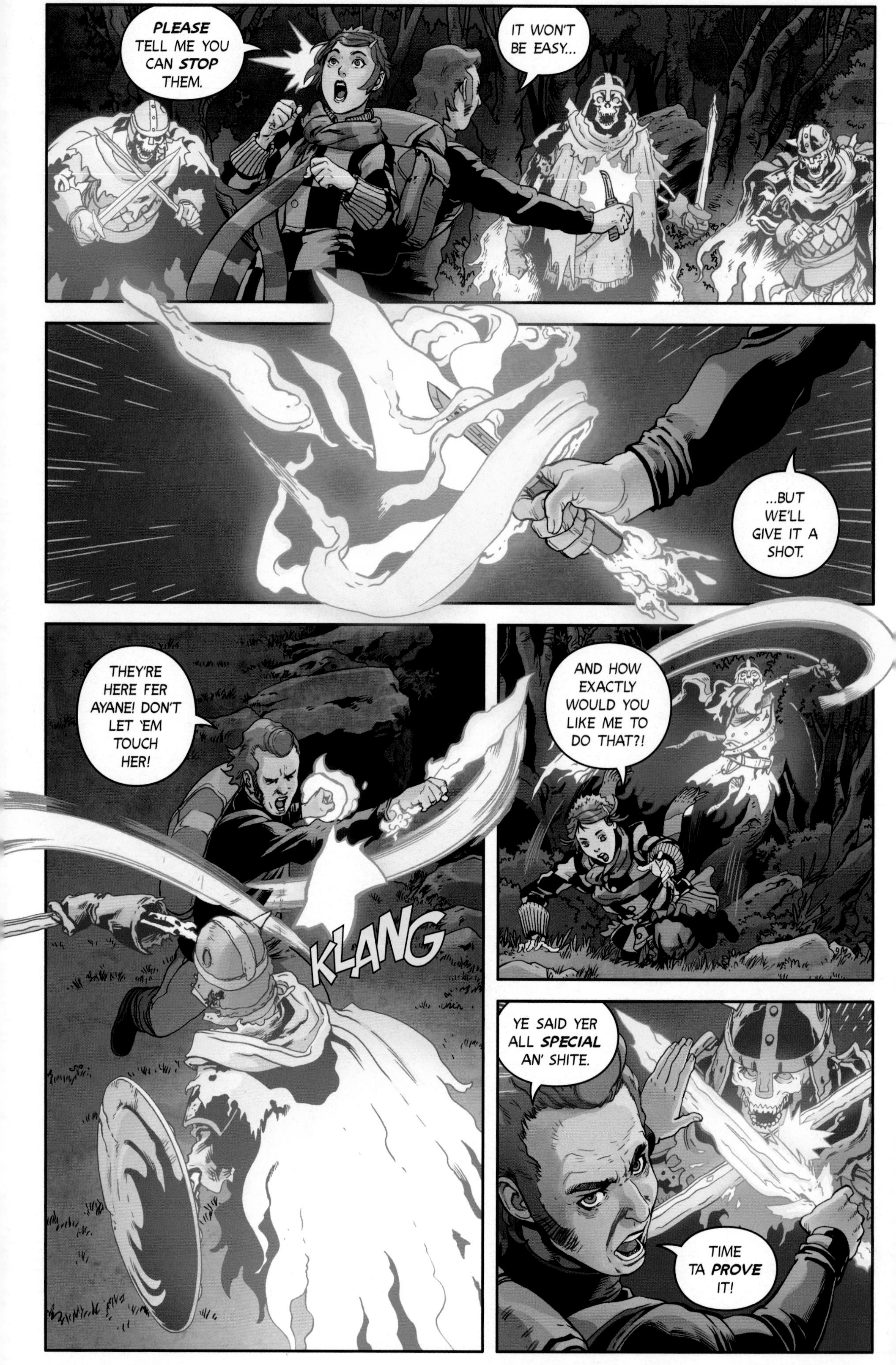
PLEASE TELL ME YOU CAN STOP THEM.
IT WON'T BE EASY...
...BUT WE'LL GIVE IT A SHOT.
THEY'RE HERE FER AYANE! DON'T LET 'EM TOUCH HER!
KLANG
AND HOW EXACTLY WOULD YOU LIKE ME TO DO THAT?!
YE SAID YER ALL SPECIAL AN' SHITE.
TIME TA PROVE IT!

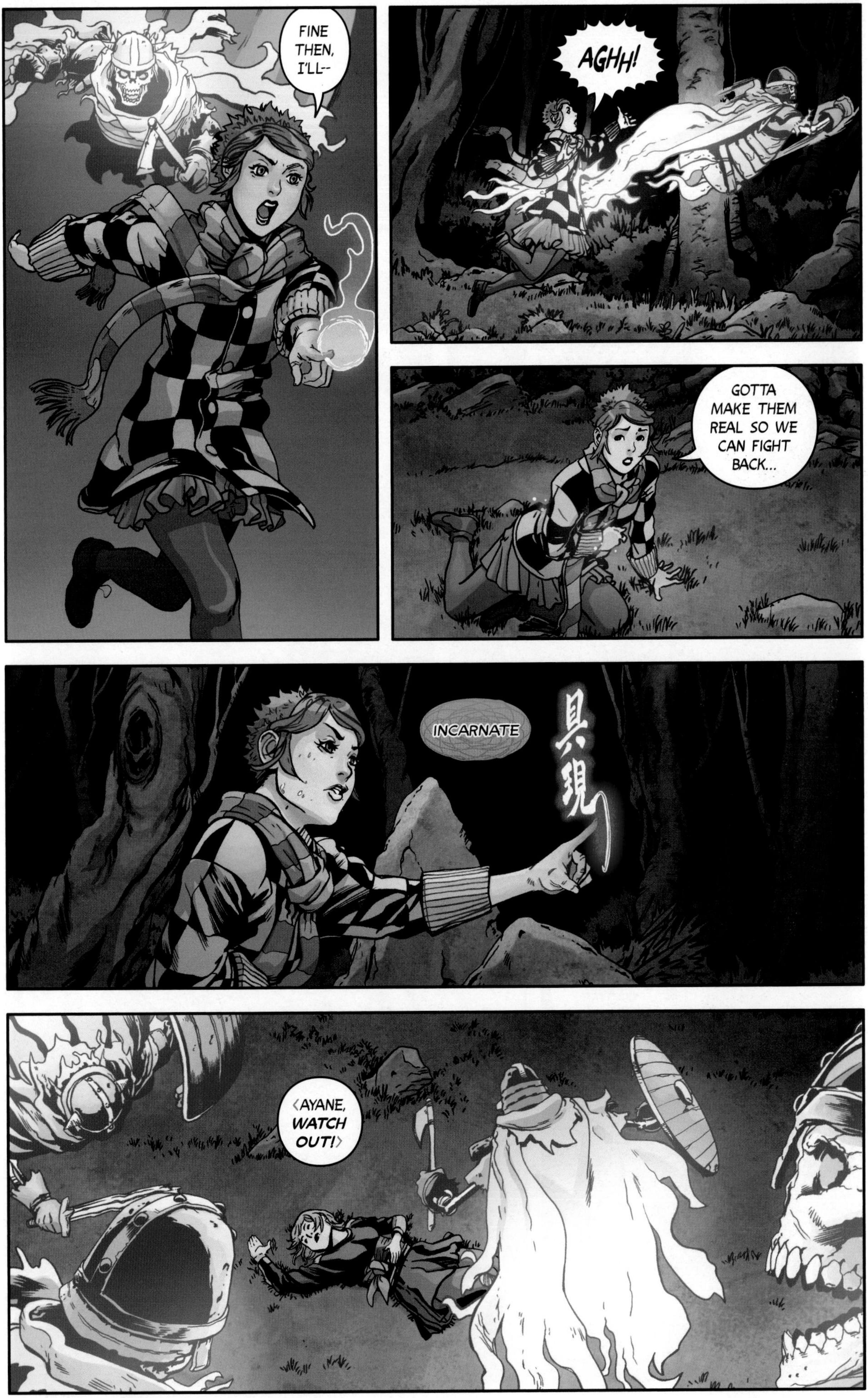
FINE THEN, I'LL--
AGHH!
GOTTA MAKE THEM REAL SO WE CAN FIGHT BACK...
INCARNATE
具現
<AYANE, WATCH OUT!>

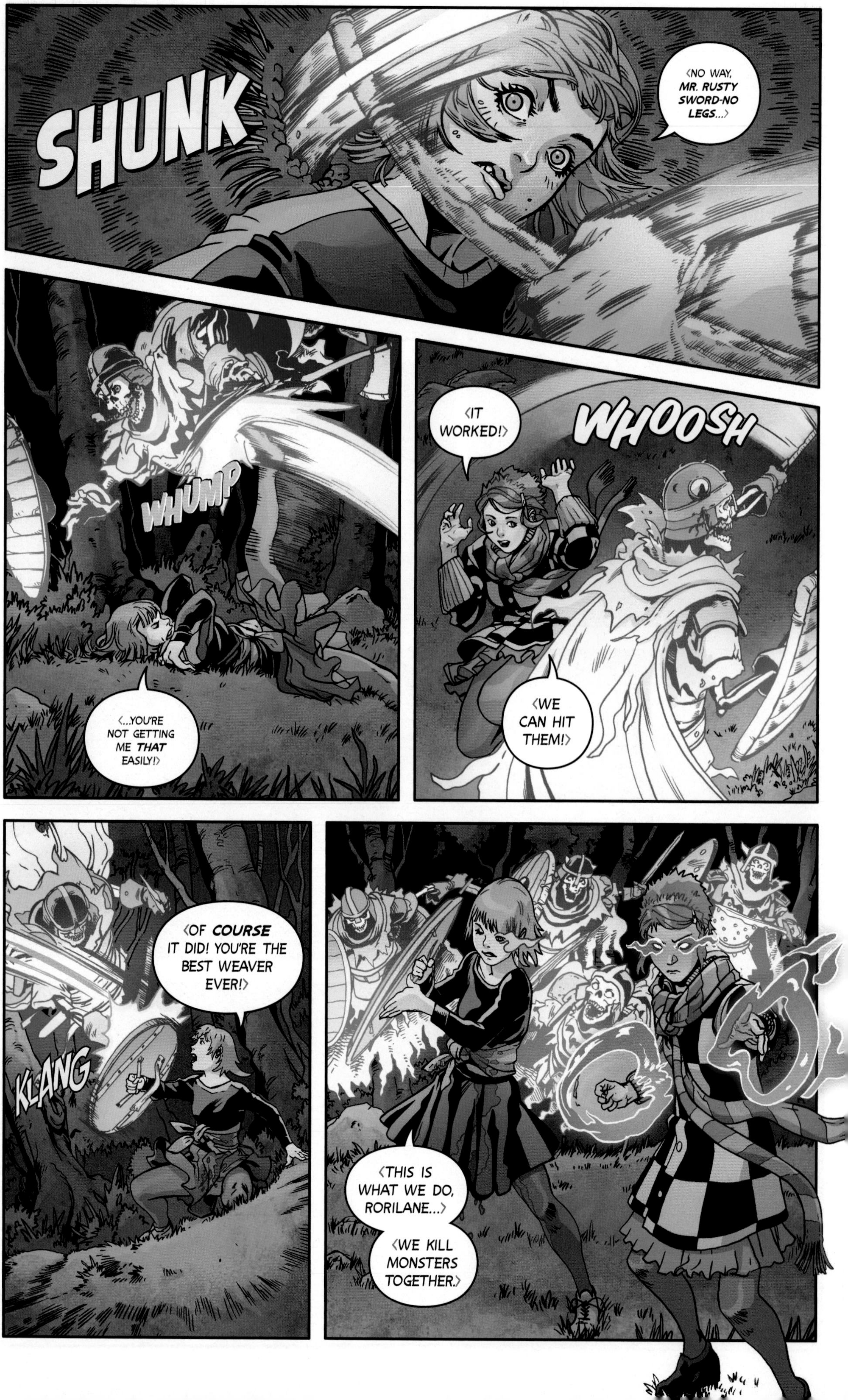
SHUNK
‹NO WAY, MR. RUSTY SWORD-NO LEGS...›
WHUMP
‹...YOU'RE NOT GETTING ME THAT EASILY!›
‹IT WORKED!›
WHOOSH
‹WE CAN HIT THEM!›
‹OF COURSE IT DID! YOU'RE THE BEST WEAVER EVER!›
KLANG
‹THIS IS WHAT WE DO, RORILANE...›
‹WE KILL MONSTERS TOGETHER.›

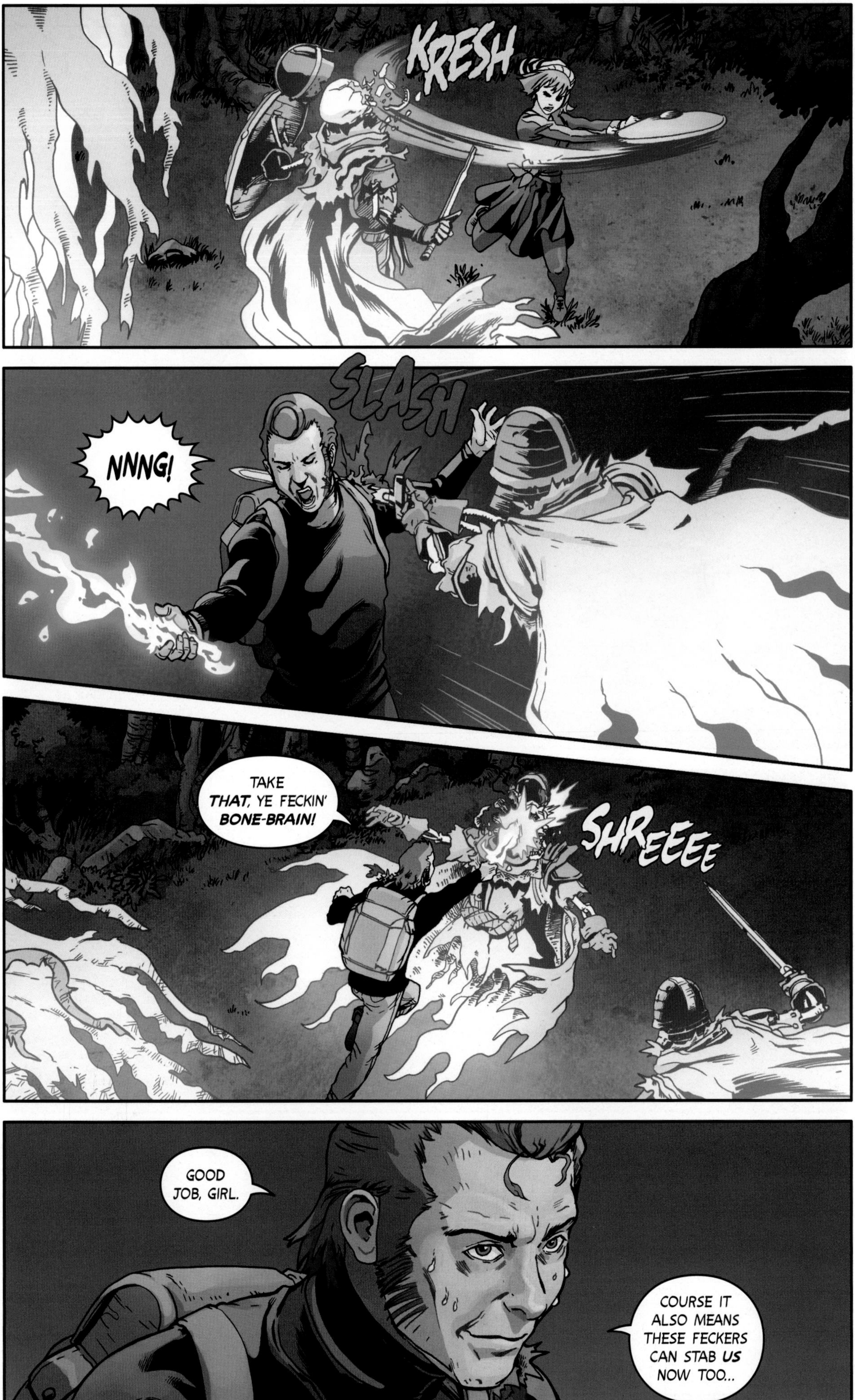
KRESH
SLASH
NNNG!
TAKE THAT, YE FECKIN' BONE-BRAIN!
SHREEEE
GOOD JOB, GIRL.
COURSE IT ALSO MEANS THESE FECKERS CAN STAB US NOW TOO...

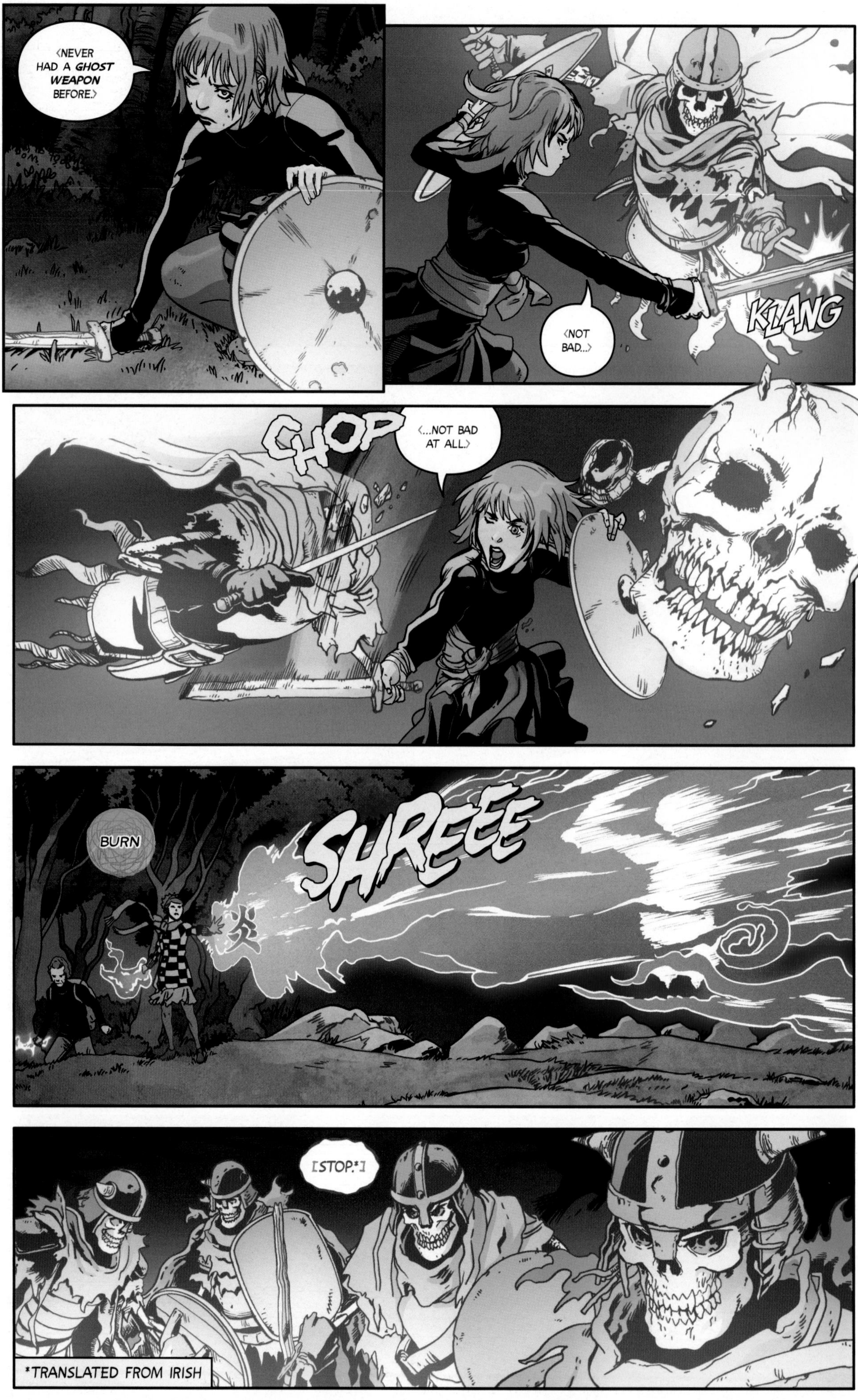

‹NEVER HAD A *GHOST WEAPON* BEFORE.›
‹NOT BAD...›
KLANG
CHOP
‹...NOT BAD AT ALL.›
BURN
SHREEE
[STOP.*]
*TRANSLATED FROM IRISH

[YOUR MAGIC TAMPERS WITH THE **NATURAL ORDER.**]

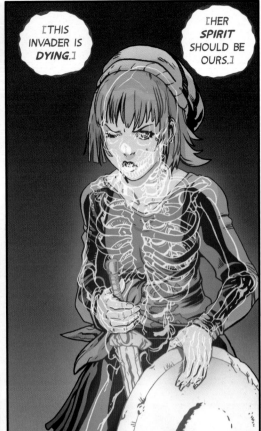

[THIS INVADER IS **DYING.**]

[HER **SPIRIT** SHOULD BE OURS.]

[IF YOU WANT IT SO BAD, THEN COME AND FECKIN' GET IT.]

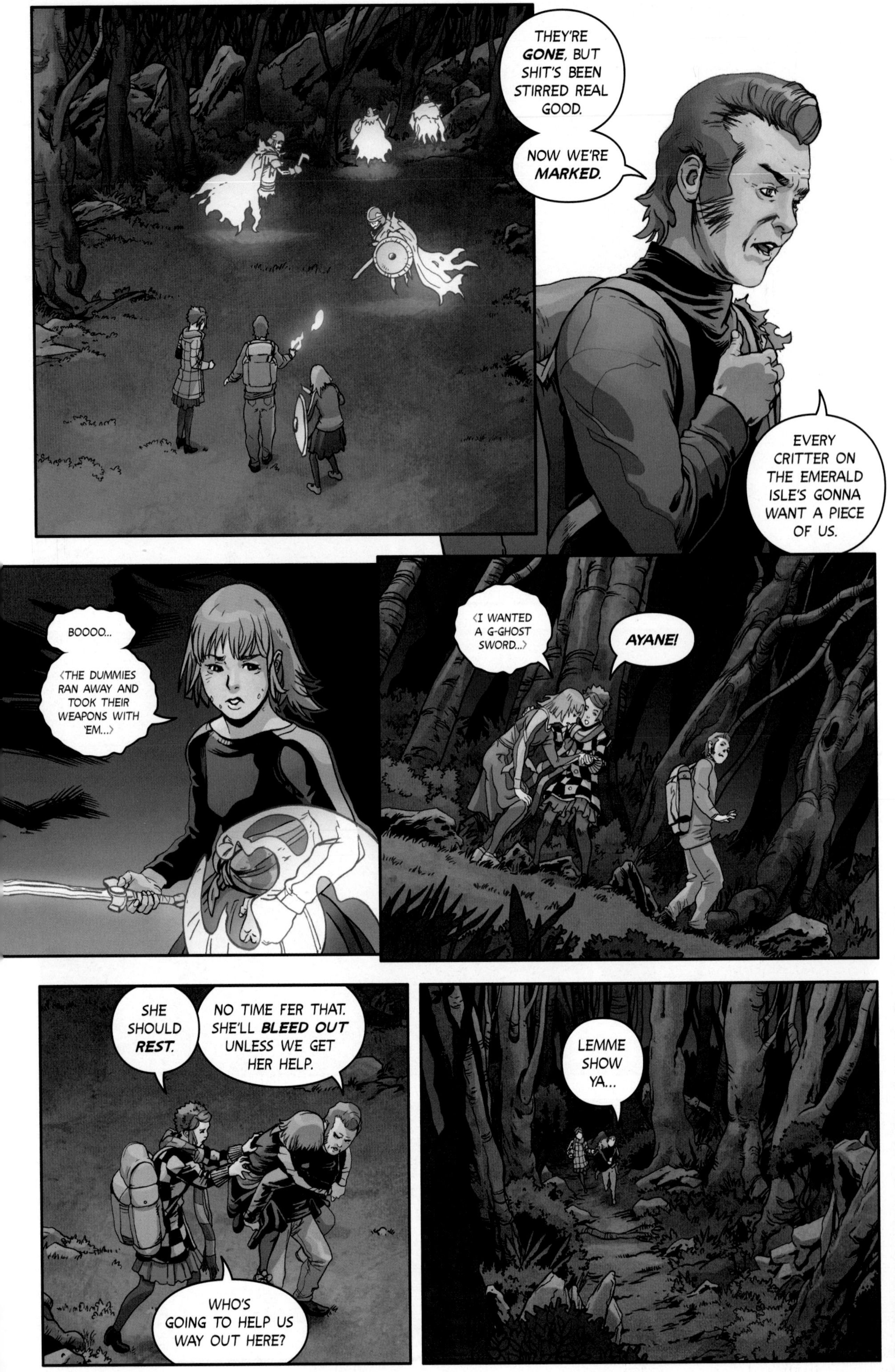
THEY'RE **GONE**, BUT SHIT'S BEEN STIRRED REAL GOOD.
NOW WE'RE **MARKED.**
EVERY CRITTER ON THE EMERALD ISLE'S GONNA WANT A PIECE OF US.
BOOOO...
‹THE DUMMIES RAN AWAY AND TOOK THEIR WEAPONS WITH 'EM...›
‹I WANTED A G-GHOST SWORD...›
AYANE!
SHE SHOULD **REST.**
NO TIME FER THAT. SHE'LL **BLEED OUT** UNLESS WE GET HER HELP.
WHO'S GOING TO HELP US WAY OUT HERE?
LEMME SHOW YA...

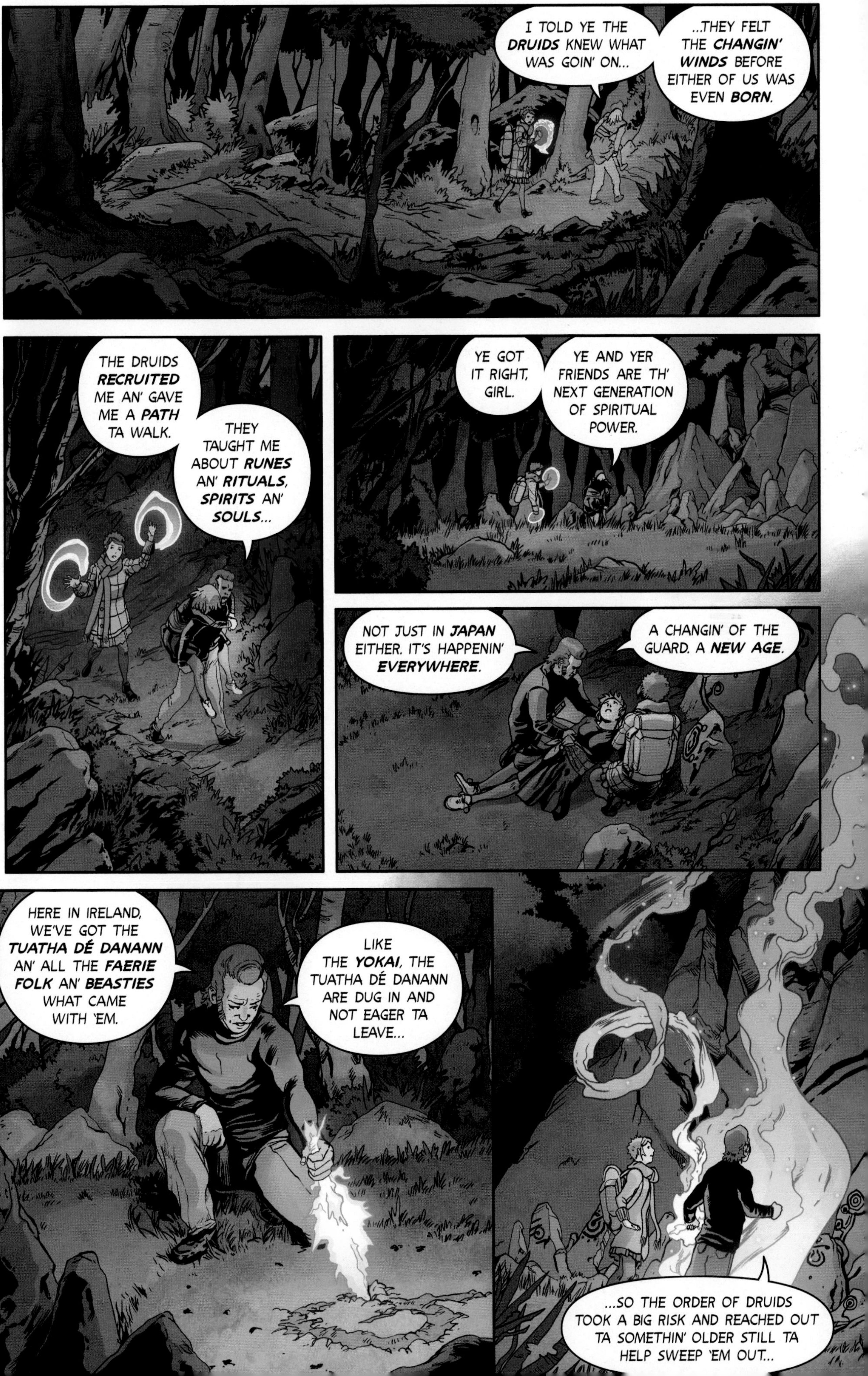
I TOLD YE THE DRUIDS KNEW WHAT WAS GOIN' ON...
...THEY FELT THE CHANGIN' WINDS BEFORE EITHER OF US WAS EVEN BORN.
THE DRUIDS RECRUITED ME AN' GAVE ME A PATH TA WALK.
THEY TAUGHT ME ABOUT RUNES AN' RITUALS, SPIRITS AN' SOULS...
YE GOT IT RIGHT, GIRL.
YE AND YER FRIENDS ARE TH' NEXT GENERATION OF SPIRITUAL POWER.
NOT JUST IN JAPAN EITHER. IT'S HAPPENIN' EVERYWHERE.
A CHANGIN' OF THE GUARD. A NEW AGE.
HERE IN IRELAND, WE'VE GOT THE TUATHA DÉ DANANN AN' ALL THE FAERIE FOLK AN' BEASTIES WHAT CAME WITH 'EM.
LIKE THE YOKAI, THE TUATHA DÉ DANANN ARE DUG IN AND NOT EAGER TA LEAVE...
...SO THE ORDER OF DRUIDS TOOK A BIG RISK AND REACHED OUT TA SOMETHIN' OLDER STILL TA HELP SWEEP 'EM OUT...

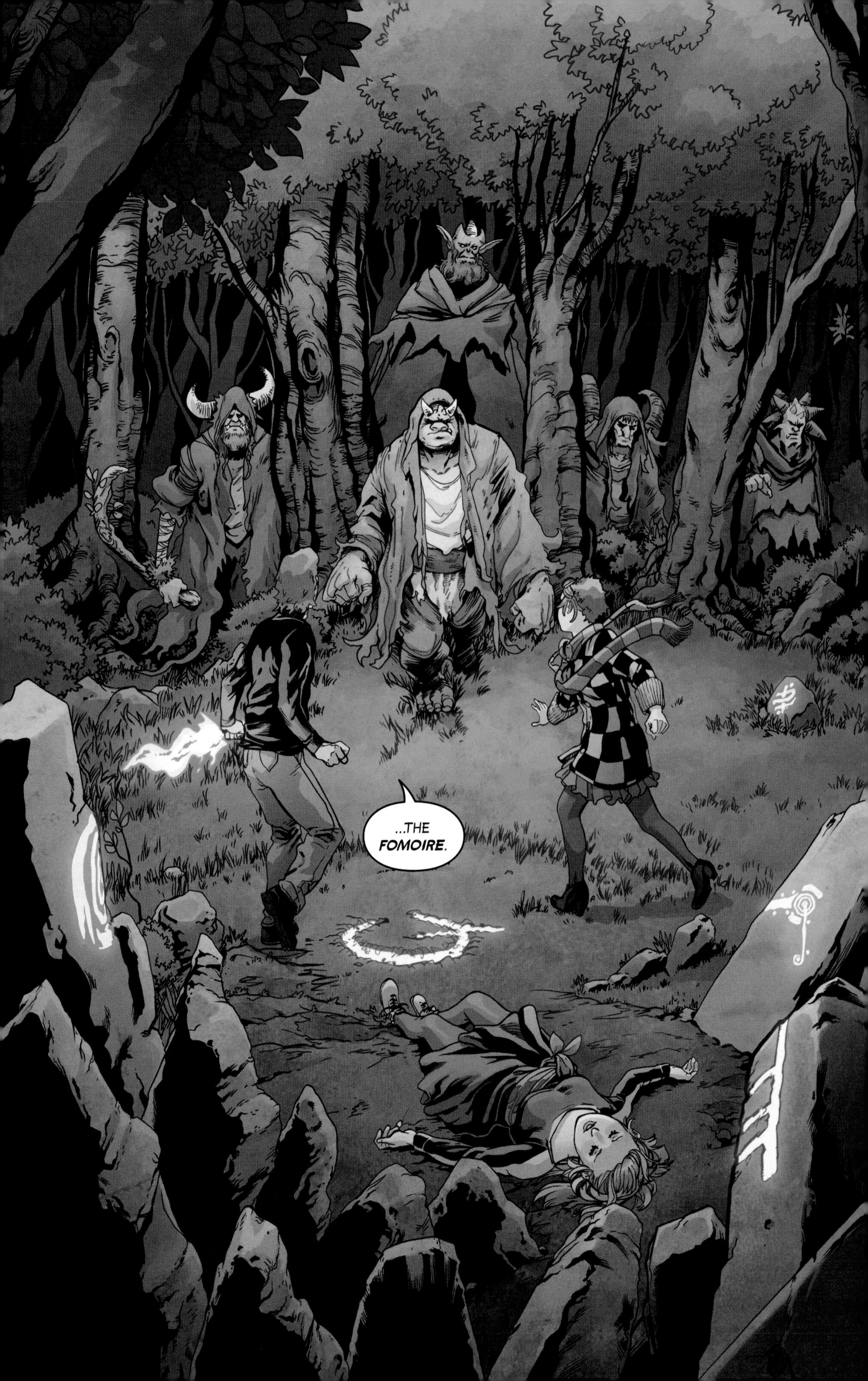
...THE FOMOIRE.

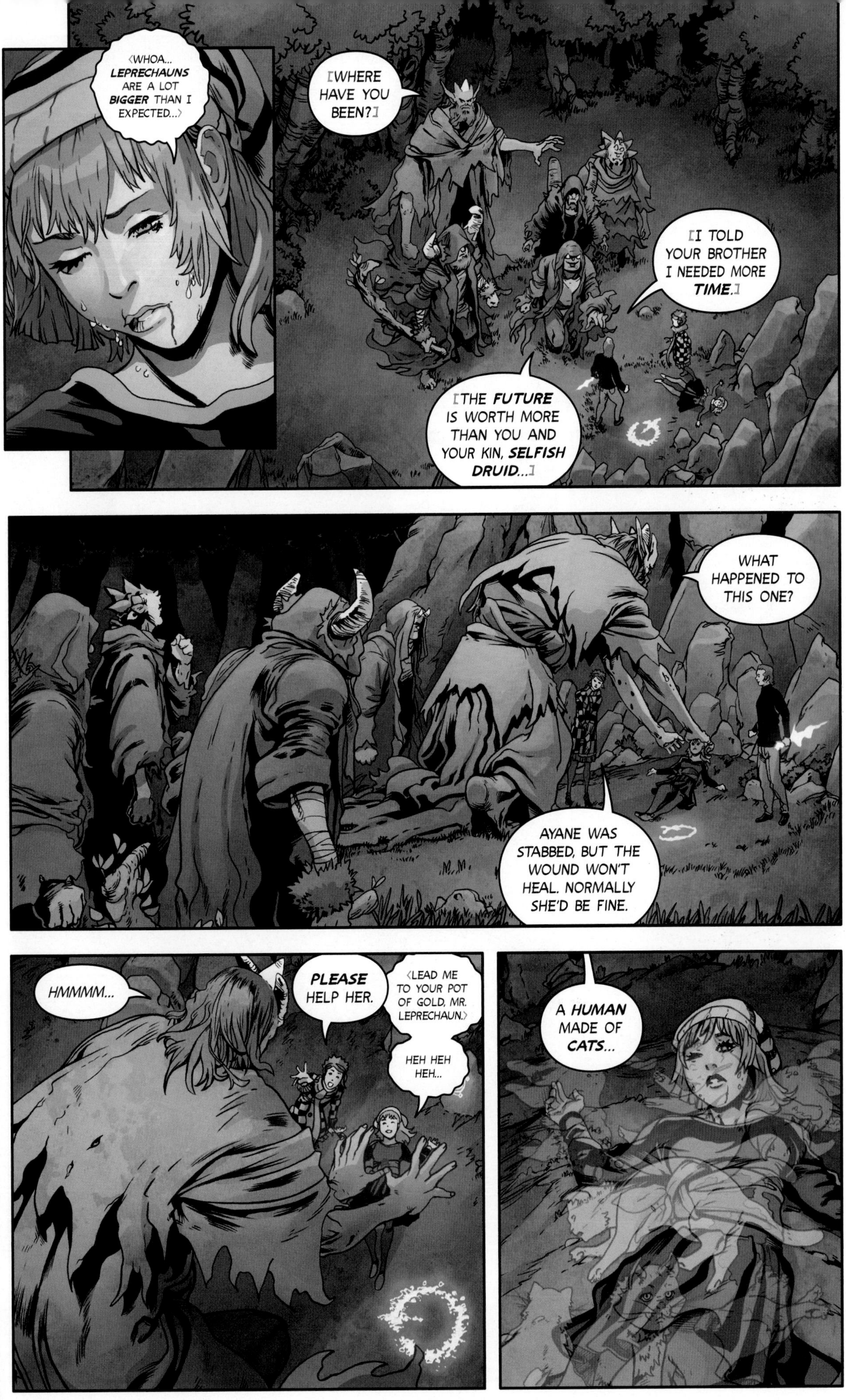
‹WHOA... LEPRECHAUNS ARE A LOT BIGGER THAN I EXPECTED...›
[WHERE HAVE YOU BEEN?]
[I TOLD YOUR BROTHER I NEEDED MORE TIME.]
[THE FUTURE IS WORTH MORE THAN YOU AND YOUR KIN, SELFISH DRUID...]
WHAT HAPPENED TO THIS ONE?
AYANE WAS STABBED, BUT THE WOUND WON'T HEAL. NORMALLY SHE'D BE FINE.
HMMMM...
PLEASE HELP HER.
‹LEAD ME TO YOUR POT OF GOLD, MR. LEPRECHAUN.›
HEH HEH HEH...
A HUMAN MADE OF CATS...

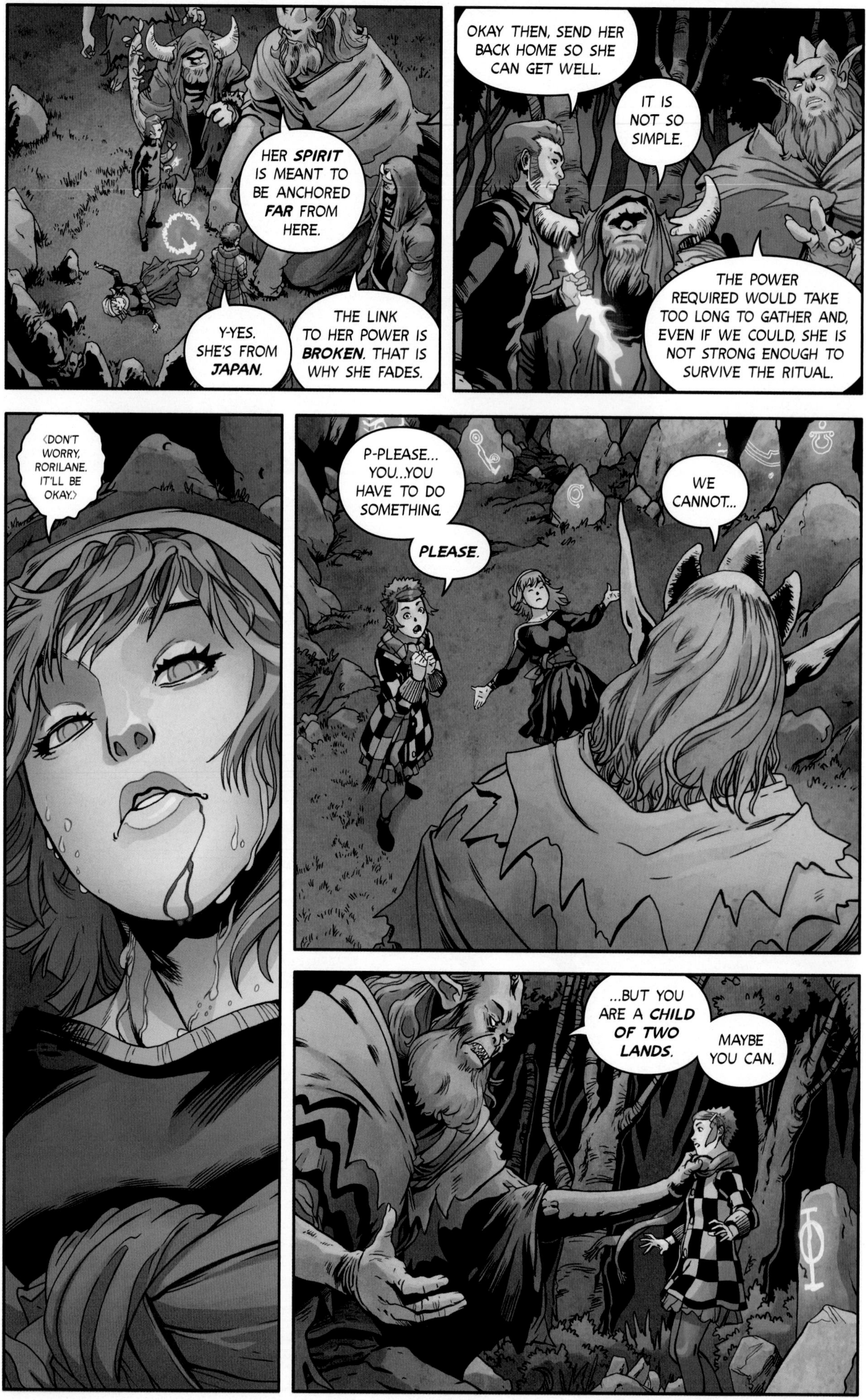
HER SPIRIT IS MEANT TO BE ANCHORED FAR FROM HERE.
Y-YES. SHE'S FROM JAPAN.
THE LINK TO HER POWER IS BROKEN. THAT IS WHY SHE FADES.
OKAY THEN, SEND HER BACK HOME SO SHE CAN GET WELL.
IT IS NOT SO SIMPLE.
THE POWER REQUIRED WOULD TAKE TOO LONG TO GATHER AND, EVEN IF WE COULD, SHE IS NOT STRONG ENOUGH TO SURVIVE THE RITUAL.
<DON'T WORRY, RORILANE. IT'LL BE OKAY.>
P-PLEASE... YOU...YOU HAVE TO DO SOMETHING.
PLEASE.
WE CANNOT...
...BUT YOU ARE A CHILD OF TWO LANDS.
MAYBE YOU CAN.

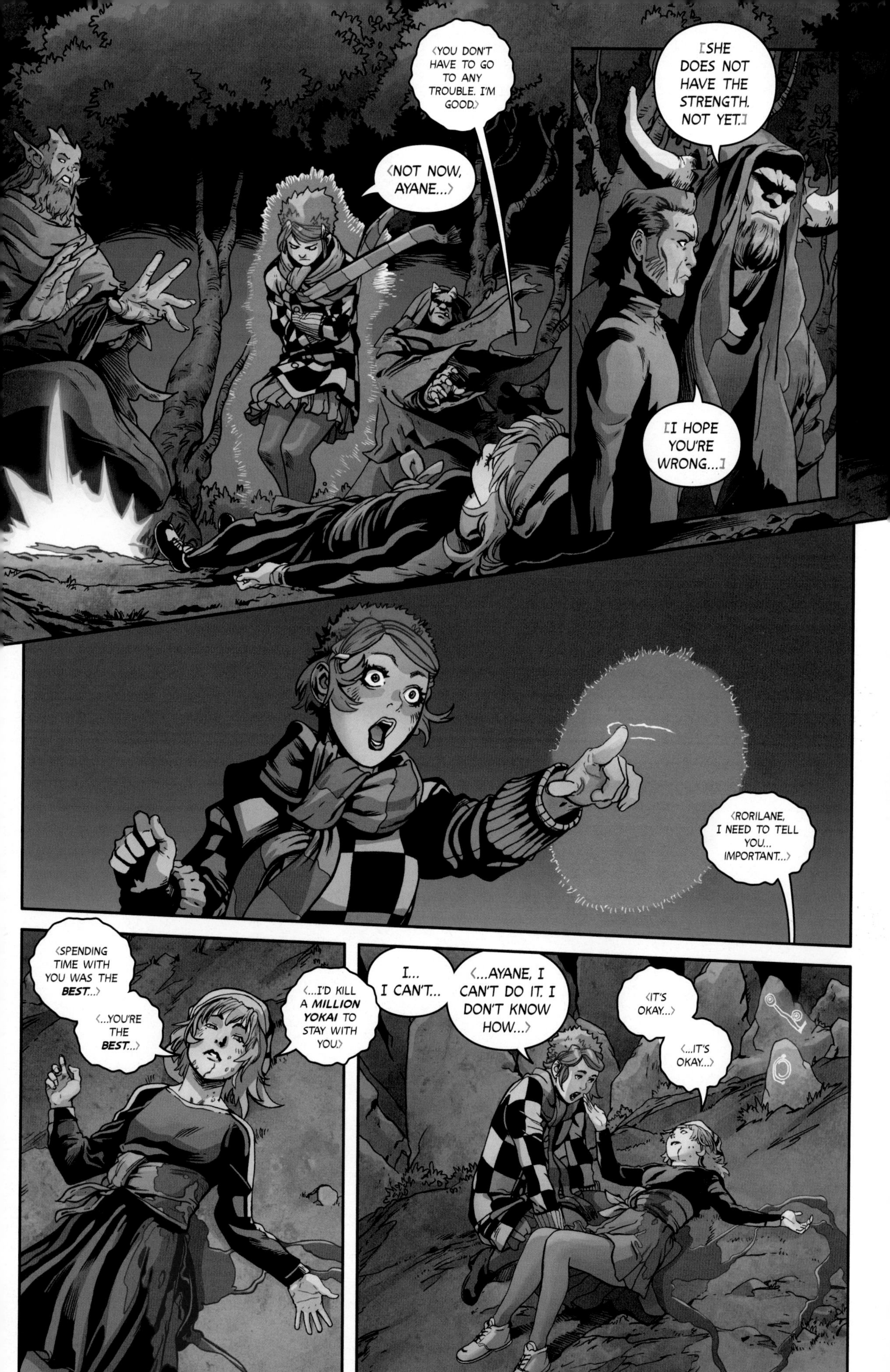

<NOT NOW, AYANE...>
<YOU DON'T HAVE TO GO TO ANY TROUBLE. I'M GOOD.>
[SHE DOES NOT HAVE THE STRENGTH. NOT YET.]
[I HOPE YOU'RE WRONG...]
<RORILANE, I NEED TO TELL YOU... IMPORTANT...>
<SPENDING TIME WITH YOU WAS THE BEST...>
<...YOU'RE THE BEST...>
<...I'D KILL A MILLION YOKAI TO STAY WITH YOU.>
I... I CAN'T...
<...AYANE, I CAN'T DO IT. I DON'T KNOW HOW...>
<IT'S OKAY...>
<...IT'S OKAY...>

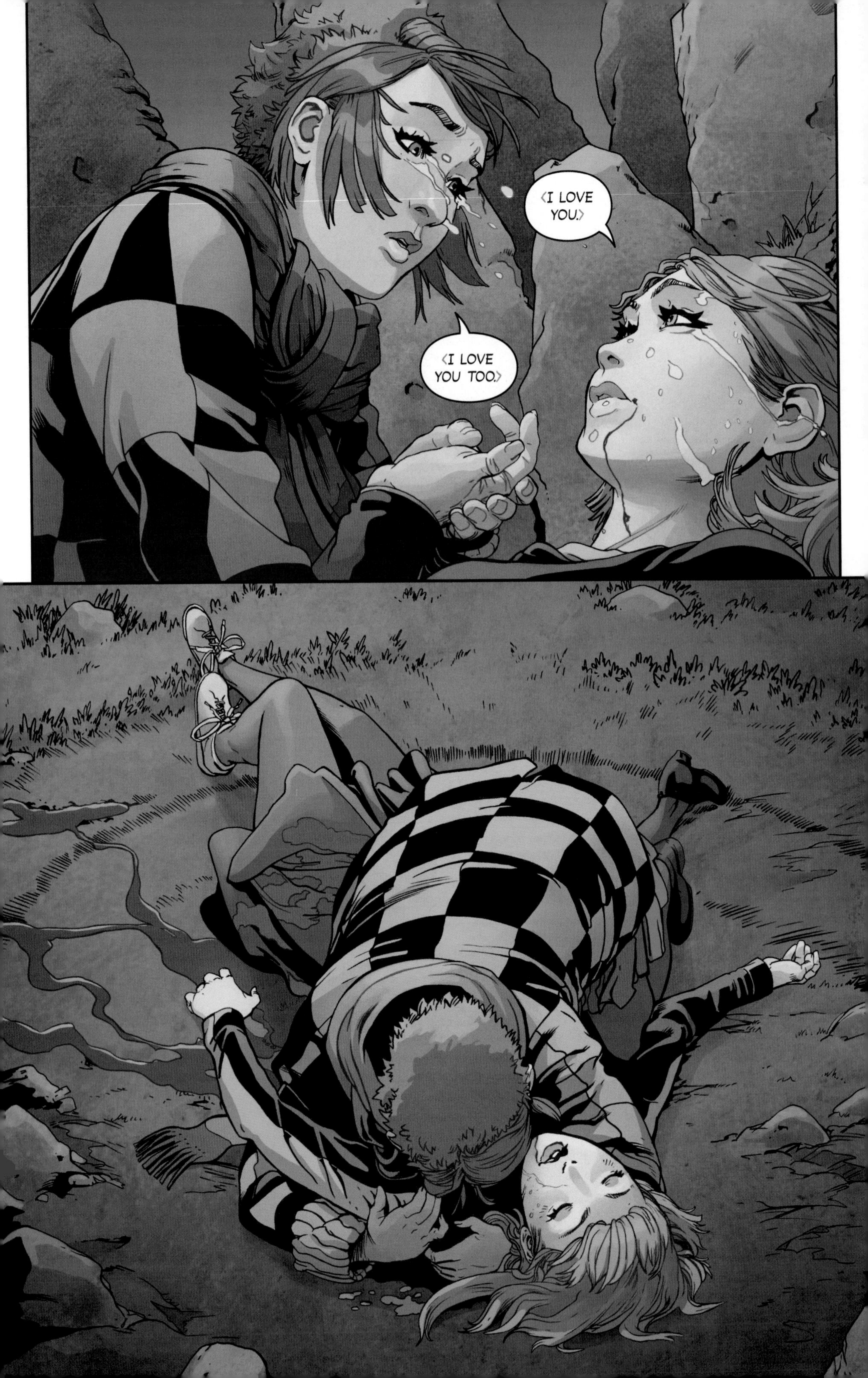

‹I LOVE YOU.›
‹I LOVE YOU TOO.›

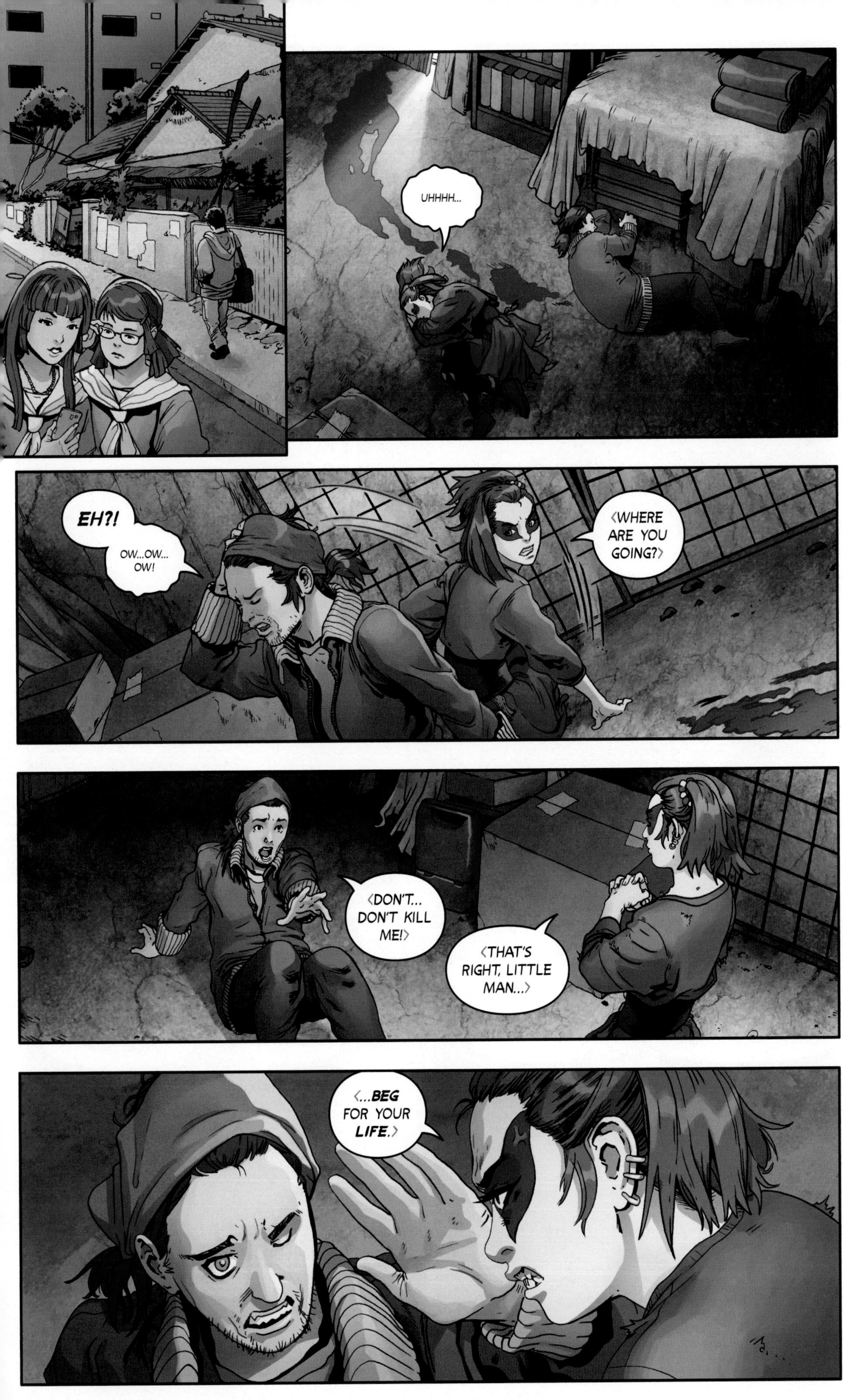
UHHHH...
EH?!
OW...OW... OW!
‹WHERE ARE YOU GOING?›
‹DON'T... DON'T KILL ME!›
‹THAT'S RIGHT, LITTLE MAN...›
‹...**BEG** FOR YOUR **LIFE**.›

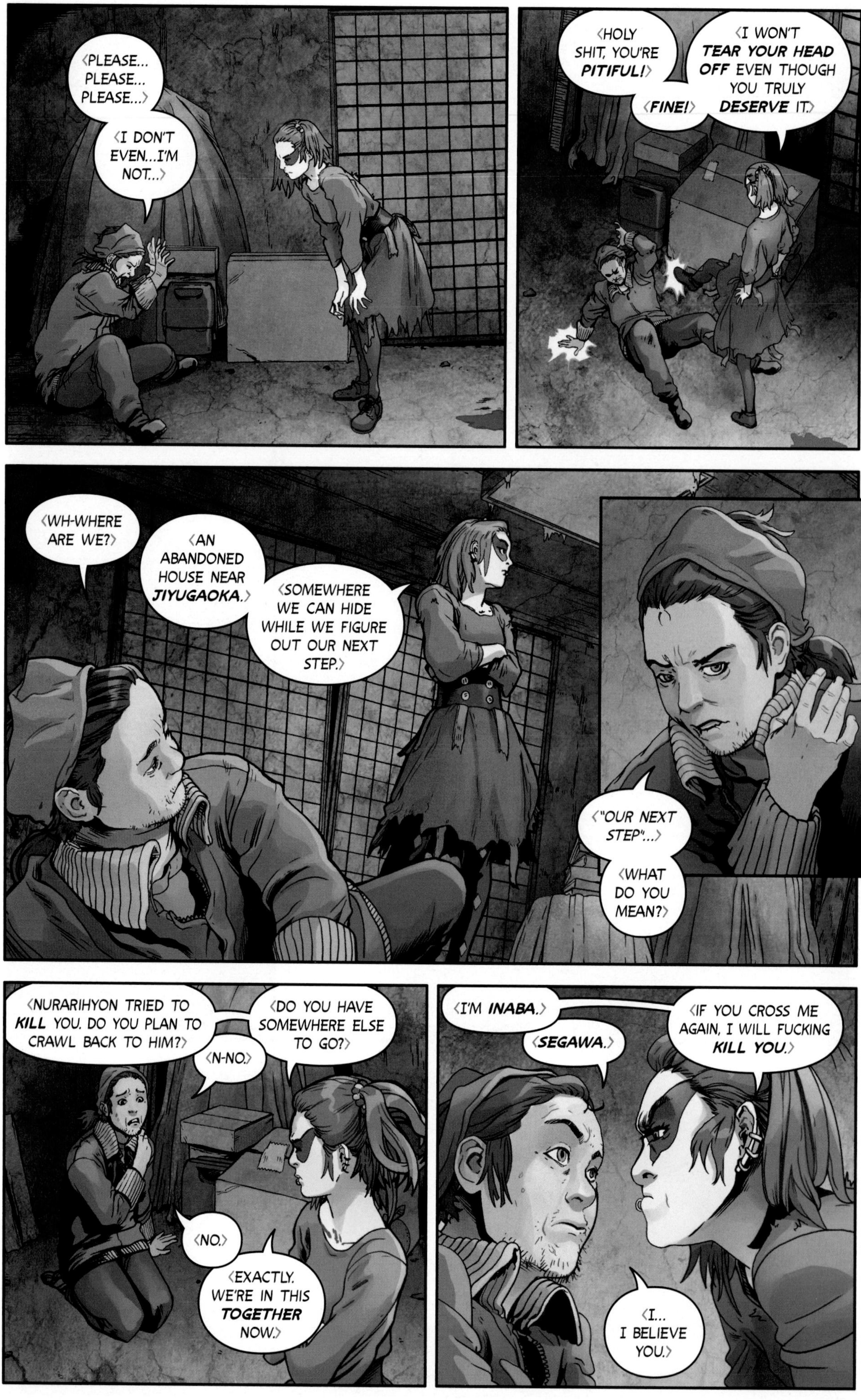
‹PLEASE... PLEASE... PLEASE...›
‹I DON'T EVEN...I'M NOT...›
‹HOLY SHIT, YOU'RE **PITIFUL!**›
‹**FINE!**›
‹I WON'T **TEAR YOUR HEAD OFF** EVEN THOUGH YOU TRULY **DESERVE** IT.›
‹WH-WHERE ARE WE?›
‹AN ABANDONED HOUSE NEAR **JIYUGAOKA.**›
‹SOMEWHERE WE CAN HIDE WHILE WE FIGURE OUT OUR NEXT STEP.›
‹"OUR NEXT STEP"...›
‹WHAT DO YOU MEAN?›
‹NURARIHYON TRIED TO **KILL** YOU. DO YOU PLAN TO CRAWL BACK TO HIM?›
‹N-NO.›
‹DO YOU HAVE SOMEWHERE ELSE TO GO?›
‹NO.›
‹EXACTLY. WE'RE IN THIS **TOGETHER** NOW.›
‹I'M **INABA.**›
‹**SEGAWA.**›
‹IF YOU CROSS ME AGAIN, I WILL FUCKING **KILL YOU.**›
‹I... I BELIEVE YOU.›

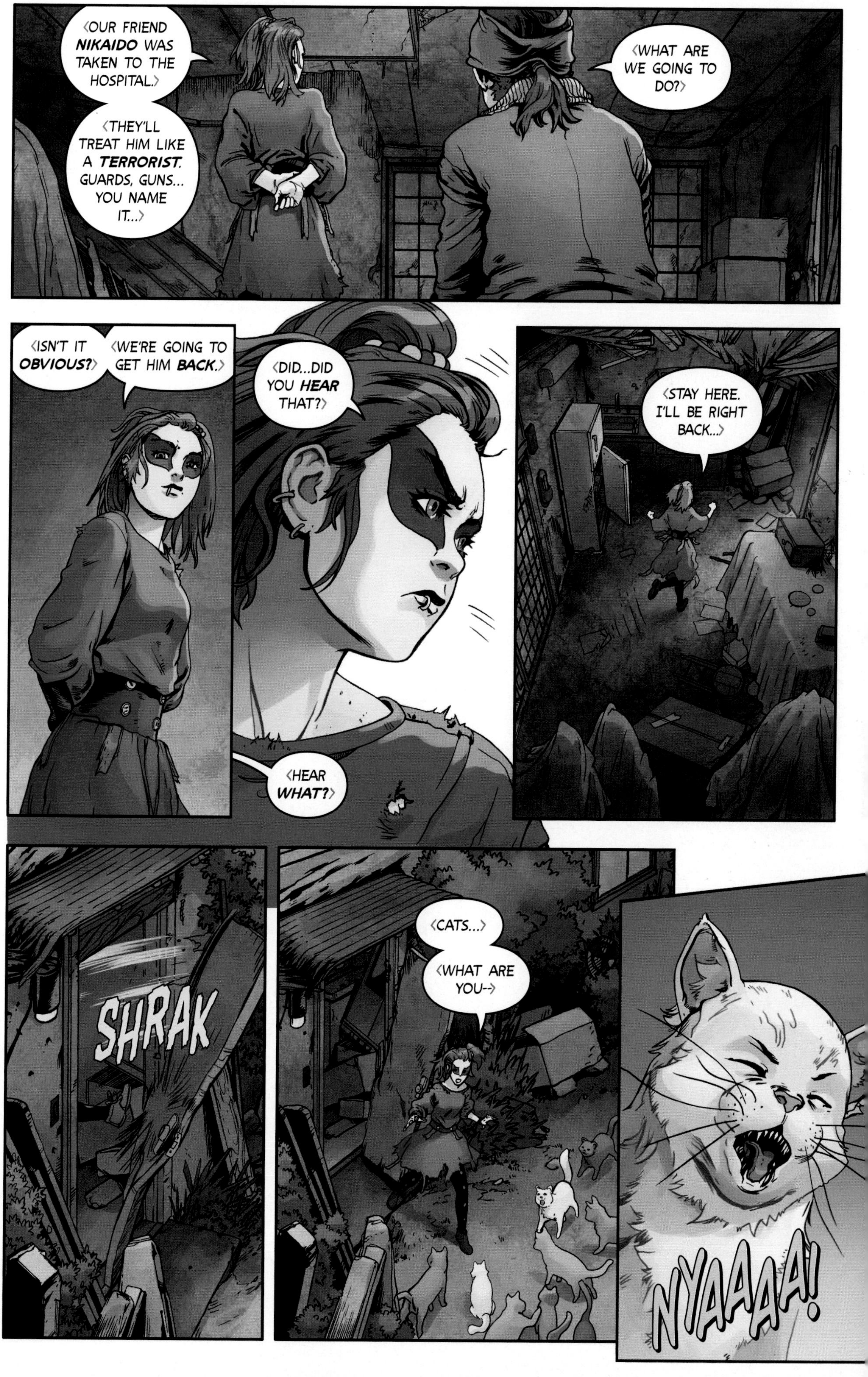

‹OUR FRIEND NIKAIDO WAS TAKEN TO THE HOSPITAL.›
‹THEY'LL TREAT HIM LIKE A TERRORIST. GUARDS, GUNS... YOU NAME IT...›
‹WHAT ARE WE GOING TO DO?›
‹ISN'T IT OBVIOUS?›
‹WE'RE GOING TO GET HIM BACK.›
‹DID...DID YOU HEAR THAT?›
‹HEAR WHAT?›
‹STAY HERE. I'LL BE RIGHT BACK...›
SHRAK
‹CATS...›
‹WHAT ARE YOU--›
NYAAAA!

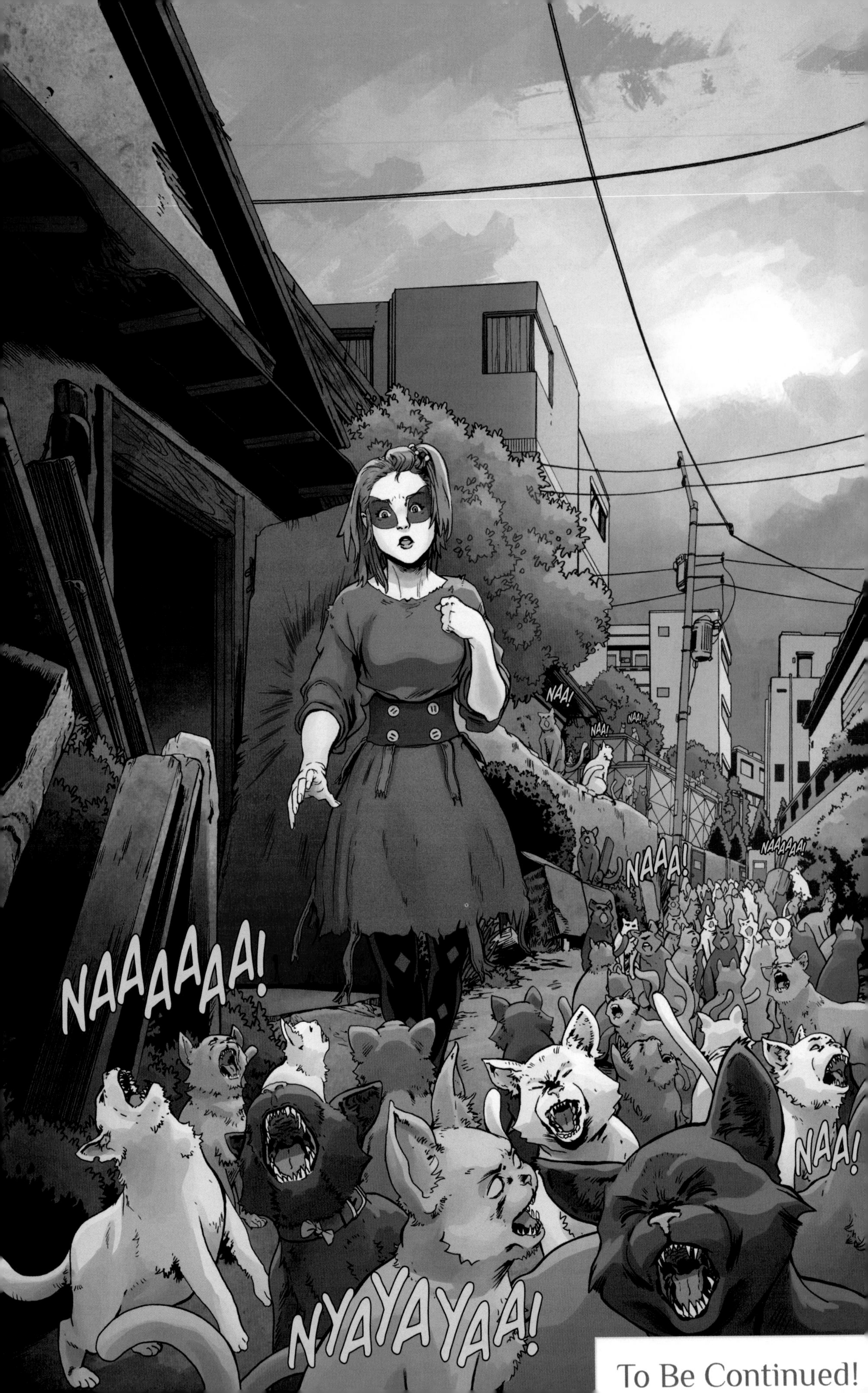
NAA!
NAA!
NAA!
NAAA!
NAAAAAA!
NAAAAAA!
NAA!
NYAYAYAA!
To Be Continued!

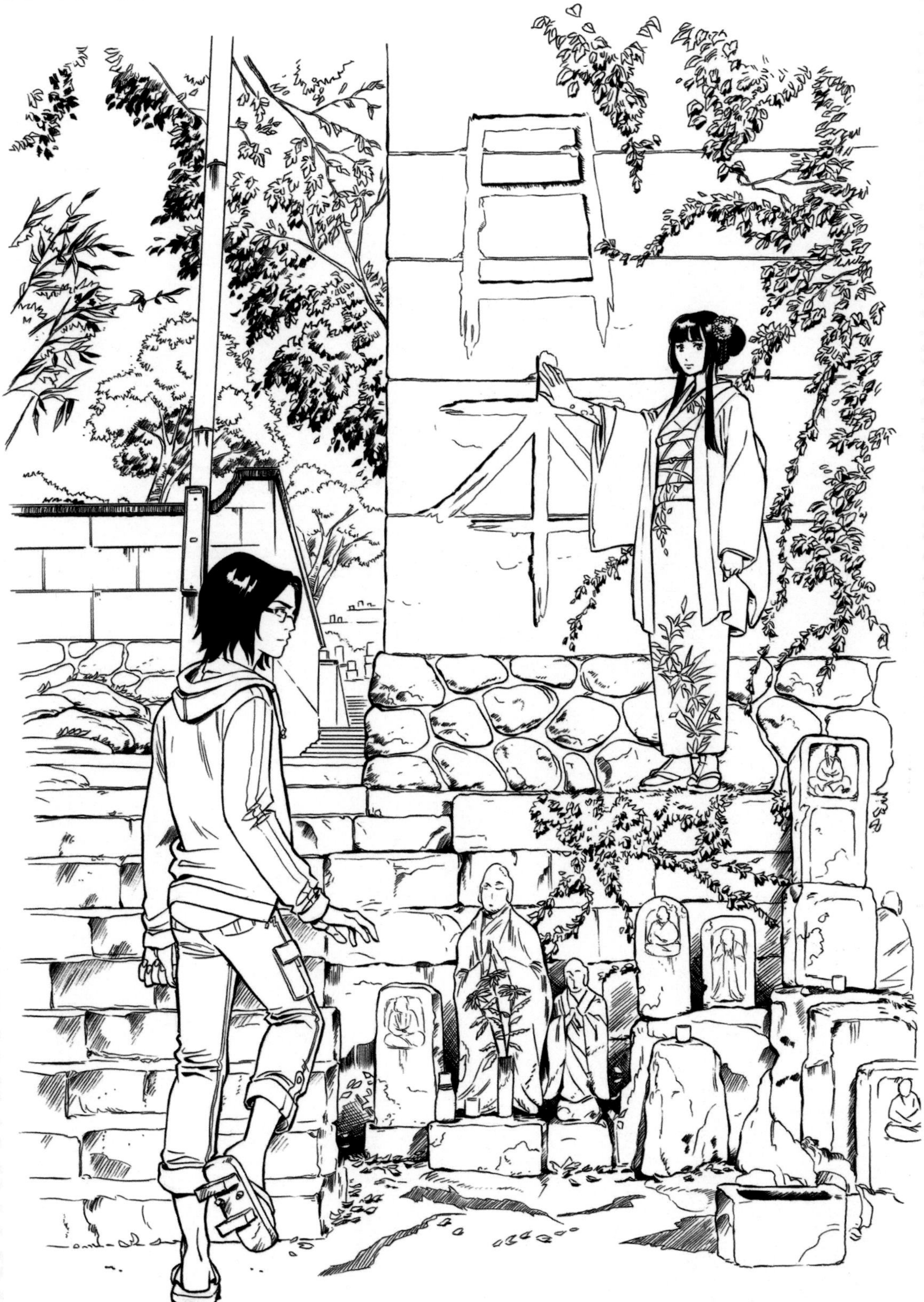

WAYWARD #11 (Cover C)
Line Art by Danica Brine

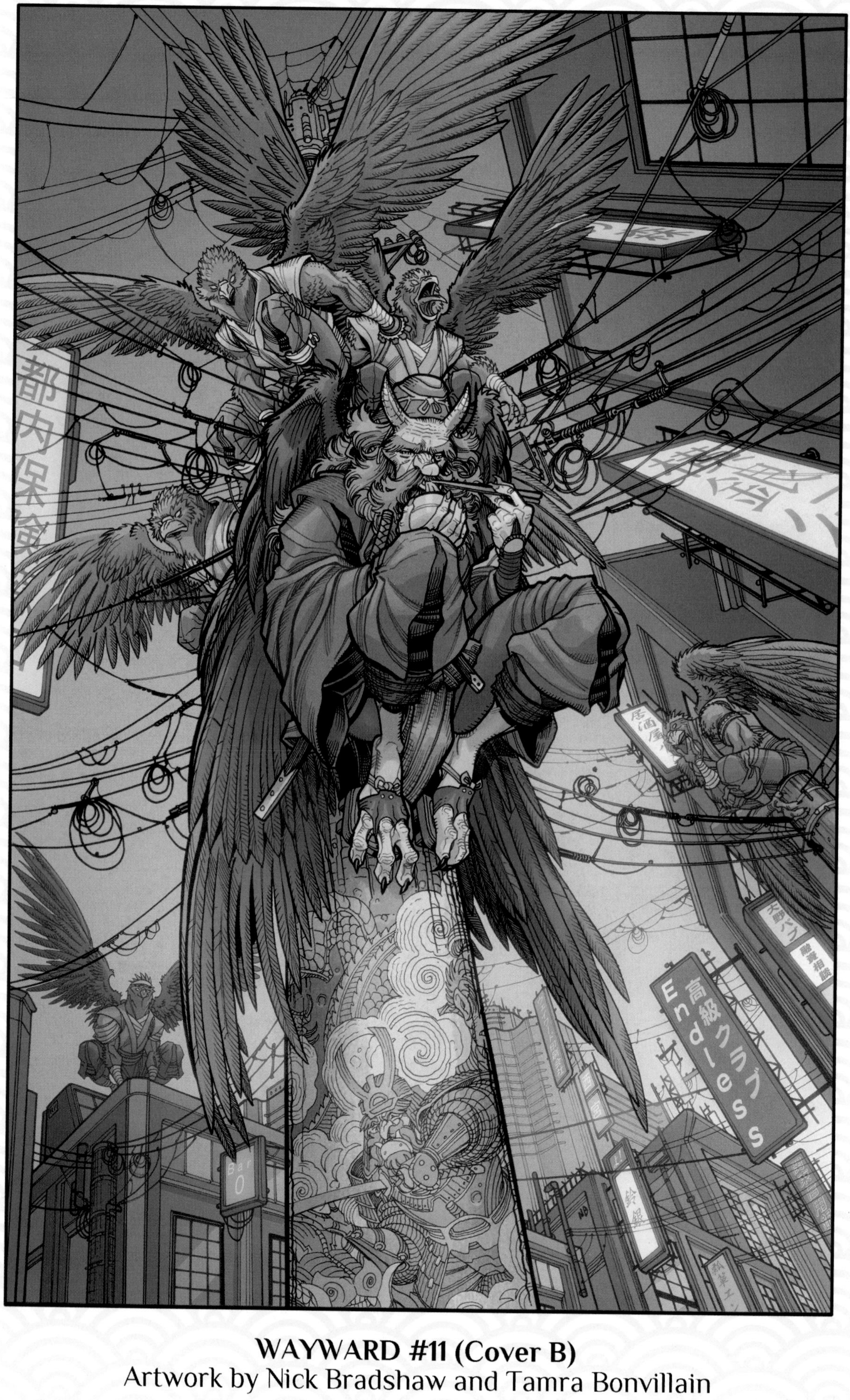
高級クラブ
Endless
Bar
0

WAYWARD #11 (Cover B)
Artwork by Nick Bradshaw and Tamra Bonvillain

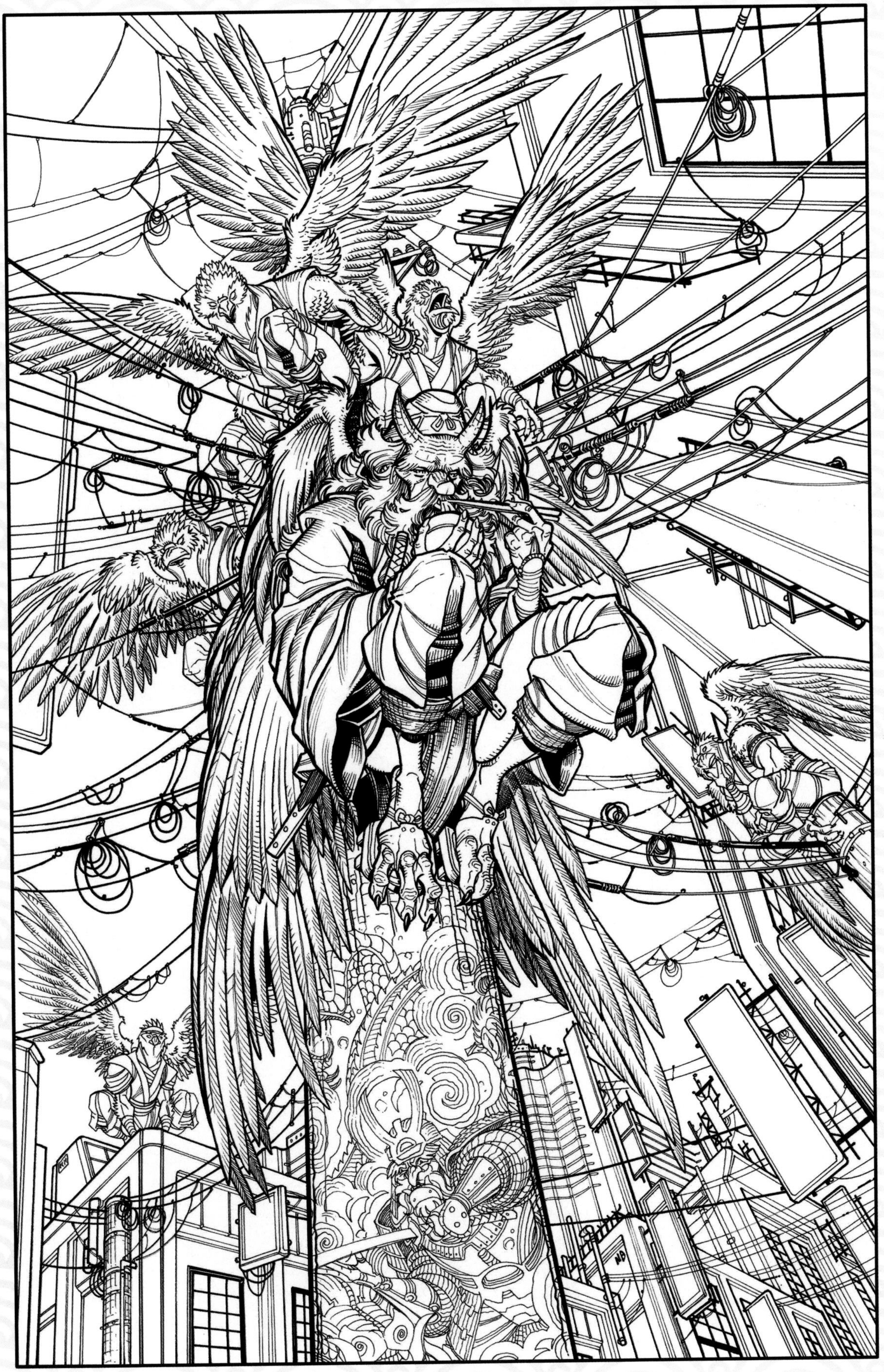

WAYWARD #11 (Cover B)
Line Art by Nick Bradshaw

Wayward
COVER GALLERY

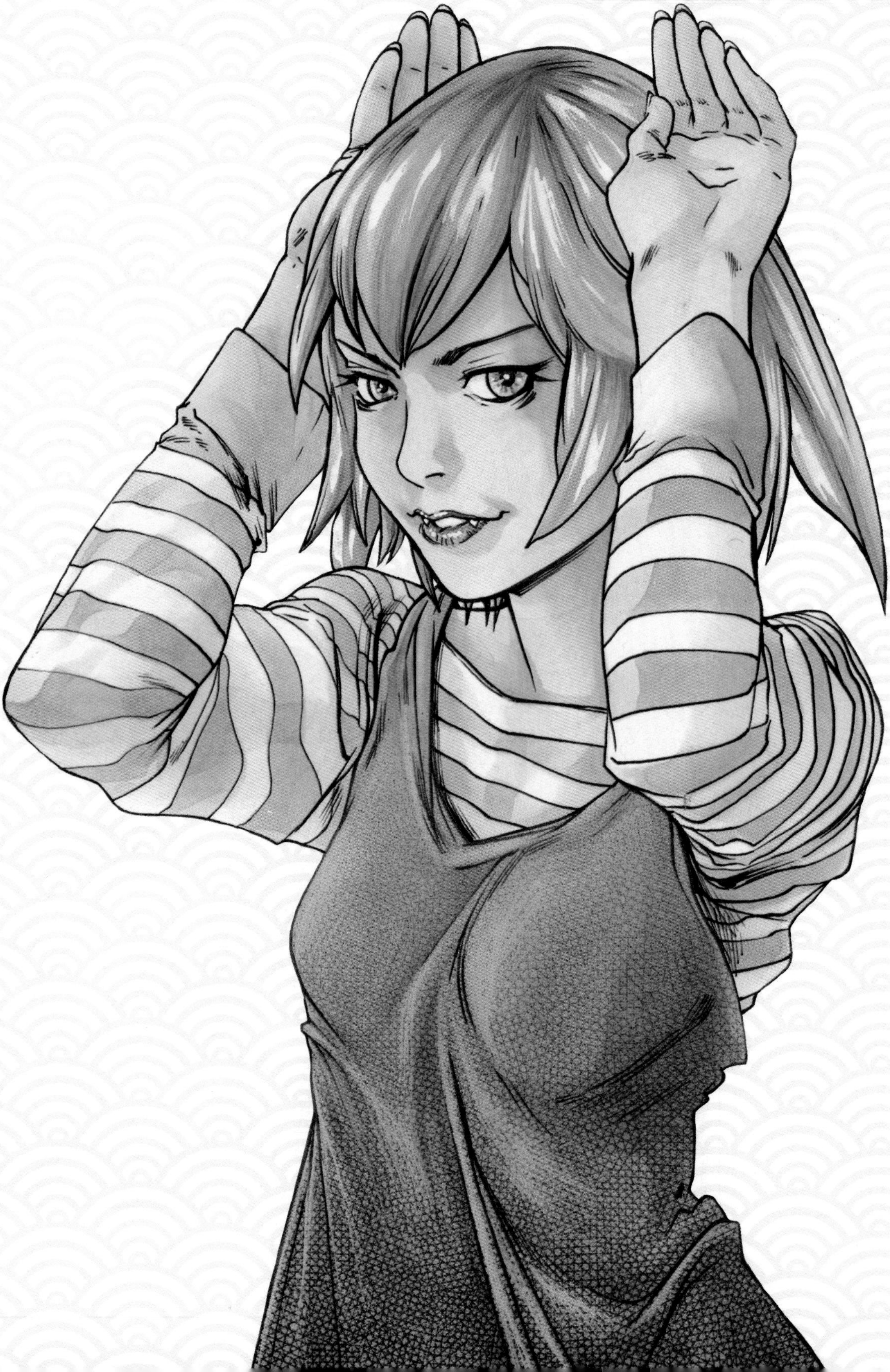

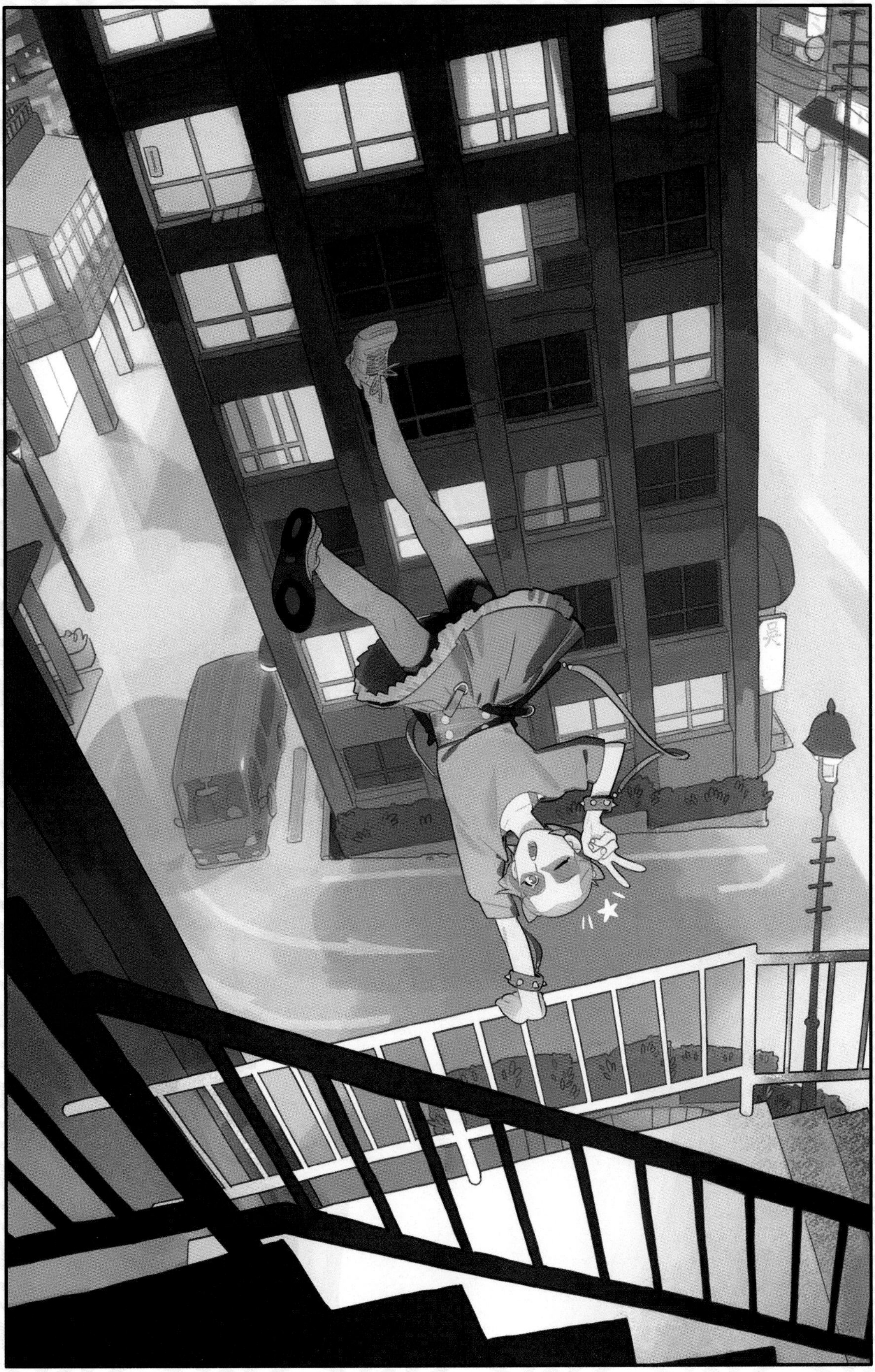

吳

WAYWARD #12 (Cover B)
Artwork by Vivian Ng

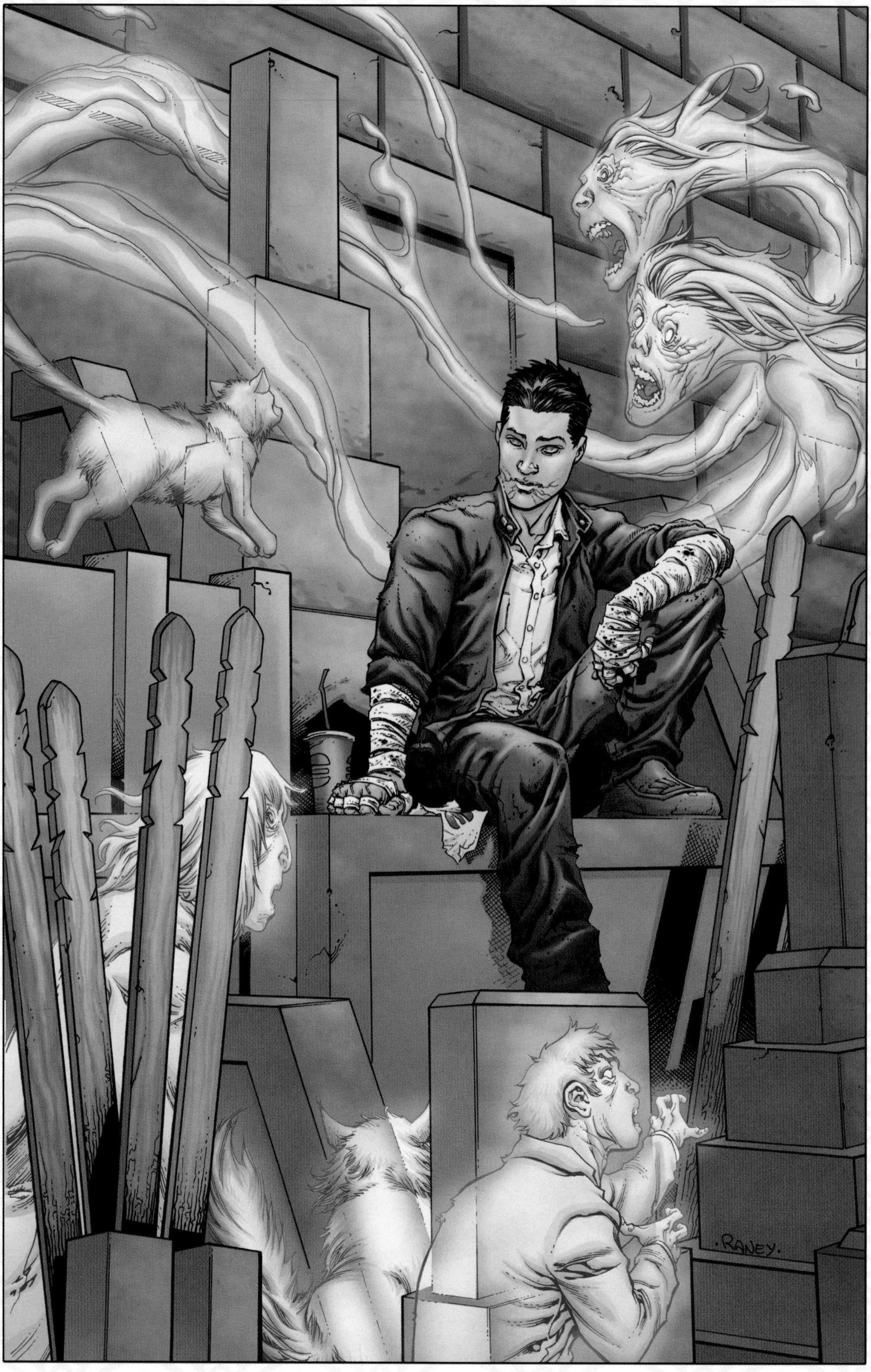
RANEY

WAYWARD #13 (Cover B)
Artwork by Tom Raney and Gina Going

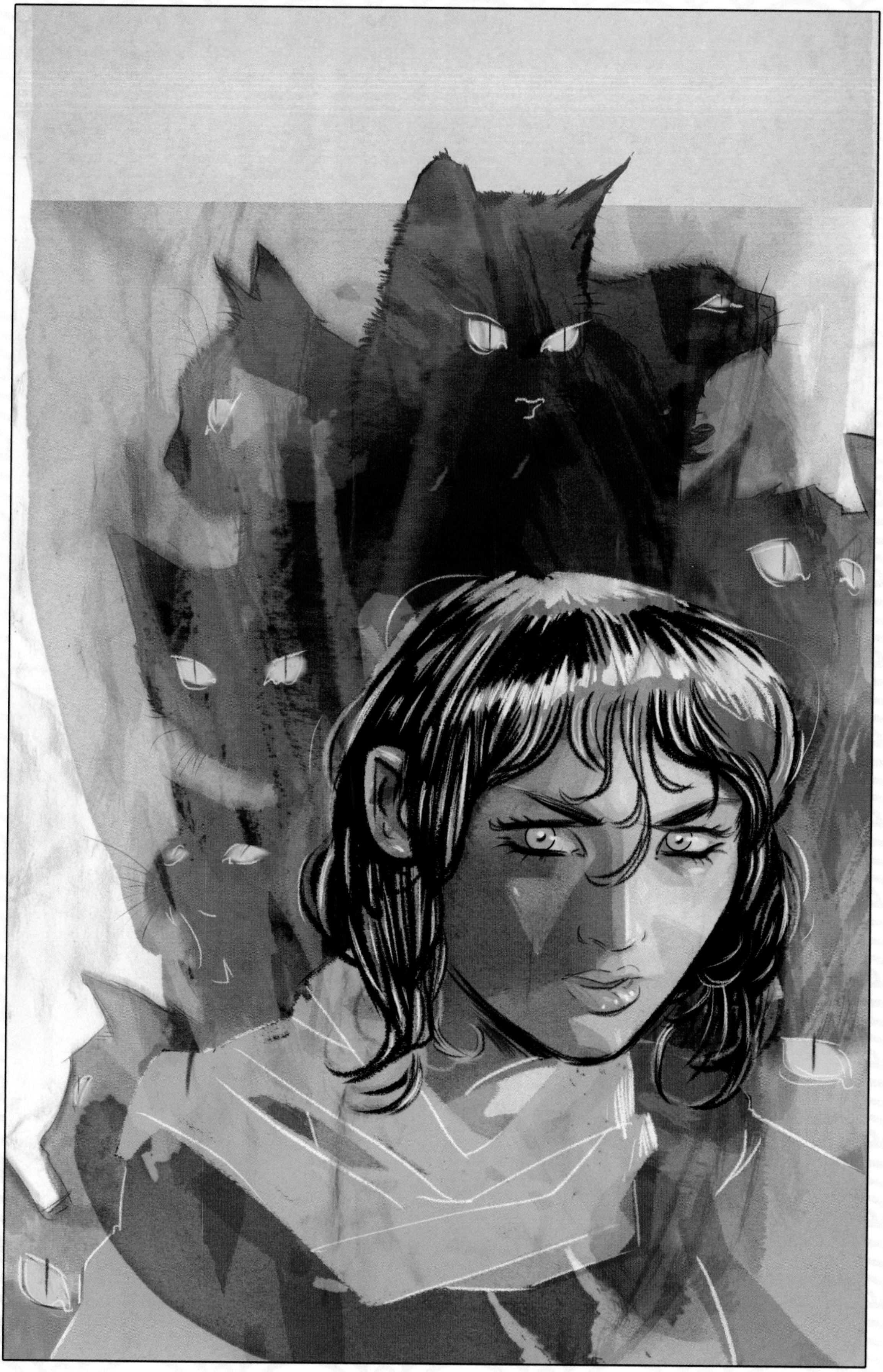

WAYWARD #14 (Cover B)
Artwork by Tula Lotay

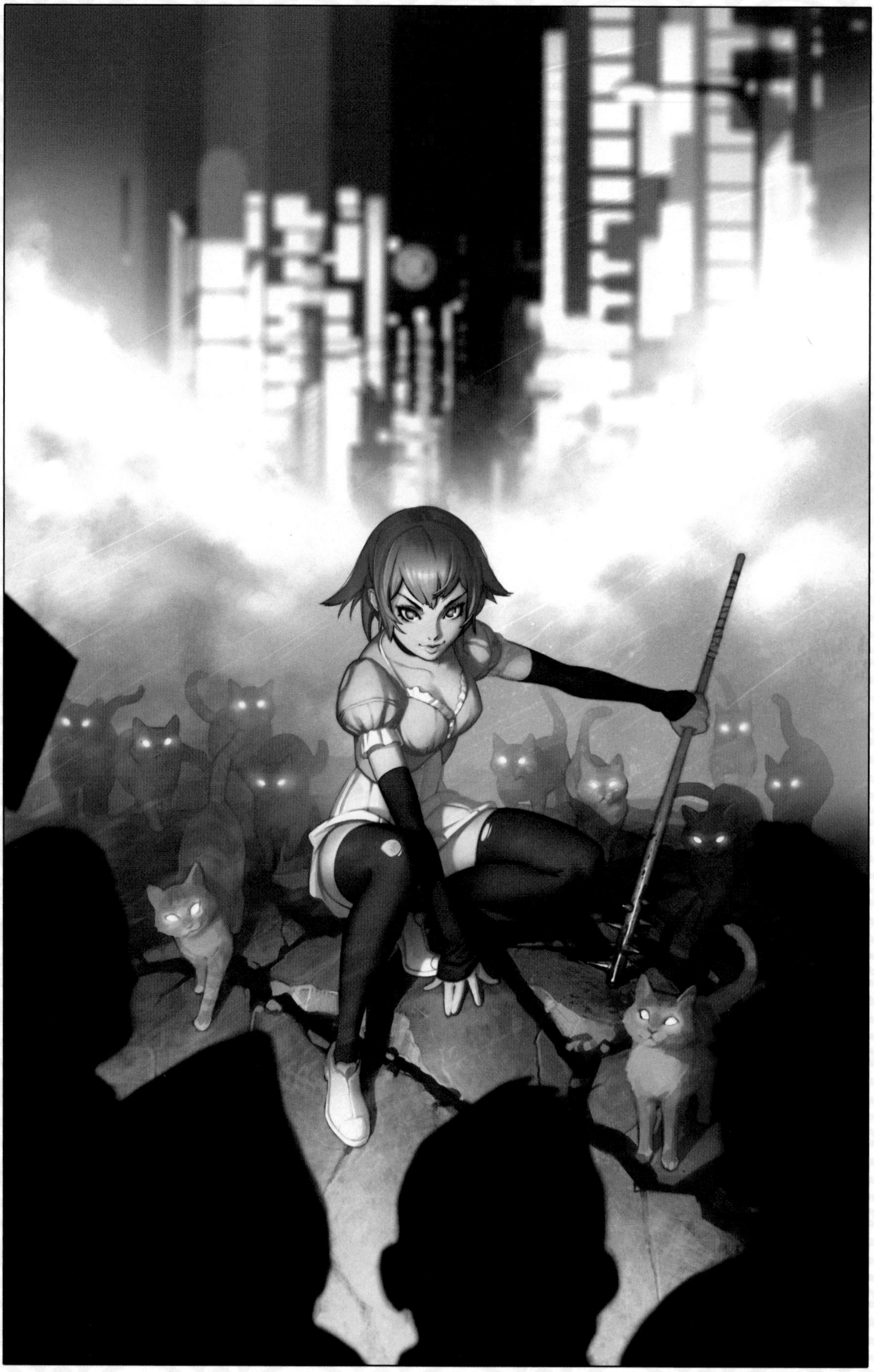

WAYWARD #15 (Cover B)
Artwork by Ilya Kuvshinov

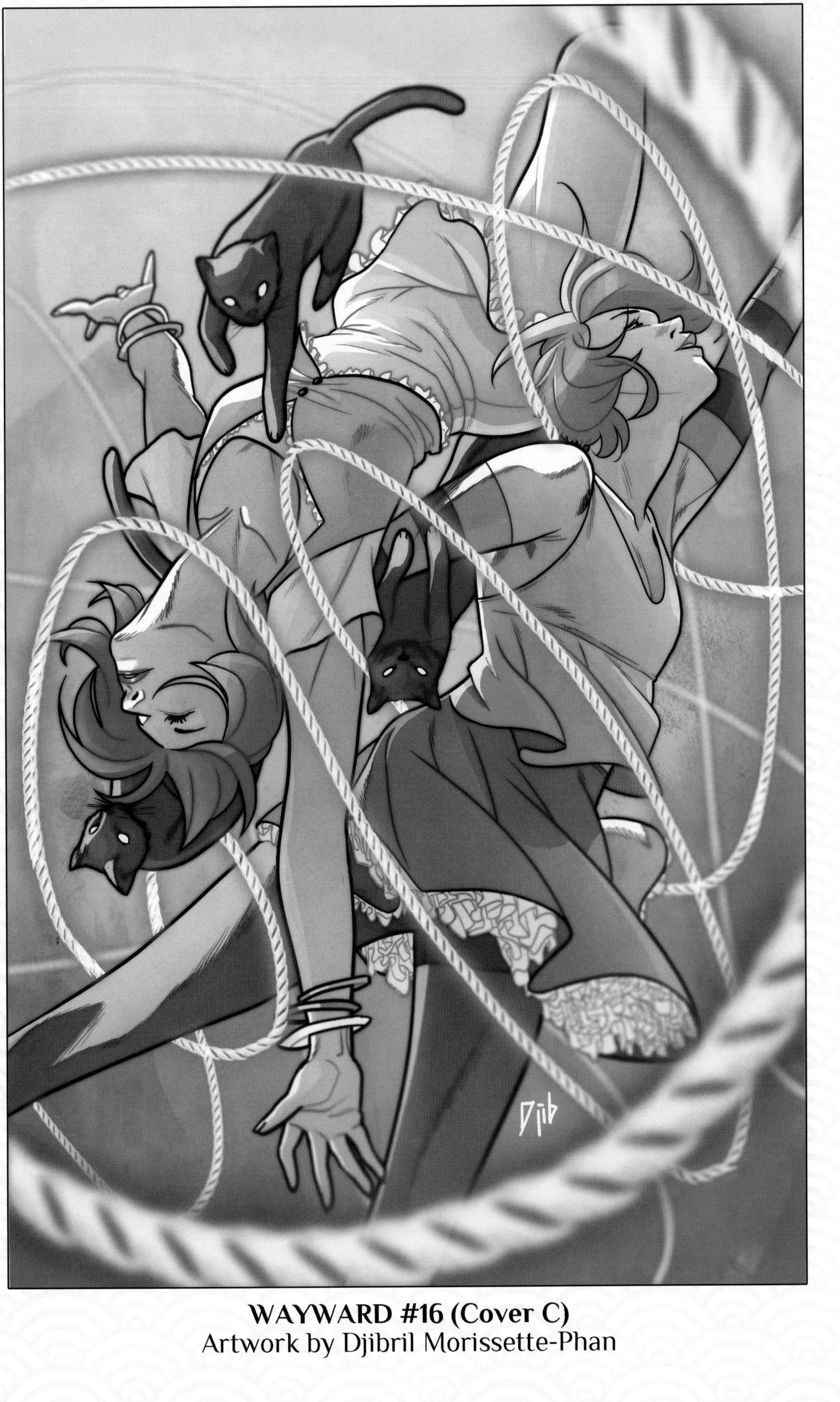
Djib

WAYWARD #16 (Cover C)
Artwork by Djibril Morissette-Phan

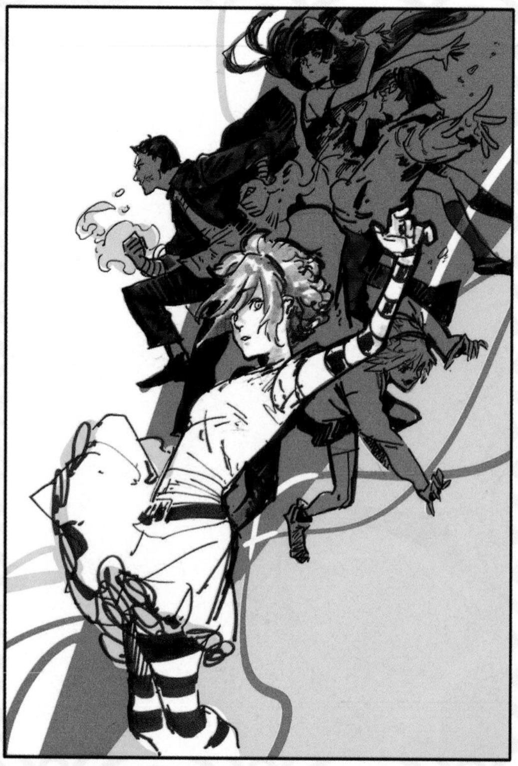
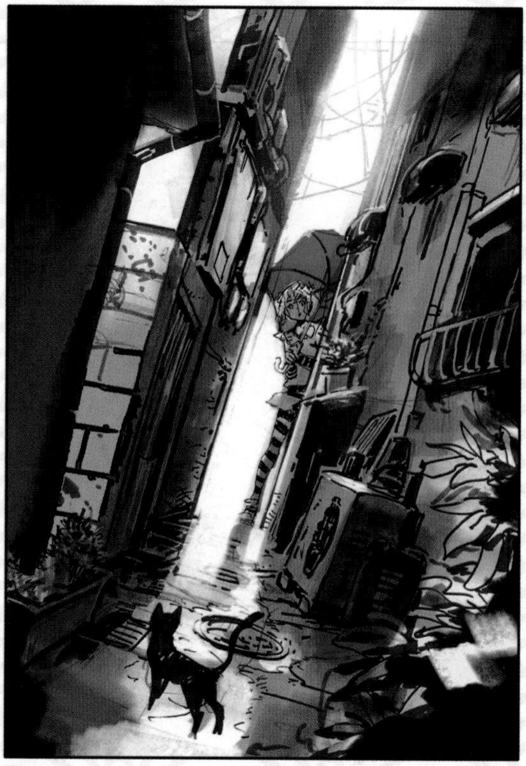
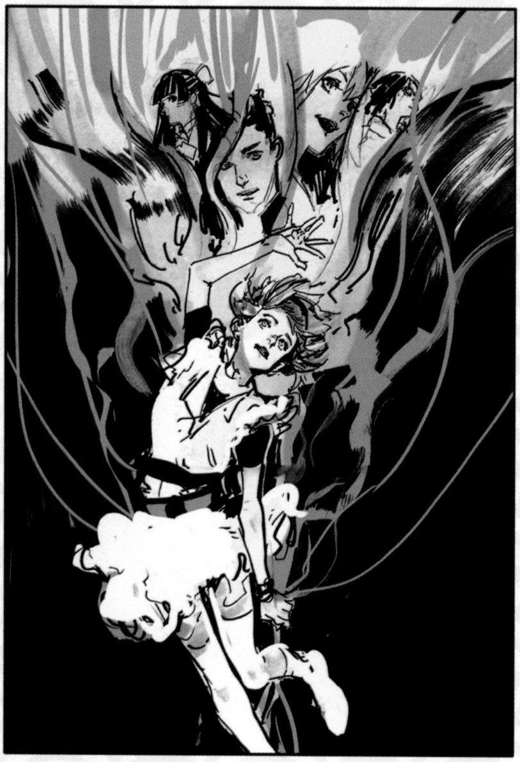
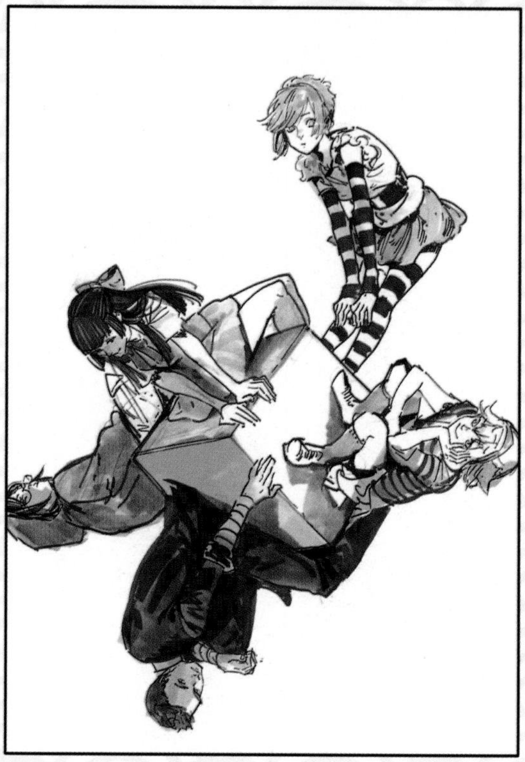

WAYWARD #16 (Cover B)
Roughs by Kamome Shirahama

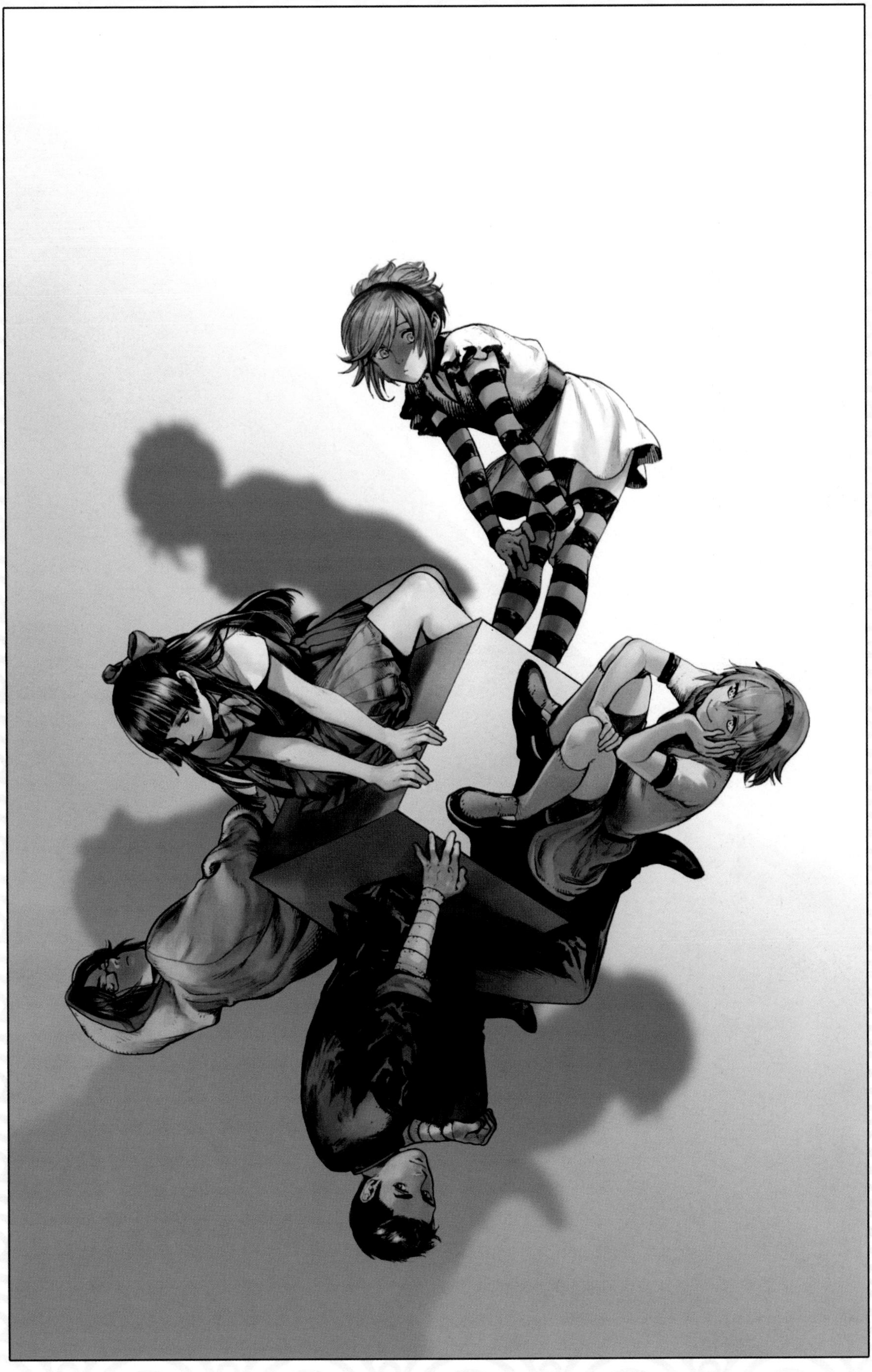

WAYWARD #16 (Cover B)
Artwork by Kamome Shirahama

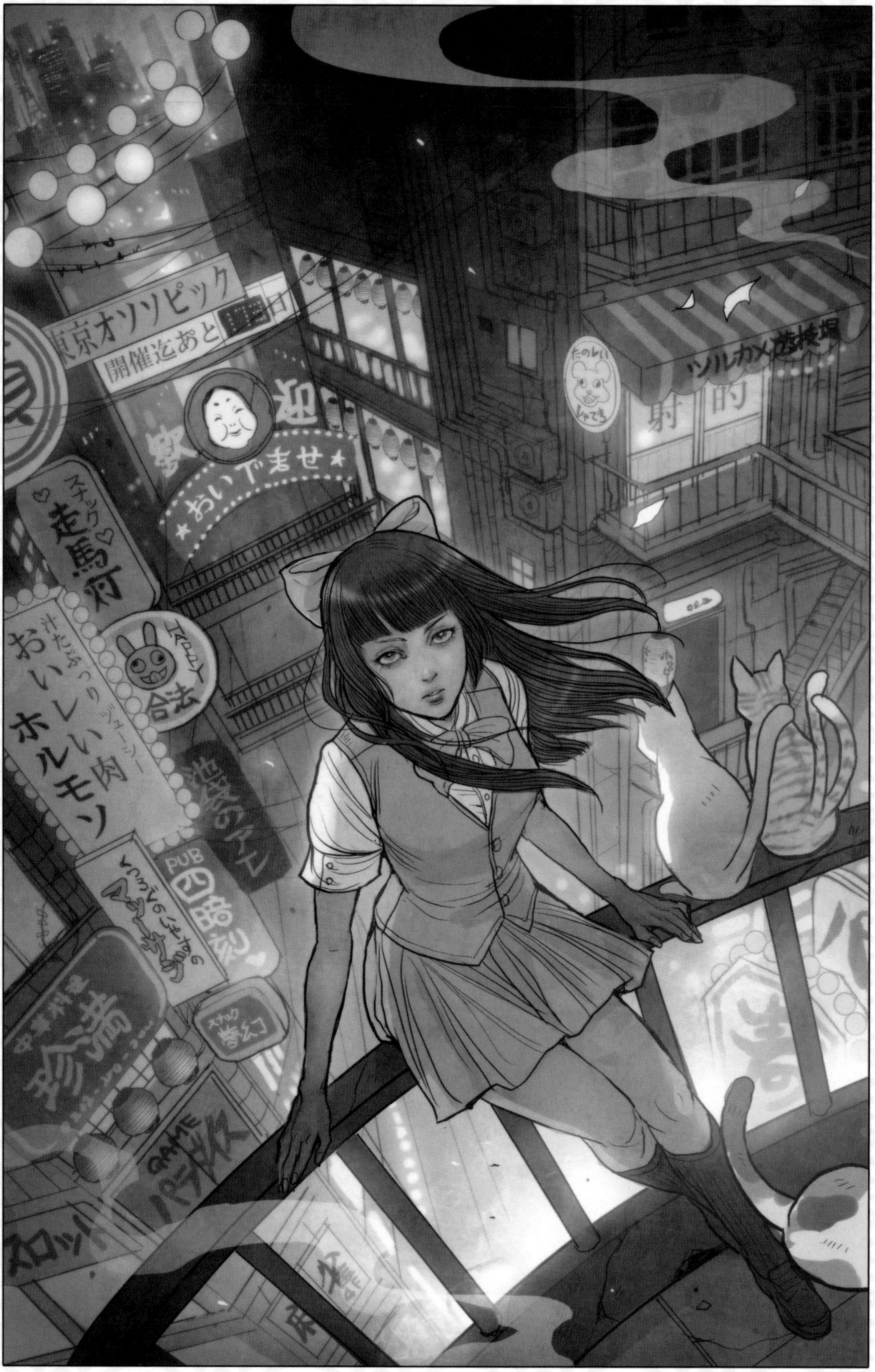
東京オソソピック
開催迄あと
迎
おいでませ
スナック
走馬灯
汁たっぷり
おいしい肉
ジューシー
ホルモン
合法
PUB
四暗刻
射的
GAME
スロット

WAYWARD #17 (Cover B)
Artwork by Sana Takeda

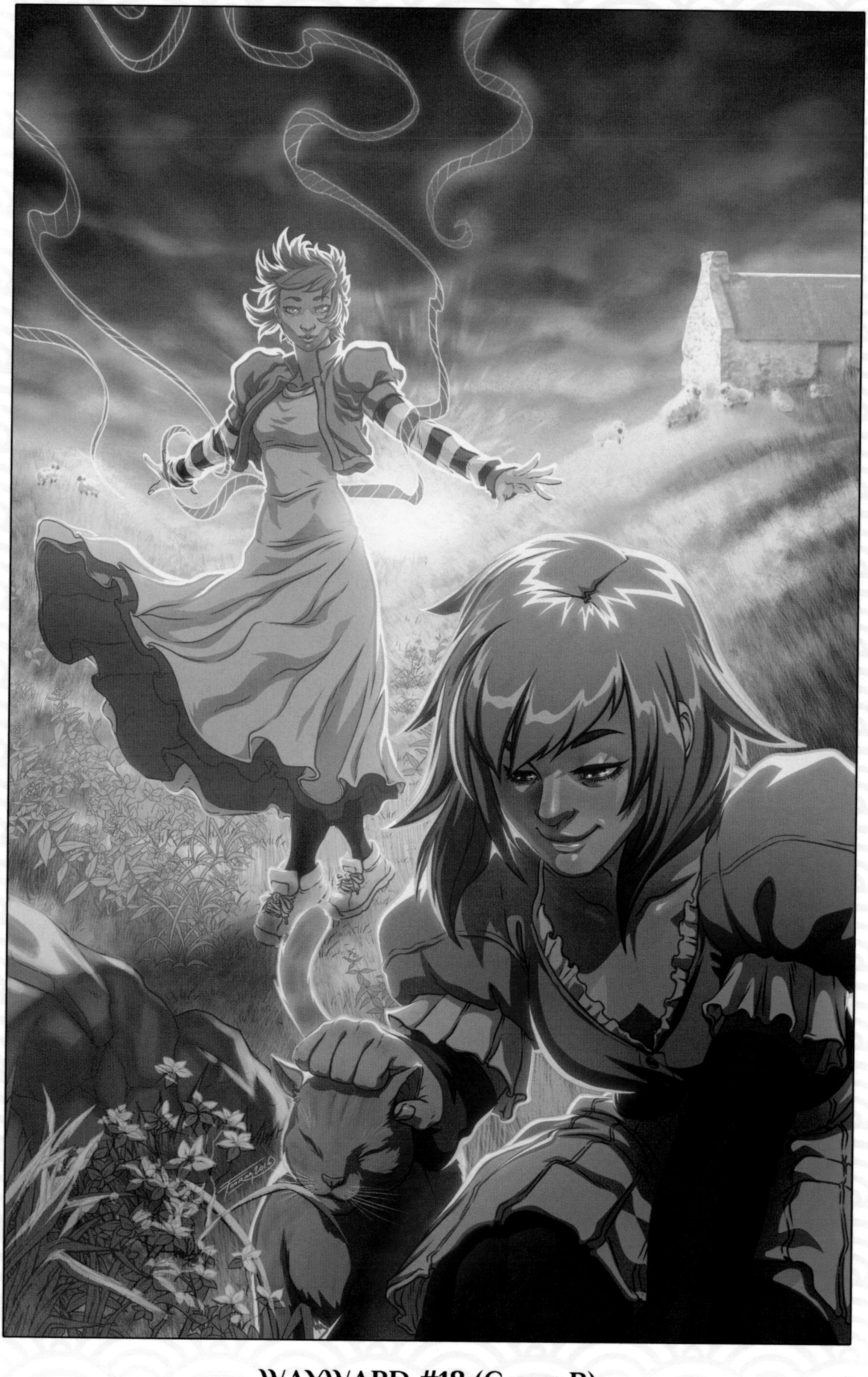

WAYWARD #18 (Cover B)
Artwork by Royce Southerland

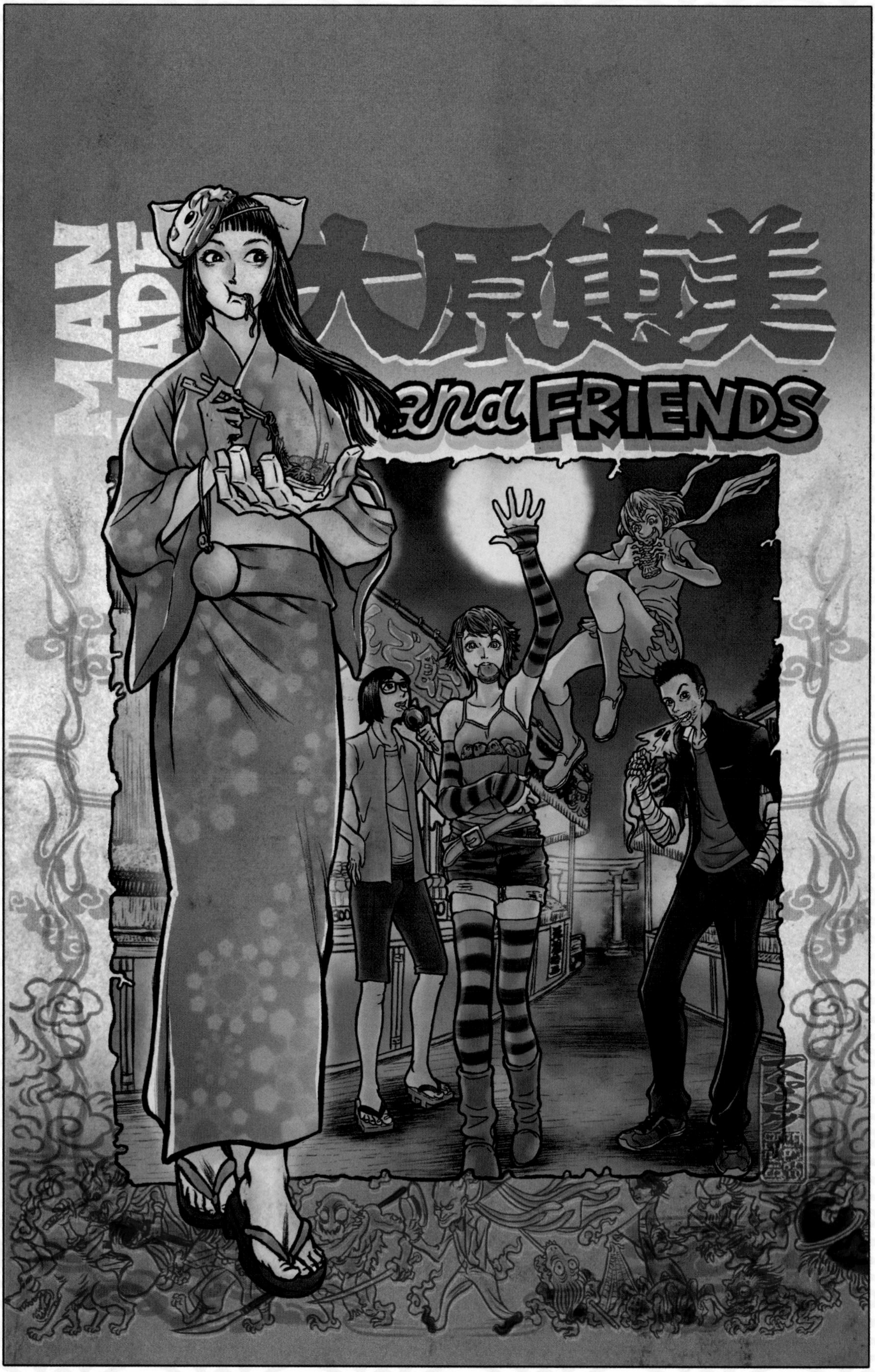
大原恵美
and FRIENDS

WAYWARD #19 (Cover B)
Artwork by Superlog

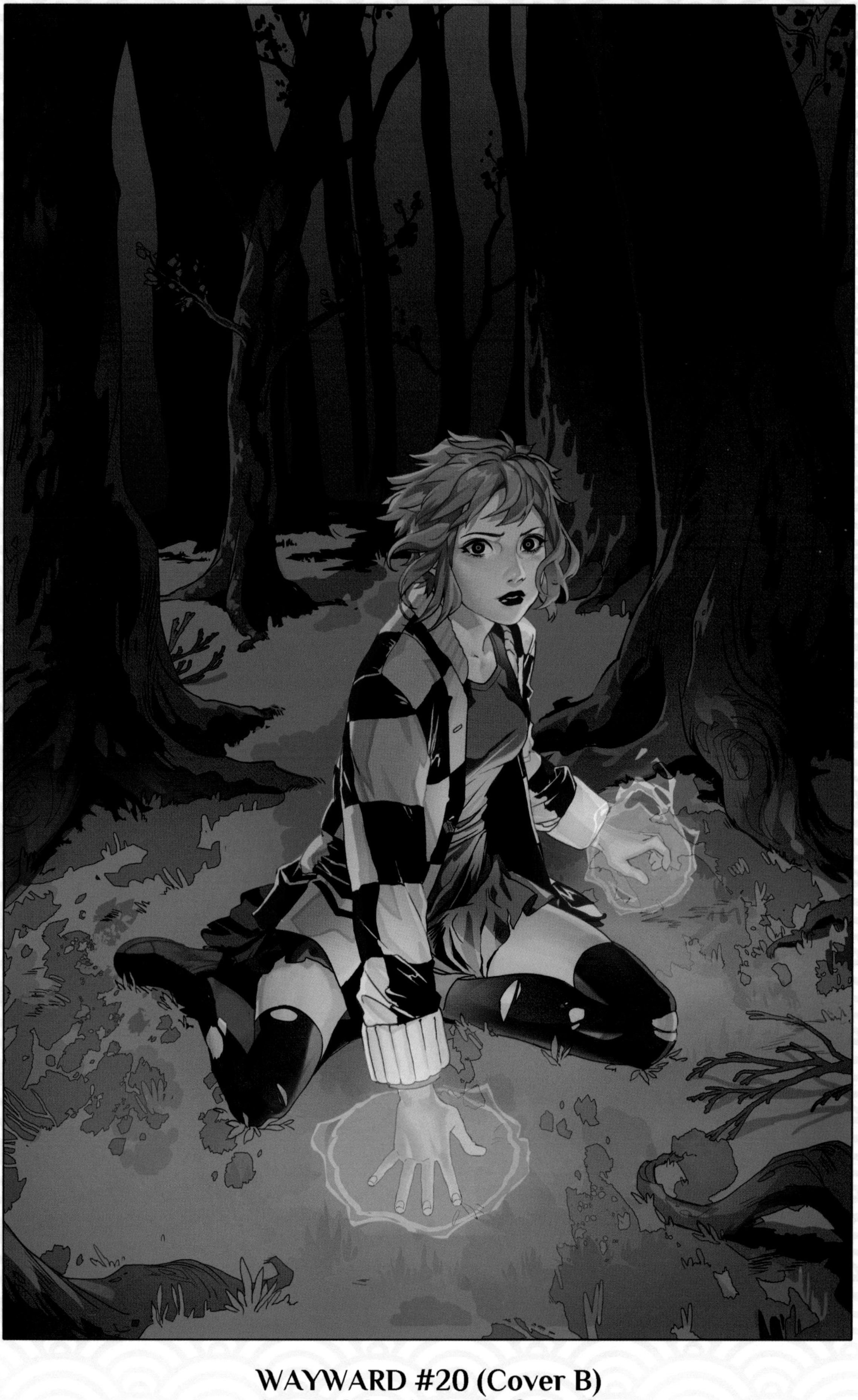

WAYWARD #20 (Cover B)
Artwork by Amanda Schank

Segawa Touru

瀬川
Segawa

The Hacker

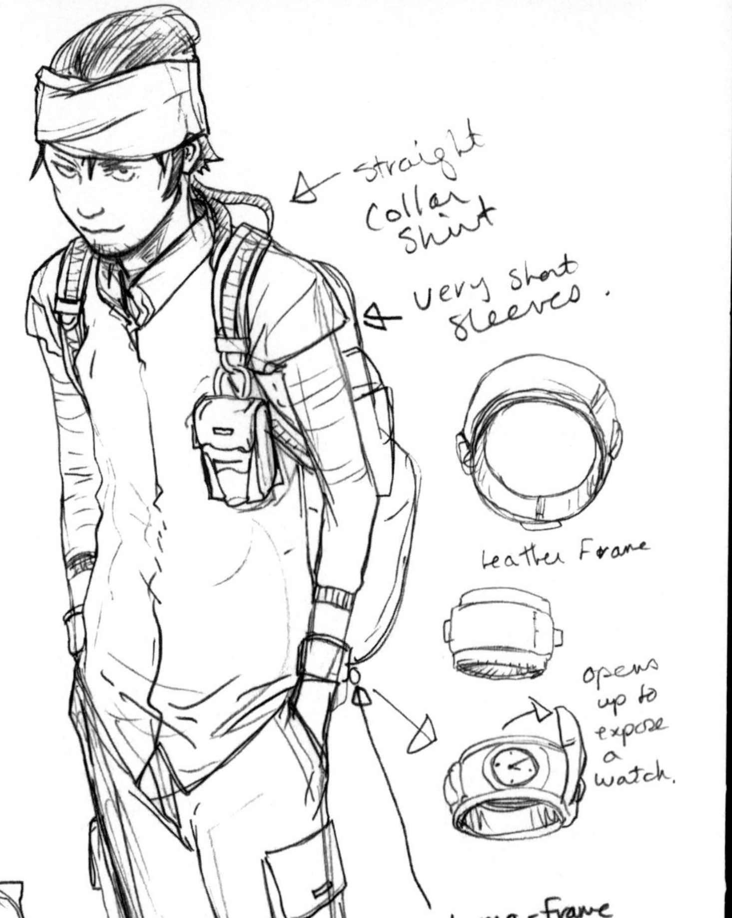

straight Collar Shirt
Very short sleeves.
Leather Frame
opens up to expose a watch.

Segawa's arrival in the series grew out conversations I had with Steven about modern life in Japan.

Ohara can affect manmade materials, while Segawa connects and controls networks – electricity, data, all kinds of good stuff.

In the first arc we avoided mentioning manga and anime, but with Segawa it seemed appropriate to have him be more of a fanboy, absorbed in both online and pop culture.

-Zub

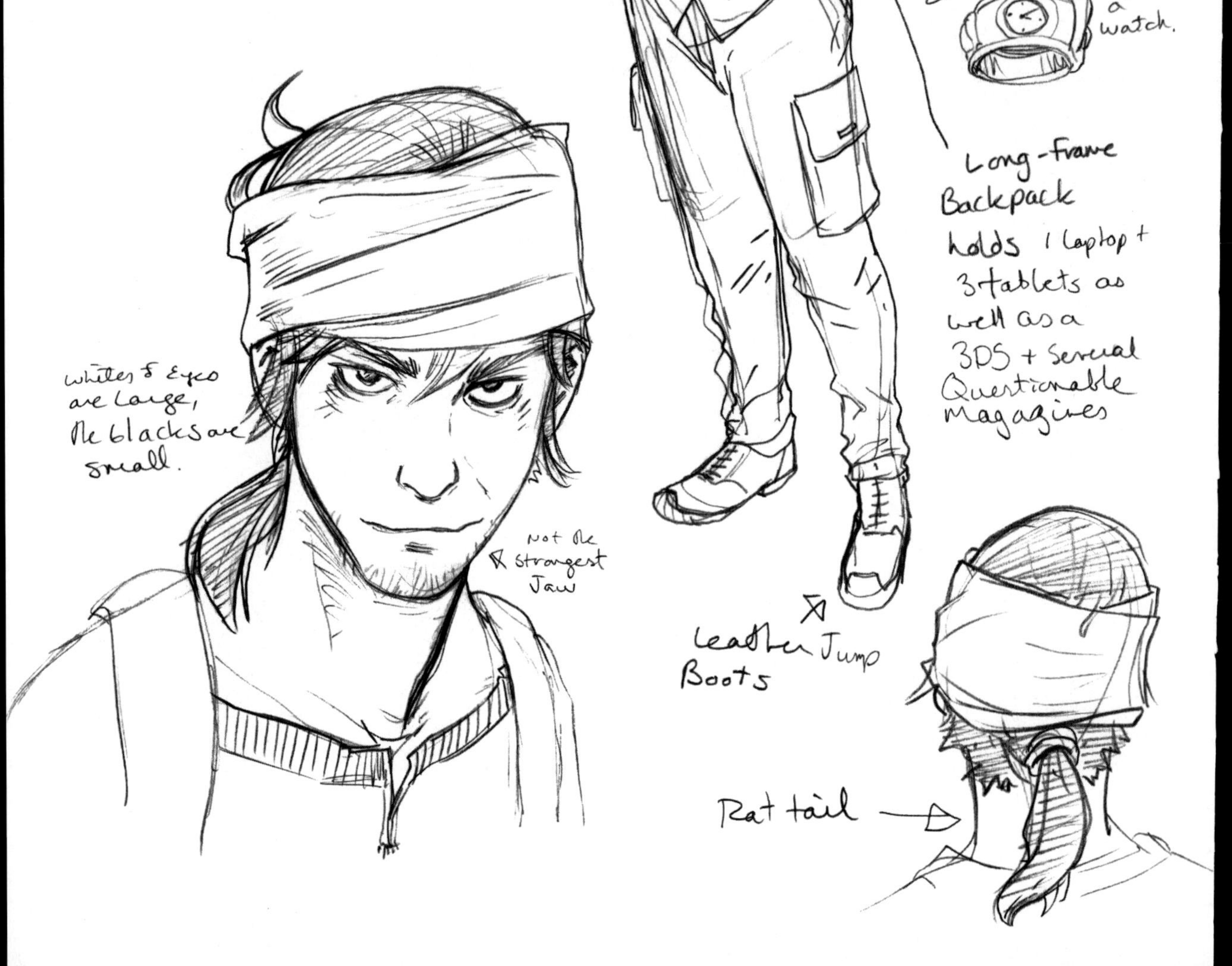

Long-Frame Backpack
holds 1 Laptop + 3 tablets as well as a 3DS + Several Questionable Magazines
whites of Eyes are Large, the blacks are small.
Not the strongest Jaw
Leather Jump Boots
Rat tail

Inaba means “place of the grain” and is related to Inari which is a name for fox gods/spirits. Kami means beautiful fragrance but phonetically sounds like 上 or 神 which mean respectively "above" or "deity".

-Steven

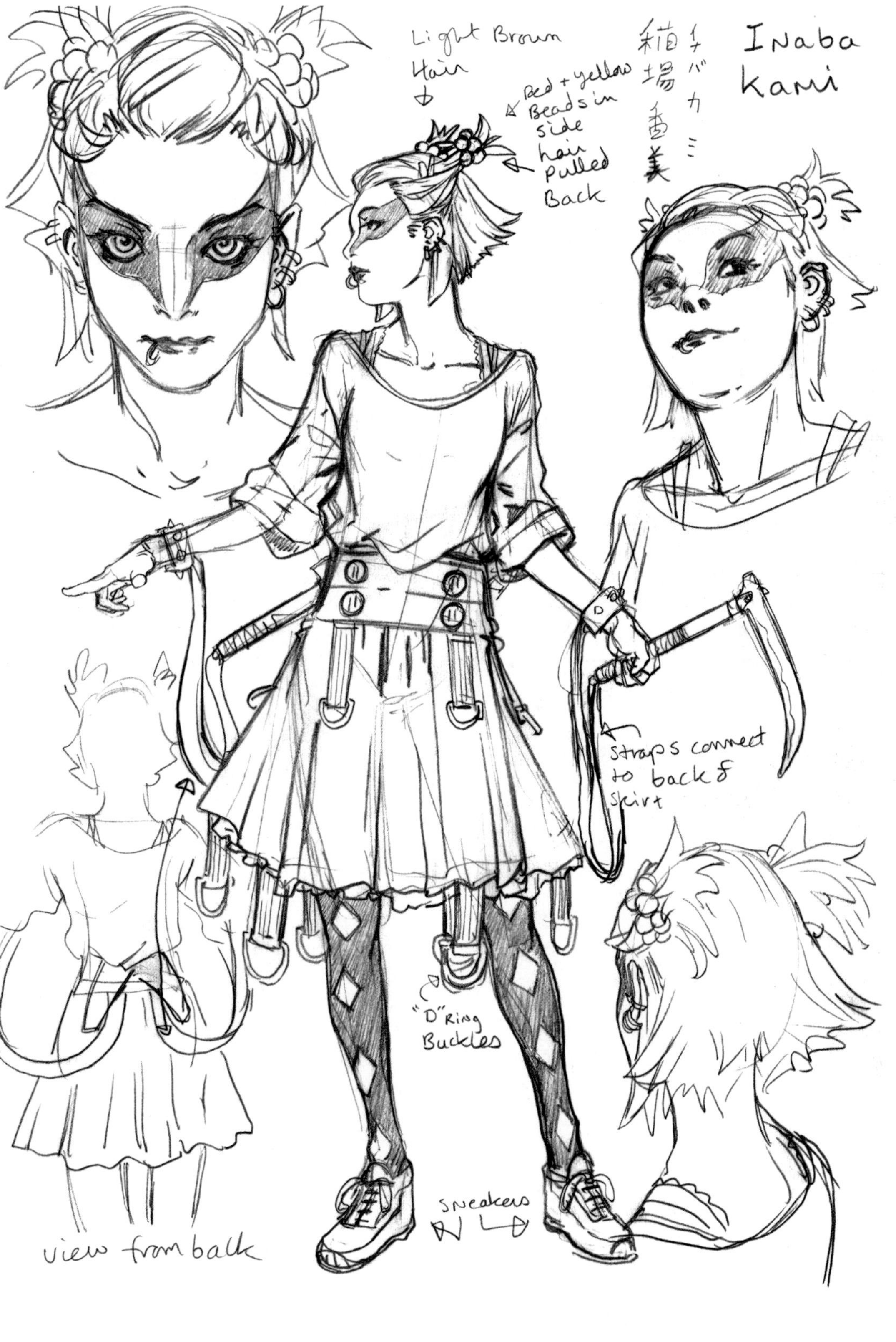

Light Brown Hair
Red + Yellow Beads in side hair Pulled Back
稲場 香美
イナバ カミ
Inaba Kami
Straps connect to back of skirt
"D" Ring Buckles
Sneakers
view from back

During the Meiji period, the Japanese government declared war on yokai. Not a traditional war—they didn't attack with bullets and bombs. Instead they used more effective weapons. Politics. And ideas. As Francisco Goya said, "The sleep of reason produces monsters." In the 1860s, reason awoke and banished the monsters.

First a little context:

Japan is sometimes described as a "unique country." It's a controversial statement, wrapped in Japanese nationalism and the study of "Japaneseness" called *nihonjinron*. But political points aside, there is one defining aspect of Japanese history that is highly unusual, to say the least.

When Tokugawa Iemitsu—third shogun of the Tokugawa shogunate—takes power in 1623, he has a problem. His grandfather's compatriot Oda Nobunaga allowed Jesuit missionaries and traders to gain a foothold in Japan. They occupy the southern island of Kyushu and the port of Nagasaki, where they actively attempt to subvert Japanese culture. Missionaries encourage Japanese people to take "Christian names" and abandon kimono and geta sandals in favor of "proper" clothes. On top of this, local lords are too powerful, growing rich on Western trade and technology. Iemitsu's solution is swift

and absolute. He expels all foreigners from the country, and slams shut the gates of Japan. From 1633, he institutes *sakoku*—the country in chains.

Foreigners are banned on pain of death. Any Japanese person outside the country is forbidden reentry. Trade is limited to the Dutch, and contained on the artificial island of Dejima. The rest of Japan is hermetically sealed and preserved. For 220 years, they incubate in insolation. Japan turns inward—a self-contained microcosm focused on the endless refining of the arts. Also called the Edo period, most of the *things Japanese* —like artisanal geishas and woodblock prints—are developed during this period. And yokai. As told before, the country is consumed with belief in the supernatural.

Fast forward to 1853. The American Commodore Matthew Perry knocks on the locked doors of Japan with cannon fire. Using his four black warships in an act of Gunboat Diplomacy, Perry gives Japan the choice to open its gates to trade—or be conquered. They relent.

Japan is a time capsule. The country has not advanced technologically for two centuries. Perry and his shipmates might as well be spaceships landing, complete with laser guns and robot butlers for all the wide divide between Japan's spears and rowboats and Perry's canons and steamships. The leaders of Japan are deeply ashamed when they see the scientific accomplishments and ideas of the Western nations, compared to their own backwards, superstitious people. It's a rude awakening.

Change happens rapidly. Civil war. Strife. By 1868, the shogunate is overthrown. Sixteen-year old Mutsuhito returns imperial power to Japan when he is enthroned as Emperor Meiji in the Meiji Restoration. The last charge of the samurai in the 1877 Satsuma Rebellion proves the folly of bringing swords to a rifle fight. The Edo period is finished. An age of enlightenment dawns; and the attack on yokai begins.

Leading the charge is "yokai professor" Inoue Enryo. A crusader against superstition, he declares that the "unknowable" nature of yokai can be elucidated using the twin tools of science and psychology. In his 2,000-page magnum opus *Lecture on Yokai Studies*, he rigorously dissects and defines the various types of yokai, categorizing them as celestial phenomena, terrestrial calamities, natural species of plants and animals, or delusions of the mind. In further books, such as *Tenguron (Study of Tengu)* and *The Dissolution of Superstition*, he labels belief in yokai as a psychological disorder. Inoue is no atheist; he believes deeply in the shinkai--the True Mystery that lies beyond the borders of human perception, smaller than atoms and larger than the universe. Inoue espouses that petty folktales and ghosts distract from this more important mystery. They must be swept away.

Inoue's influence is pervasive. Eager to shift the populace towards the modern miracles of science and industry, the new Japanese government also wants to eliminate regional cultures in favor of a controllable, national identity. Key to this is demolishing belief in local guardian deities and shrines and refocusing the population on a single religion of worshiping the Emperor as the God of Japan. Using Inoue's writings, they institute several *Imperial Rescripts on Education*. Included is the absolute statement that yokai do not exist.

The government campaigns to remove all references to yokai. The supernatural is stripped from art, literature, and the theater. Famed storyteller Sanyutei Encho is forbidden to use the word *kaidan* and forced to write a prologue to his new work *Mystery of Kasane Swamp* saying "... there is no such thing as ghosts, they are all merely neurosis..." The dread haunter Oiwa is reinterpreted as her husband's guilty conscious. The yokai side-shows of Asakusa are banned. The government is almost as effective at expelling yokai as Iemitsu had been two centuries before in removing foreigners from Japan. What was once invisible, but became visible, is made invisible again.

The attack on yokai is not an absolute success. There are safe havens. Yanagita Kunio gathers and shelters yokai in the protected towers of academia. The opposite side of the coin to Inoue Enryo, Yanagita focuses on commoners. Known as the "*Japanese Brothers Grimm*," he hikes the countryside with fellow researcher Sasaki Kizen. They collect and preserve vanishing beliefs and narratives like kappa and the child spirts *zashiki warashi*. Recorded as *Tales of Tono (Tono Monogatari)*, they wait to be rediscovered by later, less skeptical generations.

Another man, a foreigner living in Japan named Lafcadio Hearn, is equally fascinated by ancient legends. He writes the stories his Japanese wife tells him in his 1889 book *In Ghostly Japan*. In 1903 he publishes his masterpiece *Kwaidan: Stories and Studies of Strange Things*. With Hearn's books, yokai travel abroad.

And in the isolated fishing village of Sakaiminato, a withered old nurse named Nononba tells stories remembered from her childhood to a young boy named Shigeru Mizuki—who will grow up to reintroduce yokai to Japan through the modern entertainment called *manga*. And the country will fall in love with its monsters all over again.

If you find yourself on the losing side—if your lord to whom you have sworn fealty lies bleeding in the dirt—what do you do? Do you hold true to your ideals, your training; do you choose honorable death, even if it is by your own hand? Or do you turn tail on everything you have ever lived for, throw down your flag and run fleeing into the night, to live on as an honorless deserter—a ronin.

The word ronin has meant many things over the centuries, from farm workers to laid-off businessmen. But it has never meant anything good. The translation is a weird one; the kanji that make up the word (浪人) read as "wave person" and are meant to invoke unreliability. Loyalty is one of the core factors of Japanese society, especially loyalty to a superior. Switching teams is frowned upon. Social harmony demands that everyone knows their place, and does what is expected. By contrast, ronin are flotsam and jetsam, adrift on the tides of an inconstant ocean. Wanderers, vagrants, vagabonds, drifters—they are people without foundation, without loyalty or respect.

The term originated during the Nara period, where it labeled peasants who fled their master's lands. Unable to return home, these wave people drifted the countryside as migrant laborers, rarely staying in one place and scratching out a meager existence. As Japanese culture evolved, masters assembled armies, built castles, and declared themselves lords. They took personal bodyguards whom they called *samurai*—a word which literally translates as "servant." With the rise of clans, ronin applied more and more to freelance fighters and sellswords, those without loyalty who fought for the highest bidder.

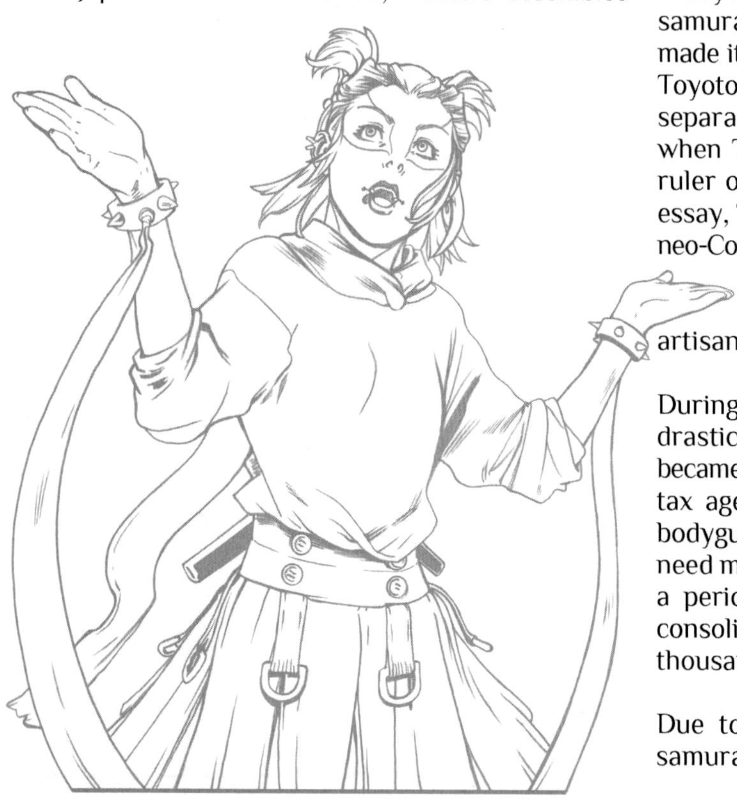

The golden age of ronin was the Sengoku period, the time of Warring States when Japan was engaged in seemingly endless civil war. With all of these lords vying for power, they needed bodies and weren't too particular about where they got them. Any disgruntled farmer's son could throw down his spade, pilfer a spear and armor from one of the multitude of dead bodies, and present himself at some castle walls ready to fight.

Some of these ronin did well for themselves. The lord Tōdō Takatora famously served ten different masters before allying himself with the future shogun Tokugawa Ieyasu. Saitō Dōsan was a wealthy shopkeeper who put down his balance book and picked up a sword, seizing power at Mino province and becoming known as the Viper of Mino. This was a rare time in Japanese history when social mobility was possible.

One of the most famous ronin of all was Toyotomi Hideyoshi. A peasant's son, he fought his way to samurai rank and status—and then immediately made it so that no one could follow in his footsteps. Toyotomi enacted laws establishing samurai as a separate noble class. Things got even tougher when Tokugawa Ieyasu seized power as the sole ruler of Japan. As you will recall from a previous essay, Tokugawa instituted societal controls using neo-Confucianism. To ensure stability, he established the shi-nō-kō-shō system where everyone was sorted as either a farmer, merchant, artisan, or samurai.

During the Edo period the role of samurai changed drastically. No longer necessary as warriors, they became bureaucrats—middle managers, accountants, tax agents, scribes, and occasionally ceremonial bodyguards. Great lords realized that they didn't need massive armies anymore. They went through a period of downsizing. Pretexts were made to consolidate castles and fiefdoms, and hundreds of thousands of samurai were effectively laid off.

Due to the strict rules of shi-nō-kō-shō, these samurai could not seek an occupation or even a new master. They had only two options available; the expected path of suicide to cleanse their shame, or throw away honor completely and turn ronin. Generally this meant finding employment as a robber, thug, or swellsword. It is estimated that under the third shogun Tokugawa Iemitsu, close to half a million displaced samurai wandered the country as ronin. This lead to the Keian Uprising in 1651, and an eventual relaxing of the strict laws that forbade seeking employment. It turned out that putting ronin back to work was a more equitable solution than demanding mass suicide.

The final bow of the ronin took place in 1703, in what is called the event of the *47 Loyal Ronin*. A minor country lord Asano attacked the court official Kira Yoshinaka in the shogun's palace. Asano was clearly in the wrong, and sentenced to suicide. His lands and clan were disbanded. Asano's three hundred samurai were turned ronin. However, forty-seven of them remained faithful to their lord, and in an incredible display of loyalty plotted over two years to take revenge on Kira. Their actions moved the country deeply, and their story has been called Japan's "national legend."

One of the keys of the 47 Ronin tale is precisely that Lord Asano *did not deserve their loyalty*. He was a hot-headed jerk who sacrificed the lives of all who depended on him just because he couldn't keep his temper. What so impressed Japan, and why these forty seven are venerated to this day, is that even in the most harrowing of circumstances they stayed loyal— a loyalty that was given, not earned. On a darker note, these forty-seven were held as ideals for soldiers during WWII, when absolute loyalty was commanded at the cost of their own lives.

In modern Japan, ronin has changed again with the times. It still refers to vagrants, but now it is those lost in a society that no longer needs them. Japan's modern ronin are students who failed their college entrance exams, or downsized business people. Like the wave people of old, they drift through the world trying to find their place. As ronin have always been, they are looked down upon and disgraced—even if it through no fault of their own. They discovered that loyalty given doesn't always result in loyalty returned. A lesson that is by no means unique to Japan.

Left: Inaba Kami design sketch by Steven Cummings. Colors by Jim Zub.

"The future always starts with Fire," Nurarihyon says, and nowhere is this more true than Tokyo. The name of the capital of Japan translates as "Eastern Capital," but perhaps *Fushicho*—Phoenix— would have been more appropriate considering the number of times the city has been burned to the ground and then risen again from its own ashes. Seeing their city burning was so common that people used romantic nicknames for the conflagrations. When blazes sprung up, Edoites would say that the "autumn leaves" had come early. Fires were said to decorate the city and were called *Edo no Hana*—the Flowers of Edo.

Edo—the former name of Tokyo—began its life as an obscure fishing village of no importance. The name translates as "Door to the Bay" or "Estuary." There was little to mark the place on a map: some good fishing; a few huts; a shrine dedicated to the magical head of the samurai Taira no Masakado that had landed there in 940 CE after flying around Japan—the usual sort of thing you found in any coastal Japanese town of the time. But then Edo's fortunes changed.

In the late 12th century, the warrior Edo Shigetsugu fortified a local hill to use as his home. His successor, Edo Shigenaga, allied with Minamoto no Yoritomo, the first shogun of Japan, and was granted a castle. Shigenaga built Edo Castle on that same fortified hill. It sat still for a few centuries, until it was chosen by Tokugawa Ieyasu as his power base when he was an upstart lord. After winning the Battle of Sekigahara in 1603, Tokugawa—now the new Shogun—established Edo as the center of his military government and gave a name to the 265 year span known as the Edo period.

Almost overnight this sleepy village became an urban center. The city sprawled and bulged at its borders—people did not move to Edo so much as they were crammed in. New buildings of tightly packed wood structures were hastily put up to meet demand. Dozens of families packed into tiny, single-room apartments stretched out in *nagaya*, meaning long houses. Windows were little more than paper screens that did nothing to shield from the elements. Japanese winters are bitter cold, and heating these shacks was done with charcoal braziers called *hibachi*. As you know from basic science, oxygen + heat + fuel = the necessary ingredients for fire.

The city of Edo burned to the ground forty-nine times between 1603 and 1867. Aside from the great fires, there were uncountable smaller blazes that only took out sections of the city. Most of these were accidents; a spilled hibachi, a candle left carelessly untended, a cooking fire out of control. But many others were purposeful. Disgruntled peasants suffered in bitter poverty while the shogun and samurai lived in luxury. Due to the strict laws of Neo-Confucianism there was no escape from their situation; they were people with nothing to lose. Other arsonists had a more bizarre motive —entertainment. The Flowers of Edo were a diversion from dull lives, and scholar Matsunosuke Nishiyama wrote *"It is not unthinkable that in Edo, probably many residents simply rejoiced in the great fires."*

At least one fire had a supernatural origin. In his 1899 book *In Ghostly Japan*, Lafcadio Hearn recounted the story of the Furisode Fire, also known as the Great Fire of Meireki that destroyed 70% of Edo. According to legend, there was a young woman who caught a glimpse of a beautiful samurai walking down a crowded street. Instantly in love, she had a special kimono commissioned, and went out day after day hoping to catch the object of her obsession. He never appeared, and the woman wasted away, dying in her beautiful kimono. Her parents donated the valuable clothing to a temple, but everyone they gave it to died, haunted by the lovelorn lady. After killing three girls, the temple priests decided to burn the cursed cloth. Setting a torch to it, the kimono exploded. Flame leapt from rooftop to rooftop like something alive until the entire city was consumed by the woman's loneliness.

Counter-measures were eventually put into place. The shogunate established Japan's first official firefighters, which were organized like a military and put under direct control of samurai lords called *daimyo*. Fire towers were built, and flammable thatch roofs were replaced with fireproof ceramic tiles. But no amount of protection measures would help against other menaces.

In 1923, the Great Kanto Earthquake shook Japan, devastating Tokyo. The name had been changed in 1869, when the last shogun Tokugawa Yoshinobu stepped aside for the young Emperor Meiji in the Meiji Restoration. But emperor or shogun, Edo or Tokyo, the city gave way to the shaking earth that struck almost exactly at noon, causing millions of cooking fires to blaze out of control and allowed the Flower of Edo to blossom once more. Over 100,000 died and almost 40,000 of those were incinerated by fires that swept through downtown where people huddled for shelter.

The final time Tokyo burned to the ground was due to neither cursed kimono nor earthquake. On April 18, 1942 James H. Doolittle flew a small squad of modified B-25 bombers over Tokyo, dropping sixteen incendiary devices. While the Doolittle Raiders did minimal damage, they set the stage for later B-29 high altitude bombers. The B-29s carried special cluster bombs filled with napalm that ignited thousands of small fires, merging into an all-consuming firestorm. A single bombing run on March 9, 1945 killed more than 100,000 people, making it the single deadliest air attack of all time, more devastating than Dresden, Hiroshima, or Nagasaki.

Even still, Tokyo rose from the ashes again and remains a vibrant, incredible city. The Flower of Edo blooms only for a time, clearing the path for something new. Although not everything is lost; the shrine to the head of *Taira no Masakado* remains intact, more than a thousand years later, proving that no amount of fire can destroy some of the oldest gods of Japan.

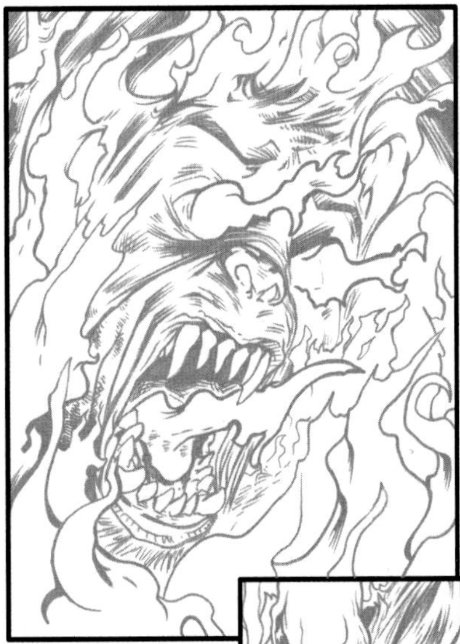

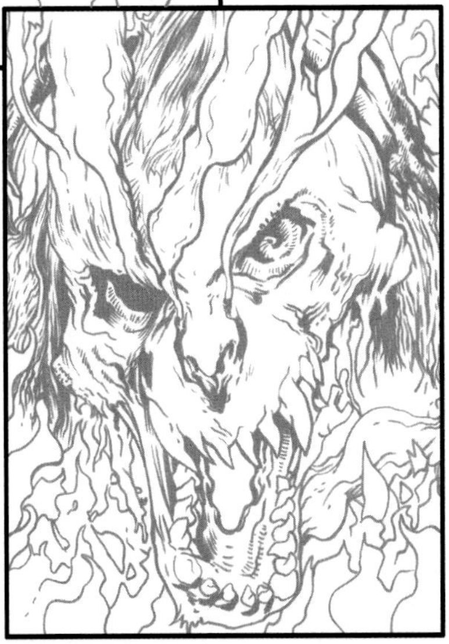

Don't get arrested in Japan. Trust me on this one: Just don't. Don't break the law. Don't put yourself into the court system. And don't ever, ever, ever wind up in a Japanese jail. Because if any of these things happen to you, well... Japan is a lovely country, and one of the safest, most welcoming places I have ever been. But that security comes at a price.

When the justice system of Japan brings down the gavel, they bring it down hard. Police and prosecutors have almost unlimited power. Under the *daiyo kangoku* system, they can imprison anyone in a holding cell for up to 23 days—for any reason. You are not entitled to translators, food, visitors, or assistance of any kind. Your embassy can't help you. Daiyo kangoku is an oubliette. The police don't even need to accuse you of a crime.

During this time police can and will do almost anything to get you to incriminate yourself. They interrogate in shifts, making sure that while you never sleep they are fresh and ready. Appointed lawyers press you to confess, promising it will go easier on you. They lie and cheat. Stories are told of non-Japanese speakers presented with documents they were told were release papers, only to discover they had signed themselves into jail with detailed confessions. And should you be officially charged the assumption is guilty unless proven innocent. There are judges who have been sitting the bench for thirty years without delivering a single "Not Guilty" verdict. There are no juries. There are no mistrials. Everything goes on behind closed doors.

This is a surprise to many. The public face of Japan's police is the ineffective "officer friendly" sitting at the *koban* police box, the smiling *omawari san* (Mr. Walkaround). You find omawari san all over Japan. They perform the taxing duties of offering directions to lost tourists and holding on to missing items until the owner comes to retrieve them. They bust kids smoking and skipping school. Trusted and beloved members of the community, omawari san make neighborhood visits, and check in on the elderly to make sure everyone is OK.

I think the only conflict I had with omawari san in Japan was when the local patrol officer would stop my wife and I for riding two on a bicycle. He would smile and laugh, saying "Didn't I just talk to you two about this yesterday? It sure looked like you... it's pretty dangerous to ride like that, you know!" Then with a wave of his hand he would continue on his way, and we would walk the bicycle for a respectful distance before hopping on again. It was a game we played together.

But it was just a façade.

Behind the harmless face of the omawari san is another police entirely. The National Police Agency is a large, military-style organization, overseeing several prefectural bureaus and specialized forces. Instead of simple domestic crimes—of which there are relatively few in Japan—squads like the Security Bureau face off against radical political and religious groups like the Cult of Aum Shinrikyo, or the highly organized gangs of the Yakuza and Chinese Triads. They fight secret wars away from the public eye. The nature of these wars are carefully hidden by news outlets and reporters who collude to obfuscate crime waves in order to maintain the perception of safety that is so important to the country.

This military police has deep roots. In old Japan, laws were enforced by private military and citizen groups. Each town and village was responsible for its own security. With the centralization of power in the Edo period, the aristocratic warrior class of the samurai were organized into a strict system of control, becoming what some historians call the world's first police state. These samurai police enforced morals and societal behavior as well as official laws. Showing disrespect to a superior was as much a cause for a beheading as murder and robbery.

The samurai organized squads of citizen patrols, as well as utilized extensive networks of informers and ex-criminals to act as spies. The *okappiki* and *gōyokiki* were a special class of outcasts and ruffians utilized by the police. Any distasteful duties that would mar the honor of a samurai could be outsourced to those willing to get their hands dirty.

With the end of Edo, Japan modernized and the police did as well. In 1874, the first government police force was created in imitation of Western law enforcement agencies. However, while the uniforms and titles changed, they remained enforcers of public morals. With the rise of the military government that led to WWII, police became more concerned with thought crimes. The Kempeitai secret police were formed, the equivalent of Nazi Germany's Gestapo. Under various Peace Preservation Laws like the Safety Preservation Law and the Public Order and Police Law, disagreeing with the government became a capital crime. College professors and free thinkers were rounded up. Everyone feared a night visit from the Kempeitai.

Japan's defeat in WWII saw the Kempeitai disbanded. Occupation forces served as police until 1947 when the new Police Law was passed. This law severely limited police powers and held them in check. This served well until it was amended during the 1950s. It was a time of civil unrest, so greater and greater powers were ceded to police and prosecutors; powers which they retain to this day. In his book *The Japanese Way of Justice*, author David T. Johnston says "it is difficult to find a state agency—inside Japan or out—that wields as much power..."

This unchecked power—what Johnston calls the "benevolent paternalism" of the Japanese criminal justice system—is both demonized as remnant of a fascist system and lauded as the reason behind Japan's ridiculously low crime rate. And it is both. I was shocked at friends who thought nothing of sending their seven-year old daughter to walk to the convenience store several blocks away at night, clutching a fistful of cash. The country is that safe. I also had a friend who worked as a police informant until his face was slashed in a knife attack. He told me, "There are two kinds of police in Japan. The friendly omawari san—and the others. Make sure you never have a reason to fall into the other's hands."

I offer you the same advice.

Make War No More – Japan's Self-Defense Forces

Countries fight wars. They raise armies. They attack and defend. They invade. That's what they do. Waging war has been one of the main occupations of countries ever since the first nation states emerged. Threat or actuality of war is a key factor in international negotiations. When Commodore Matthew Perry opened the locked gates of Japan and ended the Edo period, he did so with loaded cannons in an act of Gunship Diplomacy. History is written in such conflicts, and war is part of the dialog when countries speak to each other. Except Japan. Of all the nations on Earth, only Japan is forbidden by law from going to war.

Article 9 of the Japanese Constitution states "Aspiring sincerely to an international peace based on justice and order, the Japanese people forever renounce war as a sovereign right of the nation and the threat of use of force as means of settling international disputes." It also states that "land, sea, and air forces, as well as other war potential, will never be maintained." This means Japan technically has no army, no navy, no air force. They have no tanks, no warships, no missiles. It is illegal for Japan to amass armaments that could potentially threaten other nations. Which doesn't mean the country is entirely toothless. As with all political maneuvering, the language of the law does not define actuality.

The truth is much more complicated.

Anyone who knows history understands that Japan is not an inherently pacifist nation. On the contrary, for most of their history the Japanese have been a warlike race, in continual conflict with their neighbors—and with each other. Much of the country's history is defined by civil wars. After all, there's a reason Japan is synonymous with warrior classes like samurai, ronin, and ninja. Renouncing war was not something the country did willingly; a Japanese Gandhi didn't come along, preaching the power of peace and convincing everyone to lay down arms and be the only country on Earth to forever surrender the right to war as a sovereign nation. In fact, Article 9 was intended to be punishment; a muzzle on a rabid dog.

At the end of WWII, Japan suffered a defeat more total than most can imagine. And not the flash bang of Hiroshima and Nagasaki that usually comes to mind. When I was translating *Showa: A History of Japan*, I dove deeper into the war from both sides than I ever had before. I had long believed in the established American mythology; that Japan was a vicious country determined to fight to the last man, and only the technological marvel of the atomic bomb forced a preemptive end to WWII. The bomb, says the official victor's narrative, saved hundreds of thousands of lives —both American and Japanese—in a war that would have otherwise dragged on for years.

In truth, Japan was defeated long before *Fat Man* and *Little Boy*. The nation had depleted itself of all resources. Its warships were dead in the water, lacking oil to move them. Their soldiers had no bullets. No one had food. Everyone was starving. The country was hollow, projecting only a thin veneer of strength that needed the slightest prick to reveal the rot inside. When American occupiers

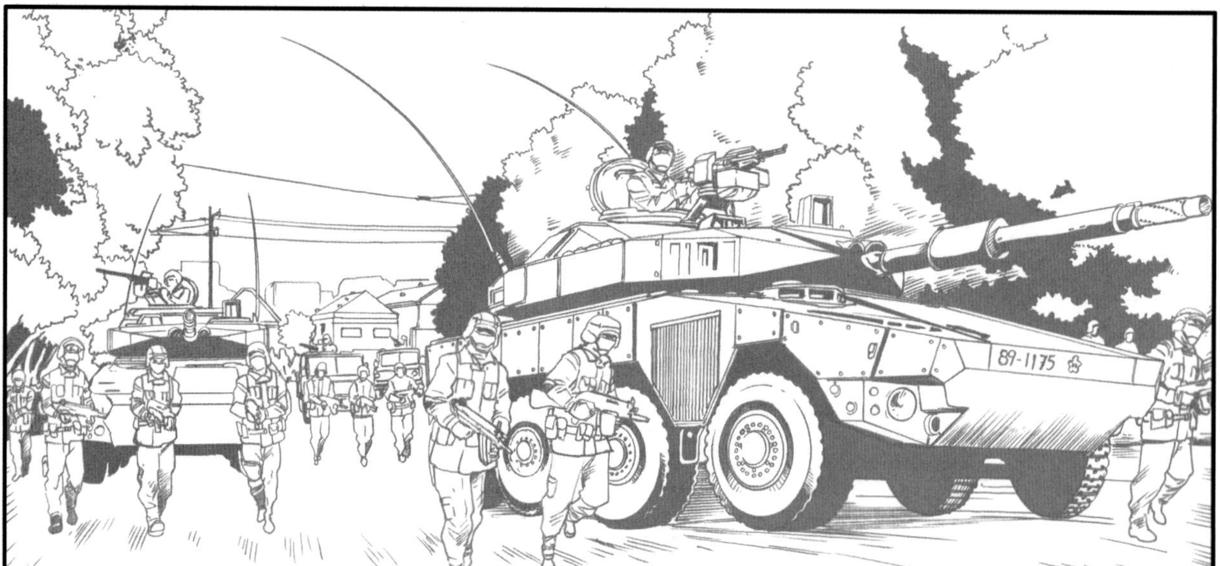
89-1175

came in, Japan had been drained of all opposition. As Supreme Commander of the Allied Powers, General Douglas MacArthur was given full authority to shape Japan into whatever country he saw fit. He executed those he saw as a threat; pardoned those he thought he could use. When his team wrote Japan's constitution, it was ratified by the other Allied powers. The Japanese themselves were given no say in the matter.

Similar controls were put on Germany and Italy, but when those occupations ended and control of the government returned to the people, Germans and Italians voted to overturn those clauses—to take off their muzzles. Much to the world's surprise, Japan found that it liked its anti-war position. As shown in the Pulitzer Prize-winning book *Embracing Defeat*, Japan turned its punishment into opportunity. Militaries take a lot of money, after all, and without the burden of supporting armed forces Japan was free to focus on economics and industry.

So how does that leave Japan today?

When Buddhism came to Japan from China, it brought with it foreign concepts like vegetarianism. Japanese monks wanted to be good Buddhists, but they also wanted to eat yummy meat. The solution was to rename certain animals as plants. This way they could obey the letter of the Buddhist strictures, if not the intent. And it's why to this day when you order a nice bowl of "peony" what you get is a tasty dish of wild boar. Japan's armed forces use the same strategy.

Instead of an army or navy, Japan has "Self-Defense Forces." They do not have tanks or other war machines, they have "special purpose vehicles." The fact that these special purpose vehicles look a lot like tanks is beside the point. For decades now, Japan has been growing its military capacity, always careful to hide it under euphemisms and political camouflage. Theoretically, their only role is to defend Japan from outside invasion. How else can they protect themselves against Godzilla? But a bomber painted like *Hello Kitty* still drops a bomb as powerful as one painted like a regular warplane.

In an odd twist, the country that pressures Japan the most to amend Article 9 is the country that wrote it. The U.S. found themselves in a new war in Korea almost immediately at the close of WWII, and looked to Japan to assist. This situation repeated with the Vietnam War, and more recently with the Iraq War and potential conflict with North Korea and China. As its most powerful Asian ally, the U.S. wants Japan to join in on international conflicts. But Japan points to their U.S.-made constitution and politely declines—although they are more than happy to sell supplies to American troops and make a bundle.

This *"Get Out of War Free Card"* won't last forever. The current Japanese Prime Minister, Shinzo Abe, has been lobbying to reverse Article 9 for years. One day Abe or a similar politician will succeed. The switch will be flipped, and Japan's Self-Defense Forces will get a new coat of paint and emerge as full-fledged armed forces, able to fulfill their role of defense and attack, waging war on the world stage.

Eyes meet across a crowded dance floor. Sweaty bodies move to the music. Drinks are drunk. Skin meets skin. By mutual consent they depart hand in hand. Fortunately, our couple does not have far to go. They are in the Minami area of Osaka; a few blocks will take them from bars to a district reserved for—something else. Whether in the mundane rooms of Green Gables or the more eccentric playgrounds of Gang Snowman, Japan's love hotels stand ready for whatever goes on behind closed doors.

Unlike many of the sex myths about Japan—sorry, used-panty vending machines don't actually exist—love hotels are real. Any city of size has a district. There are 37,000 across Japan, and they can be found in surprising locations. I did a bicycle trip with some friends across Shikoku, and as we crested a lonely mountain pass we discovered a castle-shaped love hotel. Yes, we totally stopped. We had to. Because love hotels are as vital a part of the "Japan Experience" as karaoke, sushi, tea, Shinto shrines, or any other wonderment that make up the cultural landscape. And they are a hell of a lot of fun.

It's no surprise that Japan's relationship with love hotels—and sex—is long and complicated. Turn back the clock 1,000 years and Japan was a land of enthusiastic coupling. Shinto is an earthy religion; orgies were an important part of fertility festivals, ensuring a good harvest. Nudity was no big deal; mixed bathing was the norm. It took Western missionaries to convince Japan that sex and nudity were shameful things that needed to be covered and controlled. Japan reacted in a pragmatic way. In the 1600s, they cordoned off sex into walled pleasure districts.

Pleasure districts were a vital part of the culture.

Like the *Moulin Rouge* and the prostitutes of Paris, the freedom of the *ukiyo*—the floating world—generated a robust arts scene. Most of the Edo period art and theatre we know was inspired by this floating world. Pleasure districts remained active until 1958 when prostitution was officially outlawed.

As society changed, the business of sex adapted. In her book *Rabu Hoteru Shinka Ron* (*The Evolution of Love Hotels*), Kobe Gakuin University professor Kim Ikkyon shows how in the Showa period hoteliers started renting rooms called *enshuku* (one-yen dwellings). Instead of rooms for the night, guests could pay an hourly rate of one yen. Hotel owners noticed enshuku were rented by regular couples as much as by prostitutes. As the country prospered in the post-war economic recovery, hotels offering hourly rates saw huge profits. Entrepreneurs created inns specifically for this purpose, called *tsurekomi* inns, meaning bring-along hotels. These were frequented by married couples as often as less formalized lovers. Japanese homes are small and crowded, and tsurekomi inns offered a rare chance at privacy.

By the 1960s, traditional Japanese inns had fallen out of fashion and tsurekomi inns began to transform. Lots of money and a passion for Western extravagance led to flashy exteriors and escalating themes. The first true love hotel, called *Meguro Emperor*, opened in Meguro, Tokyo—the same area as one of the Goshiki Fudo temples. Raking in 40 million yen a month, the *Meguro Emperor* spawned many imitators. *Hotel Love* in Osaka lent a name to all similar establishments. From there any theme would do. Hotel *Chapel Christmas*; the Japanese castle-themed *Kuchinashijo Togenkyo*

Atsugi; the ostentatious *Geihinkan*. Something for everyone.

I was an enthusiastic patron of love hotels during my years in Japan. It took a while to learn the ins and outs, the etiquette and policies. And where the best ones were. In truth, the vast majority are unspectacular—standard-issue hotel rooms with maybe the addition of a karaoke machine and some mood lighting. Finding the good stuff takes dedication and research. And patience. You can get a room for either a "Rest" (an hour or so) or a "Stay" (the whole night). There are no reservations and the best rooms book up fast. If you have your heart set on any particular room, get there early or be prepared to wait out whatever couple is currently using it.

It's worth it. I stayed in hotels with starlit skies and grotto-style hot tubs complete with faux cave walls. My wife and I spent our anniversary in a rooftop palace with an in-room swimming pool. There are hotels ready for any fantasy, mimicking the inside of classrooms or subways, or...bumper cars. Whatever. I don't judge. And neither does Japan (most of the time).

It's not a perfect illusion. The walls are thin. The corridors dingy. The veneer gaudy. Love hotels are like Disneyland—you have to decide in advance to buy into the imperfect fantasy. If you're going complain about long lines, expensive food, and cheap effects...you might as well not go. And like Disneyland, who you go with makes all the difference. An enthusiastic partner is essential. Fun will only be had by mutual agreement.

(And I know it's hard to hear, but be prepared to be turned away. Love hotels are shockingly conservative. Most take a hardline one man/one woman stance for guests. Don't expect to go on a lark with a group of friends. And yes, homosexual couples will often face discrimination and be denied. It's Japan; there are lots of rules to be obeyed. No accommodations made for foreign tourists. Some won't allow non-Japanese to stay at all. It happens.)

The hunt for wild love hotels becomes more difficult in modern times. The era of massive sex fantasy castles is fading. Part of the shift is that women now lead in relationships. It is reported that in 90% of visits the woman picks the room. Hotels have changed their appeal, offering hot rock spa treatments instead of garish jungle settings. Also,

the Japanese just don't have that much sex anymore. In 2016 Japan's birthrate dropped to its lowest of all time. Love hotel profits are declining. By the 2020 Olympics, the government plans to convert 10,000 love hotels into ordinary hotels to accommodate tourists. If you want a last chance to experience this unique, fascinating, and ridiculously fun culture, you had better go quick. And bring someone with whom you can make the most of it.

Tsukimono – Yokai and Spirit Possession

There are eight million gods and monsters in Japan, and more than a few of them ride around in human bodies on occasion. Yūrei, kappa, tanuki, tengu, and kitsune. Snakes, cats, horses, and spiders. Almost any yokai can possess a human. When they do, they are known by a single name—*tsukimono*.

The concept of spirit possession is an ancient and ubiquitous belief in Japan. In his 1894 book *Occult Japan*, Percival Lowell wrote:

The number of possessing spirits in Japan is something enormous. It is safe to say that no other nation of forty million people has ever produced its parallel...

Spirit possession alone is nothing unique. Cultures with a history of ghosts or supernatural beings (that is to say, all cultures that have ever existed) have near identical traditions: mediums enter a trance, clear their minds, and willfully draw spirits into their bodies to serve as oracles. In Japan, these mediums tap the power of kami or ancestor spirits in a process called *kamigakari* (神懸り; divine possession). The kami can be singular or plural, ancestor spirits or a merger of deities. Because of the obscure nature of kami, it can be difficult to tell exactly who is speaking from the medium's mouth. But they all know it is a voice from beyond.

Where Japan really gets wacky—where it takes a giant leap sideways from most supernatural traditions—is tsukimono, yokai possession. If it gets pissed off enough or is willful enough, pretty much anything can take control of your body. As Lowell wrote:

...there are a surprising number of forms. There is, in short, possession by pretty much every kind of creature, except by other living men.

Tsukimono are rarely a spontaneous event. Often the yokai possesses as an act of revenge—perhaps a human killed one of the yokai's children, or destroyed their home. Or it could be simple greed: a fox wants to eat a delicious treat that it otherwise can't get its paws on. The reasons are as innumerable as yokai themselves. But as opposed to kamigakari, it is always involuntary. No one invites tsukimono into their body.

Tsukimono effects come in various forms. In most cases, the victim takes on the attributes of the yokai or animal. All you have to do is take a yokai, add *–tsuki* (possession) to the end of it, and let your imagination go wild.

A victim of *tanuki-tsuki* (tanuki possession) is said to voraciously overeat until their belly swells up like a tanuki, causing death unless exorcized. *Uma-tsuki* (horse possession) can cause people to become ill-mannered, huffing at everything and sticking their face into their food to eat like a horse. *Kappa-tsuki* (kappa possession) overwhelms people with the need to be in water and develop an appetite for cucumbers. *Yūrei-tsuki* (ghost possession) leaves people to wither away and die as their life force is slowly snuffed out. Almost any bad or unusual behavior could be blamed away as possession by some yokai. A very convenient bit of folklore.

In general, the only way to free someone from a tsukimono is through an exorcist. Usually these were the wandering Shugendo priests called *yamabushi*. They were the great sorcerers and exorcists of pre-modern Japan, roaming through the mountains and coming down when called to perform sacred services and spiritual battles.

Not all forms of tsukimono follow those same rules. *Kitsune-tsuki* (fox possession)—by far the most common type of tsukimono—is unique in that it resembles classic demonic possession in Western culture. Instead of the possessed taking on fox attributes, kitsune-tsuki feels like a bodily attack. The victim experiences shortness of breath, phantom pains, speaking in strange voices, and epileptic fits.

Up until WWII, kitsune-tsuki was treated with deadly seriousness by both mystics and scientists. In his 1913 book *Myths and Legends of Japan*, F. Hadland Davis wrote:

Demonical possession is frequently said to be due to the evil influence of foxes. This form of

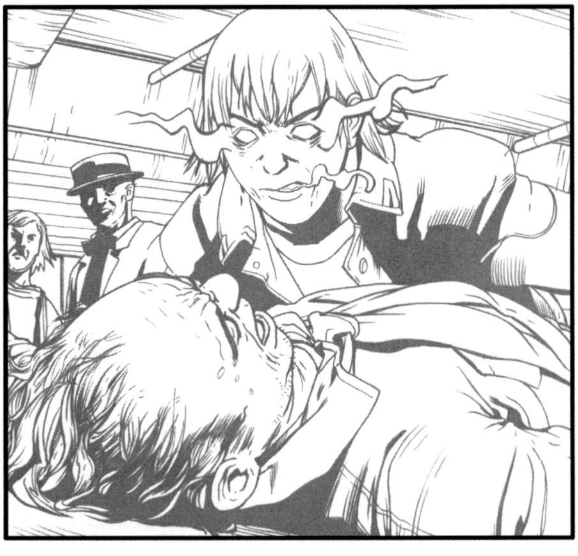

possession is known as kitsune-tsuki. The sufferer is usually a woman of the poorer classes, one who is highly sensitive and open to believe in all manner of superstitions. The question of demoniacal possession is still an unsolved problem, and the studies of Dr. Baelz of the Imperial University of Japan seem to point to the fact that animal possession in human beings is a very real and terrible truth after all. He remarks that a fox usually enters a woman either through the breast or between the fingernails, and that the fox lives a separate life of its own, frequently speaking in a voice totally different from the human's.

Another unusual type of possession was by *inugami* (犬神), the god dogs that moved throughout the Shikoku and Chugoku districts. Inugami possession was less direct than other forms of tsukimono—it was a hereditary taint that affected an entire family line. Inugami-possessed families were called *tsukimono-tsuji*, meaning something like a witch clan. The invisible dogs acted more as familiars than invading spirits. Tsukimono-tsuji families were able to command inugami to spiritually attack others.

Victims of kitsune-tsuki and tsukimono-tsuji were actively discriminated against. Possession was a stain that lasted forever. People carefully checked the family backgrounds of potential marriage or business partners to ensure they had no hint of yokai lineage. To bind your family to a possessed family was disastrous—you and all your heirs would now carry the taint. During the Edo period in particular, people were vigilant against possession. Accused families would be burned out of their homes and banished.

With no surprise, tsukimono discrimination is often linked to the untouchable caste known as *burakumin*. These were the outcasts of traditional Japanese society: undertakers, butchers, tanners, and the like, those who worked with blood and corpses. Many burakumin families were accused of being tsukimono-tsuji; people said that when you walked through a burakumin village, you could sense the invisible foxes and dogs, waiting for their master's commands.

Of course, in modern, more enlightened Japan, no one believes a word of it. Or do they? While you can probably no longer get away with blaming your expanding waistline on being possessed by a tanuki who is forcing you to overeat, there are still rumors of inugami families and those with kitsune-tainted bloodlines. Folk beliefs die hard. Like the tsukimono themselves, they never completely go away.

Lafcadio Hearn: Man of Ireland and Japan

There is something about island cultures that makes for rich folklore. I don't know if it is the lack of neighbors who potentially alter and diffuse traditions, or if having the ocean on all sides makes islanders feel the power of the dark. For whatever reason, island cultures run deep veins of magic. Some of the most bizarre, most fantastic folkloric gods and monsters can be found on islands, in places like Ireland and Japan. And no one walked the ley lines connecting these traditions quite like Koizumi Yakumo, known better in English by his birth name Lafcadio Hearn.

Hearn's life began on the Greek Ionian island of Lefkada. His mother, Rossa Kassimati, was a Kytherian aristocrat, and his father Charles Hearn was an Irish Surgeon-Major. Rossa's seven brothers objected to the union. They attacked and stabbed Major Hearn one night, leaving him bleeding on the road. But the assault did not have the desired effect. Instead of dead or divorced, the couple got pregnant. Patrick Lafcadio Hearn was born June 27, 1850.

Hearn's early life was as tumultuous as his parent's marriage. He did not stay long in Greece; at the age of two he was taken to Ireland where his father promptly abandoned wife and children, leaving them with relatives. Homesick and lonely, Rossa returned to Greece. Hearn was left behind in the care of an aunt. At age seven, his parents' marriage was annulled. They both went off to remarry and have new families. Hearn would never see them again.

Calling himself "Paddy," Hearn spent the next ten years of his life shifting between Ireland and Wales, absorbing the culture and the stories of the Tuatha De Danann and Formorian fiends. He also discovered a passion for Greek mythology and pored over whatever tomes he could find. A childhood accident blinded his left eye, leaving him self-conscious and withdrawn. But Hearn's aunt loved him. They saw to his every need, and sent him to school in France to be educated. When he was nineteen, however, a bad investment left his beloved aunt in poverty. Unable to continue to pay for school, she brought him home and told him he would have to make his own way in the world. As a final gift, she put five dollars in his pocket, gave him a one-way ticket to America, and wished him good luck.

In America, Hearn became enamored by Edgar Allen Poe, earning himself the nickname "Raven." Following in Poe's footsteps, Hearn became a journalist and writer. He gained fame in Cincinnati writing about gruesome murders and seedy places. He next moved to New Orleans, where he explored local magic, even befriending the voodoo queen Marie Laveau. He mingled with the immigrant populations, writing the first articles on Filipino life in the U.S., and publishing the book *Some Chinese Ghosts* in 1887. After ten years, he wished to see more of the world and worked for two years as correspondent in the West Indies island of Martinique. Then in 1890, Hearn accepted an assignment for *Harper's Weekly* to explore the newly opened country of Japan.

Whatever he had been seeking, Hearn found it in Japan. He felt connections between Japan and Ireland, and even an idealized version of his birthplace in Greece, seeing similar threads of paganism and animism, of a world alive with the supernatural. Japan's yokai and yūrei fascinated Hearn. He was eager to dive into the folklore and stories, but something vital kept him back.

Lafcadio Hearn could not speak Japanese. He never learned. Fortunately, his new wife Setsuko was an understanding and patient woman. Every night Hearn would ask her to "tell me a story," and in her halting English and gestures she would relate half-remembered legends from her childhood. If Hearn liked a story, he would make her repeat it over and over, then he would write it down. He made no attempt to be faithful; Hearn would happily rewrite characters and plots to make a better story.

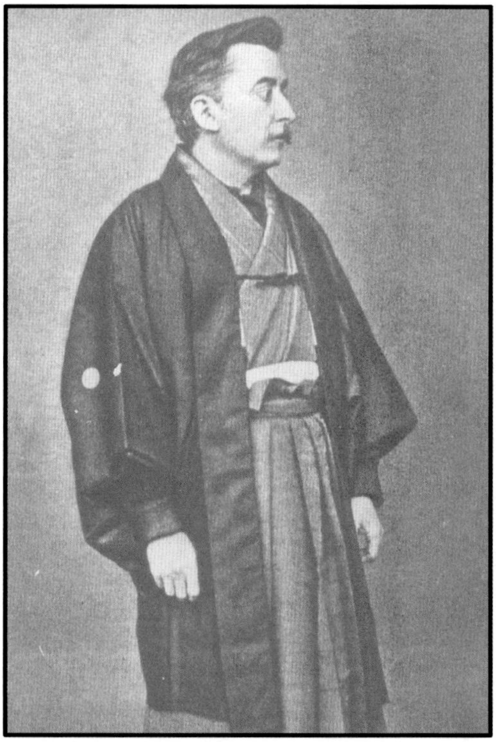

He published his first of these re-worked fairy tales in 1897, as *The Boy Who Drew Cats*. Part of the Hasegawa *Japanese Fairy Tales* series, Hearn then included adventures like *The Goblin Spider* and *Chin Chin Kobakama*. He put his stories into books as well, and in 1899 published *In Ghostly Japan*. Several books later, in 1903 he published his most famous work *Kwaidan: Stories and Studies of Strange Things*.

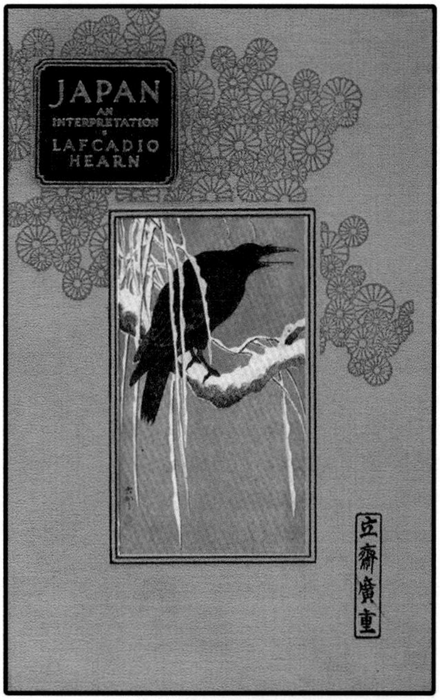
JAPAN
AN INTERPRETATION
LAFCADIO HEARN

Hearn was not the first to write about Japan's supernatural. But perhaps he was the first to do some from an artistic rather than anthropological point of view. He cared first and foremost about writing a good story. And because of this something remarkable happened. Hearn's stories were translated into Japanese and published under his Japanese name of Koizumi Yakumo. They became immensely popular. In the modern world Hearn's versions have completely supplanted the Japanese originals.

To this day children in Japan grow up on *The Boy Who Drew Cats* and *Kwaidan*, thinking they are authentic Japanese folklore. When you ask someone to tell you about the yuki onna snow woman, they are guaranteed to tell you Hearn's version, that exists nowhere other than his books. Hearn's *Earless Hoichi* has completely replaced the original, and become one of Japan's most famous ghost stories. Several of his *Japanese Fairy Tale* entries are considered to be original works created by Hearn, although you will now find them in Japan in books on Japanese folk legends.

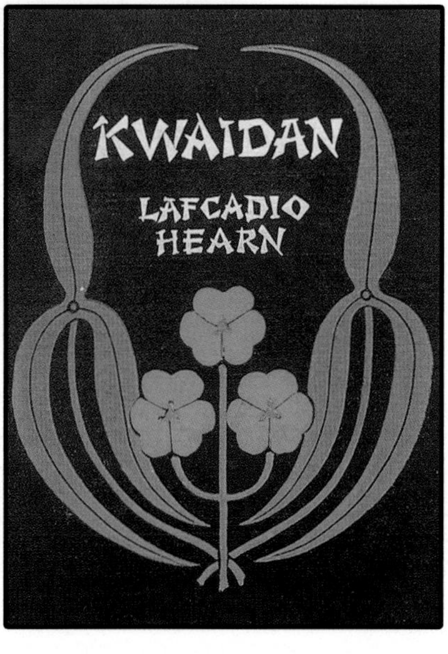
KWAIDAN
LAFCADIO
HEARN

Many scholars find influences of Irish and other folklore traditions in these tales by Hearn. There are elements that are certainly syncretic. You can see traces of the unseelie court in the ghostly nobility of *Earless Hoichi*. And Hearn's yuki onna stalking cold winter nights in search of prey perhaps has more in common with banshees than with the elemental nature goddess of Japanese legend. But they have become Japan's stories now. A subtle influence crept into the thread of the yokai legends, slowly altering the weave until the pattern changed completely.

Perhaps Lafcadio Hearn was the first Wayward.

While grammar and vocabulary can be a twisting, winding, endless staircase—especially the Chinese characters called *kanji*—one of the ways the Japanese language is much easier than English is in pronunciation. There is no coarticulation, elision, intrusion, or aspiration. What you see is what you get—with a few exceptions. Most Japanese words use consonant/vowel pairs, so pronunciation is simple. Just toss a hyphen after every vowel and you are good to go!

Oh, and remember that every vowel gets its own beat, even when next to another vowel. Take a word like "yokai." In English, you blend the last two vowels together into a single sound, pronouncing it "Yo–Kai." In Japanese, it is a 3–syllable word. "Yo–Ka–I" (Yoh–Kah–Ee). See? Easy!

The Wayward
Ayane – A–Ya–Ne (Ah–Yah–Neh)
Emi Ohara – E–Mi O–Ha–Ra (Eh–Me Oh–Hah–Rah)
Inaba – I–Na–Ba (Ee–Nah–Bah)
Nikaido – Ni–Ka–I–Do (Nee–Kah–Ee–Doh)
Rori Lane – Ro–Ri (Roar–Ree) * *Lane is pronounced... "Lane." And I'm not going to get into the R/L pronunciation thing. Consider that the advanced class.*
Segawa – Se–Ga–Wa (Say–Gah–Wah)
Shirai – Shi–Ra–I (She–Rah–Ee)

The Yokai
Akaname – A–Ka–Na–Me (Ah–Kah–Nah–May)
Gashadokuro – Ga–Sha–Do–Ku–Ro (Gah–Sha–Doh–Ku–Roh)
Hitodama – Hi–To–Da–Ma (He–Toh–Dah–Mah)
Hyakume – Hya–Ku–Me (Hyah–Ku–May)
Jorogumo – Jo–Ro–Gu–Mo (Joh–Roh–Gu–Moh)
Kage Onna – Ka–Ge O–N–Na (Kah–Geh Oh–N–Nah)
Kappa – Ka–Ppa (Kah–Pah) * *Another oddity, the double consonant. You have to kind of pop your lips for this one to do it right. Like a glottal stop, but with your lips.*
Kitsune – Ki–Tsu–Ne (Kee–Tsu–Neh) * *Note that "tsu" is a single sound in Japanese. Try saying "su" with your tongue in the "t" position and you will get near the target.*
Kyokotsu – Kyo–Ko–Tsu (Kyoh–Koh–Tsu) * *All the tricky bits in one name. If you can say this one, you can say any of them.*
Neko Musume – Ne–Ko Mu–Su–Me (Neh–Koh Mue–Sue–May)
Nopperabo – No–Pper–A–Bo (Noh–Peh–Rah–Boh) * *The same double–consonant as kappa.*
Nurarihyon – Nu–Rah–Ri–Hyon (New–Rah–Ri–Hyon) * *Did I say "no coarticulation?" Sorry, a bit of a lie. There is "some" coarticulation, like the H and Y here that make up "hyon."*
Suiko – Su–I–Ko (Sue–Ee–Koh)
Taka Onna – Ta–Ka O–N–Na (Tah–Kah Oh–N–Nah) * *Same again with the "n." It's the only free–standing consonant in the Japanese language. "N" never comes at the start of a word, only the middle or end.*

Tengu – Te–N–Gu (Te–En–Gu) * *That one's weird, right? But yeah, the "n" in the middle totally gets its own syllabic beat. It's pronounced..."n". Think of how an "N" sounds without a vowel, and you got it.*

Sorry...I lied a little about that "easy to pronounce" thing at the beginning....I also skipped over long vowels to make things a little easier. So this guide isn't 100% accurate, but should give you enough to approximate the accurate pronunciation!

When Rori casts one of her powerful kanji spells, our friend Nishi Makoto is the one using traditional brush and ink to make the sweeping strokes you see incorporated into the comic page art. Here are some of the ones he's done so far:

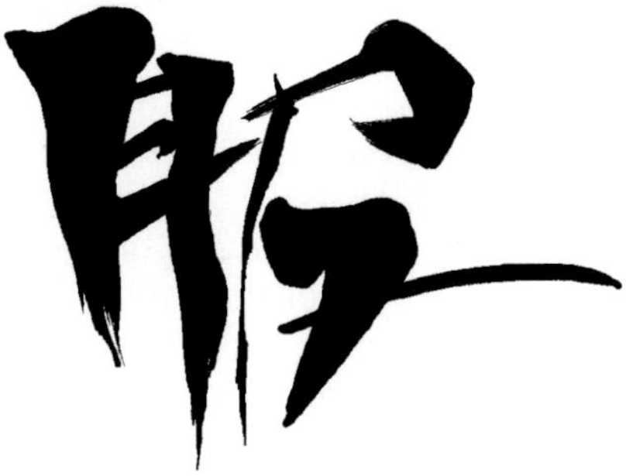
脱

Chapter#9: "Clothes"

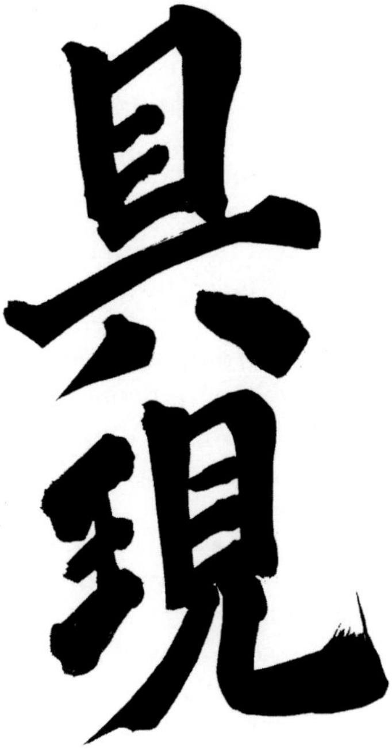
具現

Chapter#20: "Incarnate"

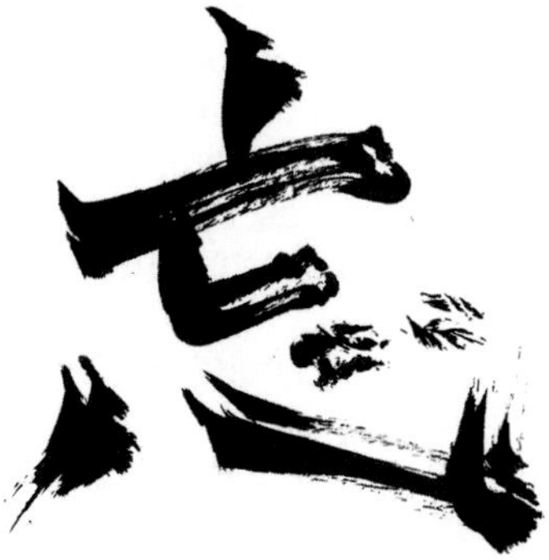
忘

Chapter #9: "Forget"

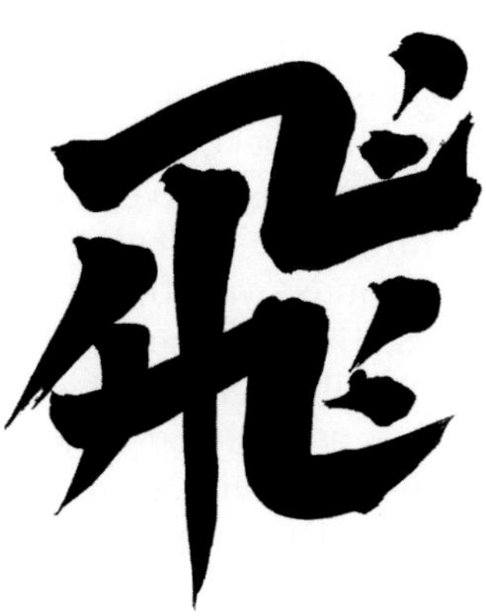
飛

Chapter#13: "Fly"

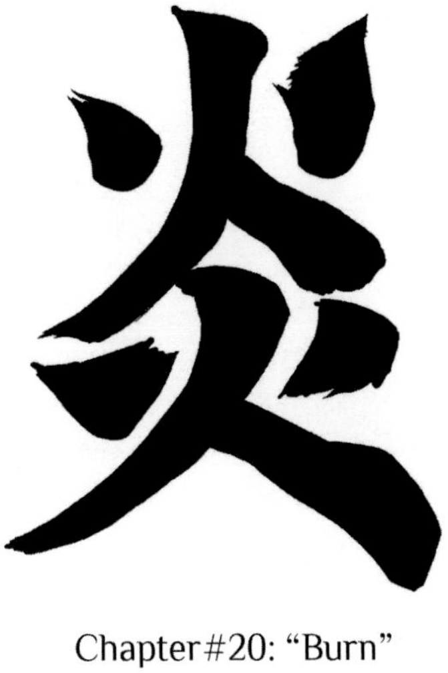
炎

Chapter#20: "Burn"

For generations, children of Ireland have been reared on mythology and folklore. Of course to us they are far more than the tales of ancient legends, they are where we are from and define who we are now. From Cú Chulainn to Fionn mac Cumhaill and the Salmon of Knowledge to the triple goddess The Morrigan, giants, demigods and creatures from the ethereal realm have always been a part of our lives.

Most of Ireland's regional and national festivals evolved from the gods and goddesses of ancient times, especially from the Tuatha Dé Danann, deities deemed as the forefathers of Irish culture and civilization. Of course the Formorians, a wild and altogether darker and more sinister supernatural race, still have their part to play.

The goddess Brigid is immortalized in the spring feast of Imbolc and Saint Brigid's Day, while Lughnasa is the harvest festival in the name of the god Lugh. Lugh was actually the son of a king of the Tuatha Dé Danann and his mother a Formorian. His games known as *Tailteann* were a test of strength and agility among his people. Today these games have become known as the Gaelic Games, played in every village, town and county throughout Ireland.

Fear is at the source of the majority of folklore tales and practices, particularly in relation to death and the protection of the soul as well as safeguarding against the ethereal creatures of darkness. The festival of Samhain is a prime example, taking place at the end of October intertwining the light and dark, shielding against bad spirits and misfortune,

but also welcoming back the dead with open arms.

The fear for celebrants was that of course malevolent spirits and evil entities could also cross with their loved ones as could the Devil himself. As well as the dead, homeowners had to contend with the fairies travelling abroad to create mischief. Gifts in the form of food or milk would be left on doorsteps to guarantee a fairy blessing. Anyone foolish enough to not do so would be subject to pranks by the cheeky wee folk at best and victim to a fairy curse at worst.

Of course most terrifying are the harbingers of death. Crom Dubh was the sacrificial god associated with death and slaughter and his incarnation was The Dullahan, a part of the 'Unseelie court' of the fairy realm. The Unseelie fairies are those deemed the most evil and malicious of all the otherworldly entities. Also known as *Gan Ceann*, meaning 'without a head', The Dullahan hunts the souls of the dying in the night.

Banshees have forever been known as portents of death, and the goddess Clíodhna was the very first of these wailing spirits seeking death for revenge and torment as well as calling on those due to die, with individual families often having their own Banshee heralding a death to this very day.

From these gods and goddesses an entire culture and belief system has grown, with Ireland being home to a myriad of ethereal creatures and spirits, from both the good Seelie Court and sinister Unseelie Court.

Once again fear is the driving force behind the behaviour and response to these creatures and their accompanying threat, with fortification rites being fundamental. Druidic runes, for example, focus on strength, energy, health and protection. The markings on runes tend to come from Ogham, an ancient language of Ireland uncovered by archaeological finds over the centuries by way of Ogham Stones. These Stones have been found all over Ireland, usually associated with burial stones of ancient kings and warriors; however, they are not of the past — Druidic practices are not just ongoing in modern Ireland but growing in popularity.

Of course in previous centuries much of the population of Ireland couldn't read or write and hexes, protection spells and rituals involved symbolism to get the point across. A *Piseóg* is a curse, placed on feuding neighbors, competing farmers and so on. Often recognized by a circle of eggs found in the hay or a talisman placed on a wall, they are set to bring misfortune on the home.

The power of the Piseóg lies in fear, and a farmer would be so terrified of the curse he would destroy his own crops and cattle. But these curses can't still be happening today, can they? Tell that to the terrified man in Kerry I spoke to recently, who found a circle of eggs on his boundary wall and hasn't slept properly since, his mind trying to figure out who would curse him and why.

What of the cute and friendly leprechaun? Don't kid yourself! There are several types of leprechaun and not all of them guard a crock of gold! For over 1,000 years, the leprechaun is descended from the Tuatha Dé Danann and are a part of the Sidhe or Fairy family. The name *Leprechaun* has two sources, both from old Irish. The first is *Leath Bhrogan*, meaning 'shoe maker', and the second is *Luacharmán*, meaning 'small body'.

Leprechauns like to keep themselves to themselves and really don't like mortals — or each other. Very much loners, they are happiest in their own intoxicated company; however, there is one you should be afraid of and that is the *Fear Dearg*, which translates as 'Red Man'. Recognized by his blemished yellowy skin, Fear Dearg is dressed head to foot in red, and his greatest delight is your fear and dread. He has the ability to make your nightmare a reality.

Of course this is all just the tip of the iceberg. We have Fairy Shock Troops riding the wind, devastating farmlands and cattle just for kicks, spirits of the eternally damned wandering the earthly realm looking for Irish souls to steal, serpents, mermaids and hellhounds. We have the *Púca*, a shapeshifting creature who terrorizes the night and ghosts, demons and the Devil himself.

If you thought Saint Patrick had driven all the paganism and darkness from Ireland, you would be wrong. Far from Christianity banishing these beliefs and rituals, the early monks actually documented these mythological events into such manuscripts as the *Book of Leinster* and the *Annals of the Four Provinces*. Instead of turning the Irish away from their gods and goddesses, the clergy fashioned their stories into those of saints such as Saint Brigid. This is why Christian and Pagan stories are intertwined in much the same way Irish history and mythology can never be separated and why we are great storytellers — it's in our blood, heritage and very essence of being.

Ireland is a land rich in mythology and folklore, mixed with dark history and truth, bound neatly in fear, magic and excitement. Welcome to the Emerald Isle!

When it comes to Irish history, there is a point where 'fact' takes a backseat and tales of legendary heroes and villains take centre stage. What did you expect? We are a nation of storytellers!

While the races of the Tuatha Dé Danann and the Fomorians are known worldwide, many forget that the Fir Bolg, or *Men of the Bog,* were long settled on the desolate Irish landscape. Do not let the translation of the name fool you—it simply means they were able to turn rocky, barren fields into fertile, arable lands. These literal and figurative ground-breaking men also established the sacred Hill of Tara and were the first of the High Kings of Ireland.

It is little wonder, therefore, that a race of demi-gods, descendants of the goddess Dana, mother of the land, would take an interest in conquering a domain of such opportunity. So it was that several decades after the Fir Bolg were settled, the Tuatha Dé Danann rode on the wind and came down from the sky and set foot in the Emerald Isle.

The number four is paramount throughout any doc-umented accounts of the Tuatha Dé Danann. They created four cities: Falias, Gorias, Finias and Marias. They had four wise men to teach their youth both skills and knowledge, for without both they could not know wisdom. Each city had its own treasure, the keystones of the Tuatha Dé Danann—the Stone of Virtue which called to the King of Ireland, the Sword from which no man could escape once drawn, the Spear of Victory and the Magic Cauldron which left no appetite unsated.

Nuada was the King of the Tuatha Dé Danann. Around him he had great men such as Ogma, teacher of the written word, Dian Cecht, an incredible physician, Goibniu the Smith and Credenus the ultimate Craftsman. Also on the great warrior's team were his own gods—Neit, the god of battle and *The Morrigan,* triple goddess of war, fertility and sovereignty.

It is said that the mighty Tuatha Dé Danann arrived in the Province of Connaught on the first day of the feast of Beltaine. The Ancient Druids told the King of the Fir Bolg, Eochaid, that his dreams fore-told of a powerful enemy approaching. He sent his Champion, Sreng, to meet with the emissary of the Tuatha Dé Danann known as Bres (an interesting sidebar is that Bres was of mixed race, Tuatha Dé Danann and Fomorian, a fact that will become of much relevance soon).

Sreng informed Bres that the weapon he carried was called *Craisech.* It could cut through flesh and bone, no shield could defend against it and the wounds it inflicted would never heal. An offer was made to the Fir Bolg that they could settle in one part of Ireland and leave the rest to the mighty Tuatha Dé Danann, an offer that was refused. And so began the First Battle of Magh Tuireadh.

The Fir Bolg were strong, led by their hurlers, spearmen of immense strength and agility. They were pitted against the triple goddess Morrigan, who rained down fire and cast great mists and clouds of the darkest night.

Despite the demi-god status of the Tuatha Dé Danann, they were driven back by the Fir Bolg; however, their king fell and the indigenous race conceded defeat and took Connaught for their home, leaving the Tuatha Dé Danann the rest of Ireland.

Now around this time, the King of the Tuatha Dé Danann, Nuada, lost an arm. Under the doctrine of the Tuatha Dé Danann, no incomplete man was able to reign. Nuada lost not only a limb but his crown, which went to Bres, foster son to the Tuatha Dé Danann but his father a Fomorian. Bres was a poor leader and showed none of the hospitality and social skills required of a king. While Bres began his reign, Nuada was gifted a silver arm from his physician, Dian Cecht. The son of the healer was impressed by the gift of alchemy shown by his father and studied harder and reached into darker magic. It was the son of Dian Cecht who created living tissue over the silver arm of Nuada, thus enabling him to be restored to power. Was Miach the creator of the first Cyborg? Regardless, his work drove his father to jealous rage and filicide.

Incensed by his deposition, Bres sought sanctuary and assistance with retribution from his paternal family, the Fomorians. His grandfather, Balor of the Evil Eye, agreed. Balor was so called because he has one eye that would cause death upon his penetrative stare. I often wonder if Balor was the inspiration for the Eye of Sauron, but I digress—the great battle of Magh Tuireadh had begun.

Bres went to war against his former kinsmen, his power in the form of his grandfather. Balor slayed his opponent Nuada with a single gaze from his evil eye. Undeterred at the loss of their king, the Tuatha Dé Danann were unrelenting in their attack and intent on winning the battle.

The new leader of the Tuatha Dé Danann was brought forth. Lugh, who like Bres, was of Tuatha Dé Danann and Fomorian birth. His loyalties were firm, however, and he killed his grandfather Balor with a single slingshot into his eye of poison.

Lugh found his half-brother Bres unprotected on the battlefield. Weak and defenseless, Bres begged for both mercy and his very life. In a moment of pity for his kin, Lugh agreed in exchange for Bres teaching the Fomorian people agriculture.

It is interesting to note that King Nuada had previously rejected Lugh, who had travelled far to the Court of Tara to be accepted as one of the Tuatha Dé Danann. When Lugh had asked for a place as either a blacksmith, wheelwright, swordsman, king's champion, druid, magician, craftsman or wordsmith he was refused. It was only because he excelled at all that he was accepted.

Lugh's power and influence went on to the creation of the festival of *Lughnasadh*, a Druid celebration held on the first of August every year. Such were his strengths and abilities that a test in the form of games was set up in his mother's name and became known as the Tailteann Games. These have progressed over recent centuries to become known as the Gaelic Games, played throughout Ireland to this day, growing stronger in popularity every year.

So what became of the Fomorians, the Tuatha Dé Danann and even the Fir Bolg? Well, we are talking demi-gods, supernatural races and magic—they may have been driven underground, back to the ethereal world of the Sidhe; however, they are not truly gone. Maybe there will be a third battle and the wars of Magh Tuireadh are not yet over. We will just have to wait and see...

Many a conversation in Ireland starts with 'do you know who's dead?' Death is a normal topic of discussion any self-respecting *Seanchái* (Irish Storyteller) will include death and haunting in his tale. In modern day Ireland, the customs of old still remain and the event is treated with weighted respect and tradition. We seem to have a fascination and fear of our own mortal demise that stems back to our ancient roots and the safeguarding of the soul.

For the majority, it isn't so much the dread of death itself, but what happens to the spirit and where it goes afterwards. There have always been the takers of souls in the form of demons, fairies, spirits and other ethereal beings. Over the centuries, the Irish have gotten wise and found different ways to repel or hide from those looking to reap the soul and cast it to eternal damnation – or worse.

In order to find the right protection from these creatures of darkness, you have to know who they are and what they want. Some are merely harbingers; others seek to harvest your very essence of being. Those such as the *Banshee* will (mostly) just warn you that death is imminent, however, there are two terrifying beings you should avoid at all costs.

SLUAGH

Once thought to be Angels that have tumbled from the grace of God, the *Sluagh Sidhe* actually have a far more sinister origin and purpose. Can you imagine how evil you have to be for your soul to be deemed too tainted for the fires of Hades and rejected by Satan himself? Well that is who the Sluagh are– souls of sinners not wanted by Heaven or Hell, destined to roam the Earth and take the departed for no reason other than the thrill of the hunt and to add to their ever-growing number.

Unlike other *Sidhe* (fairies), the Sluagh are unable to walk this mortal coil. They ride on the wind as a host, unable to touch the ground. They travel as a flock and, for all intents and purposes, look like a conspiracy of ravens, which is probably one of the reasons the raven is seen as a portent of death. As the howling wind and darkening sky take hold, they close in, and it becomes quite clear they are not bird like at all. With wizened, leathery wings and gnarled, skeletal frames, these twisted creatures fly in from the west and seek out the homes of the dying. This is why one of the traditions that still holds today is to close any westerly facing windows when a loved one is taking a last breath.

Sadly, not every innocent (or indeed not-so-innocent) soul escapes the clutches of the evil Sluagh, and these misfortunes are caught up in the host of the soul hunters, not to touch the Earth again or reach Heaven or Hell for all eternity.

THE DULLAHAN

The *Dullahan* and before him *Crom Dubh*, are descended from the god Crom Cruaich and are synonymous with dark rituals, death and folklore.

Crom Cruaich was first introduced to Ireland some time before the arrival of the *Tuatha Dé Danann*. Tigernmas was one of the first High Kings of Ireland, and, as a Milesian, brought the worship of this deathly idol to Ireland, building a shrine at the top of Magh Slécht in County Cavan in order to win favour from his god.

King Tigernmas and most of his troops mysteriously died on Magh Slécht on the night of Samhain, now known as Halloween, as they worshipped their dark, sacrificial deity. As the centuries passed, Crom Dubh evolved from Crom Cruaich and became a worshipped figure in his own right. He is still left 'offerings' in rural parts of Ireland today on Crom Dubh Sunday.

The darkest incarnation of the sacrificial god, however, is the Dullahan, also known as *Gan Ceann*, meaning 'without a head'. Crom Dubh did not want to be denied human souls following the introduction of Christianity and so disguised himself as the one without a head, a tribute to the sacrifices by beheading that gave Crom Cruaich/Dubh his power.

For centuries, the Celts have believed the head to be incredibly powerful as both the sacred and physical resting place of the soul. Warriors would decapitate their foes and keep their heads to ward off evil and gain more power. Those believed to have died as deviants would have stones placed in their mouths to stop the evil soul escaping. It is no surprise therefore, that one of Ireland's most feared unearthly beings incorporates all of these Celtic beliefs over the ages.

Gan Ceann is a part of the 'Unseelie Court' of the fairy realm, filled with the nastiest and darkest of the Sidhe, and his job is to reap souls. He carries his head in the crook of his arm, black eyes darting from the mottled, decaying flesh stretched thinly across his skull, searching for his prey.

The Dullahan carries a whip made from the spine of a human corpse as he stands on his wagon. The wheel spokes are made of thigh bones and covered with dried human skin, and the coach is pulled by a jet black horse with eyes of glowing embers.

The headless horseman has supernatural vision, and when he senses a soul for the taking, he holds his head high, seeing across landscapes, through windows and into the darkest corners of the most remote homes.

The soul taker does not stop for anyone and all locks swing open, no one is safe. If you get in his way, at best your eyes will be lashed out with his whip or the Dullahan will throw a bowl of human blood upon you. The stain cannot be removed and you are marked as his next target.

Certain festivals increase the power of The Dullahan and this is a time to stay in and draw your curtains tightly. If you are out in the still of night, there is no protection from this agent of death. He does however fear one thing – gold. Throwing a piece in his path may make him back off for a while and may be the only thing that will save you.

The Dullahan is only permitted to speak once on each ride and that is to utter the name of the person who is going to die. When he finds his quarry and speaks their name aloud, their spirit is brought forth to be devoured.

So we closed our west-facing windows and turned mirrors so our souls would not be trapped. We paid Sin Eaters to take our transgressions and clear a path to Heaven. We left food as offerings to the Sidhe and the departed that they may look favorably upon us. We hired Keeners to cry at wakes so as not to invoke the Hounds of Hell, sent to collect the dead and take them to eternal torment. All in the name of saving our souls.

The fate of the spirit is of more concern to the Irish than death itself, and, over the centuries, protection of the soul has taken precedence over anything else. Sometimes it doesn't matter what protections are put in place however, as the malevolent search for souls by the Dullahan and the Sluagh is too powerful and relentless. All we can do is the best we can in this life, maybe close the odd window at the right time, oh, and carry a bit of gold in our pockets – just in case!

Irish forms part of the group of Celtic languages and is also known as Gaelic. There are several languages including Scottish, Manx and Welsh. Irish is most closely associated with Scottish Gaelic and originated more than 2,500 years ago.

Although English is the predominant language, Irish or Gaelic is the official language of Ireland and you cannot become a police officer or 'Garda' (pronounced 'Guard-ah') in Ireland without having passed Irish language exams. It is tied into our culture, history and folklore in such a way it can never die and the language itself is being revived and taken to new levels through the arts, music and literature. There are also still several parts of the Emerald Isle where Irish is widely spoken day to day such as areas of Connemara, the Aran Islands and Kerry.

Although Irish follows the same alphabet as English and many European languages, we have our own unique traits such as our accent known as the 'fada' which changes the pronunciation of words by elongating the vowel. As an example the name Séan. Without the fada it would simply be pronounced 'Seen', however the fada changes the pronunciation to 'Shawn.'

There are some set rules and order to speech and pronunciation, however with regional dialects changing sounds and spellings, it can all be a bit of a challenge!

The Races and Warriors
Cú Chulainn – Coo Cullen
Fionn Mac Cumhaill – Finn Mac-Cool
Fir Bolg – Fear Bowlg
Fomoire – For-mora
Partholóin – Par-ho-lowen
Tuatha Dé Danann – Tooha Day Dan-ann

Feasts, Battles and Fairy Curses
Bealtaine – Bell-ta-na
Imbolc – Im-bol-cha
Lughnasa – Loo-nas-sa
Magh Tuireadh – Mog Tiera
Piseóg – Pish-owg
Samhain – Sow-ann
Tailteann – Tell-ten

Fairy Folk (good and bad!)
Aes Sidhe – Ass Shee
Crom Dubh – Chrome Dove
Dullahan – Doo-la-han
Fear Dearg – Far Darrig
Gan Ceann – Gone Ki-oun
Ganacanagh – Gone-canack
Púca – Poo-ka
Sidhe – Shee
Sluagh – Sloo-ah

As you can see, we rarely spell a word in Irish the way it actually sounds! My advice? Have a bit of craic trying and, after a bit of practice and a drop of fine Irish whiskey to loosen your vocal cords, you'll be a natural! *Sláinte!*

Ogham is the ancient language at the heart of Pagan Ireland and is shrouded in mystery and magic. Believed to have been created by the Druids, it was a cipher designed to confuse those unfamiliar with the ways of the Pagan.

The language is based on the Druid beliefs associated with trees, which is why it's also known as the 'Tree Alphabet'. From these tree meanings, the Druid spells, protections and 'runes' were created and they've stood the test of time.

Ogham Stones are markers discovered all over Ireland, with Ogham carved into the stone itself. Believed to be everything from gravestones of warriors to warnings, they are most prevalent in Munster, with one being found on the Mountain of Truth, portal to the Fairy Realm.

Although runes are associated with Norse mythology and magic, the Druids created their own protections using Ogham and borrowed more than one symbol from their Germanic counterparts. Runes tend to be positive energy, divination and magic as opposed to a symbol of strife.

For example, the yew represents being solitary, standing alone but the mark itself means accepting the inevitable, destiny, new beginnings and contact with the past.

The Ogham symbol for the Rowan tree (Irish word 'Caorthann') represents Strength, Healing, Health, Protection, especially against enchantment and Psychic Energy. Delicate enough for baby Rori's forehead!

For extra strength and protection, it was very common to combine the symbols for extra potency such as a combination of the Elder and Holly Runes. The Elder is an overall tree of protection casting a great shadow of protection over those in its shade. The Holly is very much used in Paganism even now as it survives even the harshest and cruellest of winters and thus is a symbol of hope and protection against evil.

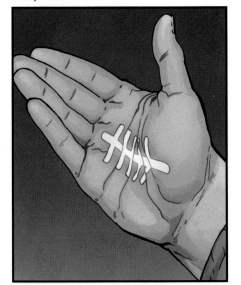

Letter	Name	Tree		Letter	Name	Tree
B	Beith	Birch		M	Muin	Vine
L	Luis	Rowan		G	Gort	Ivy
F	Fearn	Alder		NG	nGéatal	Reed
S	Sail	Willow		Z (st)	Straif	Blackthorn
N	Nion	Ash		R	Ruis	Elder
H	hÚath	Hawthorn		A	Ailm	Silver Fir
D	Dair	Oak		O	Onn	Gorse
T	Tinne	Holly		U	Úr	Heather
C	Coll	Hazel		E	Eadha	Poplar
Q	Quert	Apple		I	Iodhadh	Yew

When it comes to Fairy beasts, there is much debate as to whether they should be categorized as animals or just transfigurations of other fairy creatures. Regardless they are mysterious, powerful and, in many cases, deadly.

The Cat Sidhe (cawt-shee) or Cat Sith is one of these very beings and is one of the most enigmatic and little known of the fairy realm. Although more widely recognized in tales of folklore from the Scottish Highlands, as with much of Celtic lore it also appears in the traditional tales of the Emerald Isle.

The size of a dog, the Cat Sith is jet black except for a white spot upon its breast. Synonymous with death, the feline fairy is feared around the bodies of the deceased as it is a taker of souls. Traditions include putting out fires so as not to entice the Cat Sith with warmth and distracting it from the corpse with

games of jumping and tussling or setting riddles and not solving them.

On the feast of Samhain, many homesteads would leave out a saucer of milk so that the Cat Sith would bless the home for the coming year. Those who didn't would be cursed and the milk from their cows would run dry.

One of the most interesting theories is that the Cat Sith is, in fact, a witch. It is said that certain witches have the ability to transform into a cat shape up to eight times while retaining the ability to change back. Should the witch decide to change a ninth time, she is destined to stay in cat form forever. Could this be the source behind the legend of a cat having nine lives?

Regardless of its origin, the Cat Sith is a formidable creature with all the tricky attributes of its feral cat counterpart. Add in the fact this beast can steal your soul, and I imagine it would be very bad luck indeed for you to cross the path of this particular black fairy feline.

The Fomoire or Formorians were a race of demi-gods who arrived in Ireland from across the seas and were some of the very first settlers on the shores of the Emerald Isle. In fact, the name is sometimes believed to derive from the sea, however it is more likely it relates to being of the Underworld.

Unlike their supernatural counterparts, the Tuatha Dé Danann, the Fomoire were wild forces of nature, embracing chaos and shunning order. Some believe the ways of the Fomoire were so feral and dark that they bordered on the demonic, which reflected in their appearance and references to the Underworld. This could be misconstrued as a reaction to their unsightly form. They were generally ugly creatures, some part-man, part-animal, others with limbs missing or with one dominant eye, such as the King of the Fomoire know as Balor of the Evil Eye.

In *Leabhar Gabhala Eireann* (The Book of Conquests of Ireland) dating back to the 11th Century, the Fomoire were described as '*crowds of abominable giants and monsters*'. The women of the Fomoire were no exception to this rule. There were some Formorians, such as Elatha, who was looked upon as a human-shaped creature of beauty.

Fomoire were beings of the land. Farming and breeding were their specialty. These skills were unknown to the Tuatha Dé Danann and they were desperate to get their hands on them. That talent for working with the earth may have been because the Fomoire had been a part of Ireland since long before their rivals and were spiritually one with the land and sea in ways other settlers could only dream of.

In truth, the Fomoire are an enigma. No one quite knows from where or when they came. They dipped in and out of history and the annals of Ireland and never decisively left. Nobody can tell if they were good or evil and no one knows for sure their ultimate goal. Perhaps they slipped quietly into the shadows, watching, biding their time, waiting to rise once more...

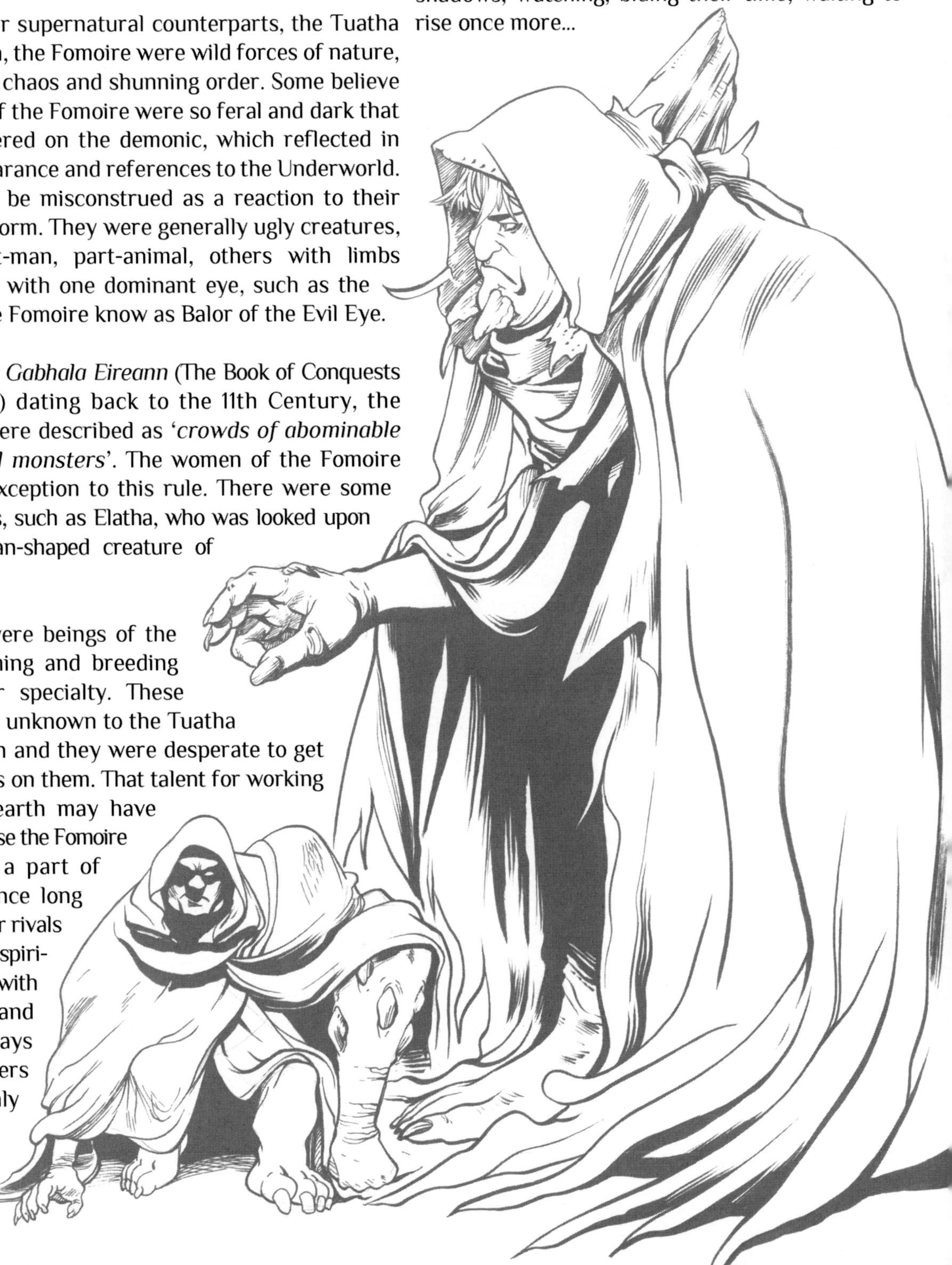

If you wondered why Irish males have a reputation for being smooth-talking, tall, dark and handsome strangers, then you need look no further than the Gancanagh (Gawn-canack). The name has a literal translation of '*Love Talker*' and the title is no word of a lie!

One of the solitary fairy folk, the Gancanagh is part of the leprechaun family, although you wouldn't think it to look at him. Tall, wiry and very easy on the eye, women are drawn helplessly to this ethereal being before he even begins to weave his intoxicating magic.

Tales of this mystery man stealing hearts and sanity date back over millennia. Likened to the Incubus, the Gancanagh is more subtle and much more deadly. Traditionally, his target would be the women of rural areas such as milkmaids, devouring their chastity and casting shame on the family, but he moves on with the times as much as he does with locations.

He is dressed stylishly and oozes charm with his distinguished pipe or 'dudeen' pressed between his lips. The Gancanagh is nonchalant on the surface and appears lazy, but don't be fooled. He will charm, lie and ultimately seduce his target - once that happens, their deadly fate is sealed.

I may have misled you by painting a romantic picture of this fairy. Trust me, this is just a façade. He isn't looking for love, he seeks complete control using his intoxicating touch and, when his prey is completely dependent upon him, he callously withdraws his affection and leaves. The victims of the Gancanagh fall into a lovesick frenzy, and, like any drug addiction, it takes over their minds and bodies with disastrous consequences. Isolated from family and friends, pining for the touch of the Gancanagh, they spiral into madness until death becomes a welcome release.

There is one way to protect yourself from this seductive creature. An amulet made from the twigs of rowan and mistletoe, pinned together with an iron nail and bound with a blood-soaked thread.

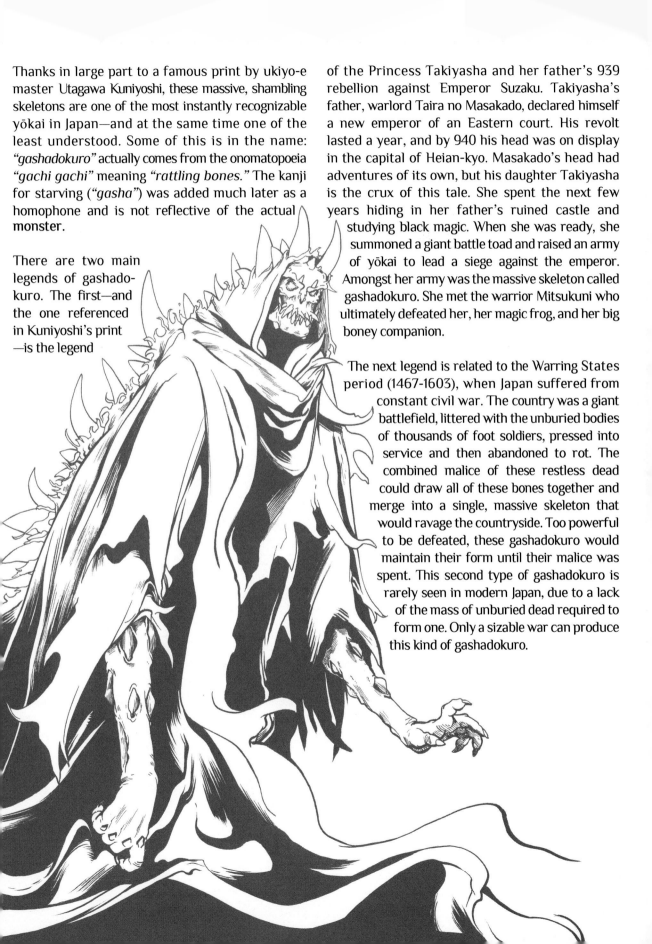

Thanks in large part to a famous print by ukiyo-e master Utagawa Kuniyoshi, these massive, shambling skeletons are one of the most instantly recognizable yōkai in Japan—and at the same time one of the least understood. Some of this is in the name: *"gashadokuro"* actually comes from the onomatopoeia *"gachi gachi"* meaning *"rattling bones."* The kanji for starving (*"gasha"*) was added much later as a homophone and is not reflective of the actual monster.

There are two main legends of gashado-kuro. The first—and the one referenced in Kuniyoshi's print —is the legend of the Princess Takiyasha and her father's 939 rebellion against Emperor Suzaku. Takiyasha's father, warlord Taira no Masakado, declared himself a new emperor of an Eastern court. His revolt lasted a year, and by 940 his head was on display in the capital of Heian-kyo. Masakado's head had adventures of its own, but his daughter Takiyasha is the crux of this tale. She spent the next few years hiding in her father's ruined castle and studying black magic. When she was ready, she summoned a giant battle toad and raised an army of yōkai to lead a siege against the emperor. Amongst her army was the massive skeleton called gashadokuro. She met the warrior Mitsukuni who ultimately defeated her, her magic frog, and her big boney companion.

The next legend is related to the Warring States period (1467-1603), when Japan suffered from constant civil war. The country was a giant battlefield, littered with the unburied bodies of thousands of foot soldiers, pressed into service and then abandoned to rot. The combined malice of these restless dead could draw all of these bones together and merge into a single, massive skeleton that would ravage the countryside. Too powerful to be defeated, these gashadokuro would maintain their form until their malice was spent. This second type of gashadokuro is rarely seen in modern Japan, due to a lack of the mass of unburied dead required to form one. Only a sizable war can produce this kind of gashadokuro.

A lingering shadow cast against a wall when no one is there. The silhouette of a woman in a window coming from an empty room. These are all signs of one of the shyest, most ellusive yokai of all—kage onna, the shadow woman.

Very little is known about the kage onna. It is said she appears on moonlit nights, and that the shimmer of moonbeams reveals her true form. She is never seen in detail, only the outline of a woman cast against an illuminated surface. What she wants, who she is—nobody knows.

Like many yokai, she can be traced back to Toriyama Sekien's Konjaku Hyakki Shūi (今昔百鬼拾遺; *Supplement to The Hundred Demons from the Present and the Past*). The third volume in his yokai encyclopedia collection, by this time Toriyama had run out of traditional folklore yokai and begun inventing his own. Toriyama often started with a frightening or evocotive name, then imagined a yokai to match. That is almost certainly the case with the kage onna.

However, in her book Tohoku Kaidan no Tabi (*Travels through the Yokai of Tohoku*) novelist Yamada Norio said that the kage onna is a traditional yokai from Yamagata prefecture. She tells the story of a man visiting his friend's house, and seeing the shadow of a women in the garden. When asking his friend who this mystery woman is, the friend laughs it off, saying he must have seen the kage onna who haunts the place. So is the kage onna a haunting spirit or just a convenient excuse for a man attempting to cover up an illicit love affair? In the world of the yokai, the answer is most likely both.

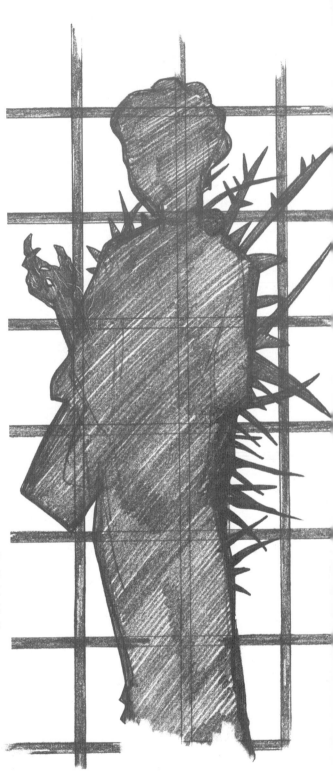

In a story that could be repeated by every Japanese child, a man coming home late at night encounters a stranger whose face is as smooth as an egg. Fleeing in terror, he meets a police officer (or a ramen seller, in some versions) and screams out his story. The police officer then smiles, raises a hand to his face and wipes down, asking the man if it looked "something like this"–revealing himself as another of those self-same monsters, a faceless apparition called nopperabo.

Nopperabo are one of the most well-known of Japan's yokai. Almost all encounters are variations of the above story, with slight variations. Tales first started to appearing in the early Edo period, appearing in kaidan collections like the 1663 *Sorori Monogatari*. Nopperabo were one of the first wave of new urban yokai that accompanied Japan's shift from villages to cities. There stories always contain some element of city life, from police officers to ramen shops.

Accounts vary as to whether nopperabo are a unique species of yokai, or just one of Japan's many prankster spirits playing games with hapless humans. When Lafcadio Hearn told their story in his 1903 book *Kwaidan: Stories and Studies of Strange Things*, he titled it *Mujina*, which are one of Japan's shapeshifting animal yokai along with tanuki, kitsune, cats, and weasels. Whatever the case, nopperabo are relatively harmless—they seek only to startle, not to harm.

Nopperabo are one of the few Japanese yokai to travel outside their native country. Sightings have been reported in Hawaii as recently as the 1950s, leaving many to believe that when Japanese immigrants went to Hawaii to work, not all of them were exactly human. It looks like a few yokai went along for the trip as well.

No face

Flat skull/face. No bridge of nose or anything that can be seen in profile.

Slightly muscular

Armed with a minimum of a medium blade.

If you think you are safe from prying eyes on the second story of the house of pleasure, you haven't reckoned with this yokai's abilities. The taka onna can stretch her body as far as required to peek in on the illicit goings-on. Her own horrible face keeps her from joining in on the fun inside, but the taka onna has a different fetish—she likes to watch.

Toriyama Seiken was either not feeling particularly creative when he drew the taka onna for Gazu Hyakki Yagyō (*The Illustrated Night Parade of a Hundred Demons*), or he felt her story was so well known that she needed no explanation. In either case, all we know of her origins are Toriyama's picture and her name. Unlike other yokai in the collection, Toriyama supplied no backstory or further information about the tall woman.

That hasn't stopped people from filling in the blanks. In his book *Yokai Gadan Zenshu* (*Complete Discussions of Yokai*), folklorist Fujisawa Morihiko first recorded the story of the taka onna as a woman peeking into brothel windows. Fujisawa speculates that these stories were most likely inspired by Toriyama's picture, and not the other way around. In *Tohoku Kaidan no Tabi* (*Travels through the Yokai of Tohoku*), novelist Yamada Norio added the detail of the taka onna being a woman consumed by jealousy and lust but too ugly to get a man. She then transforms into the taka onna and menaces anyone enjoying the pleasures of the flesh she was denied.

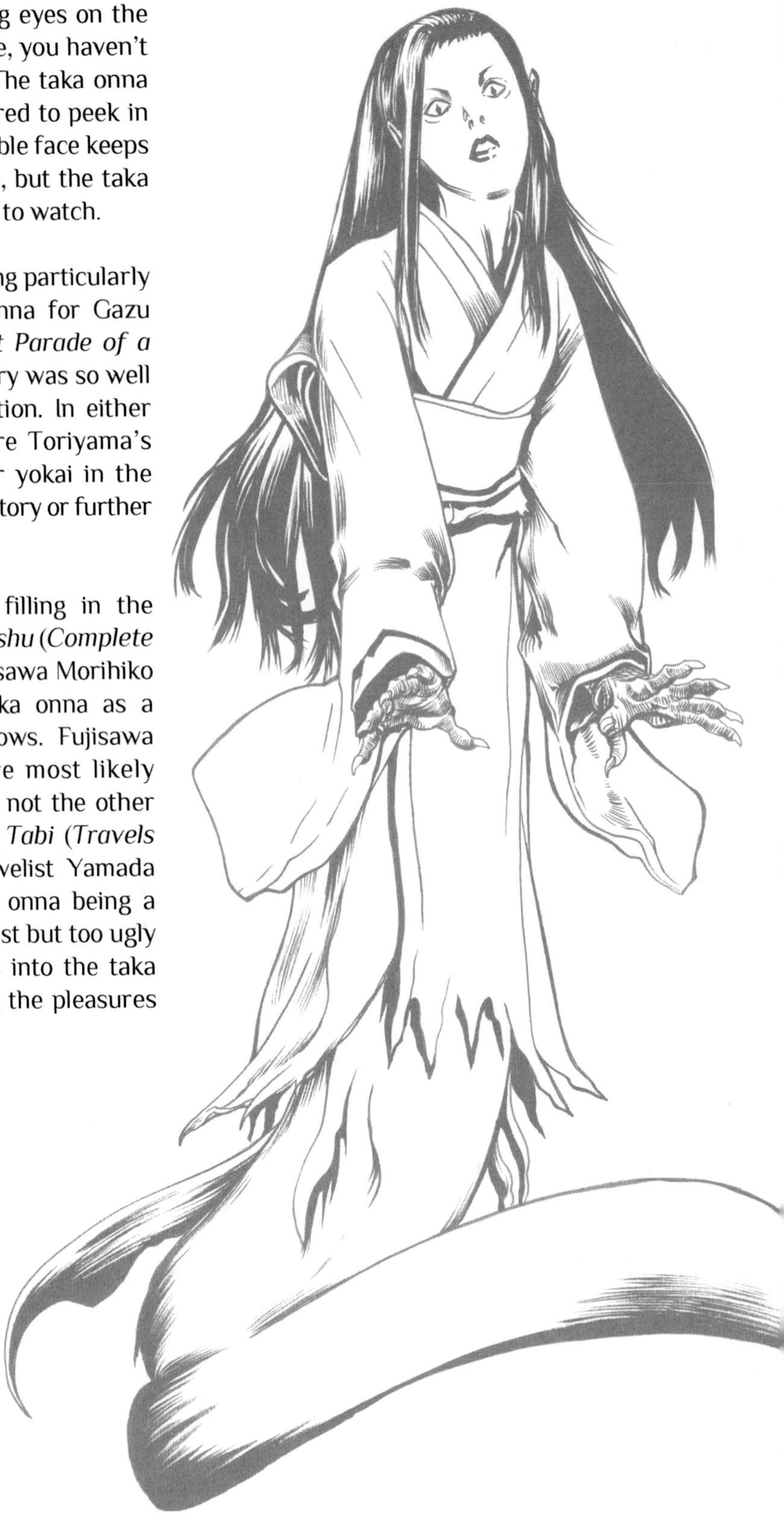

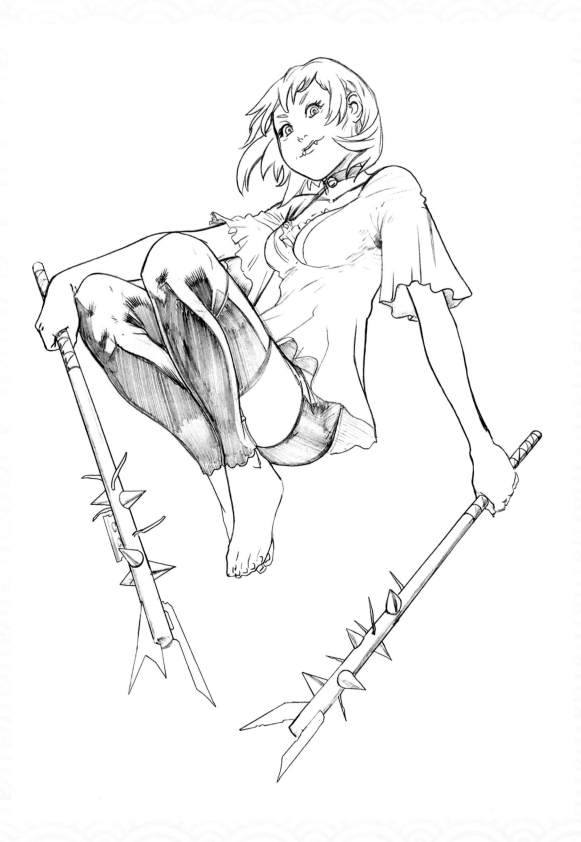

AYANE SKETCH
Artwork by Steven Cummings

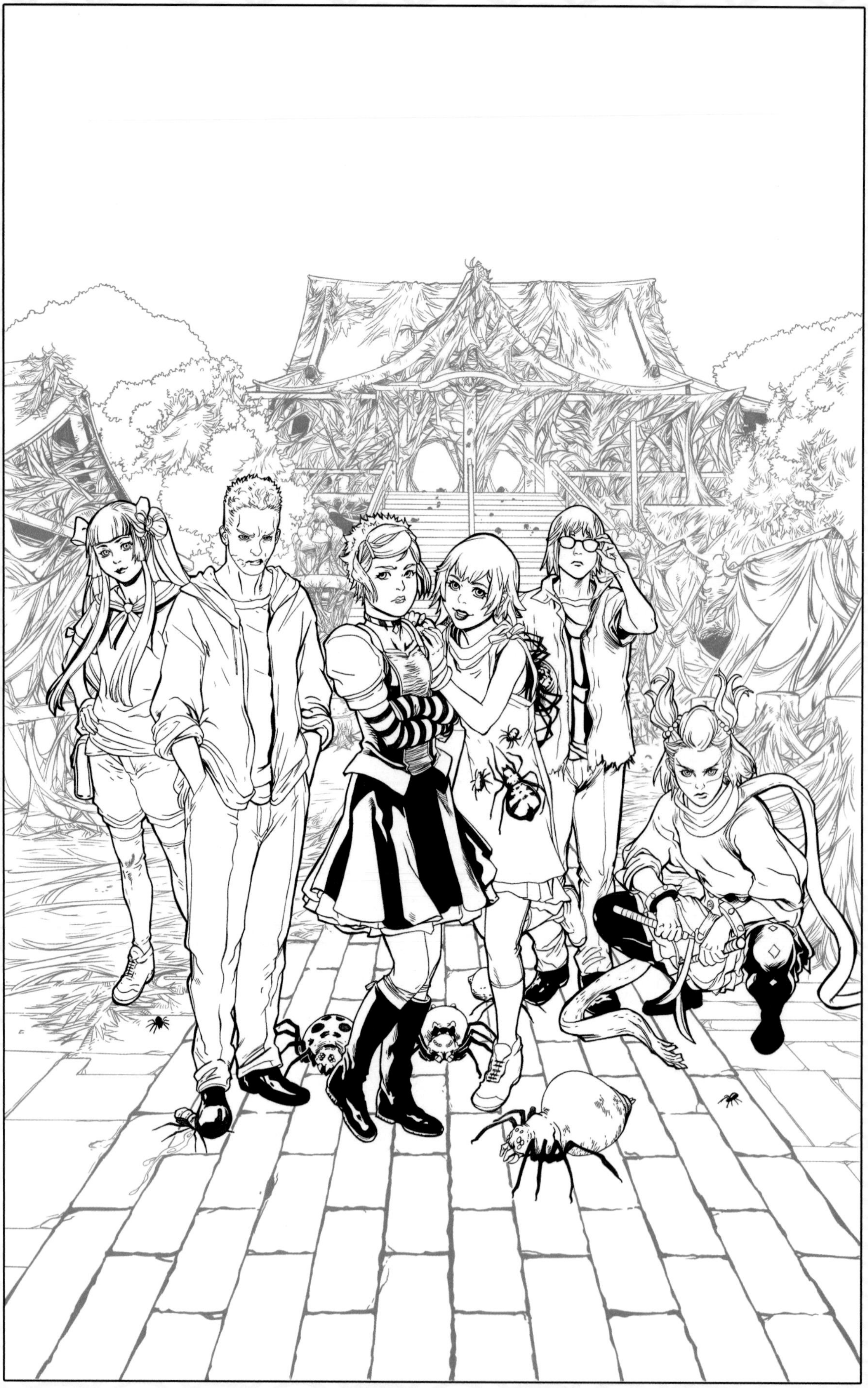

Wayward Deluxe Book 2 Cover
Line Art by Steven Cummings